D0053207

COBBLESTONE

A Detective Novel

by
Péter Lengyel

**translated from Hungarian
by John Bátki**

readers international

The title of this book in Hungarian is *Macskakö*, first published in 1988 by Szépirodalmi Könyvkiadó publishers of Budapest.

© Péter Lengyel 1988

First published in English by Readers International Inc, Columbia, Louisiana and Readers International, London. Editorial inquiries to the London office at 8 Strathray Gardens, London NW3 4NY, England. US/Canadian inquiries to the Subscriber Service Dept., P.O.Box 959, Columbia LA 71418-0959 USA.

English translation © Readers International Inc 1993

Readers International Inc gratefully acknowledges grants given by the Central & East European Publishing Project, Oxford, the National Endowment for the Arts, Washington DC, and the Wheatland Foundation, New York, to help with the translation of this book.

Cover illustration: *Head of a Tramp* (1908-1910), by László Mednyánszky, courtesy of the Hungarian National Gallery
Cover design by Jan Brychta
Printed and bound in Czechoslovakia

Library of Congress Catalog Card Number: 91-60883

British Library Cataloguing in Publication Data:
A catalogue record for this book is available from the British Library.

ISBN 0-930523-86-5 Paperback

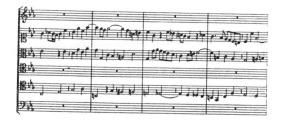

JOHANN SEBASTIAN BACH

Author's note from the Hungarian edition:

The author wishes to thank

the Soros Foundation, for its support ensuring these years of undisturbed work,

Zsolt Csalog, Mrs Ferenc Demendy, Katalin Dezsényi, Andrea Kmety, Mrs Endre Liska, Gabi Kerényi, András Neszmélyi, Géza Ottlik, Mária Pataki, Zoltán Tárnok, Daniel Ternák.

My Publisher.

My First Reader.

COBBLESTONE

PART ONE

THE SETUP

STEEL JIMMY

"You have sixty seconds until the night watchman gets here," I said to the man with the auburn locks as I stepped out of the shadows by the great strongbox of the Zara (for you, Zadar,* Yugoslavia) First Hungarian-Italian Credit Bank. Prior to that moment I had been absorbed by the delight of watching him lovingly pry open the outer steel plate with a long-handled jimmy. "Gentlemen," I nodded. I was speaking Hungarian, there by the distant shores of the Adriatic.

The three men stared at me as if they had seen a ghost by the light of their acetylene flare lamp. I grinned at the sight of their dumbfounded faces, I couldn't help it. It was an hour before sunrise, when night's silence is darkest, battles are begun and the burgher's sleep is deepest.

It was on the afternoon of this day that back home, on the Pest side of our city, the first automobile put-putted past the thieves' dens of Cemetery Road, turning onto Outer Kerepesi Road (possibly along the lines of the fallen stone walls around King Matthias' deer park**) where the smoke of puffing steam locomotives floated overhead. Eventually it would reach the traces of the lesser branch of the Danube, dried out in the course of time, already called Grand Boulevard and with good reason; where, as it turned, a guardian of the law, with the feathergrass in his hat, attempted to arrest this suspicious contraption speeding by without the aid of visible horses.

The trees of the Grand Boulevard are still slender and the cobblestone cubes of the roadway have not yet been worn smooth by our feet. In faraway Amsterdam a diamond cutter is examining, through his magnifying lens, a South African stone to determine the direction of the crystal's cleavage planes. The

---

*The narrator frequently updates changes in placenames for his late-twentieth-century audience. In 1896 Zara was part of the Dalmatian province of the Kingdom of Hungary within the Austro-Hungarian Dual Monarchy.
**Matthias I., Hunyadi (1440-1490), king of Hungary, Transylvanian-born son of János Hunyadi. Statesman, soldier, patron of scholars and artists; many feel that during his reign the Hungarian state reached its acme. [All notes are by the translator unless otherwise identified.]

gem is less than one hundred carats, and it may end up weighing half as much after it is cut and polished. It is a completely transparent, flawless diamond of the finest water, so-called. It is not large enough to be one of the world's fabled diamonds, but its fate will be worthy of our attention. Blue Blood is its name and a client has been found for it already.

A girl called Bubbles shows up at the infamous Mrs. Tremmel's brothel on Outer Kerepesi Road, seeking employment as a housemaid. In the evening at this same establishment Special Investigator Dajka's glance becomes mesmerized by one of the "madame's" protégées who has almond-shaped eyes of a deep fire, and whose former fragile dark beauty shines through her fear-trampled face with a wonderstruck innocence even in the morass of her current environment.

At a later, sensitive point of this story the girl, now star singer at the cabaret Silly Kitty, will testify that she saw the new piano player wash his hands. And her eyes will grow round at the denial, "No, I was not washing anything. Not at all." After that moment all she will murmur to herself will be, "But why is he saying that? Why?" It is a kind of pre-AIDS era story, and time will tell why that makes a difference.

The first time I heard the name Blue Blood pronounced I was sitting on the box of a hackney coach, and I instantly chose a new profession. Ever since, I have often had occasion to reflect whether the final outcome followed any natural law. After all, there were a few things I did correctly: I kept a secret hideout; I knew how to keep my life private. But there were things I bungled. More than one. Since then I have had occasion to reflect on my ambivalent moral and professional position at that time, on the callous, stupid irresponsibility of youth. My two or three obvious mistakes led to a bloodstain that could have been avoided. And to a medical history at a prison hospital. And to that hot lamp cylinder which I can never forgive myself.

It all started so perfectly.

It was not by chance that I found myself in the vault of that bank at dawn by the shore of the Adriatic. All night long I had walked the quiet streets of the port. Earlier that afternoon at one of the bars of the Porta Marittima I happened to overhear a few casual, softly spoken Hungarian words. Since then I had been looking around and searching for them until this moment. There was no one else about at this dark hour.

At the barred windows of the Hungarian-Italian Bank I heard a characteristic noise of metal scraping on metal. I found them, the ones I had been looking for. I turned into a side street, turned again into a back alley on the right that was faced by the bank building's barred windows. Next to the hinges of a small iron door the wall had been opened and the doorframe removed. A veiled light filtered out from the direction of the front rooms. I strolled in. Half a minute later I was watching from behind a dusty curtain as the handsome brown-haired man whose beard was blond sweated and wrestled with the side panel of the strongbox. If I know anything about the world, this man was working behind schedule. Another man whose face remained in the dark held the acetylene lamp, and the third, with curly hair, was handing the tools like a surgical assistant. I liked the gesture.

I pulled back without a sound and hurried out into the street.

In front of the building I could hear the footsteps of the municipal night watchman from a distance, and could envision the inevitable: the guard hears the noise, and turns back toward the bank building. Pulling my hat down over my eyes, I set out for him. To gain time I had to confuse him somehow. I timed it so that we would meet beyond the light of the streetlamp. I gestured silently that my cigar needed a light. As I moved off I could feel his gaze on my back, and I could hear him walk on, then hesitate. He was thinking about turning back. At top speed I walked around the block and went into the strongroom again. And then there I stood in front of the three professionals.

"Sixty seconds. If that much."

They can only stare at this stranger dropped into their midst. It could have been the law. Maybe he is the law. I place my hand on the auburn-haired man's shoulder.

"Shh...Gentlemen, you better disappear." Spoken in

Hungarian, there by the shore of the Mediterranean.

And immediately I committed my first blunder in this affair: I removed the steel jimmy from the man's hand and put it down. This gesture was to cause me much grief in the course of the years.

"Let's go, quick," I propelled my man toward the door.

A heartbeat later I added in a soft but clear voice, "You will find me in the evening at the Porta Marittima."

Outside, the dawn was russet-red toward the sea. There was no time for them to pick up their tools: lamp, rotary drill, steel jimmy were all left behind.

THE SIGNATURE

That afternoon at Budapest police headquarters on Franz Joseph Square, Dr. Dajka receives the first brief report of the Zara break-in. The wireless telegraph never sleeps, not even on Saturdays; messages come and go between the law-enforcement authorities of central and southern Europe and our city where the continent's roads and railways crisscross, meeting place of scientists, artists, aristocrats of high finance and high birth, and burglars.

There has not been an unsolved break-in for over a year within the Doctor's jurisdiction. The telegram, however, does have its precedents. In recent years there were two instances of safe-crackers leaving the scene without a trace. At the Sonnenschein furniture warehouse on Idol Street the thieves found only a few worthless lottery tickets. At the Péterffy shipping office on New World Street their haul was a hundred thousand forints in cash and securities. At both places they arrived unnoticed and departed without a trace. For a year now Dr. Dajka has been routinely requesting his colleagues abroad for any information about safe-breaks not only in the Dual Monarchy but all over Europe. He considers unsolved cases to be encysted ulcers and intends to do all in his power to keep them from festering.

He rapidly scans the report from Zara, re-reads it more slowly, then leaning back in his high-backed chair he slips one hand into the slit of his vest, the fingers of the other hand drumming a lively tattoo on the desk. Soon he is starting to nod his head, with more and more vehemence. He needs facts, as many facts as possible. He shouts for patrolman János Suk, who stands guard outside.

"Suk! Su-ukk!"

At this point we must go back two years, to the time when the Budapest underworld grapevine tingled with an unexpected message at two places on the same day.

A lanky figure wrapped in a dust-cloak knocked at the one-storey house on Bush Street in Old Buda belonging to the well-known fence Rókus Láncz. All he said was:

"The Safe King is out early." That said, the midnight visitor sped on, but Láncz did not slip back under his warm eiderdown. Just as he was, in his shirt and underpants, he descended into the cellar where he shifted a hundredweight of logs from the firewood stacked by the back wall, to remove a package. He carefully unwrapped the two horseblankets around a yellow pigskin suitcase which, by virtue of its expensive material and fine workmanship formed a sharp contrast with every other aspect of the environment, Rókus included. One could imagine on it hotel stickers from luxurious spas, but there was no name, address, not one letter that could have provided a clue. The fence, having pulled on a robe, peeked out at the street before opening the suitcase on the kitchen table. From among the clothes, theater props, makeup and wigs he picked out a fat morocco leather wallet, and having made certain of its contents, returned to his bed.

By then the dust-cloaked messenger, this lean foot soldier of the criminal orders, was well on his way, loping along with a thief's stride toward the far-off Cemetery Road. He had to make a huge detour until he reached the Chain Bridge, and an hour and a half later he was softly, persistently tapping on one of the doors in a row of single-storey slum dwellings. "The Safe King is getting out early," he whispered to the sleep-sodden, tousled face of a woman peering at him from behind the rough-hewn door opened a crack. Then he was gone in the dark. The woman returned to her lair and pulled out, from under a pile of ratty clothes in a corner, a bright package bundled in oily rags. The Special Investigator would have given much to see the sight of the young woman's hands fondling the gleaming nickel-steel tools, one by one.

In the South African Jägersfontein mining district a nearly naked black man had been standing for five hours in the riverbed next to his tilted board when his searching hands discovered the stone in the alluvial deposit. Never in his life had he seen one this large, never had he dreamed of anything like this. For the past four months he had not found any diamonds at all. It must have weighed a hundred to a hundred twenty carats uncut; its color and clarity could not be determined as yet. The value of a flawlessly clear stone increased exponentially with size. Until the end of the workday the Sotho man, poorly fed, clad in a loincloth, contemplated swallowing the stone and bolting. His dream was buying a coalblack stallion with shiny new accoutrements.

As far back as he could remember the fugitive's fate was to be caught or to perish in the wilderness.

When he turned in the as yet unnamed diamond, he received a special bonus of twenty pounds sterling. It was common knowledge that the price of a nobler steed at the Kimberley market started at twenty-four pounds, not including the harness.

Veron Czérna, daughter of a ropemaker from the municipality of Pest, received an orphan's tuition-free education at the Ursulines, where she learned to embroider and did housecleaning, washing and homework for her more well-to-do classmates.

The youngest judge in the city receives his appointment launching him on a career that was to make such a fateful impact on ours.

In a stone quarry on the north shore of Lake Balaton the basalt seemed to split smoothly by itself under the hammerstrokes of a tall swarthy man. It was volcanic rock, articulated by transverse joints so that you only had to hit it in the right spot and it was a regular hexahedron. Cube. Cobblestone for the new streets of the capital city.

On Rose Square the cabaret Silly Kitty was being built. When Agnes Vad - whose claim to calling herself Baroness was based on unknowable memories and desires and on one very knowable gentleman - when she dreamed of this realm of hers she had envisioned a respectable institution and significant profits. The inherent contradiction was resolved by the uniquely duplicitous construction of the finished building.

The Baroness had arrived at the capital after a strenuous youth in a brothel at Bártfa in the northern uplands (for you, Bardejov, Czechoslovakia) where a stout man, who had a mill at Topolya and who made the girls do filthy things, had loved her - that was the only way she could think of him. He died the way he lived. When he found out that he had only a few weeks left he invested his fortune in gold nuggets and willed it all to the prostitute, strictly observing legal formalities. The Baroness guards these original notarized court documents with her life, just like her gold nuggets. (Among the papers is her certificate of legal change of name; her real name had been Erzsike Csorba.) "I didn't do this," the miller panted asthmatically, "for your sake. I did it so they all won't be glad I died. Because that's all they are waiting for." And he grinned from ear to ear: he would have the last laugh on his relations.

Without even waiting for the funeral she made for Budapest to realize her dream: a cozy establishment where the girls did not have to struggle and where the gentlemen did not get overly familiar with her. She soon found a building to her liking in the inner city. Having sketched out her special requirements she began to look for a master builder, and found him on the platform of the Eastern railway terminal in the person of a Bosnian journeyman builder on his way home, along with his whole crew. For good pay they were willing to renovate her real estate. She herself purchased the building materials, getting as much enjoyment as a fishwife out of bartering and belittling the merchandise. She bought bricks, lime, velvet wall paper, from here and there and everywhere. Boards to plank the inner corridor on the first floor, plate glass for the raised cage in the downstairs café that would be her front office. An Italian opera designer from Vienna came for a week-long consultation. At the Visegrád Street depot of the Gutjahr and Müller metal factory she placed an order for four identical steel doors with peepholes. She had visions of stacked banknotes representing her net daily take, and heaps of gold nuggets in which to invest her money once the business got going. She was anticipating a considerable profit. The service entrance was an inch-thick oak door with a lock. For this back door she would need a reliable man, she thought, when the Bosnians unloaded the four steel doors from the delivery wagon and hung them. Yes, she would need a strong, trustworthy man. And then not even a mosquito could get in here uninvited.

In two months all the building supplies were gone from the front of the house: the four-handled troughs, basins of lime, gravel, every last plank. The Bosnians went back to their godforsaken mountains. The Baroness' apartment was on the first floor. The rear entrances opened on a neighboring courtyard, and she volunteered to pay for the right of way. As part of the beautification of the whole block a continuous row of new business signs was installed on both facades. A gigantic image of a Thonet chair. A huge hand pointing in the direction of the Sáfrán furniture showrooms around the corner. And at last, on the Leopold Street facade, next to the "Glass-Mirrors-Porcelain" sign of the neighboring store, between the first and second floors there appeared the sign of the Silly Kitty, *Café Chantant*. She herself wrote in her curlicued hand in chalk on a blackboard posted at the carriage entrance of the back courtyard: WANTED, cooks, waiters, cashier, cloakroom girl, kitchen help, cleaning woman, door-man-factotum. She interviewed each applicant. She personally recruited musicians, dancers, artistes, hostesses from nightclubs and cabarets or even from the street; she had the expertise. After a week only the doorman's position waited to be filled.

On the eighth day a swarthy man was perusing the notice at the Kitty's rear entrance. He wore a black suit, a bowler on the crown of his head, a not quite white starched collar, shirt, vest and tie; he could have been a factory worker, a coachman

or a bank messenger. The clothes of anonymous city folk differ
as little from each other as do humble villagers'. Just before
that he had been sightseeing in Snake Street, going past the
glass-roofed Bazaar of the Paris Emporium: engravers, dealers
in eiderdown and gloves, remnant shops, Gersits and Kuhn's
linen goods warehouse, Sáfrán's Furniture Department Store.
Then he stopped in front of the shiny windows of the Kitty to
inspect his appearance. He hunched up his left shoulder and,
affecting a limp, walked past the long plate-glass windows of
the establishment. He dropped his shoulder slightly, created a
somewhat more authentic limp, and passed by once more. He
nodded with satisfaction, went around to the service entrance
and energetically rang the bellpull, twice. Half an hour later it
was he who took in the blackboard.

Blue Blood. I first heard those two words on Váci
Boulevard. My station was in front of the National Casino on
the former Rabbits' Island, a Baron Vay having retained my
coach on a permanent basis. Before that, to assure my position
I was obliged to fight a minor brawl for the job with a fop of a
hackney coach driver famous for his yellow checkered
trousers. In the coach the Baron as a rule was blithely
oblivious of me sitting in the box, and habitually discussed the
most delicate election issues, blackball proposals, debts and
affairs of honor. And one fine day, the fact that the stone
known as Blue Blood has been delivered into the hands of the
finest Dutch diamond cutter in Amsterdam. It was destined for
a member of the House of Hapsburg, for delivery in the
Hungarian capital where the owner's new palace was being
built to be ready for the summer festivities of the Millennial
Exposition. The stone's name seized my imagination, ripening
adventurous plans in my brain. In any case it was time to quit
driving a hackney cab; no one would remember my face
hereabouts.
    That was the year when a Slovakian glassworker on a
Boulevard construction site taught me how to make a
kaleidoscope out of leftover windowglass strips. Up on the
sunsplashed higher floors the carpenters' adzes tapped out a
merry beat. German girls carried basins full of mortar, their

skirts had a thousand pleats and their blouses were white. The trowel-wielding master mason I lugged bricks for wore a black hat and vest. This was the time when a significant portion of your world was made, the world into which you will arrive at a later moment in time. People were swarming over the Grand Boulevard. Its unprecedented width was surfaced with cobblestones, what we call "catstones".*

(While a cat has nine lives, our stones have seven: as they wear out, they can be turned five times. When the sixth facet of the cube becomes worn, the stones will still barricade with their basalt bodies the death intended for us.) Horse-drawn drays were hauling bricks, door- and window-frames for the third floor. They passed on the left-hand side, reloaded and turned on the empty side streets. The electric tram's angular solo cars rolled by on rails on either side of the boulevard. The young trees on the sidewalk were watered by a mustachioed man wearing duck pants. Mills were still standing on our side of the Grand Boulevard. Pedestrians streamed past the hoardings: men sporting waistcoats and bowlers and carrying walking sticks, and ladies wearing bell-shaped skirts.

The united twin cities of the capital, Budapest, could already boast of the seamier sides of metropolitan status: in three years there had been thirty-six safe-breaks in the capital.

As usual, various parts of the truth were known to various individuals. On the December eve of the safe-break at the Idol Street furniture warehouse, the lodger at the watchmaker Lápos' on Váci Boulevard took his leave. The unusually handsome young man with auburn locks was off to visit his fiancée in Vienna. He even showed a photograph of his girl. On January sixth, the night of the Epiphany, burglars broke into the strongbox of a fashionable lingerie store on Esterhazy Street in the Leopoldstadt district of Vienna. The thieves got away with a rich loot. Dajka was duly notified.

Two days later the Lápos family received their lodger's greetings from the imperial capital on a postcard depicting a

---

*The literal translation of the Hungarian for cobblestone, *macskakö*.

Viennese idyll, and signed Márton Jankó, Postbox 107, Leopoldstadt, Vienna. This is what the watchmaker and his wife knew. But the connection between the two events was to be noted and found significant only in the light of later happenings.

There had been a rash of safe-breaks all over Europe. Dr. Dajka spent an inordinate amount of time in his office poring over French and German reports of criminal investigations, studying figures and evidence. In a small black pocket notebook he kept his annotations in a handwriting that resembled an engineer's diminutive, precise lettering. He was not interested in cases where the perpetrators had been apprehended.

He recalled one safe-cracker who had most brilliantly eluded the dragnet of the Austro-Hungarian police in the south, without ever revealing his identity. He has not been heard from since. Anything was possible at the depths of human existence inhabited by these gentlemen: a bar-room knifing may end an illustrious career, consigning the victim to a shallow ditch in some Levantine cemetery where he lies, in anonymity, pretty much as he had lived. Or he might end up in America. So that this particular man was most likely not the one behind the present cases.

Every policeman knows that the criminal sooner or later leaves his signature on the job. It is an unbroken law for every criminal, as certain as death and taxes. This is what the Special Investigator was counting on.

That week when in Zara I first encounter the gentlemen who rob safes professionally, back here at home the Eiffel-designed building of the Western railroad terminal is already completed and stands the same as you and I see it today. One summer night there are two midnights in Budapest: at sixteen minutes past twelve the clocks are set back to zero hour and the Central European Time Zone takes effect nationwide. Ever since then, the local time indicated on our clocks and watches has been sixteen minutes off.

Around this time the girlies cruising Leopold Street in Pest (for you, Outer Váci Street) are likely to be humming the current hit song, "Alfred Nobel Swedish chemist / Mixed some glycerin with flint." The Millennium is approaching at a rapid pace. It is already here, according to some of the knowledge-able historians researching the era of the Magyar Conquest. However, the ambitious construction projects and large-scale preparations for the celebration were not going to be completed in time. The authorities have therefore decided retroactively to alter the year in which the seven Magyar tribes (eight, according to others) entered the Carpathian Basin,* and, by doing so, delay the Millennial anniversary for a year. The rescheduling not only bespeaks the audacity of bureau-crats but also reveals something about the nature of time, which after all is perhaps not the primeval liquid flowing merely in one direction as some of us would believe. By now Baroness Vad's Kitty, with its twofold operation, has become an established nightspot on the corner of Leopold Street, and the main hall of the groundfloor café is the meeting place I gave to my safe-cracking new acquaintances. At the time I still knew nothing about the Baroness, her dreams, and the other services offered by The Kitty.

"Sir!" Patrolman Suk stands at rigid attention by the office door.

The recently appointed Special Investigator Dajka has been assigned to deal with any and all acts of criminal violence, murders, break-ins, robberies committed within the city limits of the dual capital. In addition, he is authorized to act according to his own best judgement in matters that might interfere with the success of the upcoming Summer Festivities.

He has a large stack of papers old and new brought up to his office.

He examines the material until late in the afternoon, when he strolls over to the recently opened Café Nicoletti on

---

*The "Basin" refers throughout the novel to the land encircled by the Carpathian Mountains surrounding the Hungarian plain. At various times in history, and up until the end of World War I, the "lands of the Hungarian crown" included most of the Basin. After the Treaty of Trianon, Hungary's territory was reduced to one third of its former extent.

Octagon Place where he can sit incognito until the evening police raids call him to self-imposed duty. He spends as much time as possible at the most diverse public places of the city; he likes this and the nature of his work demands it, he reassures his conscience. And so everywhere, at all times he keeps his eyes open, notes everything in an attempt to keep his fingertips on the pulse of the growing metropolis.

He is enjoying his cigar in the mellow summer evening on the terrace of the café when the dust-cloaked and begoggled automobile driver turns off Elizabeth Boulevard and pulls up right in front, to the accompaniment of clatter and a series of backfires. The ladies and gentlemen of the audience applaud and bottles of champagne are popped in honor of the sportsman who happens to be a champagne producer and who proceeds to give an entertaining account of the vicissitudes of his journey which began at the Municipal Park. As the Special Investigator listens to the adventures of the single-cylinder Mercedes-Benz, including the incident with the police officer at the street corner, he has occasion to wonder if this newfangled horseless carriage will not indeed be a source of concern for the police. Little does he know that these vehicles powered by the internal combustion engine will, within one or two brief generations, play a greater role in the control of human population than those global rituals of wholesale human sacrifice, World Wars One and Two; that eventually a whole new industry will arise, so that Little Kovács will be able to make a living and support a family simply by preparing optical documentation of the population decrease thus brought about. By that time the Nicoletti will be called the Savoy, although, miracle of miracles, it will still be functioning as a restaurant.

Dajka's work soon catches up with him in the form of a police messenger with the first detailed report from Zara sent by Captain Gioielli, the local colleague who is an outstanding guardian of the law and a personal friend of the Doctor's.

On first receiving the news of the Zara break-in he had temporarily assigned it to the current rash of safe-breaks all over Europe. Here, however, something extraordinary happened, there was no doubt about it. Again the robbers were not seen by anyone but were evidently interrupted by an approaching watchman. Two days previously the strongbox of the Hungarian-Italian Bank had been replaced by the newest type Wiese-Wertheim safe, and this proved an unexpected difficulty for the thieves. They left behind a complete set of tempered steel tools next to the half-opened safe. Gioielli's report gives a complete and detailed inventory, together with a description of the method of entry and the results of the investigation. The clues indicate the presence of four men; the method employed is traditional European.

Dajka pauses over some passages in the watchman's testimony, according to which just before discovering the forced entry he met a thin foreigner whom he had never before seen in town. This fact in itself of course has no significance; two thousand ships arrive at the port annually. But the unknown person positioned himself, obviously intentionally, in such a way that his face remained in the dark. He was smoking a fragrant, thin cigar. He wore a hat and a threadbare sailor's jersey with blue stripes, all too common around the docks, and his jacket lapels were turned up. He did not say a word. In hindsight the watchman realized that the unknown individual had probably wanted to detain him. Finally he ventured the opinion that the stranger's walk suggested a very young man.

A curious twist is provided by the fact that the newly acquired safe was not yet in use by the bank; it stood empty while the older strongbox in the far corner of the room contained a significant amount of valuables that remained untouched.

When the Special Investigator reaches this part of the report, he stops and stares at it without noticing that the cigar in his right hand has developed an inch-long growth of ash ready to drop and soil his suit. Four men; the new safe, although empty, is the newest of its kind. Here is the gang's signature, what he has been waiting for. All along it had been there in front of his eyes. And in the wake of the frustrated robbery one side of the equation is suddenly revealed to him.

From that moment on, because he knows what he is looking for, the signs will become more obvious.

He can say goodbye to his siesta. Without wasting time to look for a hackney coach he hurries on foot to police headquarters and once again has the pile of documents brought out. He skips over two insignificant Balkan robberies, but from the rest of the unsolved cases he draws up a chart on two facing pages of his notebook. Location, date, method of entry and of safe-break, type of safe. For the next rubric he needs international train schedules which he has Suk obtain, with some difficulty, from the National Railways. Saint Petersburg, Königsberg (for you, Leningrad and Kaliningrad, USSR), Bucharest, Nagyvárad, Belgrade, Constantinople (for you, Istanbul), Munich, Hamburg, Prague, Budapest, Vienna. He looks up only international express trains with sleeping cars. You don't become an international safe-cracker in order to crawl along on local trains in the company of peasant women going to market. And in each case the distances and dates correspond and are in agreement: *it could just possibly be* one extraordinarily productive international gang of thieves behind most of the continent's unsolved cases. So right away his attention is focused on us.

And the signature is there.

New World Street: outer door picked with a skeleton key, careful neat work, thorough cleanup, no traces left. Idol Street: wall opened up, skeleton key, neat work, no traces.

New World Street: a hundred thousand forints in cash and papers. Idol Street: empty safe.

In each of the foreign cases fitting into the series: first, flawless professionalism. Second, meticulous cleanup, no scraps, no cigarette butts, no dust or shavings from the wall of the safe. Their results show extreme fluctuations. Their reconnaissance leaves something to be desired; more precisely, it is one-sided. On the one hand it seems as if they chose their targets in a hit-or-miss fashion. And yet: the steel-plating is always the most up-to-date, presenting the greatest difficulties. As if they were drawn by the sport, attracted by the challenge of the technical problems. The outset and the goal were similar in Zara too, but this one time the safe triumphed over them; they could not crack it, they ran out of time and had to escape in a hurry, leaving behind a mess, their first-rate tools, and in the metal filings and dust, four sets of footprints. They did not even touch the more easily accessible strongbox.

On the basis of a few facts he knows quite a lot about these superbly successful burglars and feels there is a good chance that he may again expect to see their calling card on the occasion of the Summer Festivities.

He prepares index cards for these four men. For the time being most of the rubrics will have to remain blank. Name, description, nationality, age, religion, languages, special distinguishing marks, crime, favorite methods, signature, comments. He places the cards in an empty shoebox, with the word Album on its top. There is plenty of room left in it. Dr. Dajka's eventual contribution, one that would change the history of criminology, is thus beginning to take concrete shape in the chase to catch the elusive safe-crackers.

On the same day he launches a correspondence with all of the Austrian and Hungarian prisons, police headquarters and other places of detention, as well as with the police chiefs of foreign cities, with many of whom he is personally acquainted. He asks for information and likenesses of certain known criminals.

At the same time, on the basis of the two Budapest cases he requests warrants to be issued all over the continent for apprehension of the unknown perpetrators, given the few available facts. About the only thing he expects of this gesture is that it might lead to further information.

NIGHTCLUBS AND BROTHELS

At ten p.m. Dajka sets out with a splitting headache on Chief Inspector Axaméthy's Saturday night raid. Supervision of nightclubs and brothels does not officially fall within his mandate, but they are so closely intertwined with violent crimes that he is duty-bound to be familiar with them. The two key stops of the raid are the first and the last. The Silly Kitty in the inner city and Mrs. Tremmel's brothel on Outer

Kerepesi Road.

The Kitty occupies a two-storey building on Rose Square
(for you: today one of the two Klotild palaces stands in its
place), only a few paces from the Inner City Church, which
like some medieval bridge has been lined on two sides by
vendors' stalls; a hop and skip away from the Vindobona
Hotel and Café and from the teeming Grand Bazaar, and a
minute's walk from the County Hall itself. If you go down the
brief length of Danube Street you are at the city's finest open
air market, on Fish Square. By this era the cheaper, open-air
varieties of sexual traffic have been exiled to the outlying
districts; the more refined bourgeois sensibilities of the
capital's citizenry will not tolerate it in the Inner City. Right
from the start the Special Investigator thought it odd that the
Baroness, who had gone to so much trouble to make sure that
her café and dance hall should not be associated with the
low-class joints on King Street, could not do without the *Kitty*
when she devised her club's name. However, the establishment
makes up for it by an air of impeccable respectability that is
essential for survival in such an irreproachable central
location. For breakfast each morning in the hall of the *café
chantant* coffee brewed from fresh-roasted beans is served in
pint mugs topped by an inch-thick dollop of whipped cream
from whole milk delivered from the crown lands at Gödöllö.
The price of breakfast, coffee complete with spongy raisin-
studded cinnamon bread, is eighteen kreuzers. At noon the
place becomes a restaurant wafting cozy domestic aromas, and
gentlemen may at any time of the day amuse themselves with
billiards or the two Szeifert-type revolving skittles boards.
Toward evening the great window displays advertise the
night's program for the citizenry. The police inspection does
not take long for the family-style dance hall of this *etablissement* and moves on toward the deeper waters of the city.
Dajka is aware of the house's other, unadvertised function. He
simply does not want to disturb it without good cause.

He wants to know about everything that happens in the city
at night, in the streets, in dives, in brothels. At such places the
heaviest toughs congregate like moths fluttering around a
lamp. So he watches the heartbeat of the night; on more than

one occasion this has made his task easier.

The police squad leaves the Inner City behind and moves on to neighborhoods where pedestrians and streetlamps are fewer, the streetwalkers are more down at heel, and the sights more hard-core at each successive nightclub, gambling den and bordello. Ladies' orchestras are playing, hatcheck girls are smiling and nymphets are selling flowers, using this pretext to loiter about the nightspots. Such female personnel provide the most assured lines of supply as candidates for the public houses of prostitution. Deep into the night the raid reaches the most infamous of the forty-three licensed houses, Mrs. Tremmel's. This is where the Special Investigator takes note of the raven-haired girl whose face still retains traces of resplendent smiles and a lively intelligence. A fine cobweb of crow's feet clings to the corners of her almond-shaped eyes that reflect the imprint of some early wave of Mongolian influence. She is conspicuous in her environment; Dajka is convinced that she has seen better days; he will remember her. As he accompanies the police raid on his own initiative, we are entitled to say that he will be entangled in this woman's complicated affairs as a victim of his own conscientious love of work.

He spends Sunday at the office, busily writing up the events of the previous evening.

A seventeen-year-old boy reports before noon at police headquarters, stating that he found the dead body of the day laborer Lajos Lebovics, nine years of age, on Sturgeoncatch meadow. Lebovics had been a pinboy at the bowling alley of Radics's Inn, and his Saturday night's earnings had amounted to ninety kreuzers. His pockets are empty now. A single depressing hour is all that the investigation takes. The corpse's neck shows traces of strangulation by means of a leather belt, which turns up under a bush. The face of the guttersnipe who made the report is covered with fresh scratches and the belt belongs to him. Dajka is left mulling over the question of who is more wretched: the pallid, puny nine-year-old who had died for ninety kreuzers, or the dull-witted murderer, who had killed for small change.

In a New Pest bar Ferenc Kordé, ship's blacksmith, lost his

ppatience and ordered Lajos Princz to leave the premises as
he wanted to drink alone. Since Princz was unwilling to leave,
the blacksmith hit him on the head with a piece of iron; he
died on arrival at the hospital in the morning. Kordé did not
resist arrest and has been crying continually.

Keleti, the manufacturer on Crown Prince Street (for you,
Sándor Petöfi Street) offers rubber and fish bladder prophy-
lactic devices, promises discretion. One, two or three forints
per dozen, and so on. Safety and harmlessness guaranteed by
Mr. Keleti. It is up to the Special Investigator to decide if this
constitutes punishable fraud. Since the unmentionable subject
cannot be brought up in an official context, this decides its
fate. Dajka is hard put trying to imagine how the guarantee
could possibly work - unless the manufacturer maintains a
home for unwed mothers at his villa.

In the forenoon two urchins, Jenö Németh and Ferenc
Schwartz, playing ball at the Field of Blood, found a sack by
the side of the Devil's Ditch, the said sack containing a man's
pair of worn shoes and two human arms and two legs. The
sack bore the mark of Dr. Alfred Loydl, university professor
and embalmer. He testifies that the sack must have been
stolen from him; he deals only with the dissection of animals.

The authorities are preparing for the Festivities. Monday
morning the city police commissioner summons to his office all
the district police captains. He begins by calling to their
attention the benevolent legislation soon to be introduced in
the Lower House, proposing the forcible settlement of
nomadic Gypsies. He requests observations in writing to be
submitted by the following day. Then he conveys His Majesty's
Highest Wish: the Millennial Festivities at the capital must
proceed without criminals or crime. It is the duty of those
present to ensure that nothing should dim the splendor of the
Festivities when the Emperor, in his capacity as King of
Hungary, visits the eastern capital of his Dual Monarchy. And
he takes this opportunity to present Dr. Dajka, who has been
appointed by the Minister of Justice from among the members
of the judiciary as Special Investigator for the duration of two
years, and who is to have their full cooperation.

For some time now the Doctor has been anticipating a

never before experienced crime wave in the capital on the occasion of the Millennium. The brilliant pomp and splendor will attract not only the crowds of wide-eyed sightseers from all over the country, the continent, and from overseas. This will also be an extraordinary opportunity for the underworld, who no doubt are already making feverish plans. The solution lies in keeping the domestic criminals under observation, scaring them into lying low, and at the same time keeping the foreign elements out. Existing dens of crime must be wiped out while the creation of new ones must be prevented. Raids and large-scale cleanup operations have to create a counterforce against the crime wave. The extraordinary situation demands extraordinary measures. And he already knows what those measures will be.

On the following day he receives an additional, and surprising, shipment from Zara. It is a sheet bearing a fingernail-size spot of parallel, curling, hair-thin lines. According to the accompanying letter, it is a fingerprint from the long-handled steel jimmy, one of the tools left behind at the scene. It was photographed and prepared according to the most up-to-date methods of identification proposed by the British professor Francis Galton. The Special Investigator makes a face; he is a man of conservative, traditionalist outlook who makes an effort to keep up with recent advances in criminology. Still, he has a higher regard for the minutiae of everyday investigation than for the newest laboratory procedures. Besides, the very person of this Britisher is somewhat suspect: he happens to be a cousin of that infamous buffoon Charles Darwin, whose wild theories have long since been refuted by science.

"Not so," says Dr. Komora, the police surgeon, who is of another opinion. "Not so fast. Let us keep these things separate. The relationship of those two men goes only as far as the family tree. Intellectually they are not akin, and they subscribe to diametrically opposed views on the same issues." Dajka, who holds the surgeon in the highest regard among his colleagues, listens to what he has to say.

As far as the fingerprints go, says Komora, the Chinese for

thousands of years have kept records of the tiny lines on the
fingertips of their convicts. Galton has the right idea. He is a
genius who learned to read by the age of two. His basic work,
however, has to do with the theory according to which there
exist different races of humankind, with different qualities,
forming a pyramid-like order. Of course this is not really news:
in the Kalahari desert lives the Stone Age tribe of the !Kung
San who call themselves *Zumvasi*, meaning real humans, while
their name for neighboring tribes means "non-humans". The
same holds true for the Yanomami Indians of the Amazon.
Only Sir Francis expresses these ideas in a more scientific
manner. He too places at the head of the pyramid his own
tribe, the British. He most graciously includes the ancient
Hellenes, who, being extinct, offer no real competition. In
every instance it is one's own tribe that occupies the topmost
position. According to Galton's theory of eugenics, in the
future systematic efforts need to be made to promote the birth
rate of the higher orders of mankind, pretty much as we
already do by breeding Holstein cows that produce the highest
yield of milk. Now here you have a genius of the harmful kind.
For we may yet see the arrival of a practical kind of prophet
who might not have the wits to create a theory like this, but
who might on the other hand possess the armies to carry it
from the arid sphere of science into the steaming field of life.
From our more distant vantage point we may add here, these
armies did indeed arrive, from among the descendants of those
so-called white barbarians speaking the Teutonic tongue who
had crushed the remnants of Hellenic civilization. For them
the peaks belonged to the Teutons, while the depths were
relegated to the descendants of those so-called white barbarians, the Hebrews, who had filtered into the Egyptian New
Kingdom from the no-man's lands of North Arabia. Well now,
you have to breed selectively to improve the milk yield of the
Holsteins. Likewise, humans were bred. But, as we have seen,
the offspring twenty years later would rather be an ordinary,
accidental, unscientific product like the rest of humanity. The
philosopher always fails to realize that the human harvest
never ripens in his own lifetime. And one day there would
come, operetta-style, a practical prophet who, in the name of

the religion of the racial pyramid proclaimed the coming enslavement of the white man (was he himself white or non-white? only the believers could tell).

Whereas consider the cousin, Charles Darwin. According to him a species consists of those individuals who are able to produce fertile offspring. Not so the horse and the ass, for the mule is sterile. But humans, yes, white, black, red, yellow or green - their offspring will give birth to other humans. No, the man is no buffoon. As yet no one has disproved his theory.

(NOW: SAND IS SAND. OCTOBER 23, 4004 BC, 9 A.M.)

I placed the period, stood up from my old Continental Silenta and opened the window. You were not back from school yet, although I had emphatically reminded you to be back on time, we had to be at the dentist's by four.

Of course we are not the first ones who have had to wrestle with the technical problems of telling a story. *Someone* did have to be the first, though, and that person must have had a tougher time. He did not have zoom lenses, paragraphs, words. Nor did he reckon with galactic superaggregates, bosons, baryons and the Third Wave of Immigration in America (right now the Second is in progress). He happens to be our hatchet-jawed, one-hundred-forty-centimeters-tall progenitor, the first one that we have knowledge of, these days. No doubt human prehistory may be approached in ways that differ from Charles Darwin's. For example, the way Bishop Ussher in an earlier age had gone about it: he took the Scriptures and added up the ages of Adam, Seth, Mahallaleb, Jared, Enoch, Noah, Methuselah and all the others, including his own, and pronounced the last word of science. According to his findings the moment of the Creation, from which follows the age of the earth and of humankind, was at nine in the morning on October 23, 4004 BC. Period. We happen to possess, again, a longer perspective, so that, along with Charles Darwin and

Doctor Komora, we may start out by hypothesizing our black great-grandfather standing there at the beginning of things in some gully behind a barricade of thorny brush, yelping about his great adventure, *zzzz, drrr, mmmm.* That would be about three million six hundred thousand years ago, on the basis of excavated fossil finds and potassium argon dating techniques. I had promised you that we would talk about great-grandfather.

Africa. Not far from the future Afar-triangle, in the Pliocene epoch. The rainy season has arrived. A male, holding a club, and a female with a kid clinging to her hip are hurrying across the wide savanna, in the direction of the sheltering hillside. Two flashing pairs of eyes ceaselessly scan the horizon; nostrils flare and ears strain toward noises. Brute survival takes up all of their time and energy. Grandpa's fine sense of smell indicates that the moment is favorable and no sabertoothed tiger hunts for prey here. They may cross the open plain. He senses shelter by the river, far from the watering hole of the great beasts.

On the horizon, the volcanic basalt uplands of the future Ngorongoro. The air is humid and hot, the equatorial sun is setting: its nearly horizontal rays cast improbably long shadows of acacias, thistles, clumsy primeval elephants, bustards, apes. Black and white rhinoceri and antelopes are heading for the watering hole, along with baboons and a kind of buffalo. Beasts of prey, herbivores, and carrion-eaters coexist in a tight order, occupying their separate niches and coming in contact only for occasional bloody moments. Guinea hen and boar, giraffe, hyena and a giant cat share the water of the same hole. Hippopotami live in the river. Our distant grandfather, trotting through the tall grass, has to be aware of all of these creatures, that is why he is still alive at the advanced age of sixteen. They are hurrying across the volcanic ash-covered plain, lit, in addition to the pallid sun, by the sooty crimson flames of the live volcano at the edge of the horizon. Their skin is black, their nostrils flare upward, their jaws jut out; at first glance you might not be too proud of grandpa, you might find him repulsive. But the S-curve of his spine already differentiates him from all other creatures on earth. He scurries along on two feet with unhindered steps, head raised, posture erect: our direct ancestor, who will give rise to all of humankind and all of history. According to our current theories. Grandpa's roving eyes alight on a flat stone which he kicks away to snatch with a lightning-quick gesture the escaping centipede. The insect disappears into his mouth. Again, you wouldn't be too proud of him. The female receives not one of the centipede's hundred legs. She has to look for her own stones, slips in the warm mud, quickly regains her balance. Her brat snuffles at the mother's nipple but gains nothing. He falls asleep.

With a final rush they arrive and plunge for cover into a hollow in the riverbank where they can spend the night in safety. The male grabs some thorny branches to block the opening, and then in the safety of the shelter he starts to pant and grunt, excited, as he tells the story of how they got here. He specifies his topic:

- *Lalalla, lala.* - He refers to the manner of his narrative: - *Drrr-brrr* - , then: *Shhh* - he starts, in the middle of things. He points, gesticulates, makes magic. First the red volcano: - *Hoo-hoo!* - The grasses swaying in the wind: - *Shhhh.* - Now they have reached the middle of the savanna, and found food under the stone: - *Mmmmmmmm.* - The female slips: - *Oooooh* - , and she regains her balance: - *Lalall.* - The horrible great cat beyond the horizon: - *Drrr, mrrr.* - The dumb beast is snoring: - *Khrrr-sss, Khrrr-sss.* - And there is sweet water at the river: - *TchTchTch* - , shelter: - *Bababbabb.* - Satisfied, he tells the tale to the end, amidst much excitement. The common ancestor of all of us, I can identify with him, he is an earlier version of me - and it is I grunting behind the thorn barrier - and of you. His motivation is the same as any popular novelist's: to hold the audience's attention by means of his narrative, to arrest the unstoppable flow of time, to recall a piece of it, to tear it out and store it away for all of us, so that we may refer to it at any time, while it remains in its original place, a crystal with its thousands of sparkling facets: take it or leave it, now you see it, now you don't.

You were always able to spend hours looking at some

drawing depicting imagined spear-wielding Stone Age hordes. Our early ancestors always interested you. So I told the story of grandfather, at this point in my tale. You did come home in time, Auntie Pálma gave you lunch, we got the dentistry taken care of, and afterward we loitered in the city. We went down the escalator. After listening attentively to the story of the black grandfather, you wanted to know more.

"But *how* did it happen? That you didn't tell me. How did he learn to put up a barrier of thistle and brush. To swing a club. To tell a tale. *How* did he change? The father did not know how to make a club and then all of a sudden the son knew, and from then on everyone did?"

That was one hell of a good question. It included many things, such as:

From unequivocal single movements, ones that we can grasp with our five senses, how does the general emerge, the trajectories of biological evolution, of history, of astronomy? How do shifts on the scale of an inch become continental; changes of a moment, geological; how does Gibraltar seal up and the Mediterranean dry out every few million years? Or for that matter, how does our city turn into a metropolis at the time of Special Investigator Dajka? How are we able to pronounce words when we do not see-smell-taste-hear-hold that which we are speaking about?

I did not talk during our subway ride from the Grand Boulevard to the Southern train station. You were waiting patiently. And there life intervened so I would not have to leave your question without attempting an answer. (Ever since I began this story, no matter what I see or experience has sooner or later proved to be related suggested reading matter, instant illustration: the engineer Eiffel's terminal at the Western train station, standing in line for bread in the city of Kolozsvár,* Kornél Vargha's physics experiments, a ball of string in your drawer, the closing down of the former Palatine Street by the Grand Boulevard, vendors on the Square, the old gypsy on the muddy floor of streetcar No. 6, the concert,

*Cluj, Transylvania

the cross-country race, the largest square in Europe near the Municipal Park, the bomber pilot and drug-store owner Vellay on the Las Vegas strip, the interview given by an imam, fake detectives at the Eastern train station, an American quilted bedcover, the subway escalator. Wherever I happen to be at the moment. Who can understand this?) As we strolled past a two-foot strip of corrugated aluminum, you regarded it with initiated eyes: behind it lay the entrance to the nuclear bomb shelter. And then the neighboring escalator was carrying toward us the beautiful and ugly faces of the population of the Carpathian Basin. Floating downstream were:

One blue cotton jacket.

One staggering drunk, in broad daylight.

Four adults, one mother and child.

One red synthetic jacket.

A man's worn jacket fastened with a safety pin on a stylish, well-off girl.

Nine adults, one baby in a carrying bag, a miniskirt, a toothless dazed drunk, yet another drunk, five adults, one sheath gown, one schoolkid. I called each one to your attention separately: blue, drunk, adult, adult, adult, adult, mother, red. Man's jacket. Adult, adult, adult, adult, adult, adult, adult, adult, adult, adult, baby, mini. Drunk, adult, adult, adult, adult, adult, sheath. Schoolkid.

The escalator merely condenses, serves it up for us on a platter, turns it all into a moving picture, the situation as it exists.

We paid attention to all perceivable phenomena, as precisely as we could. Only a millionth part of reality, but a true sample.

So that, with our earlier, similarly rigorous observations in mind, we may in good faith state the following:

These days in Hungary there exist a number of eclectic, loose fashions.

The increase of the population has slowed down in recent years.

Alcoholism in our parts is an endemic disease. It is as obvious as saying that sand is sand. It is as real as my fist.

The escalator came to a sudden grinding halt so that everybody, child, adult, drunk and mother stumbled grappling for the handrail. Whereupon from the Olympian heights, out of ten loudspeakers, thundered an unschooled girl's voice:

"Zoli, goddamn your guts!" It was only Whistling Zoli, our city's unique clown, who stopped the escalator by means of the emergency button about thirty feet downstairs from us. "Please hold on, the escalator will be moving in a moment."

On the street he was walking in our direction, slamming display windows with his rolled-up newspaper. He even followed us into the snack bar where he smacked all the counters, and loudly rattled the radiators so that everyone jumped in the place and then he was already on his way. Zoli has received considerable attention by now; like actors and novelists, he uses his own means to achieve some sort of recognition of his existence.

37 MEN: THE SOCIAL CONTRACT

After their one-sided conversation about the pyramid of humankind, Dajka takes leave of the surgeon Komora and retires to his office to draw up, as required by his special assignment, his recommendations for the prevention of the anticipated crime wave. He will submit these in the weeks to come, and he will receive the predictable responses. Those that need only a signature will be approved; those that need money, rejected.

It is recommended that special police outposts be established at the customs checkpoints around the city, at the train stations, shipping docks and at the Exhibition grounds. Approved. The Pest District Royal Court House jail should be moved from the County Hall because the four to five hundred inmates crowding it create an unnecessary risk of epidemics. For this the funds are not approved and the jailhouse remains as is. Eventually this will turn out to be in our favor.

All possible measures must be taken to fight the covert forms of prostitution, as part of the war against everyday crime; nor is this a mistake. Dajka is not laboring under illusions of superiority, or making a moral judgement; he is aware that prostitutes will continue to exist as long as there are people languishing in sexual starvation. But let the street-walker be identifiable as such, for then she may be governed by law. Covert prostitution presents the greater danger, for it passes for something else. A man who steals, burgles or embezzles does so for a reason, and this reason, in most cases, is a woman. Chief accountants, city and county officials, rich peasants, horse traders, young aristocrats, bankers' sons and thrifty petit bourgeois, and safe-crackers as well, are to the last man defenseless against the more camouflaged aspects of love for sale. In the nightspots of the metropolis they encounter the dream of a careless, playful sexuality: lady musicians, waitresses, hat-check girls to flirt with, women whose lives are surrounded by a luxurious, insouciant aura of perfume and the popping of champagne corks. And if you don't care to face the fact, you don't have to admit that your lady's charms are available for hire at anyone's behest. So at the Special Investigator's recommendation, a single stroke of the pen proscribes all waitresses and female personnel from Budapest nightspots, save for nightclub artistes and cashiers, and even these are prohibited from joining the guests.

The city's new police commissioner takes full credit for the ordinance, but Dr. Dajka is not the least bit perturbed. He knows very well that strokes of the pen cannot solve such problems; at each establishment there will be some sly old madam who will know how to wriggle her way around the law. Too many things will have to change for an ordinance of this kind to be more than a mere scrap of paper. And accompanying the next police raid, he notes whatever will need attending to. They start out early at the Kitty on Rose Square, before opening time; in the family-style groundfloor dance hall the waiters and musicians are all men, and only the old woman in the coatroom will be required to go.

For this evening all of the city's plainclothes detectives are

called on duty. Before the raid, when Chief Inspector
Axaméthy, a colleague in charge of nightclubs and brothels,
divides the men into groups, the Special Investigator makes
sure to keep in the background. His special assignment has
somewhat blurred the borderline between jurisdictions, and he
does not want to ruffle any feathers. His tactic pays off, for he
is assigned his own group, whereupon he proceeds in good
conscience to request Axaméthy for the district that includes
the Outer Kerepesi Road.

He arrives at Mrs. Tremmel's establishment early, around
ten o'clock, and only then does he realize that he is impatient.
Suddenly unable to resist the memory of a pair of eyes with
that certain Mongolian cut, he is eager to know how it goes
with this girl whom he had glimpsed Saturday night. He wants
to make sure she is there, safe and sound.

Bubbles, who happens to be the cleaning girl at this time at
Mrs. Tremmel's, witnesses the incident, and later she would
describe how the Special Investigator, who was well-known for
his even temper, and respected or feared by everyone,
depending on which side of the law they walked, had
completely lost control of his temper on this occasion.

Dr. Dajka's father had been a policeman on the beat who at
home by the kitchen table had often talked about the service.
Later the son would spend years in judicial work. He felt that
he had been prepared for anything. He knew what suffering,
misery, greed, violence, blood and death looked like. He
thought himself a simple man; he had been a practising lawyer
before being appointed to the bench, and after ten years he
was no longer able to accept the most universal credo of his
enlightened century, the belief in an unbroken line of human
progress. As a judge and as a Special Investigator his task was
the same as his father's had been all his life: to provide
protection for others, to help in the attainment of a more
humane existence, to ease the troubles that were bound to
come anyway. He had always endeavored to discharge his duty
with honor.

· But he had never seen a sight such as the face of this girl
forty-eight hours and thirty-seven men later, her almond-
shaped eyes reflecting the squalid horror she had been

through, modified by the solace of morphine.

He stops abruptly and stares for long seconds in silence at her delicately angled eyes. Behind him, in a traffic jam, the surgeon, the assistant inspector, detectives and policemen, and Madame Tremmel, who was showing the gentlemen around. The Special Investigator's eyes from one moment to the next narrow into dangerous slits, and Bubbles, who in her incurable curiosity is pretending to be busily sweeping the floor nearby, observes how his two hands clench into fists and turn white as they hang by his side. In the silence you can hear a fly buzzing. Bubbles thinks, whew, I would not like to be in the shoes of the person this man is mad at.

Sixty seconds, each weighing a ton, drag by. Dajka, having inspected the meticulously kept private books, is already familiar with the fact of the thirty-seven men; they appear neatly numbered under the girl's rubric. This is how many clients she had to satisfy Saturday and Sunday, night and day. In these two days she has aged considerably. After each weekend she would visibly age, the people who saw her said so, Bubbles would whisper in awe to the man who would help her to escape from this place.

From the way Bubbles narrates the story I would clearly understand why she was there at the time. It was only her third day as cleaning woman at the establishment. I nod my head, I can see why. It is her curiosity and thirst for adventure. She wanted to know what went on there, to experience the Life of Sin first hand. And for the fact that she does not get badly burned, she can thank the man who stands by her all the way, who cares for her and knows how to protect her. He was the first to visit Mrs. Tremmel's, as a guest. By chance he happened to end up in the room of the dark girl with those Mongolian eyes. He sat down by the side of her bed, smoked a slow-burning cigar and gave the girl ten forints. To Bubbles he said only, "I won't let you. Not even for one day." Her stubborn will at last found a way: she applied as a cleaning woman, showing up in the role of a naive village girl who had just arrived from the train station with her little bag and who sort of knew what kind of place this was, dazzled by lace and velvet, the music and the lights. A timid little soul, she even seemed slightly hesitant. The madame received her with kind smiles; these fresh arrivals always pay off well in the end. She would have hired the girl even if she had twenty cleaning maids at the place. Their numbers tend to melt away like ice cream as they are promoted. But Bubbles will tell her tale most convincingly after her one weekend's experience, after which she flees in panic, hoping she would never again have to go near Outer Kerepesi Road. She has had the inside view and knows the whore's life.

On Mondays sharp, deep, vertical creases would show, plowed into the face of the almond-eyed girl, purple-black hollows surrounded her eyes, and her expression reflected the acquiescence of a hundred-year-old Oriental sage. But her eyes led a separate, disquieting existence, with their unnaturally distended pupils.

After the passage of some seconds the madame stirs to speak.

"Your Excellency..." But the Special Investigator cuts her off with a single gesture.

"I am not Your Excellency." Then with a voice like a rifle crack. "Marton! A complete search. Go through the whole place. I want to know everything that goes on here. *Everything!*"

The plainclothesmen scatter throughout the two floors of the building, putting heart and soul into the search. The stunned, stuttering madame is ordered to stay in the doorman's cubicle by the entrance. A uniformed guard stands in front of the building, no one may pass. Dajka brushes aside the half-dressed clients who are spouting all kinds of lies and decides to interrogate three other girls, no need to torment the one with the Kuman eyes.*

Within a quarter of an hour the assistant inspector escorts a well-dressed, white-haired gentleman from the second floor. He leans on a walking stick with a silver fox-head for a knob. By his side Marton, without the least sign of respect for age,

---

*The Kuman were a nomad nation whose tribes settled in eastern Hungary in the 12th century. The region between the Danube and the Tisza is still called Kumania.

has a tight grip on the old man's fine English tweed lapels.

The group is completed by a skinny little girl whose face shows no emotion. Dajka asks the child how old she is.

"Twelve."

And that will do it.

He did not have to inquire too deeply to discover the basic story of the girl with the almond-shaped eyes. Such stories are always so depressingly similar. She calls herself Bora: her stage name. The day she rented a room by the month on the Grand Boulevard her fate was sealed: she was bound to end up in a place such as Mrs. Tremmel's house, in the shape in which the Special Investigator finds her. In consequence of this meeting she will find herself in the Red Salon of the Baroness Vad, where she will have a direct bearing on our affairs.

One year ago she was still paying a hundred forints a month for her room. Like most brothelkeepers, the landlady had a criminal record. According to the law, prostitutes could rent rooms only with a separate entrance. The same laws specify that no one needs to tolerate a prostitute as a neighbor; she may consequently be evicted on the basis of a single complaint. Dajka is aware of the relentless reality of numbers: six hundred such rooms are available in the city, and there are thousands of women competing for them. The rents reflect the conditions. Bora's hundred forints a month may be seen in the proper light if you understand that at the same time I was paying twenty kreuzers a day - six forints a month - for a similar room.

Each month Bora sends a money order to a certain Frau Bábi near Vienna, who is taking care of her two children. After a while the inevitable process typical of the profession sets in: the earnings begin to decrease in inverse proportion to age. Her first response was to give up the idea of putting something aside for her old age. One month she missed her rent payment; because of her daughter Natalie's illness, she had to send all her available money to pay the doctor in Austria. On the first of the month the landlady inspected her wardrobe, confiscated the two best suits for the amount owed and placed the steamer trunks plastered with Parisian and

Saint Petersburg stickers out in the corridor. She could not even afford to pay the one-forint fee for a health certificate required at the time of registering at a new address. She panicked, and rented a room by the day in the outer King Street district, just until she could redeem her suits from the landlady. With the loss of her clothes, she dropped instantly into a lower wage category, and her price kept plummeting. Now she had to pay seven forints a day for her room. She had to service more men. She aged faster. When her face with the fine network of crow's feet could no longer attract enough to earn the daily rent, the circle was complete. If she wanted to keep sending money to her children, and if she wanted to avoid the lowest depths of street prostitution and the attendant constant police harassment, her only hope was admission to one of the open houses of prostitution.

"And the little dear was making such good money!" squeals Mrs. Tremmel indignantly, flanked by two policemen. She is too dense to comprehend. "Among all my wards, she was earning the best money!"

Social conventions are a peculiar thing. (Maybe I have touched on this before.) For the thirty-seven-man weekend that was so clearly etched on the face of the woman called Bora, the Special Investigator could not have laid a finger on Mrs. Tremmel. All of that was perfectly within the laws regulating the life of our civilized European homeland. But the moment the intensified search came across the little girl who was two years younger than the arbitrarily legislated, if equally juvenile, age, the situation became radically different. The Doctor fired his orders in rapid succession.

The detectives call off the search. Mrs. Tremmel is handcuffed. The police reporters of the larger papers are notified, and if they have to be roused from their sleep, all the better. Tonight, as an exceptional gesture, the Special Investigator himself is going to serve up the sensational news. Make sure that those Socialist scribblers are on hand; they have been spewing all too many muckraking articles about the helplessness of the royal police in apprehending the perverters of minors.

He personally takes the journalists on a tour of the premises where the old man and the girl were found. Let them see the cozily furnished love nest with its silken lampshades, let the readers of the morning papers find out that the widow of Elias Tremmel, residing at No. 67 Outer Kerepesi Road, is nothing but a common procuress who enticed eleven- and twelve-year-old girls into the softly-padded viper's nest of her own apartment to serve them up to the whims of lecherous old men.

The old lecher is brought in and led away.

The little girl is taken to her home by Inspector Marton, who makes a point of frightening the mother.

Afterwards Dajka sees to it that the doors of Mrs. Tremmel's apartment and establishment are locked and sealed.

You cannot take in a stray cat out of the rain without facing certain consequences. From this moment on Special Investigator Dajka is permanently untangled in Bora's chaotic life. However, he thinks he may have the possibility of a solution: the Café Kitty on Rose Square.

He stops in the midst of the crowd of onlookers assembled in the dawn and asks the girl with the almond-shaped eyes,

"What is your name?"

"Bora...Clarendon... That is, my real name is Veron... Veronica Czérna."

"What can you do?" And he is not inquiring about the tricks of a *fille de joie*.

"I'm...I'm...I'm a singer," stammers Veronica Czérna, alias Bora Clarendon. "I can sing."

A MATERIALISTIC ENTERPRISE

Two days later Bubbles turns up at the service entrance of the Kitty. She asks directly for the Hunchback who, by taking personal responsibility for the girl, is able to persuade the Baroness to hire her in the capacity of bread-girl.

It is pure blind chance that takes me there a few days afterwards. And it will be the memory of a beef *pörkölt* * with

---

*"Dry-stewed" diced meat in a thick gravy.

red wine that eventually recalls the name of the place as the rendezvous I give to the safe-crackers at the Porta Marittima in Zara.

Not only the police were making preparations for the Summer Festivities.

In far-off Amsterdam the most outstanding young master of the art of diamond-cutting studies the Stone in his well-lit workshop. Today he will decide the fate of nature's gift in the rough. His heart rejoices at the sight of this perfect gem that is flawless in the clarity of its water: it is not feathery, cloudy or sandy and it has no foreign particles whatsoever. Because of the shape of the rough stone he has decided to cut it as a rose, with an elliptical cross section so that all of its facets will be triangular. Using an industrial diamond he has already notched it in the desired shape, and now takes up his hammer and chisel. His efforts are well rewarded: Blue Blood proves every bit deserving of its name and cleaves perfectly along its octahedral planes - and at this moment its brilliance grows manifold.

And now follows the meticulous, time-consuming labor of shaping and cutting by means of another diamond - this most noble carbon can be shaped only by itself. And then at last the polishing, which might take up to six months to accomplish, using diamond dust.

A week went by; I wanted to give the safe-crackers enough time to track me down through their own clandestine channels.

At the Kitty, I could tell at a glance that they still had not been able to figure out why on earth I had warned them in the first place.

I want to get this initial conference over as fast as possible in order to proceed to action, I am aware that our time is limited. The date of our appearance in the footlights is still far off; there are still nine months left before the sale of the great diamond, but until then I intend to hide our tracks in a curtain of mist, disappear for a while and cut all of the domestic threads that could eventually be traced back to us. I am already sensing the outlines of a vague plan, a way of disappearing and utilizing the intervening months. It has been a long time since I lived in a tent or traveled in a covered wagon or slept by a campfire or heard the inebriating applause of the ladies and gentlemen of the audience as I took my bows as a fire-eater with the taste of kerosene in my mouth. It is the kind of inebriation that always pulls you back for more. If I could put together a carnival troupe and go on a foreign tour, just barely past the borders, there would be enough time... But there is a lot of work to be done before then. I head off the elegant but time-consuming exploratory skirmishes of mutual mistrust and plunge straight into the midst of things without waiting for them to reconnoitre me. I had given them advance notice that we would speak Greek, in case someone were to overhear us. It is a trick I lifted directly from them. So I say, you gentlemen wish to know if I am an *agent provocateur* working for the police, or merely a gentleman crook governed by materialistic considerations. What I need are money and the leisure to enjoy it. I decided to obtain these with your help when I overheard the two of you conversing in Hungarian on the Dalmatian coast. What I have in mind is a suitably ambitious collaborative enterprise, a single coup after which all of us could retire in peace. The place and time are here, next summer. I happen to know of a certain worthwhile target; the details still need to be researched. I have to rely on you gentlemen for instruction in the rudiments of professional expertise. If we can have an understanding, well and good. If not, that's fine too. We'll take leave of each other and that will be that.

That said, I wait. Jankó is a master of his trade. He knows full well the weakness of the gang, but has not been able to overcome it until now. The missing link has been the mastermind to plan their operations.

He decides to follow his instincts and offers me his hand in a slow, firm gesture, a slender but strong engineer's hand. The Greek goes along with him; they are used to working together.

All right, I say, let's begin then. What happened in Zara? How could it happen that there was no lookout? How did they operate until now, and what will have to be done differently?

In the course of our conversation I happen to look up at the glass cage under the ceiling, its window facing the dining room covered by a thick curtain from the inside. That is all I am able to see, but on the basis of subsequent events one may calculate with precision that the Baroness must have been standing in front of the credenza that locks with her key, smoking a slim black Havana cigar and reading aloud for the benefit of the doorman, who is standing by the desk:

"...*une interessante, jeune spirituelle Parisienne désire protection d'un monsieur sérieux, très distingué, chiffre Musette...* Do you understand that?" Here she looks up into the deep eyes of the doorman. "Like hell you do, dummy. A Parisian girl is seeking the protection of a serious gentleman, code word Musette. Here." She sighs. "I am afraid, *ma petite*, that you will be willing to settle for less. But as long as you have decided to take the fatal step..." And she snaps at the doorman, "What are you waiting for? You're staring at me." But her voice lacks that edge of anger and severity; barely perceptibly her green eyes are misting over. The doorman makes his move, hulking toward his mistress.

If the proprietress were not otherwise occupied, and would peek out from behind the two wings of her curtain as is her wont, she still would not see anything worth noting. Three men dining at a table by the window would be nothing out of the ordinary. Almost all the tables are taken, business is good, imagine how well the place will be doing next year!

On the ground floor I am the one who asks the questions. I am disturbed by a certain amateurish touch. It is a holy miracle that they were not caught. For the time being I want to find out about safe-cracking, everything that can be told in words, down to the smallest detail, like a curious child. How do they choose a target? How do they prepare for their move? How does the operation itself take place? I intentionally hold back questions about their personal histories, they will tell me all about themselves soon enough. It feels good to come clean from time to time about matters that must always be kept secret. They sketch the outlines of their activities for me.

Jankó has never been caught here at home. During the first years of his career the nascent sensationalist press created the figure of the mysterious Safe King who comes and goes without leaving a trace, taking his booty through walls of safes and strongrooms. No one has ever seen him, no one knows what he looks like, his nationality, his creed or breed. Only force of habit made the presshounds assume that he was a man. He made sensational news - and always incognito. Well, that was the nature of the game. Little by little, though, the police began to catch up with him. So one fine day when they got too close for comfort, and the publicity became too heavy, he left the capital and the lady cashier of a King Street café, without any goodbyes. He had already made sure to leave behind a base of operations in the capital; his cheerful, patriotic optimism foresaw a great future upswing in safe-cracking in his homeland. He left a supply of cash with the fence Láncz on Bush Street in Old Buda. He stopped by at the flowergirl Karola Gombocz' place in Buda. (The lady cashier had not been aware of a rival's existence.) Here he deposited a complete set of burglar's tools, and having done so, departed for the South. By Zimony below Nándorfehérvár (Belgrade to you), where the Sava flows into the Danube, he managed to give the slip to his pursuers, and one week later he turned up in Istanbul, where he set up temporary headquarters. In the dark depths of the Bazaar he purchased a Turkish passport in the name of Hajji Daoud, which was his identity when the local police arrested him a few months later. That he was no Hajji became apparent after the first words but he never let out his real name and nationality. He spoke only German. He had it all planned far in advance; he simply wanted to allow the personage of the notorious Safe King to sink into the murky waters of oblivion. He stuck by his plan throughout his imprisonment. At this point in his story I had a feeling that here was a man you could count on if you had a long-range enterprise in mind, and a new methodology for the great coup. A man of foresight and perseverance, made of the rare stuff that giants are carved from. In a word, a king. He had one terrible but understandable weakness: women, and this would return to haunt us. He sat in jail for two years while the

Austro-Hungarian police could keep track only of his disappearance. He was released, but after six months the risks of
his profession caught up with him again; he was the guest of
the Romanian police in the Regat for the autumn, as a
Prussian prisoner, according to his plan. He had a gift for
languages. His cellmate was Socrates Andronicos, a Greek
merchant born in Rhodos who had opted to supplement the
slow profits in carpets with an income from tobacco smuggling.
He spoke French. Now the King thanked his lucky stars for
the French mamzelle imported by his father, who had been an
assessor to the orphans' court in Pest, and who did all he
could to provide the finest education for the future success of
the bright son who possessed such outstanding mechanical
skills. Soon a warm friendship grew between him and the
Greek, and they began to make plans for working together
after their release. In the meantime, while there were no safes
to crack, he gave Hungarian lessons to Socrates, who in turn
taught him Greek. They did their time and were released early
because of good behavior, whereupon they headed straight for
Hungary. He picked up some of the cash left with Láncz the
fence and spent a few lovely days with Karola Gombocz,
incidentally helping her to open up a second-hand clothing
shop that would thrive in the fertile humus of the slums near
Cemetery Road, from where the girl would eventually emerge
into public light. He grabbed his tools, and having left behind
a small box of gold Napoleons for an emergency supply, he
moved on. It won't hurt to have piles of all kinds of
second-hand clothes around the house. He warned the woman
not to expect him, security was first and foremost now; they
must sever all contact. She accepted it all without a word; she
was grateful and docile. That is the only kind of woman for a
burglar, though the King was not aware of this. The time for
the Idol and New World Street break-ins had arrived.

Márton Jankó took a room with the family of the
watchmaker Lápos. Some day they would describe how
liberally their lodger spent his money left and right, always
coming home in the wee hours, and frequently boasting of box
seats at the opera. There was no shortage of money.
Meanwhile Socrates stayed at a small hotel on Bath Street and

amused himself in the company of dancing girls. The only reason he did not keep a permanent hansom cab, like bankers and journalists, was that the King disallowed this as too conspicuous. Women, champagne, caviare, flashy chariots - this is what burglaries, and somewhat further afield, hijackings, the taking of hostages are all about, no? Back then they had set out from Budapest to conquer the continent. On their first outing they came across Haluska, an ex-bricklayer who would be their lookout; he had golden hands that could take walls apart much faster than they were built. He made an excellent lookout. They traveled frequently; sometimes the loot was plentiful, sometimes not. Professional vanity always directed the King toward the latest, most up-to-date models of safes; he was an aficionado of metals who loved his work. After a while there was no steel safe he could not open in less than an hour. They were well on the way toward speeding up the redistribution of the continent's wealth.

By now the King has warmed up, setting out on a colorful and informative improvised lecture on the major brands of steel safes, their locks and walls. I keep thinking, if only the city's police chief could hear this. I am not yet aware of Dr. Dajka's special assignment that places us under his jurisdiction. The King is fascinated by the latest Wiese-Wertheim safe with its inch-thick walls and hidden lock mechanisms. At Zara it took them by surprise; the old model across the room was a familiar acquaintance. He was delighted by this new challenge and became entangled in the pleasures of unexpected difficulties. So they had to call in Haluska from outside, and that was how they forgot about the time and the night watchman. He knew he would come across this new safe again; he had never before left a safe locked that he had started to pry open. We cannot know what was in that Zara safe.

Over the semolina pudding and noodles with sour cream and cottage cheese we evaluate the procedures. I can promise him that we shall certainly come up against the new safe. It will be in all the better places, and will mark the royal prey; our loot will be in it. But we need to plan out and research our great coup. This is our main task for the time being. We cannot waste our time on taking down walls - too slow and too messy. We shall get inside using our brains. The lock is concealed on the smooth face of the new safes, probably in a different location on each one, presenting a greater difficulty than a double-tempered steel wall. I suggest that maybe we should first rattle it a bit with a Chicago-style explosion. Then we could surely see where the lock was hidden. I am counting on a single coup; the chances of being caught increase on multiple exposure. We are going to need a new set of tools.

Before we leave the café I look around unobtrusively, taking note of the glass cage under the ceiling; it is an individual touch. From several tiny, barely perceptible signs I conclude there is more here than meets the eye. I keep my observations to myself.

I conclude by saying that we need some capital to start out.

We'll have it, nods the Safe King, and here I am about to make my second mistake in this enterprise. Even one would have been enough to sow the seed of our downfall.

In the late night hours of the same day I sit back dead tired, contemplating the final four sheets of paper with the drawings for the new tools we need to have made to order: the steel jimmy, the fox-jawed pliers, the rotary drill, the crowbar. A midnight train had brought Haluska from the direction of the Banat, in the south. The mistake was to hold the planning session in the drawing room of Rókus Láncz' house on Bush Street. The drawings were created by my asking repeated questions, uncertain, feeling my way, and the King giving the answers. I had some previous experience in metal-working and was able to appreciate fully his extraordinary engineering talents. He had the ability to transpose the most fleeting thought, hesitant wish and haziest of goals into steel the way a composer jots down the score of a melody heard in the innermost ear. We kept sketching and re-sketching all through the night. All the while he told stories of his stormier years. The unused drawings were immediately burned in a small iron stove. We worked on, as if we had known each other for ever. The Greek and Haluska kept going outside to keep an eye on the street. In the end the King said to Láncz, "Well now, old thief, take out that wallet, we'll be needing what's inside it."

The cellar was under the back part of this old peasant house that was farthest away from the street. A passerby would have concluded that the wavering light in the backyard was occasioned by a sanitary outing. On the way I note that the stable is chock-full of dark-green, thick military horseblankets heaped in piles. From under a stack of wood out came the pigskin suitcase and the stuffed morocco leather wallet. The Safe King holds it in his hand, weighing it, then he reaches in, takes out a bundle of banknotes about a finger's thickness and gives it to me, uncounted. Once he trusts somebody he trusts him completely. He gives me his gold cigar case to use; it is a purchased item, not hot. Three days later he only smiles at the Greek's anxiety when they still have not heard from me.

By then I have plunged into the burgeoning nightlife of the city. Taking my well-stuffed wallet I frequent the *cafés chantants*, clubs, hotels, gambling dens and casinos.

THE MORAL CODE

The Special Investigator's day is off to a chaotic start. A report came in from Old Buda that a caravan of Gypsies, forty strong, has been partying at Arpád Unger's tavern. It was the tribe of the Voivode, or Chieftain, Shashtarash from Transylvania, with eight wagons, which stopped in on the way back from the fair at Ujlak. Around noon, the report went on, the city police captain sent out two patrolmen to drive out the Gypsies past the city limits. Oh no, for heaven's sakes! exclaims Dajka. He immediately mobilizes all available men and has the horses prepared. In half an hour a thirty-man flying squad aboard wagons with bells clanging is racing toward Old Buda. Where, in the meantime, what the Special Investigator had feared, has happened: the tribe's *maiulo*, (voivode) called Bershehero (Shepherd in the Romany tongue), did in fact lose control over his men. The Gypsies, having been disturbed in their noisy but harmless revelry, had grabbed clubs and staves to fight off the officers of the law.

Soon they pushed the two policemen back out on the street where patrolman Török panicked and fired his sidearm. It was his great good luck that he was a terrible shot, quite unsuitable for the force, but this actually saved his life. He and his partner were not torn to pieces on the spot. The Special Investigator, on hearing the shot as he rounded the corner of Willowdale Street, gives the order: port arms, shoot only above their heads, charge. He leads a frontal attack at the head of his men. Further bloodshed is thus prevented and nine Gypsies are arrested. In the confusion one fourteen-year-old Gypsy lad named Ferke (called Kodel, in his Romany tongue) makes his getaway together with his sweetheart Murikeo, the Pearl.

Dajka knows nothing about the pair, and he drops the affair, having restored law and order. He hands over the prisoners for interrogation and orders his lunch brought to his office.

At last he finds time in the afternoon to go for Veron Czérna, alias Bora Clarendon, to the pension where he had deposited her like so much luggage for the few days until he could find time for her. He calls for a cab and has a patrolman take down her steamer trunk with all the labels on it. He pays for the room and for the cab out of his own pocket. This is how rumors will start circulating at headquarters. He tells the cabdriver to proceed to the Silly Kitty at the corner of Rose Square and Leopold Street.

Accompanied by Bora - let's call her by the name she preferred - he enters the café by the door under the sign of the pointing index finger. The Baroness is sitting in her glass cage from where, through an opening in the velvet curtains, she can check on the waiters arranging the hall for the evening dance. When she glimpses Dr. Dajka, her instinctive panic lasts only a moment, and she hurries to meet him with a broad smile.

"Are you able to provide work and a room for this girl?" the police officer asks. "She's a singer."

For a fraction of a second the Baroness suspects a trap.

After a moment's hesitation she raises her head. "You have never before asked a favor of me. From this moment consider the girl to be under my personal protection."

From now on the Baroness will have a certain nagging sense that something is amiss. Nonetheless she at once takes Bora under wing, and the girl is assured of as much security as any penniless person may hope for in the night life of the capital.

In this wilderness, the Baroness is a strange phenomenon. In running her business she blends a sober evaluation of the market with theories of social progress, as if she were trying to carry out the ideals of a Schultze-Delitsch cooperative within the medium of the restaurant and nightclub. Her hostesses are more or less partners who receive their shares of the profits. The employees are on salary. As a matter of fact Dajka for some time has known more about the Baroness than she would have suspected, and he is willing to overlook certain matters. Every day and every night he is in contact with the seamier side of life and time has taught him much. This woman, too, is basing her calculations on human nature; her clientele come from that portion of the male population of the capital which boasts of an impeccable reputation by day. And if she contrives to make the almond-eyed girl's life somewhat more bearable, as she does for the victims of the flesh-market, then this will be dear to the eyes of her Lord and Maker. So Dajka considers Agnes Vad to be a part of those new forces that are at work to bring the fresh breeze of a more humane future into the Budapest night, here on the corner of Leopold Street.

"I wish we had more like her," he had said to the silent girl in the cab on the way over, and he smiled as he tried to imagine what His Excellency the Minister of Justice would have thought.

He takes his leave of Bora in a corner booth of the café, the same one where earlier in the day I and my new business partners had discussed our professional future.

"Don't ever touch morphine again," he tells her gently but firmly, in lieu of saying goodbye. "Because then I will have nothing more to do with you."

This is when Bora realizes that her guilt and deepest secret are written plainly over her face. It is with considerable fright that she stares after the man on his way to the exit.

The hunchbacked doorman with the broad shoulders bows deeply as he lets out the officer of the law. "We hope to see you again, sir."

Dajka stops for a moment. He looks the man over; he had not seen him here before. Was that a trace of mockery in his voice? The Hunchback looks him straight in the eye and dispels any doubts. The experienced lawman's eye takes note of the face and figure and files it among thousands of other miniscule memorabilia.

French champagne cascades from a little ballroom shoe down the gentleman's chin, past his bowtie. The cards are being dealt and in the background the throaty laughter of the tough girls hits raucus notes. Enterprises are set in motion and bloom, trusteeships in bankruptcy are awarded and forfeit moneys are paid. The stock exchange is played to the hilt. After a dazed dream comes the morning of cold, smoke-bitter awakening and the news of unexpected audits. And at noontime, revolver shots ring out as the gray matter of petty clerks and wealthy dealers and brokers splashes over the linen and silk pillowcases. The city lives and dies.

The morning I take my leave of the safe-crackers I direct my steps to Landerer's tiny basement printing shop, to order one hundred visiting cards on cream-colored stock. The cards will carry the name I am using at the time, as well as the schematic design of a neat little coat of arms that I sketched out for the engraver in a moment of inspiration: in one half of the divided field five diagonal bars, in the other half, a man leaning on a drawn sword. I will have about as much right to this device as to my name. From there I proceed to Kamarás, "Tailor for Gentlemen" on Seminary Street, where I am measured for one pure wool overcoat, two suits, a jacket, tails and a tuxedo, with a surcharge for rush delivery. I take my lunch at Pompl's inn and use the remaining time to purchase a few small but indispensable items: cigars in a cedar box, winged collars, various trifles.

In the afternoon my calling cards are ready; the clothes are delivered the next day.

And the day after, I plunge into the nightlife rife with the sound of crisp banknotes. I walk the city night, just like the Special Investigator. And just as he does, I take an ardent interest in the stews, in the dens of vice, in all the frailties of my fellow citizens. And I see the same things. Humans live for and off each other, as do the Nilotic crocodile and the tiny watchful plover that picks out the leftover food particles from the open jaws of the monster, whom it also relieves from the leeches feeding on its gums.

Within a few days I visit, on King Street, the Black Cat, the Blue Cat and the Spotted Cat (where once upon a time the King's girlfriend had sat on the throne by the cash register). I try every nightclub and clandestine gambling den; I sit down to play, win some but mostly lose. At a gaming house on Prophet Street a girl with a cigarette holder points out to me the Special Investigator who arrives incognito, accompanied by a dozen gentlemen wearing derbies who are all looking rather discomfited in civilian garb. My retreat takes the form of a stylish departure that no one notices. For the time being let our acquaintance remain one-sided; I will do all in my power to keep it that way. I make sure that no one is following me - at this point no one should have any reason for doing so. The hackney cab takes me toward other dives. I engage doormen and porters in conversation, and indulge in short whispered exchanges with certain shady customers and giggling girls. A discreet banknote or fine cigar always has its effect, and little by little I begin to find my way in this closed world. My eyes are always scanning the room and I play without concentration. Most of the time I rise from the table early and move on.

One night as I step out of the cab in front of the brilliantly lit hotel entrance, I feel in my pocket the wallet stuffed so generously by Jankó the King: neither gambling, nor the cost of my sleek, brand-new top to toe black elegance has put a perceptible dent in its impressive bulk. The metropolitan night's debauched pleasures flood me; the city is at my feet, waiting to be possessed.

Fashionably dressed gentlemen come and go in droves; aromatic Havana-smoke rises in the night air, and inside, the orchestra plays a popular Viennese waltz.

I do not go in at once. Lingering outside I offer a cigar from my gold case to the liveried doorman. Go ahead, my friend, don't be afraid to take one, put it away for later. We chat for a while.

A little later my doorman nods imperceptibly in the direction of a wiry man who has stepped out of the playing casino for a breath of fresh air and to dab his bald head with a handkerchief.

Inside I approach the Maitre d' and fifteen minutes later I am seated at the gaming table facing the bald man, and losing in a big way. I am playing in a progressively wilder and wilder fashion, completely irresponsibly, in fact. I am impassioned, wealthy and foolhardy. I place my new, gold cigar case on the table. My opponent's eyes light up as if he had seen the promise of a new life just when he was about to abandon all hope. And indeed, that is exactly what is about to happen, although not in the way he would have imagined it.

Toward dawn I do what I have to, and ask for pen and ink. I place one of my cards on the table and dip the steel pen in the ink, and write on the back of the card: 100, that is, one hundred forints. I blot it, and it is all set. I make a mental note to get this little piece of paper back. I spread my arms.

"I am terribly sorry, but that was all the money I had on me. Where may I send what I owe you this morning?"

The card I receive in exchange reads: Gottfréd Abraham, Mech. Engineer. The address is that of the Michaelson Steel Foundry and Machine Works plant on Váci Road. And all the while I have several thousand in fresh banknotes in my pocket.

I spend the morning at the steam baths and have the fatigue soaked and massaged out of my muscles. I catch a few winks in the barber's chair while I am being shaved, then I am driven back to my lodgings. There I burn ninety-nine calling cards in the fireplace, change my clothes, and after an ample brunch at Nicoletti's Café I am able to show up at the Michaelson Foundry in the Angel-land district with an appearance that at one glance promises major orders. I ask to see the chief engineer as the noon bells are ringing.

I hand over the hundred forints; we are alone in the office. He returns my card. I take out matches, light one corner and carefully turning the card burn it over the ashtray. The engineer watches attentively. I open the window, throw out the ashes, and even as I watch them scatter in the wind over the empty lots, I casually remark:

"I have a business proposition for you, sir. I believe it will interest you. My cab is waiting outside."

The hook is set; I feel an electric charge in the air.

"To Prugmayer's beerhall," I instruct the driver.

"Yessir, on Andrássy Avenue."

Andrássy, of all things! I pretend to be outraged, for the engineer's benefit. It used to be Radius Avenue, and for me, it will remain Radius Avenue forever. A street ought to have one name in a lifetime. To think of the cheek of those bureaucrats. They dare to pull the names of *ministers* over the city's fingers, until finally there won't be any natural names left. (This sort of thing has a certain timetable. First comes the populace - the people. Workers, citizens, taxpayers, natives. In a word - us. A road that runs radially from the center toward the outskirts is naturally called Radius Avenue. With a capital letter; this is the first, and true name. Hatvani Road leads to the Hatvan Gate; Váci Street goes to the Vác Gate.

And then there are those who believe that if they have the machine guns on their side they can do anything. Along comes some bureaucrat and Radius Avenue receives the name of the prime minister. At first Palatine Street lost its name only on the section from the House of Parliament to the Grand Boulevard, and the rest went later. A Streetnames Sub-committee is formed to revise its own ordinances. Globe Street in the Angel-land district was renamed after the head of some department. Little Globe Street, no doubt, will be renamed for his deputy chief. They do not seem to realize that a name must be natural and easy to pronounce. It is part of the popular tongue, it belongs to the people, to workers, citizens, taxpayers, natives. But the bureaucrats will never learn; any day now they will pre-empt Lehel Street or Váci Street, once they feel like naming streets after themselves. Just wait and see.)

I have lunch with the engineer. We chat and I feel him out, to make sure. I have found our man. He is a rather unworthy *landsman* of the factory-founder Abraham Ganz. This Hungarian gentleman from Switzerland happens to possess his own well-equipped gunsmith shop at home in the converted stables of his summer villa on Stefania Road, with its own diminutive foundry and lathe. For gullible collectors he fabricates authentic sabers and dirks of all periods, which are then rapidly aged by being buried for a few weeks, to be eventually marketed by shady dealers in antiques. They are splendid specimens. He happens to be under exasperating financial pressures. He is a master craftsman; his sabers cut and the muskets actually shoot. All this I had found out before; this is what made him worthy of our attention.

I flash the well-stuffed wallet at him, to see the eager hopes arise in his eyes over the steam of Turkish coffee following our lunch. Within the wallet I separate the banknotes into a smaller and a larger bundle, and discreetly let him see them all.

That night on Bush Street I lay out the four final drawings in front of him. Rókus Láncz looks with obvious relief at the wallet and me, as if he had given up ever seeing us again. His single-storey house with its tiny windows is one of the few places in the rapidly growing city where outlaws on the lam may find shelter, food and clothes.

The engineer accepts our offer, which seems to be tailored just for him. The smaller bundle of notes finds its way into his pocket, and then the drawings undergo one last transformation. Abraham questions the King, he expostulates and argues, and eventually modifies the drawings with a few expert strokes. The fence listens with horror and disbelief as I discuss the intended purpose of these tools with an outsider.

My associates will have the opportunity to place their blind faith in me for another three weeks.

For whole evenings I have the King tell tales of the good old days when he was circulating in Viennese society. These are trial drillings into the deepest layers of his memory. He had dropped a casual remark in the course of the hours spent designing our tools. Somewhere in his head resides the information that could now resolve one of the last imponderables in our enterprise.

On the third day I hit paydirt. He is fondly reminiscing about one night with a certain gentle blonde lady when his lips pronounce the two magic words: jeweler and Millennium. In the course of his amorous adventures and the ensuing bedside smalltalk he had managed to amass a wealth of information about the clientele and business practices of the major jewelers of our city, whose trade is so closely linked with the imperial capital. I keep at him with a bulldog tenacity until I am so exhausted I can barely see. He senses my drift and cooperates willingly. The findings: information about those particular transactions for which the merchandise is secretly imported directly from London or Paris, so that the collections may be shown to the client. The King is able to recall the name of the firm, a conservative and by no means flashy one, that happened to be among the most fashionable in this field where rank is measured out in carats. I imagine that the stone, before being shown, will be kept in the latest model double-walled Wiese-Wertheim steel safe. A transaction of this magnitude could dwarf an entire year's volume for even the largest jeweler. For the Millennial summer Budapest will entertain a convocation of the Dual Monarchy's highest aristocracies of blue blood and finance, and great purchases will be made. The guests of the National Casino, I am well aware, will occupy the front ranks, and among them the foremost will be those members of the ruling House of Habsburg who will be residing in their own recently built palace. These individuals will be identifiable, and eventually the date of the delivery may be pinpointed.

Three weeks later the engineer Abraham arrives with tools that are masterworks of the finest Chicago quality.

In the cellar the lantern's light reflects with a dull gleam on the head of the finely worked steel jimmy. I watch Jankó's face: a deep involuntary sigh, a lover's sigh, escapes his lips. He picks it up with reverence, lifting, testing its weight and balance, how it feels in his hand. He even licks a finger and draws it along the edges, before he nods in approval. I am more interested in the man's mystique than in the tools. The King fondles the tools of his profession as passionately as the most fulfilled artist handles his brushes.

The ritual is repeated eight times. After the King nods for the last time I hand over the thicker wad of notes to the engineer, who then hands over the yellow pigskin shoulder-strapped *étui* in which he carried the set. This is the lagniappe.

"Well?" asks the gentleman burglar, nodding in the direction of the departing man.

"Don't worry. I'll take care of him," I reply. The meaning is obvious: the engineer knows too much. And noiselessly I slip out into the dark night in Abraham's wake.

I am not thinking about doing away with him; you should know that. Murder, around this time, is resorted to only by political anarchists; no decent safe-cracker would sink so low. The world will have to become a much drearier place for that to happen.

I catch up with the engineer on Vienna Road. I hand over the full wallet itself, and remind him that it is for safekeeping only.

The man knows what's best for him. After we part, he hurries home and tiptoes across the hall so as not to wake up the little woman and the two children. Here our reconnaissance proved somewhat spotty; we had not known about the family. (But it would not have made any difference.) He packs underwear and clothes in a suitcase, writes a farewell letter to the wife, puts money in it. He takes a cab to the villa on Stefania Road; he had already cleaned out the workshop. He makes sure to pay all of his gambling debts; he leaves separately addressed envelopes with the casino's porter, for he is careful about his reputation. He leaves a huge tip and Peter, the porter, even in his retirement, generations later, and after upheavals that turn the whole country upside down will still reminisce about him: this is how a real, "peacetime" Hungarian gentleman acted at the hour of his death.

In the dark before dawn Abraham takes a cab to the factory. There no one knows about his night life, his debts or his home workshop. The watchman lifts his hat in greeting; the office buildings are still empty at this hour. He uses his own keys to open the gate, the doors and the safe of the executive offices, as befits the factory's guiding soul and de facto manager. Ten minutes later he lets himself out and locks up after himself. At dawn he leaves behind his coat and wallet as well as the keys to the safe neatly placed by the handrail of the Chain Bridge, along with a shred torn from his trousers caught on an outer bolt. He puts on the clothes from his suitcase. At the factory office none of the clerks find anything amiss when they arrive at eight-thirty. The chief arrives around noon and takes fifteen minutes over his usual pre-lunch cigar before he reaches into the safe for a pile of papers. He retracts his hand in horror as it touches something silky and soft. His fright foreshadows trouble. Instead of papers and cash, he has touched the chief engineer's silk shirt awaiting discovery.

Dr. Dajka receives the news through the usual channels. In her first panic the lady typist reported a burglary, which would have been the Special Investigator's province. It soon becomes evident, however, that there is no sign of forced entry. A while later the report of the Chain Bridge patrol arrives about the suicide whose personal papers were found. After a few days' investigation light is shed on the seamy underside of the chief engineer's life: women, cards, gambling casinos, and the payment of all debts on the dawn of the suicide. The picture is clear. Too clear. Had they not accepted it so easily, it would have become apparent that our man paid up, but only hours later did he turn up at the office safe. The investigators talk to the wife, the teary-eyed mother of two. Her sorrow is genuine, she had loved her deceased Swiss-born husband; he was a colorful, well-mannered, refined man, a gentleman to his last breath, who knew his duty and killed himself. So the affair is forgotten; no one can touch the widow's property, she can even draw on Michaelson's handsome pension plan, according to English law. The family name remains unblemished. For the moral code is merciless. Had Abraham chosen to flee to America, all would have been different. In this case the engineer outwitted the social consensus that would have indirectly condemned him to death. But he could not spare his family the grief; that much of the drama had to be authentic.

Mrs. Abraham and the two children move back home to the family estate at Zenta. She tells no one about the money, and the King's banknotes pass all scrutiny, I have checked them over myself. The police conclude that the affair has nothing to do with the safe-breaks; it is simply a case of misappropriation of funds coupled with suicide, like so many others. The case is closed. By then Abraham, under a carefully chosen identity, and in possession of an expensive fake passport, is aboard a ship to America, where he arrives three weeks later.

(NOW: UP, DOWN, STRANGE, CHARM. STONE DEAF ANGEL. GOAT TITS)

When I got this far a moment ago I heard a tenor clangor and a gentle crack: a car crash six floors below, at an intersection of the former Valero Street. It was raining, and rush hour traffic was getting into high gear. The sudden silence down there was replaced by the noise of the gathering crowd. Just about every day there is a car crash at this blind intersection. At such times I think of the bureaucrat whose sole job is to prevent accidents here, whose speciality this is. The rain-saturated atmosphere transmitted each creak of the supermarket door with a startling immediacy into my room.

I could hear sounds of the water squished on the asphalt by tire treads of cars and buses in the traffic that was starting up again.

Auntie Pálma called to me from the kitchenette. "Imre dear, what do you think? Should I put the child's food on the range to warm up?" Imre: I have gotten used to my name. I said to her that maybe it should be heated only when you are home. And the countess agreed with me. She always does; she is an angel. A seventy-year-old, stone deaf angel with a fractured femoral neck. *Bone*?

I was waiting for you to come home.

In the course of the months of work everywhere: on the bus, before going to sleep, I have given a tremendous amount of thought to the question you asked on the escalator: *How* did it happen? Everything. How did it all happen? There is no simple answer.

Let the story be a roomy, breezy hall, where one will be able to live, walk around and inspect everything.

Particles of matter take shape, move around. According to our current state of knowledge the smallest among them is the quark, which is, as they say, the building block of the world. It was discovered in the Second Great International Year of Physics. Six different varieties are known.

Up, Down, Strange, Charm, Bottom or *Beauty*, and *Top* or *Truth*. They remind me of the seven dwarfs, sans Sneezy. A meson, for example, is made up of two of them, a baryon, of three. (According to current hypotheses.) And just as no one has ever seen an atom, no one has ever seen a quark, a meson or a baryon, either. In this they resemble the Almighty of the three monotheistic religions. Unless, indeed, they are It.

If only we were able to answer the questions about these particles, in a *precise and humanly understandable manner:*

- When?
- Where?
- How?
- What is it that moves? - then we would be able to give an account, with unwavering fidelity, of everything that happened.

We are almost able to say something about the direction of their movement. According to the Second Law of Thermo-dynamics, the probability of a decrease of entropy in a closed system is zero. In other words everything is inevitably heading toward the all-consuming uniformity of a deep freeze when/where each cubic kilometer of space would contain a single atom of gas.

We are almost able to say something. Almost.

Very well then, we narrate. We have no other means but language, language that we have been creating in our own image ever since Great Grandfather's days, language that is flexible, language that adheres. One sound follows another, one word, sentence, paragraph after another - that is how it has an Up, a Down, a Charm and only this way can it have a Top. However, the moment we relate something strung out in a yarn, in a linear fashion, we are already endowing the cosmos (that had existed before humankind, and will continue to exist after us) with our own qualities, as if it had a beginning, middle and end. We pretend that existence is one well-ordered story, where the bad guys are made to stay after school and the good kids are promoted into the next grade. Or if you prefer the darker version: the well-poisoners rule the world, true patriots always bite the dust, the armies plough through the adolescent girls, and the pure in soul are choked to death by the stench of the latrines. A is followed by B, aleph by beth, one by two. But the world is not like that.

Let us use language, by all means. But we must realize at the same time that what we produce this way is only the outer shell of the story; it is a trick that has been available to us ever since that first black grandfather's world-shaking discovery: *drrr-brrr, lalallall*. Painters and sculptors are able to command one or two additional dimensions, which places them that much closer to nature. The musician makes music, like a bird, and comes closer still. But even they do not think that enough.

Let's see now. The structure of that great hall is outlined, sketched out in the murkiness of one-dimensional time by the pure lines of light beams in which dust motes dance. I know what I intend to relate. I have an inkling of what will be in the story and what will be omitted, and by the time I tell it, I will know exactly. Its task will be to help us understand what forces, as held in what kind of balance, sway the scales of our existence.

But plenty of the craftsman's problems remain.

Right away, the question of the beginning: to announce boldly how far ahead we are to reach. An ideal solution occurs here.

At last you came home. You did not get soaked, you had raised the hood of your North African jellaba. You told me about the playground where the kids were talking about being in love. Every time you raise your eyebrows the scar on your nose whitens. It grows pale at the most unexpected moments. You had once banged into the glass door, back in our Spindle Street apartment, when you were playing hockey on the floor.

You went to your room to eat your dinner.

The apartment here on Valero Street is another backdrop.

It fits in with the others.

The rain had finally stopped. At the open window the air was clean, fresh, edible. And little by little the shishtering of the automobile tires on the rough asphalt was fading away. (After the defeat of our revolution in '56, the cobblestones were left underneath; always be aware of that as you walk here.) And I knew that now gradually the street would become abandoned.

I lowered the blinds and lit the lamp in the early dusk. I heard you rustling next door, preparing your schoolthings for tomorrow.

You took some of the grapes that I bought at Pannika, the private stall-keeper's stand on the former Palatine Street; it is the variety of grape we call "goat tit". That phrase always reminds me of Mátyás, the Fráter. He has a way of using the expression like no one else, his personal way, full of love, as when, seeing a bunch, he moans: oh my God, so many tits! He had lived in a village for some years after the war. So I asked for the "goat tit" grapes.

I looked at the street down below. This is where the muddy walking path passed on the outskirts of town once upon a time, from the Tüköry embankment, covered with grass and flowers, across wet marshy meadows past the lumber yards, and as if undecided on which way to go, at this spot it wavered to the left. When it became Valero Street, it still turned at the same place, in front of single-storey houses that used to hum with other sounds. At that time too there must have been some bureaucrat in charge of this intersection. And every time when two coaches nearly collided here, you could hear many a loud "Whoa!" and the grinding of wheel hubs and the snorting of horses through the ground-floor windows of the silk factory located at today's number 26/30, and then the factory girls would look up from their cretonnes and taffetas.

THE CROWDED FAIR IN THE TOWN OF LONDINIUM

At the final trial scheduled to settle the affair of the battle between the police and the Gypsies, all the free members of the tribe led by Bershehero the Shepherd appear. The flagstones of the courthouse corridors are teeming with half-naked Gypsy children and with women smoking pipes. The fourteen-year-old Ferke or Kodel, who will become my friend, is there, together with his sweetheart, the Pearl.

The august court accepts that the Gypsies had no malevolent intent, and that the patrolman's injury did not prove fatal. The men found guilty of the violence are sentenced to the four weeks' incarceration that they have already served awaiting trial. They are free to pick up their infants and women and go wherever they please.

Kodel is all for getting away now; he is already aware of the legislators' kindly intentions for improving the Gypsies' lot and the proposed plan for their forced settlement.

One thousand years after the last nomadic groups had settled here in the Carpathian Basin, his people are still nomads. For about the last hundred years the law has required that they have first and last names, but among themselves they still use only their Gypsy names. In brief, the proposed enlightened law aims to settle a few Gypsy families in each village. The Gypsy chiefs would lose their absolute authority. During the first year they would be permitted to erect tents in their backyards. Kodel has been keeping his ears open during the trial. Now, taking his beloved Murikeo by the hand, he is ready to flee. For the oral tradition of the tribes still preserves the story of former attempts, generations ago, at improving their lot, when tens of thousands of Gypsy children were taken from their parents in order to give them the benefits of education, and everyone who could sought shelter in caves and forests. Kodel wants no part of such an improvement of his lot; he reports what he knows to Bershehero, and the tribe at once sets out toward the wilderness of the Hargita Mountains, where they can weather these oppressive times. I accost the boy on the sidewalk right in front of the courthouse, and then and there hire both of them to join my future traveling troupe. I am looking forward to good times, roaming the world in my covered wagon and living the life of a wandering comedian. Due to a fortuitous array of circumstances there will be enough time, for I and my safe-cracking colleagues will have to make ourselves scarce on this scene for a while. I intend an important role for Kodel in my troupe.

In fact I attended the trial for this very purpose, and, after some time with the tribe, I picked out the young couple from among the throng camping on the stone floor of the corridor. I had overheard their quiet conversations. According to one of our social conventions, the ethnic makeup of lists of criminals wanted by the police, of street vendors and bootblacks, and of itinerant entertainers, is always as follows: out of ten, three Gypsies, three Jews, three Slovaks. In America, *we* (the Hunkies) are included in this group, along with Polacks, Dagos, Kikes, as the Polish, Italian and Jewish immigrants were once dubbed. Their latterday equivalents exist, with the additions of more recently arrived groups: Mexicans ("Greasers"), Cubans, Vietnamese ("Gooks"), Russians, Jamaicans. Along with the latest ethnic migrations, new gangs arise from the dust; it is always the latest arrivals' turn. In the metropolises of Europe there are Kurds and Turks, Arabs and West Indians, always labelled with their respective German, French and English sobriquets.

At the end of three weeks the engineer will send us a telegram. And in the meantime there is plenty to do. During these weeks I must recruit the artists for my troupe. I have always found the cheerful aspect of the world in the multitudes. This has been a long-time passion of mine, not merely a flash in the pan. More precisely stated, suddenly I am in the grip of a desire that goes back to a former time. Long ago. After we traveled on from Wittenberg toward the Belgian and English universities, it happened at the marketplace of the Town of Londinium, during that strange time when, owing to the adoption of the Gregorian calendar, on the day after the Fourth of October we had to write the Fifteenth of the same

month. The two of us being my young master Bali, itinerant
scholar from Transylvania, and his factotum, myself.

Having sojourned in one and the same place, my young
master began to gain weight from all the beer consumed, and
it had seemed meet to move on. I benefited by acquiring some
words in the German tongue that stuck to me like burrs in a
sheepdog's fur. Now all those words are mine own property,
no one can ever take them from me, nor whatsoever I
overheard and mastered of writing and Latin usage. For many
days we had to lie in waiting at Dünkirchen, for lack of a fair
wind. As soon as we arrived in Londinium, and put up at an
inn, and having visited scholars, we went to pass the time at
the marketplace in jolly good humor, watching the multitudes
attending the performance of a merry comedy.

In front of our amazed eyes a dog performed on hind legs
to the sound of a flute, while the dance master cut capers.
Hard by were the booths of vendors, whose heaps of velvets,
jewelry, and feathery lacework were laid out on canvases
spread before their tents. Here they offered old clothes for
pennies, and ink by the potful. Here one repaired chairs,
another mended kettles. Itinerant coal-pedlars offered their
goods from sacks, a barber excised corns. "Fair lemons and
oranges," a snubnosed little girl chanted in her native tongue.
A burly, rough seafaring man, wearing a bandanna and a ring
piercing one ear, recited tales for a penny each in English or
in pig Latin about endlessly rolling grassy plains, treasures of
gold, and savages with copper-red skin. And myriads of
well-fleshed beasts called bisons, free for the taking. For the
first time it was impressed upon me that while we, back at
home, were still engaged in fighting the bald-pated Janissaries,
over here a whole new world had been opened up across the
Ocean. And my wandering heart drew and rent me in two. For
I at once decided to travel to that great unknown New World,
even if only one half of what the old pirate related were true.
And at the same time I was drawn back home toward Buda.

A pound of grilled beef was to be had for a ha'penny here.
We appeased our hunger and devoured slabs of delectable hot
roast leg of mutton bought at a roadside stand, and washed it
down with fresh water from the pitcher of a pale thin child.

Then having purchased a loaf of bread, we gave alms to the wretched prisoners whose donation bag hung in a corner of the marketplace. A dusky Gypsy girl with flashing eyes read cards and told fortunes. Who knows, she may be Kodel's relative, for the tribe of Bershehero had also wandered in England before arriving in our land.

There is no written source. Only the oral tradition is available to us, according to which the tribe that battled the police in Old Buda, under the leadership of their chief Shashtarash the First, had passed through the British Isles in the course of their wanderings across Europe on their way to the Carpathian Basin.

And all that time we lived on mutton and watched the comedians. They shewed a colt that could distinguish a lad from a lass, and a newborn calf with two heads and eight legs. And while the singer sang, and the flautist played, and the reserved English picked through the motley merchandise with an uncharacteristic, ardent Mediterranean eagerness, I was suddenly enlightened by the recognition that the two-headed calf must needs be an assured livelihood for its master, no matter where you go. And I suspect that you may not even need a prodigy of nature for this, for everyone cheats in this business.

At one glance from the diamond eyes of a slender Italian girl in the comedians' troupe my heart is on fire and my very marrow is ready to melt. And that pair of eyes marks my innermost betrothal to the restless life of the itinerant comedian and wandering storyteller. That is why I spend all my free moments in the study of fire-eating, horn-playing, beggars' songs and the showing of pictures, in the hope that she should glance at me once again. I am familiar with the camp at the forest's edge, the inns and hamlets where I can make my living, and now even with the august buildings of the courthouse at Markó Street.

And now within two weeks I have gathered my troupe. My most brilliant catch, and a sure-fire attraction, is Hannah Savannah, equestrienne, born Rachel Mendelsohn, who will work with her two budding daughters. The others are: the Brothers Schordje, trapeze artists and illusionists, old man

Rupucz the tightrope walker with his wife, and Lajos "Scrambled Eggs" Kocsis, strong man and factotum. Kodel and Murikeo the Pearl can still take on any role; they are the blank pages in my book. And last, Vuchetich and Sárosi, animal trainers, with forty little black and white dogs, and Sárközi the Minotaur; plus eight small children belonging to one or the other. The Misses Mendelsohn can also double in the roles of Lilia and Alma, Snake Girls; Rupucz and the Schordjes as The Paprika Vaulters; and Hannah's horses will pull one of the covered wagons. The poor comedian's horse must also shoulder the yoke. Fire-eating and cornet-playing is my domain; I will regain my old skills soon, for they have become second nature to me. We are leaving in a month, in the direction of old Muscovy.

WORLD PEACE

One afternoon an expensively dressed Levantine gentleman appears at Hácha and Keresztes' hardware store (next door to the Two Lions pharmacy) and inquires about the most recent models of safes equipped with double walls of high-carbon steel plates and concealed locks. Speaking excellent French, he claims to be a carpet dealer from Constantinople, and having made his selection he pays for his purchase in gold, with good old Napoleons. He has his own men collect the safe. This is an everyday occurrence; it often happens that various Orientals, meaning Greek, Turkish, Serbian, Russian and Armenian merchants, travel this far west in order to buy here. These East-West dichotomies are not so hard and fast; they may shift from time to time and our country tilts with them (*et nos agitamur in illis*).

Mr. Hácha in his hardware store on Radius Avenue does not have the slightest reason to suspect the two porters who, in a matter of minutes, whisk the safe up the ramp into a giant closed van. And, since there is no reason to be secretive in front of these men, one of the owners comments in a clearly audible voice to his partner, "We are ordering more of these.

The next one is going to the Odessa Savings Bank." The two porters superstitiously spit on the money they receive from the Turkish gentleman and, with an eagerness that is standard for the lower classes, they head for the nearest bar. The carpet dealer instructs the drayman in clear and loud, if broken German, "To the central train terminal!" and they drive off northward on Radius Avenue.

The irreproachable hardware merchants will never know that Haluska, the driver sitting on the box, having reached Factory Street (for you, Franz Liszt Square), takes a righthand turn, then another right, into the thick traffic of King Street, and ends up on Saracen Street (Paulay for you), heading toward the Chain Bridge.

By the time they pay the bridge toll (with a shout of "Thonet furniture factory!") and cross over to Buda, the roles have changed; Haluska the villager wears a vest and gives loud orders to the Gypsy-like driver wearing tattered clothes, whom nobody, not even his own mother, would take for the prosperous carpet merchant. The King and I, who were porters a while ago, are now hiding in the dark interior. The wagon and the two dun dray horses are no different from the thousands of others that rumble through our teeming commercial-industrial city.

On the other side we pull up for a leisurely, substantial dinner at a fishermen's tavern beside the Danube teeming with master craftsmen and burghers. Outside, the horses are provided with plenty of oats; who would ever guess that our Gypsy-like driver's name is Socrates. Only after dark do we drive on toward Old Buda, where the double gates of the courtyard on Bush Street close after us in pitch darkness, sheltering us from the eyes of onlookers. We emerge from concealment, and all of us, with the help of the landlord, see to it that the safe is rolled down into the cellar with the least amount of noise.

And now comes the experiment itself, which aims to combine the working methods of the finest professionals from two continents. We proceed to cut, drill and blow the safe apart - it is, after all, our lawful property. We first turn our attention to its side wall. Using an oxyacetylene blowtorch,

Socrates and Haluska take turns, proceeding inch by inch, to fashion a circle of red heat about two handbreadths wide on the outer wall. Like a surgical assistant, I hand them the tools one by one. These blowtorches can work wonders; their flame is capable of melting even platinum. Meanwhile, I light up one Trabuco cigar after another; I am thus able to clock the time, for it takes fifteen minutes to smoke each cigar. I catch the ashes falling through the opening on a folded newspaper. It takes an hour and a half to cut out the circular piece. That is too long. Now it is the star attraction's turn: enter Jankó, the lead actor of the drama. He picks up the metal disk after it has cooled and puts it away. Modifying the now familiar procedure, he moves the torch around the circle in a steady sweep, and cuts out another disk in forty-two minutes. This is only the first phase; we are not inside the safe yet.

I open up the front using our two keys. From the inside you cannot detect the slightest sign of our attempt to break in; the cash would still be secure.

I relock the safe and we ignore the lock. Now it is time we resort to the finest of Chicago-style tools, dynamite. ("Alfred Nobel, glycerin and gunpowder...") I ask Láncz to bring down a pile of those old horse blankets from the stable. First of all I do a trial run to find out how loud a smaller, localized explosion would be. When the explosion is detonated under three layers of horse blankets, Haluska, who is monitoring outside on Bush Street, reports that he was unable to hear anything. The King sets the charge and a one-minute fuse on the inner wall exposed by the circle that he cut out. Having made sure that everyone has taken cover, I light the fuse. Before the dust of the explosion is settled, we are already on our way toward the safe. I see my companions' faces smudged with soot, looking like so many inquisitive demons; I surely look the same. When we remove the shreds of the green horse blanket from the safe's door, the results surpass our expectations. Whereas the explosion did not rip open the wall of the safe, it did loosen all the screws and bolts around the lock, whose outlines are clearly visible on the smooth surface of the outer wall.

Again, the oxyacetylene torch, then the rotary drill, then the auger bit. I hand them over, learning the order in which they are to be used. Then comes the long-handled steel jimmy. The wall around the lock is pried open, its pieces like flower petals, which the King covers with white linen as he bends them outward with the needlenose pliers, to break off the intrusive parts one by one using duckbill pliers. All in all, the operation consumes ninety minutes: the amount of time the King needs to open her up. By now dawn is breaking.

"Whatever happened to our Chief Engineer?" he asks. I look up at him while packing our things away.

Twenty-one days after the engineer embarked by ocean liner, a telegram arrives from America at the Budapest Central Post Office. It reaches us in time.

In the New World, on the occasion of the New York Electrical Exposition, at precisely eight in the morning on this day, the telegraph machine that stands on the east side of the hall sends a message into the ether: "GOD CREATED NATURES TREASURES AND SCIENCE NOW HAR-NESSES ELECTRIC POWER FOR THE GLORY OF NATIONS AND WORLD PEACE STOP". Whoever com-posed the text - in all probability Thomas Alva Edison himself - saw no contradiction between the two goals. The words fly to London, and around the world via Lisbon, Gibraltar, Malta, Alexandria, Suez, Bombay, Madras, Singapore, Shanghai, Nagasaki, Tokyo, Vancouver, San Francisco, Los Angeles and Chicago. The clock on the wall reads five minutes past eight when on the western side of the same table another telegraph machine taps out the following message: "God created, etc..." The American post office charges one hundred fifty-two dollars for the delivery, faster than anything conceivable, of this superficial and grandiloquent bit of information. The former Chief Engineer pays much less for the telegram he sends us from the Western Union office of the same city, the largest one in the New World. On the other hand, the message sent to us *poste restante* has a much higher message to noise ratio. "MERCHANDISE ARRIVED STOP ALL CLEAR STOP WAREHOUSE FIREPROOF SUTRUROY 20156416 PIROSKA."

The engineer paid eight dollars and seventy cents for the cable. You may observe here that society in this epoch has not yet reached the highly organized state at the time of your arrival. Telegraph offices the world over instantly transmit all sorts of vague messages, codes and signals - as long as you fork out the eight-seventy. The central post office does not yet contain a certain dark room (no water faucet or photo equipment for developing and enlarging, but plenty of phone lines manned by an attentive crew that does not draw its pay from the post office). Letters and packages are handled exclusively by postal employees, and even to state this would be to belabor the obvious. When it reaches London, the engineer's message changes direction, and comes to us via Amsterdam, Cologne, Prague and Vienna.

I look for it daily at the Central Post Office. My instinct for survival had made me reluctant to give my address to the King or to the engineer. And when I rented my twenty-kreuzers-a-day room, I made certain it had a rear escape route through a window facing the courtyard. (By the way, the meaning of the message is as follows: Abraham has arrived. 2-0156-4-16 signifies: Second Avenue, number 156, an address that contains something of interest; and the day, Thursday, the fourth of the week, at sixteen hundred hours in the afternoon, local time. Sutruroy has no significance at all.)

DRESS REHEARSAL

At last we are all set. I feel good about heading east with my traveling troupe. We have four covered wagons and five tents for all of our belongings, including humans and animals. Outward bound, we are giving no performances; our motley crew can make good use of the time for practice and rehearsals. Wishing to be out of the country as soon as possible, I find us a Romanian boat that is returning home without any cargo and whose captain, for a small charge, is willing to take us down the Danube to the delta. It will take four or five weeks, floating downstream on the slow boat.

From the Danube delta it will not be too difficult to find passage to the nearby port of Odessa. From there we will return by following the Lesser Circuit, stopping wherever we are able to perform in the Russian Empire, Romania, Transylvania and Hungary. I will be grooming Kodel as my successor, with Murikeo's fiery eyes flashing by his side.

It so happens that Agap Kevorg, an Armenian subject of the Tzar, who regularly travels all over the Continent on behalf of his multifarious business enterprises, arrives in Budapest just before our departure, to transact some business that is part of his cover. His merchandise is Armenian cognac, purchased with prospects of a healthy profit, so that his conscience at the moment is snow-white, and the excellent King makes use of this opportunity to bring all of us together. He is a handsome, cosmopolitan man with dark hair and dark eyes; his handshake is warm and firm. He looks more like an international chess master than an international dealer in stolen goods. He is styled *Amber* in a dozen languages by his business partners all over Europe. Here is the missing link in the unfolding of our well-organized enterprise; one whose role is to be played later.

In the course of our rambling exploratory conversation it turns out that Kevorg knows Odessa very well, having lived there, and that in fact he had recently embarked from that very port. I recall that not very long ago I heard mention of this city. I think of our adversary, the police officer who will eventually be on our case, and some devilish imp suddenly taunts me to drop certain clues for the man, to give him a fighting chance, and thereby make our contest somewhat more equal. In my juvenile overconfidence I am convinced that our little band, with the King on our side, is invincible and would be able to get away with just about anything. "How many savings banks are there in Odessa?" I ask. The answer, just as I had suspected, is: one. Where is it located? What kind of building is it? How well is it guarded? How do they transport cash? Without any hesitation Agap Kevorg provides professional, precise and essential information, and even draws a little map showing the port, the bank's neighborhood and layout, entrances and guardposts. The King and I memorize the map so that we could recall it even in our dreams, whereupon we promptly burn it. So that a manager's stray remark at Hácha's hardware store turns out to have been our starting point for this caper which will provide us with a chance to test our methods. In Odessa the great Russian shipping companies transact millions' worth of business, a fact I know from the systematic perusal of the daily press. (You would be surprised how much you may find out about the life of a nation and about the world at large, from a real newspaper.) And we can count on the presence there of the double-walled Wiese-Wertheim safe by the time we complete our slow downstream passage on the Danube. I am anticipating no special attention to us from the Tzar's police; there are hundreds of European troupes similar to ours all over the highways of the Russian Empire. The Greek has been to this Black Sea port before, and on the basis of the little map, we are able to arrange a rendezvous two months hence. My three associates will travel on a luxury liner via a southern route. Ask me no questions; just be there with the dynamite on time.

I slip the flat, yellow pigskin bag under the straw in my wagon. During our first stopover I begin Kodel's training, to make sure he will be ready to take over as soon as possible. He is smart as a whip, strong and reliable, with a sense of humor to boot. I teach him everything in the business, so that when I am no longer with the troupe he will be able to run the show. He is up to the task; I was right about my man.

The King and the other two will transport the dynamite, divided into three small flat parcels, inside portfolios. We shall meet only on that one night.

This is our dress rehearsal, and it goes smoothly indeed. Like most of the significant steps in the progress of humanity, our procedure is the simplest possible. The Greek cuts, the King sets the charge, I hand over the tools, Haluska is the lookout. We complete the job in seventy-five minutes. Jankó insists on saving the steel disk that we remove from the safe, and slips it into a side pocket of the leather case. I make sure that we rob only the drawers belonging to a private shipping company. The others are marked with the Tzarist treasury's coat of arms, on bright copper panels inscribed with Cyrillic characters. We don't touch those. There is no need to rouse a whole division of Cossacks chasing us for taking the Tzar's gold in a land where even local peasants need a pass to enter town. So I tell my colleagues to calm down.

Which is not an easy thing to do. Carried away by our success, Jankó and the Greek are all for finding another safe to crack. I cannot allow this. In the ensuing silence I suggest that they continue their pleasure cruise, maybe sojourn a while on the French Riviera, wherever they like. They can take the whole loot, consisting of rubles in high denomination banknotes and gold jewelry that can be melted down; such stuff must not be found on us, poor wandering Gypsies and comedians, in case we are searched in Russia or at the border crossing. My colleagues are also to take the *étui* with the tools inside it, and may they enjoy their life of leisure within the confines of the law. When the time arrives, and their presence will be needed, I will place advertisements in the international papers. Any notice that mentions double-entry bookkeeping and Biarritz will mean a noontime meeting at Muratti's Viennese beer hall one week after the date of the notice. They will find the address of their new quarters waiting for them *poste restante* under the name of István Tóth, at the Central Post Office. In the meantime my troupe and I will be slowly wending our way home by way of the Lesser Circuit.

The three gentlemen's brief absence passes unnoticed on the luxury cruiser, and by the time the steamer casts off to sail south on the Black Sea, all three of them are sipping cognac in the Salon. The yellow pigskin *étui* travels along with them. On board they are oblivious of one another's presence. After Odessa we feel confident that there is no safe extant or about to be invented that can withstand us.

But it also means that now our future great coup would become a kind of a return performance, which is something that I would just as soon have avoided. We had now served notice to the police throughout Europe that a comet of the first magnitude had appeared in the skies of the Continental criminal world; and would be duty bound to pay attention to where and when we would show up next. With the benefit of hindsight I will readily admit that I indulged in Odessa out of sheer arrogance, pure orneriness. Our proper target was still nine months in the future, awaiting us in the capital that was about to celebrate the Summer Festivities.

The air of the Odessa carnival is rife with legends; circus performers from a hundred nations exchange grapevine news and rumours; opportunities are plentiful and everybody is making ambitious travel plans. My nights are afire with the torrid and tender threesomes so generously offered by my little darlings Lilia and Alma, whose unselfish love and budding womanhood are mine to enjoy on the straw under the tarpaulin covering our wagon. Our time is short, not even enough for a brief visit to the Crimea. The Greater Russian Circuit is a glittering dream of promises; the elegant watering places of Evpatoria and Simferopol are only a short boat ride away; there is Saint Petersburg of the white and windy nights, and the capital, old Muscovy, city of wooden houses; then, further afield, Poland and Galicia. A winter journey on sleighs drawn by small hirsute horses, endless fields of snow punctuated by the occasional Cossack outpost. If we had enough time, we could attempt to visit our distant cousins up north, we could entertain the Voguls of the River Ob and visit the peninsula of the Samoyeds, from where we could turn back south, toward Barnaul, Semipalatinsk, and the territories of the Tatar prince, Orenburg, Saratov, Tsaritsyn, Astrakhan and Kherson. But the great event awaits us back home, so that we have time only for the Lesser Circuit, which leads us home through Transylvania.

Back in Budapest Dajka receives the report from Odessa after a delay of two days. He glances at the details. He has an inkling that something is stirring in the folds of the underworld. The safe-crackers have appeared out of nowhere; a gang working with such up-to-date American methods has not been seen on the Continent before. They had left behind the payroll of the local garrison and other valuable papers they had no use for, and left no clues for the Tzarist police to give pursuit. All the smooth copper surfaces had been left untouched.

Dajka concludes that he is faced with a gang that works intelligently, maybe too intelligently. He does not like it, but he will have to wait. In the meantime he reaps the harvest of his busy correspondence, and, by doing this busy-work merely to pass his free time, he makes a lasting albeit anonymous contribution to the history of criminology. In the course of the past several months, in response to his inquiries, he has received the personal data of three thousand five hundred individuals with criminal records. From the index cards he will prepare a directory of criminals, complete with meticulous cross-indexing that provides all names and aliases; where one can identify the murderers and robbers, the giants and midgets, the lame and the one-eyed. Each entry lists, in German and Hungarian, everything that may be useful for a police investigator: name, place and date of birth, religion, languages, personal description, special identifying marks, known crimes with detailed results of investigation, and the criminal's signature. And side by side with the helpful portraits sketched by police artists are the new-fangled photographs. Listed under the B's is Isaac Israel Baumgarten, railway cutpurse; under the H's, Julia and Maria Haldek, alias Diri and Dongó, twin thieves and *filles d'amour*. Under T, Mrs. Elias Tremmel, brothelkeeper. Certain entries are listed only under an alias, such as under L, Lajos the Lisp, the notorious highwayman. And closer to home, the entry K-039 covers the Safe King. The others receive two capital N's and a three-digit number. The card for the criminal identified as NN 124 contains the data of the Zara bank job, the method, Captain Gioielli's sketches of the tools left behind, and the fingerprint preserved using Francis Galton's method. (Dajka saves the fingerprint only because one of his colleagues had taken the trouble to send it.) One of the unknowns at the Odessa job receives the number 210.

Since I had decided to take up this profound and exacting profession, I ought to have been aware of Sir Francis Galton's discovery.

Within a matter of weeks the Directory becomes an international success. Police departments the world over (including quite a few from the Western Hemisphere) show keen interest in receiving one of the two thousand copies printed.

THAT WAS THE YEAR

Summer turns to fall, fall to winter. This is an eventful year. Mankind discovers an invincible enemy far more potent than the saber-toothed tiger: microbes. And the knowledge that uranium ore has its own radioactivity dawns on us - knowledge that shall prove most fateful. Former slaves in North America publish a New Bible in which the devil is depicted as white, whereas Adam and Eve, and Jesus of Nazareth are black, in confirmation of the relativity of social conventions. Explorers set out on new paths to unveil those areas of the globe that are marked white on the maps of Euro-American civilization. In the engineer Tesla's Prague laboratory small glass bulbs have been lit up continuously and with unwavering intensity for the fourth year now since the inventor had created a vacuum inside them.

In the recently erected building of the Budapest House of Parliament a Bill is introduced, proposing the celebration of the Millennium, the one thousandth anniversary of the founding of the state. The Bill is passed for the kind consideration of the Upper House.

Just before the springtime of the year, far beyond our borders, in the land of Wallachia, I nourish fond fantasies of all the riches pouring into the capital, ready to fall into the laps of a few well-prepared safe-crackers.

Bora Clarendon is employed as a singer at the Baroness Vad's club. Dajka sees the girl only on Mondays, when he is the private guest of the management at the Kitty. As a result of their conversations and mutual silences a new liveliness has appeared in the girl's eyes. Now that she no longer has to earn a living by selling her body, her eyes have acquired a more natural glow. She has become stronger, and seemingly younger as well. And she has not touched morphine since she moved here, to the corner of Rose Square.

Dajka, over a casual lunch of fresh goose cracklings in his office, has occasion to reflect on the lengthy hiatus in the series of safe-breaks. He tends to attribute it to the resonant silence before the breaking of the storm. The available information would seem to indicate that the new gang has taken early retirement at the peak of its success. And he knows all too well that such things do not happen.

The preventive measures taken by the police prove to have their effect. Though trickling in slowly, reports eventually arrive at the Budapest police headquarters: foreign criminals are staying away, and even the better-known of the domestic malefactors are clearing out of the Dual Monarchy.

Dajka pays a series of solitary visits to the Black, the Blue and the Spotted Cat to check if these clubs are obeying the law prohibiting night waitresses. For the demand is there. There are more than a thousand registered prostitutes in the city. The police officer can see the new generation of fresh candidates for the brothels walking the streets in broad daylight: the *bonne* who had just been dismissed by her mistress, or the wide-eyed peasant girl newly arrived in the capital. With the approach of the Great Events there is an influx of refugees from the provincial brothels. The newcomers drive up the price of available rooms, thereby fattening the brothelkeepers' profits and adding to the responsibilities of the police. The decree about night waitresses will of course remain a mere scrap of paper here at the various Cats and at other nightspots. Motivated by greed, the human mind is capable of devising the most intricate dodges around the law.

We are on our way home along the Lesser Circuit. Our itinerary touches on Kishinev, then Iassy in Romania; then we are at the Hungarian border. Kodel is by my side, watching me deal with the official formalities. After a thorough inspection of our caravan at the border, we set out for the Transylvanian towns: Kézdivásárhely, Marosvásárhely, and Kolozsvár. If we happen to be near a regional fair, we make a detour for it. We cross the Carpathians at the King's Pass into Hungary proper, and here in our descent we catch the first true breath of springtime. We shall be on the outskirts of Budapest by early summer. At Nagyvárad I part from the troupe, entrusting it to Kodel. I travel ahead, supposedly to find quarters for the troupe. But in reality that is the least of my worries. I must prepare for my other associates and establish a base of operations. Then send out the classified advertisement, so they can be on the way. And our target must be pinpointed and properly cased.

I cannot yet know that here at home an earthquake of an encounter is awaiting me, a meeting that will in an instant make me forget about all the safes in the world, a meeting that will change our lives.

(NOW: BEING BLACK. TRAIN STATION WATCHERS. HERMES AMBASSADOR)

The last two lines - "make me forget about all the safes in the world, a meeting that will change our lives" - were already hunted and pecked on an electric typewriter. It is Swiss, a grass-green Hermes Ambassador, and I bought it yesterday from the Fráter.

Earlier in the afternoon I had gone to pick you up at the kindergarten. The latest craze in the district's schools is playing with rubber bands. I had to buy five yards of pyjama elastic for you yesterday at the store on Ferenc Deák Square. And when I went to collect you, I saw the white-haired teacher sitting on a tree trunk in the schoolyard, stretching one end of the rubber band on a rickety thin leg sticking out under her white smock. You were so engrossed in your rubber band game that you did not even notice me. On the way home you told me how the teacher, Aunt Piroska, read out the names taking attendance after lunch, "Vargha. Vargha... let's see, which of you children is Vargha?" (You were rolling your r's clearly. We had to work on this quite a lot; you used to speak with a burr...) Then the teacher remembered you. "Oh yes, that black-haired little girl." Things always happen in bunches: that was the third time within as many days that someone called you "black". This made you happy. "It feels so good to be black," you said.

You have inherited this from Imola, this enjoyment of being

just what you are. She was like that. From her you have received those easily offended freckles around your nose, and the whiteness of your skin through which your veins show blue. You resemble her in a myriad tiny details; for instance, the way your nose wrinkles up in an unexpected grimace. That's something you couldn't have learned from her. I looked at you and thought that you are going to be a very attractive woman. (And a wave of anxiety seized me: it will be at least another ten years before you and I can move on, whereas even yesterday it would have been already too late.) I mused over your straight long hair, your expressive mouth. It is clear what you inherited from whom. You got your hair from me. Another trait you and I have in common is the ability to enjoy a quiet time alone, which you possessed as soon as you were able to stand on your flat little feet. I too had to make friends with solitude early in life. Once I requested you not to disturb me because I was working. You were three at the time. You took aside five cherry pits, placed them in a plastic dish, and you kept moving them around and talking to them; the six of you had quite a good time, until suddenly it was evening. I still remember that you could recognize each pit by the way it walked, each had a name and occupation, home address, and its own bad habit. Your flat feet came from Imola, as did the set of your mouth; your green-gold eyes are hers. But the single most important thing came from the both of us.

At home you pointed at the styrofoam bulletin board on which I had pinned up the meat ration ticket sent by Zoli, your uncle in Kolozsvár, Transylvania. "Aren't we going to visit him?" We show the ticket to all of our visitors. On its watermarked yellow banknote paper are the outlines of the ox head in red, the pig in black, and stamped on the back, in a foreign tongue, "Unit No.17". In case I would forget about it, all I have to do is look up from my desk. The egg ration is orange, the chicken ration is brown. "Yes, we shall visit him."

I was able to buy the Fráter's typewriter because he received an IBM electric from abroad. This Hermes is twenty years old, I would not have believed that electric typewriters had been around that long. He loved this instrument and wanted to make sure that it went on to a responsible new owner. It made me feel good, naturally. And we bargained quite hard.

"Three thousand forints," said the Fráter. "You can buy a brand new East German one for as little as eleven."

"No way. I insist you take at least four thousand." I wasn't going to be had that easily.

"Well, what the hell, make it three thousand five hundred," he conceded at last. We shook hands on the deal.

Afterward, to celebrate the spectacular purchase, I took you train-spotting, to the Eiffel-built terminal of the Western Station. Some day we shall depart from there. First the glass superstructure was raised over the old building, which was taken down later, so that the trains could run without interruption. Recently you remarked, "I'm really afraid of being bored some day." I had to reassure you, that you need never be bored. There are plenty of amusements, things to do, and worries to keep us busy here. Look at the Western Station, it is being renovated now. We walked around the four new pairs of rails under construction in place of the former long row of tracks, and it was a sad sight. I simply could not believe that they were capable of leaving us only four tracks. But the reason is not so obscure, you merely have to look at it from the other end of the tracks, from the vantage of Byzantium. When the international express trains arrive, the visitors will see platforms of an unprecedented width and spaciousness. The commuters of the black trains, we the natives, will have to trek out past the terminal, far into the freezing cold of the outside tracks. So we trekked out there. Meanwhile I was telling you how often Imola and I used to come here. She would copy for me the graffiti in the women's lavatory. You could see here all sorts of bag-people, plainclothes cops, beggars and thieves. You could see at first hand how tasty and nasty the hustle and bustle of a metropolitan train station could be, with all of its human and inanimate trash.

A MOVABLE FEAST...

So our time is slowly approaching. Meanwhile, the nation is flourishing, and the thriving twin cities of the capital provide the emblem of this spurt of development.

By now two thirds of the city's population of half a million people are Hungarian. We are more and more at home in our bustling, rapidly growing Budapest.

Nowadays we conjure up this period with a loving exaggeration and a kind of bias that are produced by an absolute attachment to one's home, but the fact is that back in those days our city was one of the most unforgettable as well as most comfortable cities in Europe. And the city was preparing for the festivities of the year 1896, the year picked by the bureaucrats with the same death-defying bravado with which they so love to discard old street names.

All around, we may observe the uninterrupted rampage of so-called history that always finds its ultimate fulfilment in human sacrifice (this is a law that has not yet been recorded in the books). The "telephonograph" - a pioneering news service - invented by Tivadar Puskás is humming with all the news it brings home from all over the world. In Constantinople, the Porte orders the public execution of two members of the Armenian committee: Toros Oussept, an Istamboul coffee broker and Baselio Kalpakian, bootmaker, who have been charged with sending threatening letters to prominent Turkish officials. Their bodies are left hanging for two days in public view on the gallows by the Bosporus. (This particular chapter of so-called history is going to spring into full flower hidden behind the complicitous cloud cover provided by the global war. For that is the time when even at home, stores will be looted and some of the neighbors will be made to disappear; one had better be aware of these things. About a million Armenians will be massacred, just because they happen to be Armenians.) Both Mother Nature and plain old ignorance do their job in controlling population levels. The news from Egypt has a depressing effect on the stock exchange. Ten thousand dervishes are massed in the Nile Valley, threatening to advance. There is an outbreak of cholera and the populace is taking its revenge on the European doctors. In Yokohama a tidal wave drowns ten thousand. In Berlin experiments are conducted to investigate the healing effects of Roentgen-rays.

Meantime your forefathers dare to dream of building a city and a nation, in the midst of inconsistent compromises and a semi-colonial status within the Dual Empire, they are engaged in making real history (in contrast to those heroes of so-called history whose greatness is measured by the magnitude of their contributions to controlling population growth; chalk up fifty million souls for the politician with the little moustache, sixty million for the politician with the big moustache, rough estimates. May their names be ground to dust!).

Vienna, the imperial capital upstream on the Danube, is watching us with jealous eyes, and tries to maintain its supremacy over our awkward, growing giant by resorting to rule through repressive laws.

And still the City belongs to the cutting edge of the world at this time, one of the few places where humankind may catch a glimpse of what tomorrow is going to be like, if things go well. Our city is interlaced by a network of electric street cars, the speedy dark-green cars representing the most advanced technology of the day. Local trains serve all points of the outskirts and suburbs; in addition, a rack-and-pinion railway and a funicular go winding into the Buda hills. The first electric subway trains in Europe are in operation here in our city - at a time when the London underground is still relying on steam engines. After Boston and Paris the third telephone system in the world is installed here. And since the spring thaw melted the ice on the river, the construction of the new bridge with its bold arching lines has been proceeding full speed at the Tollhouse Square. The basic layout of a large-scale system of avenues already exists, comprising the Grand and Small Boulevards, Radius Avenue and the giant quays hugging both sides of the river. These will define the shape of the City for centuries to come.

(Of course all of this could have been even better. Like every other metropolis, ours too has its share of irreparable mistakes: in the course of time we do away with Reedy Lake,

Willow Lake, the Fire Well. We could still be enjoying their cooling waters within the ring of the Grand Boulevards. In fact, in place of the Grand Boulevard, where the former Tüköry embankment held back the waters of the Lesser Branch of the Danube, we could now have a canal encircling the inner city of Pest, and instead of the screeching wheels of the No. 4 or 6 streetcar, we could be conveyed by the chuffing *Vaporetto* No. 4 or 6. We could sit down on a bench under a willow tree and watch the merrily cavorting coots, the quacking ducks and hear the whistle of the reed-buntings of Pest. Or listen to the frogs of Leopoldstadt: brek-kek-kek-kex, co-ax, co-ax. But we have done away with our woods. There could be kindergarten classes on outings traipsing about the shady groves and walking paths along the swan-studded canals. Then Amsterdam would have to be called the Budapest of the North.) Yet in spite of all, we never built so much in so little time. The Tunnel under the Buda Castle Hill is completed. The new Podmaniczky Street is opened to traffic. In two short years, at a veritably American pace, a whole new district has sprung up in back of Theresa Boulevard. Its new apartment buildings give two hundred thousand people access to nine times as much air and living space as the Budapest average up till then. And they call this new quarter "Chicago". The city has a thousand streets and squares; at this period it becomes so impressive that even its remnants at the time of your arrival (after a war, the bombings, a peace, another war and a revolution, plus the map of our part of the world totally redrawn) - even this leftover city will be acknowledged as one of the most beautiful of this densely historied, jutting land mass of a Continent. In the course of the most recent years and months, even as I am writing this, a hundred years' soot and grime has been scrubbed away from the Grand Boulevard and its façades have been newly stuccoed; as you can see for yourself if you walk down on Valero Street and turn right.

You step in from the heat under a cooling gateway, or walk under the plane trees that give shelter to tens of thousands of sparrows, feeling that all this has been here for as long as the hills, as if this were a part of the natural order along the banks of the Danube.

The City and the nation of which it is the crown jewel and the sewer are both fabulously wealthy and impoverished, magnificent and petty, at the same time.

In a settlement on Tide Street in the Angel-land district, seventy-two families live in converted stables that are unfit for human habitation. Everyone uses the same well, which freezes in winter; in that season the tenants are obliged to make do with melted, sooty city snow.

The Bishop of Vác establishes a hundred-thousand forint foundation dedicated to benefit the homeless.

The government budget is burdened with the expenses of three hospitals for the treatment of trachoma.

Moth, vermin and pest control services are provided by reliable experts.

The Rákospalota line of the electric train system is opened, with trains running every ten minutes.

In Transylvania Street there is a settlement of sixty one-room hovels converted from what was originally a shed. The tenants are unemployed day laborers with many children, and servant girls (the ones who are liable to drink lye at moments of desperation) - these are the sediments of the flood of people streaming into the city. They subsist on potatoes, horse meat and cheap plum brandy. In the midst of filth and stench, prematurely aged, withered children sleep on the bare floor at night, wrapped in the same rags they wear in the daytime. When the Special Investigator goes to visit these cockroach-infested labyrinths, he concludes that you could not do any worse even if you had deliberately set out with the intention to propagate scrofula, consumption, starvation, moral and physical turpitude and crime.

The Exposition holds its own with anything available in the civilized world; one American visitor exclaims, "Great! A Second Chicago!" But in reality the scene cannot be compared to anything other than itself. The swirling, colorful crowds form one unending Fair, life is a movable feast. Rushing or loafing about on the streets of Budapest are ten times as many inhabitants as a hundred years earlier.

And of course so-called history is proceeding full-tilt here at home too. A great public meeting turns into a demonstration, whereupon the government begins negotiations with the Independence Party and with the Socialists. A sort of Truce of God is concluded, so that work continues in the factories even on May Day, to ensure the scheduled opening of the Exposition. It is a way of celebrating the occasion through work. New business enterprises mushroom or fail every day, and entire fortunes are made and lost on the stock exchange each afternoon. On the commodities board the price of coffee plummets upon the news of a rich harvest in Brazil. The price of cocoa also sinks, as if in sympathy.

At the Olympic Games the Hungarian champion Gyula Keller, member of the Budapest Athletic Club, runs from Marathon to Athens in three hours and six minutes.

...AND THE BLACK LAND

It is easy for Hungarian citizens to think that all roads lead to scintillating Budapest. Anything was possible in that period. But do not despair.

In the pursuit of happiness, adventure and a new life, all sorts of people flood, flee, and gather here, coming from all of the sixty-three (for you, twenty-four) counties of the kingdom, and from halfway across Europe. Since that year we occupy a more prominent place on the map of the world.

If you were to compare this new Budapest to the ill-repaired, Turk-occupied Buda of two centuries earlier, or to the former Islamic Pest with its mud-plastered windows, you would not recognize the place. The city is fully alive again, and well on the way to become one of Europe's pearls, as it had been during the time of Master Vespucci's (Amerigo's brother's) trading days here.

There are two kinds of migrations in progress, away from misery toward sunlight. Shipping companies employ agents to tempt the peasants to emigrate to America, and the latter are able to move to the City without passports or boat tickets. So there is a folk migration from the Hungarian countryside on foot, on horse-drawn wagons, and aboard the trains arriving in the new glass-roofed terminal of the Western Station. They are arriving on the six-twenty. They are coming from the boondocks. And they are migrating here from the east, the way people are migrating to America in the First Wave of Immigration: Swedes, Italians, Poles and Hungarians. We are the Promised Land of this era: this country, this City is a Little America, next to the greater Eldorado of America itself, where any of the tired and poor may enter.

Servant girls and off-duty soldiers promenade hand in hand. It is a make-believe America on the freshly built, recently opened Grand Boulevards. Here you may find peasants and counts, swineherds, shepherds, princes, tinkers and ploughmen, coachmen, sandaled Wallachians, great-hatted Slovaks, Armenians, assorted Jews, lords, gentlemen and Gypsies.

In bright or musty homes and apartments, facing the street or the courtyard, in Buda or Pest, in offices, dens of vice, factory rooms and empty lots, or trudging on the cobblestones and mud and asphalt of the city are the forebears of the folk whom we will get to meet during the year of the Little Bear Bar. And if they are not yet here, then they are back in the sixty-three counties getting ready, driven by murky passions and drawn by misty hopes to migrate to the city, as people of the Earth have been doing ever since the walls of the city of Ur were erected.

In the village of Kunadacs, Little Kovács' great-grandfather is preparing for the Summer Exposition. This will be his first visit to the capital. He will be swept along in the seething throng of sightseers, and after his return home, he will have tales to tell his gaping village audiences that will be transmitted from father to son, will motivate periodical visits to the capital about every twenty years, and will catalyse a ferment that will, four generation later, and along with the twin disasters of war-widowhood and the loss of land, tear the family in the person of Mother Anna from its centuries-long residence in the village, and transplant it to a small street, bombed to rubble, in Old Buda where Little Kovács will grow up to be jeered for being a hick by the future "Brick", or police informer, Lali Gere.

And while the tribe of Bershehero is already roaming the Transylvanian Alps, back here the bill aiming at the forced settlement of Gypsies is introduced in Parliament, proposing that they be regarded as wards of the state, no matter what their age, a condition that would eventually lead, upon their final settlement, to their assuming the full rights and responsibilities of citizenship.

In three successive votes the House of Representatives grants tolerance to the Jewish religion. The Jewish community establishes a foundation for five scholarship students at the Ludovika Military Academy.

The teamster David Edelman, great-grandfather of Olga the Whale, lives in the Orczy apartment building. Back in the time of his grandfather, Jews were not permitted to settle in the city of Pest. Back then what is now the Theresienstadt district was still the countryside. When delivering a shipment of virgin tobacco to the capital, the teamster was permitted to sojourn for up to sixteen days at the Häusler farm at the outer end of King Street; there was a Jewish inn there. During the Revolution of 1848 he was a member of the National Guard, and his family at the Transdanubian hamlet of Baracska was counted in the census that aimed at granting Jews equal civil and political rights. That was during the few months of liberty when, having overthrown the occupying Austrian rule, the revolutionary regime was trying to put into practice the most high-minded ideals of the age.

Now for the maternal ancestry of the Whale. They are dirt-poor tillers of the soil in the village of Cibakháza near the town of Szolnok. None of their relations have ever been to the capital, and they cannot even conceive of such a visit.

The maternal lineage of Dani Kovács sheds light on the far-reaching process rooted in the mists of the past that will push his father the photographer into a domestic war at a time of peace. His maternal great-great-grandmother, Elvira Hannauer, housewife and self-proclaimed lady, is a resident of the city. Theirs is a matriarchal family; its essence is perpetuated on the distaff side. We shall have more to say of them.

From coarse gray cloth Elvira sews a nightgown for her

daughter. The neck opening is closed off by a drawstring, as are the two sleeves, which may be tied together. It is all in the best interest of the child. The family doctor told the mother about the perils and about the various degrees of preventive chastisement. She in turn informs her husband. The child that puts her hand under the blanket at night must surely be fondling her genitals. And this is an affliction that must be combatted at all costs, according to the prevailing opinion of medical science. Although it breaks her heart, she will have to resort to corrective measures. From now on the little girl will have to sleep in her new gray nightgown. Elvira keeps passionately stabbing with her needle at the coarse cloth. The gown is closed, wrapping the trunk and the thighs, while keeping the two hands away. It should definitely tame the most stubborn sinful tendencies. "The child is secretive, sulky, loves to laze around in bed, and morning after morning she persists in keeping her hands under the blanket," Elvira sums up for the doctor. What's more, *she loves to be alone.* So that the upstanding old physician, a longtime friend of the family, is able to pronounce the diagnosis in no uncertain terms: self-pollution.

"This is the most insidious disease in the world," he goes on to enlighten the mother, who soaks up every word. Not the bubonic plague, not cholera nor black typhus, as formerly (and latterly) believed; these diseases merely ravaged certain places at certain times. The contagion of self-pollution on the other hand is totally universal. Its victim frequents the toilet. When she emerges, the face is flushed, the eyes are strangely bright, heartbeat and breathing are accelerated. Later the face is livid, the lips turn white, and the eyelids become swollen. Deep purple shadows form under the furtively darting eyes. In time the victim loses weight, becomes enervated, her skin hangs flabby and she perspires profusely. Then come the dull aches in the back, the thigh and the calves. Eventually her speech becomes halting and her voice grows faint. The hair loses its luster, develops split ends and begins to fall out.

Elvira lists the preventive measures that must be taken. An austere and plain diet. Dinner at six p.m., a cold bath every day, plenty of exercise, fresh-air gymnastics. A healthy, tiring walk in the evening, sleep by open windows, in light bed-clothes, on a hard board for a mattress. She will continue to oversee the child's reading matter, ditto for her playmates, lest they direct her attention in sinful directions. These peasants, she murmurs. They live in poverty, in filthy, smelly places. They possess nothing because they do not work, they only drink and wallow in sin. Some of those peasant brats actually *see* what those farm animals do. That's the way they are raised.

If these measures fail to be effective, she will have to turn the child over to the physician.

Her husband withdraws, in terror of her tongue, and does not even realize what is being said to him. He is a bookkeeper, quiet and meek. All his life he had to make do with his mother's family name. He is illegitimate, according to the social consensus of the moment, the decade, the century. *Some people are born illegitimate.* He is branded for life. His pedigreed spouse of pearly virtue reminds him of this often enough.

In the maternal lineage of this family, generation after generation, the same situations, scenes, *sentences* repeat with a bleak hopelessness. Little Kovács' wife Klári received her patterns from her mother, who got them from hers, and so on back through the murky ages they have been handed down from mother to daughter. These women possess great talent for finding the proper mates for themselves. The husband's qualifying criterion is long-term blackmailability.

The coarse gray nightgown is inherited by the daughter's daughter, who becomes Mrs. Hirling. It will guarantee that she will never in her life take pleasure in a man; she will never dare to love man or woman. This is the essential message that is handed down from generation to generation until the chain is at last broken by Little Kovács' son, Dani.

Kovács, in his youthful innocence, got Klári pregnant, and thereby got himself involved with this lot at an enormous cost of his time and energy.

(But when you think of these sexless women and these Bricks - informers "built into" the system - give them the credit they deserve.

They are most useful for one purpose: by their mere existence they serve as reminders of the seamier side of the human universe. Kovács, from his close vantage point, actually values his wife for her help.

Help, in making sure you will not form, all by your brave self, the mistaken notion that the world is a movable feast, a great big green sunny meadow where colorful balls keep bouncing high into the blue sky. Of course you are right, the world is a holiday; I want to believe this, even after all the Turkish and Tatar invasions. Or at least it can be a holiday, that too.

However.

This is where they all become useful, these "Bricks", these Masters of the Universe and these Icicle Women who are thrown into our lives in the course of our days, who raise a pyramid of skulls beneath the walls of our fortress, kick old men off the streetcar and sew up their children into coarse nightgowns for the night. They are reminders that the chasms of the Black Land always gape in front of our feet in the middle of the meadow. You will need all your courage and all your strength for mere survival. For we would be terribly lost if we did not know this variety of the human species and believed that life is *only* a holiday. Let us be thankful for them. Let us thank them the way Olga the Whale will give her thanks one day at the Little Bear Bar for all of the "Brick's" bitter taunting.)

And the long overdue task of breaking the chain falls on Kovács. He is a taciturn, even-tempered, decent man whose gentleness is mistaken by Klári for weakness. Klára senior, the mother-in-law, instinctively opposes the marriage, and she is right. Since all her efforts are in vain, she next attempts to harp on the lower social status of the photographer. "Peasant." But Kovács refuses to feel inferior; he was not born to be a servant. As hard as he is on himself in every respect, he proves to be just as tough an opponent in the war that is forced upon him; for the sake of his son he will not shirk any struggle.

It makes no difference from our, or Dani Kovács's, or humanity's standpoint how the pale little girl's life passes through this period of natural sexual maturation, whether she masturbates or not. The results are the same anyway. And, as a matter of fact, Dame Elvira does not remember her earliest years; a taboo mechanism as powerful as a nightmare has repressed the fact that she rocked herself to sleep each night with her fingers sweetly wandering into the folds of her pre-pubescent mound of Venus.

So here are one or two forebears of Alva Ráz.
And Ballsy's.
The "Brick's", the cop's, Mr. Rudi's and Mia's, who will call out "half past eleven!" at the Little Bear.
Forebears. There is Emil Gomba, ministerial counsellor, who, by virtue of my later adoption may be said to be your pre-dated great grandfather. He conducts trial measurements and inspects the riverbed of the Lower Danube. The regulation of the Iron Gates takes a giant step forward this spring, when near the Jucz Rapids he has thirty thousand cubic meters of hard serpentine rock blasted out and directs the cutting of a channel thirteen hundred meters long and sixty meters wide in the rushing waters of the riverbed. He is obliged to purchase a second-hand Hungarian ceremonial costume in which he receives his latest decoration, this time from the Russian Tzar. (Which is only one of his seventeen medals that we were able to view in my nephew's collection. For his work on the Iron Gates he eventually received decorations from the rulers of every Danubian state, as well as from numerous non-Danubians, such as Vittorio Emmanuel the Second and Tzar Alexander.) He is the grandfather of your great-grandmother Vargha, that wiry matron dressed in black, who, in her ninth decade when I got to know her, was spry and curious, aware of everything that was happening in the world, and who read in three languages until she became blind and deaf and was only able to listen to the radio through a special hearing aid, in order to keep up with events from day to day. I should have kissed her hand, but I shied away from it. I have long regretted that I did not. You arrived just in time to meet her.
This family of ours is a chaotic bunch. On my side there are

only the adoptive parents. In addition we have a gunrunner, from after the war, an American uncle and a physicist, Grandpa Elek, the storyteller, and a boxing champion. First the great-grandmother: out of their single apartment on the Belgrade Quay they created two during the early Nineteen-Fifties, and I lived in the remainder thereafter, when they adopted me. On the dividing wall of the room, above the sofa, as a joke not without a certain element of danger in those years, hung the family's patent of nobility recorded on the original dogskin, surrounded by portraits of ancestors wearing ceremonial outfits and boas. A kind of diminutive family "Red Corner", in blue. You never got to see it, for the remnant of the apartment was traded away last year by great-grand-mother's daughter Sarolta, the biologist.

(NOW: SWEDISH GIRLS, SWEDISH SUMMER)

Last week I rambled through a white night in Stockholm. I was there for Midsummer Night.

I strolled down Kungsgatan under a milky white sky after midnight. In the bright dawn I came across a bum wearing worn out shoes as he staggered off with uncertain steps toward the new day in the richest country in the world. Since long hair happened to be in fashion, the police and the army have been issued orders to wear hair nets. In the underground labyrinth of the Hötorget (which is pronounced with a y, as Hötoryet) the long-legged female police officers were rounding up drug addicts and drunks. I was ambling through this night of festivities without darkness, and I was yearning for those tall Swedish girls, blondes and brunettes. They hurried past the underground department store's barred windows with the lapels of their multi-colored short linen jackets raffishly turned up. O Swedish summer. Personally I was yearning most palpably after my cousin Kerstin (pronounced Shershtin. And this is another part which I would not be able at this time to share with you, so that I had to tell you about Stockholm without mentioning her).

She is a native Swede, and not really a cousin by blood relation, of course. We have acquired her in a most roundabout manner, even for our complicated family. Barna, the son of your great-grandmother Vargha, is the one who adopted me. He has a younger brother Kornél, the American Uncle, who had emigrated before the war and became a professor of physics. His second wife in California is Ulla, a Swedish-American lady. Well now, from her it is only a short sparrow-hop to the daughter of her younger sister back home.

Kerstin Lannegren. "I will never be able to remember how we are related," you said yesterday, when I mentioned her. Don't worry, it is sometimes difficult to keep track of even one's blood relations more distant than your first aunt.

She came to meet me at the airport, of course. She gave me dinner at her place, and talked about the middle-aged business man with whom she has been carrying on a protracted affair. She would like to have a child, but not by him. It was as if we had known each other forever.

She dragged me all over town; she loves her city as much as I love mine. We went for boat rides in lagoons, made an excursion to the lake district where her mother had a house; in the photo on the card table Pekinese palace poodles were licking the face of the father who was a ship's captain; we sailed among islets of reed. We went to the cinema, walked around in the old town, in the midst of carefree bands of teenagers on a Saturday night. We stopped at the Club Bolaget, in the back, by a wooden handrail, holding beer mugs. I had heard about the place from Sándorka and wanted to see if the jazz drummer about whom he had told me at the Little Bear was still there. The Club is located on a narrow, quiet little street in the old town and sure enough Malcolm the Red was still at the drums. I *saw* his drum solo. I also heard it; but he has a move at the very end, when he tosses his sticks up in the air, catches them and hurls them straight out over the heads of the audience. The two sticks stop in midair, thrown some two or three meters, and after a moment of stunned silence they fly back into his hands like magic wands and you realize they are tied to rubber bands. I will try to tell you how

Sándorka got to see this.

I was staring at Kerstin, I could not get my fill of her. Each time she spoke, her voice created an irresistible tingling inside me; the attraction of the forbidden fruit stirred in the subdued dawn, as if I were skirting the whirlpools of incest just by listening to her. As for her, not for a moment did she seem to realize that her, in every respect, distant cousin from exotic Hungary also happened to be a man.

GEMSTONE AND CESSPOOL

From Nagyvárad I take the international express train so that I arrive in the city in high style. Our day has come. The city is a steamship on the point of departure, its boiler at a red heat, ready to burst.

My traveling troupe had arrived at the city tollgates earlier that morning. Kodel, as he later tells me, was able to handle the situation perfectly. A police check ascertained that nobody was on the wanted lists and that no one was carrying jewels, money or children belonging to other parties. After receiving permission to camp in the People's Park, they set up their tents near the tollhouse until my message, carried by an idle Gypsy lad, arrives with instructions to advance.

On the train I am already able to find out a good many things. It is crammed with people, all of them going to the city. They say that a monkey circus is performing on Arena Road, and that the People's Park, behind the pond by Hermina Road, is crammed with all kinds of sideshow booths teeming with buffoons and barnstormers. That is where, in the fine summer weather, all the common folk are heading, as are some of the sophisticated ladies and gentlemen out for a glimpse of lower-class amusements.

I get off the train at noon. It is a cloudy, breezy and warm day. The whole country is streaming into the city, tens and hundreds of thousands getting off the noontime trains. The police detachment at the terminal pays special attention to the train from abroad. My documents show that I have spent the past several months as manager of a traveling circus in the lands of the Russian Empire and the Kingdom of Romania. They let me go in peace, reminding me not to neglect to register with the police once I am settled. Somehow I will manage to skip that formality, however. My luggage is picked up by a porter wearing a clean new uniform designed especially for the festivities.

Everyone is back home by now, and here I come, the future piano man.

The Baroness is home, and Bora. And so is the hunch-backed gatekeeper, and Bubbles the bread-girl, near the man who will take care of her.

And all around us, the city, with its poverty and glitter and chaos.

In a private apartment on Főorházuu Street in Buda, licensed midwives offer their services and counseling, absolute privacy guaranteed. The eighteen-year-old daughter of a janitor is dreaming of an elderly gentleman from the country who would become her mentor.

Young virgins and ripe matrons are the recipients of perfumed notes in the shuttered rooms of apartments both in the Inner City and beyond the old town walls. Amanda. My sweet darling. Karolina! I yearn for the delights of the past few days. Be careful, control yourself. A good-looking young *masseuse* offers her services for lonely gentlemen. Will come to your apartment. Jozefina! Each moment of the day my lips murmur ardent prayers for you. The one who lives only for you. I will know my duty, Anton. I love you. And you? A.B. If you are not there at 4 p.m. you will never see me again. Pál. Please let me know in writing when you are coming out again, I will meet you halfway with open arms. Until then I will not even ride out. For what is my life without you? I kiss your little hands. Your handsome lieutenant.

The Special Investigator's working hours are filled with petty criminals. He discovers the vulnerable point of the emigrant-recruiting racket: since the tempting advertisements flood the countryside via the Royal Mail Service, that is where they can be controlled.

An issue of *The News Courier* costs two fillérs, standing room at the National Theater eighty fillérs, and the price of admission to the public baths is thirty-eight fillérs. At the Folkhostel a bed is sixty fillérs, eighty for a private cubicle. The whole city is outraged by the astronomically inflated food prices at the Exposition.

The electric-powered subway trains are in service late into the night, until half past midnight. For the grand parade in homage to the King (not the Safe King, but the Emperor-King Franz Joseph the First) there are still some first-floor window seats available on Bath Street, and bleachers at the pub at Number 10, Leopold Boulevard (for you, St. Stephen Boulevard; this morning I asked you to go there and verify if I am right: nowadays that is the address of the automated post office and the Espresso Dupla).

I exit the glass-roofed Western Terminal that still smells of fresh paint, and begin to hunt for a cab. A teeming crowd floods the environs of the train station, everyone here for tomorrow's parade in homage to the reigning monarch.

I review what I must do. First I must find living quarters for all of us. Then I can set out to roam the paths of the exhibition area in the People's Park. I am amazed by the seething, jabbering human potpourri; all these strangers are my people. As you will see, this is the best part of traveling: each return home is a fresh cause for wonder.

My troupe, as it happens, is the least of my worries. I will send word to them soon.

It takes forever to find a cab, so I seize the opportunity to look around, and re-orient myself to home again. To the left and right the newly finished Grand Boulevard's cobblestones reach out in graceful arcs; you may still see some left here and there in Old Buda, a few late survivors along the route of streetcar No. 18. Between rows of fragile young trees on either side of the wide Grand Boulevard flows the traffic of the metropolis: cabs, streetcars, vans and carts, something to see on every side.

Black and white are the sights of a city street, the moving shadows of time passing, in the corners of shop windows or across the sidewalk.

An elegant lady, her waist tightly corseted, sails by, a threefold light cape thrown over her shoulder. Well, well, fashions have become simpler. I am aglow with life, with the spirit of enterprise. I clink the pieces of gold in my pocket that I have been saving for this day. (I cannot count on our loot from Odessa; that will have to be saved as an emergency reserve.)

So I hum a song to myself. Coo-coo-ri-coo, the rooster cries...

From now on, we are going to be living the high life here at home.

It is two in the afternoon. Thunder rings out and a slow rain starts to fall on the crowd, the streets, cabs and showmen's tents. The temperature, according to the thermometer at the train terminal's entrance, has dropped to 17 degrees Centigrade.

At long last I find a cab. There is no way my former colleagues could recognize me. My suit, as a result of the tailor Kamarás' artistry, has been cut to fit me like a glove. The knowing onlooker can recognize that certain air of careless elegance conveyed by work of this quality.

But not on me. On me even the most perfect cut appears as something foreign and awkward.

There is a star on the horse's forehead.

From here on I am following a closely worked-out procedure.

Under no circumstances am I to put up at a hotel or inn. I tell the man to drive on in the direction of the Inner City, where he will receive further instructions.

I change cabs at Gisella Square in front of the Magyar Commercial Bank, making sure that the former driver does not see me. At the first tobacconist I change my pieces of gold. I notice the coxcomb cab driver pulled up waiting by the sidewalk of the Haas palace; he is still wearing the same well-known checkered suit, yellow boots and black derby. He is the prince of cab drivers, accustomed to being hired by the day or by the week by crazy counts and journalists. The work of Mr. Kamarás and the one-forint banknote produce the desired effect. I tell him to drive wherever he feels like. Giving him enough time to simmer until he is steaming with curiosity, I eventually start up a conversation. He proudly points out to me the newest wonder of the Inner City, Sándor Street (for you, Bródy Sándor Street - see how insidious the street-namers can be?) where the road surface has been covered with a layer of asphalt. Gone are the worries over sewage, water and gas pipes and electric power lines, and, in addition, the new miracle surface will be easy to keep marvelously clean. As you may see for yourself, any day.

On this day there are half a million people out on the streets, the entire population of the city. That certain Princess of the House of Habsburg has not arrived yet, but except for her, everyone is here for the festive occasion. And no one has gone home yet. The crowds are enormous.

After fifteen minutes' jovial conversation we casually touch on the fact that the driver has heard of someone likely to have two furnished rooms for rent - a tailor in a new apartment house, past the Grand Boulevard. It will be easy to find one other room somewhere for Haluska, our lookout. I ask the fop many questions, mostly about hotel accommodations. I have him drive in another direction, away from the Grand Boulevard, and get down at the Golden Eagle Hotel. I do not need a witness for what follows.

The rain has stopped. My suitcase is heavy, but I am no laggard. I walk over to Leopold Boulevard and after a brief inquiry at the first tailor shop I find out what I want to know: the man I am looking for is Emil Knorr, gentleman's tailor, at the corner of Pannonia Street. The apartment is on the top floor; there is an elevator. From two blocks away you can hear the rumble of the Pannonia Steam Mill, and there is a circle train line that follows the curve of the street. My man asks two forints, twenty kreuzers a day for the rooms. As I view the place, opening all of the doors, a shy girl's figure flits by; the family has three young graces. I spend somewhat more time in the bathroom, from where a door opens into one of the rented rooms. I open the back window and find the prospect reassuring: an outside gallery encircles the inner court, with an exit to the loft. A short leap from a loft window leads you to the rooftop of the neighboring building, and through its attic and staircase there is access down to another street.

Back in the salon I nod in agreement; I will take it for the entire duration of the Exposition. My business partners are very particular and require peace and quiet.

I dictate the data for the police registration form to the tailor. Inn and hotel keepers are required by law to notify the police of their guests' names and occupations on the day of arrival. I give one as Aga Sadegh (taking care to be consistent with the monograms on those soft French shirts and suitcases); Turkish citizen, occupation: wholesaler, residence: Istamboul. Likewise I provide a name corresponding to the King's initials. I do not know the exact date of their arrival, I tell the tailor, so why not wait with handing in the registration forms. Placing my walking stick on the mantelpiece, I sign for the two gentlemen and pay for the first two weeks. They will arrive soon.

The instinct for hiding is in my blood; I continue to lead a dual existence. I rent Haluska's room near the New Market; I find it on foot. And now for my own quarters; these various addresses must not be connected by any cabdriver's memory. I set a rule for myself: to and from my lodgings I must always travel on foot. Little do I know how soon this rule will be broken, as all rules are. I do not ask any questions. I check my innocent-looking luggage with an aged cloakroom woman at a coffeehouse, then set out in the quiet neighborhood around the new House of Parliament, where, making the most of my appearance, that of a fine gentleman, I try my luck knocking on the doors of several carefully selected old houses. Diver Street. A cart stands in front of a small house, its wooden gates nail-studded, a red mailbox on the wall. The tiny windows are almost at pavement level. On the wooden shutters of the window next door there is a hand-painted pub sign. If you wanted to find the street today, it is not far, only a block south of us, but you would find in its place Báthory Street, and a larger building that used to be the Ministry of Produce Collection (in the days when such ephemeral entities still existed). The back window of the room gives on to the street at the rear of the house, and I am able to ascertain at a glance that after an easy vault over a fence I could escape handily toward the new House of Parliament and to freedom down by the river quays. It is convenient to have the pub and the small store next door. My wizened, stone deaf landlady has not even heard of such new-fangled practices as police registration forms. She is happy for this chance to pick up a few crumbs of the current prosperity. I rent the room and go for a walk. I wire my notices to the major French, Italian and Austrian papers: large Biarritz hotel needs accountant, fluent French and German, double-entry bookkeeping. References required.

I mail a letter to the Budapest Central Post Office, *poste restante*. Then back to the room with my luggage. I ask for warm water, and wash away the long day's fatigue. Having shaved and changed into fresh clothes, I go out and by way of Palatine Street I find myself on Leopold Boulevard in a few minutes. My lodgings are ideally situated: close to the Inner City, yet in the midst of a modest single-storey anonymity. I cross the Boulevard, zig-zagging in and out of the thick cab traffic. I am not far from the abutment of the Margit Bridge, going past pubs, empty lots and palings, where today's Comic Theater stands. I catch a fiacre heading in the direction of Pest.

Evening is falling. Well then, let us have a look at the festive city. At last I am able to light up my remaining fragrant Virginia cigar, and, puffing it at leisure, I lean back in my seat. So far so good.

The cab stands still, moves a little, comes to a stop again: ahead of us the road is filled with an unending line of noisy cabs and coaches that start, then grind to a halt.

One horseman moves suddenly, whereupon another horse rears, rolling the carriage backward. Screams fill the air left and right, and up ahead. The ladies out for a ride are given a scare; the gentlemen swear or laugh it off.

At the intersection I look down the narrow canyon of a new side street.

And now on each side of the long line of coaches thousands of firebrands as thick as my arm flare up in the air along the sidewalks next to the rows of modern apartment buildings that flank the Boulevard. In every window oil lamps and candles are flickering; here and there one may see the platinum glitter of electric lights. The street lamplighters are responsible for presenting this honor guard, these blades of flame: the lampbowls atop the dark pillars having been unscrewed, they light, one after another, the freely streaming jets of natural gas.

As we turn toward the park, I glance farewell to the Grand Boulevard, where the string of façades of gigantic three- and four-storey apartment palaces turns into mist and vapor behind the gold and diamond glimmer of that wall of flame.

PART TWO

STUDS AND FILLIES

A MAN

Another weekday dawns for the owner and staff of The Silly Kitty. Another day of hard work. A Friday, to be precise, which is, after all, different from the other days of the week: there will be fish for dinner tonight. Keeping a meatless day changes somewhat Baroness Vad's morning routine, going to the market. Her two purses filled, she sets out with her doorman, and on the way to the market she enjoys the pageant of children at play; this has become a regular morning pastime for her. The little ragamuffins in kneepants are all over the place, they are on their vacation, out on the cobblestones of the streets in the midst of dirt, refuse, fruit peels. On Leopold Street, right next to The Kitty's outer wall, a war of marbles rages, while over on Hat Street they are playing stickball, pitching pennies, playing tag. Down below at the ferry station (for you, the Elizabeth Bridge) on the gently sloping bank of the Danube they are fishing with worms for bait, using bent pins as hooks.

Women are thronging to Fish Square (for you: non-existent; now a block of buildings on the quay, where everything has been built over). They are wearing flannels and checkered linens, kerchiefs covering their heads, shawls knotted across the chest.

As the Baroness reviews the list of things to do today, an unpleasant task comes to mind: she will have to let go one of the cleaning women from the village of Pilisvörösvár, and this kind of thing never goes smoothly. No matter how much she loves what she does, it seems that all the world's problems come crashing down on her in the mornings. The contributions from her girls must be stretched to cover food expenses and the upkeep of the rooms. And then there are the salaries for cooks, waiters, charwomen and the rest of the staff, not to mention the costs of providing hot and cold running water and electric lighting. The one thing that is sacred to her is the sum of money she puts aside each month, as down payment toward the price of her dreams for the future, assuring that her brown

velvet bag weighs more on each successive first of the month.
It is usually in the mornings when doubt assails her each day:
how long will she be able to keep the secret of the dual nature
of her establishment from Dr. Dajka? This dark cloud is
relatively easy to disperse; the Special Investigator is, after all,
benevolent and even fatherly toward her. His protégée, the
singer Bora, has been doing very well since last year; she has
managed to stay away from morphine. She is a quiet girl who
knows better than to gab about things her patron and mentor
need not know. No, the police are not the Baroness' greatest
worry anyway. As she winds her way among the market stalls,
the Baroness confides her worries to the doorman, almost as if
she were talking to herself. Ever since his hiring she has been
bringing him to the market; it is his job to carry the shopping
basket. They usually set out after the delivery of the fresh
cream for breakfast. This way the service entrance can be kept
locked from noon until the next morning; there is no need to
admit into the building those ne'er-do-wells who loiter about
the market. The doorman always takes the keys with him,
wherever he goes. By the time the provisions she purchases
are delivered, the two of them have returned from their
shopping.

She has not yet admitted this to herself, but she is rather
proud to have this hunchback with her. As a rule he is dressed
in an indigo linen coverall equipped with enormous pockets
and snap fasteners. The mistress likes to rest her eyes on his
bear-like head and the bulging musculature supporting the
sloping shoulders; he reminds her of the dwarves and
blackamoors who accompanied ladies of the royal courts in
days of yore. Ever since he has been escorting her, even the
loudmouthed fishwives have shown her more respect.

Oh, she would have enough problems on her hands even if
only the public part were all that there was to The Kitty.

So her mornings have become prime billing in her day. This
is when she has to purchase provisions for the noontime and
evening menu of the *café chantant*, and, in addition, food for
the large "family" staffing her establishment. It is a lot of
work, but she has a profit to show for it. Meanwhile, the secret
of The Kitty is hers to enjoy and cherish. His Excellency the

Special Investigator can rest assured about the welfare of his protégée, who is safe and sound under the Baroness' care - and yet here she is, still needing to keep two sets of books. That is why she comes to market with two purses. There are some things that she prefers to select herself, such as raisins for her coffee cake, the cuts of meat or fish served at dinner. In front of Mrs. Fanda's booth she decides to splurge, for once. The days of the Festivities are upon us, and her large iceboxes are empty. She is going to buy tenderloin at eighty kreuzers a pound for Saturday night's "family" dinner. The rest of the meat is separated into several packages by the Hunchback: one for the choice, and one for the second-class soup meat, and another containing the heaps of marrow bones. Mrs. Fanda is to wrap it all up and have it delivered at the gate under the archway on Hat Street; you can reach it through the back courtyard of Number 2, Leopold Street. The marketwoman sells her pullets by the pair, and the doorman lifts these straight from their large cage, into his baskets. It is amazing how strong this man is. When her new steel safe was delivered, he carried it upstairs into the inner office all by himself, supporting it on his head and shoulders, after the Wiese-Wertheim firm's men hoisted it up for him. Before she found him, she used to go marketing with the cook and one of the kitchen maids, and they still had to have the poultry brought back by one of those loiterers at the market.

They stop at the soapseller and chandler's shop. House-keeping simply devours supplies. Kerosene is needed for the lamps, never mind that all the guest quarters are lit by those expensive electric lights. And it seems at least a dozen lamp cylinders burst each week. The Baroness keeps up a litany of complaints while her doorman follows after her like a faithful beast of burden. At Fanda's, the fishmonger's, Agnes Vad picks out two enormous carp. At the furniture warehouse on the corner she deliberates over some tables and chairs. She lives to the hilt each and every minute of her day; this moment in somnolent Danube Street infuses her with its dense concentration. A wavering one-horse cart approaches, over-loaded with a tower of wickerwork and sieves. Under the canvas awning the doorbell of a shop starts ringing. In the shadow of a pushcart little girls wearing large straw hats are chasing each other. The steeple of the Franciscans' Church casts the morning shadow of its cross on the bumpy old cobblestones down the middle of the street; the tip of the shadow points at her feet. On her right stands a row of two-storey houses; their windowpanes scatter flickers of morning light, their white wood lattice fences weave a flashing web.

In the end she buys a giant twin-compartment wicker hamper for fifty kreuzers. This will make the marketing a bit easier for her hunchback; he can keep separate the two kinds of purchases. As he looks back at her, the dark depths of his eyes reflect something other than gratitude: is it amusement, or forgiveness? She cannot decide. Somehow she feels as if it had been the servant who had purchased something for his mistress. The mystery surrounding this man of hers thrills her, makes her shiver.

"Get going," she shoves him with a certain rough tenderness. They are homeward bound.

They enter the courtyard through the arched gate on Hat Street. All around lie the scattered belongings of the master cooper who rents the workshop: broken-down wheelbarrows, piles of lumber, axes. A small apprentice, looking forlorn in his oversized apron, is stacking staves, lugging them from one side of the yard to the other. The Baroness glances upward at the palisade fence of the first-floor passageway; it reaches all the way up to the second floor, so that from the small hovels in the courtyard one cannot see who goes up there, day or night, and that is how she wants it. They step in under the passageway. In front of the service entrance a packing crate awaits them, with straw sticking out between its boards: this must be the new set of porcelain coffee pots and mugs from the Zsolnay factory in Pécs. Across the courtyard the three tiny huts hug the base of the partition wall as if they wanted to shrink away in their utter insignificance. Up above, a patchwork of dovecots, and beyond those, the spire of the parish church. Here, at the steel door of The Kitty, she goes through her daily ritual. From her voluminous bosom she pulls out the small leather bag, and takes out the key to the four steel doors. She opens the door. The Hunchback precedes her with his load. They stop for a moment; the Baroness lights a kerosene lamp and locks the steel door to the courtyard. Together they inspect their peculiar steel chamber. Its shape is a regular square, each side consisting of a Gutjahr-Müller steel cell door equipped with a peephole. This is a veritable sluice chamber on dry land: no two doors may be open at the same time. The Hunchback puts down his load. The Baroness turns her key in the door on the left and opens it to the steps that lead up. "Wait here," she says, as always, and, taking a second lamp, hurries up to her inner office. From the small metal safe she removes her velvet bag, making certain that it is heavy, and getting heavier. She shakes it to hear the clink; opens it, reaches in and for a moment stands with her eyes closed: she envisions her many-storeyed dream mansion in its own park. As she is locking it away again, she experiences a shooting quiver of anxiety: perhaps she should not keep it here at home, after all. The doorman is waiting for her. His cubicle is behind the right-hand door; this is where he sleeps. The only other key to the doors is with him at all times, and there are no other copies. No one passes through this steel chamber without his knowledge.

He takes down a white apron from its hook on the door. The Baroness' eyes wander to the neatly made bed in the cubicle, and she quickly turns her head.

"Let's get to work," she spurs herself on aloud. The Hunchback, who is bending down, grins up at her. He locks the door with a practised hand, and tries the doorknob. He opens up the door leading to the ground floor. Ahead of them lie the service areas of the coffeehouse: kitchen, pantries, cooler and wine cellar entrance, and the spacious dining room for the employees of the establishment. This is the world of the service entrance. Beyond it lies the greater realm of the café. The Baroness' apartment is on the first floor; the smaller rooms occupied by the staff are on the first and second floors.

She lets the Hunchback pass on his way to the kitchen and she herself heads for the deserted main hall of the café. She oversees the cleaning women as they remove the cover from the billiards table, roll up the outside metal shutters and draw open the draperies. As morning light floods the café, she inspects the table settings, and makes sure that the Vienna, Berlin and Paris newspapers have arrived. The first guests are expected any moment. She nods in greeting as she passes the throne of the elderly daytime lady cashier, then mounts the serpentine stairway to her glass cage perched under the high ceiling. First she replaces in her cabinet the key to the service entrance; the entryway will be under observation from here on. The key to the steel chamber hangs around her neck. She sits down at her escritoire. She places the cash from the two purses in two separate piles, and counts it; then, going past her canopied brass bed, she opens the cabinet and places the money on two adjacent shelves. Only now does she draw apart the pale green silk curtains in front of her writing desk to survey her coffeehouse realm from on high. Month after month, and she still marvels at the vulgar elegance of her clientele. All the lords and gentlemen. And she already has her sights on higher goals. She sets out in front of her the main accounting book, as well as a smaller one bound in red leather.

She calculates, makes plans, does her bookkeeping; her morning passes in busy-work. Her tasks are numerous, her worries an ocean, but she takes to it like a duck to water.

At the apartment of the tailor Knorr near the circle railway, where I had reserved their rooms, my two partners arrive one morning.

The youngest of the three Misses Knorr watches the arrival from behind the curtains of the parlor and catches her breath on glimpsing the auburn-curled, Apollonian good looks of one of their tenants. Their elegant luggage boasts gilt-tooled monograms as would befit world travelers for whom distance is no obstacle. And even though she has heard that the handsome gentleman is Hungarian, he seems to be chatting quite fluently with the foreigner in the latter's language.

Our third associate and I are conversing in the middle of bustling Hatvan Street at high noon, soon after he checks in at his lodgings on Newmarket Square. His time has come. Starting tomorrow he will show up daily at the Grand Bazaar, dressed as a workman. For his role he needs to produce a conspicuous blue scar on his forehead, and he must stop shaving. And it won't be a bad idea if he neglects to wash for a day or two. He will hang around until he finds occasional work, odd jobs. His task is clear: to reconnoitre, to infiltrate.

THE VENGERKA

Breakfast and brunch having gone smoothly, the waiters are setting the tables for lunch in the grand café. Agnes Vad is done with her books by noontime. She gives praise to the Lord - ever since her Kitty was built she could count herself among the lucky ones of this world, who do what they love to do twenty-four hours a day. Her prayer is interrupted by a misty image of the Hunchback as he looks up at her with his smoulderingly ironic, dark, dog-like eyes. She is roused from her reverie by a knock on the door of her glass cage. With a quick movement she slips the still open red-bound book under the larger ledger.

"Come in." It is the Special Investigator, who arrives at a well-calculated hour. He likes to drop in, and he has the Baroness' standing invitation to join them at the long dining table used by the staff. The highly placed gentleman frequents the premises on behalf of his protégée. "Just a moment, let me put away my bookkeeping." Dajka turns away toward the café, drumming on the window pane with his fingers, tactfully pretending that he does not see the two books replaced in the cabinet. Agnes Vad does not notice this unusual courtesy on the part of the law enforcement officer.

The window panes of the glass cage tremble as the bells of the Inner City Church strike four. The proprietress wipes her pen nib and makes sure to stopper the alabaster inkwell. She draws the curtains of her cage and motions to Dajka, "Please follow me."

With a regal bearing she leads the way into the dining hall next to the kitchen, where her employees and business partners are already waiting for her. It is dinnertime for anyone who is at home now, dress is casual, and there is an abundance of hair curlers and mustache presses. In the Baroness' system these common meals have an important role in binding her extended family together. Aladár, the head waiter, jumps up to hold the chair for his mistress. He is indispensable; the smooth flow of the two kinds of night-time traffic depends in large part on his social sensitivity and tact. Here are the scullery maids, the waiters, and the daytime cleaning women who commute. And of course the girls - her hostesses. Also in attendance are the artistes, the exotic dancers, Kink and Kalkasa the Indian illusionists (although their birth certificates identify them as the brothers Kanalas, Gypsies from Small Saltpeter Street), as well as Muhammad Abdelkader the unicycle artist, better known as "Oily Nate". The Baroness holds her head erect; she knows full well that she is the one they can thank for the roof over their heads and the steaming plates of soup on the table. A flash of her eye is enough for the bread-girl on her right to yield her place to the Doctor. His almond-eyed protégée, who is neither dancer nor hostess, is seated next to him. They all stand while Agnes Vad says a brief grace, and takes her seat as Aladár assists her with the chair. The grande dame claps twice, and immediately the two cooks enter carrying giant tureens of steaming fish soup to put an end to all formality. A quiet trickle of chatter begins, and soon giggles may be heard from the end of the table; spoons are being lifted with great frequency and the slurping becomes less inhibited. Since the Doctor first started to visit his protégée, the staff has become used to having the Special Investigator in their midst, and the Baroness, in a bold turn, invited him to join the staff at their meals, if he would like. No one needed to be cautioned about secrecy.

The Doctor converses with Bora in low tones. In the course of these meals and during the occasional Monday dinners, he has become almost unsure of what constitutes the borderline between his private and official capacities.

The lady of the house is scribbling numbers with a pencil on a paper napkin by her soup bowl. Then she raises her voice to address the whole company, and the whole table grows silent.

"For two months now the market prices have been steadily rising."

The Special Investigator comes to the conclusion that Baroness Vad would talk about the same topics if he were not here, perhaps with a different selection of words. He listens carefully. She had early on decided that her menu would not reflect the spurious inflation of prices caused by the festivities. She knows that the workaday weekdays will return, and the steady clientele upon whom her business is based will remember that she did not extort high prices at a time when she could have, and everyone else did.

Lately she has been giving much thought to appliances that would make housekeeping easier. She has decided what they need.

The Doctor can enjoy an unexpected treat: to witness the actual, real-life application of the Schultze-Delitsch theories of a co-operative. The faces at the table, by their relative attention or indifference, reveal who are business partners, (mostly the various artistes and hostesses) and who aren't, such as Bora, or Bubbles, who is only a bread-girl. Agnes Vad counts off the items on her stubby fingers.

"First, a Sweeper Vac brand vacuum cleaner. It does not need that pesky electric power. Second, a washing machine with a floating washboard. Third, and fourth, a clothes press and a centrifugal drier. I have gone around and inquired, made my calculations, added and subtracted until I figured it out. All in all, the daily two-forint contribution from everyone will be sufficient to cover the expenses. The weekly wages will remain as they are, and we'll be able to reinvest the increased income from the Festivities into the business."

So he can see that his singer is in a good place. The Doctor is able to speak to her here any time he wants. For the Baroness knows that she might easily come to be in a position where she would need the personal goodwill of this powerful official. And if fate will have it - even though Agnes Vad breaks out in a cold sweat at the thought of a police officer beyond her steel doors - then he would have to be told about the upstairs, too.

In the course of the long conversation after the leisurely meal, Dajka has repeated occasion to nod in approval. Bora, this humble yet complex woman, has made quite a recovery;

she is at last able to face the realities of her life without hiding
or varnishing the truth. She has trusted him all along, and little
by little she has lost that hunted look in her eyes along with
her timidity, so that talking with her is no longer like pulling
teeth.

The ropemaker's daughter has a delicate network of
premature crow's-feet around her eyes, on her temples and
forehead. Still, hers is a strangely attractive face, with that
porcelain complexion and those Asiatic eyes. At times she lets
drop a word or two about her past life, for the benefit of the
Special Investigator, who is listening with fatherly interest, and
at other times she chatters on like a child who is happy to
have found someone who is kind enough to listen to her with
obvious interest. Her little Natalie had diphtheria, but she is
getting better. And her son Miklós is a growing boy. Bora's
ramblings pretty soon wander off into her past. Little by little,
in the course of the past year, from Russian and French
placenames she has dropped, and the occasional foreign
expressions, names and minuscule odds and ends, the Special
Investigator has been able to piece together the story of her
life.

Little Veronica, the apple of her parents' eye, had grown
into a slender, delicate maiden by age twelve, one whose dark
beauty and bright intelligence shone like a lamp out of her
surroundings. Her father, a hard-working ropemaker, had the
will, but lacked the means for his daughter's advancement.

Fate had hurried the resolution, although by way of
misfortune: that same spring the girl's mother was confined to
bed with galloping consumption and died within six weeks. The
father confessor of the family, on the basis of the girl's
outstanding school marks, was able to place her as an orphan
with free tuition at the Ursulines' school in Szentmihályfalva.

There she did laundry and ironing, housecleaning, all sorts
of menial work in addition to her schoolwork, and even found
time to do her more affluent classmates' homework, for cash.
The French teacher, whenever she felt indisposed, always
asked the tuition-free scholar to take over her classes. Paris,
City of Lights, began to feature prominently in the adolescent

girl's dreams. She embroidered ornamental boxes and whenever she earned a little extra money, she put it away next to her maternal inheritance, the thin gold chain and the crucifix.

On her eighteenth birthday she took out her treasure box, sold the chain and cross, and in the middle of the school year said good-bye to the Mother Superior and to a kitchen-girl who had been her friend. She kissed her father on the cheeks at his workshop, purchased a white dress with a pelerine at Zsuzsanna Krak's; at the Magyar Fashion Bazaar she bought a muff, a fan with artificial flowers and a silk parasol, and, taking her small wicker suitcase, boarded the train that took her to Paris at Carnival time. She had intended to find employment as a governess, but had no luck. When she spent the last of her small savings, she accepted the long-standing offer of the proprietor of the café that was in the same building as her pension. Adopting a stage name, she sang Hungarian songs in the evening for the middle-class public. Ever since then she has called herself Bora. What she lacked in vocal range or in singing ability was more than compensated by her lovely face, her innocent charm and her refined convent upbringing. To her father at home she wrote that she found employment as a governess, teaching German to her landlord's children.

At night the bodice of her Hungarian costume was sprinkled with crystalline glitter that reflected the hall's lights like a myriad sparkling stars. At the end of one short month she was offered a contract at six times the money, at one of the great *cafés chantants* with enormous plate-glass windows facing the Champs Elysées. And she was still a woman of spotless virtue.

The men of the Parisian night-life were captivated by this exotic Hungarian flower hailing from the westernmost edge of the Eurasian steppes. And yet the first one to invade her bed was the landlord mentioned in her letter, the fat, sniveling husband of her landlady. She woke terrified on the iron bed in the dormer, a filthy paw over her mouth. A silent scuffle followed, then nausea, and blood stains on her bedsheet in the bleak dawn light above the rooftops. That day she asked for and received a double salary at the café so that she could move to a hotel. Night after night the local gilded youth and nouveau-riche bankers offered her their lives and fortunes -

but never their names. Theater directors and aristocrats, manufacturers and obscure foreign princes approached her, only to disappear into the void.

One fine day, as in a fairy tale, the prince of her dreams arrived in a white automobile, to take her away to the sparkling realm of eternal snow and ice. With his sleek black hair combed straight back, he sat in his stage box; he was Russian, slender and young; a colonel and a prince. Bora went weak in the knees as she sang. In the fall they traveled to Saint Petersburg.

The girl's tragedy had been inscribed in the book of her fate at the moment of birth. She matured early; her fate was to fade early as well. Her almond eyes glowed with a dark fire, her stature proud, her waist as narrow as a reed, her complexion a pale glimmer of mother of pearl. At eighteen she stood at the height of her beauty. She was the queen of that Saint Petersburg season, hovering at a certain precisely delimited demi-mondaine depth or height. For the young prince did not *quite* take her away as in the fairy tale. Fairy tale princes do not have to heed the social consequences of legally contracted marriage, nor do they have to reckon with the at times one-sided relationships of love and life on a grand scale.

Prince Nicholas purchased and furnished for her a small mansion by the banks of the Neva. Life was an unending party; the troika sped on the glittering powder snow, the three bells jingled, the birch woods were left behind, the horses' breath steamed in the frost, the French champagne bubbled, the Russian Gypsies sang, the Hungarian Gypsies played the violin.

By the time the white birches had new leaves and the tight-fisted Russian summer arrived, Bora was carrying a little princely bastard under her heart. When he was born, she named him Nicholas after his father, and when they were alone, she whispered Hungarian endearments and called her baby Miklóska. The father of the child hired a nurse and increased the monthly allowance. On the sly, *tout Petersbourg* applauded the lovers, with a malicious sneer.

Two years flew by, and *tout Petersbourg* now had a new

favorite in the person of a leather-clad Cherkess danseuse sporting blonde braids. A second child was born on the banks of the Neva and received the name of Natalie in the holy rites of the Russian Orthodox Church.

A first early harbinger, a single white hair appeared in Bora's raven locks after the birth of her second child. For hours on end she would sit at her vanity, trying to assess the meaning of this blow. She came to a decision. She thought she should read the message as nature's alarm, warning her that it was time to make arrangements for her own and her children's future. She took the step that she had been cautioned against by her friends, the ageing cocotte who had first-hand experience of social conventions, and the wetnurse who had native peasant good sense. She gathered her little daughter in her arms, while her small son waddled beside her, holding on to her skirt in the slushy snow. This is how she rang the bell at the door of the princely palace on Nevski Prospect, to demand her rights. Let Nicholas make her his princess before the whole world and let his children carry his name. The prince could only ask, in tender regret, "Why did you have to do this, my Bora? *Oh, pourquoi?*" But she was determined not to give up her just struggle under any circumstances.

In the afternoon the unwed mother was visited by a plainclothes detective from the Saint Petersburg police. Over the black slushy puddles of the small riverside street, the grapevine had it that he was from the dreaded Ochrana itself, but this was not the case. In the name of the government of the Tzar of all the Russias he offered her a free choice: the Mademoiselle, with all deference to certain high connections, had three days to depart of her own free volition from the territory of the empire, never again to return. On the fourth day at sunrise she would be forcibly deported by the police as a *Vengerka*, back to her homeland, where she belonged.

That was the word that crushed her, and drained all her fighting spirit. You see, many girls and women of our homeland had, for a long time, traveled East as dancers or chorus girls, just as nowadays they travel to the West. It is best to face the truth and hang our heads in recognition of our national misery, or else raise our heads in bitter defiance, proud of the beauty and desirability of our women; but be that as it may, we have to acknowledge that this word "Vengerka", which means a Hungarian of the feminine gender, had come to designate a whore throughout the brilliant snowy spaces of the Russian Empire. Bora had always believed that it could apply only to the others, to those common little dancing sluts. Yes, the word is a cruel instrument, sharp as a razor, weighty as a guillotine: think it over twice, before playing with it. All of a sudden, without warning, the daughter of the ropemaker from Miller Street had to face the facts, and wake up in the grim light of a single word to find that even in her little mansion, with her troika, her Mumm's Cordon Rouge and her truffle patés, over the years she would amount to nothing but this, a *Vengerka*. She would have taken her own life that very minute, had she not her two innocent ones to consider. And so she merely went in search of a buyer for her little mansion, any buyer she could find at a day's notice - and the butler of the Cherkess dancing girl's patron was willing to pay one third of what the house was worth, in cash. It occurred to Bora that perhaps Nicholas, too, had obtained the property at a bargain price. But by then this no longer mattered. Giving wide berth to her homeland she traveled to the nearest metropolis, which happened to be Vienna.

Here she was taken under wing by a sixty-year-old landowner from the County of Udvarhely. Bora, who was still hopelessly and irrevocably in love with her prince, now found, for the first time, the expensive solace of morphine. An old woman, an abortionist-midwife, administered it to her intravenously, so that she could put up with the sour breath and sweaty siege of the ageing paramour's flagging desire. By the time he grew tired of her, she was injecting her own dosages of the poison, with hands that had acquired an evil expertise.

The first wrinkles on her face sketched the outlines of tomorrow's fuller map. The price of her mansion was quickly melting away.

What followed were chance encounters, mostly for daily bread: a lieutenant of the hussars, a bank teller. Her last liaison was with a cab driver; that was how low she had slipped on the social scale. She spent more and more time sitting on the edge of her bed staring away into nothingness in a pleasant stupor. Unaware of her two small children crawling about like little animals, she would wonder what this snuff-scented stranger was doing in her room, who would not even understand when you spoke plain Hungarian.

By early winter the abortionist was arrested and her confession led the police to Bora. She was expelled from the imperial capital. Hard-pressed to find a home for the barely weaned Natalie and the four-year-old Miklós, she entrusted them to Frau Bábi, a Grinzing matron who weighed two hundred sixty pounds and who specialized in caring for the offspring of unwed Hungarian mothers with similar fates. Her charges were well fed, clean and playful, but the monthly costs were steep. Bora paid for the first quarter and boarded the express train for Budapest.

The ropemaker left no house or inheritance, not even debts. Within two weeks Bora began her descent down the predestined path. A young count, who fancied himself a perennial law student, rented an apartment for her on Váci Boulevard (for you: Bajcsy Zsilinszky Road). When the flash in the pan relationship fizzled after a few months, as a generous quittance he purchased for her the lease of a coffee shop in the outlying Stone Quarry district.

The shop meant waking at the crack of dawn, and back-breaking work lugging huge milk cans all day long. A hundred liters of milk were sold each day. Her small apartment in the back reeked of buttermilk and whey. Less and less of the income was left after her monthly payments to Frau Bábi. By now Bora had forgotten that she ever sang. She saw only one course of action for herself. She sold the coffee shop and rented her first room in Pest, on her way down the road that led to Mrs. Tremmel's as the last stop, where the Special Investigator came across what was left of the one-time star student of the Ursulines, the former toast of Saint Petersburg. You know the rest of her story.

RAGS, MUGS, AND DOLLS

Dajka thanks the hostess for the long luncheon as he slowly rises from the smokers' table in the staff dining room. This afternoon the story of Bora Clarendon has finally taken shape for him. He sets out for headquarters in a gloomy mood. He is somewhat perturbed by the ambiguous status of the café; whether the Baroness is breaking the law seems to depend entirely on his view of things.

He intends to clear his desk before the onrush of the weekend. It has been well-nigh a year since he has had news of the safe-breakers, but each morning he wakes up with the feeling that this will be the day he will hear about their latest exploits.

The Baroness stays in her office. She pulls the curtains and contemplates her coffeehouse with quiet satisfaction. Now that Dajka is gone she can breathe freely. Business is thriving, the place is more crowded than ever; ninety to a hundred lunches are sold daily instead of an average of twenty-five a year ago. At night, when the place turns into a dance hall, the band goes over well, and so do Kink and Kalkasa, and the ageing soubrettes. As for the upstairs program, which she had recently revised, it seems to be just right, and will not need further changes until the end of the season of Millennial Festivities. Again she has succeeded in accomplishing the impossible: attuning the two different programs that are as far apart as earth and sky, heaven and hell, although their music is the same. On the ground floor night after night Bora sings her one and only love song to lukewarm applause. Dajka comes at times to hear her, so that she can account beautifully for keeping the singer around. As for her real act upstairs, it has worked out phenomenally; when she sings that number, the corners of her eyes with their fine network of crow's-feet somehow suggest untold mysteries; her mere presence attracts men of all ages and types. Since that final weekend at Mrs. Tremmel's she has not had anything to do with any of them, and still, each guest stays later because of her and big spenders spend even bigger.

This is the hour when waiters, illusionists and dancing girls can relax a while in their rooms. These few hours of the day are truly their own, until the evening, when each will resume his or her role. The mustache presses and hair nets are taken off now, another dab of brilliantine is applied to the hair, and the men set out like lone tomcats on their early evening prowls. The women remove their hair curlers; some remain at home to chew the cud, or do a bit of needlework, or play cards; others go out on the town to shop, or stroll, or ride a carriage and look around, pretty much like any idle middle-class lady with nothing to do. The bread-girl puts on a full white blouse and a high-waisted organdie skirt that sweeps the ground. She elects to take her scarlet red Lyons silk parasol, fatefully, as if she had intended to mark herself so that I would be able to follow her all the way home. The service entrance is locked until the morning, and she can only go through the restaurant if the doorman is not in his place, so she leaves by the back exit. The Hunchback lumbers out of his cubicle, opens and shuts the steel doors and gives her a leer of mysterious complicity. If someone were to see him now, it would be hard to mistake him for a man with a deformity. The girl flashes her gamin-like smile at him, revealing the glow of the snow-white enamel of her teeth. Out past the carriage gate she takes Hat Street to Leopold Street and looks up at the windows: the shutters cast long shadows on the facade. At the hackney stand on Rose Square she takes a cab and has herself driven to the Exhibition grounds. She has been longing for some time to see the sights all by herself, to take in all those marvels that the whole country is so excited about, to enjoy all the entertainment and sideshows in the Municipal Park. She heard they even had a real fire-eater.

The generously thick brick walls of the building exclude the noise of the hoofbeats of the hackney horse from the all-glass office installed under the ceiling. Having finished the letters ordering the selected appliances, the Baroness puts down her pen. With a superfluous gesture she dusts the letter with writing sand, and seals the envelope. She tugs at the copper handle of the bell pull above her escritoire. Then she indulges in a long and luxurious stretch so that she can hear her bones crack.

A moment later the Hunchback enters, without knocking.

"Béres," she calls out to him, drawling the name by which he goes these days, "draw the curtains for me."

She carries her hefty blonde body so lightly that she nearly passes for slender. But she is not slim; even her face is broad and somewhat flat. She has prominent cheekbones, and a pug nose. Her grey eyes are far apart. Her throat is full and has a milky sheen. Hers is a facial type that can be seen all over Europe. Her flaxen hair is so light that even if she had begun to have gray hairs they would not show. The rosy tinge of her sensual mouth, her carefully tended complexion flecked with gentle wrinkles that are like hairline cracks in the dry soil - all remind the doorman of the words of the Gypsy voivode Bershehero, whose greatest praise, his hymn to life, went like this: "Now she is so fine, all woman." And that is precisely what the Baroness was: fine and clean, and a woman through and through, down to her toenails. Smart enough to know what she wants and honest enough to admit it.

A tiny crack of light streams in through the middle of the glass wall from the direction of the hall of the café where only the daytime lady cashier keeps watch in the afternoon.

"No, you're not getting any," the Baroness says slowly, her voice cracking. She pushes aside the finished letters. She stands up from her escritoire, takes two steps, and with a single motion of her short, round arm she gives an open-palm shove to the doorman's chest so that he lets himself drop like a bowling pin flat on his back in the middle of her canopied brass bed, where he disappears from view. She bends over him. His mute canine gaze again makes her eyes all misty. She takes one of his arms and extends it toward the corner post of the bed, and likewise adjusts his feet to the two posts at the other end. Without a word the man lets her do as she pleases; he merely looks on. Now the other arm is placed next to the last post. Then she peels herself out of her layers of clothes, down to her last, daring knickers that are fastened with ribbons below her knees. She kneels by the doorman's side, and moves over him. She casts a hungry glance at the abundance of towels by the sink. She has a penchant for tying his extremities to the four posts with knots that can be easily undone.

"You're not getting anything now. Do you understand, you big brute?" Slowly, sensually she throws her right leg over the fully clothed man who is stretched out, and kneels astride him. "Don't you dare move." She grabs a handful of hair on his sturdy nape and draws the wide-eyed man's head toward herself. With languorous deliberation she rubs his nose against her armpit, then draws his face to the warm hillocks of her breasts. Her ecstatic smile seems to say, "This is what I am; inhale me, devour me." She snuggles and wiggles against him. Her grip tenses on his head as she carefully wraps her legs around his neck. "Princes?..." she asks. "Do princes have it this good?...Tell me." With quiet mirth the doorman shakes his head, drawing his mouth and nose side to side over her crotch wrapped in soft silk and moist with desire. "Would you like some?" asks the Baroness. And now she is caressed up and down by the eagerly repeated nods of his head. "Me too. Me too, you animal!" she croaks in a husky voice. Her eyes are melting with desire. "This is only an appetizer. You'll get the whole thing when I tie you up. But not now, you beast. You know we can't, not in broad daylight. Now get going and mail those letters."

The paths, willy-nilly, are converging.

Haluska the lookout is lugging things all day: gramophones, salmon, ballroom footwear and shotguns. About the only thing he does not carry is the remontoir clock the gentlemen insisted on taking home themselves. Afterwards he always holds out his hand very humbly. His services are constantly called upon at the hunting equipment shop, at the store for devotional articles, at the shoe store and at the delicatessen. He is always hanging out at the Bazaar. He has become a slovenly, unshaven but friendly person, exactly as his role demands.

After a short time spent at headquarters, the Doctor has himself driven to the Exhibition grounds. In the cab he skims through the circulars on the most wanted criminals, something a police officer must keep in mind if he is to help maintain the city's peace during these hectic times. He sees portraits of escaped convicts, and vagabonds who, after the completion of their sentences, were ordered to return to their villages but never showed up. Here is a rogue's gallery of cutpurses, cat burglars, pimps and fences, notorious vagrants and murderers. He scrutinizes the portraits until his experienced eye commits them to memory. After the period of rehearsals and dry runs the Millennial siss-boom-bah has been in full swing for a month now. Exhibitions, processions, parades. The city is full of wealth and splendor, which is bound to attract that Chicago-style, dynamite-using gang of safe-crackers. For the duration of these Festivities every police officer and detective must keep watchful, especially in the quarter of the predictable targets.

He blends into the crowds at the Exposition grounds. Derby hats and flowery feminine headgear are streaming by under the breeze-driven clouds of the sky. This is the day on which Krishna Gopal the Indian fakir is going to commence his trance. It is not a punishable fraud; let the gullible public beware. But the fact that the city is able to support two sleeping fakirs at the same time is evidence for the man of the law that the traffic is thick and a lot of money must be changing hands.

Mosque Square, where the national orchestra of Rudi Rácz is playing, is a veritable paradise for pickpockets. In the thick of the audience Dajka recognizes one of his plainclothesmen. The cry of the barker rings out on the small plaza in front of the wax works show. Inside, a special glass case displays the moving scene of an officer dying on the battlefield, in the course of which you may observe the doctor, his arm moving up and down, attempting to stanch the bleeding gunshot wound, even as the head of the sapient surgeon sways with knowledge of the fatal hopelessness of his efforts. Also to be seen: Louis Kossuth, the father of our country, lying in full state on his catafalque, life-size.

This is where the hot air balloon ascends, piloted by a personal representative of M. Godard.

Just a hop and a step away is the Komédia World

Panorama, with its own barker, trying to outshout the others. Panoramas of foreign countries! See the blind horse, railroad carriages, battles, scenic landscapes! Under a gigantic magnifying glass the view of Naples, with fierce Vesuvius belching smoke! The public execution of horse thieves and malefactors in the streets of Stamboul! The Occupation of Bosnia, complete with Hajji Loya himself, the leader of the Sarajevo resistance! The conquering Spanish Armada scattered by the storm and the cannonade of the English ships! Napoleon Bonaparte in his melancholy exile! An old-time whipping post, polka-dot scarves, the machine that can write and the Minister of Nourishment!

Dajka keeps his eyes open and observes everything around him; for a long time now he has been unable take a single step in a private capacity. He is soon past the official Exhibition grounds and enters the so-called Municipal Park, a much more interesting arena for him. This is obviously a far, far livelier scene. The place is crawling with itinerant clowns; it is one vast hurly-burly of entertainers, illusionists, high-wire acts and fire-eaters. Dajka has been through this area countless times since its opening in May, and his interest has never flagged. He witnesses how bumpkins are hooked by vendors of whetstones, matches and miracle glues. He picks up a pottery mug. He handles a wooden spoon, inscribed with burnished letters: "I love you Mariska". He replaces it, carefully maintaining his incognito. Hearing the ragman's spiel is a connoisseur's treat. "Rags, ladies, for rags I'll trade you plates, cups, give me your odds and ends, I'll give you mugs, dolls, all kinds of Juliska, Mariska, Boriska dolls."

There are Italian street singers, Albanian and Gypsy dancers; in the distance there are donkey, camel and mule races for prizes. The ponies are trotting. Proceeding past booths, tents and canopies, the officer of the law reaches that end of the grassy turf where my troupe is camped out, near Hermina Road. All paths seem to converge. He recognizes neither pickpockets nor detectives in the encircling crowd that is four and five deep. But before he has had enough of the cheap entertainment and decides to move on, having cast a coin on the tarpaulin, he wriggles through the crowd to the front row. And so he will be able to see clearly, although without understanding its significance, the sudden, inexplicable hitch in my well-practised routine during the fire-eating act.

Dajka is still standing in the back row when I lower my upraised palms and lower on to the tarpaulin the girl clad in sky blue. She is Murikeo, the Pearl. I am wearing a worn, brown striped suit and a soft hat. The pockets of my jacket stick out, for they are stuffed full of odds and ends. My shirt collar is folded out over my lapel, and boasts a line of ingrained dirt, and my face sports a two-day growth of beard.

ALLEY-OOP!

Murikeo hands me the trumpet. I play a cheap honky-tonk melody, some military marching song, and meanwhile, as always, my eyes are roving all around, scanning everyone. I am always on the lookout for her, it has become second nature to me over the years. I am still unaware that it will happen today, that my life will take a whole new turn. I wipe my mouth on my jacket sleeve and put down the trumpet. The Pearl takes a bow at the side and with trivial little ballet flourishes gestures to introduce the main attraction. Kodel holds up high the one-liter green bottle for everyone to see.

"Alley-oop!" At my softly voiced command the bottle flies in a precise arc into my hand. Only my associates can hear me. "Now watch this," I hiss to Kodel from the side of my mouth. "You might have to do the next show." And behind my back Gyuri Schordje's drums begin to roll.

Showmanship... With a circular gesture I carry the bottle around, in front of the ladies and gentlemen in the audience. I throw my head back and tilt the bottle to my mouth. I suck my cheek pouches full, taking care not a drop goes down my gullet. The drum roll keeps up a steady monotone. The Pearl picks up from the tarpaulin the front page of the government daily, shows it all around to the general merriment of the groundlings. She rolls it up into a torch. Kodel lights it and hands it to me. I throw my hat down on the tarpaulin. Here comes the moment of carburation, the crucial instant.

And at this moment, when my mouth is full of the horrible taste of kerosene, it happens: life throws a handful of sand into the machinery of our safe-cracking operation. As if struck by lightning, I am pierced by the vision of a pair of bright eyes and a tell-tale feminine mouth, in the first row of the audience. I become completely oblivious to everything else that is happening around me. My lips create a mist of tiny droplets of kerosene which, as I bend forward, I blow toward the audience and light up in front of my mouth. The onlookers have the distinct impression that I am swallowing the flame, instead of exhaling it. I look her in the eye as I blow out a roaring tongue of flame, nearly six feet long, such as I have never before produced, in the direction of the human ring encircling me, so that it shrinks back in fright. She wears a white blouse and a white skirt and is twirling a closed red parasol on her shoulder. She is enjoying the fire-eater's show. Remarkable. Most remarkable.

When the flame goes out, Murikeo, with sprightly blue strides, hastens to pass the hat around at once before they get a chance to recover, for the more tight-fisted ones will start slinking off as soon as the show is over. I rattle off my spiel at lightning speed. "Ladies and gentlemen, give if you please, give if you liked and give if you didn't." The crowd is already breaking up, you simply cannot talk fast enough for them. The girl with the red parasol tosses a coin into the hat, and looks back at me once before being swallowed up by the crowds. I recognize my moment of decision: this is it. Alley-oop!

"You take over," I snap at Kodel without a moment's hesitation, and put the bottle down. "You're the boss now."

My move is the last straw; our downfall becomes unavoidable. Our painstakingly prepared heist is going to be rudely crossed by the unpardonable drama of lovers' jealousy. From here on I needed absolute and total security in every move, and yet: I would still do the safe-job all over again even with full knowledge of what was about to happen.

I take my hat from the Pearl's hands, and, lifting the hem of her blue skirt, I tip the small change into it. I kiss her, pat her on her sweet little behind; I even have time to kiss Lilia and Alma farewell on the lips before leaving my troupe forever. I put on my soft hat and with gliding steps I take off in the wake of that girl with the tell-tale mouth in the crowded fairgrounds. I am not going to lose her.

I jog along the length of Hermina Road, my eyes flashing left and right like a lynx prowling. I am not surprised when the summer clouds are suddenly scattered by a breeze and a burst of sunlight floods the teeming sidewalks. In this new light, far ahead, a red parasol opens, as naturally as a flower. That is Today, glowing red in the distance. That is She. All is well in the world; lady luck is with me from now on and the sun is shining for me. This is the Lyons silk parasol she will leave behind forever in her room, along with her other proud possession, her pearl-grey dress. There is no rush now. I can follow her at a more leisurely pace, allowing a safe distance between us.

Entrance to the Exposition grounds costs thirty kreuzers. I would like to rinse out my mouth. Whew, the taste of kerosene is the one thing I hated in this line of work. The girl is really taking her time, she doesn't have to start work until nightfall, but I am not aware of this as yet. I know nothing about her.

And we take in the Exhibition quite thoroughly, she leading the way, with me in tow, according to the rules and regulations of trailing a person. From Barnum's Seven Wonders of the World here is Thompson Wilkins, a gentleman who is seven feet six inches tall. And the Bearded Lady. And Aelvona, the beauty with only half a body, growing out of a card table. And a sad couple: the last Aztecs, from faraway Mexico City, who are now being dragged all over the world. And the Elastic Man. And Melanie, the Magnetta Lady, whose flesh is illustrated with tattooed portraits of Schiller and Mozart, as well as the image of our New House of Parliament. At the Oriental Theater, we see a *danse du ventre* featuring Namura and Zorak. In the grand mosque, a Muslim service is in progress. Whirling dervishes whirl, and howling dervishes howl. These True Believers have been attracted here from the last European vestiges of the Ottoman Empire. Here is the

Bazaar's public scribe, also a lapidary and a potter. The tailor
is ironing with his feet, Turkish style. In the recreation of Buda
under Turkish rule the delicate little Gothic and Renaissance
buildings are immaculately clean, each with their tiny toy
balconies, towers, and thickly latticed Turkish windows. The
gentle citizen will find here many a charming, cozy nook and
such merry entertainment that he may even become reconciled
to a couple of hundred years of Turkish occupation.

It is easy like this, when all that is so far away in the past
and we are no longer a territory of Islam - for once upon a
time, we were such. - It is heavy, the yoke of the heathen
lording it over us, whenas with my hard-saved pennies from
years of mendicant singing, impatient of waiting any longer, on
the seventh day of the month of All Saints around noontime,
in the guise of a Dutch merchant I approach on the wide open
highway toward Pest, plying my trade, wondering whether I
would be recognized or would I be allowed to earn a
livelihood as a minstrel and public scribe in the Bazaar? To
the chiaus standing guard I complain in broken German about
the horrors of those Netherlandish winters. I had thrown away
my triple lute, my livelihood. At this time the Blue Planet is
going through a little Ice Age; the Baltic Sea freezes like a
small puddle; on the island of Greenland the Viking
descendants of Erik the Red die of starvation and frostbite;
Alpine glaciers advance far south into Europe, and in my
minstrel travels I had occasion to see wee Dutchmen bundled
in scarves skating on the Amsterdam canals that froze to the
bottom. The world-famous Second Chicago, our unified twin
capital city, is still far off in the future; for that matter, the
original Chicago has not been founded as yet. It is in quite
another aspect that hilly Buda awaits me now: as the main
western outpost, along with the flatland town of Pest, in the
Mahommetan empire of the East; having fled from here once
upon a time, and now having returned from foreign peregrinations, I cannot forego the sight of my native town. Round and
round I circumambulate the walled town like a moth at night
flying around a lamp, well aware that if they recognize my
face, they will seize me, their former captive slave, and
dismember me with their handjars and drag me around tied to

a horse's tail. Still, I fall helplessly into the flame of the lamp. It is a Friday, the holy day of Islam. Back home, I suffer the piteous wounds of my nation, invaders on all sides battering, smiting the Magyar hosts. I cross the watery outer moats of the walled town of Pest. By the old gate I dip the cup into the icy well water awaiting the thirsty wanderer. Bread, pilaf and candles are handed out, this being the heathen's holy day. I take it all under my robe, I am home at last.

Saint Peter Street in Pest on the river's left bank (for you: Petőfi Sándor Street - University Street - Kecskeméti Street) is lit by one solitary flickering oil lamp. In the middle of town a rivulet gurgles in a stinking ditch, sending steaming miasmic exhalations upward (for you: Ferenc Deák Street). Slipping and stumbling I make my way from one row of hovels to another. They are all plastered with mud, and possess the tiniest windows; the rains have ruined some, and pigs root about in puddles where houses once stood. Following the mud-plastered, ramshackle fences that keel over tottering, I arrive on the boggy and miry bank at the footbridge that leads to the other side - roughly about where the large store is where I bought the elastic waistband for you today, and where, as you browsed through the store's treasures - ribbons, buttons and fasteners - you came across those small glass stars, that are the latest rage at school: everyone is sticking these sparkling thingamajigs on sweaters and clothes.

Neither do I find my solace in the crumbling houses of Buda as I reach its marketplace across the cemetery of Our Lady. For a spell of sleep I find a chamber in the back of the old cathedral. The churches are empty and without priests, their roofs crumbling. The fallen tiles are not replaced, the rain leaks in and the wind blows through the walls. Cinders of houses consumed by fire. Swayback walls are propped up with large joists from the outside. Alongside formerly resplendent palaces all sorts of ragtag additions and vendors' stalls are stuck on with lumps of mortar. Older and once proud houses have disappeared without a trace. Others have been divided with stone and wooden partitions into wretched little holes in their Levantine fashion by the janissaries and other Turkish warriors. Elsewhere they have broken through the walls of a row of burghers' townhouses to create improvised armories, mosques, stables or medreses, schools for the Turk.

Alas I find the Church of Our Lady; woe is me, it has been turned into a djami, cleansed of all graven images and pagan idols, obeying the Second Law of Moses. The grand old bell that must have weighed sixty quintals has been cast down from the tower, and in its place they built a balcony out of wood; at the pinnacle of its spire, instead of the cross, they planted a crescent and emblems of the Turkish sultan; within, they put up minbar and mihrab and they read aloud the Mahommetan Bible, the AlKoran, much to my sorrow and shame. - The girl, thank God, by now has had enough of this doll's-house Turkish Buda, in this day and age that saw our new House of Parliament recently finished. She twirls her red Lyons silk parasol on her shoulder; I cannot tell if she is laughing or crying at what she has seen; she shakes her head, murmurs something and moves on.

So on we go. She does not want to miss anything. She inspects the one and only, true Edison cinematograph, Doctor Candiani's Venetian glass blowers, Abdullah's carpet bazaar. The Italian tarantella, the promenade boats, the regatta, the Turkish *café chantant*, the Parisian panorama and the Arab fortune teller. By the Saxon house and the Gypsy tent from Fehér County, on the corner of Arena Street, she leaves the park and finds herself on the former Radius Avenue.

Today this street is darkened by a swarm of humanity. The girl sets out. The sidewalk is a mass of flags. To cross to the other side would be to tempt Providence. Four lanes of carriages are rattling and careening over the famous wooden boards of the roadway, in an endless procession of elegant parade coaches, carriage and fours, speedy landaus, and light fiacres. I have to walk two city blocks before I can cross. In the outer traffic lane an omnibus is lurching like a mastodon, displaying a Bensdorp Dutch cocoa advertisement on its giant billboard. It stops on the corner of Mulberry Orchard Street and she gets on; I reach it just in time. Today is that kind of day.

The wind has scattered the clouds, and it is uncertain now whether it will rain. Both of us get off at Izabella Street.

(For you: still Izabella, this lucky one has survived.) The tawny walls of aristocratic mansions are covered by the national tricolors and endless buntings. In the roadway pass cavalcades of parade escorts from the various counties, the hussars all equipped with powder pouches. The brilliant white sleeves of the coachmen billow up on the boxes of magnates' resplendent equipages.

At Octagon Place, where Radius Avenue intersects the Grand Boulevard, between four fountains a paunchy mounted policeman is trying to control his large, unruly horse. A white plume of feathers flutters in a sudden breeze. Here only the zig-zagging velocipedists can wheel about, sunlight gaily flashing on their peaked caps. The larger vehicles are stopped in a traffic jam as far as the eye can see; horse-drawn trams, a yellow Court phaeton carrying one of the royal princes of the House of Hapsburg (with which House, as you well may imagine, we shall have some business in due course). We are witnessing that exceptional moment when the traffic of the united twin capital cities comes to a complete and prolonged halt. The girl crosses the street, and I likewise, in her wake.

At last she sits down to catch her breath on a bench where saplings fresh from the nursery stand behind her, each young tree protected by a strong stake and an iron cage turned inward at the top. The greenery on Factory Street provides rest for the eyes. These trees are here to stay, making this one spot where the asphalt, and all its pimps, will not triumph. I make use of the occasion and pay a hurried visit to the public lavatory, "second class", where for a fee of thirty kreuzers I can at last rinse out the kerosene taste from my mouth. Once and for all: I am not going to gulp that stuff ever again.

I hide behind nuns dressed in black, peasant women wearing scarves and many petticoats, and ladies with parasols until the girl moves on. I cannot as yet know where she is heading. Only premonitions stir within me. We pass new four-storey buildings with the scaffolding still in place. The planks, sand, and mortar have already been carted away, so that not even a single loose brick remains on the ground.

We are at the terminal stop of the King Street electric tram, near St. Theresa's Church. This lively, colorful, much-trafficked yet relatively orderly street hardly resembles its former self, when it was the chief thoroughfare leading from the Country Road (for you: Council Boulevard) to the Town Park, the most unswept of our streets, while being the main commercial artery of the town that rose from its ashes after its occupation by the heathen.

At a first glance from the sidewalk by the church, all one sees is chaos.

Yet we are only a few steps away from the serenity of Radius Avenue. Here fiacres run amok, omnibuses rage; an absurd, leftover dogcart convulses, a throng of carts and wheelbarrows clatter, shove, surge, thud and plow into each other, overrunning the littered street, at times even straying onto the sidewalk if no other means of passage is available. Little Jews wearing silk yarmulkes unload mysterious packages, bales, crates and sacks from arriving vans, oblivious of the late hour. As I amble along on the opposite side of the street, submerged in this Mediterranean-flavored teeming, I manage to get closer to the girl. I observe that whenever she stops in front of one of the numerous nightclubs, she takes her time to read through the entire program, and pouts. This is where all the Cats are lined up side by side, the Black Cat, the Spotted Cat, and over there, the infamous Blue Cat at No. 38 King Street, the high-life nightclub, an establishment not recommended for lady guests. So what?

We reach the Orczy House at the end of King Street, where Olga the Whale's forebear had once been simply referred to as the "Black Jew". When Emperor Joseph, the "Hatted King" (because uncrowned), issued his edict requiring Jews to adopt family names, Olga's forefather became Edelman. In this quarter the streaming crowds thin out somewhat, and we face the open square ahead. For once it happens to be empty and our eyes can roam freely. A slight gradient leads a yellow double-decker omnibus out of the bay formed by the sidewalks. (Perhaps this is the granddaddy of our yellow Budapest streetcars, among all these dark green electric trams.) Fragile young trees stand enclosed in their cages, and gas streetlamps hang in florescent clusters from poles planted in the wide sidewalk. Striped awnings, like so many thick eyebrows, project over shop windows and cool entryways.

I hide in doorways, shop entrances, behind advertising pillars. Up ahead the girl has embarked on the sea of cobblestones covering the square: brave navigator whose vessel is launched across turbulent waters. A horse-drawn street car arrives from the direction of Váci Boulevard. A hansom cab passes, its top pulled down. A peasant cart approaches, laden with long timber spars that jut out in the back, and a constable glares at the carter. It neither rains nor shines, but the girl's red parasol, left open, is a pirate sail floating by the Two Turks House into the estuary of Thirtieth Street. I break away from the safety of the shores and plunge in after her, enchanted traveler on the wings of salt breezes.

The master tailor Emil Knorr is a law-abiding citizen, a pillar of security and strength for the homeland (the Dual Homeland, a duality that will one day disappear). So law-abiding that, in the strictest obedience to rules and regulations, he personally delivers the registration forms of his gentleman lodgers to the police station. They are subsequently recorded and filed where they may be duly retrieved from among the many thousands here for the Millennial Festivities.

Back at home the auburn-haired guest completes his prolonged, somewhat womanish toilette amidst much splashing and loud gargling and emerges dressed in formal evening wear from top to toe, even though the sun is just setting.

He has himself driven to the central post office where he sends a cable in German referring to certain grain purchases, to Agap Kevorg, Russian subject residing at a Saint Petersburg address: "PREPARE FOR DELIVERY OF MERCHANDISE STOP LETTER ON THE WAY STOP". From the post office he heads toward King Street, and not far from St. Theresa's Church he settles in at one of the red cloth-covered tables of the Viennese beer hall. For an aperitif he orders a Zara Maraschino from Muratti, the Greek manager, who hurries forth in person, and then he orders dinner, consciously passing the time as the rest of us arrive one by one. He is prepared for a long wait.

By now we are on the diminutive streets of the Inner City, within the limits of the former town wall, at Gizella Square. The girl's cheap shoes are beating a rapid tattoo echoed by the walls of the houses, where only the diagonal layout of the cobblestones marks the sidewalk. In front of the King of Hungary Hotel, where I spot the arrogant "upper-crust" cab driver waiting at his stand, I slip by hugging the wall.

We leave behind us the entrance to the electric subway train, a splendid little cast-iron construction. Nearing Small Bridge Street (for you: István Türr Street) the character of the public changes again: we see upper-class ladies wearing hats with large rims, and maids in their Sunday best. I lose sight of the girl with the talkative mouth. At the corner of Christopher Square I bend over as if I were fussing with my shoelaces. From under the brim of my hat I look around and am at once reassured: the red umbrella is still sailing up ahead. As my glance glides past the statue of Saint Christopher, who carries a plump angelic child on his shoulder, I am overwhelmed by the superabundance of signboards, their continuous wealth of information. I tie my shoelaces. Across from me are the signs of the Gränichstädten Brothers, of Jakab Rothberger, who sells camelhair havelocks; Malvin Putz advertises his tailoring institute, and Testory his pharmacy. All along the way I am confronted by these signboards of this, until recently, mostly German city now becoming Magyarized, where the beer was Dreher's, the seltzer factory belonged to Ries and Berkovits, and Johanna Schlick owned the women's hats and fashion salon. The cocoa was Bensdorp's, the department stores Dietrich and Son's, Schopper's and Schmolk's and Homolka's; the language school was Berlitz, the shoestore Agular's, the stamp shop Manó Fantó's. The delicatessen king was Gyula Meinl, who figured as "Julius" at the Imperial capital, Vienna. The photographic studios of Földváry and György Klösz are still open, as are Keresztes and Hácha's, Viczián and Wittman's, Hajosz and Hohejl's, and Professor Ent's language school, Merényi's mechanical engineer shop, József Máté's beer and wine house, Károly Pál's venison shop, Doctor Bárán's dental offices and Gábor Eröss' hotel. So this is today's order of business: in our own capital city, having weathered the Turkish occupation, we are to rout the language of the current world power, and in the process, teach the very stones to speak the Magyar tongue, which may not be a major world language, but is still a great language - and it is ours.

(NOW: IMOLA'S FATHER, YOUR GRAND-FATHER; TRIBAL FEELINGS; JIGGLING ROTUNDITIES)

The day before yesterday, a get-together by Lake Balaton revived the sleeping demon of tribalism within me. It is an unworthy feeling, I know. But who among us has not stumbled on certain occasions.

We were visiting your grandfather, your sole relation on your mother's side still living in Hungary's present-day territory. This alone is reason enough to pay him occasional visits. In addition, he happens to be one of those rarities, a great man. He is something else, a rare bird in these parts. There was a time when, in addition to a certain Puskás, (who by then had emigrated to Spain and who was known for his agility in kicking a soccer ball), grandfather's name was becoming famous in the world. He is a scientist. His specialty is such that his mother tongue has limited him, but not much. With superhuman perseverance and fortitude he pioneered new paths that did not exist before, at a time of adversity in this part of the world. Perhaps it was the scientist's eternal faith, his working tool, that child-like wide-eyed wonder at the world, that helped him surmount the impossible. He maintained his independence in a field where you cannot work without a politicking boss and plenty of money. Budget approvals. He was well known for five years, maybe ten - and then the radical free-thinkers of the salons found new mascots, like that Cherkess girl back in the Saint Petersburg demimonde. And all of a sudden - I will say this slowly - he grew tired of it all. He ran out of determination. Now he resents not having had enough so-called success. He is embittered by life's calculable injustice.

Perhaps it was that initial, chance recognition he received; it misled him, made him believe that the "world" demands deep thinkers and world-shakers, that genius will out, as the headlines of illustrated papers promise, and that it has something to do with noisy press acclaim, prizes, rank and pomp. The reasons are many. The exaggerated power of circumstances. The exhaustion of a historical intake of breath in our long-suffering country. Human frailty. And this much in advance: I love him. I cannot accept his resignation, even in words.

He ended up quite drunk, but I feel this is no extenuating circumstance; I realize that the law applies in this instance.

"What we have here doesn't count," he said.

You were sleeping the sleep of the just inside the house. The girl who is his wife nowadays had also gone to sleep.

These few days gave a paradisical taste of their summer vacation. The villa was lent to them by one of the old man's admirers. They went around naked in the house, garden and water. Márk, together with his curvaceous little wife, and their pale little baby - who is your six-month-old uncle, just to make sure that your relations will not be simple on that side either. We all went around naked.

At night Márk set about making us a meal. He is a great chef whose instructors had been wonderful French and Italian women. He was pouring red wine into the soup, half a bottle at a time.

The two of us sat under the willow tree.

"I made a mess of my life," he said, looking at his plate, "by staying here at home." This was how he explained his troubles.

It was the first time I had seen a red vegetable soup.

"Who needs the things we fevered intellectuals perish for, over here? Who benefits from them?"

Among his ideals you would never find pictures of bearded, bereted guerrilla leaders, bomb-throwing murderers or airplane hijackers. Only the boring, usual faces of those who revolutionized the human lot: Newton, Thomas Aquinas, Edison, Einstein and Archimedes. You know, the ones whom I call leaders.

"In science you must travel. The way in the old days a young journeyman would. To see the world. That is the only way to accomplish something, by making it available to four billion people. Among all those people there might be a few for whom it would make sense. But for the ones here? They are bums.

"I think that was where I made my mistake. I should have gone to America right at the beginning. Twenty years ago."

That was when his career took off.

Suddenly there I was, facing an emigrant soul who had missed the last boat.

"Think of Kornél, he went away," I tried to argue. "And still he keeps returning home to his dying day. For him it is not enough to have the recognition of two hundred fifty million Americans and three hundred million Europeans - he would still like to show it off at home. And so would the others."

He did not even hear me. "Look around this row of villas. On the left, a bum, he sells vegetables, all he cares about is his fifty grand each month. On the right, another bum, an engineer, he is worse yet, all he does is sail and he hasn't read a novel since his graduation." And here came the steep conclusion. "We have not accomplished anything in this country for a hundred years."

Márk's spoon, in a vague wandering gesture, went around to include the Balaton region and the entire Carpathian Basin. I realized this was not the wine speaking. It was an intellectual desire to shock. It was his desperation at having run out of steam. He was acting up, as they say somewhat loosely these days. Strutting his stuff.

He displayed an original variation, by placing his own tribe lower than any other.

"They are bums, you are right," I agreed. That much was obvious. "That is exasperating of course. But I don't think they are any worse than French bums or New York bums, for that matter." I had gotten used to attaching weight to every one of his words. Now I was simply unable to accept that this man, of all people, was unable to distinguish what was important. This thing called success, there is ludicrously too much talk about it already. An Austrian professor tells my friend that every man has his price; we'll get to that later. Money, success, power or women. For your grandfather money never had much of a purchase. An overwhelming generosity, that should be taught in school, made him leave behind his material possessions with the women he abandoned. (Starting with your grandmother.) And fame had just about caught up with him after all the neglect. By then he had started to drink. He attended international conferences.

"And anyway," here we came to the nub, "this nation is going to be absorbed, it has to disappear. How many of us are there? Fifteen million: less than New York."

"Why must you say these idiotic things?" I asked. I had a fleeting vision of a time when we would no longer be here in the Basin, replaced by some other folk who would eat fried snails with couscous sitting in the lotus position under the willows. After all these years I could thank the old man for an enlightening moment: the realization that it was not only our personal extinction that we are unable to visualize. Truly, deeply, we cannot imagine it for the ethnic entity to which we happen to belong. The human organism is not capable of this task. "Sorry, I cannot believe you. You don't really mean it."

Imola had learned her songs from her father, "Black Kite", and the others. "*Lapatyomba*". I believe in the old man's accomplishment. It had interested the people in New York, naturally. And inside him was that little boy on Tordai Road in Kolozsvár (Cluj for you), and that youngster in a small town west of the Danube, after Kolozsvár had been moved abroad. And the dense, smoky, dusty Chicago of our city, where he as a young man fled from the smalltown asphyxia. The way tumbling tumbleweed goes, driven by the wind. Those songs. They would have been inside him even if he had been a professor of physics - as illustrated by Kornél, our American uncle. Both of them had grown to manhood here at home, and ones like them are grown only here among us. They are no better and no worse than those from elsewhere. Only different.

And they are not even like each other.

How could all this disappear?

In the course of the years Márk had come to accept that

writing books was my business, so I could argue from that position.

"For better or worse I cannot make a choice, retroactively, to have been born, say, an American. And I don't think that is bad. When I tell a story, I am working under the assumption that it will never get past the borders of our fifteen-million-strong, inflective language - at least there has been no precedent in seven hundred years. But I feel all right about that. This is my own, and only in this tongue can I say *brekkancs (froggy), plajbász (pencil), skiró (scooter), cseréptörés (Ollie-ollie-oll-in-free)*, for example.

"It is not all that hard to accept facts.

"And, sorry, I maintain a heretical creed: we are not going to be absorbed. Some day the sun will grow cold, but that is another order of magnitude. We shall be here in our place for a very long time; I don't think we can live believing otherwise. We have survived until now, even though the odds were against it."

One morning the little wife, radiant like a Rubens Madonna, hovered above the water on the long plank of the dock, on her way to the garden, to give your little uncle a suck, and her rotundities jiggled, jounced and bounced from side to side. There I stood rooted, amazed at how beautiful humankind is; the female half, at least.

HONKY-TONK PIANO

My shoelaces have been tied. The red parasol is bathed by the gentle horizontal rays of the departing sun. The most jubilant crowds are found on Váci Street, where the populace overflows from the asphalt-coated sidewalks into the street. White lamp globes hang overhead on wrought-iron braces. The parasol passes on its way past Town Hall Square, on to Huckster Street (for you: Paris Street); it goes past Knitter Street and in front of the House of the Piarists (for you Barnabás Pesti Street; we used to loiter in the university corridors in its back building on our way from Marxism lectures to Leninism seminars in those fine days when the Piarists were no longer allowed to drug the workers' susceptible minds with the opiate of religion).

In front of the Bazaar's entrance the last remnants of traffic consist of a few hansom cabs and fiacres and the occasional elegant landau. I make my way through a crowd of men and slow down for a moment, wishing to look around. I am obeying the call of duty. Inside one finds the European equivalent of a Near Eastern Greek-Turkish bazaar, complete with mosaic floor, fountains, palm trees and caryatids. The jeweler's window display is being emptied for the night by a gentleman sporting long side whiskers à la Franz Joseph.

But I have more urgent business at hand, now and forever. I hurry on after my prey. Up ahead the swing of the parasol signals a graceful ambling stride, it sways, leisurely, with all the time in the world, before gliding into the darkened canyon of a side street between the old Town Hall and the four-storey corner palace on Serpent Street. In the bay formed by Rose Square, she sails past the cab stand by the main entrance to the Silly Kitty grand café and nightclub, casting a familiar glance up at the windows and shutters.

She sails down one block of Leopold Street.

We are home now. A grocer's delivery boy rides by on a tricycle, hurrying in the twilight. I look at the upstairs windows with their open shutters; drying towels exhale their stale secrets. I imagine the scent of curling irons in the sunset. I hear the sounds of off-key singing, and the splash of a basin of water. The girl turns into Hat Street and by the time I round the corner to peer after her, she is gone. Not to worry: there is only one arching carriage entrance in the stone wall, which leads into the courtyard of one of the Leopold Street buildings, and the rear entrance of the Silly Kitty (which fronts on Rose Square) opens on to the courtyard. A small doorway is cut into the carriage gate. Above, a noteworthy palisade shields the gangway of the first floor. This is where the girl was headed. This is where she lives. Where else could she belong? What else have I been looking for everywhere? This is where my life is centered from now on.

I've got her.

O my God.

What a truly beautiful street corner, what marvelous towels, glorious curling irons, lovely splashed water and unique arched entryway.

Dazed with emotion I stagger in front of the building and examine the façade anew. Ground floor plus two storeys, colorful large billboards that reach past the corner. An ordinary building in the heart of the Inner City, one that will disappear without trace around the time when the cobblestones of the Grand Boulevard are being shifted for the first time on the occasion of the construction of the bridge at Pledge Square, when the whole quarter will be demolished until not even the outline of these streets that have survived so much destruction, construction and deconstruction will remain. I linger over the signs posted at the nightclub. Breakfast, Lunch, Home-style Cooking. *Etablissement*, Silly Kitty, *Café Chantant*. Solid, middle-class, family entertainment, recommended for ladies no doubt. Dance, songs, Pupilla, the Siren of the Adriatic, Kink and Kalkasa, illusionists from the wondrous far-off land of India, Mamzell Bora Clarendon, *chanteuse excentrique*. See the animatograph, the invention for the coming century; plus numerous surprises each and every night. The charming tableau of the Kitties, and the spine-tingling melodrama of the Contest of the Ladies, to test your nerves. The first show goes on at ten-thirty, the second at midnight.

I have to leave to meet my associates at Muratti's for the last time. On the way I stop in at my place for my cape. It will not be conspicuous, for the weather is turning cooler again.

For dinner the manager moved my partners to a table with white tablecloth in a separate section maintained in a side room for the more distinguished guests. The others have already arrived. I sit down with them and we converse in low voices and at length. I order *pörkölt* with macaroni. The others are already on their desserts. They report that at their lodgings they have already set up in the attic without the landlord's knowledge. The time has come to acquaint them with the anticipated fruits of our labors, and for everyone to get to work.

This is the first time I pronounce the name of the Stone in front of them. They become respectfully hushed. Now it is obvious why the lookout had to produce that blue scar and haul all those goods in front of the fashionable firm of jewelers whose name the King had heard in Vienna. If someone were observing us, he could see me sketching something for the others. Streets and squares. A front entrance. A rear entrance. Doors. Locks. The rounds of the night patrol. The three seasoned rogues mumble their lessons with eyes closed. Afterwards, having torn the paper to shreds, I playfully burn everything in the ashtray, just like any slightly pyromaniac customer would.

The separate room would prove to be no help in the end. The manager would recall our supper, the burned paper and the four men whose clothes do not harmonize. After the fact, our presence there would gain significance for the world at large, the head waiter would recall that in the back room four unknown men drank Schwechat beer from tankards. The blond-whiskered, auburn-haired, elegantly dressed one had boiled beef *flanken* Viennese style with horseradish; the poorly dressed one and the curly-haired one both had sour lungs with dumplings. The fourth one, of medium build, sat with his back to the entrance and remained wrapped in his cape all that time indoors. At the time no one would have thought I was trying to conceal my features, but under expert interrogation all they could come up with was that the fourth individual had piercing black eyes and ate his *pörkölt* with macaroni. (On this occasion I could have ordered the usual dumplings; I did give it some thought, but rejected the notion. I felt secure about our situation.) The dinner cost about eighty kreuzers apiece and they left generous tips. These generous tips would become a recurring leitmotif.

The die is cast, our enterprise is under way.

"Let me have some money," I casually ask my hand-picked companions, "I am going to the Silly Kitty." To scout out the place, to pass the night away. I should not have disclosed this gratuitous information.

"The place where we had our first meeting?" asks the King.

"What do they have there at night? It is a café, a small tavern. A dull place."

But I am going anyway.

I have no need to bask in their loyalty, the way they hang on each of my words. Since this afternoon all I can see is a red parasol, and those blood-red lips. I am following another star.

The *chanteuse* opens the show with a feeble little song; hardly any of her is showing under the cat costume. Then respectable, middle-aged artistes perform their charming tableau; Tzitza in a white headdress, Mitza in a black one; and they all shuffle about on this humdrum stage. Next, drearily, the Pearl of the Adriatic and the Contest of the Ladies.

I watch the show. I had emerged from my fiacre in front of the Kitty just before ten-thirty, my hair freshly combed, clad in the formal evening garb tailored by Kumarás. Anyone who had seen me earlier in the day unwashed and unshaven, picking up loose change from the tarpaulin along with my Gypsy colleagues, would not have recognized the essential underlying identity: I wear the impeccably tailored formal evening garb with the same awkwardness as the sloppy jacket of the fire-eater. By means of a banknote folded lengthways I persuade the headwaiter to give me a side booth. Like the other gentlemen and ladies in the audience, I patiently endure the song, the charming tableau and the painful melodrama, casually musing over the no longer slender ankles of former chorus girls revealed during the show. The music is provided by a band seated underneath silvery ventilation cowls of unusual proportions. The wildest spectacle of the performance is a droll and inoffensive circle dance performed in ensemble by Pupilla the Siren of the Adriatic, Tzitza and Mitza, and the embattled ladies, to the unsettling rhythms of what must be a Parisian number. They perform numerous sprightly and generous encores of this dance. By now the *chanteuse* is no longer in evidence. The girl with the telltale mouth, the one I am looking for is not to be found here. Waiters, coatroom attendants, bread-boy, musicians - all are males. The high cashier's seat is fashioned like a throne, a piece of stylistic bravura over which rises the owner's glass office cage. The cashier is the only female employee, a hag of about seventy, no doubt hired for her looks, so perfectly in line with the spirit of the ordinance curtailing female night staff.

My eyes take in each and every detail. The head waiter carries a covered tray laden with dishes and wines up the winding stairs to the glass cage. Up there, a broad female face may be glimpsed between the parted velvet curtains, observing the café.

At last the stilted circle dance is over and the lights go on. The color scheme of the hall consists of somnolent, tired greens and beiges. The back of the café is set off by a row of pillars painted silver, and in front of these, above the dance floor maintained for the clientele, bell-shaped chandeliers multiply the brilliant light in their thousand tiny glass prisms. Waiters are carrying Maraschinos for the male customers and raspberry sodas in cut-glass carafes for the ladies. Middle-class women and girls, in search of a predictable, titillating and safe evening's entertainment. In this overheated environment the bourgeois matron, duly accompanied by her lawful husband, may display splendid indignance at the depravity of the music and the dancers while biting a corner of her mouth in the stifling atmosphere. ("That sly old Theodore, he certainly knows the smart nightspots.") Here and there may be seen a solitary and very elegant gentleman, or a military officer in shako, observing the middle class fare of night life. In the entire dance hall there is not a single gesture or detail that could be objected to by the most puritanical stickler for propriety. The café is a masterful blend of slightly titivating but essentially innocent borderline genres, dished up at an excellent Inner City location. And yet, a voice inside me keeps insisting, there has to be something more.

Meanwhile I see no trace of the girl anywhere.

After a brief respite the musicians start up the strains of a Viennese waltz, and the dance floor in front of the pillars is soon full of dancing couples. One glimpses high black lace-up boots as the ladies are obliged to raise the hems of their whirling skirts. Masculine palms are sweating on female waists, and starched petticoats flash by. They sway to the *pas de patiner*, the waltz and the polka.

Young waiters cater to every need of the crowd, so that there is no need whatever for the distinguished, silver-haired head waiter's presence down among the tables. Yet he reminds me of someone, the way he circulates, and all of a sudden I realize what it is: he has the air of a strolling streetwalker waiting to be picked up. Soon he is summoned by a gesture from a hog-faced, bristle-mustached, prosperously attired country gent. The headwaiter strolls over and bends down to attend to the request. Hog-face takes a surreptitious look around as if he were poaching, and whispers in the headwaiter's ear. The latter nods, and with another gesture of his head indicates the other end of the hall, beyond the row of pillars. It is remarkable how unobtrusively the customer makes his way to the back, where he and his guide are swallowed up in the crowd of dancers. Two minutes later the headwaiter is again strolling among the tables. He deals exclusively with well-dressed, solitary gentlemen. I am able to pick out the next client even before he does, and keep a careful eye on the proceedings. The customer does not pay his bill as he leaves with the head waiter, and yet the young waiters clear his table, put on a fresh setting and seat a new guest there.

A naughty, honky-tonk, cobblestone street song keeps echoing in my inner ear. That jingle-jangle, honky-tonk piano. In a kitty-cat house. Waiting for us. Why don't we take a look.

I wait until the second show is well under way, just before the inoffensive dance number is about to begin, and when the silver-haired head waiter passes by, I gently clink my champagne glass. He bows and smiles, at my service. My hands happen to be fondling the King's morocco leather wallet.

"Tell me, my good man, is this all there is to the place?" I wave the wallet in a circular gesture. These are the accepted conventions: I address him familiarly, calling the white-haired head waiter "friend". My gesture includes the patchouli-scented females, their brilliantined, sweating dance partners and the faltering stage show. My man is the very image of a dignified eagerness to serve, standing there with torso slightly inclined over my table. His posture seems to say: "I do not have the honor of knowing the gentleman." Therefore, it is high time that I introduce myself, by passing into his hand the wine list on my table. I do not know by what legerdemain he spirits away the crisp banknote I placed there, but it is gone.

"My name is Aladár," he reciprocates the introduction without missing a beat. "Please ask only for me." With his left hand he gestures behind him to one of his assistants. "Would you be so kind and follow me," he adds, and we are on our way. We pass the musicians as we go, and I take a good look at the band energetically playing the notes of the can-can under the unusually wide, oversized ventilation cowls. As I glance back near the pillars, my table is already being cleared.

We come to a corridor in the back corner of the café. Sinuous music accompanies us as we leave the dance hall. The performers are beginning to dance to its hectic rhythms. Aladár has the knack of walking in front of one as if he were following - the perfect lackey. At the end of the corridor we confront an ordinary door with the sign, No Entry. We must be in the right place. He tugs at the copper lion head of the bell-pull. From here we can still hear the music and hubbub of the dance floor. The door opens, worked by some clever system of pulleys and wires, for there is no one behind it. As it clicks shut in our wake, we are enveloped in silence. A few steps on, the corridor takes a right angle. At its end, another small passageway leads to a black metal door. As we approach, the peephole rustles and the key turns in the lock. We are in a very small, square metal chamber; a pair of eyes watches us through the peephole on the left. I cannot see the face; this Cerberus has a strategic guardpost, commanding all three directions. Aladár leads me through the door on the right, which immediately closes behind us.

I follow him up twelve steps. On one hand, a row of doors, on the other, a palisade reaching up to the ceiling; behind its planks I sense the evening cool of the outdoors. A labyrinth of turn upon turn follows; the narrow passageways go up and down in a chaos of levels. It is a struggle between me and the builder, whose intention had been to disorient me. Finally nine steps down to a heavily padded door. And if I have kept track correctly we are somewhere above the dance hall, on a level higher than the ground floor. We have arrived here in less than a minute; I can still hear the bouncing measures of the café orchestra. Aladár disappears behind me as the last door opens in front of me and I see the red salon for the first time. Thrust under the oppressively low ceiling with its inlaid gold stars, I can feel its weight. I am enveloped by the mélange of smoke thick enough to cut, steam, sweat, eau de cologne, wine, cigars, and something else that my confused senses cannot quite identify. I pause in the doorway and after a momentary bewilderment I know what it is: the dance hall music. The honky-tonk piano. The same number, and in the identical rendition as downstairs, even continued at the same strain where I had left it. Here it is accompanied by a song, a woman's solo voice; she returns to that snippet of the refrain I had heard earlier: "Heeya hey! ... Heeya ho!"

A squeal pierces the dim recesses of the salon. A champagne glass smashes against the wall behind my head. I duck, even though the missile was not aimed at me, but at the worries and cares of the world at large; Hog-face wanted to do away with them all in one fell swoop. The bubbly liquid is absorbed by the deep crimson brocade of the well-chosen wallpaper. Dim points of electric lighting struggle in vain against the smoky clouds of the chamber, casting a livid glow on the stage across from me. The music is the same as downstairs and yet different. In this atmosphere, and heightened by the singer's anguish, the music that was droll and lighthearted in the café now becomes a sensual, torrid chant accompanied on the tiny stage by that unsurpassably lewd dance, that epitome of the new times and new morals, the authentic Parisian can-can. A semi-circle of fillies, heads bedecked with light aigrettes, broad black straps and white horsetails on their buttocks, are kicking legs clad in black net stockings and garters up at the ceiling, as if they wanted to flaunt that fabled third armpit.

I am still standing dazed in the doorway when one of the upstairs waiters, attired in red tails, hurries forward. Meanwhile the dance reaches its triumphant climax. The girls, through clouds of milky white cigar smoke, gallop around like ponies on their miniature stage. Closer up I can see their legs stamping in unison, and the dark straps straining on their thoroughbred cruppers.. The soloist is motionless in front of

the chorus. Her costume is more seductive than any naked-
ness: on top a severe, tight blue parade coachman's suit with
gold braids buttoned up to the neck, closely hugging her
slender waist as only a woman's waist can be hugged, and a
long deeply slashed skirt in the same colors. She is singing the
refrain: "Little horsie... Little horsie..." Up here the honky-
tonk piano has its cover on. That jingle-jangle sound.
Absent-mindedly I pull on the glacé gloves I hold in my hands.
Following the waiter, and affecting confusion, I manage to end
up in the corner by the small piano. My cat's eyes adapt to the
impenetrable smoke and darkness. My second glance discovers
what I had been looking for: the female staff here, where the
authorities and their ordinances are flagrantly flouted. There
stands the bread-girl, modestly, wearing a white apron and
white head-dress, holding a tray suspended by straps from her
neck.

Soon the waiter in the red tail-coat calls out to her, "Over
here, Bubbles." Now I know her name.

And there sits the Safe King, in the seat of honor, at a
banquette table near the stage. This is why I should have kept
quiet. I should have known. Now he thinks he understands.
Well, it's all right. Perhaps I may need him here. He could
keep an eye on this house for me, if he becomes a regular. We
still have some time left, it will have to be spent somehow. He
is very elegant, carefree, having a good time. As I pass in front
of him he does not bat an eyelash. He is a professional
through and through.

On the way over I absent-mindedly draw a finger across the
red plush cover of the piano, as a sergeant of the hussars
would, after dressing down the horses. There is dust on my
gloved finger and a visible streak is left behind on the cover.
Hmm, an unused instrument.

Ignoring the waiter, I select a strategically situated table in
the middle of the floor with only two chairs next to it,
commanding a good view in all directions. Along the wall
facing me three steps lead up. A thickly pleated velvet curtain
flaps open; near it, behind the stage, I see a narrow
passageway, a couch; in the corners, diagonally placed, two
doors with frosted glass windows, the circuit board of the

electric system, and the edge of a white sink. All of this has the appearance of having been constructed on a reduced scale because of the tight space. The red-coated waiter stands by my table. His name is Abris, he informs me in a low voice. Up here, for the chosen and initiated few, everything is cozy and comes with a personal touch. Here everyone is of the better sort - as long as you have money. I order champagne, the very best, and caviare, with a cocky, safe-cracker's nonchalance. I try to see as much as I can. That will be all, I wave to Abris, as he glances in the direction of the house girls sitting on easy chairs lined up along the wall.

Whoever created this world tucked away between floors was well aware that in the thick of smoke, sweat, alcoholic fumes and music a different color scheme is in order than the one employed on the respectable ground floor. The various shades of rich reds in the wallpaper, carpets and velvet curtains are set off by the slender gilded columns, and it is as if the penguin tones of evening wear and the waiters' crimson coats had been designed into the ensemble. The same goes for the stage: black straps, black stockings and white aigrettes, pink lacy costumes, blue coachman's outfit. Each table is tiny, and each is occupied by a gentleman, with or without one of the girls. Nothing is taken for granted.

"Giddy-up, little horsie... Giddy-up." The second stanza of the song is over when the hubbub of the audience rises. Hog-face is making his move. He is an outstanding specimen of the subspecies *Homo sapiens sapiens*, whose adaptability has enabled it to spread from the poles to the equator: the previously respectable bourgeois of the ground floor, in less than an hour, is down on all fours, his collar askew, shirtfront and tails hanging out. His face bathed in sweat, he grunts by the side wall, his teeth champing on a bridle made of garter ribbons, as his meaty jowls are squeezed between the knickers on the slim thighs of the girl riding on his back. The little hostess waves her empty glass in the direction of Abris, the waiter.

A husky man lugging a crate of champagne crosses behind the curtains that are always slightly open near the stage. He disappears in the direction of the washroom; I get a momentary glimpse of a broom closet, behind which, I guess, there is a pantry. The man's gait is uneven, one long, one short step; either the load is too heavy, or possibly he has a limp.

The red-coated waiter, a napkin over his arm, topped by ice bucket and champagne, is making his way through the thick goulash of the salon toward the couple playing horsie. Life is proceeding full tilt here.

Hog-face smashes another champagne glass against the wall. The rose pink lingerie jerks her boar-headed mount's suspenders, urging him to a double turn. He has to concentrate with all his might just to stay on all fours. He manages to dodder past me toward the curtained wall, so that the ice bucket is unable to reach him in time. He and his rider thrash up the three steps in a spectacular fashion. The girl draws the curtains apart, and since the couple's movements are not very coordinated, for a few moments the view is clear. At the top of the steps there is a wide brown door through which they disappear and, I believe, keep on ascending.

The salon is peaceful now, in its own crimson mode. I have seen enough. I know what I have to know.

At the table by the piano my auburn-haired accomplice raises his glass in a toast to the chanteuse on stage.

Meanwhile the bread-girl circulates among the tables, wearing her plain little head-dress, modest and inconspicuous.

(NOW: UPPER FOREST ROW)

Sunday we set out for the former Folk Park. We were going to see those dark green early electric tram cars, the yellow cars of the horse-drawn trams, and the single-cylinder Mercedes Benz automobiles at the Transport Museum. The Fráter's makeshift apartment happened to be on the way, on Upper Forest Row (not street, but, yes, row) so we rang his doorbell. He is always there when you need him. He cannot obtain a telephone so you can only drop in on him. His attic apartment is crisscrossed at the most unexpected angles by rough-hewn brown rafters across two of which he laid the large door on which he writes his books, and ever since then, his old desk has been mine. We found him in his pyjamas; he works at night and it was barely noon. Ever tactful, like all great men, he lied that it was time for him to get up anyway. He washed the sleep from his eyes, wet down his beard, gave some milk to the cat, smoked two dark cigarettes that go by the name of Workers and downed one mug of hot, bitter coffee. And then he was awake, ready to chat. You busied yourself with the tabby cat while I spoke about my problems. Earlier in the morning we had been roaming in Buda, and we took the new subway on our way here. The escalator delivered in front of our eyes a veritable motion picture, featuring various coats, drunks, children, adults; this reminded me that it was at this spot, when you were in your second year at school, that we had discussed the story of the Black Grandfather and how it could best be told.

On Upper Forest Row I could consult a specialist; for, as you know, the Fráter is a pro. He told me that his ill-fated first novel, written before his first published work, may be about to appear. The editor, who will make the decision, has telephoned to petition the "other person", who had been responsible for holding back the publication for nine years. In principle, it has already been approved. The text is the same as nine years ago. In the meantime his first book was published. "Comrade Secretary has a few comments to make on your book," the editor in charge of the manuscript said at last, reluctantly. She was doing her job and yet she was not in charge. This was precisely the kind of situation that made her want to quit and take a job as night janitor at the Central Train Station, where help is always wanted. Principles are principles: the Fráter's text has been handed over to two more top level security controllers. "Anyway, he would like to talk it over with you in person." My friend gave her an idiotic look. "He can veto it but he wants to discuss it with me? I don't think there is any room for further discussion here. This manuscript has been around for nine years. The worst that could happen is that they will not allow it to be published. And that is already the case." "Wait, wait, please don't do anything hasty," begged the editor. "Please do this for my sake, call me the day after tomorrow. I am going to try to talk to the Secretary." And two days later: "Won't you sit down and talk with him... He has already given written authorization for publication." "That's different, then," said my difficult friend.

Later, at a coffeehouse table, he turned to the top level controller, addressing him in the familiar mode, as convention dictates, "You know, if what we say here could influence the book's publication, I would not be able to make any concessions, if for no other reason than this: how would I know that I am not doing it out of weakness?" And he made sure to pay for his own coffee.

That man has no love for the Fráter's book, nor do any of his confreres. And yet: they approved its publication. "It is no easy matter for them," my friend related with sympathy. This field is perhaps the last remaining republic, and its citizens recognize no authority other than quality. You can't fake it here, as a certain Sándorka, the sometime drummer at the Little Bear Bar would say, you can either do it or you can't. What happened in the coffeehouse that day was strange and unpredictable. There is some kind of unadmitted process of loosening going on here. The comrade actually had a personal, or, if one may put it this way, private observation to make. "Oh," my friend replied. "But after all, this is a novel, the whole thing is made up. It is unbelievable, but our purposes are at one on this point. The less that character resembles your one-time acquaintance, the better. I am going to change him even more radically. Instead of a gynecologist, he is going to be a ragpicker, instead of a short squat man he will be a gaunt giant, his dark eyes will turn blue, and if he acts up too much, I might give him red hair and a lightbulb for a nose." So that my friend's first novel, which, in his complicated chronology, precedes his first published novel, is at last all set to go to print.

As we were on our way out, he gave me some good advice about my own problems. For he is a true pro.

"Well then, what are you going to put into your book?" You asked me with your inexorable logic. You had been listening to our conversation.

"That is what we are going to have to sort out," I said, grabbing the leather strap in the old subway. "Perhaps the whole book is going to be about that. The Fráter suggested that we get off at Arena Road. Maybe that will be of some help."

BEFORE THE STORM

This is the season of surveillance. When I followed her from the park was not to be the only time; my fate from here on is snooping and hiding. Completely exhausted after a long day, I call for ice cream on the terrace of The King of Hungary Hotel when I discover the pair of lovers in the midst of their happy tryst. It is the bread-girl, whom I had not let out of my sight since the park, and who will now become the incidental cause of a love drama, along with her beau who carries a walking stick. He is preparing to take possession of the girl this evening, and I am going to have to tail them, or more precisely, to follow that third party who has been tailing them for some time.

Three weeks have gone by since my first night at the Kitty, where I encountered the Safe King and found Bubbles. Since then we have had three weeks of African climate in this capital of ours, located as it is in the temperate zone. Ever since, a torrid heat wave has been steaming over the cobblestones, macadam and asphalt of these streets. Our preparations have been completed by this date, but we still have to decide about our exact timing.

I have already received the results of the assignment given to our lookout, Haluska.

Even though in his role as a poor village vagabond he was not able to seduce some upper-crust lady's maid who moved in high enough circles to be a source of information, he still found his opening. One day he was entrusted to deliver a sealed note to the targeted elegant address on Crown Street. He knew what to look for there, and he found it in the person of the unimpeachable servant of the family, whose furtive glances, as well as the patch of purple capillaries in the wings of his nose, betrayed him. By now the servant has become his secret drinking partner, with whom he consumes time at the rough-hewn tavern tables of the Outer Kerepesi Road district, in deep conversation.

The sooner we make our move, the better it will be, but the timing does not depend entirely on us.

On this day the big news in the capital concerns the typical hussar-like jest played by the officers of the riding academy: they rode their horses from the lower quays up the steps near the Chain Bridge and galloped over to the Pest side of the capital. And on this day the first piles are driven into the Danube riverbed at the site of the Tollhouse Bridge, which will be dedicated as Franz Joseph Bridge (for you: Liberty Bridge, after having been blown up by the Germans and rebuilt by us following the Second World War); I am sorry if I have the same story to tell about our other bridges; in this respect our history possesses a certain monotony. And the Hungarian Africa at the zoo welcomes a new arrival on this day: a vigorous male child is born to one of the village families encamped there. He receives the name of Ofelioko according to pagan rites. Three hundred of our dark-pigmented fellow humans may be seen there from nine in the morning until ten at night, in the habitat of the lynxes and Nubian lions. Here they live and give birth, and we keep them... in the zoo. Here, in the middle of enlightened Europe. I still blush when I think about it. And what had become of dear little Ofelioko?

Dr. Dajka has had a busy day: the Summer Festivities of the Exposition are in full swing, and unlawful activities of all types have been flourishing. In the morning he represented the municipal police department as witness at the trial of the Schlezinger brothers, who had shoved their blind sister into the Danube to be rid of her. Soma got six years in the penitentiary; Adolf was acquitted.

He spent the afternoon at home, resting up for the eight o'clock police raid. There is still a chance for a catnap before an early dinner.

To work properly you need time; which is as true for telling a tale as for cracking safes.

The diamond cutter comes to a decision: the Stone will receive a platinum setting. The client may command all the crowns of the Imperial House, the jeweler may possess all the money in the world, but this is still his area of expertise. He would not even have considered the commission if they were going to interfere with his work. The setting will be of the so-called *à jour* type, around the plane of the greatest diameter, separating the lower *culasse* from the upper crown. It would be a crime to hide any part of this diamond.

These past three weeks I have spent a lot of time loitering outside the Kitty, like a hound on the scent. The structure of the place is obvious: the ground floor café is a front for the upstairs salon. It serves as a larger pool from which they can skim the goldfish - the well-screened, moneyed male public of the capital, attracted here by a word-of-mouth, open secret. Ergo, the cat in its name. For were it not for the secrecy, the Baroness would find herself booted out in no time from this refined Inner City quarter.

I watch the girl: this turns into my main activity. And almost unintentionally, I become well versed in the ways of the establishment. I know their schedule: when they go shopping, when they expect clients, daytime and night, burghers, magnates and figures of the demimonde. I know about their weekend peak traffic and their weekly day off on Mondays.

Like incense, the scent of paints, varnish and enamels from fresh building sites floats over the city. We are almost ready for our great coup. The portents gather all day, foreboding the impending storm. Events are rolling inevitably toward the dramatic climax of the night.

Outside of the capital many places in the country had rainfall during the day, with thunderstorms and hailstones. Here in the city an electric tension hovers in the air under the tremulous cirro-cumulus clouds.

I am still yearning for an ice cream cone as they sit there, a stone's throw from me at the other end of the terrace. I turn my back; they have not seen me. The slow-footed waiter carries a small glass of raspberry soda to their table. I watch them as the man with the hat and walking stick gestures to the waiter to place the drink in front of his lady. His gesture reeks of the jungle impatience of amorous passion. The girl downs her cooling draft and rises with an inimitably graceful movement. Her knight assists her, removing the metal chair with one hand.

She is wearing her serene dove-gray outfit, a light summer jacket over her arm, as if already, in the heat of the day, she had prepared to roam the cool evening streets with her lover. They march past the Haas Palace and cross the estuary of Music Hall Street, heading toward the Danube. I can see the man looking back at the corner of the former Main Street (for you, Ferenc Deák Street). And I observe how the mirth leaves his face. I follow the direction of his glance toward a woman in a long skirt drawing back into the shelter of an entranceway at the lamp factory warehouse. Despite the summer heat she wears long black gloves reaching to her elbows and carries a silvery webbed reticule as she steals after the lovers. She seems familiar from somewhere.

My innermost alarms sound. I cannot wait for my tardy ice cream, and jump up with parched throat, tortured by thirst, to set out after them. I must see what is about to happen, and intervene if possible. I cannot identify the woman with the silver handbag, but the possibilities are not many. I must save the bread-girl from any danger.

The man with the walking stick is herding his lover toward the Danube so that she is unaware of what is going on. I too take care that the woman trailing them should not notice me. The sun is setting over the river. On the other side rises the new spire of the former Church of Our Lady.

The Music Hall arcades are a man-made system of caverns. We near the zigzag white line of the Buchwald chairs on the lively promenade, the cast iron figureheads on the railing by the Danube bank. (You know these: blooming buds alternating with putti raising their oafish iron heads between the closely spaced rails. And when in that film *Kalimagdora's Lover*, about the Prague Spring, the scene is set beside a nameless riverbank, they could not hide the Budapest location from us who recognize our cast iron putti, even if there is not a single Hungarian sign, even if that is the only detail of our city's face.)

I follow along that iron-putto'd railing, at a safe distance. We make up a convoy of sorts: the two of them up front, the woman with the long gloves stealing after them, and I trailing unobserved in her wake. She snatches up the sweeping ends of her long skirt and breaks into a run. She is wearing gray chamois boots with buttons.

Across the carriage way, where nowadays the No.2 streetcar passes, and down to the lower quays.

A steamship puffs by on the Danube. Across the river in the Buda hills the Citadel fits snugly into its landscape, an excellent vantage point for foreign cannon, from where the flesh-tearing and bone-rending cannonballs may reach us anywhere in the twin cities, as they did in 1848. Eventually our Nazi occupiers would make use of this location to that same end - and they were occupiers, remember that.

We are at the bridge entrance now. Horse-drawn carts and drays. Iron curbs under a Drive Slowly sign. This is where we had crossed with our van, shouting "Thonet Furniture Factory" at the toll booth. The giant square flagstones of the quay. I am past the bridge when the first cool breeze from the Danube wafts across my face; it is the first tiny harbinger of the great thunderstorm about to come.

The police detachment setting out on the evening raid is at the Salt Square town house of the Countess Szirmay. That afternoon there had been a break-in and a theft of silverware. The report was made by a certain Hlavnyai, the super-intendent. The Doctor inspects the premises in person, accompanied by two policemen. He finds contradictory clues: the entry was effected by means of a skeleton key and a crowbar, efficient work that appears to be that of profes-sionals. But in the apartment itself he finds an amateurish mess, superfluous damage and upheaval. The countess had traveled to Karlsbad for the season and had had the Salt Square apartment temporarily closed up. Make note of everything and obtain all the information on the staff. He makes sure that the men left behind thoroughly search the premises and secure any clues if possible *in natura* and deliver these to headquarters. He himself goes on with the raid squad; he has a long night ahead.

Right at the outset, passing along the Tollhouse, Museum, Charles and Váci boulevards he is forced to cite seventeen individuals for begging on the open street. On the sidewalk at Rottenbiller Street he dictates his report to his assistant Marton, commenting for the seventh time, that since its completion and opening, this street has become an unsuitable site for the Homeless Shelter.

On this weekday night his objective is the inspection of the city's slum apartments that are overcrowded in violation of the letter of the law. He begins at the outer Leopoldstadt district as a wind arises from the direction of the Danube.

I stop to stare down at the steps of the quay, where iron-banded girders lie about, above the barges fastened below. Their ends are carved sharp, making them seem like a handful of pencils flung down there awaiting the fumbling fingers of titanic school children to be chewed by shovel-sized giant milk teeth at the school for behemoths. I see warehouses with long tiled roofs. Under the great gray tarpaulins covering them, magic shapes are outlined by stacks of crates, barrels, staves, door and window frames. This riverside stretch serves as storage shed, food pantry, attic and cellar for the city that has grown into a giant with a population of half a million.

Suddenly a few drops of rain begin to fall, and stop just as abruptly.

Sailors in striped jerseys. One of the barges carries a sign advertising a book and stationery store. The raw strands of huge coils of rope. The smell of distant ports, hawsers, chains and knots - I hear a brief snatch from Turkish flutes and tambourines. In the meantime, while I was submerged in my brown study, my prey had almost slipped away.

I run in the direction I last saw them, by Parliament Square toward Váci Boulevard. Here I find empty lots and crumbling wood fences. These are the single-storey buildings of old Pest, where my own low-slung lodgings are to be found with the red mailbox, wooden gate and tavern sign. I follow them behind the new House of Parliament.

The wind arises again. On the corner of Sailor Street the Berlitz School of Languages advertizes instruction in French, Russian and German. Young trees raise their heads, each in its own iron cage along the rails of the horse-drawn tram: these new trees, new streets, new buildings are awaiting the inhabitants of tomorrow's city - such as Imola, and you. It is getting dark. The man stops at the horse tram station. But Bubbles shakes her head, so they continue on foot.

Evening is falling. The police raid squad goes from tenement to tenement: the dens of Transylvania Street, the remnants of the old Saxon Houses on Bem Street. The realm of a slum landlord behind the Wool Scouring Works. It is impossible to nail each moneybag at the same time, thinks the depressed Doctor; we could not cover that much ground in one night. In two single-storey houses he finds eighty-two wretched apartment units. The landlord charges nine kroner for each little hole, and his miserable tenant can raise this amount only by taking in night lodgers, making the tenement's population grow in a geometric progression, like the price of a diamond of the first water. And the landlord had even set up sheds under the eaves and rented those. The Doctor marches on, relentlessly.

In the vicinity of the Western Railroad Terminal I suddenly surmise where they must be heading, with the woman trailing them. Across the river there is an undisturbed view of Buda, where a single castle crowns the hill with its many wings. The entrance of the Dairy Farmers' Association is covered by a drawn, corrugated iron shutter. They stroll on along the northern side of Leopold Boulevard. The girl does not have a notion of what is going on at her back.

I don't even turn my head as I walk past the street into which they had slipped. I must stay far behind so that the woman does not see me; my sixth sense whispers to me that this might be very important some day. (Little do I know that it will be this very night.)

As far as the eye can see, factories, steam mills, breweries and granaries rise on both sides of the still unfinished Grand Boulevard, and beyond, in the back streets, the dark stumps of factory smokestacks loom black in the evening; this part of the city is still undecided in the heat of construction whether it will become an industrial district or a genteel residential quarter.

I cannot follow them to the gate of the apartment building. Possibly this is the moment when our carefully prepared masterwork is being broken in pieces. Good God, I say to myself, what is this going to lead to? The truth is, of course, that it is not very difficult to predict what will happen.

My feet carry me on, down toward the lower quays, among the rows of tent awnings of the warehouse depots. Long planks lead out of open barges, and the unloading goes on nonstop in the evening. On the roadway a large cart is waiting, and men wearing leather aprons are loading it with huge plates of glass in wooden frames, moving with extreme care. Down below, the deck of the barge supports pyramids of basalt, wood, copper, glass and bricks.

This segment of the quays is the entrance gate to the city, which admits bit by bit the parts that will go into the construction of its boulevards and radial roads, apartment buildings and stockyards, prisons, factories, streetcar sheds, pensiones, theaters, music halls and grand hotels.

Like a line of ants, day laborers are approaching with wheelbarrows laden with bricks. The end of the line is balancing on the plank above the water. Their shirts and trousers are white, their heads are dark, inverted exclamation points in the settling darkness. Their faces carry the load of their fatigue, as they trudge upward through a layer of light mud that has been dragged by wagon wheels and human feet from the waterside up to the road. Crisscrossing the regular latticework of the cobblestones is a labyrinthine pattern inscribed by random wheel tracks. Among the hundreds of millions of bricks piled up in pyramids, a maze of paths leads in all directions, and planks reach from one pile to another. Between these miniature streets are squares, an occasional sentry box, then another district of a myriad passageways, the piles reaching over my head, cutting off my view.

I have to scrape the whitish mud from my shoes laboriously, as I head back toward the paved civilization of Leopold Boulevard. I whistle as I muse on my way back to my lodgings, where I metamorphose into a gentleman in evening wear, from my upturned collar down to my patent leather shoes. Tonight I must be at the Kitty; this is my most important task.

It has turned completely dark. Cool winds blow from the direction of the river. The three weeks of African weather in Budapest are coming to an end.

By now the police raid squad has reached the temporary lodgings rigged up on Cemetery Road. Here the Doctor's brow darkens once more. He sees row upon row of tiny cabins, each accommodating a dozen human beings. By nightfall, when they are all at home, one can see that in some instances it is three people to a bed. There are tears in the Special Investigator's eyes, produced by the acrid fumes and smoke exhaled by so many human bodies. And this is the summertime, when life is supposed to be relatively easier here.

To close the circle, the landlord here is the city itself, the very recipient of the policeman's reports. In the morning Dajka will file his notification about each and every overcrowded slum. Thank God, it is not his responsibility to see to the evictions.

"If only they could all fit into my living room."

In a smelly cellar two adolescents await him under guard. They were found to be in possession of a gardener's knife, supposedly only for self-defense. The usual story: two ragtag outfits, two identical beatup hats pulled down over the eyes, two identical pug noses. Village lads, the inhabitants of the city of tomorrow. Soon after their arrival their money ran out. Then came the room rented by the week, followed by lodgings by the night. These two have descended all the gradations and have been thrown out into the street. They have not committed any crime. But they have to be hauled in for vagrancy. He is well acquainted with this type, which will turn to crime eventually. In the workhouse they will be educated - by the real criminals.

From here and there the constables have collected fourteen

street urchins, and have locked them in the paddy wagon. If Dajka had his way, he would open the barred door of the horse-drawn wagon and let them all go free. But he sends them off to detention. He sighs deeply: at last the raid can proceed toward the inner districts of the city. For a change of air, he craves the district of the night dives, where he will not have to deal with crowded slums, and will face only murderers, robbers and whores.

My showman's instinct senses trouble, there in the innermost of these inner districts, in the red salon.

The storm that has been hanging over our heads has moved another step closer and is rumbling over the hills of Buda, where it stirs, hidden by the benevolent cover of darkness.

The start of the show finds me in my usual place near the tiny stage and the covered piano.

To all appearances I am quaffing champagne and inspecting the two-legged horsies on stage. I shrug off Abris' unspoken offer, and the girls seated by the wall respect my solitude. No one is pushy here, nothing is obligatory. The Baroness, through her novel concept, her hostesses, has found that murky never-never land between open and clandestine prostitution. She has an excellent eye for these border zones. All of us seated here are sharing an exclusive secret that may be broached by any of us under the right circumstances. I expect something to happen at any moment, but I don't know what. I have not had a drop to drink; I must keep all my senses quite keen. The bread-girl is here, safe and sound, strolling among the tables or standing at the back; with her white head-dress on and the tray suspended from her neck, she is the very image of stability. From the corner of my eye I keep a glimpse of Bubbles.

The night is still young, the air is relatively thin; there are still several empty tables, and it is time for the first show.

A gong sounds. From behind the velvet curtains the horsie chorus giddy-ups onto the stage, all harnessed. Everything seems to be going well. The music surges, the covered piano stands in silence. The gentlemen are trickling in, the red-coated waiter Abris is kept busy, carrying full trays and ice buckets, directing girls to some of the tables. Cigar smoke billows towards the grillwork of the rectangular vents above the stage.

The time of the "Grand Tattoo" scheduled to close the Exhibition grounds tonight is still far off, but already one can see uniforms here and there through the smoke of the salon. The traffic between the outer and inner rooms is filtered and unobtrusive, as ever. The person who designed the workings of this place did not make provision for murder.

Champagne bottles are popping; one Excellency, who had already had too much to drink, is guzzling from a golden high-heeled shoe while the owner of the shoe giggles. All goes as if on schedule. And still, I can sense a tension in the girls like that preceding a storm, even as they kick up their black-stockinged legs at the stars like so many high-strung thoroughbreds. I recognize the introductory bars of the "Little Horsie" number, the one I had first heard not so long ago in the family-style dance hall downstairs.

The blowzy music forges ahead on its own path, unstoppable, as if we were approaching a spectacular triumph. The Baroness is fidgeting in the back, I can see that she is nervous, and would like to delay the music, but cannot. In the smoky, dank atmosphere there trembles an awareness that here every moment is sacred, for the program must proceed like clockwork. The tempo is merciless; the chorus begins its restrained pony-like nodding as their aigrettes sway on their heads, and they circle the stage showing off their alluring, strapped cruppers. This is the dance motif that introduces the "Little Horsie" number. The girls are casting sidelong glances in the direction of the door of the dressing room.

"This is the last time she'll do this to me!" is all I can hear. The proprietress is standing near the stage, by the artists' entrance. Her head is twisted backward, her face is red with impotent rage.

"This is it. She's fired, I'm done with her!"

The introductory bars are almost over and her soloist is still not here.

She hisses out from behind the curtain; the leading chorus girl, who wears a double aigrette, dances over to the edge, her head ornament askew; she is exaggerating and trying to disguise each movement, making it all the more obvious that she is listening to her employer.

The Baroness is whispering instructions through her hands covering her broad face.

One of the guests snatches up his glass and downs its contents.

Still no vocalist, and the scandal is unavoidable now. My eyes cannot afford to miss the tiniest detail. The fillies set out to gallop around the stage one more time. A high-ranking officer with a gold-braided collar buys a cigar from the bread-girl. She circulates near the front tables, surveying the situation on stage.

(NOW: THE LARGEST PUBLIC SQUARE)

We exited the subway and took a look at the traffic lanes of Europe's largest public square. This was where we were going to find the answer to your question about what was to be included in the story. And we did not have all the time in the world for it.

This largest public square had acquired considerable significance in the education of our nation, although not at all in the manner the so-called leaders during the megalomaniac early 'fifties envisioned when they ordered its construction.

Our task was to take the difficulty in hand and keep twisting and turning and manipulating it until it became easy. Pay attention now.

Should we proceed as the wind, or as thought?

This Square seemed to have been explicitly created as a learning ground for discoverers of Vitamin C, developers of information theory, inventors of the hologram and various and sundry storytellers; a learning ground closely related to the existence of our ethnic entity here in the Carpathian Basin, as empirical proof of the usefulness of limits. This was the largest construction project of that brief historical epoch of the early 'fifties which lasted, for us, about as long as the most recent organized global bloodbath (No. 2), and left nearly equivalent scars. The construction consisted of the demolition of a round church in perfectly good condition, the clearing away of thousands of trees on an entire section of Arena Road, and the pouring of a lava of thick concrete over grass, flowers, and roots so that no life could break through. The nothingness thus created received the name of a thick-mustached foreign politician, the same after whom the whole era was eventually named. His bronze statue once stood there, but later only his boots, the rest of the body having been cut off by oxyacetylene welding torches, yanked out of its boots by cables and four dumptrucks. For a long time afterward the two boot-holes were stuffed with large bundles of straw, in accordance with the as yet unstudied rules of etiquette governing such a yanking from one's boots. In those days we the survivors called the place Boot Square. Afterward all the concrete continued to lie there with unshakeable indifference. Its role in the city's structure had been to serve as the breezy marching ground for parading crowds and for mustering those administrative instruments that can most efficiently wipe out crowds, such as machine guns, five-megaton tactical nuclear weapons, and rubber truncheons.

Now, not long before your arrival, during the second birth of Hungarian automobile traffic, by which time there was not a trace left here of even a worn bronze boot heel, cars could race about all over the square. Never such limitless freedom. In fact the rattletraps had too much of a good thing, because they kept crashing into each other with greater frequency than on the narrowest, most crowded Inner City streets.

Then one fine day lines were painted on to delimit the traffic lanes. We went to take a look, just outside the subway exit. As a consequence, what was road was defined, and all the non-road around it. And ever since then there have been hardly any accidents. That great mass of demolition, clearing, and lava of concrete began to be of some use.

This is the learning ground. You can easily see its relevance to our problem: limits are needed. So that we can know at once what are the things we don't have to worry about.

You know what, let us proceed so that neither of us will have problems.

I had a rash notion, perhaps it will not work. It is not very practical, but I will tell you anyway. Our task is to scan everything: merely a few billion years. I toyed with the idea of setting out, as the fairy tale boy, asking his mother to sew him a knapsack, to bake him some *pogácsa*, those small round unsweetened cakes, and not stop until we reach the end of the world, where children are running in a flowery meadow, chasing the flying ball. There we could sit down with our legs dangling over the sheer cliff at the edge of the space-time continuum. We could watch the movie unfolding before us, from beginning to end. Our procedure would not be totally unprecedented, for after all, the Earth has already been viewed from beyond our atmosphere by human eyes, seen for what it is, a ball, on the Christmas before your arrival (in the summer of 1968, when our basalt cobblestones were all being coated with a layer of asphalt). We would never have believed that to be possible. So we could sit down at the edge of a suitable rock ledge, under a mulberry tree, in the grass and weeds. And our legs would be swinging in the ether, like clappers in a bell, ding-dong. So much for my rash idea.

And then we would start out. Our first order of magnitude would be astronomical. We must include it, because it suits the Beginning (and won't the history of the Universe slip in here? It has a great resemblance to fairy tales; it is endless and finite at the same time. Its complex extensions are incalculable, in the literal sense of the word). About those orders of magnitude, we'll have something to say later.

About the beginning of time, more later. That belongs to the field of ultimate questions: the beginning, the possible extensions, the infinite series of newborn space-time bubbles emerging from the tissue of the universe. We shall ask questions about everything, just have patience.

Every living thing exists in a world such as can be perceived by its sensory organs and comprehended by its brain. Our story cannot be otherwise, either.

Why don't we take a peek, what would it be like if the

Thundering Dragon, commonly known as Brontosaurus, were to tell its tale?

The Seven-Headed Dragon flings its mace from seven times seven leagues away, to the kidnapped princess back at his cave, so that the earth shakes. He flies home with seven-league strides and thunders, "Who goes there? I smell a human."

Nor was this creature invented by anyone. For dragons exist. More precisely, dragons have existed. We have fossil evidence. Facts. Some of them had three spines on their mace-like tails, others had a single, fifteen-foot horn; some flew on thirty-foot wings, others had six horns protecting their bony, armored collars. There were dragons with two and three brains. The Tyrant Dragon King (Tyrannosaurus Rex) had a twelve-foot stride, it has been measured.

The Thundering Dragon was sixty feet long and weighed twenty tons, but its forebrain was the size of an apple. It was awfully stupid.

The hot sun of a tropical climate shone down on it. The atmosphere was humid and stifling, and enormous dark green ferns and reddish horsetails - the ancestors of the red-trunked sequoia trees - towered over the giant's head.

But for our dragons these colors do not exist. Our Earth is not their Earth. You have had dreams in black and white - that is how they see the world. Dim, blurry and flat. Their world contains one dimension less. No, the young Earth is not for them, nor the lush riverbank, the bubbling swamp or the steaming geyser. This beast's chief intellectual achievement is that his thighbone does not collapse under his immense weight, for he wades mostly in swamp water. That is where he lives, belly deep amidst steaming marshes and putrescent miasmas, sloshing around in the wet darkness. His brain is programmed for food, enemy, female. If something small moves near the rotting treetrunk at the swamp's edge, he strikes out and chomps it up. The chief task of his forebrain is to synchronize clamping of the creature's teeth. A large shadow stirring on the hillside signals an enemy. Our Thunderer's reptile brain is flooded by dragon furor, he rushes with seven-league strides to stamp it out, whatever it is. The smaller brain in the back, near the waist (the second head of the Seven-Headed one) coordinates the tail strokes that are capable of cracking an opponent's back. This is his fighting style, not too fancy but effective. If he sees a beauteous dragon maiden (in murky, two-dimensional black and white), he roars and rumbles over, accompanied by a splashing flood tide of swamp water while the ground shakes as he takes possession of her, buries her with melting love as one mountain would another. The dragon mom drops her eggs in the sand and forgets about them; she is too stupid to care for her offspring. But even the little brains she has are enough for survival, her broods multiply and flourish for an unprecedented one hundred forty million years.

Until they vanish from the surface of the Earth.

There are many theories about the cause of their extinction. A change in diet produced a thinner eggshell. The early mammals - the poorman's smallest child who outwits the dragon - preyed on their eggs. Catastrophe struck in the form of a giant meteor, cosmic radiation, flooding. Perhaps the most plausible is the theory that parallels the migration of continents, for their surprising extinction took fifteen million years. South America breaks away from Africa. The Atlantic and Indian Oceans are formed. North America is still one with Eurasia, and Australia with Antarctica. India moves on through the shallows toward Eurasia. Great land masses wander away from the equator. The tropical dragons one fine day find themselves in the inclement temperate zones and the common cold finishes them off.

And the mammals inherit the kingdom of the earth.

I am unable to make up anything. And I think this holds true for others as well. Or to put it more precisely, every tale has its origins in perceivable reality. (Is this reality broad or narrow? We have no grounds for comparison.) Our world is superior to that of the Thundering Dragon by virtue of our increased capacity of perception.

We cannot even dream otherwise - for the congenitally blind dream in sounds. And we can grasp only a fraction of the world - this is proved by the gifts we have received on this difficult terrain, every time we happen to be listening to music from thousands of miles away, or looking at the greenish phosphorescent image of a living person's skeleton. We did not have the ability to sense these phenomena prior to the inventions of the pioneers: Professor Roentgen's X-ray machine, and Tivadar Puskás' telephonograph. Both are simple devices - once they have been devised. These are the people I call pioneers, leaders.

Our reality therefore is what we perceive. It is a lot, but it is also too little.

For now, we have struggled for this bit of headway: we may omit things as we see fit.

We shall find the right tools, we'll get it done somehow.

Plenty remains to be included in our story. We have already started to tell about this and that. This brings us back to the year of the Silly Kitty again. On this day the highest temperature in the country was registered at Zimony, near Nádorfehérvár, thirty-six point six Centigrade, and the lowest at Késmárk, eleven point eight degrees Centigrade (for you, respectively: Novo-Belgrade, Yugoslavia, and Kezmarok, Czechoslovakia). The weather is shifting, tending to be stormy, and the barometer is dropping. When we left off, I was sitting toward nighttime in the red salon that was built hidden between floors so that it is undetectable from the street.

Outside, the first lightning strikes with a terrific crash. Indoors the music is lighthearted, the ponies are nodding their heads and swaying their tails, and in the midst of this tense merrymaking the sudden fury of violence is about to be let loose. From where I sit I can hear, through the wall and the wallpaper, the wind blowing with increasing ferocity on distant streets, driving clouds of dust and grit, smashing windowpanes. All of the preliminaries are set for the event that is about to change our lives. It is not a very notorious crime, and the daily press will not be able to make much of its confusing details, so that attention to the case will subside and fade. But then soon enough it will pale by comparison to the eventual great sensational news of the summer. We are almost there.

"HEEYA HEY, HEEYA HO!"

Like a fury with streaming hair, a woman bursts into the red salon from behind the curtain of the stage.

"Second stanza!" I can distinctly hear the Baroness' loud hiss. From the moment the disheveled cabaret singer swings onto the stage, all eyes are held by her. Everyone stares: the proprietress, the chorus girls, the distinguished audience. Without a doubt, she is this evening's star; she is the one proclaimed by the crescendos of the hidden orchestra, and the beam of the spotlight is focused on her. This is her Grand Entrance.

She is in her street clothes; the reticule with its silvery web still hangs from her arm. "Giddy-up, horsie, giddy-up." Outdoors the wind before the storm is howling, and it seems that I can hear the creaking of the boards in the passageway's palisade. It must be my imagination. "Giddy-up... Heeya ho, heeya hey!" My earlier premonition has turned into a certainty: that afternoon I had seen Bora, the star singer of the café. Today she arrived too late to sing her cat-costume number in the dance hall downstairs. She raises an arm sheathed to the elbow by the black glove.

The chorus girls are wound-up figures in a clockwork.

Like some music hall goddess of revenge, the singer takes center stage, in front of her horsies, who are all lined up. She sings with murderous playfulness: "Little. Tiny. Horsie. Giddy. Up. Heeya hey, heeya ho!" She does not stop there but runs across the stage, with a strange convulsion in the middle of her movement. This single gesture combines the nodding, parade dance with a spasm of raging fury. She leaps down to the floor, swinging the heavy reticule in her hand.

Agnes Vad steps forward to see what is going on.

I can make out the whitish mud caked on her gray buttoned boots. I know everything that needs to be known. I could intervene and stop her at this instant. But I run short of attention; I am suddenly pressed for time, literally. I may not be alone in this, but there is no way to know. It is the other woman who is important, the one in the back, holding her insignificant tray. Each of my muscles is taut; this is the moment I have been anticipating all night, in fact ever since I saw that strange threesome earlier in the day. Of course I could not have foreseen precisely what trouble would follow. Only I can block the singer, I am the only one in her way. I rise from my seat. But I move in the direction of the bread-girl. I know very well what Bora's reticule contains. Bubbles stands placidly between two tables, holding her tray, watching the events with head held high.

Right in front of me the singer takes out the brick from her reticule. She lifts it high above her head. The moment stands still, stretching into infinity; the silence weighs on us. Then Bora takes one more step forward. "My love!" I can hear her clearly. "My last, one and only love," she says gently before smashing down at the temple of the handsome man who is looking up at her in amazement.

After that I see only the champagne and the blood, gold and red, the colors of the sun. The bottle of champagne lies on its side at the edge of the choice stageside table, and the golden droplets of Törley's Talisman slowly blend with the blood into a sinuous rosy rivulet. The victim's body lies on its back by the brocaded wall that casts enigmatic, grim patterns on his livid face. The blood runs down his high pale forehead, down his face and neck, and starts to soak through the flounced, lacy shirtfront of his evening attire. Drops of blood are splashed over the wallpaper, where it meets the bare stucco; blood drips onto the floor where the carpet drinks it up, turning it a deeper shade of crimson.

Everything happens with lightning speed. The aigrettes are fluttering. The jouncy music blares. The chorus girls cannot stop at once; in winding down their movements they grope about awkwardly, taking a few more steps atop the high little stage along the trajectories of a role that belongs to a previous universe.

The singer stares in stunned incomprehension at her beloved lying there in his blood. It is impossible to anticipate what will happen next. I can sense only that the tension has been discharged. The fury's passion is spent.

The black-stockinged legs have come to rest now; the

underarms are no longer on display. The white aigrettes give another hesitant, limp flutter or two; the horsetails droop under the black straps. In the back of the room there is a clattering of glasses, a tipsy girl titters, and grows silent. In the waiter Abris' hand the tray tilts, the champagne bucket slowly begins its slide, and he keeps tilting it back in place with a swinging counter-movement.

The music is still jingling, jangling. The Baroness reaches into the grillwork and pulls a hidden handle, cutting the music off in the middle of the beat. Only the helpless shuffling of one or two feet can be heard now. In a flash the mystery of the music is revealed to me. I can recall the slight jag as the music continued when I was first led up here from the dance hall downstairs, and I also recall the oversized ventilating cowls above the orchestra. The music is conveyed upstairs by the excellent acoustics of an ingenious system of ducts that transmit sound in only one direction. And so, depending on the nature of the dance, the lighting and vocal style, the music that was merely silly downstairs becomes torrid up here. We are indeed located right above the dance hall. That is why the two programs have to begin at the same time; that is why · everything has to go like clockwork up here.

All of my senses have become keener: I can see from the corner of my eye with full peripheral vision, I can see with my temples, with the tips of my ears and the back of my neck; my angle of vision has grown to three hundred sixty degrees, nothing in this room can evade my attention.

And as the silence descends, the singer Bora Clarendon lifts her head triumphantly and looks in the direction where the bread-girl is standing, as if to say, Now he'll never be yours. Perhaps she is thinking about her two princely bastards in foster care near Vienna, and what will happen to them. This enchanting auburn-haired dream lover was her only joy, and these, her own white hands, have just done away with him. With high theatricality she flashes a radiantly beautiful leg, once the wonder of Paris and Saint Petersburg, as she plants her foot on her lover's chest, like a noble beast of prey placing a paw on the felled gazelle. Her many-buttoned chamois boot leaves a small, whitish mud print.

She looks over the disheveled row of aigrette-bearing chorus girls, bobs her head twice and starts to sing. "Giddy-up... Heeya hey, heeya ho!" Never before did she sing it with this much feeling. "Giddy-up, horsie, giddy-up, little horse." Her voice rings out loud and crystal clear.

PART THREE

ON A NEW JOB

ADRENALIN

"Heeya hey, heeya ho!" Bora's singing voice resounds loud and clear in the salon. "Giddy-up, horsie, giddy-up..." An instant later the final notes of the song flow over the lifeless body on the floor. The singer's face turns deathly pale, and her straining body goes limp. She sinks into an empty chair.

And throughout, the rumble of distant thunder.

Chaos and helplessness reign. No one in the room can fathom the primal emotions that have ripped the scene of revelry in the brief span of one hundred twenty seconds.

And so, because of an infatuated woman, we became entangled in a violent crime that would drag in the police. It was a love triangle that brought about this fatal kink in our affairs. We were powerless to do anything about it. And whatever had to happen, was going to happen.

A tremendous storm was brewing.

I was prepared. Ever since I caught that first glimpse of the lips of the girl called Bubbles in the fairgounds throng, I should have been able to foresee my future encounters, in a time when the world would be a meadow full of dancers.

According to my calculations the great day at the jeweler's is one month away, at most. On this very night the Dutch diamond cutter is contemplating with rapt gaze the results of his work, the finished stone. Reduced in weight to forty-eight carats, it is now embraced by an ethereal platinum setting. Everything is on schedule. Nonetheless, the unexpected is going to interfere with our meticulously prepared plans. It has already interfered, although we are as yet unaware.

For who could foretell that the singer's hair would turn completely white in the course of this one night. That she would demand for herself the most severe punishment, the dungeons, the gallows. That her accountability would become the key issue of a trial that would never take place. That I would not be able to restore her sanity, ever again.

After the Huckster Street affair, we shall expect the heat to descend on us. But even then, we shall not be able to estimate the eventual significance gained by a rip in the shoulder of a used cloak, or its home repair.

Bora's song is done. Her victim lies beneath the sole of her small chamois button boot. And the momentarily suspended animation in the room stirs into full activity again.

Once again, after long years of patient waiting, I face that sudden, violently physical moment of action. I must make a move now, otherwise my life will elude me.

Now is the time to summon up my finest abilities from reserves as deep as some Mindanao Trench.

My inner processes speed up by a whole order of magnitude. Suddenly my system secretes adrenalin. Blood vessels constrict. Blood pressure rises, the pupils expand. Sugar is pumped into the muscle tissues, other bodily functions slow down, as only in those rare moments that shape the future. I know from former occasions that nothing can stand in my way at such times.

I am surrounded by a series of frozen tableaux:

The waiter Abris. His ice bucket, teetering at the extremity of its slide on the tray whose plane is almost vertical. The napkin over his red-clad arm shines, a white flag of surrender. The bucket is poised for its catastrophic denouement.

A disheveled girl at the back of the room. Solicitously peering over her is the fat blockhead of a drum-major in the Dual Monarchy's army, a brick of flesh that looks remarkably like the head that will, after several turns of history, in the early Nineteen-Fifties, fill all election posters wherever the eye can see, with images of the bald-pated Fearless Leader of those times, the butt of nationwide witticisms. Here one chubby hand clutches a shako, the other is spasmodically trying to tidy the disarray of the girl's drenched curls.

The bread-girl. Having put down her tray on an unoccupied sofa, she is smoothing her apron with a slow downward gesture; her face is a study in dreamy, dumbfounded curiosity. I know that her name is Bubbles.

The Baroness in front of the stage, her arms outstretched in bewilderment. Behind her, in the deeper shadows, the crooked shoulder of the workman in overalls flashes past; I catch a glimpse of his wild dark head of hair.

In an array of interrupted gestures, the girls are grouped around the focal point of the prostrate body; some on the stage, some in the laps of guests, others on the floor.

I must find a solution, and at once. To tangle the threads. To bedevil the opposition by creating uncertainty and confusion, to dampen the gunpowder of his diligence. I cannot at this time know that the adversary, because of that stray cat of a protégée he chose to take in from the rain, will turn out to be the very person doggedly following the trail of the safe-breaks for the past two years. The man whose odds I helped to improve by the Odessa affair. The man who could frustrate all of our designs, in a very ugly way.

Now I have run out of time. The simplest truism flashes through my brain: to press a murder charge, first and foremost you need a corpse. If the authorities are given a chance to track down the identity of the felled man, the bread-girl could fall foul of the law. And the police would sift through the past until they would find out who we were - and everything else along with it. You will get to hear the whole story. But back there, I had to take the risk, for my own as well as the girl's sake.

This is when I need all the help I can get, even if it comes from the devil; and I have a feeling that assistance is on the way.

A man's hoarse voice cries out: "Short circuit!"

And it appears that darkness was the only missing ingredient for things to start happening in a hurry. The swinging tray tips over, and a loud shout from the direction of the head waiter signals that the contest between the red-coated waiter and the Earth's gravity has been won by the Blue Planet.

The first screams are already leaving the throats of some of the girls.

Within minutes there will be more cops here than customers. And that will spell trouble for us all.

Bora Clarendon clutches a rosary from her reticule now relieved of its heavy load, and I imagine her telling her beads. Around her the infernal noises of darkness are descending.

The energetic drum major has straightened out his uniform,

and, snapping soldier-like orders all about him, is gradually
sidling toward the exit of the salon. He would no doubt prefer
to be elsewhere by the time pandemonium breaks loose in this
dubious locale. Halfway to the exit he becomes entangled in a
maze of overturned furniture and shouts, "*Licht!*" followed by
the Hungarian word for "lights", fully in the spirit of the
Constitution guaranteeing the use of both languages in the
Dual Army - for this achievement we may thank the blood
shed by the heroes of the 1848 Revolution. The Baroness is
wringing her hands and moaning for her doorman, "For God's
sake, Béres, where are you now when you are needed?"

At this moment Dr. Dajka, the Special Investigator, is with
the police squad raiding one of the gambling dens on King
Street, in the midst of dealers in stolen goods, embezzlers and
thieves. He is tired, but the worst of the night is over; after
this, he is headed for the relatively genteel Inner City, and a
walk at dawn followed by muscle-loosening exercises.

Thunder and lightning over King Street. Dajka pulls a
curtain aside. As the thunderstorm bursts directly over the city
of Pest, streaks of lightning flare in the sky, flooding the streets
and sidewalks in a daylight brightness. The parched cobblestones smoke under the downpour's fusillade. The edge of the
sky and the buildings that glisten in the rain are painted red by
the glow of a millhouse set on fire by lightning on the other
side of the city where rows of warehouses stand, in the
neighborhood of Tollhouse Square and Salthouse Street. Next
to the raging elements, human figures appear to be mere ants.

As shuttered windows are torn open by the wind, the
residents of the capital jump from their beds, and peek out of
their windows, so many nightcapped heads terrorized by the
Godforsaken turn of the weather.

The police officer consults his pocket watch: it is five
minutes before eleven. Clicking the lid shut he slips the
chronometer into his vest pocket.

Inside the windowless salon the downpour goes unnoticed
while I feel my way in the dim candle light to the washroom by
the stage. Behind my back the hunchbacked doorman appears,

equipped with a screwdriver, wires and a branched candelabra. He is groping toward the row of porcelain insulators.

"At last!" The Baroness' sigh of relief may be heard all the way to the washroom. The darkness is lifting. More and more candles are being lit in the hands of waiters and hostesses. "I must take a look at the small safe," says the proprietress to the Hunchback. "As soon as the lights are on, you come with me. Hurry up."

The doorman putters around, and at last the electric ceiling lights come on. These fixtures are meant to be used only for cleaning up, and they do not show the place or its guests in a flattering light.

Soon everyone present is staring in disbelief at the bare carpet: the victim's body has disappeared. (Please be patient.)

"Where did it go?"

"My God, what could have happened?" Squawks and squeals; general consternation.

"It looks like he's flown the coop," growls the deep basso of one of the guests. "While the lights were out!" And I swear he gives off a sigh of relief.

The leaden weight of the unknown settles over the salon.

Bora stares at the carpet, at the slightly darker, twin stains of an uncertain outline, the only evidence that blood has been shed. "They took him away," she murmurs. She sets out toward the red velvet curtain, as if she were a sleepwalker. The Hunchback catches up with her and grabs her shoulder.

"That's all we need, to get the guest rooms involved in this," he says, his left hand still clutching a bit of electric wire.

"My dead lover," moans the singer, for whom each word is a struggle.

The strong sinewy hand of the Hunchback forces her to sit down on the sofa.

For an instant, I am flooded by light in the washroom; I had failed to draw the curtain behind me rapidly enough. My evening outfit is immaculate. If someone were to witness my actions now and later testify about them, there would be one fewer unsolved crime burdening the annals of the capital city's police. Behind me, I hear the Hunchback taking charge of things.

"We must call the police," he tells the Baroness.

"The police? Up here?" In panic she casts her eyes around her red salon. "No policeman has ever set foot inside the steel doors...or been upstairs. If the police come up here, we're finished."

The Hunchback places a hand on his mistress' shoulder. He is now acting more as a supporter than as a mere servant.

"There has been a murder; at the very least, manslaughter. And anyway, they will find out everything. It's going to be hard times for the Kitty. But Madame has done nothing wrong. We must not hide anything." For the taciturn doorman, this is quite a lengthy speech.

It is of the utmost importance now to stave off a noisy scandal, and to keep the hyenas of the press away. Not to allow the nightclub to acquire a bad reputation among its clientele. Because then they might as well close up shop.

"You could ask for the Special Investigator. He will come, because of the girl. And he might be inclined to treat us leniently. I have posted one of our waiters at the main entrance, with orders that no one is to leave. At midnight the second show is going on downstairs as scheduled, but without Bora. The steel chamber is locked."

So Bora will never again sing that song in her cat outfit. The proprietress nods, in surrender. "Do what you think is best. But first you must come to the office with me." And on the way there, the Baroness states, for the very first time, the leitmotif that will recur so often in connection with this case, sounded in various tones of hope, annoyance or helpless resignation: "If the body is not to be found..."

The doorman walks by her side, without a word; there is nothing to say.

He is told to stand guard at the office door. She takes out the velvet bag from the small safe, and calms down only after she has ascertained its weight. She unties the string and pours out the contents into the pen tray on her desk. Her future shines and sparkles there. A heap of real American gold nuggets. The doorman is the only other person who knows about her pet project. Only four or five more years and the Kitty will have provided the needed capital. That is, if the

Kitty is to survive this night.

Back in the salon she heads for the lever that regulates the vents. In the downstairs café the music has stopped. She is intimately familiar with the meaning of each little noise. These vents transmit sound in only one direction, from the downstairs up. The designer did not plan on the present situation; the present situation was inconceivable.

Downstairs there had been no power failure. There the public goes on flirting and courting and dandling, blissfully unaware of what happened. It is intermission time, the dance music will soon start up, signaling the beginning of the second show. I was filled in about the details later.

When Baroness Vad shuts the listening vents, I reappear. As it happens, (and for the second time tonight) Bora is the only one who sees me. She is there next to the stage, like someone for whom life has lost its meaning, looking around with lusterless eyes.

The Hunchback is taking charge. I feel a certain peace and satisfaction as I watch him. He steps on stage and strikes the gong. In the sudden silence all heads turn in his direction. Here is a man, self-assured, calm and collected, clad in his indigo work clothes and apron, in the midst of all the assembled evening outfits and uniforms.

"No one can leave until the police arrive," he announces, to an uproar of outraged exclamations. With a broad gesture he motions for quiet, and his voice overrides all others, "In the name of the state police." Here is a man who knows how to find the right words.

Downstairs in the café the burglar-proof iron shutters roll down with a rumble. A waiter holding a black umbrella has taken up his post by the front entrance.

"Gentlemen, I thank you," the doorman concludes. There are no ladies in attendance. In addition to the gentlemen, only employees or partners of the establishment can be found in here. "The waiters will be serving hot frankfurters with horseradish. You are all guests of the house."

Back in the small office he presses pen and paper into Madame's hands.

"Why don't you write, 'Please come at once. We've had

some trouble.' Sign it. No need for the writing sand. Aladár must take it immediately at full speed to Police Headquarters."

Now that she is doing something at last, the Baroness feels better.

This is the moment when I recognize and seize my opportunity. It will enable me to stay here by Bubbles' side. Though of secondary importance, this also happens to be the best place to hide: right here, in front of everyone.

I manage to dig up a feather duster from the broom closet. Right now there is no music; a chaotic, hysterical hubbub is rising in the salon.

"Shall I play something?" I ask the Baroness, pointing in the direction of the small piano. I have business elsewhere, but it will be hours before I can leave here. She nods her head energetically: go ahead. I remove the cover and dust off the piano. Just as earlier I had quit my sideshow career with a single flourish, so now, with one gesture I find myself in the midst of a new job where I can earn my bread, and make myself useful in society. I lash into the keys. The honky-tonk piano. And, let us not beat about the bush, at the kitty-cat house. A few weeks ago, when I recalled this song for the first time, I had still envisioned myself as a guest here.

At Police Headquarters the corporal on duty takes delivery of the Baroness' note. It is addressed personally to Dr. Dajka, Special Investigator. The scented paper and its envelope quickly remind the corporal of the rumors circulating in the hallways at headquarters. Perhaps it is, after all, personal business. He despatches a patrolman into the thunderstorm to deliver the note to Dr. Dajka, wherever he is with the raiding squad.

The downstairs guests at the café cannot understand what the rumbling of the lowered shutters is all about. The night is still young, no one is getting ready to go home.

In the doorway of the salon the stocky drum major is shouting and turning red in the face. How does such a...menial dare to prevent him from exercising his right to free movement!

"The doors will open only for the police," the Hunchback informs him. And the doorman stands his ground, turning a deaf ear to curses. His calm face is somehow, inexplicably, superior. The high-ranking officer stops short in the midst of a stream of oaths, slinks back to his table and starts to stuff his face with salt peanuts.

And here I go, plinking away at the piano, in a poor semblance of business as usual. I will just have to wait out the arrival of the police.

The messenger catches up with the raiding party at the Orpheum on Sailor Street. Fortunately the place happens to be equipped with a telephone apparatus, and Dajka promptly places a call to the Kitty on Rose Square. The telephone rings right next to my ear, in the corridor to the dressing room. The singer is still sitting in the same place, absorbed in her rosary. The doorman lifts the receiver from its yellow copper hook.

"Excellency, it would appear that someone died here; he was hit on the head. One of the guests, we do not know his name. It was Miss Bora who did it, I regret to say. They say she did it with a brick. And there is a problem. The body of the victim is gone." Obviously this cannot be dealt with on the telephone.

"You must leave everything untouched. Son, are you sure you are sober?" It is as if the Special Investigator would like to cling to that last straw of hope. "I'll be there immediately."

He recalls that enigmatic smile on the doorman's face when he had let him in, that first time. Now he can only give his approval to the man's actions. But first, one more question. "Are there any blood stains? Well then, place a basket or box directly over them. Block off the area with chairs and make sure that no one walks over it."

The Baroness must indeed be a clever woman to have hired a man who has such presence of mind.

In the café downstairs the second show is underway. Here in the salon the last straggling hostesses and guests appear from the direction of the upstairs rooms. Aladár has returned.

The Baroness sets about to do what she can for her nightclub. She has Abris clean up the spilled champagne. Then she mobilizes her reserves: the food to be served. She delivers a short exhortation to her staff: the waiters and the girls.

The police are on the way toward the Silly Kitty. Whether the place will stay in business and keep providing a livelihood for all of them will be decided in the next few hours. It's finished for the secret of the upstairs salon. However, if someone is not absolutely *certain* about what happened, about what was seen, then it is best to keep quiet.

She herself serves a small cup, a finjan, of Turkish coffee at each table, urging it on both girl and guest alike, in a manner that refuses to take no for an answer. Let everyone be sober. I sip the coffee and taste the sweet coffeegrounds on my tongue.

Later the Baroness Vad signals in the direction of the kitchen and a procession consisting of dancers in horsetails, coatroom attendants, and the bread-girl files out carrying steaming bowls of cabbage broth and platters of frankfurters with horseradish. And lemonade as a thirst-quencher.

After the corporal's order to saddle up, a police detachment rides at breakneck speed toward the nightclub to secure the premises. The horses' hooves splash through ankle-deep puddles that cover entire city blocks.

Dajka is soaked to the skin by the time he reaches his carriage. Having ordered the raiding squad to follow him, he speeds through the deserted streets in the direction of Rose Square. The cloudburst is at its height, but the storm will have abated somewhat by the time the two police detachments reach the club, almost simultaneously.

The Special Investigator, who is in dire need of sleep, is about to confront the most difficult case of his life. An initial inspection and subsequent investigation, in the course of which the most factual finding for a long time to come will be a raving, unsubstantiated self-accusation. He orders the waiter with the umbrella at the front door to be replaced by an armed police guard. Then he storms into the establishment.

Upstairs the doorman is keeping his ears to the vents.

Meanwhile the charming scene of the Kitties is being performed below.

Upstairs, at the piano, I am giving a rousing rendition of

"Little Horsie", as long as we are all together here, as if I had
been doing this all my life. I have picked up the tune in no
time.

Downstairs the Special Investigator stops the music and the
dancing with a single imperious word.

Madame signals to me to stop playing.

I am able to visualize the downstairs dance floor, where
large, messy amoeba-like puddles are being left by the boots of
the drenched policemen. The severe figure of Dr. Dajka, well
known all over the city, generates alarm among the citizenry
being briefed downstairs.

Through the vents comes the sound of an opening door and
the rattle of the metal shutters going up and down.

Dajka has just sent the first of his men to catch up with him
back into the storm to fetch a forensic expert. The visit of the
police doctor can wait until morning. Dajka would prefer to
work with Dr. Komora.

The sound of heels clicking, the clatter of a sword dragging
along the floor, running steps receding, door, shutters, door.
The clanging iron-shod steps of half a dozen men rumble by
the stage and can be heard approaching the row of columns at
the back of the hall.

The din of the captive audience mounts one notch higher.

The police boots are heading directly towards the red salon.
The Baroness' face grows white, and she is close to fainting.
With bated breath I am pulling for the House, already feeling
myself one of the insiders.

"Did you tell him which way?" she asks the Hunchback,
who shakes his head. He grabs the branched candelabra and
runs down to meet them at the steel chamber.

The Baroness shakes the singer, who is still sitting in a
stupor.

"Did you ever talk to him about the upstairs?" She does not
have to specify to whom.

Bora shakes her head. By now she has no motive to lie
about anything.

That the salon hidden between the two floors has never
really been a secret to the Special Investigator, friend of her
establishment, is a fresh blow for the Baroness - and there will

be several others tonight.

I start to play the piano again.

The Hunchback leads the Special Investigator through the steel chamber. He locks the steel entrance door with its peephole and opens up the one on the right.

"This way, your Excellency."

"I know, I know." And indeed he does. "You just lead on with that candelabra as long as we have no other light." The doorman decides to risk it and guides the police officer through the maze. In the morning, when Dajka will have familiarized himself with every nook and cranny until he knows the place like the back of his hand, he will recall this minor deviousness. He will realize that the Hunchback had intended to gain time. But for whom? And for what purpose?

And so the police officer gets the same introductory view of the place as I did three weeks ago, on my first visit upstairs.

(NOW: RAZORBLADE, POLKA-DOT BANDANNA. LECSO. THE BEGINNING)

We went for a long walk in the hills of Buda. On the way back we took the streetcar (formerly No. 83, for you, No. 56) down to the Square. We seem to be unable to avoid this place, no matter where we are heading on our cross-town jaunts. For the last year or two this is where homeless youths have congregated. I saw two of them all over each other on the streetcar. A boy and a girl, sporting fatigues and camouflage colors. They were scrawny with malnutrition and grimy with what seemed like weeks of not bathing. The girl was about fifteen, not yet fully developed but she already appeared used up, wasted. Around the neck each wore a bright naked razor blade on a chain, and a red polka-dot bandanna tied in a knot. Yet another razor blade appeared to be slicing into the boy's earlobe, and the girl had a safety pin apparently piercing her lip. An old-fashioned safety pin, such as your various great-grandmothers kept around the house, along with the sewing box, by the fireside where apples were quietly roasting. These two wore their military colors, the razor's edge and the pin's point somewhat like those other kids who used to wear faded blue denims not so long ago, when it was fashionable to stick flowers into the barrels of rifles. Nowadays the popular rock groups are named Air Power, Carpet Bombers, Counter-intelligence. This, apparently, is the current method of baiting the middle classes and of selling the most hit records. I know this because I always make a point of reading the graffiti on the city's walls. They like to scrawl swastikas next to their messages. For they are ignorant of history, and have not learned what went down when the German politician with the little mustache announced his plans for a New Order in Europe. All they know about the swastika is that it is just something forbidden. But I am still rather old-fashioned, the same as I was in the face of that New Europe, and so I am skeptical and unreceptive toward this new wave. I preferred the flower children. And I do not admire military virtues.

In the wake of the Second Great Organized Butchery, the remnants of old Europe were full of orphans, whose fathers and mothers had died at the front, in the bombings, in prison camps, or were incinerated as sheer waste, in efficient ovens. But these kids here are merely unwanted children. This age has created a new phrase, one that we would have believed to be self-contradictory, back in the days of carpet bombing: "orphans of the living".

They spend their nights on the top landing of heated staircases in apartment buildings. They are the crowds at the concerts of the rock group Beatrice, and they are the ones who buy up the supplies of Technokol Rapid and plastic bags at the stationery stores, they sniff glue to get high; they steal prescription blanks and swallow forty vasodilator tablets and wash them down with red wine. Theirs are early and lingering deaths.

At the time I did not want to call your attention to them. The city has its new dangers; these are the ones you are going to grow up with. Intoxicated twelve- and thirteen-year-old kids collapsing on the street. You are almost at that age; in fact, you are there already.

On the Square we decipher their messages on the aluminum-clad advertising pillars. "What the fuck's with you? Laci the Bear and Onion. Where's the great Calvin Square gang? Lecsó and Ivan. HETESI you prick, why weren't you here at three? Laci the Bear and the Thief. Tibi, Carthage on the thirtieth. I'll have the record for you. Police is the best. What's up for New Year's? Lecsó and Laci the Bear. Violin! What's your problem? Why do you always split when we find you? Please reply, or eat shit. Ann and Chick. Going to hear 'Rice. First Monday, Railroad St. at four." (They adore the rock group Police, and tear gas on the rocks. 'Rice, that's another rock group, the ones with the polka-dot bandannas.)

And then there we were again on that escalator. That was where once, a long time ago, you had asked me how it all happened, with grandpa.

Since then, we have looked into the matter of what to include in our story.

The next question is: at what point do you begin?

And anyway, who would have the insane gumption to lay down the law: you must paddle forward to such and such a point in time to come to the beginning of the story?

Our object is to find out whatever we should know while still staying within the bounds of the humanly possible. (As far as we are able to penetrate; for no one is claiming that the story must suddenly end at some point where it can be cut like a piece of string. A point where the next thousandth of a second, or next Angstrom unit, means facing the great Nothing.)

One possible beginning still seems plausible, from our high vantage point: if only we could begin at the beginning of all that happened.

We have a tendency to believe that what we perceive is the whole world in its entirety.

But if the Dragons were to write novels, their world would not have any red or green or depth in it. So we might as well recognize at the outset that our version is also bound to omit one or two things.

Let us follow backward in time the movements of the galaxies observable through our telescopes. Inevitably we reach a moment when the cosmos was all one mass, a tremendously hot and dense sphere of gases. This mass must explode with an unspeakable force, and this is the birth of the universe. This explosion is still going on in front of our eyes, constantly. Observe. (And, while observing, keep in mind that our task is precisely to relate it, to put it into words.)

For openers, the Big Bang. Twenty billion BC, plus or minus these two thousand years. Supposing.

Blare, light, heat. What takes place here cannot be conceived by the human mind; the makeup of our brain is inadequate for that. We shall have more to say on this point; in fact, one could claim that this is all we shall ever speak about, no matter what our subject. But to go on.

We are talking about the period of time after the passage of ten to the minus thirty seconds (that is, zero point thirty zeros followed by a one): *that* minuscule fraction of one second. Whatever happened earlier than that is perhaps unapproachable for Humans, in terms of measurable consequences.

At this point, the Universe is pervaded by extremely hot radiant energy.

After the first million years - a mere blink of the eye - the temperature has decreased to a trifling few thousand degrees Centigrade.

Vortices. The first atoms are born. We are made of them. There. Each grain of each of our cells, but in a form that is some stages earlier than the present. We are there, even as we sit here at the edge, swinging our legs. We are what we contemplate. Down to every last one of our baryons.

At this time all is gas and star dust, shadows of swirling gigantic plate-like forms. Assuming the basic laws of physics have not changed in time. Assuming Einstein's General Theory of Relativity is a true account of the effects of gravity. Assuming in the beginning all Space was taken up by a single hot and homogeneous gas that was expanding. There are additional assumptions that must be met, without which there can be no Big Bang theory.

There, among the plates, you can already find the first traces of order. Non-existence asserts itself as that finite black nothingness, from where matter has been extruded.

In the witches' cauldron swirling gases condense into clouds of atoms. Around the nuclei whirl electrons; capricious by nature, they are at the same time both particles and waves. The atoms in that cloud will eventually go into the making of each and every drop of water, rock cliff, coffee grinder and block warden. You and me. We contemplate ourselves.

We revel voluptuously in this vision of the observable universe. Its full baryon count is about ten to the seventy-eighth power. A one followed by seventy-eight zeros: that is how many particles; this too has been measured, calculated, it is a fact. Physicists have postulated a residual background radiation that had probably cooled down to about three degrees Kelvin in the course of twenty billion years. Twenty years later a measurement found it to be two point seventy-four degrees Kelvin. So that this instant seems so certain; there seem to be no unanswered questions.

If only we could forget about that little snippet of time, that ten to the minus thirty seconds we have neglected to account for. That does not fit into the theory. And so, there are some unanswered questions left, after all.

For example, we have no adequate explanation for the force of gravity.

It draws together myriads and myriads of galaxy-size disks. Malleable formations are shaped in the midst of birth pangs that wrench the universe.

Nor will our story include speculations about the future history of the universe, billions of years without humans when in the winter light of dying infrared suns, beings mightier than gods will bask in order to let their organisms soak up a little bit of vitamin C.

(Human civilization has existed for one millionth of the duration of our Milky Way galaxy, so that its order of magnitude is negligible. The evidence for the evolution of species is convincing - we have the photographs to prove it, so to say. But nowhere does it say that the process has to end with us. So far, evolution has not stopped with any other species.)

We said that the direction of changes - toward nothingness -
is something we can predict. Almost, but not quite. For the law
of thermodynamics we are basing this on has two key words in
it: closed systems. But what if before, behind, past the
Universe and even, God knows, concurrently in the same
space-time continuum but along different dimensions, there
exist other universe-aggregates and other super-aggregates? Is
there any sense at all in speculating any further along these
lines, where a few more steps and we come up against the
white-bearded or close-shaven individual who happens to
dwell up there to the left of the angular ceiling light fixture at
the Spindle Street apartment? (Where I used to look up in
despair, even a year or two ago: can you see, old man, what
this kid is doing to me? "Daddy, I touched the 'pinach," you
would announce, proud of your achievement. We had creamed
spinach for lunch. And you helped yourself to it by plopping
down your spoon so that green flecks covered the table, the
wall, the ceiling, the father, the child. That was when I looked
up, with a sigh, "Oh my God!" I was dead tired trying to be
mother as well to you. "Is that where he lives?" you asked me,
pointing in that direction with your chubby arm creased
around the wrist - an unmistakable sign of the local
superabundance of food allowed under the current draw in
the political chess game of Central Europe. You pointed at
the light fixture. "Who lives up there?" I asked. "Daddy's
God." That light fixture, at times yellowish, at times opalescent
- its milky, hazy square did intimate something not quite of this
world. "Not only mine," I said. "Everyone's." I waved my
hand vaguely toward the left of the light, to indicate greater
distances: "But way up there. If he is anywhere." In this
matter I adopt a holding position until more information
becomes available.)
    So we skip those dimensions we are unable to perceive.
Leave them out. Space has three, time is the fourth. One
German physicist found that he could unite gravitational and
electromagnetic interactions in one theory if there were a
fourth spatial dimension. Its structure is very peculiar, like a
very long tube, that is infinitely extended along one axis, and
infinitesimally small along the other. With nine dimensions we

could account for all known interactions in one theory. And, in theory, altogether twenty-six dimensions are conceivable.

We are unable to experience twenty-two of them, dimensions every bit as important as depth, or time. At least twenty-two, for the theory itself is subject to human limitations.

Supposing the Old Man - Spindle Street, square ceiling lamp, up there to the left, *supposing* - were to tell stories to an audience similarly long-bearded or close-shaven, he would most likely be preoccupied with the technical problems of the work of creation. The way it stutters and putters all around: here a Big Bang, and over there an even bigger one; here an expanding universe, and over there a smooth, pulsating, or an overblown one (to paraphrase the poet Weöres: "We create one, blow up another / we fiddle with various You-niverses"). The ordinary, everyday subject matter of such a story would naturally be the passage of another billion years, and this scintillating turn of events would be signaled by a reformulation of the laws of nature, the crumbling of the walls of civilization raised in blood and song, the clash of matter and antimatter, the elaboration of a twenty-seventh dimension, and the painful contraction and joyous re-expansion of the next series of universes.

Their kinds of stories are unimaginable for us, by definition. That is why we made an attempt to tell the Thundering Dragon's tale. We looked in the other direction to find a scale for comparison.

So on the first Monday of the month I went to Railroad Street to hear the rock group Beatrice, without you. This was easier than doing fieldwork at the top landing of a heated apartment building stairway. We stood right next to the stage. The crowd of children swayed as one continuous wave, like a field of wheat in the wind. They screamed in their delight; one girl fainted for lack of air, and a boy passed out from sniffing glue. Neither fell to the floor, for the crowd was too thick for that; they were floated to the exit of the hall on a sea of upraised arms. An arm's length away from me a skinny dark-haired young girl was making out with a bald forty-year-old sitting on the edge of the stage. She threw her head back, shoved her hips forward, straddled the man's knee, and kept rocking and swaying more and more vigorously to the rhythms of the 'Rice songs. I was paying attention to the intensely public-spirited poetry of the lyrics, when, at last, right on the beat, she came, with a long, exhaled cry.

Our visit to the Largest Public Square has taught us how to omit. So for the time being let us be satisfied with what our current state of knowledge accepts as fact, based on measurements and the rational processes of our limited human understanding.

We could begin with the birth of the universe twenty billion years ago. We would pan across the cosmos, with careful attention, but rapidly. Don't forget, I gave you my word.

Our goal is to reach as quickly as possible the conceivable beginnings of our story, our recognizable places and times and characters.

That streetcar stop in front of the Little Bear Bar. The vicinity of the Fifth Buda. The back passages of the Silly Kitty, where the Special Investigator has initiated his endeavours to solve the murder committed with a brick.

And meanwhile, we shall try not to get lost in the process of striving for completeness.

BUSY HANDS

This is crazy, but I could just as well have begun the story at this point.

"I want to know what happened here!" The Special Investigator storms into the salon. I now recognize him as the man I successfully evaded a year ago, that night at the gambling den, when I was still looking for the bald engineer. He has not changed. But he cannot identify me in my formal evening outfit, having seen me only once in the City Park, when I was wearing the rags of an itinerant fire-eater.

At first glance he cannot detect any sign of a crime. There is no corpse. And even though he has already received a quick briefing about the night's events, the salon (its ambience and clientele, including produce dealer and foppish young bank clerk) still takes him by surprise. The air is stale and thick with cigar smoke that cannot quite obliterate the bouquet redolent with alcohol, cabbage soup, cosmetics and perspiration. The most jarring note comes from my earsplitting, provocative piano playing. He is about to turn in my direction when the singer, having caught sight of him, drops her rosary and sweeps him away.

"My benefactor!" she screams, clutching his arm.

"Baroness!" Dajka calls out as he shakes off the girl.

"This girl..." the proprietress indicates Bora with a nod, "I am very sorry, Your Excellency."

"I want to hear all about it. Just *what is going on* in this establishment?"

"Oh, we have never..." But she cannot finish her sentence.

Bora points at the bare floor; her stiff-fingered hand seems to have aged suddenly.

"I killed him!"

Dajka grabs her by the shoulders.

"Let me see your eyes." His voice is ominous. "Show me your arms!" He inspects her arms, but finds no evidence of using morphine. Suddenly relaxed, his features now reflect nothing but sadness and resignation. The woman he brought here for shelter has, in all likelihood, killed a man.

Again Bora screams. Dajka, who finds my persistent, insolent piano playing a nuisance, intends to wave me off, but stops halfway through the gesture. With all this happening he can pay attention only to Bora. From past experience he knows how to handle hysteria, guilt and morbid delusions. To begin with, lovingly and attentively, he slaps the girl full in the face, quieting her at once.

"Calm yourself, all right? Listen to me. Why don't you sit down, and we'll take care of everything."

A patrolman leads Bora back to the sofa, where she sits beside the Baroness. At last the Special Investigator is able to turn his attention to the piano player.

"How dare you permit this mu-sic?!" he shouts at the Baroness. "Who is that clown? Are you in your right mind? Stop it at once!"

"It was better this way, your Excellency." I look him in the eye while I close the piano cover. "The Baroness thought it would prevent panic." I find it more convenient to credit her with the idea.

The Doctor's eyes glint. He takes note of me; I can tell he dislikes my face. He is a superb policeman, with a scent as keen as a bird-dog's. And this business with Bora has already upset him. Later, much later, I would learn from Marton, his assistant at the time, that it was at the moment of seeing my face, a mug that made his fingers itch, that Dajka decided to take charge of the investigation personally, and not rest until he got to the bottom of the matter. (Oh, the best laid plans...) This is the only way he could help the girl, by seeing to it that, whatever she had done, justice would be served.

"Start the inspection! At once!" He barks at one of his detectives. His professional duty is to establish the facts, which can be obtained only during the first few minutes, by interrogating everyone present. He turns to the proprietress. "I will need a quiet room."

The Baroness nods in the direction of her office.

Bora now flares up again.

"Let me see him!" She waves her arms. "That red-headed slut stole him away from me!" She points at the velvet curtains; past them are the upstairs *chambres d'assignation*. Dr. Dajka's eyes follow her pointing hand. So it is inevitable now: one more second and this girl is going to drag the upstairs into this affair, once and for all.

The Baroness steps in front of the triple steps.

With a sinking heart Dajka watches the almond-eyed girl. (*"Slut." Possible motive?*) Lately those dark shadows have disappeared from around her eyes - and he has almost begun to expect her to show some *gratitude*. He turns aside to hide his confusion. I observe each and every nuance; at the moment this is all I can do in the battle of wits that I have been anticipating so eagerly. Nor would I want him directing his anger at me, the way he had vented his anger at

Mrs. Tremmel on account of this girl. I can see the profound sadness in his eyes, and in his posture. But he shakes his head abruptly, turns, and is once more his usual self. He uses work - which is a far cry from morphine - as an opiate to soothe his brain.

With a nod of his head he directs Marton up the stairs. Each and every statement, no matter how implausible, must be checked. Standard operating procedure. After all, somehow a body has been spirited out of this place.

With all the delicacy of a shunting locomotive, Patrolman Suk pushes aside a wildly gesticulating Baroness Vad, and the detective advances up the three steps.

Meanwhile the night is not getting any younger. Dajka and his men have much to do, and all of it immediately.

Secure the scene of the crime. Scrutinize the whole environment, including every object or routine involving Dora, and anyone else who might be a suspect. And, until the accomplice has been identified, anyone may be a suspect.

Dajka must find out who saw what.

"Is that the stain?" he asks, pointing at the darkening twin ovals on the carpet, at the spot where the blood and champagne had spilled. The Hunchback used a wicker basket to cover that spot in a corner of the salon which he has had cordoned off by a line of chairs that resemble so many huddled police guards. The doorman points out where the customer had been siting, and how one could leap off the small stage. He himself had been in the passageway in the back at the time, working near the pantry. The show had begun. He had just let in the singer. Her breathlessness did not seem remarkable; after all, she was late. He saw no sign of a weapon on her. After locking the door he hurried upstairs. He was in the middle of unloading a crate of Zara Maraschino onto the shelves when the lights went out. It was a blown fuse, and he was able to replace it; afterwards he made sure that his mistress' note was despatched to police headquarters. For a simple working man, this hunchbacked doorman speaks in a most clear and articulate manner. Still incensed, the Doctor peevishly reflects that in this den of vice nothing is as it appears. But he controls himself, resolving not to be unfair toward anyone; that is a luxury he cannot afford.

From where I sat I had a ring-side view of all that happened. That was why I had selected my table in the first place. But others were less clear about the events. Several guests stated that the singer leaped off the stage. Some thought they had seen her strike a blow in the direction of a nearby table. According to others, she had been singing on the stage. The victim was standing up in the front. No, said others, he had not been standing. There was no victim to begin with. In fact, nothing out of the ordinary had happened. The drum major thought he had caught a glimpse of a brick in the melee just before the salon was plunged into darkness. But no, he could not swear to it. Miss Máli, the lead chorus girl, noticed that Madame Bora's handbag might have been weighed down by some heavy object. Possibly. The waiter Abris had been busy in the back of the salon - take a look at the spot where he spilled the champagne. Nearby, between two tables, was where the bread-girl had stood. The Baroness had waited at the exit of the dressing room by the stage. She can lie without batting an eyelash: she claims she saw nothing, because her attention was focused on the back of the salon. Her soloist was late, the show was off schedule, everything was in total confusion.

She is defending her life's work and achievement, with the fearlessness of a lioness sheltering her cubs.

The chorus girls were unable to see anything with certainty, for a thousand different reasons. They had their own act to perform. They were frightened. The light was poor. The smoke obscured everything. One of the hostesses claims that she saw a man who might have been carrying a body. But her candle was knocked from her hands and she fell down. She points uncertainly toward the center of the salon: somewhere around there. Dajka has all the men, starting with the staff, pass in front of her, and asks her to try and pick the one, by build, whom she may have seen carrying the body. It is soon my turn in the line. She is a meek blonde, and as soon as she lays her bovine eyes on me she nods energetically.

"He's the one." The blood freezes in my veins. But the Special Investigator merely waves a hand, "You may go." And he tells the patrolman to send in the next.

I manage to leave the office with firm steps. Abris sidles over to me.

"She is not going to be much help to the Special Investigator. You are the twentieth man she has fingered. Anyone over five feet and not as fat as a pig. Only with the doorman did she have an easy time: one look at his crooked shoulder and she shook her head: Not him."

Marton returns to give a report in a low voice. He has combed all the rooms; not a trace of any person, object, or clue relating to the crime. Dajka is torn by conflicting emotions. He casts a glance at the singer with those Tatar eyes: poor girl, her mind has been deranged by the pain of her loss.

He questions the proprietress about the possibility of a robbery. In the glass cage over the coffeehouse he checks the locked cabinet; its metal bolt is secure. He picks up the two account books one after the other, then lets them drop back onto the table. The wheels are turning in his head. The double-walled small steel safe between the two floors is quite another matter. Baroness Vad can sense some profound and basic sympathy in this man whose face is so severe, and knows at once that she can win him over only by baring her soul to him. She requests that he send everyone out of the office. Then, without any further ado, she opens her velvet sack and spills her stash of rough American gold nuggets on the pen tray on the table in front of him. She is with her confessor now. It all started when her father's small fortune melted away in the failure of a local Eperjes savings and loan bank. Ever since then she has refused to put her faith in banks; whatever she has, she keeps at home. This is *one* of the reasons for her cardinal rule that the only time the steel chamber may have two doors open is when the doorman stands between them. The secrecy is not solely because of the upstairs salon. She tells about the intolerable, filthy demands made on her by the nouveau-riche mill-owner back at Bártfafürdö (where his nephews eventually inherited only enough real assets to pay the mortgages, which had metamorphosed into her gold nuggets). She tells about meeting the Prussian Baron Ormund

Freiherr von Berchtesgaden zu Neumannthal on the train, in whose memory she titled herself Baroness. And she tells about her fondest dream: some day to build in the hills of Buda an internationally ranked health resort hotel, exploiting the Danube's water basins that are so rich in carbonates and hydrogen sulphide. There would be an institute of hydrotherapy for the treatment of scrofula, chlorosis, and dropsy, equipped with blood-cleansing tincture of iron cures and the most modern twin-celled electric baths. Entertainment would be provided and she would not charge treatment or music fees. With patriotic fervour she describes how the rich foreigners would flock here, much as the affluent Hungarians flock to Karlsbad or the French Riviera now. She has already looked into all the angles. She was planning a high-rise palace hotel with several wings that would open like the pages of a book. Therapeutic halls, promenade concerts, pavilions, and eventually perhaps a refined roulette casino, such as at this time may be found only in Monte Carlo. (Where we too shall visit.) To leave behind once and for all the shadows of the brothels of the past. She takes the Special Investigator's hand in her own, gently, and looks up at him, her eyes wide open: all of her plans depend on the income from her salon. And Dajka stores away all this information on the credit side of the Baroness' account. The conversation lasts three minutes.

Afterward he extracts his small black pocket notebook, sits at one of the coffeehouse tables and inscribes, in his punctilious engineer's handwriting, at the top of the first blank page: *When? Where? How? Who? What?* (Crime is no different from storytelling, as you may see; both have to be unraveled.) Some of these rubrics will remain blank for a long time.

Then he turns to the Hunchback. "What are the exits to this place? Show me all of them, one at a time." He leaves Marton in charge of the salon.

He is already familiar with the entrance on Rose Square. The doorman first leads him once again through the steel chamber, by way of the staff dining room and the kitchen, past the pantries, down to the service entrance, which also opens on to the courtyard. It provides direct access to the kitchen and service quarters. This is where supplies are brought in; servants and cleaning women pass this way from early morning on. Every day it is locked after lunchtime until the following morning. The service entrance boasts an enormous padlock; the key is at all times in the Baroness' office. Dajka tries the sturdy lock, giving a few tugs. The thick oak door is as secure as a fortress.

Now the time has come to explore the means of egress through the famous steel chamber. Dajka has himself led out through the back door, across the courtyard and out through the carriage gate to Hat Street. He notes the direct passage afforded by the palisaded gangway, and realizes that on his arrival here he was needlessly taken a roundabout way, but he does not say anything. Béres holds the umbrella over the great personage's head. Under the open lean-to the blade of an axe left outside reflects the pale glow from the windows facing the courtyard.

"And those?" Beyond the thick curtain of the rain huddle the dark shadows of the three adobe huts attached to the wall of the neighboring building on the other side of the yard. Each one is a neat, free-standing rental on its own, with access to the well in the yard. The landlord appreciates the extra income he is able to squeeze out of his property. All three are occupied by poor folk, who pay the rent regularly. One of the tenants is a monkish bookworm, a regular ascetic; another, a sour old bachelor, is manager of the nearby Sáfrán furniture store, and the third is a legal clerk, sort of shabby genteel. By the time the nightclub opens for business, they are all sound asleep. Dajka makes a note for himself; they should all be questioned. But that can wait until daylight, along with an inspection of their hovels.

The entrance and carriage gates have been kept open, because of deliveries. Dajka has them locked; he asks for the keys to the steel chamber and posts an armed guard there. These keys have been dangling all along from the doorman's belt; he has let no one in or out since the singer's arrival.

On the ground floor the clientele's hubbub subsides when Dajka is guided into the owner's glass office cage. The keys are in their place in the cabinet. Nor did the elderly dragon lady at the cash register see anyone ascending to the office. She did, however, have to leave her post once - the call of nature - at which time she asked the busboy to keep an eye on the entrance. The youngster does not recall seeing anyone go up.

The front exit can be reached only through the main hall of the coffeehouse, which was filled with hundreds of customers. The Baroness is ready to vouch for her till lady and for her doorman.

And who will vouch for her?

It happened in the dark. But there are other witnesses who say they saw something suspicious in the wavering light of that candle. Some of them think they could sense something bumping and dragging against objects during the blackout.

Cui prodest, the Doctor murmurs to Marton, his assistant. That good old time-tested principle of Roman law. It is first and foremost in the perpetrator's interest to get rid of the corpse. But the perpetrator has confessed and insists on being punished. Her culpability would be proved beyond doubt if and when the fact of the killing is established by way of a post-mortem. But it could be in some other party's interest to do away with the evidence. Everyone present is, potentially, an interested party.

Patrolman János Suk has been listening like a stone-faced statue to the indignant sputtering of the gentlemen crowding around the guests' exit. They are all of them eager to leave as soon as possible, and all have been pressing claims entitling them to special treatment. By now they have all resumed their impeccable evening appearances, and yet, one keeps tugging at a slipped collar, another brushes non-existent motes from a shako, or wipes an imagined stain from a patent leather shoe.

No one goes near the washroom, and no one is able to witness a pair of busy, clever hands rapidly washing, then thoroughly rinsing, a hand towel.

In most cases the criminal, wishing to destroy evidence, overlooks some apparently trivial detail. The policeman's task is to find it.

The neglected detail in this case happens to be a spot of

blood. At this very moment it is drying and turning brown on a rug in a first-floor room, and the good Doctor does not have the least suspicion of its existence; neither do I.

He asks for a candle, and in its light examines the underside of each and every table and chair. (Only in the course of my inexcusably belated criminology studies will I learn that people deficient in manners have a habit of wiping their greasy or otherwise besmirched hands on the underside of the table; ditto for bloodied hands.) He is also looking for smooth, shiny surfaces, even though he places no faith in the new-fangled procedure. He is, nonetheless, meticulously thorough in his methodology. I do not know at the time why he does this; later, when I find out, it will be too late. However, there are no shiny surfaces to be found here.

He shines the light in every nook and cranny, and on sharp edges; just beyond the upper border of the wallpaper, about eye-level of a seated man, he discovers a speck of blood. He marks the location on his diagram of the scene. He asks the doorman for a piece of sturdy windowglass. He uses pure gum arabic to glue the glass over the droplets. He takes a look around the room: when a policeman cannot avoid treading on high-ranking toes, it is useful to know whose toes they are. A certain gentleman from Town Hall sits near the wall. Over here is a general of the Dual Army, with a red stripe on his trousers. A few tables away, a well-known newspaper publisher. And in case he were to have an attack of sympathy for these pot-bellied civilian and military personages, all he has to do is recall the image of Bora Clarendon's face that Monday back at Mrs Tremmel's house, and the sight of that slender, pale flower-like child escorted by the old man who sported a walking-stick with a silver fox-head knob.

The adhesive has dried. With his pen-knife he scrapes off the outermost layers of wallpaint behind the speck.

Marton draws a broken outline on the carpet to indicate the supposed position of the supposed victim. The forensic expert photographs the floor. Magnesium powder flashes in the pan, and the skinny girl, who three weeks before had been riding on the back of her porcine guest, gives a little scream. Patrolman Suk of the bristling mustaches, a man who is not afraid of his own shadow, calms her down, with a surprisingly delicate touch.

It occurs to Dajka that the piece of glass may have something particular on it. From the hackney cab outside he has a detective's bag brought in. He spreads a sheet of tracing paper on the carpet and on it outlines the kidney shape of the twin blood stains. He is quite proud of being such an old-fashioned officer of the law.

He has not forgotten about the upstairs rooms of the establishment; he will, unavoidably, have to trample upon delicate sensitivities there, so he leaves that task for last.

He commandeers the office space for his interrogation room. The door with the frosted glass inset opening on the corridor is the only entrance; that is where I will soon come face to face with an uncomprehending Bora. Behind the Doctor's back is the small wall safe. He is flanked by Marton and a detective.

He starts with the singer. First and foremost he would like to know what she had done, how, and why. He fears for her; he is afraid.

To begin with, he examines the girl's nails, her scalp and hair roots. All clear. But this proves her neither innocent nor guilty. Blood may spurt in haphazard directions. On her shoe soles he finds no traces of blood; he does not know what to make of the encrusted layer of whitish gray mud coating the uppers. When Bora arrived at the club, the rain had not started to fall yet. He makes a note of this; the singer is unwilling or unable to discuss it.

Her confession, by the way, turns out to be not only penitent but downright gushing. She demands the gallows; solitary confinement in the dungeons, bread and water, the coarsest prison garments. She repeatedly mentions the Márianosztra Prison. One need not be a physician to realize that she is in a state of shock. Whether she is punishable or not depends on her accountability at the time of the crime. Unasked, out of the blue, she mentions a trivial detail: a man recently washed his hands here. Dajka has no way of telling whether this is merely another phantasm. If someone, in the midst of all this confusion, had time to wash his hands, then he had something to hide.

This is the last time we hear Bora speak articulately and coherently. She is calm and soft-spoken. She is able to provide only scraps of information. Someone stole her lover from her. And she killed the unfaithful one. With a brick. A man has washed his hands. She does not give the name, occupation, or address of the man involved; she cannot waste her time with such trivia. She will not say who the slut is. She stubbornly insists that the body is here, somewhere upstairs.

Dajka looks within, and asks his conscience: could he be biased in favor of, or possibly even against, this girl?

Upstairs no corpse is found. Bora, a frail woman, could not have spirited it away all by herself. But no accomplices have been found.

Nor does the brick turn up anywhere in the nightclub, as if it were no bulkier than a proverbial noodle. At last, about to dismiss her after the lengthy interrogation, Dajka rises from the desk and steps up to the girl. He realizes that tonight was the first time he had ever touched her, and how rough he had been with her. He places an encouraging arm around her shoulder, and tries to calm her by offering to help, promising that he will not rest until he has investigated every aspect of this case as thoroughly as possible, no matter what other matters might arise. (And they will.) He cannot guarantee her solitary confinement at the Márianosztra Prison; that will be up to the sentencing judge. The fact that she is ready to confess is not deemed sufficient proof in the eyes of Roman - and, praise the Lord, of Hungarian - law. The accused cannot testify against herself. He tells her to respect herself, accordingly. (And she should respect her era as well, we may add, from our greater historical vantage. Our country's laws would not always be this enlightened. As we have seen in the early 1950's, in the year of the Newtown Festival, the confession of the accused was held to be sufficient proof to justify judicial murders. May God rest the victims in peace; meanwhile the judges go on enjoying their pensions in their sheltered villas in the hills of Buda, to the end of their days. Well, in this world of ours it is not always the littlest prince who wins the hand of the beautiful fairy queen.)

This is when Bora Clarendon meets me in the hallway to the dressing room. I am loitering there in the hope that they will let me go sooner. Dawn is breaking outside. It takes all my strength to disguise that I am a vibrating bundle of nerves. I have things to do in a hurry.

And in fact Dajka calls for me next.

I have committed my share of blunders in the course of this affair; and our whole gang of safe-crackers had to pay for these. Blame it on my lack of experience. But all of my blunders will be dwarfed by the wrong I am about to do in the next moment, against the singer. I will do her a grave injustice, in order to save my own skin.

In Bora's head at this moment all is still intact. Her values are clear: man and woman, old and young, money and love. Saint Petersburg is the past, and the future is Márianosztra, bread and water, rough prison garb. This was the day when she learned that her lover has been deceiving her. Her own hand held the brick that struck his head, and she saw his red blood spill. Now even his corpse had been stolen from her. And she has seen me washing my hands.

In the doorway she turns back toward the Special Investigator and tells him that it was me she had seen.

Without missing a beat, and looking her squarely in the eye, I say, with a soothing smile, "You must be mistaken."

I cannot do otherwise. But the singer's nerves have reached the snapping point. The old Hungarian adage, "There's always room for another forkful on the haycart," is nonsense. In the universe as perceived by Bora my four words have no place, they cannot be accommodated; they constitute precisely that final forkful of hay that cracks the axle and breaks the wheel. How will the gentlemen of the jury believe her guilt now? She asks me in a dreamy voice, "But how can you say that? You know I saw you. How can you?" Her head turns back and forth from the Special Investigator to me. Perhaps at this point I could have still saved her. But I have no reserve of concern left for her. I am thinking of Bubbles, and of myself.

Now all her howling emotions break loose.

"He has blood on his clothes!" She accuses me with outstretched arm, as if pronouncing an ancient curse. "He has blood on his hands!"

Her eyes grow dim, and never again will they regain their former clarity.

I could just as well have begun our story at this point.

(NOW: CELLS, FACTIONS, HOT-DOG VENDORS. LIZARD)

Two weeks ago you contracted a mysterious virus.

The day before yesterday the brothers-in-arms of the Istamboul rooftop machine-gunners massacred eighty-five people at the Bologna train station in the name of some glorious cause — there are plenty of slogans to be found for it: oppression, liberation, truth, faith and morality - eighty-five people, old women, men, children, cripples, at random - merely because they happened to be waiting for the train. The perceived reality around us has suffered yet another change. In our day it will no longer be possible to live out our lives in bitter exile, if we do not happen to share the ideals of the State (of the less tolerant type). In one year state-sponsored assassination squads have murdered fifteen refugees, among them teachers and doctors, in London and Rome alone. They tie schoolchildren to bus seats, pour gasoline over them and set them alight. And our so-called world is gradually getting itself used to such revolutionary new developments in the field of human relations.

The day before yesterday Auntie Pálma unexpectedly did not show up.

By yesterday the cells, factions, fronts and armies have already started to bicker over who could claim responsibility for the murder of babies in Bologna. In vying for the honors they will lie and swagger. "The action was carried out by armed men" - say the journalists, the ones who are paid to put these things into words. Nor are they paid for nothing: they will call murderers *youth*, or possibly *students*, *armed men*, *fighters*, or better yet, *patriots*. Blowing up train stations and department stores is labeled a *commando action*. The newswriters are doing a great job: they manage to create the impression that nothing has changed since the days when commando action meant a few dozen uniformed English soldiers blowing up a heavy-water plant in Nazi-occupied Norway. (And thereby possibly preventing the politician with the small mustache from developing an atomic bomb.) Nowadays, refined intellectuals the world over applaud every explosion all the more. They call themselves radicals, and non-parliamentarians. I may be mistaken, but it seems to me that this complicated world is at times so very simple: you are either on the side of the victims, or on the side of the murderers. The rest is just words.

Until yesterday you stayed at home in bed. I went out to sign you up for a children's sculpting group called LIZARD. A baggy-eyed, bloated, toothless whore was leaning against a newsvendor's stall on the former Calf Square (Rákóczi for you). I was heading toward a neighboring street that houses the old Bodograf Cinema (for you, Coalminer Theaters A and B).

Since I began this tale, a horrendous new world has sprung up around us, and we didn't even notice it happening, over the past four winters and three summers. A world made up of baksheesh-people: repairmen, waiters, shop assistants, chief resident gynecologists. Their mustaches are like those hot-dog vendors', a fashion spreading like leprosy. They wear glistening cream-colored jackets of nubby raw sateen. Bluejeans, spark-plugs, restaurant tables are to be had only for a bribe; the hot-dog vendor makes a hundred per cent profit on each bottle of soda by keeping our deposit. His kind are multiplying like weeds.

And if we fight back, or dare to ask for the return of our deposit money, the same old surprised, manly, wounded look appears on their sensitive faces: "But this is not what we were told!"

For the time being I have adopted a procedure against murderers of children and hot-dog vendors. On the one hand I keep in mind that the person who pours gasoline is also a victim of history and of his elected politicians - his drama is a valid tragedy in which two *truths* clashed, originally. On the other hand, I refuse to participate in it. I refuse to call those who set children on fire, *youths*; to call a murder a *judgement*, or an execution; to call a hand grenade an apple, or call what is black, pink. It is all a matter of language. I do not buy bluejeans. I do not drive a car and I do not drink sodas at the hot-dog vendor. But what am I to do at the doctor's, where the weeds of corruption prove stronger than human frailty. That is the heart of the problem. At the doctor's, our very survival is at stake. So I join the corruption, awkwardly.

It will take centuries, once we are able to start rebuilding.

At LIZARD I filled out a form for you in a corner of the room overtowered by a paper-máché giantess with six arms and two mouths, somewhat resembling the lady I saw waiting out on Calf Square. Across from me children were painting an exercise in color harmony on a thirty-foot strip. You will come here next week and see how you like it.

When I crossed the square on the way back, the baggy-eyed fat woman still had not found a taker. Is there a man sexually starved enough to want her? I wondered, somewhat rhetorically. And immediately I heard the answer uttered by Piros' voice: Just take a look at those men. They don't have too many teeth, either.

At home I confronted the piece of raw meat that Auntie Pálma was going to roast for our dinner. I screwed my courage to the sticking place, and following a remembered trail of observed gestures - much as I had learned to play the lute, and to bandy about images - I prepared our dinner. We are surviving. You are getting better. For a side dish, I cooked cauliflower in a breaded batter.

The Countess was unable to come because Uncle Ferenc, her husband, had died. She had telephoned and you spoke with her. I know this because you told me afterward, obviously. She was crying. It is better this way, she blurted in a smeared voice. In the end he had to be carried from the bed to the chair.

THE SANDOR ROZSA SYNDROME

Dr. Dajka decides to send a patrolman to rouse the police surgeon Komora from his bed after all. He will be needed to attend to the singer.

When asked, I show Dajka my hands; I raise and turn them, all cooperation, let him handle them. Without too much conviction, he examines my nails, my hair, my clothes, the soles of my shoes. Luckily I had left the muddy shoes back at my room. Their resemblance to Bora's could have started a disturbing train of thought.

When I stepped into the office, past the screaming singer just now, I came face to face with Baroness Vad's small steel safe. Wiese-Wertheim, double-walled, with concealed locks. The whole thing measures no more than twenty inches square.

The good doctor raises his eyebrows on seeing my clean hands. Later he will tell the surgeon that this in itself would be suspicious in an individual of the lower classes, on a weekday. But with an itinerant entertainer, a mountebank, how can you tell which class he belongs to?

He sees that my papers are in order. Now that he knows who I am, and what my business is in the city, he does recall seeing my fire-swallowing act. But something still bothers him. How can a person who, back at the park, was a common sideshow comedian wrapped in a ragged jacket now afford to drink champagne in an evening outfit that looks like it came from a top tailor's atelier? "Oh, these are my work clothes," I explain, prevaricating with an inspired modesty. "How else could I have gained entrance here? I also happen to be a musician and am looking around for employment in the capital."

He wants to know what I saw earlier that night. With newfound loyalty toward the woman who, I hope, will be my new employer, I manage to obfuscate matters further. I heard a scream, then there was a disturbance, then it got dark. How could I have seen anything? Even asking a question I am telling a lie.

This excellent officer of the law most definitely does not

take to my dubious physiognomy. He will be sure to remember my face. He raises a cautionary finger in farewell.

"Take care, my mountebank friend. Tread softly. And don't cross my path."

As far as I am concerned, I am done with wandering for a while; I intend to stay right here near Bubbles.

But I have little patience for petty or timid roles. I tell him that whether our paths will cross again is in the hands of fate.

He is done with me and I am dismissed without further comment; he is not used to being answered back in such fashion.

On the way out I cast a fond farewell glance at the squat little safe.

Striking while the iron is hot, I then and there come to an agreement with the still dazed Baroness, who hires me as piano player for the salon. I will not be needing a room. Agnes Vad switches to a piano solo for her upstairs entertainment; anything to avoid what happened here tonight!

"You're hired - provided the place is not closed down - and I am not in jail," she adds, exhausted.

I have no fear of that happening, as long as the police do not produce a corpse...

And I have no worries on behalf of my former troupe, either, now that I have arrived at this new and brilliant stage in my career, which promises to be certainly no worse than the wandering minstrel's lot. Like a billiard ball on the green baize of society's table, I roll into a small pocket that is waiting for me. I found a niche where my talents are needed: as a piano player in a brothel. I still have to visit a music store to buy some scores, because, even though much depends on individual interpretation, bawdy-house music is a distinct genre nonetheless.

The Special Investigator is well aware that he still has to check out every one of Bora's statements, and all of her belongings. He scrutinizes the hand towel hanging on the rack in the washroom. Every night a new towel is placed there. He finds no trace of blood. Nor has the towel been recently replaced; it has the marks of having been used. He does not stop to wonder or speculate; over the years he had trained himself to accept facts without hesitation, and to make use of them as givens. He saves the hand towel in the state it was found.

There is a stir at the main entrance. The police surgeon has arrived. In a low voice Dajka provides him with a rapid summary of the events. One of the witnesses says that the singer had ended her performance with a foot placed on the corpse. It is imperative to determine whether she can be held accountable for her actions. They have Bora lie down on a sofa.

She has not said anything since her encounter with me. Komora, the surgeon, calls her by name, takes her pulse, looks under her eyelid, examines her pupils, her reflexes. He passes a finger in front of her eyes.

"She has not survived the ordeal with her faculties intact," he pronounces the verdict in a low voice. He draws some Valium into his syringe and gives the girl an injection. He believes the collapse of her rational mind occurred at the time when she struck down her lover. My God, he is far from the truth!

It is all my fault, but too late now. I feel awful; I am haunted by a vague sensation of uncleanliness.

Now that I am at last allowed to leave, I hurry off to attend to my urgent business. The least I can do is to honor these obligations. We have had a poor start. In the meantime the rain has begun to pour again in endless streaks and torrents over the city, and within minutes out on the street I am drenched to the skin. We are having a summer of tropical extremes this year; here I think of Ofelioko's Hungarian Africa at the Zoo, and the heartaches this humid, hot, rainy weather must cause there, recalling memories of the homeland. The solid black wall of rain, falling in vertical sheets, hides the diminutive adobe huts; the wind has stopped.

For Dr. Dajka the exhausting work of inspection and interrogation stretches into the morning. What happens is exactly what I had counted on when I took my daring, albeit unavoidable step. The girl had struck in front of everyone, and yet even that fact has not been established unanimously. The people assembled here from all walks of society are an alliance of accomplices united by the most diverse motives. And it seems that the sole purpose of this alliance is to tangle the threads, to cover up what happened. This is what the doctor is up against. Some mysteries he will not be able to unravel, not even with all the dedication in the world. But you will hear everything, be patient.

For the the gentlemen guests trapped here, the wafting clouds of smoke carry visions of the faces of their superiors at the office, or the stern, holier-than-thou visages of wives and mothers-in-law. They refuse to accept the testimony of their five senses, and prefer to believe a wished-for reality. The result is that each and every witness' deposition is blurred and uncertain, One obfuscation breeds another.

Dajka promises that no journalist will expose anything that does not come before a jury. The presence of the well-known press baron ought to be a powerful guarantee, with additional support from the general and the town-hall bigwig. But the overall picture is no clearer after the interrogations.

No Hungarian is going to volunteer information to a lawman or a magistrate; it just doesn't happen. Dajka has a name for it: he calls it the "Sándor Rózsa syndrome". October 1848 is not that far in the past. Rózsa, the highwayman wanted in seven counties, together with his freebooters, was granted a pardon by Governor Kossuth four days after the victory at the battle of Pákozd. Rózsa and his band were freedom fighters now. After the defeat of 'Forty-Nine the occupiers persecuted all and alike as common criminals, no matter if they were militiamen, soldiers or generals in the national army - or former highwaymen. Ever since then, whenever the authorities have been after someone, our first impulse has been to consider that person to be one of our freebooters, and hide him in the nearest haystack. The syndrome is a lasting one, as ever-newer 'Forty-Nines keep recurring for us. (Let this be some consolation, when you review our history.) "You know, my friend," Dajka says to the surgeon, "it may be because of this Sándor Rózsa syndrome that I became an officer of the law. I hope that some day we shall arrive at a time of peace when, as in the civilized West, it will be easy to distinguish freedom fighters from common robbers."

Now only the staff remain to be interrogated, one by one.

Bora is no longer telling her rosary. She is no longer confessing, nor is she denying; she speaks no more. Never again will she speak. Dajka sighs, and calls in the next person.

It is the girls' turn: dancers and hostesses. Night-duty chambermaids, coatroom women. Hazy recollections, meaningless outbursts of consternation.

The vanished client was a great admirer of Bora's. No one knows his name or address. Yes, most likely he was her lover. Auburn hair. In the salon, as in the entire Dual Monarchy, just about every second man or woman has auburn hair. Yes, he was a handsome man, the little bread-girl admits with a sigh. She reels off the usual story. She says she used to be a lady's maid (which is a lie). But she takes care to mix in a smattering of facts, and admits to having also been a cleaning woman at Mrs. Tremmel's. But *only* a cleaning woman. There came a strapping private from the Csongrád garrison, and he seduced her; at present he is serving in the occupying forces in Bosnia. She fails to state how brief her employment had been at Mrs. Tremmel's; she forgets to mention that it was the Hunchback who got her a job at the Kitty. The Special Investigator's practised eye can tell that she is not a prostitute. He suspects that she has not been telling the whole truth, but that in itself does not mean she must be guilty; at a place like this everyone has good reason to omit certain facts. Why deny it, the handsome client was sweet on her, and she had responded to his ardent courting. When the turmoil broke out she was carrying her tray at the back of the room.

Some of them must be telling the truth, but which ones?

Just about the only fact on which the town councilman, the publisher, the drum major, the Baroness and the bread-girl concur is that in the confusion prior to the blackout Bora Clarendon sang her song, the "Little Horsie". This was a crazy thing to do, but it does not explain why the lights went out.

The Doctor has not forgotten about the alleged handwashing. But there are no witnesses.

And now comes the difficult part.

Dajka puts down his pen. "Baroness, I can no longer avoid this. I certainly do not wish to be ungrateful for your hospitality. Therefore, I will not insist on seeing the salon's account book, which you are even now trying to hide from me with such touching eagerness. But to conclude our investigation here today, it is essential that we see the remaining rooms of this establishment." He starts out toward the triple stairs and the velvet curtains. The proprietress makes an attempt to stop him; after all, nothing of importance is up there. Her entreaties, tears, and curses are all in vain. The key to tonight's events must be up there, the policeman tells her.

A murder is a murder.

He takes a few moments to explain the situation to her.

"I am going upstairs. Baroness, you are childishly naive. Did you really imagine that I, a regular visitor to this place, was not aware of the salon over my head? There must be at least thirty people working up here. Your clients probably include half the city. How can you still believe that only the police are ignorant of your activities? Upstairs it is one girl per room; that alone speaks volumes. You are able to operate because you are *tolerated*. I brought that girl here precisely because of your clandestine salon. I realize that your artistes have a *choice*. I am willing to look in the other direction, and allow this establishment to stay in business. I am aware of its larger role in the city's night life; I am not a journalist. However. I am a policeman. My task is to find out what happened. And if I were to see a cigar butt that could be important evidence lying on the ground in the gateway to hell, then you can bet your life that I would harrow all hell to recover it. I will harbor no qualms about anyone or anything. Your naiveté is evidence on your behalf - up to a point. But from this day on your Kitty is going to be an ailing creature; her fate will depend on the findings of our inspection and on your willingness to cooperate. So take care, and think it over twice if you are going to hide something from me. And now get out of my way."

As a concession, he inspects her apartment alone. The colors here are pastel; armchairs bearing antimacassars yawn with somnolent bourgeois rectitude.

Following that, with Marton's help he turns the waiters' and the girls' rooms on the top two storeys completely inside out. Up here there is no running water or electric lighting. He can tell at a glance which rooms are inhabited by women who receive no visitors. He does not find any clues.

A mute Bora has already been taken into custody. He sends her over to the basement cells at police headquarters. The police escort seems to have a calming effect on the singer; she is prepared to face her punishment.

It is dawn. The interrogators and the interrogated are both tired. Dajka tries to summarize the facts in the presence of Marton and Dr. Komora.

Of course everyone is telling lies here. It is to be expected. We are looking at a capital crime - *if* a corpse can be found. To lay the foundations for a charge, three factors must be established: motive, occasion, method.

For a possible motive, we have jealousy. But in a nightclub, that's no more than sand in the desert. The occasion: the dissolute atmosphere of the place, the smoke, the confusion - all that is not enough. As for method: first of all, a bloodied brick has to be found.

And in order to have a crime, we must also come up with an injured forehead that matches the brick.

ENCOUNTERS

By the time I complete my business and am on the way home, the night is over. I whistle as I stroll. After all that happened tonight, one theme keeps mischievously recurring in my mind: my encounters. The nightclub and the affair with the brick no longer count for anything, and even the preparations for the great safe-break pale into insignificance.

The early morning summer sun plays hide and seek behind the clouds as I round the corner of Váci Street. The streets are still empty. Here is the Grand Bazaar, once more. I stop in front of it. The job is still waiting there for me and my fellow robbers. There will be difficulties. But I dispel the thought like a cloud of smoke; what are difficulties for, after all, if not to be overcome. The more arduous the circumstance, the grander the adventure. I light up a Partagas, but cannot inhale it, as I burst out laughing at the reflection of my figure sporting drenched, wrinkled evening clothes, in the mirror of the corner window display.

For a moment I am afraid that all the pent-up tensions of the night are going to explode, and my laughter will turn to hysteria.

Those encounters of mine. O my goodness. At first it seemed an impossible undertaking, to haul a body across the salon occupied by so many people. But inside me I could hear the sirens of a far greater calamity starting to wail. I uttered an Alley-oop! in the soft undertone of showmen, and the right person had heard me and understood.

My accomplice appeared out of nowhere; I had not even been aware of his existence; all of what I have said about him so far in this story came to me much later. Out of the corner of my eye I noticed a small movement he made which reminded me of something, then I instantly forgot about it. Our eyes met for a fraction of a second. I raised my hand to my temple, in a hesitant and yet rapid gesture, as if to sweep away a cobweb - or the one-way flow of time itself.

He recognized me. I could count on him through thick and thin; he would help me, blindly risking everything. He too has been looking after the girl up till now, and he too has been instinctively avoiding the authorities, or being identified. Our minds work in similar ways.

I shot a glance at the body lying on the carpet, then I looked up and away. As if propelled by steel springs I was suddenly in the dimly lit zone behind the stage. No one saw me. I looked on at my hand slithering up toward the main switch of the electric circuit board as if I were seeing an alien creature. One jerk, and the salon and the corridors were plunged into darkness.

(I was not aware at the time that the darkness also electrified a third person into action.)

I felt my new companion by my side. As I lifted the heavy

body, he snatched up a waiter's napkin and laid it over my arm, to prevent bloodstains. He guided me toward the brown curtains.

In a doorway behind the curtains a terrified girl appeared, clad in a cheap nightgown. I was able to see fairly well by the light of the small candle she was holding. I had my back to the dim glow.

Bora was aware of murky outlines, as if someone were carrying a strangely crumpled, heavy burden. She sensed that they were taking away from her the dead body of her beloved, forever. She tried to move, but her limbs had turned to lead. She did not recognize me. Nor had anyone else, as it became obvious during the interrogation a few hours later.

With my shoulder I shoved the girl holding the candle, making her fall down. Her candle gave another flicker or two, then went out. I hauled my burden up to the top of the stairs. Then out onto the gangway hidden behind the palisade. Between the boards shone the pale light from the courtyard; the planks were creaking in the wind before the storm. I turned around, needing guidance. Then my helper caught up with me, pointing the way. On my left, at the end of the gangway planks I saw the steps, and the steel door down below.

"Hurry" was the first word he spoke, in a whisper. He was leading me to the right, toward an unnumbered door. "This way."

The body of that young dandy who a few hours earlier, around sunset, had still been twirling his walking stick now lay on an oval table in the room at the end of the corridor. His temple was deathly pale. I adjusted his collar. I blew out the night-light and peeked out on the corridor. As I opened the door, the window shutters blew open behind me, so that all the curtains fluttered and snapped in the sudden gust. My companion had shut the other window, after tossing two pebbles from the sill at the window of one of the small hovels in the back of the yard. "Let's go down in the courtyard," he said, pointing to where we were heading. A dark crimson drop of blood slowly began to roll down the bloodied temple, followed by several others, but I did not see this. The sudden draft flipped up the corner of the checkered linen tablecloth and blew it back between the table's legs, where it became stuck. Meanwhile, the head tilted back so that the blood dripped, from the noble arch of the forehead, past the folds of the tablecloth, directly on to a patch in the crenellated design motif of the fake Persian carpet, where it soaked in, spreading over the battlements. And that is where it would stay, waiting for the day when its discovery would force a turnabout in the flow of events.

The seconds sped by. The light of a candle flickered toward the salon from a distant room, as its flame was momentarily diverted by the draft. Ahead of me lay the passage toward the twelve steps and the steel doors and the courtyard.

The disheveled girl stumbled off, trailed by her lanky beau in tails, still fumbling with a trouser button. The corridor grew quiet.

I wrapped a blanket around the body, which had grown heavy with inertia, took it in my arms, and set out under the gangway, down the steps. In the process my hands became bloodied.

I went past the two doors of the steel-plated room, and found myself outside on the old cobblestones of the courtyard. Half-finished barrels and staves were lying about; wood shavings crunched under my feet. Suddenly the wind had stopped, giving way to an ominous calm. At the same moment I was confronted by my outside accomplice, the one on whose window those two pebbles had clinked. This completed the round of fateful encounters. He was a man with a bear-like build, and yet for an instant he reminded me of the fragile Bubbles, whom I had left behind in the salon.

When he saw what I was carrying, his eyes made a lightning-fast circuit of the courtyard, before he carefully took charge of the body I handed over to him. "I will need a doctor's bag," I said. He nodded. I snatched up the brick lying by the steel door, wrapped it in the bloodied napkin, and placed it on top of his load.

During a flash of lightning he looked me in the eyes. He had the air of someone who had just received news of a great celebration, and was about to embrace me and plant a manly kiss on both my cheeks. We had flashed on each other. He was there to help Bubbles, if need be. Before he agreed to let her work here, he had checked out the place. He had not known about me until this moment.

He turned around and disappeared under the eaves of the tiny house huddled by the bulkhead of the neighboring building. He had only a few meters to cross, and no one saw him. The door closed behind him and no light filtered out. I felt the first warm drop on my forehead, just as the sky resounded with a monstrous clap of thunder. I turned back to where I came from, locked the steel doors, and pocketed the keys. So far I had got away with it.

I manage to control my hysterical laughter in front of the shopwindow. My scarecrow reflection is uninterrupted by bright gleams from objects in the window display; these have been removed for the night, leaving only their red velvet cushions on which their impressions invite amateurish guesses on my part: necklaces, rings, medallions, earrings.

By now it was morning, but the sun hid its face.

Dajka takes leave of his colleagues, shuts his pocket notebook and sets out on foot in a northerly direction across Town Hall Square toward his apartment on Bath Street, near the old Stockmarket (for you it will be the New Stockmarket, the former Red Academy, and today's television station).

The incipient daylight is obscured by the gathering clouds of another thunderstorm.

At one in the afternoon it starts to pour again; the storm will rage to the accompaniment of mighty thunderclaps, with only minor interruptions, through the early afternoon. The water is again ankle-deep in the Inner City. The streets stay wet until nightfall, a thin layer of city mud coating the sidewalks. Throughout the ebb and flow of the storm the thermometer registers a steady twenty degrees Centigrade. After a three week drought the atmosphere becomes so saturated with humidity that it feels as if a strict Imam has drawn a veil over the city's face. At the Doctor's house his wife Maria sees to it that the servants speak in whispers while the Special Investigator tosses and turns on his sweat-soaked pillow, as his dreams replay the anxieties of the night before. He is now reliving a despair for Bora that had been suppressed during the course of the interrogation. In his dream he recalls that on his way home he noticed something on Huckster Street, something familiar that was out of place. He is unable to pin down what it was, and giving up, collapses into the depths of dreamless sleep.

By three in the afternoon he is back in his office at headquarters, absorbed in studying his album of criminals. He has little appetite for lunch.

A day has gone by since the affair of the brick. The tailor Knorr receives a picture postcard mailed at the Western Train Terminal in Budapest. Within the city limits, mail is delivered in one day. Their tenant has unexpectedly left for a spa, but he wishes to keep his room. The foreign gentleman confirms this in broken German, and pays the week's rent that is due.

I am biding my time. I mean to accomplish what I had agreed on with my partners in crime one year ago, even though in the meantime everything has come to be seen in a different light. Still, the adventure beckons irresistibly.

We are prepared to vacate our headquarters in fifteen minutes at the first sign of danger. I weigh the relative risks of moving and staying put. I find out that Bora Clarendon has remained silent. She is in no condition to give the police any information. So we stay.

After the passage of some days, the Knorrs' handsome tenant returns. He now frequently receives visitors. The once-in-a-lifetime Millennial summer is here, and reeling by. So much physical and intellectual power, not to speak of good capital invested, must not be allowed to go to waste.

In the daily press, after the terse and vague reports of the morning after, hardly anything else appears. One or two minor papers publish the usual stories about the latest instance of police incompetence. Meanwhile the major papers, exercising a wondrous restraint, continue to build a wall of silence around the affair and to keep the wall in good repair. In this, their policies are no doubt dictated by those few influential editors and publishers whose assiduous attendance at the salon had all along been independent of their obligations to keep the public well informed. That's the word among the studs and fillies at the Kitty.

During this week the Doctor spends long nightly hours at the club; Abris keeps a special table for him by the piano, two tables over from the one where the victim had sat. Dajka sips his lemonade, and observes the scene, with a preoccupied air; he chats with the staff. I do what I can, by being on hand.

The first week goes by. One afternoon Dr. Dajka searches the three small houses attached to the bulkhead of the apartment building at No. 2 Leopold Street. The tenants (the ageing bachelor book-worm, the store manager and the legal clerk) all pass muster. Bora Clarendon, in remand, is unable to take care of herself. She refuses to wash or comb her hair; she sits and stares at the wall of her cubicle in the prison hospital at police headquarters, where an elderly nun takes care of her. She eats the food that is placed before her, but says not a word. After repeated examinations, Dr. Komora's considered opinion is that she is not malingering.

We are still in the dark about the time of the arrival of the Viennese guests at the Millennial Exposition.

In the household on Crown Street the manservant is considered to be a piece of furniture with white gloves on; the masters of the house discuss the most private matters in his presence. The servant, in turn, after being treated to a third glass of free wine, is not even aware that he is revealing intimate matters to his drinking companion with the scar on his face. The servant describes how the firm's junior partner is personally responsible for all acquisitions; how he travels everywhere alone, how all he does is shop around, select the merchandise, strike the bargain and pay up. But how the shipments are delivered to the steel safe in the jewelry store is still a mystery. However, this does not worry us too much, for I know my associates. They are not common highwaymen. They have that certain signature, remember? We feel confident that we shall know where the goods will arrive.

I stroll over to Kerepesi Road, walk into the Paris Department store, where no one will remember me in the crowds. The selection is excellent in combs, cigars, clothes and brushes. I purchase a neat small whiskbroom and a clothes-brush.

For one final time the Stone sits flooded in light, before it is sent on its way. The young diamond cutter gazes with delight at the result of his labors, at the triangular facets that refract the cool Netherlandish light and scatter it in all the colors of the rainbow over the humble tools and tables of the workshop. He imagines it suspended on a flat platinum chainlet around a dazzling neck. But there he is trespassing beyond his station.

With a profound sigh he takes leave of one year of his life. From a drawer in his desk he removes a slightly used and somewhat dusty but sturdy grey envelope bearing the printed inscription, *"Echatillon sans valeur - Muster ohne Wert."* A free sample, without value.

A quarter of an hour later he is standing in line at one of the windows of the Amsterdam central post office. "Registered?" asks the lady clerk. "Oh no, just first class mail," answers the unshaven young man with the bloodshot eyes. The address on the envelope does not reveal much: *Société Anonyme de Paris*. And were one to visit the address, one would find an insignificant little office in an insignificant little house on the Left Bank, known to a mere half a dozen initiates as the home office of the company that controls the major portion of the world's diamond trade.

For Dajka the second week marks the beginning of a period of fruitless investigation. Time and time again he has Bora brought to his office from her prison hospital cell, and these meetings become increasingly depressing. His sense of duty, however, takes precedence over his emotions.

By the tenth day following the brick murder the singer's hair has turned completely white. The fire in her eyes has gone out.

Dajka has managed to convince Chief Inspector Axaméthy, and then the Commissioner of Police, that if there is any new development in the case, it can only turn up at the Kitty. So that it is actually in the best interest of the administration of justice to keep the club open for the time being. That means I can keep my new job.

FROST-BITTEN FRUIT

The investigation cannot be closed. Dr. Dajka has no reason to keep Bora in detention any longer, without filing formal charges. But the basic requirement for a charge of man-slaughter is establishing a causal connection, by means of an autopsy, between the behavior of the accused and the victim's death. The girl is not a foreigner. There is no reason to fear she would flee abroad. She is harmless, according to the police surgeon's professional opinion. Therefore she is allowed to return to the Kitty on Rose Square, the only home she knows. The Baroness offers to take care of her, and to cooperate with the authorities.

The unusual silence of the press regarding the case encourages the wildest speculations. The tom-tom drums of the underworld jungle are banging away nonstop. Marvelous and horrifying tales circulate among the strolling ladies of the night. There is talk of a princely husband in Russia who threw himself in the Neva for the Hungarian torchlight girl, and of Paris nights, featuring crushed pearls dissolved in champagne. And there are dark hints at a convoluted web, a conspiracy of silence, and a hushed-up axe-murderer who ran amok in the nightclub.

"And what am I to do with her?" The Baroness asks her doorman the somewhat rhetorical question. Bora merely hangs about, or sits on the edge of her bed and stares vacantly into space. The connection, however, between the Special Investigator's goodwill and Bora's welfare is only too obvious. And so the girls of the house wash and iron for her, and take care of her without a word of complaint. These bad girls are not so bad after all. Bora eats her meals at the common table. And her presence weighs on the whole place. She calls up horrible memories, as she wanders aimlessly through the house, her face still so young and her hair all white.

On the tenth night following the affair with the brick we are in the middle of rehearsals, when she happens to walk by the entryway to the lit-up stage, where a solitary chorus girl is waiting, a filly without her aigrette. Did we help her, or do her wrong, by removing that body? I am far from being able to decide for sure; I have been too busy with our own business at hand. So I keep an eye on her.

And today we find out that she did not lose her voice. Egged on by certain vague memories and subliminal hunches, I finger the first notes of her song, "Little Horsie". She is startled. One prolonged tremor runs through her body, from her grey hair to the soles of her brightly polished street shoes. She tosses her head, like a worn-out charger on hearing the notes of a trumpet call, and opens her mouth once or twice. Essential here is the extraordinary sensitivity of the Baroness, who motions to me to keep it up, and who, at the exact moment when the introductory bars end, pushes Bora out on the stage, on cue.

And Bora starts her song right on the beat, "Giddy-up, Horsie..."

We rehearse with her for two more nights, and on the twelfth night she makes her return. On each occasion she has to be shoved onstage. And each time it is a new miracle, the way the lights and the music, the same as *then*, trigger in her the refrain with a deadly certainty and set her lips singing that silly song.

Everything else has to be done for her. Dr. Dajka has informed us that he has sequestered portions of the singer's pay to send on her behalf to Frau Bábi in Grinzing, and has opened a savings account in the girl's name.

Besides that song, she utters not a sound. She neither cries nor laughs nor curses; she does not leave the house. She is not really alive. And I must always play the accompaniment for her; this is my punishment, to see her from close up every day in two shows, one after the other. My employer possesses an unfailing instinct for the psychological needs of her esteemed public. She gives Bora a raise and refuses to let the singer's hair be dyed.

The investigation does not turn up any new evidence; this helps to prolong the silence. Only a few more weeks are needed, if all goes well, until the next bit of sensational news should make everyone forget the affair. My companions and I shall have some say in that. It is now the end of the second week.

Every night the singer, young yet white-haired, stumbles out in front of her fillies, her eyes staring vacantly into the distance. Her snow-white hair remains a topic of curiosity; the questions lead to suggestive silences.

The rumor-mongers know no more than the police about what happened at the Kitty. However, their certainties are not limited by statute. They *know for a fact* that the white-haired girl, whose unchanging voice nightly performs the "Horsie" number, is the perpetrator of a bloody, real-life crime of passion - and is utterly mad. She is the talk of the town. Baroness Vad had been worried about losing her refined and choice clientele from the Inner City; well, she needn't have worried. Her Silly Kitty gradually turns into the number one draw in the night life of the metropolis.

Before, the clandestine salon had attracted by virtue of the sweetness of forbidden fruit, and its clientele was recruited by word-of-mouth, hearsay. But now it is no longer the whore-house hidden on the upper floors that titivates the public's fancy. In the wake of the first swarms of golden youth, strictly upper crust, some of the more mature members of the House of Lords are beginning to show up. Within three weeks our clientele undergoes a complete transformation, and our original orders of French champagne have to be doubled. I know what draws them here and it turns my stomach. It is that frost-bitten fruit, with its piquant, sweet and slightly fermented flavor, that makes these birds flock here so eagerly.

The Baroness suffers no pangs of conscience over the coincidence of the white-haired singer's madness and the fat daily take. From now on the money-changer with his apothecary scale and gold nuggets is a more and more frequent visitor at the back door under cover of night, making the Baroness' eyes dance with visions of the top floors of her palatial high-rise resort hotel aglimmer in a dazzle of gold. Of the girl's mute stare, only Dr. Dajka is mindful, and I, on the other side of the fence.

In the course of these weeks Dajka is fully occupied: all the busywork in the ongoing and unsolved cases that, in another year, would be left to the underlings. He is unable to catch up on his sleep, and goes about in a permanent state of leaden fatigue.

Among the Misses Knorr there is an epidemic of the heart flutters; they are constantly on the watch for their handsome tenant. But all they see is a daily stream of visitors. On certain days Marika lets in a lady who conceals her face behind a veil, and this occasions an incomprehensible pit-a-pat in her frail bosom. For this humble middle class home is now daily visited by Life and Adventure personified, hidden behind that black veil. On Sunday, as the girls will eventually, and with the greatest reluctance, confess, an unknown visitor arrives, and remains for hours closeted with the tenants in deep negotiations. Perhaps they are not even speaking Hungarian, for the girls cannot understand a single word through the keyhole.

Three weeks have passed. The long wait makes my business with my colleagues more difficult. No matter what the dictates of reason, these men are not going to lie low this long. For one thing, they are simply unable to survive for *weeks* at a time without women. And I cannot do anything about that. They are not going to renounce their highest priorities - the very thing they became burglars for, if we consider ultimate motivations.

The Greek has picked up a marvelous little dame; her name is Lori, and she is a seamstress who refers to her one-room efficiency apartment on Seminary Street as a "fashion salon". She will do for Socrates as long as the Odessa loot lasts. Their finding each other is another signal for me that time is pressing. All of us need something to do, and the sooner the better.

I ask the Greek to stroll past our target and inspect the inspectable locks. He comes back with a task ready-made for me. I am going to have to make an imprint of the outside doorlock in broad daylight.

We go through the practice motions in the attic, using an iron rod with wax on its end.

One evening at the Kitty I overhear two illustrious and solitary magnates, whose very voices hark back to my days spent waiting as a cabman in front of the entrance to the National Casino. They are discussing the preparations for the visitors expected from Vienna: a ceremonial reception at the ship's landing, a social evening get-together at the Municipal Concert Hall, a ride on the new electric subway train, a viewing of the Exposition, champagne brunch, banquet, ball at the Casino. It is between shows; I am drifting about in the salon, and at last drop anchor by a lonesome girl's table. The two gentlemen are seated directly behind me. What they are talking about is no secret so I do not have to make a special effort to eavesdrop. It is all about the upcoming visit. We still have two or three weeks left, says the older gentleman. This is the sentence I have been waiting for.

Haluska, our lookout, is notified the same day: he must be all ears, and should try to find out something concrete.

On Tuesday, the Safe King takes the stage. He and the Greek play the roles of gentlemen out for a stroll, who are to arrive casually at the target at a precisely calculated moment in the afternoon. As long as there are no physical obstacles, the King considers it unthinkable that he himself should not go there in person. They are both burning with desire to work at last. Before the appointed time they make sure to keep away from the neighborhood of that certain block of the Inner City; but trouble comes from an unforeseen direction. For it proved to be trouble, the way things turned out later, serious trouble. At the first busy intersection they are accosted by a buxom lady wearing a towering feathered hat.

"And how can this be? You in Budapest again?" she asks, beaming, as women of all classes and orders do, when the Safe King's eyes turn to them. "And why, pray, are you not staying with us?"

They are able to get rid of her only with the greatest difficulty. Eventually the Greek does manage to pay close attention to the locks on a certain cast-iron grillwork gate. By then the two of them, in the role of the interested parties, "a Turkish and a Hungarian gentleman", are conducting negotiations in a highly regarded and exclusive jeweler's inner office. The Safe King's loving glance glides appraisingly over the steel safe that stands modestly huddled by a wall. It is an impressive specimen, stronger and burlier than anything they have seen up till then. Hello Uncle Safe, he murmurs to himself, in tones of childlike rapture and devotion. The office is equipped with a water faucet, pitcher and glasses. Socrates, exuding Oriental munificence, is looking for an out-of-the-ordinary, not to say extravagant gift for one of the favored ladies of his heart, and, conjuring up visions of sandalwood-scented hareems, manages to charm the senior partner into producing the flat key to the main safe from a leather wallet. As the jeweler opens the safe, he keeps the concealed lock out of his clients' view by positioning his body between them and the safe.

The pair take their leave at closing time; their voices and manner are promising. They are able to watch the store assistant, and the gray, wilted lady cashier depart for the day in the direction of Váci Street. The doors leading to the glass-roofed arcade and to the storage room are locked from the inside.

Today the youngest of the Misses Knorr is at last able to do some house-cleaning; ever since their tenant returned from the spa, the woman in black has been taking care of housekeeping around him. If he did request something to eat, or some tea, he asked that the tray be left on the doorstep. Neither of the tenants is at home at this moment, and Marika takes a chance and pulls out the drawer of the writing desk.

She stumbles upon a fabulous treasure: the silver overflows. But luckily there is nothing else for her to discover, for we had taken the precaution of conducting our professional preparations exclusively in the attic. And so the three girls fancy their ethereal tenant to be a fairy-tale prince.

On Friday afternoon it takes Haluska a whole liter of wine at the tavern on Stonecarver Street to loosen the tongue of the house servant, who blurts out that there is a letter concealed in his pocket. Late into the night, Haluska convinces the staggering servant that the letter was mailed at the post office, first class, as he had been instructed. And since the letter will in fact arrive three days later, no one will have cause for doubt. Lifting it was child's play.

This is a real pearl, this envelope addressed to the *Société Anonyme* in Paris. We steam it open. It is the formal order for a shipment referred to as the "House of Hapsburg". Two trayloads of jewelry. Two Schaffhausen gold watches, one a man's, the other a woman's, one set with emeralds. A full selection of jewelry, necklaces and bracelets, clasps, earrings. And the Stone, called by the Budapest jeweler as such, without specifying its name. Payment to be made in person. The Stone is to be sent to Budapest in the usual manner before the arrival of the buyer. No date is given. We remain your faithful servants, etc. The letter is in French. Later that night, after the envelope is re-sealed, Haluska deposits it in the giant red mailbox standing in front of the Central Post Office.

I conclude that it will happen roughly two weeks from now, and consider that to be our terminus, distant as it may be. (Two weeks can be a long time here, in the world of action.) Therefore we must act now. I immediately relieve Haluska from his porter duty; he must not be seen any more in the vicinity of the target. I trust that his hirsute face will be forgotten, along with the many porters who come and go, and if anything, they will only recall his scar. His further assignment is to shave off his beard and mustache, and upgrade his appearance to look like a natty dresser from now on. The scar should stay, but he should comb his hair over it. Meanwhile he should still cultivate the alcoholic servant. He could make up some story about how he inherited a sum of money. From now on they should meet in distant locations, perhaps find some small taverns in the Tabán district, a different one each night. His job is to ferret out any news on a daily basis.

The third week has gone by, and the supply of silver is

diminishing in that drawer; it trickles away in work and living expenses - ending up at those Tabán taverns as well as with the charming Lori, who is just as indispensable for the well-being of our little crew.

But we leave our iron reserve untouched.

I take public transport on my way to accomplish the task involving the wax-tipped iron rod. I do this on a Saturday, traveling by both horse-drawn and electric trains.

In 1950, the year of the Newtown Festival, Little Kovács was tripped up in the classroom by Lali Gere, and, as he fell he almost smeared on the oiled floorboards a drawing of the horse-drawn train by Botond Bodnár. One of his neighborhood friends caught him as he fell, and the two of them together managed to salvage the notebook. Kovács was the new boy in the class, his love affair with the city still fresh, as was his backwoods accent from the village of Kunudacs. During these past few months he had learned to recognize these Lali Gere types by the very set of their eyes - that everpresent human type that, on seeing a weaker individual, never fails to bully him. Their eyes are as a rule narrow, suspicious, full of fear and hate, as you may verify for yourself. The new kid in the class is always weaker, as you are well aware, you too have been a new kid in the class after our moves. So naturally the whole class stood around these two, to see what would happen.

Kovács refused to accept his assigned place in the pecking order. Already in his sixth school year he made it clear that he had not been born to be a servant. He grabbed Lali Gere by his white linen jacket and slammed him to the floor. The back of the jacket showed the stripes of the oiled floorboards. The whole classroom broke out in laughter. Gere was suddenly flooded by the despair that wells up in those child-burning, store-bombing murderers, no matter how shining their faith, whenever we fire back at them. Mighty sobs convulsed him on the floor. As he was getting up, he vented all of his murderous frustration at Kovács in two words, intended to demolish him:

"Stupid hick!"

The math teacher, who was just then entering the room, heard him. Everyone raced back to his place and silence reigned. During math class one could hear a solitary fly buzz. Kovács later told me how the old-fashioned pedagogue made use of this opportunity for the enrichment of young souls. He did not inquire about the fight. He called on the top student, Zombory, and asked him where was he born. "In Budapest." And your father? "In Budapest." And your father's father? "In Fogaras", Zombory replied. (For you, Fagaras, Romania.) Good. You may sit down. And you, Bárán. Father born in Budapest, grandparents in Rákosszentmihály (today, the 16th district of the capital). He went on interrogating, always stopping when the first village name cropped up. From Transylvania, from the Highlands, from Transdanubia. Then he summed up. "My father was born in the county of Máramaros, and my mother in Komárom... Stupid hick, I heard someone say. Kovács. So you were born in a village." Only now did he turn toward Lali Gere. "And what's wrong with that? Does that make him some kind of country bumpkin? A stupid hick? And what is supposed to be preferable? Hailing from the capital city? Or from certain districts, say Old Buda? Or certain streets only, say, if you live on Louis Street? What makes you think that somebody has to come from a village to be a hick? Did he pick on you, yell at you, attack you?" The grey-haired teacher guessed what had happened with flawless intuition.

Just keep Lali Gere in mind, later when we will talk about the intolerance shared by Genghis Khan and the Brick. These two men, each in his own way, could not stand the city dweller. Could not stomach a whiff of him. They are the Lali Gere types; the specific *direction* of their geo- and ethnographic hatreds makes no difference.

"So it would appear that you, Mr. Gere, are the only one who is entitled to jeer here. As for the rest of us, we all came from the sticks," concluded the old-fashioned mathematician.

After that, no one called Kovács any names at school. Back on the street where he lived he was never called a hick; the streets are more tolerant, the streets are a republic of their own.

The drawing by Botond Bodnár, sixth-year pupil, in that endangered notebook, contained illustrations of the material learned about the city's history. About an era that saw, all within a few short years, the construction of the Grand Boulevards, the quays, Radius Avenue, the funicular to the Buda Castle, and the subway system. When the teacher reached the point in his lecture where the horse-drawn trains were electrified, Botond Bodnár's imagination lit up. He immediately illustrated the event in his lined notebook: tiny horses were pulling the long train carriages, and a power line led to the hindquarters of each animal, where it plugged in under the tail.

A wave of guffaws swept through the class as the drawing was passed from desk to desk. Back in the year of the Kitty, of course, the great switch to electric power took place in quite a different manner. On Saturday around noon I mount the horse-drawn train at the back, where an iron railing protects me on the platform, the wax-tipped rod conveniently hidden under my all-concealing cape. The oblong sign on the car's roof indicates its point of origin and destination. This is the age of the already and the not yet - pretty much like any other age, I guess. Out on the City Park line one can already see the smaller, dark viridian cars of the electric train, while on other lines the horse-drawn trains are still in use. I purchase my ticket for six kreuzers. The car is drawn by two heavy workhorses; the graceful curves of their tails parallel each other. These municipal train horses are exceptional: although they wear no blinders, they never wander from the tracks. I sit down on a side seat and peek out under the canvas canopy. I see the first single-cylinder Mercedes-Benz automobile approaching from the other direction. The spectacle of the teeming city has a calming influence on my nerves; it seems to spark my grey matter. I take the opportunity to make sure that I am not being followed.

I had set out from my rented room, where I do not keep any object that could connect me with my business. I have to take care of my own security in case my companions are arrested. I simply cannot face the prospect of being caught. If my colleagues are captured, for them it is just a few more years in jail.

I ride on the horse-drawn train and on the electric one, and

circumnavigate the city before approaching my goal. Later in
the day, the street traffic thins out.

At a stretch of the track where the former, lesser branch of
the Danube once crossed Radius Avenue, the two carriage
workhorses stop by themselves, while a man pushes a cartload
of furniture over the tracks.

I get off at the terminal station. Instead of having electric
lines plugged into their backsides, the two horses are
unharnessed and led around to the other end of the carriage
to make the return journey. And I stroll over to the tracks of
the electric train, which are deeply imbedded between the
sharp new edges of the cobblestones. This train has only one
class - a triumph for the age of the rule of the masses, which is
rapidly approaching our part of the world. It stands on a
bypass rail, this awkward, angular vehicle, the sphere of its
great bell gleaming from its front. The mustachioed conductor,
wearing his flat service cap and carrying a crank, steps off the
platform and trudges ahead. I am waiting in a group of
passengers under the young acacias of the sidewalk, and
wonder if my cape stands out among these bowler hats,
walking sticks, short jackets, vests, trousers and boots. Black,
white, grey, black. I make sure that I am not being followed.

By the time I reach the scene of the action I am able to go
about my business with confidence, as if it did not matter at
all; there is not the least room for a miscue. The siesta hour
has arrived. By now the stores have closed all over the city,
and the citizenry are everywhere enjoying the quiet of the
afternoon, digesting their noontime meals. In one hand I hold
matches, while the other is tapping my cigarillo against its tin
box. I can take an undisturbed look up and down the square,
with a clear view of Váci Street and Town Hall Street. It takes,
in all, one minute. Even the weather cooperates: a slight
breeze rises from the direction of Gizella Square. So it is
natural that I have to take shelter in a doorway that is closed
off by a cast iron gate of Oriental style, fancy grillwork, making
sure that my cape hides from view the iron rod as I fit its flat,
waxed end into the lock and turn it, ascertaining the fit. In the
same movement I light my cigarillo, carefully shielding the
match with my palm. I do not really like cigars, and that is why

I am constantly changing brands. The Bazaar is least guarded by day and night from this, its most heavily trafficked side, facing the large square. If a yawning chambermaid or cook looked out from a window across the way on Knitter Street, or if one of those porters strutting in a brand new uniform in front of the grand coffeehouse were to glance my way, all they would see was a man wearing a cape taking shelter in the doorway to light a cigar in the breeze, and, having lit up after a bit of a struggle, walk on. He couldn't be a real gentleman, smoking on the street...

As I move on in the breeze, which has suddenly acquired quite a bite, I draw the cape together on my chest, and the sudden gesture makes the material split. Lowering my shoulder, I take a look: it is not a bad tear, about an inch long, and it should hold if I walk carefully until I get back to our headquarters.

On Monday morning I purchase a pocket alarm-cum-stopwatch, for cash, in a store (in case you find this peculiar), and at night, taking shelter in the darkness of Huckster Street, I time the night watchman's circuit twice; it takes seventeen minutes, plus or minus one minute.

The next morning the Misses Knorr, judging by the sounds emanating through the door, conclude that their refined tenant must be working with some kind of metal or steel. When the inevitable comes, they will profess that they decided that he must be a great inventor, an engineer who devised clever machines. The wind that powers the windmill of dreams is once again surpassed by everyday reality.

Not wishing to attract attention by our frequent trips to the attic, we decide to cut this single key in the room. The negative imprints of the key are coated in gelatine dissolved in spirits, which hardens the wax. The rough key is lovingly cut and polished in two different versions by the Greek. We shall have to deal with the inner steel door on location.

But that will not be a problem, for we shall not be out on the open street.

It is now the fifth week after that night at the Kitty. The silver from the Safe King's drawer has been reduced to the barest of trickles into the mattress lining of the Tabán tavernkeepers.

The steering committee of the National Casino holds a meeting. Gambling is abolished by a majority vote; offenders may be subject to expulsion from membership. Personal invitations to the Exposition are sent to, among others, the young princely couple belonging to one of the lesser branches of the House of Hapsburg. The couple's new Budapest palace is receiving the final touches.

The sixth week.

The loose-tongued house servant at last utters the long-awaited words in a tavern: his master is packing for a few day's journey.

The program in honor of the guests from Vienna is published. The most brilliant event is to be the Wednesday night closing reception and ball, which will require all the space available at the National Casino, and to which the high and mighty of the capital city have been invited. Based on my knowledge of the facts and on my acquaintance with the feminine psyche, I decide that this is going to be the public debut of the Stone. Therefore its showing at the couple's mansion is to be expected at the beginning of the week.

At Vác, a special delegation from the Casino awaits the distinguished Viennese visitors with a ceremonious welcome.

"The master will be away from the store three days this week," reports the house servant. I know what to make of this absence.

The guests of the Exposition alight from their boat at the brightly illuminated landing slip at Franz Joseph Square. They are conveyed to their lodgings to rest after the fatiguing journey. Those without residences in the Hungarian capital head for hotels.

On the following Monday night the two partners will stay late at the office. They claim it is for making an inventory, but they have asked only Ernestine, their old maid cashier lady, to stay in. This news allays my last uncertainties. Whether they are making an inventory before the upcoming large trans-action, or intend to meet with a master jeweler in connection with the Stone and the shipment for the House of Hapsburg, the sale itself cannot take place any sooner than next Tuesday.

A final telegram is sent off to Agap Kevorg in Saint Petersburg. And the next day Agap leaves for the West on urgent business involving the Persian carpet trade.

The next morning, a workingman's cap pulled over my eyes, I am loitering around the sleeping cars of the Paris express to make sure that the house servant puts the luggage aboard for his master's short trip. It is the thirty-sixth day.

The tensions of enforced idleness are rapidly disappearing, only to be replaced by other sorts of tension, as the hour of action approaches.

On the thirty-ninth day the junior partner arrives back home. He again entertains his elder, bachelor partner and they pop a split of the Widow Clicquot's champagne - in advance. Perhaps they should not have. It is a Friday night.

All that afternoon there is a flurry of secretive activity around the store, and they close two hours early.

Aware of this fact, Haluska the lookout makes his bluish scar disappear and in one fell swoop the talkative house servant loses his generous drinking buddy. It is high time.

Dr. Dajka knows nothing about the Stone; as far as he is concerned, the careful secrecy of the partners is a complete success.

Sunday morning at eight a.m. the Viennese visitors gather at the Rémy kiosk, and ride the electric subway train to view the Exposition. The reception committee gives a brunch in their honor at the Hubert champagne pavilion.

It is Monday, the forty-second day after the brick affair. I am free that night.

Boarding the express train in Lyon that afternoon, and continuing via Milan and Vienna toward the Hungarian capital and royal seat is Agap Kevorg, alias Amber, Russian subject and international dealer in stolen goods.

For six weeks running the Baroness has invited Dajka to the Monday night dinners. She might as well cultivate her contact with the authorities, as long as he has become so attached to her establishment. By a quarter to nine the great hall of the coffeehouse is filled with chatting women and men. Everyone is wearing their Sunday best; these Monday dinners are not held in the service dining room. The proprietress brooks no exceptions; this is our equivalent of Sunday, and if you are not there by nine o'clock sharp you had better have good reason. You may leave any old time; the Baroness is understanding about that. I am the one to initiate the conversation with Dr. Dajka, impelled by some foolhardy compulsion to talk. Hmm, it must be some guilty feeling. He talks about my troupe. They are still working at the Municipal Park in the old location, and are doing well. I was just going to see them in person, to find out how they were doing, my friends Murikeo, the pearl, and Kodel; and the passionate, playful, and identical twins Lilia and Alma, with whom I lived in such close proximity for nearly a year. And all those little brats who, in caravans and in tents, screamed in my ears and peed in my lap.

Bora arrives, takes her seat, looks at her plate. Dajka converses and repeatedly has to snatch his eyes away from the girl. At nine o'clock sharp the Baroness makes her grand entrance. Aladár holds the chair for her; he has managed to turn this gesture into an indispensable ritual. Agnes Vad says grace, after which everyone sits down, dancing girls and non-dancing girls, musicians, cleaning ladies, doorman and waiters, Kink and Kalkasa. "A first-class act," says Dajka, nodding in approval. A newcomer in evening dress also sits down; I have not seen him before. The old cash-register lady keeps guard over the front entrance; on Monday nights this is the only way to come in; on Mondays even the Hunchback is off.

I take my seat, the piano man of the salon. The first course is already being served. A first-class act, it echoes in my head.

The police officer has gradually become a familiar figure for the staff. To accomplish this he acts pretty much the way a cowboy in the New World does, one who has to break in a wild horse, and just sits around aimlessly, whittling a piece of wood in the corral, merely to let the horse get used to his scent, his voice and gestures. Dajka chats, tells anecdotes, and jokes. But if you are guilty of something, you will soon find out that there is a system behind his seemingly random questions. I am soon on to him. He is still searching, sniffing around for a scent, with quivering nostrils, even so many weeks after the event. He is unable to rest in the shadow of an unsolved crime. He makes no secret of his annoyance with me. He interrogates me, about my former life. About the Lesser Circuit traversed by our itinerant troupe. About that evening six weeks ago. How is it that I became a piano player at this place? The second course is served. Somewhat reluctantly he drops my case, and moves to a seat next to the number one chorus girl. I find out that the newcomer is an illusionist in search of employment. He makes use of some new-fangled machinery in his act.

I adjust the napkin around my neck and start in on the succulent stuffed turkey, without the slightest trace of nervousness in my stomach.

Soon I am able to get away, and leave the premises in plain view of the ancient battleaxe who sits inexorably on her throne in front of the serpentine stairs, where they have served her dinner. After the meal most of the staff leave; this is our only free night all week.

Meanwhile Marika Knorr lies awake, unable to sleep; her thoughts revolve around their mysterious, noble tenant. In her white virginal bed she is repeatedly swept by hot flashes which she in her youthful innocence attributes to the warm summer weather. It is late at night when the entrance door of the apartment is heard to open, and within moments the youngest girl is wide awake, lying there with open eyes, alert. With bated breath she strains her ears for the sounds of the man's passage through the apartment. She is helped by the familiar noises of the rooms, which she can readily interpret. She sees nothing unusual - as she will explain at last, reluctantly, to the Special Investigator - in the late return of the foreigner. By the time of that interrogation, the Special Investigator and his men will have started out on the trail of the burglars both at home and abroad. So it did not seem unusual to her at the time, Marika will explain (and it is like pulling teeth), for their tenant always came home very late, sometimes only at dawn. But on this night something unusual happens: after his return the man is heard to be washing himself, splashing water, the way he usually does before going out, and then he retires to his room. Earlier he had laid out a clean white shirt of fine linen for himself. "And how did you know about that?" Dr. Dajka will interrupt her. He will already have dismissed the stenographer from the apartment's living room, and even Marton (in whose pocket there will be a ticket for the midnight express toward Constantinople, Cairo, Alexandria, Port Said and Salonica, enabling him to follow the trail on land and water). This way the young girl, suffering from the wounds of her unrequited, dreamy love affair, will find it easier to talk. And the sobbing girl will confess that she did not shrink from tiptoeing barefoot in order to peek through his keyhole. "God almighty!" Dajka will sigh at this point in the drawn-out interrogation. If only he had known this earlier. And if they had known, indeed, everything would have happened differently after Marika's eavesdropping. Because the little girl saw everything through the keyhole, while her heart was hammering hard enough to burst in her chest, for after all, the other gentleman could have stepped out into the hall at any moment. Waiting, spread out on the tenant's bed was a many-pleated large cape, and on it the neatest, slim yellow pigskin case with a shoulder strap. Then out he came from the bathroom, refreshed, naked to the waist, and she looked and looked, until she escaped from the keyhole, with a racing heart. This is what the police could have found out from her at an earlier time.

Marika Knorr cannot offer testimony about what followed. Forty minutes after awakening her, the tenants, together with their guest, leave the premises.

In the great hall of the Baroness' coffeehouse the most loyal and persistent are still basking in the afterglow of the festive dinner, ruminating as befits true trenchermen. These are the rewards of another hard week's work; friendly conversation late into the night, and pleasurable, leisurely digestion over cigars, cognac and liqueurs.

(NOW: "CAISSON" AND "TUBING")

Last week we traveled to Prague. Monday I came home, after making reservations, with the news that we were going to stay in a school dormitory. "That's not so great," you said, disappointed. I wanted to know why. "Because there is no valet." For a long time now, you have been looking forward to staying at a hotel, and you had your own expectations about it.

"Dark is the night, the streets are empty," I hummed a popular song about the underworld as we stood in line on Tuesday to exchange money. "At dawn they'll know what's gone, and plenty." I picked it up somewhere on the street, possibly during the times after the Great Organized Blood Bath (No. 2).

From Wednesday on we went sight-seeing in Prague. This was your first time abroad. A "real abroad", you insisted with mathematical precision, referring to Imola's relations who also live abroad in Kolozsvár and Fogaras, in Romania. Whereas this was an abroad where actual foreigners live. It was your first airplane ride, lasting one hour. So we saw Prague, without a hotel valet. They were constructing the subway; I had visions of the deep tunnel, the drill and shield, "caisson" and "tubing". Red placards rose above the parade grandstands, and there were long strips of red fabric stretching over the heaps of cobblestones in the uprooted street: "Long live the glorious days of May". In Czech. Under our feet, dirt and dust and the thudding of planks on the improvised sidewalk. On the wall, a bulletin board featuring the outstanding workers on the subway. On another board, photos of the laggards, with names and work positions. I told you that there had been bulletin boards like that in our country as well, in the early 1950's, following the influx of Russian words such as "Davay" (Give!) and "Kleba" (Bread) and "Ukase" (autocratic order), and after the second wave of deportations, when our language became enriched by such foreign imports as "caisson" (pressurized chamber for underwater construction) and "tubing" (underground construction unit with a circular cross-section). How did these words come to us from our great Slavic neighbor? By the same route as "combine", naturally, and "metro"; that is, all the way across Eurasia. "We sat on the underground express, without a word," I quoted you another hit song of bygone years. Well, all the "tubing" and all the Stakhanovite "caisson"-workers notwithstanding, that projected super subway system of the early 'fifties was never completed in our country. A few years later, in 1956, I learned from Imre, under whose name I have been living for all too long now, that this was the ideal time to build a subway system, when so many buildings lay smashed to rubble on the city's main arteries, the power lines were all down, and the existing tracks were damaged by the tank treads and fallen debris. He had been studying to be a civil engineer, he told me two days before his death. As long as the streetcars cannot function, and we have no automobile traffic, within half a year to a year we could have built underneath the ruined avenues and boulevards and quays a network of subways, just as we had built the first subway on the continent back in the year of the Kitty. It would have cost little more than the renovations, and so what if it could not be used as a nuclear fallout shelter. Two days later even more buildings fell down, additional power lines were destroyed and tracks damaged, and Imre died on the cobblestones of Móricz Circus. (We would not have believed that there were so many stones on that square; we were able to raise walls, pyramids, man-sized passageways, labyrinths, all made of cobblestones.) Back then we, the survivors, missed out on the chance to build a subway system. The construction of the new subway was eventually begun twenty years later, quietly, with fitting modesty; you were one year old at the time. And we were still not allowed to call it by its name. But back in the early 'fifties, when that abortive attempt was made, we too had these bulletin boards posted, with photos of the good and the bad, everywhere, from kindergartens to old-age homes. We were still handsome back then, thin and poorly shaven, and each of us possessed a face that had its own anarchistic contours, each one different, and not even the good workers' faces filled out the whole picture frame on the bulletin board. And what about our good neighbors, the Czechs? Will they, too, struggle twenty years for a mere seven kilometers of nuke-proof subway track?

"And I could have practised my English," you grumbled on the way back from Prague yesterday, still bemoaning your hotel.

THE SCENT OF WILDFLOWERS IN A ROOM

The feast in the ground floor hall of the Silly Kitty is drawing to a close. The night is well advanced, it is already Tuesday, the forty-third day. Dr. Dajka, a guest in a somewhat ambiguous position, swirls his cognac in the glass, which is properly shaped so that its concave surfaces concentrate and direct the aroma of the expensive imported nectar toward the drinker's olfactory organ. In the meantime the lights have been doused and everyone present is absorbed in reverential contemplation of the final treat: the illusionist, a real Englishman, is performing wonders with Professor Roentgen's all-penetrating X-rays. The Baroness had already decided at first glance that she would hire the act. But she asks for a full demonstration; let her extended family enjoy the free entertainment. Meanwhile she converses in an undertone. Bora is silent. Her eyes still attract Dajka. He tries to ignore the white hair; when he catches himself staring he looks away, feeling guilty.

Porter No. 56, who is customarily stationed in front of the Vindobona Coffeehouse, is heading home after a long day's exhausting work, when he encounters some well-dressed revelers crossing Newmarket Square (for you, Elizabeth Square). One of these midnight gentlemen, all dressed in black, stumbles on a pile of dirt left behind by construction workers, and drops a long iron bar. He snatches it up and hurries after the others. The porter twirls his mustache, and nods in disapproval. He is not going to get himself involved in any kind of upper-class hijinks.

On a New Job   247

The Special Investigator is the last to leave on this night; he finds it difficult to tear himself away. Once more he rehearses those well-worn thoughts, at the insistence of something at the back of his mind. *Motive*: jealousy. Motive? This puzzle has been nagging at him night and day for the past several weeks. He swallows the remaining cognac, stubs out his cigar, and rises. He feels he must follow the scent, and proposes to take a look at the women upstairs in their everyday environment.

"Please follow me," says the Baroness, who leads the way upstairs. Her entire future depends on this nightclub: the prospects for her resort hotel, and for a decent, secure middle-class existence in which the last traces of that hefty Highlands wench will have vanished. With an iron will she sticks to her false story, insisting that she did not see what Bora did. Other than that, she is wholeheartedly prepared to cooperate fully with the Special Investigator.

Porter No. 56 arrives home, and not even bothering to light a candle, crawls into bed, snuggling against the warm, voluminous buttocks of his wife. Soon he is sound asleep.

The police officer and the proprietress progress through the upper floors, and make their way from one end of the corridor to the other, chatting with the staff. The tone has already been set by the intimate mood of the dinner, and by Dr. Dajka's nocturnal existence that seems to hover on the border between light and shadow. Room after room, they encounter the familiar mélange of smells. The Baroness makes an effort to participate in and direct the conversations. At last they reach the final room at the end of the corridor. It belongs to the bread-girl.

Dajka is still nagged by that recurring notion, an expectation to find the answer to his questions somewhere in some cranny of this rambling house; upstairs, downstairs, or between floors. The Baroness opens this door as she did the others, without knocking. A stifled scream emanates from behind the door.

"Take it easy, honey, no hysterics, please," she advises the room's occupant, as she did the others. "His Excellency the Special Investigator would like to have a few words with us, informally." There follows a rummaging inside, then a small flame flares and stabilizes, casting its light on the palisade planks of passageway.

Here, too, the furniture is inexpensive and functional. A broad bed, a cupboard with shelves and hangers, a small writing desk. The place of honor is occupied by a tall wash-stand, with soap and a towel on its metal top, and clean water in the large basin. Greyish soapy water in the pail below. Dajka turns with bemused interest toward the pretty creature, who is somehow different from the others. She silently nods, intimidated, toward the awesome visitor.

In the middle of the room stands a large, heavy oval oak table that is out of place here. The checkered linen tablecloth is rectangular, and the discrepancy in shape makes its ample pleats bunch up in accordioned pleats that reach the floor. Dr. Dajka is on the right track here. If he were to move that tablecloth aside, and see the darker stain on the crencllations of the carpet design, and were to interrogate the girl, he would learn quite a bit about that stain. But he finds everything in order. The steel doors in the back are locked; the shutters on the two windows of this corner room are drawn tight, so there is not the slightest draft. At the window the Doctor pauses, and absent-mindedly picks up a pebble: it is lovely, white-veined, smooth as polished marble. He turns it in his fingers. Through the crack in the shutters he can see the small huts in the courtyard, their dark windows; it is late. The summer night is sweltering. The police officer suddenly feels ashamed; surely he has better things to do than to play with little pebbles. He puts it back in the small pile, and slowly lowers his body into the only armchair. He does not expect to find out very much from this girl.

"Bubbles, the bread-girl. Am I correct?" Just another chat after all the others.

An Inner City street in the dark of night. One belated pedestrian, a bristle-mustachioed country gentleman from the Bácska region, is trudging on toward the National Hotel, whistling. His footsteps ring out on the deserted sidewalk, but suddenly he notices a gent dressed in black evening wear up ahead near the square. There goes someone else returning from a spot of harmless late-night fun, he thinks. He can tell it is a tipsy young dandy dawdling around, smoking a cigar. Now he is fumbling with his bowtie, and just at the moment when our passerby goes past him, he stumbles over a manhole cover, and, wildly flailing to regain his balance, he creates a huge racket.

A noise that was sufficient - the bristle-mustachioed one will reminisce later, in a veritable pose of self-caricature, smoking his pipe back home on the porch, and savoring the details of the notorious man-hunt in the freshly arrived Budapest paper - to drown out whatever noises were emanating from behind the grilled gateway of the building nearby. He notes that the time tallies with the hour of his return to the hotel. And he chuckles to himself: what if he were to step forth with his information! But damn the police, he would never do it. To waste his time traveling to the courthouse... They will never hear from him, that's for sure.

On the corner of Leopold Street the Special Investigator calls for a cab.

The strong scent of meadows and wildflowers that permeated the bread-girl's room is still in his nostrils; even the air smelled different in her room. In the middle of the windowsill stood a simple glass vase with a giant bouquet of fresh wildflowers. The girl was snuggled in, drawing her coverlet up to her chin. Those beddings saw use only by the room's occupant. Her cheerful countenance is all that she is required to contribute to the salon's business. She forms part of the atmosphere, together with the tray suspended from her neck; she is a piece of furniture paid a modest weekly wage. She does not want to do more, and that is her privilege. It was precisely this unique quality that made him bring Bora to the Baroness back then, and on account of which he is prepared to shoulder certain personal difficulties on behalf of the Kitty. He did not learn anything new tonight, not even from the girl called Bubbles. He does not forget the pebbles, nor does he attribute any special significance to them. They are a peculiarity of the girl, as is the bouquet of wildflowers. Nor will he ever find out their true purpose.

As he is driven in the direction of Bath Street, he feels that he is as far as ever from solving the brick murder. Was it done with a brick at all? Was there a murder? There is no evidence.

He arrives home at dawn. This has been happening more and more frequently, ever since he got himself entangled with that almond-eyed girl and her night-time existence. Luckily his wife, the Lady Maria, possesses a level-headed understanding that ensures family peace. He drops off into deepest sleep, after leaving a note for his wife to let him sleep until he wakes. Even an officer of the law is entitled to sleep his fill every once in a while.

THE MORNING AFTER

Daybreak follows night on this Tuesday, like any other day. Dawn sparrows, their heads no longer under wings, chirp lusty arpeggios, advertising their affairs from the trees of the former Newmarket, greeting this new day of the Lord with loud bird-hosannahs.

The last of the well-heeled revelers vanish from the much-trafficked sidewalks of Serpent Square, Fair Street, and Hand Street. Working people are setting out for jobs that hide behind the bright facade of the metropolis, in sewage plants and engine houses, garbage dumps, warehouses and water works, from where they maintain and safeguard the brilliance up above. A milk cart pulled by two horses clatters down Váci Street. On this street, which will eventually be restricted to pedestrians, in this era vehicular traffic rages full force; only later, much, much later (around the time of your arrival) will it dwindle, when the smoke-belching, rattling No. 2 and No. 15 buses will be diverted to the former Archduchess Maria Valeria Street. Imola and I gazed at these outmoded monsters so many times: they appeared downright graceful and slender, as seen overhead from the Italian graduate seminar nicknamed *Paradiso*. A tomato tossed from the fifth floor window would spatter splendidly on a roof below, and occasionally the bus drivers would brake with incomprehensible force, and an ear-splitting screech of tires. Not so the two-horse milk wagon on this dawn; its driver does not give a fig about the early morning slumbers of the citizenry. At the cab stands on Leopold Street, and on the former Saint Peter Street (renamed Crown Prince Street at this time) fresh clumps of horse excrement are dropping with silent thuds. Sleepy streetsweepers with their whisk brooms nudge aside these steaming fresh yellowish spheres, and herd the prematurely fallen leaves; this is about the worst of environmental pollution at this moment in history. Across from the building of the Piarists, in the Grand Bazaar, the shop assistant of Hatvanger and Bócz's exclusive jewelry store is unlocking the street entrance with a loud clatter, in preparation for a new business day.

He senses, rather than sees, the first sign of something amiss: the small patch of dim light that emanates each morning from the store through the peephole is now replaced by a midnight black. He opens the door with a gesture more abrupt than is his wont. When he notices the black scarf placed over the peephole, he is seized by misgivings; the lady cashier would never be capable of such an irregularity. And then there is not a moment left for anything. Without even a glance at the counter, he turns toward the gaping door of the inner office. The great safe, wide open, stares back at him. He closes up in a hurry, and runs at top speed to notify the jeweler Hatvanger, who is enjoying the pleasures of breakfast with his family on Crown Street. The junior partner is appalled. There is no need for him to be told what is missing from the store.

If - armed by the unfair advantage of hindsight - we review the sequence of events, we may state that from this Tuesday on, until the day when a telegram from Bremen will announce the less than satisfactory conclusion of the case, the Special Investigator will not have a single free minute. That is the kind of man he is. From here on he will feel personally responsible for the solution to two major crimes, and whenever he comes to a dead end in the case of the Bazaar robbery, he will return to the unsolved affair of the brick murder.

His wife shakes him awake early in the morning. This is how it works when the wife is a true partner. She was prepared to guard his rest with all her might, yet something told her that she must wake him now. He awakes to the pangs of conscience, and fleeting recollections of last night: Bora talkative then mute, her white hair, those dark almond-shaped eyes; and Bora singing. Dajka kisses his Maria on the lips and pats her broad back reassuringly.

He despatches the patrolman who brought the news, to summon Marton. The forensic specialists and detectives are already waiting for him at the scene of the crime. He washes hurriedly, scrapes the bristles from his face; with bloodshot eyes sits down to his scalding café au lait, and sets out with a tight stomach, without having caught up on his sleep. As he flings himself down in the seat of the hurtling cab, the stale tastes of last night's cognac and cigar still mingle with this morning's coffee. The rattle of the carriage shakes him to action, and after the second sharp turn he is filled with a childlike excitement. He has been waiting for this day; now it is here. Thirty-six safe-breaks within a period of three years, and now, in the Millennial year, after a very long pause, one more. He is praying for one thing only: that it should be our gang he is up against.

News of the burglary has already spread. Several hundred curious bystanders throng to the Bazaar; the crowd overflows into the narrow side streets, and blocks the traffic passing through the Inner City in the early morning hour. This is a completely different population of the city: daytime, alert, hard-working, penny-pinching and elegant, earning and spending its money in the daylight. Only those strata of society who make up Dajka's night-time clientele are not represented here. The two uniformed guards posted in front of the grillwork gate and the steel door are holding the crowd back only with the greatest difficulty. They were the two patrolmen on duty last night. From his reinforcements Dajka soon creates a cordon around both entrances, and orders the curiosity-seekers pushed back.

In the looted jewelry store he heads straight for the safe. He gives orders that he is not to be disturbed, and proceeds to inspect everything, without touching. It is with a sense of satisfaction that he arrives at his conclusion: all of the signs are in accord. The safe is of the newest, double-walled type and the place has been swept clean. The traces left by the whisk broom in the barely perceptible layers of ash and dust are part of this gang's signature. The plates and bolts on the door of the safe have been jarred loose by the explosion, just as in Odessa; likewise, the circular hole, through which they found and reached the lock, is also familiar from the Odessa reports. The damage has been kept to a minimum. The burglars entered unnoticed, and departed leaving practically no tracks.

Huge question marks tower in the Special Investigator's mind: Why here? Why Monday night? What did these scoundrels know?

He takes out his magnifying glass for a closer look. On the open door of the safe he soon finds a shred of green wool yarn, then another; a dozen pieces altogether. Under the safe, shreds of white linen, and he finds additional green particles in the most unlikely places: on top of the wardrobe on the other side of the room, behind the spittoon in the far corner. He gathers all of these with tweezers into small envelopes, and labels them for tests in the forensic laboratories. He has little faith in the Galton fingerprint technique. Those of his colleagues who have employed the technique in other parts of Europe, recommend paying attention to smooth and shiny surfaces. There were none found in Odessa, and none will be found here. There are no fingerprints visible on the shiny surfaces.

At a glance he is able to tell that he is facing a new development in the "bloodless revolution in safe-breaking in Hungary and Europe." (His own words.)

Two words echo in his brain: inside job. From the footprints in the meager layer of dust it is impossible to tell with certainty if there were two or three intruders. Fortunately the shop assistant had the good sense not to enter the room.

The patrolman salutes and gives his report at stiff attention.

"And the two of you didn't notice anything out of the ordinary?" Faced with this question, the patrolmen are distinctly aware of how much they would like to be somewhere else. Dajka dismisses the two policemen and sends them home to catch up on their sleep. But first, someone should bring him a shoebox. Yes, a plain cardboard shoebox; no, he does not need the shoes. Within minutes they bring him one from a nearby shoestore. The patrolmen are at last free to trudge away, downcast; but the corporal does not obey the order to go home.

On the lid of the shoebox Dajka outlines the hole on the safe door, and cuts it out, using his pen-knife. He places this cardboard circle next to the one from Odessa.

Messrs. Hatvanger and Bócz, upon arriving at their store, do not take long to appraise their losses. They had already expected the worst. Their firm, poised at the dawn of a new era, has just suffered the most painful loss since its establishment.

Dajka's hair stands on end as he listens to the tale of the shipment of the diamond known as Blue Blood. When Hatvanger pronounces the words "House of Hapsburg", Dajka's mind reverberates with his original special commission on the occasion of the Millennial Jubilee: His Imperial Majesty's Highest Command, to keep these festivities free of crime. He must retrieve this loot at all costs.

"So, I take it, you have kept the stone's arrival a total secret? At least as far as the police were concerned." But he leaves off. The two jewelers are clearly in shock. For Dajka, in order to protect their valuables, information about their presence would have been essential. This burglary could have been prevented; it was predictable, he had even been expecting it; had he known about the vulnerability of the store on the corner of Váci and Huckster streets, the outcome would have been different. The Stone and the accompanying shipment were delivered as ordinary first-class mail, marked "Sample without Value", mailed by Hatvanger in Paris, without any insurance.

Dajka instructs the proprietors to prepare an inventory of all missing objects, with detailed, professional descriptions of the stone known as Blue Blood, and all other items in the shipment. They must do their best to placate the Princess, to beg her indulgence, patience and discretion, and assure her that the police working on the case have assigned it the highest priority. This is an unenviable task, but they have earned it, thinks Dajka.

Who could have found out about the shipment? And how? But it is hopeless: no one, naturally. What is he talking about? They have kept it a total secret.

On the basis of the inventory taken the day before, the list of objects missing from the large safe is rapidly drawn up. The Stone. The large trays. The two gold watches inlaid with gems, nine other watches in fourteen-carat gold, and twenty-one jewels. Gone from the storage bins and drawers are thirty-one American-made nickel Goldwyn remontoir pocket watches with chased covers, and various silver jewelry. Also from the safe: state lottery documents and paper bills, one hundred eighty thousand forints in newly issued hundred-forint bills, and about thirteen thousand forints in mixed denominations, Monday's take. From the cash register, the supply of change: five hundred forints in singles, three hundred in twenty-fillér pieces, three hundred forints in assorted silver. The perpetrators have left behind four individual savings deposit books of twenty thousand forints each, a hundred forty forints in small change, fifty thousand forints in promissory notes, and two hundred thirty thousand forints in various securities. On hearing about these, Dajka gives a knowing, almost admiring nod. Yes, it had to be them. This was their style: whatever cannot be readily converted into cash through their underworld channels had been left behind, incidentally sparing the owners further losses.

(Here let us pause for a moment's silent but unsympathetic reflection on the revolutionary blackguards who, when they see a girl wearing lipstick, wipe it off with sandpaper; or of the petty, drug-induced muggers in New York, and lately, Buda and Pest parks, who snatch the old man's wallet, rip off the old woman's wristwatch, gang-rape the young girl, but are still tormented by a sense of unfulfillment that tips their delicate psychic balance. And so, as they leave, they kick the old man to a bloody pulp.)

Dajka has mixed feelings, including a triumphant note that

he finds difficult to account for. He feels, now that the safe-breakers have made their move, that he too is launched on the path that will lead to the untangling of a string of unsolved break-ins, and eventually to his snapping the bracelets on the wrists of each member of this international gang. He is both right and wrong in this expectation: he will solve the case and yet he will not; he will handcuff us and yet he won't. And throughout this affair a vague memory will keep stirring at the threshold of his consciousness. Something that happened. Something he saw, recently, here on Huckster Street. But he cannot put his finger on just what it was.

Early-rising prostitutes are out on the streets of the Hungarian capital. Saltpeter stains sketch murky diagrams on the walls of outlying taverns over the heads of people pickling themselves in the living death of alcohol. By the rear wall of the Imperial and Royal Artillery Barracks, on a fenced-in empty lot overrun by weeds, two girls, daughters of an Angel-land janitor, copulate standing up with a platoon of new regimental recruits, at two forints apiece. And making their toilettes in the afternoon are those more elegant streetwalkers who sell their services in the Inner City districts, for a correspondingly higher fee.

A variety of tireless bawds keep public brothels and rented rooms busy twenty-four hours a day all over the city.

From hamlets, villages and small towns, folk issue in masses - the inhabitants of tomorrow's capital.

On the streets, servant girls sing the popular song, "America is one big city / Where the girls are always pretty". Later, during the early 'fifties, we all sang, "America, you wonderful world!" the *chastushka*, a type of song meant to be popular social criticism, and originating east of us. The progressive cultural workers had intended these words to drip venomous satire, but by the time the song reached the outlying provinces, the quotation marks eroded, the irony leaked away, and the bare truth of the statement remained. And so we believed it as a tenet of faith. In the year of the Kitty, Dajka himself has no illusions on this score, but the willing victims gulled by the shipping agents believe the song, with the desperate determination of emigrants. Because of the shortages of bread and land back here at home, they believe that over there, even the fences are made of sausages..

The engineer Abraham is not typical of the million and a half who stagger into emigration around this time.

We dismiss our tired, our poor, our huddled masses yearning to breathe free. That is what Emma, the poet, says on the pedestal of the Statue of Liberty. But, looked at from this side of the Ocean, it is not such a simple matter. After the police managed to restrict the misleading advertisements, the shipping agents opened their fly-by-night offices in the Hungarian capital. This enabled them, via questionable practices, to claim a regular bounty from shipping companies such as Nord-Deutsche Lloyd and Hamburg American, for every Hungarian who has scraped together enough pennies to purchase a ticket to the New World. Against this, the authorities are helpless. Gradually, the First Wave of Immigration to the New World via Ellis Island is in full swing. (As I am recounting this, the Second Wave is on, made up of Indo-Chinese and Latinos; there will be a Third Wave, from all over the place.) But now, the immigrants are greeted at the Port of New York by the words of the poet: "Give me your tired, your poor..." And the America of the next century is built by them. We shall get to see it.

On this forty-third day the Armenian, Agap Kevorg, travels through Budapest. He passes by the intersection of Holy Saturday and Bush streets.

On this day I shake out my cape at our headquarters, wrap it around a long crowbar, and shove it up on top of a tie beam in the attic, where it cannot be seen.

As it turned out, that night I went straight from Dajka's interrogation to assist with the tools at the burglary. It was at eleven-thirty when I put the last finishing touches on my wardrobe, at my humble quarters on Diver Street.

BRAZEN RETURN

Miss Marika Knorr did not get to see the King, who had donned his fresh shirt in the process of opening the yellow *étui* that lay on the bed.

He paused for a moment for blissful contemplation of the set of precision-tooled steel instruments gleaming in their snug velvet-lined pockets. We had entered the building without having to ring for the concierge downstairs; for a long time now we had had our own keys. Bódog Haluska had also arrived, and he and Socrates noiselessly exited through the bathroom window to the outside gangway. In two trips they brought down the objects needed for tonight from their hiding place in a remote corner of the attic. The landlord and his family had gone to bed early and were sound asleep, except for Marika. But she was unable to make sense of the mysterious sounds; all she could conclude was that several men were moving about in the tenant's quarters. This was only the second time I had visited there since renting the rooms. And all along, an unimpeachable gentleman had been living in a room rented from an elderly landlady in the neighborhood of the New House of Parliament. He went to work at night (probably an artist, a bit of a Bohemian), was at times unshaven, occasionally he came home rather late, but he was always quiet and polite, and paid the rent on time. And to this day he had not registered with the police.

We made our preparations behind drawn curtains. My cape had been mended; under it, on a hook, hung the bull's-eye lantern favored by thieves, the lighter in my pocket. A linen knapsack for the litter, and an oilcloth bag for the loot. "Isn't it rather large?" Bódog asked. "On the contrary, let's hope it proves to be too small." We also took along a cut-up pillowcase, from which we had removed the monogram identifying it as a dowry piece for one of the Misses Knorr; one reserve scarf, and a sheet of paper backed with adhesive.

Meanwhile the landlord's daughter, alarmed by the sounds of our activities next door, pulled the covers over her head in a futile attempt to go to sleep.

Under his cape the Greek was carrying the traditional two-foot long crowbar, a small whisk broom, a clothes brush, the knapsack full of rags, and a collapsible, elegant soft leather suitcase. He managed to fit all this under the loose cape without producing the slightest bulge.

The King checked his instruments, making sure that their tempered cutting edges were protected by the leather slipcases. Circular cut rasps, augers, a spatula with a curved handle for removing ashes, flatnose pliers, rotary drill, twist drill, duckbill pliers.

All of us dressed in black, from top to toe.

From the messy quarter around the Newmarket we hurried toward the serene heart of the Inner City, on foot, avoiding cabdrivers. Haluska, the lookout, was decked out in formal evening wear: tails, stove-pipe hat, cuffs pulled back and fixed with rubber bands, his white shirtfront covered by a black scarf, so that nothing should be flashing in the night. But all the while the dark clouds of disaster were gathering overhead. We arrived at the Grand Bazaar at one a.m., as planned.

The darkness was broken only by the lights emanating from the plate-glass windows of the all-night coffeehouse on the other side of Town Hall Square. The square and the street were patrolled by two policemen, guardians of honest burghers' dreams. And incidentally, they enabled us to accomplish the business we had in these parts.

In the distance, at the entrance of the National Hotel, the traffic was ceaseless, night and day. We did not encounter anything unexpected. "We meet here in ninety minutes, at the latest," I said to Bódog. In the interim he was to be the very image of a gentleman; he must remember not to chew tobacco, but smoke a cigar instead.

After rounding the corner I lit up my own Trabuco. The first key noiselessly opened the lock on the outer grill gate.

We waited until the police patrol passed the grillwork. In the distance, Haluska melted into the shadows of the square, as if he were a dark poster glued to the wall. We had seventeen usable minutes ahead of us.

The pinpoint spot of the bull's-eye lamp lit up the glass-roofed arcade. Half a minute. We stood in front of the small steel door leading to the storage room. Now it was the Greek's turn, being our resident expert with locks and keys. He riffled through his metal key forms, blew on his fingertips, stretched his fingers, pumped them into a fist. Ten more seconds. With three quick twists he inserted an empty key bit into the stem of the pre-cut key, without the least clink. He fiddled with it, wrists turning in surgical precision. In the spotlight of the carbide lamp he examined the scratchmarks. He screwed in a new key bit, then another. The third key turned in the lock, as smooth as butter. A minute and a half had passed since the patrol went by. I was mesmerized by this sight of a professional at work.

The King led the way, with sprightly steps, between islands of accounting books, tools, old furniture. At the far end of the storage room was the glassed door to the office; he had already visited there with the Greek, and seen it from the other side. "Adhesive," he breathed. I did my best to move in a way that would live up to the quality of work displayed before my eyes. In retrospect this seems a pious wish, for my confreres moved noiselessly, with rapid and sure gestures, like great nocturnal beasts of prey. The Greek was already squeezing out his handkerchief under the dripping faucet of the sink. I pulled out the adhesive paper and smoothed it out on a table. He plastered the paper over the door's glass with the practised movements of a lifelong bill-sticker. The paper stuck to the frosted glass; Socrates gave a push with his right palm; at almost the same time his left caught a falling glass fragment. Grass does not grow more silently than this. Then he opened the door from the inside, with the key that was in the lock; not a scratch on his wrist. Now we were in the room where the great bear-like safe squatted - and we got there without having to break through any walls. No one looked at It; safe-breakers are a superstitious lot, like sailors. Two and a half minutes. Brush and whisk broom were laid out on a table. The Greek pulled forth a gigantic screwdriver from one of his bottomless pockets. He slipped a sheet of paper under the glass door leading to the store; using the screwdriver he turned the key in the lock a little and then pushed it out; after it dropped onto the paper, he pulled the sheet and the key back under the door. I concealed the lamp under my cape. He now opened the door with its own key; we were home free. There was the counter with its glass display cases. Across from us, through the peephole of the steel door fronting on Váci Street, a trickle of light was visible. I hung my scarf on a hook above, so that no tell-tale light would leak out. Now I could use the lantern. "Chisel." I handed over the chisel. A couple of soft cracks, and the drawers were open, almost undamaged. The cash-register drawer came next, yielding the day's take in a steel box: a few thousand crowns, in all denominations; coins in sealed rolls. All this could wait. The Safe King now stepped up to the great bear. I knocked my cigar ashes onto the pages of an open accounting book. Three and a half minutes. From here on our progress would be more laborious.

"Acetylene torch." Said by the pre-eminent surgeon heading his experienced team of assistants. A typewriter table was rolled to the front of the safe; the acetylene torch was set on a pile of books. The Greek aimed the flame at the target. As the metal began to glow at a red heat, he moved the flame along the circumference of an imaginary circle. The King's instruments lay arrayed in exemplary order on the table.

I put out my cigar and carefully wrapped the stub in a sheet of foolscap. The light of the acetylene torch illumined the piece of work at hand. I flipped open the lid of my racing stopwatch, and took the oilcloth bag into the other room. The cash drawer took thirty seconds to empty; we removed bills and small knicknacks from the steel box. Then, one after another, the glass display cases of the counter, and the four drawers. My bag was beginning to fill up with rings, necklaces, brooches, earrings, pocket watches. Then back to the office. The King now spelled the Greek at the acetylene torch. At sixteen minutes I gave the signal, and we froze. Time seemed to have come to a standstill while we waited in the silence of the night for the heavy echoing footfalls of the police patrol. We could hear the two policemen laughing loudly, and even slapping their thighs.

The flame was doing its work. "Chisel." One wrenching twist, a crack, and the flatnose pliers held the severed steel disk, its edge still red-hot. The ashes fell on the pages of the accounts book. The circular opening did not reveal the location of the hidden lock. The steel disk was already cooling on top of the safe, on its way to become one of the King's trophies. He did have this one human failing: a hopeless vanity, just like a violin virtuoso's. But then he has a right to be vain. He was now spooning out the ashes, to make way for the charge.

If I had intended to give better odds to our opposition, I had succeeded. Back in Odessa and here at the Bazaar I was not yet aware of those factors which gave the Special Investigator, to be frank, odds superior to ours. He had the expanding network of international police cooperation. He had his album of criminals. Our great coup meant, as it were, a return to the scene of the crime - something I had warned against. A terrible mistake, and we would be in for our share of surprises!

"Dynamite, blankets." Everything was ready, and on hand. The King spread a green horse blanket on top of the books. We could hear the edge of the opening emitting barely audible crackles as it cooled. The charge was placed on the inner wall of the safe. We doubled up three horse blankets, just to be on the safe side in the still of the night, with police patrols around. The whole works was covered tight. With unhurried enjoyment the King lit up one of his unfiltered Egyptian cigarettes. When he carefully tapped off the long ashes of his Ibis, he made sure they fell on top of the other debris. The stopwatch. Twenty seconds of total stillness. I had counted only on the police patrol; the municipal night watch had another route, far away. Our lookout had not sounded any alarm.

The King brought his cigarette to the end of the fuse which began to burn with a nervous crackle.

"Sixty seconds," said the King. I recalled these two words from our initial encounter in Zara. "Take cover." We ran toward the street side of the room. Socrates pulled the door closed behind him, and we took cover on the outer side of the counter. There was a dull thud, as if a crate had been dropped behind the closed door. There were no residents in the building; not a soul stayed overnight in any of the Bazaar's shops, we knew that for certain. This was the moment when Bódog Haluska stumbled outside, to distract the attention of the corpulent country gentleman on his way back to the National Hotel.

The front panel of the safe was jarred loose at all of its seams. In the lower left corner, in a region that had been hidden from our observers by Mr. Bócz's wide midsection and waistcoat, we could now observe the rectangle of the lock outlined by the welded beads over the bolts. Now for a pitcher of water, and Socrates' moistened handkerchief, to wipe the soot off our faces.

"Acetylene torch. Rotary drill. Twist drill." One of the auger bits broke. I finished my second Trabuco.

The King used a pitcherful of tapwater to cool the shishtering edge of the hot metal, sending up a fine cloud of steam.

"*Krummkopf.*" Somewhat carried away by professional pride, the King could not pass up using the thieves' argot for this long-handled burglar's tool sanctified by so many perilous professional engagements. This is a specialist's term, used by all safe-crackers, but it is not a Hungarian word. Even so my tall cousin, "Little Kornél", would, much later, try to convince me about the technical need for such verbal monstrosities as *object-oriented, user-friendly software design*, to the point of insisting that this was proper Hungarian usage. Eventually you will have to deal with these and their ilk when you engage in studying the new world of artificial intelligence, so handy at a time when we will be able to disappear without ever leaving home.

"Linen." Hand's-breadth strips of the Knorrs' de-monogrammed pillow case, to be placed over the out-turned petals of the front steel plate. Using these as he cracked off each piece enabled the King to obtain a firm grip with his duck-bill pliers, and also muffled the sound. He now paused to remove the steel disk from the top of the safe and carefully tucked it away in a pocket of the *étui*. He spooned out more ashes, and only then did he reach into the dynamited hole for the steel safe's lock. While his sensitive surgeon's fingers felt their way around inside, he looked up at the ceiling; his usually smooth forehead was lined by parallel creases, when, clickety-clack, you could already hear the tiny, delicate sounds of the lock turning. Now he placed his left palm on the outside of the heavy steel door. The moment had arrived, to grasp in our hands the crowning result of years of work, the reward of our steadfast faith and persistence, the interest on the capital invested, and to enjoy the triumph of our professional pride. Now Mr. Steel Safe was at last forced to yield the jealously guarded secrets of his innards. As the pinpoint spot of the lantern moved slowly, deliciously from left to right, (the way we write in our part of the world), above the brilliant cool fire of the Stone we could all read in undisturbed peace the curlicued letters so beautifully engraved on the inside back wall: *Steel Safe made in the factory of Friedrich Wiere, Vienna. Burglar proof.*

The only thing that remained was to collect the rest of the loot. My unbroken faith in the information obtained by Bódog Haluska proved to be fully justified.

For one fleeting moment I held the Stone between my fingers: icy crystalline fire resting on its own black velvet cushion. A princely bauble. Its facets caught the pinpoint light of the lantern and scattered it in all the colors of the rainbow over the dark office. The treasure brazenly asserted itself. I thought of the Koh-i-Noor and of the Great Mogul, of the Deccan Plateau and of Sumatra. Formerly the diamond was known as the stone of the Sun - though it is only carbon.

This stone was the harvest of two years' work and preparation. I recalled my learned friend whom I had met two days before on Tollhouse Square. He was telling me how in the course of his library research he chanced to meet a well-known Viennese professor. This latter gentleman insisted, with an overwhelming self-confidence based on personal experience, that every man has his price, to be paid in one of four ways: money, power, fame or love. Money? Here it was, radiating its cold fire between my two fingers, yet my system did not respond to its temptation. It did not move me deep inside, I was blind and deaf to it. I would not trade one of my walks in the crunchy snow for this. Power? Likewise. It was so *cheap*. Just look at the people who attained it, the means they employed, *and what they did with it*. Fame? When pop singers and soccer stars got the largest chunk? People love me for what I am, and that feels good, admittedly. But to act differently for that? And then who would be the person enjoying it? Someone other than me, for sure. That's all invalid, *does not exist, by definition*. (And I would always want to be free to travel by streetcar among my fellow humans, as long as there are streetcars. Wearing the fairytale magic hat of invisibility. That's how it ought to be, for a teller of tales.) With the Stone, in its ethereal setting, in my hand, I could almost comprehend falling for that fourth option. Yes, I could be vulnerable, perhaps, to the lure of woman's love. But could I be bought at that price? Could *that* be the price of any-thing? I think I would be only too aware of it if she did not want me, but merely gave herself as *currency*.

I shook my head, and slipped the Stone into the bag. Let's see what we are going to live on. Here was the shipment referred to by the code name "House of Hapsburg". Two trayloads of jewelry. A man's pocket watch with a flat emerald set in the middle; among the ancients, this was the gem of the planet Mars and of the month of June. Rings, each with a lesser, but perfectly clear diamond of the first water. A cherry-red carnelian. Many-tiered earrings with dozens of small diamonds. Silver torques and bracelets, classic examples of the silversmith's art; three Baroque gold clasps, heavy brooches, gold hearts and crosses on chainlets, a string of pearls. Now for the cash: banknotes in thick bundles still bearing the original sealed wrap of the issuing printer; the serial numbers of these have probably been recorded. We are going to need "Amber", the Armenian, to exchange these for us. The money will be discounted, but it will be clean. Crowded on to a third shelf were the day-to-day contents of the safe, all those jewels that left their coy imprints on the velvet cushions of the display case for the night. The plainer gold watches, with chains; a small stack of necklaces, crucifixes. Two hefty piles of stocks and bonds. I leafed through these, and left the bigger one in place. The smaller one I folded in half and slipped into an inside pocket of my cape. We left the savings books behind.

We were somewhat ahead of schedule. There was a complete round of the police patrol left for a thorough cleanup. Our vanity is human and excusable: we were tempted to make our work impeccable.

The Greek carried the long crowbar back to headquarters. The oilcloth bag hung on a string under my armpit. Now the small whisk broom and clothes brush were put to work; a sheet lifted from an accounting book served as our dustpan. There we were, three men, meticulously cleaning up after ourselves, every last bit of debris, ashes, shreds from the explosion, fragments of steel chipped from the safe. We wiped every surface free of dust, from the panels of the safe to each and every glass shelf in the display cases. Our only motivation was vanity, the human striving for perfection. I was not yet aware of the special significance of smooth and shiny surfaces.

Broom, brush and accounting sheet all ended up in the flattened linen knapsack, which went inside the small suitcase that looked perfectly plausible in the hands of a man elegantly decked out in evening wear. Eighty-five minutes had gone by since our arrival. I left my black scarf over the peephole inside the front door. My cape had unavoidably picked up some of the steel filings, ashes, and settled dust of the explosion. Outside, under the glass roof of the arcade, once more we inspected one another's faces and clothes.

We had managed to stay within the time agreed upon with our lookout. He joined us on the corner of Town Hall Square and Huckster Street. There was no need for even the smallest of nods. The great coup had been executed with complete success; that much was obvious. He collected the suitcase with our litter and cleaning supplies. It was his job to get rid of these.

My head resounded with the poet Vörösmarty's words: "A man's work, sheer delight."

On Bush Street Agap Kevorg is handed an oilcloth bag, and the bundle of hundred-forint banknotes still wearing the original sealed wrap. There is no need for him to count it. The wealthiest diamond dealers conclude their deals with a handshake, and ship their goods in ordinary first-class mail; professional pride dictates that our dealings should be as full of trust as theirs.

In one swoop we have freed ourselves of the loot and the evidence. For there is going to be one hell of a to-do around here. The border crossings will be the most dangerous spots, and it will be best to carry cash, clean cash, traveling like lords, so as to avoid the least shadow of suspicion. The Armenian spends a single day in Budapest, does not need lodgings, and thereby avoids leaving a superfluous trail.

The Stone now journeys along the route taken by the Orlov, otherwise known as the Amsterdam, diamond, on its way to grace the tip of the Russian Tzar's scepter. Somewhere over the endless versts of the Tzar's realm the treasure will find the fabulously wealthy provincial landowner, or Tatar khan in the hills of Crimea, and it will be absorbed like water spilled in the desert sands. Perhaps the Stone will end up ornamenting the swan-like neck of some Cherkess beauty. But first it must make a detour on the international express train heading toward the Levant, where some of the smaller items that are not so easily traceable may be passed off. Kevorg will have to find buyers for the stocks and bonds as well. An unexpected western detour will also ensue. He will not be asked for identification papers at the borders; we are, after all, in Europe. As soon as he has the first portion of our cash ready, he will get in touch with us.

Until then, we are going to have to lie low.

That morning I thoroughly clean each and every one of our instruments up in the attic, back at headquarters. The landlord's anxious adolescent daughter does not wake from her troubled dreams at the early morning hour when we noiselessly creep back into the apartment.

The King makes a side trip that he does not tell me about. If I knew about it, I would be even more eager to get away. Taking a portion of the Odessa loot, his last nine gold napoleons, and a suitcase full of clothes, he has himself driven to the Central Railway Terminal, where he enters at the Departures, and walks out at the Arrivals. He is only obeying the rules of survival: securing his getaway funds and his own alternate line of escape, in case of an emergency. He does not tell me about this. Meanwhile I keep to my own quarters, about which I have not told him. And I too have taken the precaution to stash away my escape funds, from the same source. There is no reason to blame each other for anything.

The officer of the law, whose day had begun in such an exhausting fashion, has to face its equally crowded continuation; the ongoing cases do not let up. The investigation of the Salt Square stolen silver is still in progress; one of his detectives has interviewed Countess Szirmay, who had meantime returned from the spas. Dajka gives the order for another inspection of the house, for that is where the case is going to be cracked. The burglary must have been committed by someone other than the intruder. There has been no progress in the case of the chopped-up body; the corpse has not been identified as that of anyone known to be missing, and Professor Loydl proved to be of unimpeachable character. So the case is pigeon-holed in the unsolved file.

And he has not forgotten about the affair at the Kitty. In his mind he goes over it for the thousandth time.

But now, it seems, the daily press has at last gotten a mouthful with this newest sensation; it has sunk its teeth into the story and will not let go. But the Princess does not give interviews to newshounds. They, however, soon dig up from their files the robbery on New World Street, and pose the question that offers itself naturally: Are we up against the same international gang? The kindly editors, at this early stage of the affair, are still handling the police with kid gloves. Their patience is infinite, says Marton, the Special Investigator's assistant; at times it lasts for hours.

At this point Dajka has not yet made the connection between the Crown Street household and the jewelry store, and has not thought of interrogating the Hatvanger family and domestic staff. The tattle-tale servant would have recalled quite clearly every detail of Bódog Haluska's features, including his bluish scar, in both his tattered and in the stylishly attired versions.

Already in the course of that first morning the Special Investigator has requested permission from the Public Prosecutor's office, under conditions of the utmost secrecy, for search warrants to the premises of the better-known dealers in stolen goods of the capital, to be used whenever the time is right. He plans to mass his forces in order to surprise all of them at the same time. He is already engaged in what will prove to be a long hunt.

Some editors have rushed to insert the news of the great burglary into the late morning editions of Tuesday's papers. One overzealous pen-pusher adds his own speculations: the police are looking for a group of suspicious young men, who are probably foreigners in the city. I resent this latter interpretation. Foreigners? I ought to write a letter of protest to the editor. I am as much at home here as anyone else.

In Dajka's black notebook one notation is definite: *Hungarian*. The plural *-s?* is added with a question mark. Our Special Investigator does not share the belief commonly held in law enforcement quarters, that safe-crackers have no homeland. The gang, in days of yore, began its brilliant international career back here. And, as you are well aware, among the four of us, three are Hungarian. The Special Investigator, unburdened by any prejudice, faces his task with somewhat better odds than his less astute colleagues. The rubric "Personal" was started on the basis of the footprints found in Zara. And regardless of the fact that, in the career of a gang such as ours, dispersing and regrouping is more the rule than the exception, nonetheless there is a straight line, based on the group's signature, leading from Idol Street through Odessa to the Grand Bazaar. From now on the empty rubrics in Dajka's notebook will steadily fill up with details. There are well-defined columns and empty spaces set aside for eventual accomplices. A tentative identification is made of the Safe King - in the album of criminals, section BA *alias*, K-No. 039, "a person known solely by his familiar sobriquet". The existence of Nos. BA NN 211 and NN 210 is indicated only by the presence of footprints.

On the facing page the Doctor's pencil lists dates, places, names of tools used. He groups and regroups his facts in various orders, draws charts, rearranges, and whenever he finds one combination more convincing, he makes energetic use of his Elephant brand rubber eraser. Yes, we have returned.

The city is seized by "burglar fever". The police headquarters is flooded by a stream of hysterics and would-be witnesses. They are all interrogated and then sent home. The precious hours of the first day, when the tracks are still warm and memories still fresh, are speeding by.

Countless events transpire on this same Tuesday in the city and in the world at large. One of these, which is going to touch upon our narrative, takes place on Radius Avenue. There are several good hardware stores in this neighborhood. Past the Two Lions Drugstore, and the store of Keresztes and Hácha, where we had already visited, is Gerenday's Hardware Supplies. That afternoon an unknown inquirer drops in, and requests a demonstration of the latest Phoenix brand electric safe, reputedly capable of withstanding the assault of the most cunning safe-cracker. During the demonstration, the fashionably whiny young lady accompanying the interested party does not make the slightest attempt to hide her boredom. The man is tired, has circles under his eyes, and is very cheerful. He listens with his head tilted to one side, and his pertinent questions betray a thorough expertise. He listens for well-nigh half an hour, at the end of which time he politely thanks Gerenday and his assistant for their helpful information, and departs without leaving his card. "You will hear from me," he says, and they will indeed. He then offers his arm to his lady and the two of them proceed, on foot, in the direction of the Municipal Park. The Special Investigator will hear of this afternoon visit only much later, when it will be of great interest to him. And if one of his detectives should at this moment follow the mysterious couple, only two blocks away he would observe them entering the shop of the clothiers Viczián and Wittman, specialists in fine shirts and underwear. Were the detective to take the trouble to question the clerks, he would discover that the gentleman and his lady shopped at length and with evidence of a knowing good taste, in the ready-to-wear shirts and underwear department. They purchased three dozen shirts, assorted underwear, and some neckties, and ended up by selecting brocade and silk foulards. The lady had assisted in the selection, evincing a definite sense of style, and clung to her beau's arm all through the proceedings.

Yes, he always did possess a sureness of stylistic touch.

Late in the afternoon Dr. Dajka finds time to issue the call for a manhunt, through the thousands of official and unofficial channels available to him. The suspects may turn up individually or in a group, in Pest, Buda or Old Buda. He sends out his detectives and posts them at railroad terminals, public baths, restaurants, coffeehouses, licensed brothels, and at the tollhouses around the capital. Let them watch closely all marketplaces and street vendors' stalls. Let them interrogate every single porter, beggar, cabdriver and streetwalker of the city. Let them leave not a stone unturned. The investigators should make use of the assistance of all uniformed public servants. He wants results. The little that is known about the suspects should be forwarded to all police patrols as well.

A special effort is made to inspect the registration forms filled out at every hotel, inn and pension.

The mobilization is made somewhat more cumbersome by the fact that it has to be conducted in near secrecy, so that the birds in hiding should not get wind of how much or little the police know about them. He decides against raiding the stolen goods dealers at this time. Let them lull themselves into a false sense of security; let them think that the storm has passed. He has his own plans for them.

Five hundred copies of the description of the Stone and the other jewelry are printed up, for distribution among jewelers and pawnbrokers. Dajka has the text translated into German and copies wired to colleagues at various capital cities. A large-scale, Europe-wide dragnet has been cast.

"Look for him," he tells a gathering of inspectors, police officers and stenographers, assembled for the evening briefing at the end of this tiring and largely fruitless day. It is the forty-third since the affair of the brick, and the first in the full-scale manhunt for the safe-crackers. "Look for him, for the fourth man. The one with the sailor's shirt."

Let us leave them at this point. To be continued.

PART FOUR

CROSS-COUNTRY

WAITING

So, let us return to Dr. Dajka's investigation. "Look for the fourth man," he said. From here on, the pace of events will quicken.

Towards evening of the day after the deed, our man Amber is on a train speeding southeast across the arid, dolomitic countryside. The locomotive belches sparks, and the prolonged train whistles fill the night's black void. Eventually Marton, Dajka's deputy, will also take this train, and ships as well, in pursuit of his prey halfway across Europe.

From here on, whether the safe-breakers can stay out of jail, as well as the answer to the age-old question, does crime pay, will be decided by a battle of wits, matching the Special Investigator against Agap Kevorg. Which one will prove cleverer, more inventive, and quicker? The locale of this battle will shift from the red velvet sofas of wagons-lits, to the smoke-spewing express packet boat of the Peninsular and Oriental Shipping Company chugging from Salonica to Port Said; it will involve the dismal dives of Levantine ports; it will depend on Balkan baksheesh to expedite the crew of death-ships, as well as the occasional noiseless knife in the night.

The great Budapest Bazaar break-in is, momentarily, the most notorious heist of the continent. It is the daily topic for bank clerks and janitors, not only in the Hungarian capital, but in the most remote corners of the Dual Monarchy. The newshounds, in contrast to the exemplary self-restraint they exercised regarding the brick murder, are now having a feast, demonstrating the expertise and bilious inquisitiveness that is expected from the full spectrum of the daily press in a parliamentary democracy.

That first night is almost over. While the policeman is still in the midst of his troubled dreams, the news somehow spreads along the city's underworld grapevine, in pre-dawn hangouts, brothels with wooden shutters, gambling dens that stink of stale smoke. Among the big fish and the little fish, in this muddy backwater of human existence that has experienced the fisherman, the coral reef, the whirlpool and the rocks, the word now gets around: dangerous great predators have arrived from the outer banks. The safe-break is hardly over. Neither the damaged parties nor the authorities have yet been alerted. We will never know where the news started - perhaps in the innermost soul of a timeless underworld. The word is out: the sharks have brought unusual police activity, dragnets and raids, which will further stir up the currents already full of ripples related to all the hoopla of the Millennial Exposition.

Accordingly, naked self-interest will more and more often counteract the "Sándor Rózsa syndrome", meaning greater than usual cooperation with the police. The petty criminals of the city, unable to move to other parts, away from the Millennial police surveillance, would like nothing better than the speedy arrest of the safe-breakers, and the corresponding drop in the zeal of law enforcement. Dajka counts on, but does not relish the prospect of, this unholy alliance with unsavory characters in the manhunt that is to follow.

He knows very well that it takes a thief to catch a thief, and that night he goes hunting, in his own fashion. The lady Maria watches with wordless anxiety as her husband takes out his three-pound infantry officer's revolver, breaks it down, cleans and oils each part of the firing mechanism, loads it with bullets, and slips the awesome instrument of death into the innermost pocket of his most worn-out overcoat. He allays his wife's fears; the weapon is meant only to intimidate. In quiet resignation, Maria looks after him from the window of their comfortable apartment.

On Outer Kerepesi Road the plaster is crumbling from the walls of dubious dives.

In a tavern, Dajka talks to individuals whose personal hygiene habits leave much to be desired, individuals such as any metropolis seems to spawn in its muck and filth. He asks for a shot of rotgut. He tucks his face behind the turned-up lapels of his overcoat; around here, it gives you an aura of respectability if you have something to hide.

One after another he looks up those wretched petty thieves and street thugs who, while risking their necks, manage to survive in the primal jungle of the underworld by occasionally doing a turn as police informers. He encounters the face of Jenö the Lisp, the underworld messenger who once brought news of the King's being on the loose again. Apparently he provides services on both sides of the law.

And the police officer asks questions. Who has seen any new faces around, and where? Did anyone hear about any new-fangled burglary tools? About foreigners? About unknown big-timers, who may have been to America and back? Have there been any unusual stolen goods offered for sale? He asks around, and hands out assignments. Someone might hear of some girl who suddenly starts to spend big. Occasionally he produces a banknote and passes it under the table; he does not ask for a receipt.

The usual time-tested methods.

And he begins to see the outline of a well-defined area, where his questions bounce against a wall of secrecy.

(Only much later will he learn the most significant result of this Tuesday night hunting expedition.

At a pot-house on Inner Horsemarket Square, not far from the house of detention for vagrants, a figure wrapped in dark rags is collecting the dirty glasses from the wooden trestles. She gathers the wine and liquor leftovers in one cup, and periodically raises the cup nestled in her two hands, before tossing down the liquid in one draft. One would have to look long and hard to recognize this creature as a woman. And even longer to believe that, as attested by her birth certificate, she is only twenty-five years old. Her face, even while guzzling, is covered to the eyebrows by a scarf; her nose is partially eaten away by the "French disease". She observes the Special Investigator from a distance. Her brain, in its perennial haze of alcoholic stupor, is vaguely groping to formulate some questions.)

Around eleven, Dajka comes across the porter, No. 56, whose post is at the cab stand of the former Newmarket - a hard-working type who never turns down an occasional glass of throat-scraping wine. Soon after this man with the overcoat, who seems to be a better sort, gets into a conversation with him, the porter discloses his revelation: the night before, he happened to see some very smartly dressed gentlemen hurrying toward the Inner City across the square under construction. And now his hefty wife has read in the paper about the break-in.

"Some!" Dajka swoops. "How many?" It is too late for the porter to withdraw into the carapace of his solitude. The Doctor's experience tells him that this is not merely the wine talking. Without creating a disturbance, he takes the man back to headquarters.

(But he does not leave unnoticed. The outskirts of the city have a thousand eyes, and the first pair belongs to the noseless woman. She grapples through this quagmire of alcohol fumes, tobacco smoke and human effluvia. "Who was that?" she asks the bartender. "The Special Investigator," answers the man off-handedly, as if bestowing a favor. For it is the bartender's whim whether she will be permitted to collect her unspeakable brew here tomorrow. Meanwhile, she vaguely recollects that once upon a time she used to be a woman. The thought haunts her in semi-lucid moments.

And what a woman she had once been. Oh, she had lived it up, during that momentary flowery springtime of her girlhood, back in that year when she was the enthroned beauty at the cash-register of one of the "Cats" on King Street. Barely more than a child, the dazzling King chose her as his lover. That was how he referred to himself, once, at an intimate moment. She did not ask why, the name suited him. But then, even before she had a chance to wake from her bedazzlement, he had already left her for some flowergirl. Within a year or so, she rented a room from month to month, then by the day, which led to the brothel, and inevitably, the street corner; then, lightning fast, syphilis. How many years ago was that? A hundred? Or merely two? If she only knew that half the police in Europe were looking for her sometime lover, she would eagerly tell her tale to the Special Investigator. Not only because of the obvious self-interest, but also because the seeds of love are quick to flower into the putrescence of betrayal.)

OPEN SEASON

"All right, my good man, let's go over it once more," the Doctor thunders at the reticent porter. "You say you saw some gentlemen. How many?" "We-ell," the manual laborer drags out the word, cursing the moment that led him to seek his glass of wine at that Horsemarket Square tavern. "Not that many." "And how many would that be? Two? Or nine? How many is not many?" Silence. "What time did this take place?" "Pretty late." "Late, eh? And how late is late? What time is that? All right, enough of this." He relies on his most severe tone of voice, the Number Three Interrogation Voice. "Decide now: are you or aren't you going to cooperate?"

The porter, disgusted, is compelled to offer some details. "It seemed odd that one of the gentlemen, he had a kind of swarthy complexion, Gypsy-like... well, dropped a something that looked like a crowbar about two feet long, from under his cape... Like I already told Your Honor..."

The Special Investigator is a level-headed man. In the midst of his daily struggle with human dullness, it interests him that this simple working man had taken the trouble to note something like this. It would be an unspeakable mistake to scare him away now. "So what did you think, my friend?" he asks, lethargically. "What was your thought at the time? Where were these fine gentlemen hurrying, with that crowbar? To a tea-party?"

Let's see now. Two or three, possibly more, men dressed in black on the night of the break-in. One of them has an olive complexion and dark eyes, probably a foreigner. They seemed to be heading toward the jewelry store, toward the Inner City from the direction of outer areas of Pest. Possibly.

Taking pen and ink, he enters in his notebook: BA NN 210 (Zara. Odessa?) Dark hair, olive complexion (foreigner?). From now on, NN 210 and 211 will be two unmistakably distinct entities.

For the rest of the night, the porter will have an opportunity to go over, six times in succession, the rogues' gallery of photographs and portraits drawn by the finest police artists of

Europe. But he does not recognize any of the gentlemen.

If we get caught, it will be my fault. At this time I could not know about the early results of the chase; these will be related by Marton only much later. But I am well aware of my blunders thus far, and expect the worst. I suggest that we divide into equal shares whatever little cash we have left from our earlier enterprise, so that each of us will have something while we wait here perforce for mail from the Armenian.

The second day goes by. The more time passes since the break-in, the worse the prospects of the investigation.

Hooligans and law-abiding citizens, habitués of the night-clubs and of the street, are all laughing at the witty ditties that crucify the helpless police.

The tailor Knorr, as he will admit later, has a momentary premonition. But he decides this is not enough to go to the police. And who knows, if these people are really the ones... He is afraid. Emil Knorr is eager to avoid meeting his tenants in the hall.

Our goose is being cooked.

By late afternoon of this second day, the noise created by the journalists bears its first fruit. Dajka is able to hold in his hand an objective clue. It is but a fistful of mud on the pan of the diamond miner; it is too early to tell whether it contains even a half a carat of yellowish, industrial grade stone. Viczián, dealer in linens and fine underwear, plunks down a hard little roll of fifty brand-new nickel twenty-fillér pieces on the Special Investigator's table. Something has stirred.

Viczián remembers the man who left this in his store. He had purchased two dozen of the finest Parisian silk shirts, and it seemed odd that, although he appeared to be well off, he did not ask for the packages to be delivered. Instead he asked for the purchases to be wrapped and placed in his cab. He paid for them with crisp banknotes; these have already been deposited in the bank or sent off in the mail, and have disappeared on their tortuous banknote journeys.

The purchaser was a young man of well-proportioned build, around thirty years old. He could not recall the color of his hair. But he was certain of one thing: although at first glance the man's elegance was impeccable, he could not deceive the eyes of a gentleman's haberdasher - his outfit was put together from here and there, it was in fact, rather *vulgar*. The wearer was obviously not used to the finest in men's wear. His conversation indicated an educated individual. The lady who accompanied him was fashionable, possibly demimondaine. She had a slender, attractive figure, and laughed a lot in the course of shopping.

Dajka remains acerbic; the storekeeper understands the hint and closes by mentioning that his customer made cocky references to the bank holiday.

Ernestine, the cashier at the jewelers, identifies the roll of coins.

Those brand-new banknotes first had to be changed into used ones; the objects and papers had to be sold. Without those, the individual share of the loot is not all that great. If Dajka knew how many were in the gang, he could calculate it within a forint. The shares are equally divided. At any rate there would have been some cash, enough to buy the shirts and underwear. The Doctor is puzzled: what reason would an international safe-breaker have to spend twenty-fillér coins on the day after a great coup?

But it is no great mystery. The answer is to be found in the King's childish vanity. He could not control his professional pride. He had to rub it in, immediately, while still in the effervescent, ecstatic afterglow of the big job, hung over and not having slept. He had to show it off to the world at large: look, this is the kind of money and this the kind of woman I have. For in front of me steel safe doors and women's hearts both open up. I am free to do anything, and I can pull it off. And watch me get away with this piece of insolence.

I can understand his arrogance; I like this devil-may-care rascal whose heart is unbroken by police and prisons.

Dajka asks the storekeeper if the man had an olive complexion, or if his accent was that of a foreigner.

The answer is no, on both counts. Still, he now possesses a sort of description of one of the members of the gang. He is Hungarian, age around thirty, is of middling height, with a chaotic lifestyle, is educated (?). And under the rubric of accomplices, he writes: woman, young. (*Fille de joie?*)

He hurries over to Radius Avenue, to chat with the shop assistants before closing time. He walks around the district of the store, on the still hot trail. He strolls past the Two Lions Pharmacy, and past Keresztes and Hácha's hardware store. Later he will have occasion to think these steps over. Reaching the Gerenday store, he notices the small crowd attracted by the demonstration of the new electric safes. One clue thus leads to another. Very soon he finds out about the expert inquirer of the day before. The pair matches the description. The man had a beard and a mustache, with a "handsome, typical Hungarian face", as Gerenday puts it with the hardware store owner's simplistic view of genetics. On the basis of the kind of questions the man asked, he had taken the inquirer to be the engineer-director of the electric security system of some bank. He certainly knew all there was to know about safes. And with him, the young lady, whom the hardware dealer described as refined and beautiful. They departed in the direction of the City Park.

In a recently finished Inner City palatial mansion, Meissen porcelain dishes are flying at the Belgian cheval glass set in an ornate frame. A young princess of the House of Hapsburg is hysterical. She indulges in a fainting spell. An old muttonchops valet sets out to notify the organizers at the National Casino that his mistress - and master - will not participate in the grand ball of such a barbarous place, where the safety of the public is so lamentably ill-protected. The smelling salts! When she comes to, the princess starts to compose letters of complaint to her august relative, only to crumple them up and fling them away, sobbing.

The Special Investigator has every reason to hurry. He orders his men to produce that cab, even if they have to look underground for it. And let every man be especially alert, keep ears and eyes open, mobilize underworld contacts. They must find out who that giggling tart could be.

He updates his circulars by wire. Special attention must be given to railway junctions and to ports, where the stolen goods might be marketed. The smallest items might lead to the trail.

The roll of nickel twenties broke the ice; the sand in the hourglass is trickling at a perilously rapid rate for us. There is nothing I can do. It is the third day now, a Thursday. Knowing the planned itinerary of the Armenian, I am counting on a week's wait. We cannot stay a moment longer than absolutely necessary; it would be a huge mistake after a coup such as ours. Our man will have to penetrate the depths of the Russian Empire. Until then, the only possibility is to lie low, like a hare in the wheat, to try to blend into the background, and hope that the noisy pack of beaters and hounds will pass us by. But I know very well that the easiest target is the rabbit that springs up at the last second.

At noon one of the patrolmen who was on duty Monday night, while we were at work, shows up at Dajka's office. It is no accident that he is here; he was motivated by a subordinate's desire to make good for his omission.

He has circles around his eyes, he is unshaven, and he can barely control his broad grin. Tuesday morning he did not return home as ordered, but set out to walk all over town, visiting taverns, brothels, nightclubs, as he was, in his uniform, and he did not proceed with gloved hands. He slept three hours at a precinct station, then he was off again. He has brought his catch with him.

The man presented is a well-known pub-crawler of the twin cities, one whose special superstition is not to have more than one deciliter of wine at any one tavern. Thus the number of spots he visits each day varies from eight to twenty-one - he cannot avoid his fate. Well, during recent weeks he had come across the same two suspicious characters at more than one place - and of the two, the one with the scar on his face was no mere tippler.

"Scar? Where? What kind?"

And so the blue scar on the temple finds its way under NN 211 in the pocket notebook, with a question mark next to it. The witness on one occasion had been drinking next to the two of them at a Tabán tavern. The one with the scar was paying. Those two were constantly changing taverns. They were always busy discussing something in low voices, and they would always stop if one of the other customers sat down nearby. They could not have been up to much good.

"And the other one?"

The other one, the other one was probably not a gentleman.

"So then one of them was a gentleman?"

Sometimes he seemed to be. At first he looked like a dismissed day laborer, but later he started dressing much better. And oh yes, there was something else about the other one: one night he was wearing a weird yellow-striped vest under his jacket.

"A livery!"

A few words on the telephone to the police captain of the Inner City, regarding coachmen or male servants. Within half a day they produce the house servant with the purple nose. Desperately he tries to prove his innocent good intentions, mostly to himself. His pal was always the one who paid. His pal was quite refined. His last name never really came up. Nor, for that matter, does he have any other details about him.

The storekeepers at the Bazaar are questioned. Oh yes, the old house servant of the jeweler Hatvanger. Of course, he knew about the shipment. Was there anything wrong with that? And yes, they vaguely recalled the occasional porter: he seemed to be a humble, hard-working man, always properly grateful for each little pittance. He was of medium build, possibly fair-haired, with a beard, and of course the blue trace of an old scar on his temple. These porters come and go with fairly regular frequency at the Bazaar. They cannot identify him among the portraits in the album of criminals.

Hatvanger fires the servant, and the police are soon done with him.

Somewhere an unknown member of this gang is hiding out. Let us call him Scarface - NN 211. His identifying mark is entered in the notebook, among the other data.

Agap Kevorg, this tireless subject of the Tzar of all the Russians (and of Armenians, among others), realizes in the town of Salonica that he will not be able to travel on with the jewels toward Russia. During the spring many of the old contacts have disappeared; some steady buyers have been imprisoned. He is a full day discovering this, which almost brings us to grief.

Meanwhile back home we have too much time on our hands. It is open season on safe-breakers, and my colleagues are not going to lie low and wait. They are itching to get away. It is best if I anticipate this.

The Armenian does what he can in a night and a day. He negotiates with a shady jeweler, among others. On the second night he departs in the direction of Switzerland, without rest. There he has reliable banking contacts.

On Friday morning, while Agap Kevorg tries to nap on the red plush of a wagon-lit speeding toward the mountains and tunnels of Switzerland, back here in Budapest a lanky detective finds the driver of the cab. The couple got out with all their packages in front of No.1 Leopold Boulevard. The gentleman tipped a whole forint, and did not allow the driver to help with the cumbersome packages. They waited on the sidewalk until he drove off.

All those generous tips.

"So, young man," says Dajka to the skinny detective, who clicks his heels together. "Where should we not look for the suspect?"

"Sir, I humbly report, Sir!" the plainclothesman snaps to attention. He meditates with wrinkled brow. "At No. 1 Leopold Boulevard, where we were led by way of deception."

He is definitely one of the dimmer lights in the department; but the choice is not very great, alas. Dajka assigns the trail to the lanky detective, and this will cost him two precious days in the chase.

"This is a most responsible task. Do not leave a stone unturned in the district, on the streets or in the buildings. Check with every concierge, shopkeeper, newsvendor. Street-sweepers, tarts. Whoever is out on the streets and moves around. Or does not move around, but still has eyes. Beggars. Paralytics, the lame and the fake blind. Even the truly blind. They must have carried those packages away somehow. What else are you going to do?"

The detective shifts from one foot to the other.

"Well?" It is too late, the man has already been given the

assignment. "Well, you are going to check the hotels. You won't find them there. So what follows? What is the first duty of a law-abiding citizen, if he has a transient tenant?"

"Sir! I humbly report! I am to examine the registration papers in regard to the district in question."

"You are also looking for an olive-skinned, Near-Eastern type, who might have been seen with them. He could be an Arab, a Turk, possibly Greek, or Serbian, or Italian. Take a couple of uniformed men with you."

The lanky detective almost neighs audibly, and throws himself into the foray with flaring nostrils. His eyes can already see the document of his promotion to inspector, all framed on the wall of his furnished apartment in the "Chicago" section of Pest. Snapping a flurry of orders at the two constables, he spreads out a map, like some general before a decisive campaign. He divides the district between them, all the way down to the electric train line and the new House of Parliament. He has himself driven to the office where the registration forms are filed.

Agap, also known as Amber, has meanwhile arrived in Zürich. He has traveled by riverboat and cart, but mostly by train, at all possible speed. He checks in at his usual hotel, and after a few minutes spent freshening up, he is ready to embark on his circuitous path. Instead of the dimly-lit taverns of outlying districts, however, he is headed for bright grand cafés with huge plate-glass windows. This is where the finest high-class swindlers hang out, decked out in English tweeds and gold cufflinks.

He finds his man right away, and is able to wire us some money on the same day. In his telegram, couched in our customary code, he explains that the Stone is still to be sold, due to unexpected difficulties. He allows himself a day's rest; this will cost us dear.

Within twenty-four hours the money and the message are in our hands. Now our situation is considerably changed. We can no longer count on the original deadline; the period of inevitable waiting has to be extended. It would be expecting the superhuman for us to depart now, before receiving the price of the Stone, the true reward of all our endeavors. In this regard, I still have a few things to learn, about the importance of traveling light.

Time passes. Dajka asks for two reports per day from the group investigating the Leopold Boulevard district. The more time elapses, the greater is his certainty that they will come up empty-handed.

In the territory of the former Vilayet of Temesvár, on our eastern marches, the train heading for Budapest has crossed the Carpathians, and begins its descent along the rim of the Basin, which is edged by green forests. In a first-class compartment occupied by five travelers transpires an everyday occurrence that will soon come to have bearing on our story. Though an accidental touch, it will prove all the more consequential.

One of the travelers is a corpulently dignified nobleman of indeterminate profession: possibly a notary or a town council-man. A thick watch chain dangles from his vest pocket. Next to him, absorbed in a newspaper, sits Isaac Israel Baumgarten, a Jewish cutpurse. He is dressed for work, assuming the guise of a sociable provincial type, and he knows very well why he is sitting there, although at first glance no one could guess. Two other seats are occupied by the lively sisters, Julia and Maria Haldek. The underworld knows them as Diri and Dongó, though most people can't tell one from the other. For the record, Julie is Diri, and Mary is Dongó. The fifth passenger is Leopold Keller, firewood merchant from Máramaros, seated by chance in this compartment; he will eventually make an adequate witness. Each time the train rounds another bend the corpulent gentleman stares more and more avidly at Dongó's décolletage, which, to say the least, is most revealing, and seems to be slipping lower with each lurch.

The girl expresses a desire for some fresh air, and Israel, a most courteous young man, stands up to offer her his seat by the window. Now the fat nobleman is softly cushioned between the two sisters, enjoying a thrilling, enthralling ride over bridges and through tunnels, toward Nagyvárad, and past, to the capital.

Back home. The affair of the red salon still disquietens the realms of love for sale. The streetwalkers in the more outlying quarters are afraid to stand on their lonely corners after dark. The Special Investigator blames himself for the brick murder case remaining unsolved, and his restlessness drives him to The Kitty.

And there he sits, chewing his cigar. He watches us. We are waiting.

I am in a race against time, which is rapidly running out. For the past two days I have been walking around the environs of the various jails. I must get to know them well, for I might need this information, soon.

Night after night the Doctor is compelled to witness the flagrant violation of the edict prohibiting women employees at nightclubs. He no longer has conversations with Bora; she will not speak to anyone. She performs only her song, in her blue parade coachman's outfit, her hair all white. The Special Investigator's fury is palpable; I can feel it in my stomach. He is going to give us a hard time, I know it.

During one of the nights spent at the Kitty, his far-flung dragnet hauls in a big fish. This is when he receives the telephone message, as Marton was to tell me later.

On the phone, he appears to be weighing something, as he looks in my direction with his hand over the mouthpiece. Then he issues some orders. Later, a patrolman, his heavy saber clanking by his side, shows up with a telegram for him. Dajka reads it over, stubs out his cigar, and, as befits a gentleman, excuses himself to the Baroness, and hurries off.

I would have given a lot to know what was in the telegram. While he was here, he kept an eye on me, and I could also keep my eye on him, and somehow I found this reassuring.

This is what happened: the trail has been picked up abroad. The Stamboul police have wired concerning the list of stolen securities. The manager of the Salonica branch of the Ottoman Bank has reported that he is in possession of a bundle of Austrian state bonds. These fast-moving papers were traced through four intermediaries, before the trail was lost. The bonds are good as gold, easily transferable.

We at the Kitty are well aware that Dajka is after the safe-breakers twenty-four hours a day. Yet his persistence in the affair of the brick is worthy of Polar voyagers, or designers of rockets to the moon. His work is his only passion. (In this respect he is a twin of so many of my characters, who are otherwise very different from one another: my mountebank friend, Kodél, Kovács, the photographer, the Fráter, and Imola, most of all. This is the kind of person I want you to become when you work with your thinking machines, or whatever you choose for your profession.)

(NOW: THE MAP OF THE STORY. PLAY IN THE SAND)

I stop to pause over the manuscript of this account. It is crammed full of insertions, scribbled full of corrections. This is the only way I can do it: at first I put in everything that comes to mind, then I wear and tear, shape and correct. Later I start making a fair copy that is legible, and I start to cut.

Yesterday I went ragpicking for words discarded by my fellow humans. I would love to comb through the city, district by district, following a schedule, as some do - artists, the homeless, and whole families of Gypsies - on trash-collecting days, and bring home every word that is no longer wanted. Such as iron horse. Bawd! Stews! Counter-jumper. Carbide lamp and duck-billed pliers.

Imola once told someone, bragging:

"A lazier person never walked the face of the earth."

Meaning me. I was working on another story then.

While I preach to you about that gang leader Alva Ráz, who thinks all work stinks, I have no moral basis to do so.

Just take a look around my room. Foam rubber mattress on the floor, on it a sleeping bag, covered by a dark blue blanket marked U.S. (it arrived after Imre's death in '56, part of the foreign aid delivered together with the Mercedes ambulances. It has been worn paper thin, you can see through it here and there. But what has become of the Mercedes ambulances?) Piles of books, deposited in geological layers going back several years, some volumes left open, underlined, stuck full of slips of paper. I am terrible; I read nine books at a time, forgetting about some, leaving off others for lack of time or energy, until my work demands them. A lamp, on top of a cheap plastic chair. One old wardrobe. Collapsible Alba Regia bookshelves from Romania; when I started to buy them, they were 270 forints apiece; now they are 470, and you can't get them. Fráter gave me the desk, when he installed a new door as his desk atop two rafters in his loft on Upper Forest Row. My typewriter sits on it, Hermes, the Ambassador, accompanied by half a stationery store: pens, staplers and hole-punchers. (I tend to form emotional bonds with my tools; I am a fool for paper, or, as they say nowadays, a "paper freak". I must admit I hate this kind of usage; the other day I heard a friend referred to as a "work freak". This made me see somewhat more clearly that the basis of the material impoverishment of this country has its unshakeable foundations in people's hearts.) I also have a small radio, equipped with short wave; on the wall, a Styrofoam bulletin board, hanging in a burlap frame. Pinned on it are the seven telex paper strips bearing the map of this story, getting yellow with age - I am a terrible dawdler. And your faded photo, showing you in a sweatsuit, face all red. You are holding a numbered placard in your hands: cross-country training. A dry cleaning bill; a piece of yellow banknote paper with a black bull's head: Zoli Fogarasi sent it from Romania; it is his monthly beef ration ticket. A notification for a lung checkup. Maps on the wall: Budapest, capital and royal seat in 1896, and the city today; the two hemispheres of the Starry Sky; the familiar shape of Greater Hungary from the Silly Kitty period, printed by Manó Kogutowitz. A huge poster, a photo of the whirling Earth, with continents easily distinguishable, as seen by Neil the civilian, from out there. Coffee cups. I feel it takes too much time to maintain this whole mess. I do my honest best to get by with less and less time devoted to it. For the days when you have lunch at school, and the Countess Pálma does not come to cook for us, I have developed my canned food cookery. I have quite a repertoire. Goulash, Székely cabbage, potato paprikásh, fish stew and bean soup. The parameters of tinned food are: it should be tasty, affordable, and easy to prepare without watching. I improve on it by including additional ingredients, such as green peppers. We don't throw out much. Word has gotten out about my canned food poems; I have prepared a two-course festive Hungarian dinner for the distant relatives: Kerstin has visited here with all her light-pigmented kinfolk from Stockholm. After the meal they licked all their long fingers. When Piros, or someone else drops in occasionally, they enjoy my mess here. They say my room is very cozy. The smell is a mix of fine dust, paper, coffee. It is so Imre-like, says Piros, who has made good note of my first name, and loves to use it.

I must shower in the morning, so that the refreshing cold water will not be wasted on frivolities. I drink coffee only before work. I do not observe Sundays, Saint Stephen's Day, or April Fool's Day. I dread the year-end tumult of holidays, but I must observe them for the sake of all our relatives - your Vargha grandparents, your American uncle Kornél, Sarolta, the first Hungarian woman chemical engineer, etc. - and for the sake of the beautiful Kerstin, and finally, for your sake. The life of a bachelor with a child. Ours is a peculiar version, but no one is saying that we are all alike. I wouldn't like that.

I am willing to invest tremendous amounts of energy so that I would not have to work, in order to be able to sit down at my desk. To play in the sand, as Imola used to say.

A NEEDLE IN A HAYSTACK

The next day Dr. Dajka arranges for the special promotion of his assistant, Marton, to the rank of Inspector, and has tickets purchased for him on the Southern Express to Salonica.

He is the most qualified person to follow the trail to the Levant, and it will not hamper his investigation to have a better-sounding title.

That same morning, at precisely the same hour, police detachments arrive at the homes of known dealers in stolen goods, at more than twenty addresses. The detectives have instructions to request, politely, permission for a house search. The official witnesses are to be kept out of sight in cabs. If any of the fences insist on their legal right to a search warrant, the officers are to produce the warrant and proceed with a thorough search of the premises. This way they will not have to waste time on petty scoundrels.

Dajka expects a lot from this move, and his expectations will be justified. He will come within a hair's breadth of capturing all of us at once.

(Specifically, he would have caught us, had it not been for a woman. Everything always depends on a woman, and that is all right by me. I need that warm, curvy aspect of the world manifested in woman. Of course it is easy to solve the mystery of my yearning. Imola once told me, in a soft voice, "I am also your mother." This happened years before your arrival, years before she would become a mother. But she knew what she had to know. In women, I look for my mother, who is ever disappearing in the narrowing perspective of yesterdays; if I ever saw her, I do not remember it. So, as usual, our fate depended on a woman.)

I had already sealed our fate when, in spite of my firm determination, I did not mercilessly sever all of our under-world connections. We needed the capital. I was too lazy. And I was participating only halfheartedly after seeing that girl with the unforgettable mouth watching my fire-swallowing act.

Marton departs at noon, and Dajka conducts the rest of the day's business without him.

In the district of Kispest, there are two old-time dealers in stolen goods who prove reluctant to let in the authorities. At the house of the first, they find the brunt of the pilfered silver from Countess Szirmay's residence on Salt Square, and after a brief, vigorous questioning they are led to the source, who turns out to be Hlavnyai, the caretaker. He had tipped off his brother-in-law, who is a pro at breaking-and-entering; Hlavnyai himself had collected the silver. This explained the professionalism of the break-in, coupled with the unnecessary damage and upheaval inside the house. The household of the other fence yields only a large amount of virgin tobacco drying in the attic. The owner had counted on removing it all by the time the police returned with a search warrant. He was disappointed in this expectation.

The third place, as you may have guessed, is on the corner of Bush Street, where, at Rókus Láncz's house, the harvest is rich indeed. The detective in charge here followed his scent, literally. He happens to be the right man in the right place. In that era such a phenomenon was not unthinkable. As soon as he finds the smoking cast iron stove in the kitchen, he shuts down the damper, and reaching in among the cinders, retrieves the remnants of some securities ripped to shreds. He sends a mounted policeman to headquarters, requesting a specialist.

Rókus clams up and refuses to answer any questions. By the time the Special Investigator arrives, they will have found a large sailor's chest in the cellar. It is filled with false beards, various disguises and masks, plus some traditional burglar's tools: a set of eighty skeleton keys, drills, and key forms ready to be cut. Under the woodpile, cash in the amount of nearly 30,000 forints. It was unlikely that the old man had made so much from viniculture in Old Buda, that's for sure. The cellar also contained a piece of evidence difficult to move: a recent model Wiese-Wertheim steel safe that had been drilled and dynamited. All the details seem to match: the round hole cut into the safe's wall, exactly the same as at the Bazaar break-in. The steel disk itself has been removed and is nowhere to be found. Dajka has a cardboard copy made. The safe has been so abused that the expert can find no smooth or shiny surfaces for fingerprints. But Dajka discovers a few shredded remnants of green wool, and nearby, the whole pile of government-issue horse blankets. It all fits the pattern, linking the series of burglaries.

The elderly Láncz, who had retired several times from the business, remains incomprehensibly uncommunicative. Not only does he refuse to confess, but he insists that there is no evidence of any criminal act. To prove it, he produces a receipt from which the letterhead has been removed.

"This is mine," he states feistily. "Perhaps there is still some justice and respect for private property. Perhaps the royal police have not adopted the nihilistic philosophy as yet. Perhaps I still have the right to do whatever I want with a safe that I purchased."

The receipt is real enough. Of the dealer's name, only the final "a" remains. The purchaser's name is indicated as Aga Sadegh.

Dr. Dajka looks at the old scoundrel with a measure of respect. "Should I address you as Effendi? Have you in your old age converted to Islam? While you struggled, all alone, to move that safe down through the cellar entrance?"

"It belongs to some good friends of mine."

"Bravo. And who might these exotic friends of yours be? Where could I speak with them? And where did you purchase the safe?"

Láncz only shakes his head. "I am being harassed without just cause; I have nothing further to say." He claims to have retired years ago from dealing in stolen goods, and has been on the straight and narrow ever since. Since when is it a crime to possess theatrical props? And he refuses to answer any further questions.

Each moment of this interrogation is worth a fortune, and could lead to the recovery or loss of a fortune. Dajka knows it.

I am blissfully unaware of all these goings-on. I am in the process of sharpening my razor with long strokes on the strop, in the solitude of my rented room on Diver Street, near the new House of Parliament. I am preparing to go over to our headquarters, for the last time.

The summoned expert assembles the partially incinerated bits of paper with painstaking care. The mosaic produced is incomplete, yet much can be learned from it. There had been a letter and a foreign money order. The addressee is Láncz himself. The sender's name and address are missing, by a stroke of devilish happenstance. The amount is impossible to make out. The ink on the sender's form is less than forty-eight hours old. The letter had been written in modern Greek. Both had arrived *poste restante*; the stamp is Swiss. The Special Investigator sends a man post-haste to the Central Post Office, to inquire after any other money orders or letters from Switzerland being held there, possibly for a Greek addressee.

Luckily, my name and address have not been registered with careful calligraphy in the police forms. No one knows my name.

Dajka can now enter in his notebook, next to the Near Eastern suspect: Greek.

The recalcitrant Láncz is placed in irons. Out on the street not one policeman notices the veiled woman dressed in black, who had been gingerly treading the cobblestones rounded by centuries of wear toward that very house on Bush Street, but, on seeing all the commotion and uniforms, kept going without a pause past the officers. These latter were in the act of loading the baskets of evidence, and the handcuffed Rókus Láncz, into the paddywagon. The fence took care to look past the woman's head, giving no sign of recognition.

From here on the Doctor does not bother with the registry numbers in his album of criminals. He can keep track of his men in his head. There is the Greek, who receives letters at the Central Post Office, *poste restante*. He is probably lying low in some den of vice in the capital; possibly he is already fleeing in panic. And then there is the auburn-haired fop who paid with the roll of twenties from the Bazaar, and his little tart. And then there is the drinking buddy of the house-servant. Three, so far.

Láncz could be the fourth. Dajka adds, multiplies, divides. He is trying to bring the cash found in the chest into some accountable relationship with the loot from the burglary. But the equation contains too many unknowns. The selling price of the stolen goods, for one; then the amount missing from the impounded cash, and finally, the number of shares - the number of members in the gang.

As soon as the Nagyvárad express arrives at Budapest

Central Terminal, a corpulent gentleman runs fuming and screaming for the police. He introduces himself: he is a magistrate from the village of Jánosfalva in the County of Udvarhely in Transylvania, near the Homoród River. His perfect caricature of a figure is missing one thing from his splendid paunch: the watch and chain. He files a written report: while traveling to the Millennial festivities in the capital, his watch and chain have been stolen in the train compartment. The Goldwyn remontoir pocket watch and the long, gold chain, weighing sixty grams, were worth around seven hundred forints. He is unable to provide any information about the identity of the thief; he had been napping in the empty first-class compartment. He offers a fifty-forint reward to the finder.

"I think Your Excellency is exaggerating," thinks Isaac Israel with quiet satisfaction, while consuming his hot cocoa, *mit Schlag*, on the terrace of the Café Nicoletti. He clicks open the lid of the watch: the instrument shows seven past four in the afternoon. He slips it back into his vest pocket, together with the chain, which he knows could not weigh more than forty grams at the most.

Two men await the Special Investigator on his return to headquarters, as I learned much later, when I heard the hunter's side of the tale of this great chase. All of a sudden, after the initial silence, witnesses are crawling out of the walls. New developments from all parts of the field are breaking at a dizzying pace now.

One of those waiting is the proprietor of the tobacconist shop on the corner of Saint Peter Street. In exchange for his permit he regularly provides information to the police. Once his evidence is heard, it is only a matter of hours until the discovery of our gang's hideout in the capital, near the Circle train line.

The other man waiting is Muratti, the well-respected Greek café-proprietor, who has adopted the Carpathian Basin as his new home. The order in which the testimony of these two is heard will also make a difference. Much to my own personal good fortune, Dajka, who comes in following the handcuffed fence, sweeps past both the café owner and the informer with an impatient gesture, telling them to wait until this more important business is concluded.

But Láncz refuses to confess, and by the time the Doctor recognizes this, another half hour has passed.

Dajka, who knows very well that Láncz is not such a tough customer after all, now realizes that the fence is probably only playing for time. His conclusion is correct.

For in the meantime the woman in the black veil is riding a cab at top speed toward Pest; the horseshoes kick up sparks on the brand-new cobblestones of Margaret Bridge. She dismisses the cab on the Pest side, and hurries on foot toward an old, single-storey house just south of the new House of Parliament.

She pulls the copper bellpull, and the two words she tosses at me are sufficient to keep me from going anywhere near our headquarters today.

Fifteen minutes later Dajka admits Muratti to his office; the café owner receives priority on the basis of his social status. Muratti's report takes up another fifteen minutes, and that makes for an hour's headway, which is what we needed.

"Well, what is so urgent that it cannot wait? Let me hear all of it." The Doctor realizes that his voice betrays his impatience, and he makes an effort to control it. "Please take a seat."

By this time the woman dressed in black, displaying an instinctive slyness that anticipates the precautions observed by the black-shirted Russian bomb-throwers, again switches cabs, and is nearing the corner of Leopold Boulevard.

At headquarters, Muratti the café owner makes his deposition for the record. Six weeks ago a strange party of men dined in his private room. They burned some kind of drawing or plan in the ashtray. Having heard the news, he is following the dictates of his conscience to make this report to the police. The Special Investigator is intrigued by this, and begins to wonder whether what he calls the "Sándor Rózsa syndrome" holds only the lower strata of the populace in its thrall, or whether this immigrant from Greece has simply not absorbed the endemic ills of our nation. Perhaps the next generation, or the third...

Dajka is soon snapped out of his abstract musings by what he hears next:

"There were four persons."

"Four?" The Special Investigator is all ears now. "Are you sure of that?" And at once he has Rókus Láncz brought up from the detention cells.

"Was he one of them?"

But Muratti is firm on this point: they were all younger, lighter in style. He asks permission to call in his two waiters, who are at the café across the street. Now, under the experienced questioning of the police officer, the facts come to light: the Schwechat lager, the beef flanken, the innards, the dumplings. The auburn hair and blond beard. The man who looked like someone from the Near East. The conversation in a foreign language. One waiter speaks Slovak, the other understands French, but it was neither of these tongues. Muratti himself heard them speak only Hungarian. (Of course we held back the Greek in his presence; his Greek origins were common knowledge.) Each dinner cost about eighty kreuzers, the tips were generous. One of the four was hiding his face; all they remember is that he had piercing black eyes and ordered a *pörkölt* with macaroni.

"Hmm. Could he be Italian?"

"No, he was Hungarian." (Correct.) How did they know? From his speech; it was educated, without any regional accent, not like a criminal element. (A superficial web of prejudices.)

The café owner is an honest, sober, reliable citizen. His report is the first instance of the four burglars seen together. It is the first (and last) bit of evidence, of sorts.

So there is a fourth man, after all.

Muratti is dismissed. Now it is the petty informer's turn.

"So, what's up, old man?"

The tobacconist has an old-time customer, a certain Lápos, a watchmaker on Váci Boulevard. He is a timid man, and a terrible gossip. His modest daily entertainment consists of walking each afternoon down the corsos of Crown Prince

Street and Hatvani Street, when he usually comes in to buy a cigarillo. This past week he kept dropping dark hints about a certain "secret". If only they knew what he knew. But today he could not contain himself any longer. He claims nothing less than having been the landlord, a few years back, of one of the criminals wanted for the jewelry theft. Seeing the incredulous expression on the tobacconist's face, he produced a postcard, saying that the infamous safe-breaker had sent this with his greetings from a visit to Vienna, when he had been their tenant. And the tobacconist places the postcard on Dajka's desk. The faint postal cancellation reads: Vienna, Leopoldstadt, and the date: the eve of Epiphany, the same date as the burglary on Esterhazy Street. The facts that have led a separate existence all this time are beginning to come together. And the signature is clearly legible: Márton Jankó. (No, the King was not out of his mind. He was a gentleman in his way, and as such, having taken a liking to his landlord, sent a greeting card, when he traveled. We may explain this phenomenon in a number of ways. Social convention has changed since those days. That was a less complicated era, when the practice of keeping records on individuals had not yet developed its sophisticated forms. Today's robber etiquette is different.)

And, would you believe it, this summer the watchmaker's wife has run into the very same person, strolling on Váci Street in the company of a man with a kind of Gypsy-like countenance.

Suddenly the Doctor has a name in his hands.

He shouts for a cab. On the way out he thunders, "I want all available personnel on hand when I get back."

He does not waste another moment, but heads straight to the office where the police registry forms are kept. He calls in the skinny detective and his men who have been fruitless in their two-day search for the King's hideout. With a single move he eliminates all detours. He aims ahead of the flying bird, so that its flight will intersect with the bullet's path. He is ahead of us. The hour or two thus gained will determine the immediate fate of my companions.

He reasons as follows. He is after a gentleman burglar, who

most likely has monogrammed belongings. Underwear, shirts, cigar case, luggage - so that he must choose his alias accordingly. That includes his police registration form as well. He gives the order: look for a registration form from this summer, for a well-to-do, single individual about thirty years of age, with the initials "M.J." Occupation, indeterminate. Now, when I dictated the forms for the tailor Knorr (so as not to leave the least sample of my handwriting), I did not at all expect that the King had previously registered in town under his own name. Much less that he had been sending picture postcards, with his autograph signature.

The Doctor pulls out the three-year-old registration form at the address of the watchmaker Lápos. Given the name and the date this takes about sixty seconds. From now on he is not chasing a mere apparition.

The visitors to this year's National Exposition are myriad in number; there are many forms filed under each letter of the alphabet. They start with the Inner City districts, moving outward from there. Twenty minutes later one of the policemen fishes out the form: Mihály Jávor, age thirty-two, landowner, traveling alone.

"Pannonia Street," Dajka reads the address. He swears aloud. My God, what kind of idiots am I blessed with.

"Mr. Detective!" He shouts at the plainclothesman, and shakes him by the lapel. "Where were you looking for him? Who ever told you to look only on the one side of Leopold Boulevard?" He lets go of the man, already ashamed that he lost his temper. "Just because that safe-cracker got out of the cab with his moll on the south side of the street... That burglar is not a dullard, a nitwit... Then he would be holding some secure government job...He'd be a detective!"

And they're off. The lanky plainclothesman is reduced in rank to plain patrolman, on the spot. "Report to headquarters. Requisition a uniform. But before anything else, you are to give my order to the sergeant on duty: all available men are to gather for a raid at Pannonia Street, on the corner of Island Street and Csáky Street, near the Circle train line."

Before they leave, the other registration form is found, for one Aga Sadegh, straight from the steel safe receipt. Turkish subject, carpet merchant. The handwriting on the forms is identical; the signatures, in another hand, are illegible. Dajka does not even bother to write down the aliases, merely slips the forms into his cigar pocket. During the twenty-minute cab ride he attempts to create some sort of order in the flood of new data.

The procession of cabs arriving from headquarters rumbles past a man who is quietly slipping out in the direction of the Grand Boulevard. No one pays attention to him. He is heading toward a certain modest little seamstress' salon on Seminary Street.

Dajka divides his men quickly into two groups, in order to approach the building from two sides. He himself takes charge of the group advancing through the main entrance. A cordon of uniformed policemen encircles the whole block while Dajka, not waiting for the elevator, charges up the four flights of stairs.

(NOW: TELEPHONE PECKING. BUBBLES. GRAPE CLUSTERS)

I left off some time ago at my lighthearted idea, which was to be both inside and outside our story. Let us make use of our found instrument, the zoom lens. Here we sit at the edge of the world, our feet swinging in the ether; under the mulberry tree, on a rocky ledge; behind us on the meadow, children are shouting, and the ball with the rainbow segments bounces up into the sky. Life is a movable feast on this sunny meadow. In front of our eyes the drama unfolds: the beginning of all that happens. The Big Bang. If there was one.

These last few weeks we have been worrying about Auntie Pálma. She tires easily; she is close to seventy, although we are not supposed to know that. She fills out the social security form with her own knobby-veined, liver-spotted hand, after I had signed it. But the day before yesterday you, who are not yet a fully socialized being, stole her I.D. card, and read the year of her birth. I scolded you; it is her private affair.

Yesterday she was again unable to come. I had to report to my new workplace, so you remained at home alone. We invented the game called "telephone pecking" for days like this. The original "pecking" is a street game that I learned from Little Kovács back in the Barge Street days. From chest high, you drop a ten-fillér piece on top of another. (Nowadays, they play the game with a one-forint piece; tomorrow, with hundred-forint coins.) When we play, no money changes hands. It is because of some irrational puritanism that seeped into me, from long-ago preaching, possibly by Communists in the early 'fifties, and since then I do not play for money. It seems that we tend to hang on to these safe, basic points of reference. To play telephone pecking, instead of dropping coins, you think of a number from one to ninety nine, and the other person tries to guess it. You can come close, or you may hit the bulls-eye. We have developed this game in various ways. In the afternoon, we began to work out the living cross-word puzzle, on the telephone.

We were back at the Big Bang, at ten to the minus thirty-ninth of the first second, and moving on. For openers.

It keeps cooling, and swirling. Our zoom lens is at the universal order of magnitude, it holds in view the perceivable Cosmos. A billion years go by. Gravity pulls together plates the size of a myriad myriad galaxies.

That is one version. For in truth we can no longer be sure, now that we know more and more, whether the aggregates came first, and broke up into galaxies, or the galaxies were pulled together into plates. It is rather like the chicken and the egg.

The clouds of primal matter condense into young stars. The first generation. Thin clouds of gaseous hydrogen hover around young, hot suns that illuminate them by their ultraviolet radiation. These permeate the entire Cosmos. We were able to find out how stars were born, and how they die. The formation of life will prove more difficult to comprehend.

Let us skip ahead. Change is unchanging. Billions of years fly by, like measures from a pop song played on a piano (summer street, a cushion on the window ledge, flowery, sleepy cobblestones, smalltown ground-floor apartment).

The white field of galaxy seeds glowing thick with dense suns. Quasars ejaculating geysers of gas. Supernovas bursting with pulsating waves. Proto-stars flaring.

The three degrees Kelvin residuum of radiation has been attested to by measurement, one of the progenitors of science. The other parent is refutability. (Perhaps this is the mother, it sounds more feminine.)

And right here in the Beginning, the frailty of human knowledge is unable to account for the initial ten to the minus thirty-ninth of a second.

But that is not all. If we omit a part, this destroys the courage and confidence of knowing the whole; we shall never know if the final explanation is not precisely at that spot.

The other day scientists found dark segments of space with a diameter of one hundred fifty million light years. These are gigantic empty bubbles that contain something only on their outer membranes - that is, something that we may conceive of.

The absence of matter urges us to ask the question: is this version of it, of which we are made, the only one? And does it matter at all?

Nowadays, another hypothesis is being worked out: perhaps the Cosmos is made of an infinite series of smaller universes, each with its own physical laws and own kind of space-time. Our kind of life is possible in our universe. These Universes expanded at different rates in the Original Fragment. Like a giant cluster of all kinds of different grapes that hang every which way in nothingness, with new ones being created all the time, even as ours was. From the outside they appear to be small black holes, and they do not exclude the already extant worlds. The Big Bang fits into this hypothesis, like a small box into a bigger one. (Or, to use a reference from Slavic culture, like one Vyatka Matryoshka doll into another.)

Now as to our own local galaxy. The closer we get, the slower the movement. The rest of the universe is heading out of the picture, the direction is outward. There is no evidence that we occupy the center of the world, so that everything is moving away from everything else. It is all exploding in front of our eyes.

So here we sit at the edge of the world. It is a promising early summer day on the ledge. On the tree that leans out from the rocky cliffside the mulberries are still pale, you don't have to worry that they will stain the snowy whiteness of your denim skirt. Next to us, the veined layers of the low rocky ledge sketch out the cross section of the mountain.

The distribution of our attention is finite. Even from the fraction that we are able to perceive we will only consider that shallow envelope between two spherical shells around a yellow dwarf star, where carbon-based, oxygen-consuming life forms are able to survive: the paramecium with its cilia, equisetum, the Tyrannical Dragon King, and the dog Adu at No. 7 Spindle Street. One tiny little segment. Within it, more specifically, those areas where humans are living: Black Grandpa in his gully, Selim the Tatar, the civilian Neil Armstrong. And really and truly we are interested in the moment when we may catch a first glimpse of this, our Basin sheltered by the nearly perfect oval of the Carpathians, a place that possesses every sign of being able to support the peaceful, productive existence of the population that settles here during the age of the great migrations. Mountain, forest, plains, milk and honey. Apparently. (Other factors, not visible at the first moment: we have settled in the middle of the highway of the great migrations, and huge ethnic groups are crystallizing on either side of us. We shall have rich immediate experience of them in the course of our history, more than we would like.) This is where people like us live: the King, the photographer Kovács, Imola, you and I. We speak this language. No use worrying about how this relates to the great whole. Let this represent it all.

And we are not even interested in this mountain-circled basin at all times. We are going to be time-bound local patriots, time-chauvinists, time bigots, to boot.

But hush, we haven't the time. Let us head home, quickly. The stardust is not yet quite settled, and we are already on our way toward the streetcar stop on Vienna Road. This is somewhat in contrast to that overall view with which your grandfather saw things that evening on the shore of Lake Balaton. Independent galaxies in the throbbing, pulsating infinity. Or, to be more precise, in space. Since it has not been decided if the Cosmos is finite or infinite, expanding or pulsating, or smooth.

In this aggregate there are elliptical, wheel-and-spoke, spindle-shaped, hooked-spiral and irregular galaxies. At one edge, in a space circumscribed by the Greater and Lesser Magellan Clouds, and the dwarf galaxies of Ursa Minor, the Sculptor, and the Dragon, there is a medium-sized system, a modest, slowly gyrating wheel of light. Its diameter is a hundred thousand light years, around four hundred billion assorted stars. Red giants, yellow and white dwarfs, just like in fairy tales. We are almost home now, in Old Buda. Measured in greater units, we are in the Milky Way.

Stars are born and are extinguished in a fireworks display of immense proportions. Illuminated interstellar dust casts an aura of glory around young stars.

Our heavenly bodies are arrayed in spiral arms around a central Seed. Five billion years before Christ, A.C.A. (according to contemporary astronomy). Blue and white stars in their youth witness the birth of our Sun. We have at last come to It, let the heat radiate, the preserver of all life and novels.

It flies apart, and it revolves. We are slowing down, cycle upon cycle. Like an offshore breeze, a billion years waft by.

Fiery fragments break off from it. They condense into planets. Quite a splendid sight.

Another circle. The Planet's crust solidifies and throws off its satellite. According to the present state of our knowledge, at that astronomical moment the Moon is parked right next door, so that a human, standing underneath, could reach it with arms extended, stretching a little. After a year the moon has moved another inch and and a half away. This is how it got to be more than two hundred thousand miles away, at which distance it shone silvery and lyrical at the time of your arrival. (We made quite a stretch at the time, so that we were able to reach it, and the first man on the moon crumbled fine moondust in his gloved hand in those very days. This man was not a soldier.)

Today I learned at the office that a computer in America
has discovered a new disease based on the symptoms of five
Haitian homosexual drug addicts. It was named acquired
immune deficiency syndrome, or A I D S in its English
abbreviation. It is hard to pronounce with our Hungarian
phonetics.

Coming home I told you that I saw Aunt Piroska, your
former kindergarten teacher. You were glad to hear this, but
you could not understand why I didn't say hello to her.

The truth is, I was not alone, and I was unsure whether a
seventh-year pupil's daddy was supposed to be running around
with a woman in the subway. So I chose to lie low in the
corner and pointed her out to the girl, as your kindergarten
teacher. I told her about how you used to jump over the
pyjama elastic stretched between her skinny legs, once upon a
time.

L'ESPRIT DE L'ESCALIER

The police raid on Pannonia Street.

None of the numerous law enforcement officers notice the
hired two-horse carriage waiting on Island Street, just beyond
the police cordon. Its female passenger is well-built, of medium
height. Not much more can be found out about her later,
other than that she was dressed in black from top to toe, and
wore a black veil.

Ninety minutes after the arrest of the stolen goods dealer
Láncz, Dajka rings the bell at the entrance to the Knorr
apartment. He can hear the rumbling of the steam mills in the
district, the screeching of the Circle train.

He finds no one in the rented rooms, but that does not
surprise him. The tailor did not see his tenants leave. He has
not heard the front door close since their lady guest left.

"Lady guest?" Dajka files away the fact and storms through

the apartment, leading the way. He finds the open window of
the bathroom, and steps out onto the outside gangway. He
rushes so fast toward the attic entrance that his men have
trouble keeping up with him. Upstairs, in the back corner of
the attic, his glance sweeps over the small metal workshop. At
the other end of the loft a vertical beam of sparkling summer
sunlight pours in. He does not need to look for anything else.
Dajka is already out on the chimney-sweep's catwalk on the
roof. Balancing at this dizzying height he reaches the attic
window of the neighboring building. He lowers himself.
Another loft, a corridor, again the staircase, at a run. In the
entranceway to Island Street he bumps into my two con-
federates. They had been cleaning up the attic workshop, and
this fine, ingrained habit that had helped them survive proved
to be their undoing. Their long dust-coats flap as they turn in
an attempt to escape the police cordon, only to run into
Dajka's arms.

With this, my options have suddenly been cut. Regardless of
what happens to the Stone, I am going to have to stay here,
for thirty days at least. Whether I like it or not. Our
contingency plan is in operation, as you will see. It makes no
difference that I know that Bubbles has someone to stand by
her; I am still unable to leave without her. I need her physical
proximity for my well-being.

Outside the police cordon, the black-veiled woman steps out
of her carriage and tells the driver to wait for her, before
walking away toward the center of town. She will have
vanished by the time the police arrive.

The two men clad in the loose, long dust-coats politely offer
their crossed wrists to the Doctor, for handcuffing.

Dajka would give a lot to know why these scoundrels are so
self-assured. But he will have to wait for that information.

They were obviously in a hurry, and were leaving without
any luggage. Each one carries a wallet stuffed full of good old
unmarked Hungarian forints, which is a hard currency
well-liked in the world, at this time. (But times will change.)

The Special Investigator returns to the Knorr apartment
with his prisoners, whom he tentatively identifies for his own
purposes. One of them appears to be NN 211, the drinking pal

of the former house servant. Dajka lifts off the man's hat and sweeps his hair from his temple. There is no scar. He sends a patrolman to find the fired servant. The other captive is remarkably good looking, medium build, auburn hair, blond beard. Hmm... Could it be? Dajka's heart skips a beat.

He calls in patrolman Suk. "By the time I arrive at headquarters with these two, I want the parties who have suffered losses there, along with the hardware dealer Gerenday and his assistant, Viczián or Wittmann from the men's fashion store, the cab driver, Muratti and his head-waiter, and the watchmaker Lápos and his wife."

He would, if he could, at once wire Captain Gioielli to send the night watchman from Zara.

He turns toward the one with the blond beard.

"Who rented these rooms?"

"I did."

"I did."

One speaks in a dull tone, the other in a sweet and noble voice. For one deceptive moment it would appear that they are going to talk. But it is only to the extent of one lie - they are covering for someone, for the man who actually rented the rooms for them. After a moment's thought, Dajka decides not to force the issue. After this, the safe-breakers refuse to talk. They stand in a corner of the room, quietly contemptuous, and look on at the search as if it did not concern them at all.

Dajka shows the registration forms to the tailor. Knorr remembers now: both were signed by the gentleman who rented the rooms. Or wasn't he a gentleman? It is impossible to know anything now. The man did not live here, and never showed up after that.

I took care that, had he seen me in the course of the month and a half, he would have seen only a shabby proletarian, on the only two occasions when I went there.

The house search is a thing of joy to the policeman's heart. All in one pile, he finds clues, corpus delicti, evidence of all sorts. The youngest Miss Knorr stands in the hallway, watching this upheaval with a face that turns from crimson to pale white. The more elegant of the two men gives her an encouraging smile. In his room there are three suitcases full of suits. Eight pairs of shoes, all of them yellow. His shirts and underwear carry labels from stores in Vienna, Budapest, Prague and even Saint Petersburg. The silk foulards from the shop on Radius Avenue are also there.

"Do these belong to you?"

But the King is silent, wrapped in his pride. The tailor's family provides the information.

There is a veritable collection of photos of beautiful women. Next to the wash-stand, a glass and a blue-and-white container of Odol mouthwash. His elegance may be cheap, but it goes deeper than the surface. An additional seventy forints are found in mixed notes and silver, and another roll of twenty-fillér coins, plus six remontoir pocket watches.

Each wallet contains thirty thousand forints in cash - precisely the amount found in Láncz's house.

After all our efforts, this is the take. One cheerful shopping trip to a men's haberdashery. And even that is gone now.

Dajka interrogates the two prisoners, one after the other. Who are your accomplices and where are they hiding? Does the Greek have a paramour, what is her name, where does she live? Who is the woman with the black veil? What is her name and occupation? Her address? Who signed the registration forms? Where is he? What is his name? His nationality? Where have you hid the diamond known as the Blue Blood, and the other jewelry in the House of Hapsburg consignment? How long have you known Rókus Láncz? Who dynamited the steel safe at Bush Street, and with what purpose?

Who is your representative abroad? What happened to the Austrian government bonds? Where are your tools and who made the passkeys?

Where were you at the time of the Idol Street break-in? The New World Street break-in? The Esterhazy Street job? Saint Petersburg? Königsberg, Bucharest, Nagyvárad, Nándorfehérvár, Constantinople, Munich, Hamburg and Prague?

Who was with you in Odessa? And in Zara?

What have you done with the Stone?

But the two specialists merely look past him with blank, frosty stares.

"Well, we can do without the confessions," concludes Dajka, turning toward the King. He makes sure he has a clear view of the other man's face. "We have Rókus Láncz in custody. And soon we'll have the last one, the Greek."

And the King's eyes, undeniably, betray a flash of triumph. Dajka has what he wanted: he knows that the unknown fourth man is still at large. The Doctor is a worthy opponent.

The amounts of cash are identical. All you need to do is take the total of the loot - the value of the Stone, the jewelry, the bonds and the cash - and divide by thirty thousand, to find out the number of perpetrators who will have to be caught. A simple, logical operation. The only hitch is that the total amount is something like two million forints. This means, according to our logic, seventy burglars.

Dajka sends the two criminals to headquarters under strong police guard. As he is not quite free of the superstition that thieves have their own realm and king, and language as well, not understood by outsiders, he gives strict orders that the two prisoners are to be kept incommunicado. Yes, in the same prison where Bora Clarendon enjoyed her brief incarceration.

In the Knorr household, little Marika gets to see the burglar's tools, the stuffed wallets. She realizes that the two handsome strangers are criminals wanted in seven countries across Europe. But she chooses not to believe her eyes. In her sulking silence the Doctor quickly recognizes the symptoms of one-sided loyalty and unrequited love. That safe-cracker is quite a ladies' man. Sooner or later Marika will have to accept the facts, for she saw how the tenant stood so calmly throughout the house search and did not protest against the rudest charges.

Dajka's job is to interrogate, which he docs. Again, we are looking at the right man in the right place. He sends the stenographer out of the room. Now the girl, heartbroken by the testimony given by her parents and her sisters, and, seeing that she could not damage the case of her heart's King any further, adds her own bit to the story of that Monday night. How she had spied through the keyhole and saw their guest with his white linen shirt. He had come home at a quarter to twelve. He washed up. The men were walking around, then soon they went out again. And, with bated breath, she might as well tell all, she spills the beans about seeing that drawer full of silver. Dajka tries to suppress his urge to curse out loud.

(The Knorr household is missing one white pillowcase; not even the mistress of the house has noticed this. Cut into strips, it ended up flushed down a toilet bowl into the bowels of the metropolis. It came from Marika's dowry. Eventually Marika was to give birth to three children, and had many grand-children. In the course of her long, full lifetime, which lasted until the last year of the Second Great Organized Slaughter, she was often to have anxious regrets about these twenty minutes that weighed heavily on her conscience, until that gray December day without any snow when, near the small town of Oswiecim, located in the territory of the Third Reich, she was herded naked, along with men and children, into a room with cement floors. Her skin could feel the excrement voided by others next to her, dying their horrible deaths, before she dropped the gray bar of soap and the towel under the showerhead that sent the hissing gas into the room. Her last thought was: could her testimony have been the cause of the conviction of that handsome stranger?)

The superintendent states that he did not let anyone in or out of the building on the night of the burglary.

Naturally. For the first task of the Greek had been to make passkeys to this building for all of us.

It appears that the tenants lived high. Occasionally late-night noises could be heard from the far end of the attic. The tailor and his family believed the strangers to be some kind of engineers working on an invention, a likely possibility in this mechanical age. But they left every place immaculately clean behind them. For Dajka, this is as good as a signature of the gang.

They often had visitors. Then they would closet themselves and talk in a foreign language. There was a woman in a black veil, and a young man last week. The girls say that he was thin and graceful; the tailor's wife states that he was awkward, and wore shabby clothes. Could they be talking about the same individual? The only thing they all agree on is that they did not see much of me.

And today the veiled lady came again. A bare quarter of an hour before the police.

Oh yes, Dajka has not forgotten about her. How could she have known about the raid? There she goes, always one step ahead of him, just like that fourth burglar. The laughing demimondaine that Tuesday at the hardware store. And the lady in black so recently here to warn them.

He will have his questions about her answered, but too late, alas, so that it will be of no help. I was to hear his side of the story, much later, when we talked about the great diamond theft in the spirit of our former ambitions, man to man, in the presence of his white-haired wife, Maria, and Chief Inspector Marton, who by then was Dajka's successor, having learned both French and English, doing his faithful best to carry on the flame.

Two plainclothesmen soon bring the cab driver from down the street, as a sort of period at the end of the sentence. He had been waiting there for three hours, as indicated by the pile of horse manure accumulated. It was a lady in black (who else?) who hired the cab on Leopold Boulevard, and has been keeping him waiting for three hours now. A soft-spoken lady, the better sort. Even now the cab-driver cannot believe that she would have skipped out on him.

One of the plainclothesmen combing the quarter comes up with the all-time treasure trove of detectives, the little old lady, who, having come to the big city, has kept her village habit of sitting in a chair in front of the building, taking in everything on the street.

I still got the chills, in the far-off future, when I heard the former inspector tell me about this. For the little old lady could just as well have been sitting in front of the entrance on Pannonia Street on that summer evening six weeks earlier, when a sad woman (Bora) had stared up at a window that grew dark, hiding the two entwined silhouettes.

However, thank God, she happened to be sitting out in Island Street, so that she could see the cab arriving, the woman in black getting out, and returning. Then, moments before the plainclothes detective gentlemen - in their hard hats and ill-fitting civvies - were secretly surrounding the block, a man hurried out of the corner building's entrance. He was carrying a smallish suitcase, and went past the gentlemen of the police, toward the Boulevard. Yes, now that Your Excellency asks, there was something foreign in his appearance. Maybe it was his walk.

The third man.

For the time being the interrogations are over; the Special Investigator can hardly wait to return to the attic, in the hope of finding further traces of this gang working with such revolutionary new methods. But all he finds are traditional, bulkier burglar's tools that were too cumbersome for them to carry away: an oxyhydrogen torch, some long-handled tempered steel tools and a bulls-eye lamp. These could not have been used to crack open the steel safes at the Bazaar or at the Odessa Savings Bank, nor the legally purchased one found in the cellar on Bush Street. On the floor of the attic he discovers minuscule metal fragments. On top of a chest, there is a home-made passkey that has been used only once. It will fit perfectly the jewelry store's back door lock on Huckster Street.

The policemen gather the evidence and pack things up. The Doctor will not discover the meaning of the white linen threads until much later.

In the stairway he has one last idea and he returns to the attic. He passes a hand over the top surface of the tie beam. The tool he finds is only a plain old crowbar such as you may see in any village hardware store, but it comes wrapped in a worn cape. I had shaken it out, but that didn't do much. Once it is spread out, its function is unmistakable: worn out in use, it is full of oil stains, ashes, metal shavings. On its shoulder there is a mended tear.

The summoned individuals all await Dajka upon his return to headquarters. Suk reports that the house servant has disappeared after his dismissal, and has no known address. But it is only a matter of time before he is found. The detective sent to the Main Post Office has also returned, with a letter from abroad bearing no return address. The *poste restante* window had proved to be a bulls-eye. The addressee is Andronikos Socrates, Budapest, Main Post Office. The initials match the ones on the registration form. Could this be his real name?

Dajka immediately requests and receives the prosecutor's permission to open the letter. There cannot be much doubt that it contains evidence in the international series of safe-breaks. It is written in modern Greek. The Doctor turns to interrogating the assembled parties.

The confrontations proceed quickly and fruitfully. The jeweler Bócz recognizes the gentleman who had entered his shop to make inquiries in the company of a wealthy Turkish man. Viczián recognizes the man who had shopped for shirts and underwear on the previous Tuesday, and so does the cab driver. The watchmaker Lápos identifies his refined former tenant who was such a free spender and devoted opera-goer; the hardware store owner fingers the man who asked such expert questions. Muratti recognizes both men.

Finally Suk appears, as if on cue, and leads in the ex-servant, now a ragged man with bloodshot eyes who has been reduced to spending his sleepless nights at the asylum for the homeless on Rottenbiller Street.

The Special Investigator reminds the man that no one is obligated to testify against himself, but the former house servant still tries to prove his innocence at all costs. He stares at Bódog Haluska.

"What happened to you, old man? You disappeared from one day to the next." For an instant the lookout forgets where he is, and bursts out laughing.

Several witnesses mention the missing foreigner of olive complexion, and the café proprietor recalls the fourth man who had piercing black eyes.

"Piercing," interrupts the Special Investigator. "I know. He eats macaroni with his *pörkölt*." Indeed he knows.

The witnesses are dismissed, only Muratti is requested to stay behind in order to translate the letter.

The Greek text is all about promissory notes, endorsements, mortgages and maturation dates - obviously a secret message in some pre-established code. A closing sentence in plain language informs the addressee that the writer is enjoying a spell of fine weather by the lakeshore in Zurich.

A telegram is sent to the Zurich police captain, containing five pertinent questions, and this will set the Swiss criminal investigation in motion. Another telegram is addressed to Ritter Szevér Vidffy, the Monarchy's chief consul in Zurich, who, exceptionally, and accidentally, happens to be Hungarian. He is requested to make certain discreet inquiries in the area about a well-to-do foreigner who is sending money to Budapest. One plainclothes detective is assigned to the post office, to wait for anyone who comes to pick up the Greek's letter. Whoever shows up is to be arrested. All this happens on Friday.

Dajka has the prisoners brought in and tries my cape on them. It is too short on all of them, including Láncz. Only the Greek is left now.

"Suk, my son," says the Doctor, looking up from his desk. (He has grown used to discuss the status of the investigation with his faithful Marton, who is away now.) "Make sure you remember this moment. If this cape belongs to that mysterious fourth man, then he has just committed his first blunder."

You, too, should remember this cape. The mend on it. Something keeps telling me that we shall have more to do with it; more, in fact, than with my entire career as safe-breaker, and all its consequences.

The Special Investigator does not yet know about my earlier blunders.

In the course of the coming days a familiar scene, the clash of wills, is repeated again and again within the confines of Dajka's office. Several times a day he has the two safe-breakers brought up, always separately.

Each time he begins with the same question: "Whose cape is this?" And he fires further questions with the rapidity of a new-fangled Hiram Maxim automatic machine gun, which, firing six hundred rounds a minute, at this given moment in technological history is matched in speed only by a Singer sewing machine. In point of fact the police officer is not so much asking questions, as he is delivering a message: We know everything, there is no sense in remaining stubborn.

But both burglars stay silent. They have not had a chance to exchange a word since their capture. Obviously, they must be following the lines of some plan they had all agreed upon.

On the third day the Safe King waits until the familiar rapid-fire series of questions is over, and then he makes a request. The only food he has been given thus far is dry bread and warmed-over soup. He objects to such treatment and demands to be transferred from the dungeons at police headquarters.

For the first time in the course of this case, Dajka laughs out loud, at this peculiar mixture of cheokiness and righteous indignation. He tells the burglar that after he confesses he will be transferred to the Pest Regional Penitentiary where the inmates receive much better treatment.

Meanwhile Inspector Marton has arrived in Salonica, from where he sends a telegram. His Turkish colleagues were waiting for him at the station with the latest results: one of the smaller items has turned up in Port Said, at a dockside tavern. It is an earring belonging to the lady cashier at the jewelry store, who had left it for the night in the iron box in one of the drawers. Also in Port Said, a jeweler was offered a valuable gold watch set with a flat emerald.

In Salonica, it is impossible to find out more about the source of the watch. However, the recently promoted Hungarian police inspector is able to confront the incriminated branch manager of the Ottoman Bank, and by 3 a.m., after threats, promises and repeated questioning, threats and promises he manages to talk to the bank clerk who accepted the securities. Since this is a significant transaction, the clerk recalls the details, once authorized by his superior. The seller requested the counter value of the bonds to be transferred to Lloyd's of London in satisfaction of a payment due that day, thereby preventing a lawsuit in the case of insurance payments regarding a steamship that sank.

Because the Austro-Hungarian government bonds were valid, the bank had no cause to question their origin. The seller was obviously an intermediary. He received the market value of the securities. Marton would like to know how much of the amount reached the criminals. The bank has its own limited but functional security service, and early in the morning they contact the secretary at the British consulate in charge of insurance matters. The seller turns out to be a usurer and illegal money-changer, whose sphere of operations is centered in Port Said. (Bur Said, these days.)

The Inspector wires home again, and, instead of accepting the hotel room of dubious cleanliness he is offered, he immediately purchases a ticket on a steamer of the Peninsular and Oriental Shipping Co., which, progressing at the rate of fifteen nautical knots per hour, delivers him at Port Said in three days.

Agap Kevorg, alias Amber, who has not moved from his Zurich hotel, is still unaware of these events. In the evenings he frequents restaurants and cafés in order to renew his social contacts. He decides to spend three days scouting around to see whether he could sell the eminent Stone locally, thereby sparing himself the trip to Russia. In this he is not motivated by laziness but by a desire to advance us the much-needed funds at the earliest possible date, so we can move on. The fate of my colleagues is decided during these days.

The Greek meanwhile is getting more and more impatient, lying low in the small apartment on Seminary Street. Whenever a customer shows up for a fitting, he has to hide in an alcove behind a curtain, and his sole consolation is the occasional piquant glimpse he gleans. He ponders the situation and hesitates. By Monday evening, when Inspector Marton is boarding the steamship in Salonica, and Agap Kevorg is attending an art patron's salon in evening wear, he has had enough. He leaves the small suitcase in Lori's care.

"I'll be back for it. I won't be gone long."

And he sets out in the direction of the Inner City.

The Doctor again explains to his two prisoners that it makes precious little difference whether they confess or not. In court it will be up the the royal prosecutor, anyway, to prove their crime, and they have enough material evidence for that. The money order with the appropriate date, the cash which they cannot account for, the burglary tools, the dynamited safe. The roll of twenty-fillér coins. The correspondence between the labels on the King's clothes and the itinerary of the series of safe-breaks, from Idol Street, with a detour in Saint Petersburg, all the way to Huckster Street.

Then there are the witnesses' depositions.

The prisoners do not admit to anything; they do not protest and do not deny.

At the window of the post office where *posto restante* is handled, a man with a bowler hat sits motionlessly behind the clerk. He is nearly dozing off.

"Miss...please, for this name..." Pause. "...is there any mail?" Only after some delay is the detective's attention awakened by the puny voice. Over the past few, seemingly endless days he has heard hundreds of names and code-words, and now, nothing. He looks up lazily, and sees that the clerk is reading a slip of paper in front of her. She searches, and is already handing out the letter when the undercover man wakes up, and, almost straddling the girl's lap, cranes his neck toward the slip of paper bearing the name of Andronikos Socrates, in large capital letters. Like a rattlesnake's head, his hand darts out through the office window, grasping the thin withdrawing wrist in a vice-like grip. Only then does his head follow, his hat knocked down in the process, as he crooks his neck out through the low window, to size up his prey. It is a dusty little ragamuffin who sends up a deafening bawl upon being grabbed, thus delaying the first intelligible word that can be pried from him. While his right hand does not loosen its relentless squeeze, the detective's left hand is groping for the police whistle at the end of a deceptively elegant watch chain. The prolonged, ear-splitting blast sends into headlong flight the furtive figure taking shelter in a shadowy entranceway opposite the post office. He settles into a loping catlike stride, just another busy citizen among so many others. In two minutes he is hurrying along the sidewalk of St. Peter Street, hoping to reach the security of the dim districts around Kerepesi Road. In the surrounding streets police whistles echo from every direction of the compass. The chase is on.

The street urchin, whose face is soaked in tears, between two hiccupy fits of crying manages to stammer that he was given twenty fillérs by a nice gentleman to bring out his letter. He was wearing a monocle, and a bowler hat, and he must have had a toothache because he was holding a large white handkerchief to his face. The urchin is let go, and the detective, seeing the boy's mouth turn down when his coin is impounded, gives him another twenty-fillér piece in its place.

A ring of shrill police whistles draws in around Socrates. He panics and breaks into a run. Now the circle of beaters closes on the quarry. Another whistle, a loud shout, and a passerby starts running after him. He falls down, and two people, a stolid bourgeois and a shoemaker's apprentice jump on him, without regard to class distinctions. (They have not yet learned about those.) They are motivated only by the spirit of the hunt, which has triumphed over the "Sándor Rózsa syndrome". One sits on his head, the other on his feet, until the first policeman runs up.

As soon as Dajka has the Greek in front of him, he makes him try on the oil-stained, besmirched cape. One glance is enough to see that it was made for a shorter but more broad-shouldered figure. He is therefore in possession of concrete evidence of the existence, somewhere out there, of a fourth member of the gang. Somebody had to wear this cape at the time of the burglary.

The Special Investigator is at the point of making a prediction in front of his men: watch, this scoundrel is going to have thirty thousand forints on him. He manages to control his childish impulse, saving himself some embarrassment. The Greek has only a few pennies on him. The coin he gave the boy is untraceable.

The new prisoner will not open his mouth until a Greek

interpreter can be found for him. The Doctor does not feel like laughing now; the behavior of this customer is too much like that of the other two.

(NOW: HOUSING DEVELOPMENT. PANGEA. TYRANT DRAGON KING)

There we were, sitting at the world's edge swinging our legs, watching this movie which we ourselves were the directors of. Let us get on with it, close-ups and panoramic shots, all in strict order. The Earth fills up our screen now, and from here on the spectacle will concern us more personally. You straighten up to stretch, and I can hear your hair brushing against the overhanging wall of rock.

You lean forward, watching the show with deep concentration. I, too, lean forward to watch. The Earth is journeying, together with the solar system and the Moon, along its own quarter of a billion-year circuit. The crust is solidifying. It is still not ours. The mountains have jagged outlines, slopes drop off steeply, no soil covers the rocks, and there are no clouds. Red and orange flames shoot up from the turbulent crust, blue-white mists hover.

Two more cycles.

A thick dark layer of clouds surrounds the sphere, through which the yellow dwarf's light cannot penetrate. Vulcanic gases spread over the lifeless scene. Giant geysers spurt hot water that instantly turns to steam, which, precipitating back into the depths, eats the rocks away.

Every two hundred fifty million years we pass through the poorly heated regions of the Milky Way. By now, our order of magnitude is geological.

Four more cycles. Mountains are formed and transformed on the dry integument of the Earth, where volcanos create pockmarks and goosebumps.

We have recently matured our plans for changing our

apartment. Things have been happening around us. Certain avenues opened up, others have closed.

This city has many quarters where I feel at home, where I have lived, or had friends or family who lived there. Many of the city's faces are known to me close up.

The Inner City, once surrounded by walls.

The environs of Upper Forest Row, where the buildings date back to the first Age of Reform in the early nineteenth century (and house parties are prohibited, because the timbered ceilings conduct the thumping of dancers all over the building).

The so-called "Chicago" section of Pest, where my friend Séna lived in an atelier-apartment on the former Elemér Street.

I know all of the quays, and my favorite section of the city stands where once a sawmill burned down: Old Buda-Ujlak.

Parts of Buda I got to know with Imola, and with you I have discovered posh Pasha-meadow, which, with the passage of the pashas, was more recently dubbed "Cadre-meadow". We got to know it not as cadres, however, but as ordinary mortals, with a room-and-a-half allotment. (Which is our just share, according to the current social order.)

And lately, the former Valero Street, quarter of ministries and printers, where all is deserted after Saturday noon, quiet and airy, just like the forested hills of Buda. It is high time we tried living in a left-bank housing development, willy-nilly. So now we shall move to the legendary Angel-land district.

You are growing apace; for years now you have needed your own room, so we had to acquire two spaces. We would have preferred to live on a real street, where one house stands next to another, with grocery stores and antique booksellers on the ground floor, and where streetlife is rife - but we had to settle for a concrete block housing project in order to get the space we need. But somehow we managed to find a magic forty square yard apartment, one that does not look like it had been built now, or here. It is still only a room and a half, our allotment. But here, your have your own little room; it is soundproof, and has a separate entrance. In this quarter, we used to visit Little Kovács in the old days, and Imola had her behind slapped by a Gypsy boy.

You are going to finish your eighth year in your old school, a half-hour bus ride away. Next year, for secondary school - or, as we say, "gymnasium" - you have chosen to go to the Arpád in Old Buda, where these days men with pickaxes are breaking up the worn cobblestones on old Bush Street. The Arpád is where Little Kovács went to school, as did the other three from our old street gang who got to go to a "gymnasium": Séna, and Pityu and Arpi Kapronaky who lived down by the Danube. My friend Bread studied in the same building, but he attended the technical school (which has been gradually pushing out the old gymnasium, built with contributions by area residents; it is the same as with the street names: some people think they can be taken away from us).

I make an effort to keep up with my friends' careers, from a distance. Bread is a professor at the Polytechnic. Pityu died of an early cancer; he had been a textile engineer (your grandfather Vargha had assisted him in technical matters). Rudi is a factory foreman; recently two days in a row our paths crossed on the Square, but he did not see me. I could not call out to him, because then he would have recognized me. Séna leads an existence on the fringes of intellectual life; lately he took a job as night proofreader at the Szikra Press, to keep his days free.

Three and a half billion, BC. That long ago. We could easily drop the last two thousand - they are negligible at this order of magnitude. But be patient; they will count plenty.

Long interlocking chains of molecules are popping up in the Primordial Soup of the ancient seas: this is life.

The first bacteria.

Seven tenths of the sphere's surface is covered by water: this is the Blue Planet. Single-celled blue and green algae inhabit the shallow seas. There is oxygen in the atmosphere. From here on we shall need a deeper focus. The biological order is inseparable from the geological. (To be followed by the anthropological, the historical, and the personal, in order.)

It takes two thirds of the Blue Planet's entire present lifetime for bacteria to become multi-celled (and compared to this achievement, the rest of biological history is peanuts - if we were to stay in this same order of magnitude). Although we, being multi-celled, are related to the living things of this period, and share a common history, I nevertheless cannot say that we were present back there. Not yet. My ability to identify myself with something has its strict limits: it starts with the first human being. And of course, what actually constitutes a human being is a matter of our own arbitrary definitions.

Translucent soft globs float in the hot waters. One cone-shaped mollusc is called *elegantula elegans*. It will take only a hundred million years from here until the appearance of the first fish. The observation of the world possesses its own inimitable gradient. Greater and greater leaps will require less and less of a time span. The components of these globs gradually develop a societal division of labor. On the surface, more resistant skin cells differentiate, the ones situated in front becoming more sensitive to the environment. We are well on our way toward Little Kovács's gray, the King's brown, and your own green eyes. The path is straight. (But, mind you, I am not saying it is leading toward some goal. Anyway, we will return to this field of ultimate questions, where we are lucky if we know enough to ask the right questions.)

Yesterday's globs now grow outer skeletons. There swims the ancestor of crabs, sea urchins, insects. The brain has not been thought of yet. Not even the tiniest little germ of a brain.

Nonetheless, our time is approaching: the Black Grandpa's, and Imola's time.

But before that, the time of the primeval amphioxus floundering about in puddles. The time of the first little mammals to brave the branches and create a new biological order. The time of the tree-dwelling mammals with brains and imagination to descend to the ground of the savannahs, so that we may arise, bipeds with high foreheads. And the Neanderthal woman, whom we, Cro-Magnons, will stealthily grab from behind.

Your time is coming, inevitably.

Back in the sea our distant relations develop an endoskeleton, a row of flexible hoops against which the muscles can exert themselves, and accomplish great works.

In this late, but ever more eventful period of biological history the first plants appear, and sink their tremulous root-feet into the wet patches along the shorelines. Their spores travel in the wind, engendering future generations. They learn how to survive on dry land.

And here come the insects. For thirty million years they are the undisputed rulers of the land.

At the front end of the fish's spinal cord, the first germ of a brain appears; in times to come it will grow to weigh one or two grams.

An ice age, one of many. The first amphioxus appears on dry land.

Reptilians. They are lords of the land, and have no enemies other than their own kind.

Let's skip. A single land mass has formed, it will be called Pangea.

Fractures appear in the land mass. It takes fifty million years for the giant sphere to show cracks here and there.

At our observation point the rock ledge hurts your calf muscles, and you swing your legs once or twice over the void. Your deep suntan sets off the delicate sun-bleached down.

The northern land mass breaks away from the southern. The sheep-sized grand-daddy of the venerable dragons, (eventually someone will name it *Lystosaurus*), lives in the south, on Gondwanaland, which will split up into Africa, India, Antarctica.

The proto-mammals. We direct our lens at them, and our speed decreases as the distance narrows. They devour the sluggish reptiles after the sun goes down. They invent care for the young - we might call it love - and they shall inherit the Earth. Don't forget that ruling life-forms come and go. Eventually they all pass.

The first mammal. A warm-blooded, quick something - our distant cousin. The middle brain has been built as a second storey on top of the reptilian brain. It is the seat of intelligence. This small thing contains the germ of greatness: some day it will set foot on the road to the order of mammals, a road that leads to the stars. It still lives in a world ruled by dragons, and it can survive only because it moves by night, without disturbing the sphere of the Seven-headed grand seigneurs.

Another half a cycle. Let us lean back, put on our infrared filter, so we can see past the earth's crust. Torn-off continents swim on a sea of molten magma; this act of our play is rich in dramatic turnabouts. India separates and heads to the north.

The royal descendant of our sheep-sized lizard is called Tyrannosaurus rex - Tyrant Dragon King. Its sixty sharp teeth crowd into a mouth three feet wide. Another one has a thousand teeth, and the Super Dragon (*Supersaurus*) weighs a hundred tons. They reign supreme.

The curtain rises on another act. The more audacious descendants of a small rodent-like creature climb into the trees.

They can live by daylight now. Their color vision, in addition to scent, orients them in space. The functions of the brain grow by leaps and bounds. Since the size of the birth canal limits the dimensions of the skull, the brain begins to fold upon itself, to increase its surface. You saw a human brain when your class went on a field trip to view an autopsy. Fold upon fold, but never a kink; four square yards of surface. One girl fainted, two boys threw up, and no one in your class is planning to be a doctor.

Next, Australia breaks off from Antarctica. North America and Eurasia separate. (No matter how you look at it, our Europe - notwithstanding thousands of miles of French railroads, a superabundance of Dutch harbors, and the geographic point of intersection of European roads at Bomb Square, the natural focal point of our story in Old Buda and the South-Danubian plain, highway for the passage of the steppe nomads - our Europe is still no more than the western tip of a true continent.) India has joined Eurasia from the south, pushing up the Himalayas along the line of suture.

At the edges of the savannah something ventures to descend from the trees. With hindsight, we will call it Proto-mammal.

Africa and south Eurasia bump into each other. The Mediterranean Sea dries up and a land bridge is built between the two continents. The bipedal animal, that is neither kangaroo nor a bird, is able to migrate from Africa to Southern Europe. According to one school of thought.

We might as well establish a foothold in place. The finds are sparse; only every millionth bone survives over millions of years, and of these, only one in a million finds its way into expert hands. Our Basin takes center stage, by playing a considerable role in the adventure of human evolution. Its northern region is covered by one vast swamp, the home of Piroska (vulgo: *Rudapitecus Hungaricus*) - a shared ancestor on the stairway that leads to humankind. A few years before your arrival and Armstrong's journey, one hundred and one fragments of her skull were discovered in a bog. The well-worn molars, the ossified sutures all indicated that this was an older individual. The absence of a bone crest at the top of the skull tells us that it was a female. The frontal ridge is not prominent; the orbits are large and face forward. The coronal suture has moved toward the back of the top of the head. Together with her Chinese and Pakistani companions, she signals that we - and I use the first person somewhat hesitantly - have arrived in Eurasia, to continue our course toward the unknowable.

Rain and river waters slowly erode a channel between Africa and the tip of Europe, and more and more water escapes from the Atlantic Ocean into the Mediterranean basin. The torrents wash away the soft soil, and in one fleeting geological moment, that takes a mere century, the declivity is filled with the Mediterranean Sea, while the ocean level sinks about thirty feet worldwide. Later, the coming together of Africa and Asia pushes up new mountains; the straits between the Pillars of Hercules (Gibraltar and Ceuta) are squeezed closed. In time the sea dries up, and the whole process begins all over again. As you read this, the continents are again building up the dams, creating mountains. They are in no hurry; and, like so much around us, they have no bearing on our human-scale everyday cares.

Six million, BC. We are getting closer. The rush of time has slowed to a calibration in millions of years. A change is afoot, perhaps the most significant in our career ever since that first single-celled life-form - remember? - had floated in the Primordial Soup. We are at the threshold of the anthropological order of magnitude.

Here we come to the creature that will inexorably evolve into a human by learning to share its food and experience with its companions, in the time-honored net of mutuality. Not in the least because of speech, such as it is.

It is going to thrive, and come to dominate the remaining dry land masses of the Earth, from the Eskimo north to the Berber deserts. Although you could also conclude, on the basis of the film thus far, that our arrival had been just as unavoidable ever since the first flicker of fire in the primal explosion - insofar as anything is unavoidable. Here we again approach the field of ends and causes, and ultimate answers.

We could decide to keep count from here. Or we could keep count from the Black Grandpa's time - it is almost the same thing. We may start with the Proto-mammal, as it sets foot on the savannah: about thirty million BC. For in the actual world changes occur very gradually, the differences are minuscule, and transitions always gradual and imperceptible. Beginning with the first clouds of dust and gas. Or, to pry even further back: starting with earlier universes, back into the infinity of time. And ultimately, back into our story, of prisoners dragged on a chain, of Piros, of the Safe King, and of you; that is why we are including the Black Grandfather and right after him, Neil Armstrong, who will take a look at the neighboring heavenly body, so that we may start at the *Beginning*.

No matter how we look at it, at some point we have to decide to call the creature human. The only difference is that one way, it takes ninety-nine point seven per cent of the story from the Beginning to our arrival, and the other way, ninety-nine point nine per cent. All I am willing to assume responsibility for is the capital letter. The Beginning. That's all. Similarly, Space, with a capital letter, and a few others. Among other things, the perspective provided by our instrument allows us to see our incidental role in the Cosmos.

From there on, the grammatical usage will be in the first person, because we will be talking about us.

THE NUMBER OF SHARES

Perhaps Bora is still waiting, and waiting in vain, to be incarcerated at the Márianosztra prison. In the meantime, she sings her number dutifully and nightly at the club, decked out in her blue coachman's parade outfit. I play the piano and keep an eye on the police officer. The man adds a sour note to our busy Saturday night. When he looks at me, it is obvious that he resents my watching him.

He keeps nosing about in the nightclub. The Baroness can hardly suppress her weariness when she catches sight of the Special Investigator's husky figure, appearing for the seventh time this week.

On Monday Dajka asks the police captain of the Inner City to find the hardware dealer whose name ends with "a", from whose shop the experimentally destroyed Wiese-Wertheim steel safe had been purchased. In the afternoon the Greek is led to Keresztes and Hácha's, where one of the partners, on being confronted, soon recognizes him as one of the purchasers.

Ritter Vidffy, our Chief Consul in Zurich, welcomes the investigation as a congenial, exciting fillip to his otherwise dull diplomatic chores. By inclination he is a big-game hunter and explorer. But he does not get very far, even when he decides to enlist his unadvertised contacts in the languid local nightlife. He travels from Zurich to Geneva, and from there to Lausanne, without results. But at least his humdrum workdays are enlivened by some action.

Back in the municipal office district of Budapest, it is early afternoon. The clerks are heading home for lunch, on foot, or by cab, and the quarter will become as subdued as when you will come to know it, in a later time. (Saturday afternoons as depopulated and quiet as the wooded hills of Buda.) Occasionally at an intersection where the visibility is poor, cabs, coaches or carts collide, accompanied by Whoas and much loud shouting. Any loud crash makes the officials with gold-braided collars in the Military Transport Warehouse take their eyes off their papers in the building of the former silk factory (Nos. 26-30). Out on the street a sudden disturbance ensues; tumult, shouts, jostling. The sergeant of the patrol that arrives at the scene finds two females embroiled in a scuffle, who chose precisely this point of the sidewalk of the former Valero Street to discharge the tensions of their chaotic, dissolute lives. They create a stormy havoc crackling with snarls, oaths, and screams. At this very moment Dr. Dajka is hurrying by cab toward police headquarters and cannot witness the scene; therefore he will not be able to identify the two women whom he had seen on many occasions in the past weeks. The blonde called Máli does not know how she got into this fight, but she does not care; after the first fistful of torn hair she is into it, full tilt. By the time the policeman makes his way through the ring of bystanders who are merrily egging on the two opponents, the women are so entangled in each other's hair, wrapped and twisted around their arms, that they cannot be separated. The other combatant is Bubbles, who had suggested the impromptu shopping trip to the neighboring lace and hat shops. The two women are embroiled in such a wild stalemate that they have come to resemble two young stags with interlocked antlers, who must perish of starvation in the woods, where their white skeletons, gnawed clean over the winter, will recall the scents of last spring when the snow melts. However, Home Guard Street is no wilderness, and the guardian of the law blows his whistle. Reinforcements soon arrive, and the two unruly females are bundled up as one entangled mass into a paddy wagon, much to the merriment of the gathered public.

I follow stealthily in the wake of the interdependent party of the apprehended and the apprehenders, far enough to make sure that they are headed, as expected, toward the Pest Regional Penitentiary where there is a separate wing for women in the penitentiary that is contiguous with the County Court House.

The judge on duty is faced with a decision fit for a Solomon. He calls for a county courthouse heyduck from the guard room, and one promptly appears, his saber ominously rattling by his side. Seeing him, Máli screams and swoons. But the razor-sharp instrument of death in the service of the county merely cuts through the middle of the intertwined hair of the two parties. Máli comes to, in a hurry. The two females continue to struggle with the masses of alien hair each is enmeshed in, while the judge, without further ado, sentences each to thirty days' incarceration for disturbing the peace and creating a public nuisance. So far so good.

(Bubbles was able to forgive me for the loss of her beautiful long hair only after it grew back and was long enough to reach her waist. By then we were sailing distant seas.)

Aboard the steamer, Marton sleeps through the three-day passage to Port Said. That Friday afternoon and evening he visits four of the toughest sailors' bars in the port, and has occasion to reject advances made by nine dubious virgins of either sex. He neutralizes one knife attack in a dark alley, consumes eight glasses of resinated wine, two shots of execrable counterfeit scotch whiskey, and converses with half a dozen unshaven individuals, at a total cost of six hundred piastres to our royal treasury. But by Monday morning he has found the Saracen who had commanded the tub known as *Queen of Sheba* at the time of its catastrophe. The Inspector, who had received his early training in working with the *Apaches* of our nascent metropolis, and whose broken English at this stage (unlike later) contains dreadful infusions of mangled Old High German, manages to accomplish his task by dawn, when he overcomes the ebony-black captain's resistance. He learns that the captain had commanded what in fact was a death-ship, and that on the day of the disaster Lloyd's had received an anonymous letter from a sailor who had been beaten by the captain. The letter provided specific information about the *Queen*'s dangerous condition, even enclosing two pages torn out of the ship's log. The amount of insurance had been doubled recently. The whole case was bleakly commonplace.

The captain was lucky; no lives had been lost. But he was also unlucky, in that before the event, ownership had been transferred to his name. He had lost his commission, and as owner of the ship, was liable for the amount of damages paid out, if he wanted to avoid the penal colony. But by then he had spent half the money on cards and women. He turned to a usurer. When the three months for repayment were up, he was due for the knife that finds the defaulter, even in the most out-of-the-way docks of the Levant. The offer of the stolen state bonds at half price was seized upon as a last resort.

"How much did you pay?" Marton swoops down on him. Quickly he converts the pounds and piastres into Hungarian forints: not a very difficult task, with ten gold forints to a pound, which is worth a hundred piastres. The bonds had brought forty-five thousand forints. They were easily worth the amount, and more.

When he makes the ex-captain understand that in return for his cooperation the Hungarian police would not convey the results of its investigation to the Turkish colonial service in Egypt, the captain, with some relief, scrawls a single name on a piece of paper, using his left hand to disguise his writing. (The gesture will nonetheless prove to be unwise, and this one word will cost him his life. The harborside characters in question may be illiterate, but they are surgical virtuosos with the double-edged knife that slides silently in the night. It was purely accidental that I later heard of the captain's death, for we and Agap Kevorg did not as a rule deal with murderers.)

Next morning the Inspector wires home the amount. Dajka will know what to make of it. The telegram also requests any and all information possessed by the Austrian or Hungarian police pertaining to Agap X (last name unknown), of middle age, straight black hair, oval Caucasoid face. Goes by the underworld sobriquet of Amber, or its local equivalent. Likes to pass for a dealer in Persian carpets. Suspected of trafficking in stolen goods. More information needed.

The police are on a hot scent.

Inspector Marton stays around a few more days, hoping to find the international fence who had purchased the Schaffhausen watch with the emerald inset.

Back home Dajka places a small question mark next to the

strange-sounding name. Around noon he visits the Department of Religious Studies at the University, to see a professor
who teaches Hebrew and other exotic tongues. What kind of
name is Agap? It is a given name, answers the professor, an
Armenian given name.

Two more telegrams are sent, one to the Russian, the other
to the Turkish police. (Dajka cannot send a telegram to
Armenia, for there is no Armenia. For your information, in
case you think there is no nation with a history more
unfortunate than the Hungarian.)

I still have to notify the safe-breakers that the girl, Bubbles,
has managed to be put in jail.

The next morning the guard brings a coffee cake for the
prisoner Jankó in the dungeons at police headquarters.
According to regulations, the sergeant of the guard cuts the
cake into half-inch thick slices. Not finding any files, money or
poison, he forwards the cake to the prisoner.

The King receives the message of the 'harmless-looking
coffee cake. To make the message available to its other
addressee, he sends a few slices of the delicacy to Socrates. He
does not dare to include Rókus Láncz and the lookout, who
are thereby cut off from us at this stage of the game. Láncz
and Haluska, any way you look at it, are simply left in the
lurch. We have resigned ourselves, somewhat unjustly, to let
them serve their few years in prison. I will have to make sure
that they receive their shares of the minuscule profits of our
venture.

It will be too late when the Doctor finds out about the
coffee cake that had been sent. He will question the sentry
who accepted the package, but without result; the man will
remember only that it was delivered by a well-dressed
gentleman such as you rarely see in the environs of the prison.
But he will not be able to recall any details of the man's
appearance. Dajka thinks of the cape full of metal shavings; he
would like to try it on this mystery man.

Yes, we shall put the good Doctor through his paces. By
now he is thoroughly tired of the procedure, but nonetheless,
with the dutiful obstinacy of a great interrogator, he puts the

rhetorical questions to the King:

"Do you know Haluska?" As he is used to not receiving any answers, he goes on with the litany: "Do you know Rókus Láncz, dealer in stolen goods? Do you know the Greek, Andronikos?"

"Yes, I know him," rings out the unexpected answer. "I know him." And a third "I know him."

"Hey, whoa, slow down!" The Doctor exclaims, barely recovering from his surprise. "Where are you running? One at a time! You know him. Which one do you know? How do you know him? From where? Since when? Have you been in touch?"

"Hey, whoa..." Now it is the King's turn. "Aren't you, sir, asking too many questions at once? Begging your pardon, with all due respect..."

It is not for the first time in the course of the investigation that the Doctor has an impulse to laugh. He also feels like putting his arm around the shoulder of his handsome prisoner, and saying to him, "Look, let's drop our pompous roles, my good friend. Why don't we sit down for a glass of wine in the tavern next door, and have a good old time, just the two of us, man to man."

He cannot do it; the roles have been cast.

"You are right, you are right. Well then, let's take it one at a time, from the beginning. Have you been seeing the Greek?"

"Occasionally. But only in the daytime."

"And the other two? What else do you wish to admit?"

The Safe King is talking. And when he talks, he is fluent, he is eloquent. He claims to be an engineer and inventor who also deals in special engineering items, and travels frequently. His mother tongue is Hungarian, his home is in Fiume. (For you, Rijeka, Yugoslavia. Your post-dated great-grandfather, Emil Gomba, was obsessed by the projected enlargement of our seaport there. He founded a Magyar Adriatic Society, and authored a volume entitled *The Hungarian Navy and the Port of Fiume*).

Lo and behold, the King is confessing. The Bazaar break-in was his work, for which he had prepared in the workshop at the Pannonia Street attic. He cannot speak for anyone else, he is not a police spy, after all. The night patrol went by every seventeen minutes. One of the patrolmen wore badge No. 157. (In case they needed proof.) He knows of no other loot taken besides what has already been found. Unimpressed by any of the depositions and material evidence gathered, he denies that he did anything else that was against the law. He knows about Rókus Láncz's dynamited safe. It had been the lawful property of the Old Buda viniculturist and he, Jankó, took it apart, out of professional curiosity. He had nothing to do with the earlier Idol and New World Street break-ins. Dajka places in front of him the list of a string of earlier safe-breaks all over Europe.

"Phew." The King emits a street-style whistle of respectful admiration. "Sir, looks like you have been keeping busy."

"Well, you haven't been exactly sleeping, either."

The compliment feels good, but the meaningful confession is still missing. The King claims that he has never seen, only heard of the listed European cities.

"You mean to say you've never been to Vienna?"

"Sir, to know Vienna, nowadays, is essential for acquiring the rudiments of culture. These days."

"Where are the jewels?"

"What jewels?"

"Stop playing the fool. Where is the diamond? Where is the money?"

"I've spent it all."

"On whom? Who is that wonderfully lighthearted lass who accompanied you to the shirt shop? The woman with the black veil?"

"*Aber, Herr Doctor!* Even if we assume the said ladies actually existed, how could you consider involving the names of married ladies in my dirty affairs? Break-ins, theft. Phew!"

"Where were you staying on the day of the theft on Esterhazy Street?"

"That depends on when it took place."

"On the night of the Epiphany. When you mailed this picture postcard to the watchmaker's family. Depicting an idyll of Leopoldstadt, Vienna."

"I was staying with a young lady." And he shrugs his shoulder to indicate that there is nothing more to be said.

And so on, a good deal more in this manner. The tools found in the attic were left there by an unknown person for safekeeping. Dajka interposes that those tools could not have opened up a double-walled steel Wiese-Wertheim safe. Is that what he thinks? Why, then, Your Excellency will just have to decide, am I or am I not a burglar. For those were all the tools used.

He admits only what was already known without his help, and not a jot more. The Special Investigator would actually be surprised if it were otherwise.

"All right, let's move on. Who did the reconnoitering for you?"

"I did. Who else would have done it? And Haluska, as much as he could. But he'll tell you about that, himself. You know all about it anyway."

During this unexpectedly cooperative session Dajka is assailed by the nasty suspicion that all of a sudden, the other culprits are going to confess as well.

He has the lookout brought in, but Haluska does not talk. Could it be...? Dajka now sends for a certain Greek nightclub entertainer, just in case Socrates asks for an interpreter.

His misgivings are justified when the Greek, although he has been kept isolated from any of the others, now decides to talk through the interpreter. Dajka suspects some stratagem at work behind the prisoners' behavior, which is most disquieting, because he cannot figure out how they could have possibly synchronized their act, and what it will lead to.

All said and done, the Greek's confession is not much more helpful than the Greek's silence. He admits to having been born on the island of Rhodos, and claims to be a dealer in tobacco and suchlike products. He has traveled all over Europe, always strictly on business. His permanent residence is in Ragusa (for you, Dubrovnik, Yugoslavia). From among his belongings he even produces a tattered document, which, deciphered by the interpreter, turns out to certify that Socrates, in his youth, was employed as assistant to the caretaker of the Rhodos lighthouse. His task had been the lighting of torches for arriving ships.

He admits to taking part in breaking open the steel safe at

the Bazaar, and to having made the passkey for the outside gate. He had met Mr. Jankó when he came to Hungary to buy horses. They have no other accomplices.

After this, the confrontation is a mere formality. The safe-crackers seal their reunion with a man-size hug, and the King greets his confrère in Greek. The Doctor still has not heard about the coffee cake.

That afternoon telegrams arrive from the Russian and Turkish police. The Turkish reply is negative. The Russians indicate that a passport had been issued to one Agap Kevorg, carpet dealer from Saint Petersburg, who frequently travels to Europe on business. He is currently in Zurich, his Western business headquarters.

The Special Investigator again sends telegrams to Ritter Vidffy and to the Swiss police.

Szevér Vidffy goes to work. With a name and other data to work with, everything is done in a trice. The above-named Russian subject spent the last few days at the Hotel Lido by the lake, where he is known as an old client. He claims to be a prominent investor, is very active socially, and has traveled on this very morning.

The results are wired to Budapest, and a Europe-wide search is instituted.

The news of the capture of the international gang of safe-breakers brings a flurry of telegrams from many European capitals. Courtrooms in several countries are awaiting their appearance. Budapest has first claim, as the native soil, followed, in order, by Vienna, Saint Petersburg, Constantinople, Berlin, and God knows how many other cities.

The results of the investigation thus far are forwarded to the royal prosecutor's office. Dajka indicates that not all of the arrests have been made. But there is enough material evidence for bringing a charge in the case of the theft at Huckster Street. Meanwhile, the investigation is to be continued.

The two precious prisoners are transferred separately, under heavy guard, to the prison of the Pest Regional Penitentiary. After all, they did confess, and the Doctor is one to honor his promise. But Rókus Láncz and Haluska are left behind; our ways have parted. We are unable to do anything for them. We will not be able to keep track of their immediate fate; for a long time to come I will not even know if they ever received their diminished shares. This is how they pass from our side, mothers, childhood friends, grandfathers, sideshow comedians, caravans, each in his or her own way. It is as if our course had been set by some heavenly clockwork with its own laws of mass and gravitation, obeying forces greater than ourselves. This also holds true for those who happen to be in our lives right now. In time, you too will lose your fellow campaigners, one by one; against this there can be no remedy.

The King and the Greek are confined to separate cells far from each other; the governor of the prison keeps them under close personal observation.

The handcuffs snap close on Agap Kevorg's delicate, pale wrists in front of the ticket booth of the Berlin Hauptbahnhof, just as he is in the act of purchasing his sleeping compartment tickets to Saint Petersburg. Our international representative denies everything, with the sincere outrage of the innocent. He keeps this up until the secret compartment in the bottom of his expensive, elegant suitcase yields the remaining ten Austrian government bonds, and, lying in its own velvet cushioned box, the missing diamond known as the Blue Blood, as well as all the remaining jewelry, precisely as catalogued on the list of stolen goods.

In Budapest, Dajka predicts that cash in the amount of thirty thousand forints will be found on the Armenian. He is only 500 forints off in his estimate. He still does not know why the amount is so low, and only his instincts tell him what must have been the number of shares.

Agap Kevorg does not talk. The jewels are sent by courier to Budapest, to be identified and returned to the owners. They will add to the growing pile of evidence.

It all fits. Kevorg, the high flier, finds his way into Dajka's album of criminals, complete with file number, name, nationality, description. This is sent out to the subscribers, along with routine updates.

With the Swiss consignment recovered and in hand, Dajka

can adjust his calculations. The key is provided by the ten leftover bonds, and within minutes the picture is clear. Ninety of the bonds fetched forty-five thousand forints' worth of piasters in Port Said. The report said nothing about the rate of exchange for the stolen cash. To be sure, the banker was not motivated by charity. But we may assume that the laws of the international underworld are generally the same everywhere, and hold true in the shriek-filled nights of Port Said as well as behind the plate-glass windows of grand cafés in Zurich. Let us assume that the going rate of exchange for stolen money or securities is two to one.

The great Stone never brought them a penny.

Dajka rapidly scribbles columns of figures on the wrapping paper of the lunch that was brought in to his office by Suk, as usual.

All in all Kevorg was able to liquidate only the one hundred eighty thousand forints in stolen cash, plus the Schaffhausen watch inset with emeralds - the rest of the loot was captured by the Prussians along with his person. Counting one half for the cash, we have ninety, plus forty-five from before, and forty, approximately, for the watch. That makes for a total of one hundred seventy-five thousand.

The Safe King is one. The Greek is two. The lookout: three. The two fences, foreign and domestic, make it five. And the desired answer stares him in the face: one hundred seventy-five thousand, more or less, divided by thirty thousand, is six. Six shares.

In Zara, there were four sets of footprints in the dust. The Armenian, according to his passport, was at the time sojourning in the governorship of Radomir. (Where the surgeon Medvedieff's home had been burglarized; his gold coins will be found by the Tzar's police at the Kevorg apartment in Saint Petersburg).

One of the culprits is still at large, hiding somewhere. He wore a sailor's shirt in Zara; he smokes fragrant cigars, and eats his *pörkölt* with macaroni on the side. On him, or possibly on the Armenian, the old cape, full of metal shavings, will fit perfectly. We shall have him try it on, the Special Investigator promises, stubbornly resolute. And he will prove to be at least partially correct.

Agap Kevorg's extradition threatens to turn into a three-way international diplomatic wrangle. The Russian police want him for earlier crimes. He is also wanted by the Swiss. For the time being he is held in a German jail. It might take months before he can be tried. The royal prosecution cuts through this Gordian knot, by separating its own case against the Armenian, and calling on him only as a witness in the present trial. This concedes the priority of the Russians' claim.

For a while now, Dajka has not visited the Kitty on Monday nights. Much of the torrential influx of filth that accompanies the city's, and the country's, prosperity has ended up on his desk this year. He has been busy cleaning up the backlog of cases.

Most recently two scoundrels of unknown origin, and speaking broken French, have turned up in Budapest and have started to recruit girls for Buenos Aires and Rio de Janeiro. The Doctor will deal with them mercilessly. He has always been aware that not only our great eastern neighbor is overflowing with *vengerkas*, but also many of the more distant provinces of the Dual Monarchy rely on us for the staffing and smooth operation of their *cafés chantants* and bordellos. The recently arrived white slavers simply remind him of these open wounds in our national pride. It could be said that he considers their presence as a personal affront. Such affairs as Bora Clarendon's career produce a raw patriotic grief in him. The accidents of geography and history combine to turn this into a kind of war of independence to which he can devote himself whole-heartedly, given the colonial condition of our nation. In his heart of hearts he raises the old revolutionary standard, and, without looking left or right, he rushes straight away to defend the barricades of national honor. In less than twenty-four hours he personally apprehends the two pimps. They are placed under close guard until extradition to the officers of the French colonial ministry. The two malfeasants have grown up, weed-like, on a Pacific island possession of France, and it is well known that Marianne looks askance at those of her *citoyens*, no matter what their origins, who besmirch her reputation abroad. Her wrath is considerable; and her possessions include a penal colony where stones and guano are the only crop, under a burning tropical sun. The pair will be eligible to leave there only after two decades of stone-breaking - and there has been no precedent for that.

And other kinds of affairs. Counterfeit ten-forint notes circulate in the city, adding a sour note to the brilliance of the festive year. The notes can be recognized: one of the three "Zehn Gulden" circular inscriptions is misspelled "Zenn".

Argay, the owner of the Hotel Europe on Viceroy Street, has disappeared along with a sizeable amount of cash.

István Kovács, a baker's apprentice, and two companions attacked and stabbed to death Sándor Schiller, who was staying with the former's sweetheart at No.15 Master Street.

The royal Court of Appeals sentences the ex-banker Vilmos Györy to seven and a half years in prison for multiple embezzlement and fraud.

The Baroness is introducing a new program at the Silly Kitty.

At the Octagon Place station the conductor of the electric subway train refuses entrance to the plainclothes detective who has made the mistake of identifying himself. He was chasing a pickpocket. The conductor is proud to assert the extra-territoriality of the subway trains, on which, as specified by His Excellency the Minister of the Interior's decree, policemen are proscribed from traveling in the line of duty. And the law holds. This way, until the one-o'clock closing of the train, there will be thirteen new victims, male and female, screaming out in panic: "My wallet!" But in the end all thirteen victims will have their missing valuables restored, with a slight dent produced by the inflated prices, these days, of a good dinner with a bad girl. For that night, acting on a tip from the Haldek sisters, alias Diri and Dongó, Chief Inspector Axaméthy's raid will bag the notorious train pickpocket, Israel Baumgarten, in the "Chicago" section of Pest. He had refused to pay the girls their well-earned share, and his greed proved to be his undoing, as the two shortchanged women went straight to the police. In addition to the thirteen wallets pilfered in the subway train, the police find in his possession the very object of the disputation: the gold watch and chain of the Jánosfalva notary. That same night Axaméthy takes the occasion to read Baumgarten the lengthy list of his known crimes, a litany that the pickpocket listens to with the modest complacency of all great maestros. One of his pockets also yields the flat key with which train conductors open compartment doors.

But he denies everything without batting an eyelash.

He claims that Diri and Dongó are blackening his reputation out of sheer jealousy because he did not spend the night with them. How can Your Excellency the Chief Inspector give credence to women of their kind? He should know very well that women plying their trade are capable of any filth.

But his strategy backfires. The detectives assigned to trail Diri are led to the trio's hideout (also used by the twins as a place of assignation). Here they come across an unliquidated hoard of loot from past thefts. The police find the train conductor, as well as the firewood dealer Keller, who will serve as witnesses for the prosecution. Under the weight of amassed evidence, Baumgarten executes a well-practised collapse and contritely confesses. He even admits that he himself manufactured the flat key, having been trained as a watchmaker.

The Swiss police conduct an investigation of the Armenian's Zurich doings: mysterious nocturnal trafficking, banking contacts of unimpeachable and impeachable character. He had received clandestine visitors at his hotel. He had logged innumerable trips to every country in Europe, as well as to Cairo, Alexandria and Damascus. He had conducted a great volume of correspondence via letters and telegrams. For the past two years he had been changing Hungarian thousand-forint notes at a local bank.

After two days of brilliant detective work, the Zurich bank clerk is rounded up, and he admits to exchanging the stolen money. All of the stolen one hundred eighty thousand forints is found in his possession. He had intended to hang on to the banknotes for a while, until they were not so hot. He was prepared to be patient, for this sort of work paid much better than a conservative bank clerk's salary.

On the basis of the evidence and the testimony of the damaged parties, after a quick trial Baumgarten is sentenced to a total of fifteen months' imprisonment, of which three weeks will have been served while in detention awaiting trial. Julia Haldek gets six months, Maria one year. As it happens, the pickpocket is locked up in the same wing of the Pest Regional Penitentiary where the King and the Greek are incarcerated under the strictest security. Here is that thread which fate weaves into the texture of our lives, but we are as yet unaware of it.

The princess is at last able to receive at her mansion the jewels that have seen such vicissitudes. She had been waiting only for this, and soon she storms off to Vienna in a huff. In any case, the Highest Wish had been satisfied. Bócz and Hatvanger receive the recovered portion of their money, with the exception of two hundred-forint notes kept by the prosecutor as evidence. About ninety thousand forints have not been accounted for, and the thieves claim to know nothing about it. "Three shares", grumbles Dajka.

The preparations for the trial are proceeding along the customary legal channels.

Dajka prepares reports on two separate cases, on the basis of the results of his investigation and the material evidence of the stolen watches and cash, the money order, and the dynamited safe. The first one, involving the Idol and New World Street break-ins, and the jewelry theft at the Grand Bazaar, has already been forwarded to the Royal jurisdiction. Material evidence exists only from the Bazaar job.

The second report is merely informational in nature, and concerns the series of safe-breaks abroad, going back over the past three years, ending with Zara and Odessa, stating their relationship to the jewelry theft at the Budapest Grand Bazaar. He points out the coincidences in railroad timetables, the careful cleanup in Odessa; the missing steel disks in Bush Street and at the Bazaar, and the basic identity of method from Idol Street on. The Special Investigator knows very well that this criminological essay will be pretty much for his own benefit. The material evidence linking these scenes is a thin thread - in the literal sense of the word. The material of the Bush Street blankets has been identified by the police chemist with the shreds of green yarn gleaned in Odessa as well as at the Bazaar. The witnesses' statements, the Viennese picture postcard, and the itinerary suggested by the shirt labels are all indirect evidence that would not stand up in court. And in addition: the signature. For the criminologist, it is the authentic mark of the culprit, the answer to all questions. But for a jury, it is inadequate. And the tools used at the Bazaar are still missing.

The Special Investigator receives a letter of commendation from the Minister.

But he is still dissatisfied. His struggle goes on against that fourth criminal, who is becoming more and more shadowy, lost in the mists. He cannot mention this person in his reports. And yet he knows that this man was present everywhere, including the Bazaar, ever since the change in the gang's method. His existence has only one - negative - proof, the cape that is too short for the others. But penal law and the independent Royal Hungarian court do not concern themselves with apparitions.

(NOW: ANGEL-LAND, GLOBE STREET. EROTIC LITTLE HANDS)

Two weeks ago we at last moved in here, on Globe Street. After the days of unpacking, this is the first time I am able to sit down in peace in front of my twenty-year-old Hermes. And now you have your own separate half-room.

In our movie at the edge of the world, it is six million BC, plus or minus a few years.

Soon we are knee-deep in the Pleistocene. We are obliged

to proceed by leaps and bounds in places where we lack fossil evidence. Our instrument, the zoom lens, no matter how rubbery and elastic in speed, time, space, depth, and notwithstanding its ability to see through skin and bone, oceans, mountains and the earth's crust - can register only *facts*. Being objective, its modus operandi necessarily involves a dose of skepticism. I will concede, without beating about the bush, that I prefer it this way, because of my personal history, makeup, propensities and prejudices, and that - for other people - there exist other approaches besides the factual. Such as: astrology, spiritualism, palmistry, tea leaves, bird or cow droppings, green humanoids on flying saucers, and various co-authored works, or even a direct line to the Man with the White Beard. (One day last year, six children in a Yugoslav village claimed to have seen the Holy Virgin. *She told them* who she was. She has curly black hair, blue eyes, and wears a gray coat. She appears to them every day. At 18.40 hours. The millions making the pilgrimage to the miracle site can look on with their own eyes as the children grow silent, and all at once stare off into the air. Q.E.D. Psychiatrists have examined the youths and found them to be normal. I had expected them to be - for otherwise they might have had the crazy notion of wasting their time by tilling the land. One fine day the Church will appoint a committee, which will not accredit the miracle. A bishop predicts that this hoax will be the disgrace of the century for the Church. A professor of theology calls it the "religion of kitsch". But tourism will thrive anyway. And the state, founded on principles of materialism, will act squeamish but pocket the extra income without hesitation. The Virgin wrote the message of peace in columns of flame in the sky: MIR. Because, after all, she speaks Serbo-Croat.)

These other kinds of approaches should be resorted to when they can be measured and proved. When photographic evidence will exist.

Some of them are accepted by truly excellent individuals. Certainly, this is not a simple matter. (Take the case of my old friend, the psychiatrist, whom I have seen so often at work. All disease is psychosomatic, she told me. Including cancer? Yes, even cancer. I had asked her that question about the time I started to tell you this story, and back then her answer had sounded to me like the Virgin Mary now, wearing a gray coat, speaking in Serbo-Croat. And still, I was tempted to believe her, for she is a great specialist, with outstanding credentials, in the literal sense of the word. So I decided to wait a while. Years later, at a university in Ohio, two studies were conducted on the students, one just after vacation time, the other during exam period. During this period of anxiety, it was found that the body's natural immune system, which is responsible for killing cancer cells, does not function adequately. This is a fact, one that had to wait until now to be observed.) So that I am not so absolutely sure about certain details. One can never know if one of the above methods is not, by some chance, groping at certain facts that are beyond the pale of human perception. The only thing I resent is that air of self-assured certitude! They gaze at a crystal ball, and come up with a ready explanation for everything that the rest of humankind has not been able to account for in the past several thousand years.

The Pleistocene is the initial stage of the geological Quaternary period. Around this time, we discover how to walk on two feet, thereby liberating our upper extremities for other purposes.

This week I received a completely unexpected offer. It has at last happened: now that I have been concentrating for years on telling you this story, learning my craft, and on top of that, forced to earn a living, have published parts of it as fiction, as if it were an invention - well, now the world has taken me at my word, and accepts me as a writer. (Although we may not know much, we do know that appearances are deceptive; generally speaking, I am not what they think I am.) I received a telephone call. "Would you be interested in a fellowship in the United States? It would be for four months." Before finding this apartment I wouldn't have dreamed of going away, even if I had received the most incredible offer. Now that we switched apartments, *the very next week* I am invited to the International Writing Program in Iowa City. I have been fascinated by America for at least the past twenty-five years. I had dreamt about America. From Iowa they write me that it was they who chose me; here at the Ministry of Culture they tell me I was a local choice. That could be true as well - the kind lady with the graying topknot who is in charge has known me for a long time now. So, this fall I will be traveling to the heart of the Midwest: *Corn belt, Bible belt.*

Our friends helped us to move, especially Fráter. He had a chance to tell us about his turbulent life, about the fate of his currently rejected short story. The one whose publication was prevented for years by two words in the dedication: my first and last names. (The Lord of the Texts, the one who vetoes publication, embraced me with a cry of "Brother!" in the elevator, on the same day when he issued the ultimatum to Fráter: the story can be published, if the dedication is omitted. We later concluded that it must have been the same day.) And still, *Habent sua fata tabulae.* Yes, tales do have their own fates. Now, two years later, the piece has seen publication in the other Budapest literary periodical. For we have a grand total of two: count them, one, two. It is almost an embarrassment of riches, when an author must choose venues. For two years the story could not appear just because someone did not like my name - that is one year apiece for each word in the dedication; why, that is nothing, even for *lèse-majesté.* And then you must consider the reverse of the coin, the benefits: the prohibition generates its instant moral capital, which accumulates on its own over the years, at a high interest rate. (Conversely: the compulsory never works out, not for any amount of money.) The ten-year veto of the publication of the Fráter's book also brought some credit to the author. Now this short story of his was simultaneously published in an anthology as well, by the Ten-Year publishing house, so that my name now graces two publications. You may have noticed how tall I stand when I get on a streetcar these days. Yes, we have two publishing houses: count them, one, two.

We were moving; we brought our belongings one by one to the elevator of our cinderblock building.

In front of the building lay a pile of pipes enclosed by a wire fence; the sign on the picket gate said Pipe and Conduit

Works. Pipes thick and thin made of plastics, concrete and iron, from one foot to six yards in length, straight and with elbows, glistening and rusty, a regular horizontal jungle. Off to the side, the housing project was still being built. Children were hopping all over the pipes, crawling inside the concrete tubes, moving in. I found it amazing, how many different kinds of pipes are required by the mechanism of human habitation.

Here comes a new era. The order of magnitude becomes biological and anthropological. The speed at which our movie is played slows down from the million-year to hundred-thousand, then to ten-thousand year intervals. We have appeared on the scene, introducing a new quality. The picture becomes sharply focused and objective. We have found our earliest footprints, preserved by the volcanic ash of Afar these three and a half million years. They belong to Grandpa, of whom you might not be very proud - even though we ourselves are already in him, for he is our immediate, direct-line ancestor. We are black, hatchet-jawed, and the rain falls into our upturned nostrils. Our spine is straight. We jabber and chatter. Our brain-pan is larger than the frontal part of the skull. Our arching forehead is developing, reaching forward, to accomodate the huge mass of neurons that is the gray matter, sitting above the reptilian and proto-mammalian brain. *The third floor.* The offspring are born naked and helpless. Fact. But they grow up to be mightier than the lion, mightier even than some of our tiniest invisible enemies. AIDS may still be winning the battle, but I place my bet on humankind.
Africa and Asia approach each other, and meet.
We roam in bands of twenty-five. The males swing clubs.
We are able to hit our prey at a distance with all sorts of missiles. When you take aim and score a hit, eons of practice stand behind you. By now we have learned that by striking two stones together we may obtain sharp flints, for slicing, chopping, scraping.
We arrive in a world of settled-in carnivores. We must take what we can. We eat the sick animal, the lost juvenile, even carrion. The women gather fruit, berries, roots, and sprouts. We invent the first conveyance, twined leaves and bark, so

that we can transport food for others. This is the mixed economy of the first affluent society. We help others, and ultimately this serves us well. (He who cheats and only wants to receive, will sooner or later fail.) There is a tension, an enormous contradiction between the instinctive selfishness of individual survival, and the high-minded virtues of sharing; this burden is a challenge for the human brain. According to one school of thought, this is what turns us into humans.

About a million and a half BC.

Our uplifted heads can see farther over the grass of the savannahs, in search of prey, or watching for enemies.

We have been freed from the bondage of the tropics. We learn to survive the sharply varying seasons: summertime plenty followed by lean winter.

During the Pleistocene we become the indisputable rulers of our world, as were the insects, early amphibians, reptiles and dragons before us. We continue to flourish in the southern regions of the Black Continent, amidst a hot climate and an abundance of tubers, fish and game.

The impression one gets is that of an uninterrupted triumphal march toward today's men in neckties. But geographic variants are formed. Some of these vanish in the great game of chance; our ancestors are the survivors. Our fossil evidence becomes more abundant, and shows that the human sphere widens. We could have come from Australia, or from East Asia. And, keeping Piroska in mind, we could have come straight from here, from the middle of Europe and of our story. (It is unlikely we are descended from America, where Homo Sapiens Sapiens had arrived ready-made, some tens of thousands of years ago, if we are to believe the Diego factor analysis of fossil finds, and the evidence of marker genes. Facts.)

There is a new power at work in the visible universe.

New things arise that could not have existed without us. We change the order of the world, and the world changes us. Imagination enables us to think of things that had never existed in nature.

In the inchoate, we visualize the form of a teardrop; we dream of ultimate symmetries in stone. We chip adzes. We exist in a broader world than that of our animal relatives. We must discuss this among ourselves.

All this is supposition. But, in contrast to Bishop Ussher and Sir Francis Galton, our suppositions are based on facts.

We guard the fire obtained from flowing streams of lava, from trees struck by lightning; we braise meat and roast seeds.

It is human nature to realize what is realizable and to reach whatever is reachable. We colonize the Blue Planet, in the process populating even the arctic circle and Tierra del Fuego.

We start our own fires.

Sixty thousand BC. At this order of magnitude we might as well subtract the two thousand years of Christianity and call it fifty-eight thousand.

In the Shanidar cave of the Zagros Mountains in Iraq a dead man is laid to rest on a bed of flowers. These people looked beyond the bourn that was final and impenetrable. They are aware of their own life and death. They attempt to provide, according to their abilities, for what happens after that. Fact. And up against this barrier, our capabilities today are not very different from the humans of the Shanidar cave.

Cro-Magnon signals the leap to today's human. (And who knows when and how the next leap will come.) The first skeletons were found about three hundred miles southwest of Paris, beneath some limestone cliffs, similar to our cliff here at the edge of the world. And it took a conspicuous absence of self-knowledge and a total lack of a sense of humor to call ourselves Wise Wise Humans (Homo Sap. Sap.) - an unbiased outside observer might have named us *Animal Stultum Stultum*). We are still the same animal as then, only we have experienced more, given enough time and work; this is how we came to fly to the moon. However, take a Cro-Magnon man to the hair-stylist on the Grand Boulevard, where Ildikó, that bewitching brunette can give him a shave and a styling, massage his scalp with her erotic little hands that drip with tonic, so that his sex stirs, and blow-dry his hair; have the tailor Kamarás make a suit for him, and you won't be able to tell him apart from his direct descendants cruising on Váci Street in Budapest.

At Tata a carved mammoth tooth has been found, worn smooth by caressing hands: a talisman. Sculpture. It is the Black Grandfather of paintings and happenings; we now possess the ability to make superfluous objects.

The temperate zone. The pigment that absorbs and scatters most of the ultraviolet radiation, is only a hindrance here, because it prevents sunlight from developing vitamin D in the skin. We lose most of our melanin, and regain the rosy complexion, which, no matter how our self-respect may suffer, is what you find under the fur of present-day apes. Our lips become thinner, our hair straightens, partially, here and there. To use another system of reference, we lose our negroid characteristics.

Our frontal lobes are more developed than our elder relatives' at this period; our thought processes are more sophisticated.

According to the fossil finds, we apparently replaced Cro-Magnons so rapidly, that for a long time we believed that in the very next biological moment, so to say, we clobbered and clubbed and wiped our slower cousins out, making use of our more developed forebrain, our ability to adapt, our human skills, our words. This is one school of thought. And from here on, the variations in schools of thought assume increasing importance.

According to this school of thought, it was the weapon - as its proponents, Ardrey, the author of the popular war movie *Khartoum*, and the Nobel prize winner Lorenz, plus Dart and other gentlemen, would prefer to call the stone implement - and the act of *murder* that made us humans. This would sever our relationship to the animal world, where the majority of spectacular fights for females and territory are decided by snarls and the baring of teeth, obviating the need to kill, which would make victory biologically too costly. This school of thought holds that we humans have an irrepressible aggressive instinct against our fellow humans. This is the reason for the organized slaughter, now and forever. Scientifically put: war is built into our genes. If one of us twists the thumbscrews, well, by golly, it is in his genes. It is something you cannot help any more than you can help the color of your hair. So if I have to kill, I kill; I make war, if war must be made. Let it be.

But I subscribe to another school of thought. I admit, this may be because of my personal limitations and proclivities. Perhaps the reason I never feel like killing is that my instincts have atrophied. Or maybe I am simply too much of a coward for this manly deed.

Let us pause here for a bit. Narrow down the lens aperture, close in on the human individual, let our zoom plummet hawk-like from the heights from where you can see entire continents. The way we had focused on the first enterprising tuft-gilled fish wading out of the water. The way we focused on Black Grandpa and his family scurrying across the plains. We have come a long way since then. The remains of *homo paleohungaricus* were found in our region. A man's occipital lamella, a seven-year-old boy's lower left canine tooth, part of the crown of the second lower left molar. Fire sites, early chipped stone cutting tools. These are some of the oldest human remains in Europe, next to the Heidelberg jaw. (Piroska had been only a stage along the way.) The name of this culture is Buda. A good name. Another find, elsewhere, is a Neanderthal adult jaw with teeth, a piece of a sternum, a few vertebrae, a kneecap. Fragments from the skull of a six-year-old child, little bones from the hand and toes. In the Remete cave, two incisors and one canine. This is what we have to build on, these are the facts.

Now focus on our Cro-Magnon self, back-lit, silhouetted against his by turns barren and lush, gray and green Stone Age backdrop. A man, a Cro-Magnon man. (I will not talk to you about this, only in writing; just as I don't tell you about the graffiti on the door of the men's room at the Hello bar, informing the reader about who gets AIDS. By the time you should know about this, you will be able to read it for yourself.) And let us not forget, we are what we are looking at.

He is crouching above the bank of the stream. He had nearly stumbled onto the alien female who is bending over the water. With aroused, wide eyes he watches from the thicket the unintentional invitation extended by the woman's haunches. His is the silence of the stalking hunter. He will have to press his palm against the woman's straining mouth only for the first instant; after that, she will desire the same as he. According to the present state of our knowledge.

The scent of springtime wafts over the distant hills. The tattered, high white clouds remind him that this is the frosty north. The water is close to freezing. There are stones and dry twigs near the woman, as she wades about in the swift current, impervious to its freezing cold. Just as he had heard tell about Them. She looks at herself in the water's creased mirror. The male is curious about the sight, but he dares not move, for fear of scaring her off. No, you would not be too proud of him: that hirsuteness carries the saturated, indescribable smell and crumbs of each campfire, flayed deer, and bed of leaves, from the past winter. He cannot even scratch his beard, for the least movement would set his prey screaming, and bring her whole band running.

The watcher is filled with hazy memories of his long ahaoo exhausted half-awake sleep in the safety of a forked tree, the roar of a cave lion, forests, waters, mountains, days and nights, ever since he has been running. He had strayed this far north chasing a herd of deer; he is the first of his kind to venture this way. Where They live.

The scent of the woman is raw and arousing, a mixture of the musty essence of the poorly tanned animal skin covering her loins, and a barely perceptible whiff of female moisture. She is a slovenly, hairy mass of flesh, with rounded mammaries. Her bandy-legged, thickened calves are almost totally covered by black fur. The male is aroused from the depths of the past. *Mammammm*, he mumbles in his thoughts. Silently he licks his chapped lips.

A memory: the death cry of a young hairy rhinoceros in the mud trap, surrounded by the young and old of his band. The fresh taste of triumph.

He cannot see the front of the alien female, he can only imagine her rough facial features. (And he cannot be aware of the pain felt by an existence divorced from instinct or of the lament for the loss of unconscious animal joy.)

He waits. He must make sure she is all alone. He has already reconnoitered the campsite under the overhanging cliff, where the males are guarding the campfire. The gray-streaked mane of the chief blends into the thick fur growing on his shoulders. His ridged eyebrows are thick gray and black, his chin recedes. Our man is downwind, and can smell their smoke, while they cannot catch scent of his gnarled hair, his sweat, the wood-tar smeared on his spear. The upper lip of the rocky arch has been blackened by the smoke. They steal their fire from wherever it falls ready-made from the sky. Their brats toss gnawed bones at each other, their females give suck while they crouch, just as this one is crouching in the water.

The hunter scans the horizon, turning his head in a complete circle. He sniffs noiselessly at the air. Silently he puts down his throwing spear, his elm bow. Now he steals up behind the female, the way he would stalk the most alert beast, and his first move is to cover her mouth. He glimpses her face in the shivering water. She stops struggling; she is not afraid. He scents her feminine secretions. He lets go of her mouth and grabs her pendulous full udders with both hands. The female, as she stands bending forward, squirms, wiggles and presses backward against him.

There are no witnesses.

With each such occasion, according to our alma mater, the fitter and more resourceful Cro-Magnon genes make inroads into the territories of the Neanderthal, ultimately in the direction of Europe and Asia. This is another way in which we replace them.

The disappearance of the Neanderthals is not the only dead end in mankind's long and tangled chronicle. We gave it our attention because it is the most spectacular, and since we survived, it addresses our personal guilt. It is just that they did not die out, to put it in a simplistic manner.

We are the results of hybridization. This custom of conquering man is easily caught in the act. It has contributed to the divergence and convergence of various human types, more significantly than traditional nuptial rites. (A tumble in the hay with Ibrahim, Helmut, Sergei and Józsi.) This has created such a civilian disturbance as to make the theories of the brilliant Sir Francis - and the practice of his less naive successors - downright embarrassing, with their postulation of higher and lower orders of humankind. All we can really be sure of is that we are boys or girls. (Science is refutable. But not all that is refutable is necessarily scientific. It is one subset within a set. As if we were to say that all that is cobblestone is junk, but not all junk is cobblestone.)

Mostly because we recognized the usefulness of their females, we have, with a lewd and rapid adaptation, kept them alive - and ours have been kept alive by them, and even when we/they have killed the fathers, we/they have left new life in exchange, to put it poetically. Here we are, Neanderthals wearing jeans or shalwars, having commingled and intermixed with, and absorbing/absorbed by, the Cro-Magnons with their larger frontal lobes. The invaders did not kill as much as they raped. They us, we them, it is impossible to untangle it all now. We us.

Thirty-three thousand BC. Make it thirty-one thousand, to be precise. Throughout the long, freezing Stone-age night the fire in the cave keeps away the flashing green eyes of predators. A new Ice Age is about to begin, one that will last until the dawn of historical times. The non-utilitarian objects are increasing in number among our finds. Goddess statues, with exaggerated round teats and buttocks. Pendants. Bayleaf-shaped, paper-thin blades.

These are complex tales we are retailing, help yourself. The Holocene, the present geological period. Thirteen thousand BC - now each millennium counts. The tribe's traditions, experiences and beliefs. Armed by the power of the word alone, we receive more ready-made information than all that was contained in the genes of the populations up till now. Greater power. The liberation of our creative powers is explosive. The visible world we live in has grown more in a few thousand years than in the two million that went by since we fashioned our first tools.

We hunt in groups. With a sharpened piece of ochre stone we make wall paintings of our enemies and our food: visual art is born. Caravans on foot cross continents, snowy or sandy wastes, carrying leather bags full of flintstones, salt, obsidian and tusks - and trade is born.

We invent the spear-thrower and can bag our lunch without going near it. We throw a cape around our shoulders, our feet are shod with leather. We eat better and live longer.

The ice covering Greenland is two miles thick. In Europe, glaciers hide today's England, Poland, the Alps, and much of Russia.

We build shelters made of stone, bone and skin, whatever is on hand.

We carve lunar calendars on mammoth bone; having discovered time, we rush on, unstoppable. Soon we shall come to the era of historical time, with its pyramids, great monotheistic religions, and Genghis the Intolerant.

The seven movers came in a closed, padded huge monster of a van; it was impossible to rent a smaller vehicle in this world of megalomaniac corporations.

Within minutes they dumped all our belongings on the third floor. They were bothered by all the cardboard boxes filled with books, boxes it took us months to beg from the supermarkets around Valero Street. (We received the most from the generous Chief at the Viceroy Street store that is still known to the public as *"The Russians"*.) And we kept lugging boxes so we would have enough. A year ago the Fráter came down with tendonitis of both hands because of all the typing. So he wrapped both wrists in padded bandages, for if he strains them again, it would never go away. He helped with the lighter pieces. Somewhere he has picked up the needlessly apologetic attitude of many who live off intellectual work, and outside he kept explaining to the movers the reasons for his disability.

"Man, would I love to be a writer," said one sluggish hulk with a big mustache. "I'd just sit at home, stare at the wall, and rake in the money by the fistful."

The Fráter had always known the limits of courtesy. With a broad gesture he invited the well-fed mover, who probably made twenty times the money he made. "Sir, maybe you would like to try your hand at constructing a workable structure for a novel. The field is wide open."

SIMPLER TIMES

Flourishing prison enterprises are an inimitable feature of penal institutions at the turn of the century. In the main yard of the Pest Regional Penitentiary the teamster Wlastimir rents a stable, and his employees may freely communicate with the minor offenders.

One of these courtyard workers has lately been straying into the women's wing whenever the female prisoners are doing laundry in the yard. His heart's desire is soon granted; he is able to flirt with a girl whose bedroom eyes have been haunting him for some days now.

When he looks around cautiously, he sees that the guards choose to be otherwise occupied; they too are men, after all, their hearts are not made of stone. So that no one observes the two of them when their playful flirtation takes a peculiar turn on the second day, as the girl hands the workman a small box containing one dozen gold napoleons and a weighty little letter.

And if a law-abiding individual - and in this age, we may assume that this species is not yet extinct - were to follow the well-stuffed little package on its wanderings along the much-renovated, labyrinthine corridors of the prison, he would observe that on the following morning the same workman is engaged in a clandestine discussion with Baumgarten, the train pickpocket. This latter does not need much persuasion; after half a minute of hurried whispering he is in possession of the letter, which is wrapped around a set chisel, a Swedish steel needle file, pencil and paper, plus some of the gold. This will remain his secret, which not even Dajka will be able to pry out of him.

Agap Kevorg is delivered at the prison under tight police guard and is assigned a high-security cell.

Now the trial may proceed. The King and his two partners await in isolation their upcoming appearances in court.

During the morning yard exercise the pickpocket, having tied his shoelaces, steps back into the line behind Jankó. He whispers one word. The King passes this on to the Greek.

There is no prison guard eagle-eyed enough to detect these transactions. The pickpocket is a minor master in his own right, collaborating with other master criminals in a professional matter. I recall Rókus Láncz with a bad taste in my mouth, for he has been left behind. Yet, when it mattered most, he knew how to keep quiet. And we cannot do anything for Haluska the lookout, either.

Three napoleons find a new owner, ensuring that from here on the second-floor warden will carry the messages for my men in the pocket of his uniform. Socrates sends back drawings of two strong but crude cell locks.

Most truly daring enterprises are sooner or later helped by circumstance. Baumgarten's cellmate is released, leaving him alone during the critical days. On the first night, working steadily, he manages to cut out a foot-long piece of iron from the grillwork of his window, near the upper frame. Then, devoting another night to the task, he files three short passkeys from the piece. He does not shirk hard work when the spirit moves him.

The impatient public in both Hungary and Transylvania eagerly await the verdict in this notorious case.

The prosecutor can prove only what the prisoners have confessed. The examining magistrate reflects, with a certain reluctant admiration, that one could also say the prisoners admitted only what could have been proven against them anyway.

Whatever we have left of the money sent by Agap Kevorg will come in handy once we are out of the country. And everyone we have to leave behind will get another share.

The verdict is of interest to judicial authorities all over Europe.

As soon as the Budapest Royal Court passes its verdict, the prisoners will be handed over to the Viennese authorities. If the Vienna and Prague safe-breaks can be proved to be their doing, then they will serve their sentences at Kufstein fortress, of historical fame. Only after that will they be able to return home to serve their sentences here. After all, this is not the

Hungro-Austrian Monarchy, but the other way around. So Budapest will have to wait, pushed into second place. After they are done here, the prisoners would be extradited to foreign courts, where ofttimes the laws are not so finicky about rules of evidence, investigation, house searches, and human rights. They can look forward to long and varied incarceration in a number of foreign countries.

Inspector Marton returns from his Oriental trip, empty-handed.

I sit at my piano, in the midst of an ominous, momentary quiet that resembles the brief truce in a fierce battle. The star of the new program is the freckled and red-haired native of Britain, dubbed Sheik Serengeti Abdullah Ngorongoro. The lights go out on the miniature stage, there is a drum roll, and he begins to show off the ghostly green images of his own skeleton, after which wonder of wonders - he reappears in the living flesh and blood.

The Doctor has not disappeared entirely from our view. He merely took a brief and hard-earned respite. One day he is back, accompanied by the police surgeon Komora.

"We had better sit farther away from the stage," the latter says during the Sheik's performance. He tells the story for the Baroness' benefit, and I am able to catch every word. It appears that not long ago learned Berlin physicians had exposed a sixteen-year-old boy to these Roentgen rays for a period of two weeks, in an experiment to find out if they could turn his skin a coppery hue. Indeed they could. This was last year. And recently the boy succumbed, after six months of horrible torments, to a mysterious disease. While the good doctors were carefully noting their observations, an illness resembling some kind of cancer finished off the boy. To make this more relevant today, imagine that there were no computers in the world last year, when acquired immune deficiency syndrome was first identified. For how many years then would it have been misdiagnosed as pneumonia, or Kaposi's sarcoma, while the disease had spread uncontrollably? This is what ignorance can mean, whether it is fated, neglectful or criminal.

Serengeti Ngorongoro is not aware of the fate of the

German lad who was turned into a redskin. Neither is the Baroness; and what is worse, neither listens to Dr. Komora's warning.

Komora and Dajka take another seat on the side, out of range of the X-rays. I, too, decide to move the piano with the help of the Hunchback. The Sheik had three more years to live, at the end of which time he died a horrible death. His cancer was conveniently diagnosed as TB.

The "Giddy-up" song suits Bora as a necktie does a cow. The deathly green flicker of the X-rays matches the mood of the gray-haired young woman's weird rendition, lethargic and vivid in turns. But our well-heeled and jaded audience gobbles it up, like so many vultures.

Whenever the girl appears on stage, the Doctor's face grows solemn.

Who knows if Bora will ever learn another song in her life? Therefore the Baroness is determined to milk this one number for whatever it is worth. And anyway, only this song seems to send those shivers running up and down the spines of blueblood and parvenu alike. When Bora is not performing, she maintains her silence. I think about her every day. How long can this go on?

Dajka may cast dour looks toward the Baroness, but he has nothing better to offer his protégée, either. It is depressing even to think about what would happen if this song were to run dry.

The trial of the safe-breakers packs the courtroom every day. But the honorable public will be disappointed: the defendants are not thrown to the dogs. The King receives four and a half years.

The Greek gets three years. Agap Kevorg's trial is postponed, as he is to be extradited to the Russian courts. Haluska will serve six months for his role as lookout. The hopes of the courtroom hyenas have been confounded, for, since this is in the confusing onset of the constitutional era, my companions could be indicted only on the counts that are proved beyond the shadow of a doubt.

The lawyer assigned by the court appeals on their behalf, as prescribed by law. This procedure was not always honored in subsequent times.

I was unable to hire a lawyer for them, because I had to maintain my anonymity. When I hear about the sentences, my consolation is that, God willing, this affair is not over yet.

The trial proves instructive for the Doctor, who draws the appropriate conclusions regarding the "brick murder" case. He recommends that proceedings be halted at the investigative stage. The alleged perpetrator's contrite confession has simply not been supported by any facts. Serious doubt has been cast on the suspect's sanity at the moment of the act. There is simply not enough evidence to prosecute in this case. (That is how simple it all is, when constitutional rights are respected.)

The charges against Bora are dropped.

At the Grenadier Street gate of the County Courthouse the sentry wears a braided uniform. His task is to stand guard and to salute with his sword any gentleman who comes in or goes out.

The prison's hospital is on the second floor of the institution, facing County Street.

The safe-breakers await the result of their appeal. All signs indicate that the prisoner Jankó has grown resigned to his fate, has turned introspective, showing all signs of a humble but sincere contrition. The head warden is quite proud of his insight into human nature. To all intents and purposes it would appear that the prince of burglars is trying to avoid his former partners in crime, even looking the other way when he sees one of them during exercise period in the yard.

Monday morning he does not go for his walk.

Since Saturday Andronikos has been laid up at the prison hospital. His medical examination on admission features prominently the inch-long scar left by an ancient knife wound between the fourth and fifth ribs on the left side. His musculature exhibits weak to medium development, the lungs are good, heart function excellent. He displays the traces of a skin rash of unknown etiology on his trunk and thighs. He is expected to be able to return to his cell, cured, in a couple of days. Due to his high-security confinement, the handcuffs are removed only for examination and at mealtime.

The pickpocket is able to observe the hospital inmates being escorted to the warden's washroom on the adjacent corridor. At noon he shows symptoms of influenza, running a high fever. Without any access to chalk dust, one has to resort to stucco scraped from the wall instead - a foolproof method for producing fever symptoms. The authorities have no reason whatsoever to connect Baumgarten's person with Socrates. And what is even more telling of the period (and of its prison conditions) is that not one of the numerous prison guards finds it peculiar when that same evening the Safe King also complains of fever and other symptoms of severe influenza. The prison doctor suspects a sudden summer outbreak, and to head off its spread, he orders the transfer of the patient to the hospital.

The King's medical history is recorded on the admission sheet. He is found to be in good physical condition. The torso is especially well developed. On the scalp a half-inch recently healed scar. No evidence of flat feet. Childhood diseases: measles, diphtheria, scarlet fever, whooping cough. His right leg is slightly shorter than the left; this kind of unevenness can only be observed while swimming. He is placed in a single-bed hospital cell, and his handcuffs are retained.

Tuesday morning a uniformed warden makes his rounds at the Pest Regional Penitentiary, checking the locks on corridor doors, making sure each one is securely locked behind him. One dead end, appendix-like passageway can only be approached from the County Hall side of the building. There is no one about. He opens one lock, and goes to the door at the end of the hall. He picks out a Wertheim-type key from the bunch on his chain and turns it twice in the lock. He tries the doorknob to make sure it is open. Then, having done his work, he returns to the guard room across the courtyard.

The moment has arrived. That afternoon, in the quiet period that follows the physician's rounds, at the time when the County Hall's official hours are over, the unguarded Baumgarten, using the needle file, opens his cell door, and dressed as he is, in longjohns and without a jacket, glides down the halls and corridors, seeking shelter in doorways and around corners. When he reaches the section where the solitary cells are, the warden, a familiar face, is seen with his back turned, napping on a chair. The pickpocket sneaks past, until he finds the King's cell, where he shoves the smaller key under the door. The King takes off his handcuffs; meanwhile our cutpurse is already at work on the doorlock, using the larger key of his own manufacture. Soon they are on their way to the Greek's cell. Socrates takes off only one of his handcuffs, afraid of the clinking. His cell door is opened.

At this point Agap Kevorg drops out of our lives, even though he is not far, on another floor of the same building. We were unable to help him. But he will eventually receive his share.

Bubbles for the time being is in a safe place, in custody of the Royal Police. Sooner or later I will have to make plans for her and myself, as well.

The three prisoners pass behind the back of the dozing warden with nearly careless footfalls, on the way to the hospital's washroom. What follows is a great game of chance: everything hinges on one card, that during the half hour it takes them to cut through the iron bars of the window, not one of their fellow prisoners at the hospital will have to obey the call of nature. It proves to be a winning card - I should have been a gambler, after all. At last the King with one jerk cracks the center bar and bends it back. The rest goes like clockwork. The first to climb out on the ancient thick wall of the prison yard is the slim, feather-weight Baumgarten, experienced tight-rope walker on many a moving train. The Greek follows, and the King goes last.

The wall is topped by a picket palisade, for another nine feet. They set out, facing the wood fence, groping for support with their palms, edging by with sideways steps, not looking down. Deep below, in the courtyard, washerwomen are at work, supervised by a prison guard; among them, working side by side in sisterly fashion, Bubbles and Máli. When Bubbles looks up from her washtub, she catches a glimpse of the strange procession inching along the wall over the perilous drop, led by an apparition in long underwear.

She almost breaks out in laughter, but manages to control herself. Her heart is jumping. She does not dare to look up again, fearing the guard might notice the fugitives. Now Máli's eyes stray up from the prison wash. Her mouth gapes, about to scream *Holy Mother of God!* but Bubbles claps a hand on her friend's mouth just in time, and follows it up with a poke in the side.

They manage to pass undisturbed along the length of the palisade. Where it ends, they must balance for an endless moment over the void, before they can find firm footing on the other side. Fortunately they do not have to face barbed wire or broken glass; theirs is a simpler time. Rounding a corner, now out of sight from the yard, they inch their way along the wider ledge of the County Hall building, to the window of a certain dead-end corridor near the archives. One gentle, open-palm push against the glass, and the falling fragments are caught in the tails of a black frock coat. Then they hop inside, graceful and debonair.

At the end of this corridor they find two last obstacles, behind which remains an unknown danger: the heyducks of County Hall.

Two doors, both unguarded. The first is an oak door, a hand's breadth in thickness, with an enormous padlock hanging on iron cops deeply inserted into the wall. Its mechanism is of the Wertheim type. Baumgarten turns the doorknob, which creaks a little, and opens, and they are inside, facing a locked steel door. There follow several minutes of specialist work, employing their small collection of passkeys and the needle file. (A most expensive piece, American import, obtained from the liquidation of engineer Abraham's workshop.)

Socrates tries the key once, files it twice, tries it again, then proceeds to cut and file it at a rapid pace for five minutes nonstop. This is where you separate the master from the apprentice; when he is done, there is no need to be tentative. One turn of the key opens the door as smoothly as if he were returning to his bachelor apartment after a night of wine and roses. As the King will put it, this was a benefit performance by the great Socrates.

This is the moment when the chief warden notices that one of the cells is empty. It is his most important prisoner's.

Strolling across an unused storage room, they now step into the land registry archives. A tall, gawky clerk in striped trousers, taking advantage of the after-hours stillness to dawdle among the dusty shelves, blinks and stares open-mouthed at Baumgarten, clad in longjohns, and the two others, who turn up out of nowhere, from a direction where no one ever came from. The Greek grabs the man's lapels. The clerk will always recall the strange foreign accent of the man who addresses him at this most trying moment in his life:

"Silence now, you stay out of trouble." And that is how it was to be, unless one counts as trouble the situation in which a county clerk with an unimpeachable record of many years' service finds himself tied up with his own necktie, his mouth gagged with his stale handkerchief, wearing nothing but shirt and underpants and sleeve protectors, laid like an object on the lowest and broadest shelf in the registry. Meanwhile his worn but *still respectable* trousers and jacket, somewhat loosely fitting on the body of a good-for-nothing railroad thief, are wandering off in the direction of the outer offices.

The chief warden by now has discovered that two other prisoners are missing, including his most prized ones; he knows he is in deep trouble. Two more minutes are wasted in making sure they are not in the prison doctor's office or in the washroom. These two minutes are most useful for my men, who are progressing unhindered through deserted hallways, corridors and stairways, then across the busy courtyard. The fierce heyduck posted at the Grenadier Street gate dutifully salutes with his sword the frock-coated gentlemen leaving the County Hall. They must be on some highly important government business, for they are in an unusual hurry.

I could not wait for them outside the gate, but they know where we are to meet.

The chief warden sounds the alarm. In his panic he reports a mass prison break.

The guilty heyduck at the outer gate, chained in place by his orders never to leave his post, can only yell, "Stop, thief!"

Unwittingly, he speaks the truth. One block away on Grenadier Street a quick-thinking baker's apprentice yields to loyalty over the call of the "Sándor Rózsa syndrome", thus rejecting the historical heritage of our revolution of '48, and dives to tackle Socrates. But this time the Greek slips out of his would-be captor's grasp, shoves him back, and bounds away, like a gazelle wearing a flour-dusted frock coat, down County Street. Within seconds he is lost in the crowds on Saint Peter and Hatvan streets. At this time of the day these popular esplanades are crammed with the sauntering, well-dressed upper classes.

From here on it is three more or less regularly appareled gentlemen who hurry about their business, seemingly apart. The alarm raised by their escape precedes them, but the critical period lasts only as long as they are running, in a group of three.

The Special Investigator hears the news at police headquarters. The prize catch of his year-long labors walked out through the County Hall gate past the raised sword of a saluting sentry.

He takes Marton with him. At the penitentiary the chief warden watches anxiously as Dajka, ominously calm, within a matter of minutes organizes and initiates the manhunt. The one-time assistant to Dajka described this scene for me much later, when he was already Chief Inspector.

He is sent to collect the witnesses. A bootmaker on Grenadier Street, who, looking up from his work happened to see a group of men in dark coats hurry by. The baker's apprentice recounts his adventure, and gives a description of the Gypsy-faced gentleman. A street urchin saw a man who was wearing a coat and striped trousers that were surely not tailored for his size. No one can say which way they went, once past the streetcorner.

The Doctor decides to forget about the lines of demarcation and spheres of influence, and orders a city-wide police alert.

He composes a circular letter, so that foot and mounted

patrols can start out at once.

The Greek, with the instincts of a cornered rat, decides to double back. He rejoins his companions by the Franciscan church, where the cavernous cool of the front portal conjures up for the King the childhood security and incense of Sunday masses. Inside they can lie low for a while, until the first wave of hunters pass by, and the Greek makes use of the occasion to remove the remaining handcuff. They bow their heads in silence. Their prayers for freedom are straight from the heart and are broadly ecumenical, far in advance of the times: a Catholic, a Jew, and a Greek Orthodox, respectively. Laying their heads on their arms they take a nap in the shadowy silence of the church.

They rouse themselves around seven-thirty in the evening. On the other side of the now quiet Hatvan Street, they enter an all-night tobacconist's shop, and ask for the latest papers. In a corner of the establishment they appear to be whispering as they scan the exchange rates. They decide not to risk going for the Greek's share left at the Seminary Street apartment. After a jailbreak the police always go straight to the girlfriend's apartment.

Outside, the hoofbeat of a mounted patrol passes by. The tobacconist looks up. At this moment my men are closer to being recaptured than they realize. It is no accident that this strategically placed tobacconist's and newsvendor's establishment is operated by someone we have already met, the police informer. (This role has a long tradition in our land, under all manner of occupying powers. Its ranks are filled by building superintendents, restaurant habitués, tobacconists. Colleagues, during this era in our history when the subject of the inordinate number of reports is not the criminal, but the population at large, and at the same time human labor is cheaper than a secret microphone.) But the tobacconist knows that if he were to call out to the patrol now, his role would be forever uncovered to the underworld.

The Safe King pushes the paper aside and slaps down three twenty-franc gold napoleons on the counter.

"Exchange these for me, please."

The Greek adds, "Why you wait, we don't have all day."

The tobacconist recognizes the foreigner who has received such nationwide notoriety. But he is frightened, and holds his peace. But he exchanges the gold pieces at the rate of seven forints and forty kreuzers, instead of the going rate of nine-forty, for he is not totally intimidated.

As they depart, he leaves the shop to the counter-jumper and trails the fugitives for a block or two. The next day he will report that the criminals were seen heading across Serpent Square toward the ferry crossing at Pledge Square.

"Escaped Convicts" reads the heading of the circular issued by the Royal Police for all law enforcement agencies on this day at 16.45 hours:

- the convict Jankó, sentenced to four and a half years' imprisonment for breaking-and-entering and theft;

- the convict Andronikos, sentenced to three years' imprisonment for the same;

- and the convict Baumgarten, sentenced to fifteen months' imprisonment for theft,

have escaped from the prison hospital of the Pest District Court Penitentiary, by prying open the iron bars of a washroom window.

Jankó, alias the "Safe King" is thirty-two years of age, unmarried, Catholic. Birthplace: Zenta, Hungary. Speaks Hungarian, German, French, Greek. Height: five feet seven inches. Slender, muscular build, fair complexion. Hair auburn, parted on left. High forehead, brown eyes, normal mouth, thick blond eyebrows, square jaw, blond beard, mustache. Address unknown, original profession: engineer. At the time of escape was wearing black English wool suit with vest, soft black hat, silk socks, gaiters. No special identifying marks.

The Greek Andronikos is five feet six inches tall, round face, healthy swarthy complexion, hair and eyebrows brown, eyes black, forehead sloping, nose broken, clean-shaven. Fluent in Greek, French, Italian, speaks Hungarian with a marked accent. Religion, Greek Orthodox. Profession: uncertain.

The pickpocket Baumgarten, alias Aladár Kokas, five feet

five inches tall, thin build, native and resident of Máramaross-
ziget, original profession: watchmaker. Speaks Hungarian,
German, some Ruthenian. Face narrow, olive complexion,
black hair, brown eyebrows, eyes blue-gray, nose bent, upper
left canine missing. Wearing small hat, striped trousers and
oversized black coat. Special marks: slightly pockmarked, at
base of little finger on left hand a tattoo of anchors in foliage,
inscribed "Ragusa".

From Serpent Street they double back via Town Hall
Square, and as they slip by on Leopold Street, they are a
stone's throw from my little piano. The rehearsal is on, I
cannot leave. This is a war of nerves now.

I am testing the limits of arrogance: how long will I be able
to sit here at my piano, right under the Chief Inspector's nose?

They are heading toward Cemetery Road, where one day,
three years ago, Jenö the Lisp, underworld messenger and
stool pigeon by turns, announced that the King had been
released early from the Romanian jail. They go down Hat
Street, Grammar School Street, and Magyar Street, out to
Museum Boulevard. (These streets, by some minor miracle,
have all retained their old names, in spite of history. Make a
note of this!) And onward, with hurrying steps, but trying to
remain inconspicuous, until they are out on Kerepesi Road.

At the corner of Guinea-fowl Street they see a paddy-wagon
speed by; the guard sitting on the box has a bayonet fixed to
his rifle. This sends shivers up their spines and they redouble
their steps. The lesser mortals are tired and discouraged, but
the King leads his troops, undaunted. They now pass the
house of detention for vagrants (shivers again). The streets are
deserted. They climb over the fence of the cemetery and lie
down for a brief rest, curling up in the fetal position. But the
King is up and awake, and keeps watch until it is pitch dark
and time to move on.

He wakes his companions gently. They get up without a
word, and reach the long, shed-like row of slum dwellings
where the King raps on one of the wooden doors.

Ti-ti-ti tah-tah-tah ti-ti-ti: three short, three long, three short, the universal signal of those in need of help, on land and at sea. The lamp goes out inside, and the door is opened. A woman's hand ushers them inside rapidly. She peers out at the alleyway, and thinks she sees a shadow gliding by a wall. But her eyes must be deceiving her. She draws the thick felt curtains, locks the door, and only then does she light the oil lamp again.

Tonight no policeman sleeps in the city.

The next morning Dajka combs the penitentiary to see what he can find. The investigation is going to be merciless; heads will roll. He devotes half an hour to starting the proceedings, then someone else can continue. His instincts tell him the trail must be picked up elsewhere. He follows the route of the prison break. Looking out through the window of the prison hospital washroom, the police investigators shake their heads, amazed by the death-defying daring of the fugitives. Bubbles is again doing the laundry in the yard, and she looks away; it would not do for the Special Investigator to see a familiar face down there.

There are no signs of force on the cell doors. They soon discover the window in the washroom; down a dead-end corridor, beyond a set of bars, they find the thick oak door's Wertheim lock open - somebody must have been bribed. There are scratchmarks made by a passkey on the lock of the steel door, accompanied by the fine dust of metal filings on the floor.

In his office the chief warden belatedly lists the measures that should have been taken. The salaries of his prison guards rarely reach five hundred forints a year, he complains. No wonder if one of them was tempted by a bribe. The investigation is extended in that direction.

Dajka listens with one ear as he diligently studies some papers. He is reviewing the case histories taken on admission to the prison hospital. The physician's objective examination peels the layers of refinement hiding the burglar, and exposes the tough professional underneath, with wounds to match, on the chest or on the head.

The chief warden goes on with his report. He has already

identified the careless parties and instituted disciplinary proceedings. Two prison guards are awaiting their fate under lock and key. Three attendants at the hospital prison have been suspended. The guard caught napping has been reduced in grade and retired without pension.

(NOW: BIPEDS. LACTOSE INTOLERANCE)

Yesterday I gave up on humankind. There is just no helping them. You had a good laugh at me and the object of my scorn.

We live in a part of town where the Café has no name, and the walls are graced by graffiti featuring the three-pronged crown of the rock group Beatrice, defunct for two years now. Yesterday on the bus home we saw a poorly dressed, unshaven young man traveling with a child afflicted by Mongolism. Another passenger, a man, had been staring at the little boy. You were not staring in an obvious way; after all, you are almost thirteen. When the starer was getting off, the unshaven man, from the safety of the back of the bus, snarled and hissed after him: "What are you staring at?" And he added this year's most emphatic invective in our part of town, "You ape!"

The other one turned back. "You want something? Huh? 'Cause you could get some!" The young man had apparently exhausted his supply of words, and could only growl and sputter, and at last spat in the direction of his departing fellow man, but very unskilfully, so that the spittle dribbled down his own chest. Then he tried a final kick aimed through the closing door, a futile gesture from the start. In this three-second bout so much repressed misery and hate flared, that for long minutes afterward you gazed into space wordlessly, which is not your way at all, for, thank God, you are usually chattering. You must have been thinking that this industrial workers' district is certainly a far cry from the Valero Street quarter we moved from. True, this is no enclave of unclouded, happy human lives. But that is not my quarrel with humankind.

In front of our building on Globe Street, the Pipe and Conduit Works have cleaned up their leftovers, and the landscapers have been here. During the past few weeks, they have dragged in their behemoth trucks, and by the sweat of their brows they covered the lot with topsoil. On Tuesday the grass seeds were planted; it would take three weeks for the lawn to establish itself. Using stakes and wire, they fenced off the area of the lawn between the cinderblock buildings. They had worked hard.

At night the teenagers arrived, their instincts for vandalism well advanced. On Wednesday I took you all the way to Old Buda, to give you some perspective on the event. We went to look at what was done by an earlier generation of hooligans to the trees on the sidewalk of Turk Street, planted by landscapers in the year of your arrival. There are two trees your age left standing; the others were destroyed by young punks. The Angel-land district has its own breed of hooligans. They went to work and pulled up the stakes, running all over and stamping out the sprouting grass. Right away, on Tuesday night. Since they all live here, you could not understand why they did this. At eight in the evening they go off to watch TV. Six days a week, the grounds are emptied of them, as if a giant maid had vacuumed it clean of bipeds. On the seventh day, they have no TV programs to watch.

We went down, and, using large stones, thumped the stakes back in place, retied the wires, between eight and eight-thirty.

We did the same on Wednesday, and again the day before yesterday. Here and there you could already see the pale emerald of hopeful young grass.

Then, coming home last night, we again found the stakes torn up and tossed about, the wires thrown down. That is when I decided to give up on them. Let them fend for themselves.

For months now I have not left this story to go outside in the daytime. Yesterday I had to go out in the morning, a doctor's appointment. At our bus stop, where once upon a time Imola had received that undeserved slap on her behind, I saw a strange new breed of taxis. They did not wear the uniform of the monolithic taxi companies. They were civilians, private enterprise, a sight my eyes have grown unaccustomed to. Bureaucrats in their offices have devoted enormous amounts of care and time and energy to make clearly visible that which belongs to the people, and not to them. Therefore these taxis all have so-called "private" license plates. Last year we had fifteen hundred taxis in the city; now we have eight thousand. One of the colors has been resurrected. Who would have believed it? If you want a cab, you can have one. It has been allowed. Pretty soon we shall re-invent the wheel. But it will have to be done cautiously, almost furtively, as if somewhere up in the red sky some supreme power would erupt with tremendous wrath at the sight of our taxis, or at our freedom to take a leak, or to find a place where hot hamburgers are served.

Crossing the Square on the way home, I bumped into the Fráter. He was lumbering around the phone booths, clutching his little address book, which he periodically loses, whereupon he is forced to start collecting women's telephone numbers all over again, thereby incidentally refreshing his supply. He was trying to reach someone, without success. We sat down on a bench to enjoy the mild sunshine, unbuttoned our coats, and sunned ourselves for half an hour. It must have been too much too suddenly for my poorly pigmented skin. My head began to ache, and in front of the used book store I felt that I was suffering a sunstroke. I know the symptoms. I quickly ducked in at the Ibolya dairy bar, and knocked back two tall glasses of milk, my usual tried and tested remedy. I could feel that after all there would be no sunstroke. Indeed there wasn't; but by mid-afternoon I had an upset stomach. I had been expecting it; as far as I can remember I have never been able to drink milk by itself, my system cannot tolerate it.

In our movie at the world's edge it is ten thousand and something, BC. By this time, the geographic divergence of humankind into the major varieties has been accomplished. The African has deep brown, eggplant purple, or rarely, black skin, thick lips, dark, kinky hair. Negroid. The Asian has yellowish-brown skin, (which is closest to our skin color before divergence), prominent cheekbones, straight black hair, and the epicanthic fold in the inner corner of the eye causing it to be "almond-shaped". Mongoloid. The European has lightly pigmented, pinkish, yellowish, at times white skin, and a sharply defined profile. Caucasoid.

The ice retreats once more. (There is nothing to indicate that just for our sake geological processes have come to a stop. We can expect future ice ages.)

The climate of our Basin is dry and cold: this will be called the birch and pine period. Humans are present throughout. The Balla Cave has yielded the bones of a very long-headed child who lived out its brief year and a half in this period, according to carbon-14 dating. This is followed by the Atlantic dry and warm climate, the hazelnut period. Still later comes the oak period, which is wetter, then the cooler beech period, which is still going on today. There will be others to come.

There is constant movement, shifting and migration of people. The region of the Ural Mountains, the birthplace of the earliest Finno-Ugric tribes, the forerunners of the Magyar settlers of Hungary, is settled by Mongoloid groups from the Siberian taigas, and by Caucasoids with Cro-Magnon elements from the south. The European and Asian populations. It is a hopeless mess. (In the South Ural, we even find occasional broad-nosed, high-orbited Negroid individuals, but these had no visible influence on the formation of the Finno-Ugric group.) The relics of their existence (skates, boats, and sleds) are preserved by bogs. These are the knowable pre-historic beginnings of these tribes.

Humankind tames the dog, our first domestic animal. The ass, the sheep and the pig come later. Enormous changes, lasting to our days. We are approaching the vicinity of the historical order of magnitude.

When the first bread is baked, it is still unleavened. In the region of the Fertile Crescent we, humans, develop agriculture; and in not quite four hundred generations it will spread all over the globe. Wheat, rice. Corn, potatoes. Millet, tomatoes. An unprecedented population explosion follows. Where the land hitherto supported one, from now on it can support two thousand people.

Ownership arrives, and with it, war.

Sacrificial fires send up their smoke; stone menhirs and dolmens are raised. And we learn something that will lead straight to Neil Armstrong's footsteps on the moon in that far-off year of your arrival. As memorials to our striving upward, we erect the altar-observatory of Stonehenge and pile up the steeply stepped stones of the pyramids, our stone monuments all over the land masses broken away from the former Pangea.

Europe's agriculturists cultivate all arable land from the Dnieper to the Atlantic Ocean. They employ the plough. On the steppes of Central Asia we invent our first vehicle, the horse. And we acquire other domestic animals.

Wheels of solid oak have been dug up in Holland; the earliest carts, in our land. Because of the accident of our birth, we are most interested in the temperate zones, where the hot tropical air currents meet the polar ones, making human life possible by evening out the planet's climatic extremes. To put it provincially, this is a fairly important part of the globe. Other areas, naturally, are important in other ways. (The Ural region, for instance - and not only for us.) Within the temperate zone, we pay special attention to our continent, and within that, the smallish jutting Western land mass known as Europe, so thick with history. Within that, our eager eyes are focused on our Basin. A wave of Mediterranean migration arrives here from the south. Short-skulled Alpine types. Corded ware, Beaker culture, burial mounds. They are the ancient Alpine and Dinarian inhabitants of the mountains of Central Europe. Fennoscandians also arrive from the north. Some move on, others melt into the melting pot. All of them leave behind some physical evidence. Burial sites, bones, measurements. Because of the shortage of material finds, we know next to nothing about those who burned their dead.

The ones who will stay, and the ones yet to come. We are going to pay an unfair amount of attention to this eventual population of fifteen or sixteen million. (At a time when New York City alone has that many people, and more).

Four thousand four BC. October twenty-third, nine a.m. We have arrived at the moment of Creation, according to Bishop Ussher's system, one that brooks no uncertainties. From this point on, *everyone* may rest assured: the world exists.

At the borders of China a wall is being built against invaders. It will be one of the two man-made objects on Earth seen by Armstrong from outer space. The other one is the giant cyclotron in Chicago. In China, an imperial edict orders the destruction of all written records, to sever all ties to the past - there is nothing new under the sun. Over the centuries, slaves die by the hundreds of thousands building the wall. The situation will be different at the construction of the cyclotron, thanks to the improved architectural technologies and to the successful collective bargaining techniques of the coalition of labor unions known as the *Ey-eff-el see-eye-oh*. We create in our image the one and only God, who is disembodied. A great invention, and not merely a degenerate late variety, truly worthy of the original who, through mobility, brains, and opportunism has proven the most viable creature on the face of the earth.

On catamarans and light rafts we reach the islands of Oceania, where we prosper and multiply.

Christ. Plus-minus zero.

The eastern shores of Greenland are reached by Eskimos migrating from Asia. The great colonizing process is over: humans now inhabit all liveable places.

Our Basin is called Pannonia during the Roman period. An amphitheater is built near your future high school in the future Old Buda, which now begins its career as the natural focus of our history. It serves as the empire's eastern bastion of defense against the incursions of barbarian hordes. (The beginning of our long history as bastions of defense; this is another accident of geography.) The Roman legions also bring in foreigners by the thousands; we know of an Oriental *cohors*, and multitudes of soldiers from Asia Minor and North Africa.

Other great monotheistic religions arise. They provide their own answers to the ultimate questions. They tend to leave out the rest of humanity by virtue of their birth; their truths, by and large, are mutually exclusive. Some are proselytizing religions, in the name of love and the straight sword, or employing the crescent and scimitar. And their differences are quick to weave the next order of magnitude, which is the personal. The dark shadow of our own complexities is being projected here.

After Christ. The human population of the Basin is the so-called general Central-European type. A constant stream of nations migrate back and forth, a human tide in ebb and flow, following the vagaries of climate, drought and rainfall, the prodding of misty bodings. By selective breeding we increase the size of the horse so that it can carry an armed warrior.

Along the River Kama, the first elements of the tribes that will conquer the Basin are the Ugro-Magyars. (You will find the River Kama at the easternmost edge of Europe, on this side of the Urals. The nearest city is Perm, and Brezhnev is not far off.) This is what the textbooks tell us. Other textbooks may tell otherwise.

Around this time the Basin is turning into the last stop for folk arriving from left and right. It is the furthermost Eurasian steppe within reach of the far-ranging nomadic conquerors. From the southeast, the nomads from the Black Sea region are heading this way.

Back along the River Kama, the second component is the Turko-Magyars. The Ugric tribes are transformed into equestrian nomads by living together with Turkic groups arriving from the east.

The migrations are on. Triggered by the Huns in Inner Asia, its outermost waves wash up on the westernmost Eurasian steppe, where each group leaves behind a little bit of itself.

Right here. We all leave a little of us behind. Just think of the Tatar cheekbones and gray eyes of Little Kovács, the photographer. Human sexuality, more rampant than any animal's, and the instincts for survival shape us with the matter of fact indifference of rain, wind and sun grinding down mountains. (It is this autocratic force that will eventually compel us, against our nature, and only in the shadow of nuclear deadlock, to act with tolerance, even toward the males of the other tribe. For otherwise we should all perish.) Our components will be inseparable, like our Cro-Magnon ancestors from the Neanderthal. They are us. We are them. From West Europe come the people of the Halstatt culture. Their lack of pigmentation is striking: blond hair, blue eyes.

The hair of the Baroness, the eyes of Little Kovács could have come from them.

The availability of pastures fluctuates in Central Asia. There is more grass; a nomad nation grows, and strikes out toward the west. There is less grass, and the nomads' cattle starve; again they strike out toward the west. We arrive here as Sarmatians, with Iranian origins. There are many Mediterraneans among us, and East Baltics mingled in along the way. One simplistic theory would have us descended from the Sarmatians, period. The Alans and Goths are the first Germanic equestrian nomads arriving on the Lower Danubian plains from the grassy steppes of Eastern Europe and the Crimea. And we arrive here, the Asian Avars and Kabards.

And here are, at last, arriving in two or possibly three waves, the Magyar nomad tribes, bringing with them Ugric, Turkic and Iranian elements.

The conquerors drive before them the remnants of conquered tribes. We drive our remnants before us. We make use of their women, the way they make use of our livestock. And by the time they arrive at the gates of Europe, we are an anthropologically mixed bunch, identical only in name with the forerunners who had set out from the east.

The third component is that of place. Migrations, conquerors, conquered. Defeats. Remnants from here and there: they are with us to this day. We are with them.

And now for the significance of my sunstroke, milk drinking and upset stomach. Leaving behind a series of homelands and battles, after long migrations, carrying dried, powdered meat in our saddlebags, striking out from the Asian steppes as usual, here comes the next wave of our ancestors. Our partial ancestors, and to what extent, we shall never be able to tell, by virtue of the very nature of biology and history. Here comes that extended moment which, on the occasion of its Millennial anniversary, will be picked out retroactively, nominated by bureaucrats, the way they would promote a fourth-class clerk. Perhaps it was only the men of the tribe, about forty or fifty thousand strong, whose women and children had been overrun and absorbed by the Petchenegs back in the last old country (and who would still be thriving as citizens of a great Pan-Petcheneg Federation, if the dreaded, mighty tribe of the Petchenegs had not disappeared without a trace from the face of the earth).

Once in the Basin, the princely tribe sets up winter camp at Old Buda, the center of our story. They are reinforced by related groups who settled here earlier, and they replenish themselves in this region, in a manner that is consistent with the times. This is the theory of the "double conquest"; there are others. And so, this Basin will be our birthplace: Little Kovács's, Piros's, Imola's, yours and mine. It seems to be a fine place to settle into: there is milk, there is honey, there is plenty of pasture.

This "land of milk and honey" business is a peculiar thing. Personally I could never stand honey, and I do not tolerate milk. Still, there must be something to it.

It not only appears to be a good place, it actually is one.

Subsequent waves of invading nomads think so, too. So we, the actors in our story, acquire the characteristic color of our hair and eyes, the shape of our face, the shade of our complexion. Smooth or wavy, brown or black, flaxen or bronze red hair. Blue or black or slate gray eyes. Prominent cheekbones or oval faces, long and short skulls; light pinkish, pallid white or tawny brown complexions.

From here on this is where we are going to be melding together, in the wake of centuries of peaceable or warlike arrivals. We and they, conquerors and conquered, the violated and the violator. According to the current hypotheses. This is the land of Canaan chosen by Tatar, Petcheneg, Kuman, Slav, German, Jew, Armenian, Gypsy, and, in traces, by Turk, Greek, Romanian and French Huguenot and who knows how many others, who take a tumble in the hay to go into the making of our population. We are the result, it is all here in our genes, within the borders of Hungary and all around. We had the pleasure of meeting them, and they us. As you may see, the conjugation is not easy. It never is. Hate, bloodshed and murder are perhaps ulimately caused by grammatical laxity, that simplifying "we and they".

We simplify by lying.

Lactose intolerance. Through a whim of physiology, and perhaps because the actual has a greater power than we would dare to imagine in our fondest dreams, in this milky-haze twilight of the unproveable, unmeasurable past, we suddenly have the opportunity to quantify the proportions of the European and the Asiatic in us, made up as we are of the graceful and robust Mediterraneans, Siberian Mongoloids, broad-faced Cro-Magnons, Alpine roundheads, Dinarians, Armenoids, long-skulled Nordics, Iranians, East Baltics, Turanids, Uralians and Pamirians, mixed Europo-Mongoloids, ancient thick-set Caucasoids, and a newer infusion of Caucasoids. The mix in each of us, roughly speaking. Among us both blood types are common, the A that is characteristic of West Europe and the B typical of East Asians; the actual numbers are not known. On the other hand, consider the enzyme lactase, responsible for the digestion of milk sugar, lactose, in our digestive system. Its absence causes lactose intolerance. In simplified terms, adult West Europeans are able to drink milk, whereas in Asians milk may induce an upset stomach. A UNESCO study came up with the figures for our country. The numbers are round and elegant. We are thirty-seven percent lactose intolerant. 63-37 is the score in this genetic match on the Hungarian playing field; the direction of the change is unpredictable. This is how we are, the fifteen million of us here, individually and collectively, deep down at a level far beneath the overlay of culture and language. We are not threatened by inbreeding. On the contrary, this genetic jambalaya is often cited as a rationale for certain Hungarian virtues. I know, this is just another case of tribal self-praise.

One Persian chronicler describes the Magyars as handsome folk of fine stature, dressed in brocades, their armor wrought with silver and set with pearls.

A German chronicler on the other hand claims our faces are ugly, our eyes deep-set, our stature stunted, our customs and language barbarous.

Perhaps they were not looking at the same tribe.

Keeping our Iranian components in mind, it is conceivable that the Persian was indulging in the partiality of kinship, basking in the comfortable glow of familiarity.

The German had his own reasons for bias: the arrows of the Magyar tribes reached as far as Marseilles, and the Germans were in the way.

As for the language - I can't say, for this is the only native tongue I possess. After seven hundred years of written literature it is still *that* language. And having some knowledge of several of the great languages of Euro-American culture, I am still grateful for our language, for the crystal clarity of its images, its unequivocal manliness, the firmness of its sound, the insolent boyish fillips of its slang, its nuances resembling the tremor of oak leaves, the soft maternal warmth of its melodies. But God forbid we should think ours better than our neighbors'. We should be victims of the same primitive error that claims the Yanomami tribe, or Sir Francis Galton and the ideologue Rosenberg. Let us simply believe it to be as good as any.

This language, too, has had its clandestine intermarriages, its quick tumble of words and structures in the hay, and has adopted some chromosomes from neighboring tongues east and west, before and after the Conquest, just as the biological population did. It has withered some, but mostly it has grown. I will state arbitrarily that the Hungarian language's lactose tolerance is also 63 per cent. Such fine proportions must have their rationale.

In the world at large, after a time of ambitious buildings rising towards the sky, as part of the eternal equilibrium of up and down, a dark age is approaching, vast armies on horseback. The Mongolian chieftain Temudjin comes to power, and adopts the name of Genghis Khan, Lord of the World. His warriors do not wash, for they are pure as gold; this is the law, and they are the Golden Horde.

The Germans make a stand in front of our marauding Magyar tribal ancestors. From the setback we learn our lesson, and steer our fate in a European direction.

In South America, Manco-Capac lays the foundation of the Inca empire, as local tradition has it.

The tribe of Ottoman Turks, fifty thousand strong, flee from the Mongolians to the land of the Armenians.

The intolerance of Genghis produces consequences that touch us directly, for a new wave of Asian nomads reaches this westernmost of the steppes, only a few generations after the Magyar tribes settle here (which, in the historical order of magnitude, is a mere quarter of an hour). It's all that milk and honey and pasture. We sat ourselves down in the middle of the highway; there were no signs posted. So from time to time we get run over like a stray cat. Devastation by the Mongolians, 1241. Blood and cinders, butchery, rape. They, us. This is where Bora Clarendon's milky white face gets those slanting almond eyes.

The Blue Planet circles around the Sun a few more times.

Those of us spared by the Mongols dare to creep forth from caves, forests, swamps. We settle down again, in foolhardy trust. The same old Neanderthal story - or Cro-Magnon, depending on the view. All the slant-eyed half-Tatars left behind in their mothers' bellies by this thing called history will grow up as Hungarians; their fate is ours, and we rebuild villages in scorched places.

The Blue Planet rolls on. Tribes migrate, creating new waves of violence; here and there a copyist bends over parchment by dim candlelight in a monastic cell; a vineyard, a wind carrying the scent of flowers in girls' hair. Inventions come to Europe from China, via the Arabs. The treadle looms are at work. Gunpowder arrives on the scene. Pig iron is poured and steel is manufactured.

Two thirds of Europe's population are wiped out by the greatest plague in recorded history.

Timur the Lame scatters the Golden Horde. But he too directs his wrath against cities and people who like to wash. In his path lie Islamic territories where daily ablution is a prerequisite of a God-fearing life. He burns and slaughters his way through them. Korans scribed with ornate calligraphy and scientific tractates burn in sputtering flames; cool-fountained gardens crumble in regions that were outposts of learning in astronomy, geography, mathematics, at a time of Dark Ages in Europe. Timur Lenk builds a pile of ninety thousand skulls after the sacking of Baghdad.

Since the Lame One's passage, we thought for a long, long time that his kind belonged to an earlier, primitive age of mankind. We imagined that humanity in the course of time was becoming wiser, nobler, and better, until one fine day we would find itching bumps near our shoulder blades, about to turn into angelic wings. That is when the series of Organized Global Slaughters (Nos. 1, 2 and No.?) began, bringing the mounting piles of cadavers in leggings at Verdun and Isonzo, and the National and Socialist-induced heaps of artificial teeth, mounds of hair, and mountains of crutches in front of the efficient gas chambers, as revolutionary new technologies were invented to match the increased population.

Printing is invented in Europe, after it has been invented in China. Human experience can be expressed and shared in increasingly larger numbers of copies.

European sailors appear in America. The so-called known world grows another hemisphere. The Middle Ages are over, and the Modern begins. Although the Marxist school would have it otherwise.

The Solar System progresses another infinitesimal notch of a second of a degree in its two-hundred-fifty-million-year circuit. Now the Ottoman Turks set out from their new home, swelling with the self-assurance of the youngest monotheistic faith - proselytizing by means of the crescent and scimitar - to smite us in mid-summer. The script is written by the map and by the climate. You may calculate exactly how far they will advance. At this time, there are three to four million Hungarians populating the two lands - Hungary proper and Transylvania - that lie in the way of the Turks' progress.

Belgrade. Hunyadi's 1456 victory is still commemorated by noontime churchbells Europe-wide.

It is their God-fearing duty to conquer the non-Islamic parts of the known world. We belong in the non-Islamic part. In the fall, they return home, and leave only a garrison behind.

We build forts, walled towns. The blowing wind whispers in the ear of peasant and fisherman, and of the lute-playing chronicler that this is our destiny, here in our Canaan, to lie in the path of the conqueror, for whom we are the first, or the last, of the Eurasian steppes.

THE CART BEFORE THE HORSE

Leaving the Cemetery Road slums, three black-clad figures set out under cover of darkness. All three are clean-shaven, and their outfits bear no resemblance to the descriptions trumpeted abroad by the circular. They have divided their money into equal portions. One of them is better-dressed, and he carries luggage: a yellow pigskin suitcase, and an *étui* slung over his shoulder. From here on his ways will part from the other two, who give him a critical once-over. The farewells are brief, and manly, with a look in the eye and a handshake. One of the two reaches out and pulls the hat somewhat lower over the eyes of the well-dressed one, and nods, to send him on his way. Their comrade disappears in the direction of the Inner City.

One of the other two is fingering a small bag of paprika in his pocket, and, as a test, undoes the string with the fingers of one hand. They stand for a moment, gazing after their departed partner.

They can count on it: in the capital and its environs, and perhaps nationwide, each and every train station will be watched.

The next morning the Hatvan Street tobacconist telephones police headquarters. He apologizes to the corporal on duty for not coming in person, but he was afraid of being observed entering the building beside the Danube. God knows, no informant likes to be seen going to the police. The tobacconist's self-contempt, while historically justified, gives my colleagues a half-day's head start. Later that morning the Special Investigator receives the report indicating that the fugitives had gone in the direction of the Pledge Square ferry to Buda. They had altogether three gold napoleons' worth of funds. Considering the price of train tickets, they will not be able to get far with so little. Dajka orders increased vigilance at the customs houses and train stations. He sends a special advisory to the western border crossings.

In the course of the day false alarms and reports of

mistaken identity will be numerous. Among certain elements of the population the spirit of the hunt gains the upper hand, and burglar-catching momentarily verges on becoming a national sport.

But the fugitives are gone without a trace. Dajka must choose another route if he wants results.

Women, and women again.

At noon, orders are issued to all plainclothes detectives, and to all manner and sorts of police informers at outlying dives, flea markets, brothels, *cafés chantants*, gambling dens and other haunts of crime, to be on the lookout for women.

They must come up with a wench who was the lover of one of the safe-breakers.

And human nature interferes again, this time on the side of the law, to right the balance. It is one of those unsevered old ties. The King's nemesis.

Word of the manhunt reaches to all taverns and bars, far and wide.

By late afternoon every little bird is twittering about how the police are looking for the Safe King's sweetheart. The twittering reaches the ears of one ageless, syphilitic hag on Outer Kerepesi Road, who collects emptied glasses from tavern tables to eke out the elixir for the troubles of her life. (In those days, they do not yet call this kind of behavior self-destructive, which is what we said regarding the actions of a certain pock-marked film director more recently. Kovács and I involuntarily witnessed his last night at the Artists' Club, watching the last grains of sand drop in his hourglass. It was not a pretty sight. In the days of the Kitty, alcohol, spinelessness and idleness were the terms used.)

For weeks now hazy notions have been stirring in the woman's mind until her determination has at last ripened. Her eyes light up with a new interest and a sudden cunning. She sidles over to the plainclothes detective.

"Wait for me outside, behind the tavern," she whispers with toothless gums. "Go on now," and her hands wrapped in filthy rags push him toward the door. "I know something. But only outside." The only way the detective can get rid of her repulsive touch is by retreating to the outside.

"There was a time when the King used to be my lover," announces the noseless apparition in the shadows behind the tavern.

"You can't say things like that!" yells the detective. He naturally assumes she is referring to our anointed Apostolic ruler, and his indignation stems from the deep-rooted loyalty of a civil servant. "What you said is high treason, a capital..." He now recalls the phrase from the circular. "The King! The Safe King!" And forgetting his repulsion, he grabs the scarf on the woman's chest.

"I've seen Your Excellency at the tavern," says the one-time siren who reigned at a King Street café's cash register, in Dajka's office a half hour later. The cab ride had broken through her usual dull drunken stupor. The scales have tipped in her soul. Right now nothing would be sweeter than betraying her former lover, who had left her for another. He had left her without saying good-bye, and now, a lifetime later, this is what rankles most.

The Special Investigator has no choice; whether he likes it or not, he must use the informer.

It was a flower girl. The slut used to work the "row of Cats" on King Street.

By now it is night. On King Street, the owner of the Spotted Cat at last remembers; the flower girl became a dealer in second-hand clothing. Now for a long ride in a fiacre to Cracklings, the uncrowned emperor of the second-hand rag trade. He wants to stay in the good graces of the great Dajka, and does not hesitate to give out the name of Karola Gombocz, and the address of her business, in the slums of Cemetery Road.

In the doorway of the first hut at the edge of the slum, the police officer steps back at the reek from inside. Dozens of people are lying about on the floor, playing cards and drinking wine; this hole is their home. A skinny little boy in greyish rags is dozing by the entrance. A woman clad in burlap is staring with expressionless eyes at the two well-dressed men.

Dajka waits in the doorway until the general stir produces an elderly man, who emerges into the murkiness of the humid summer night.

"At your service, Your Excellency." If a well-dressed individual shows up here, he is either a criminal, trying to hide, or, if coming openly, a man of the law. Dajka motions him with his head to move away from the entrance.

"Is there a woman around here who sells second-hand clothes?" In the light of the full moon he can see the ooze seeping from under the black patch covering the old man's eye. The man uses a large checkered handkerchief to smear it over his face.

Karola is a good girl, and will not say a word. She may be jealous, but she will not betray her man. But nothing can prevent a thorough house search. In a corner, at the bottom of a pile of used clothes, they find the striped trousers of the archival clerk, and moments later, every piece of clothing left behind by the fugitives, except for footwear. She does not deal in shoes. There is enough to prove her an accessory after the fact, but Marton keeps up the search, prying into drawers, corners, everywhere.

"Look for a razor," the Doctor tells him. In the end he finds it himself under a respectable straw mattress. "Remind me to update the circular. No mustache, no beard."

In the same place he finds a metal box containing two gold napoleons. The clientele of Cemetery Road are hardly able to pay with this kind of coin.

Marton threatens Karola with arrest, and the loss of her dealer's license. She does not deny anything; it would make no sense. Yes, they changed here. But she is unwilling to tell into what, and how much money they had - information which would speed their capture.

Dajka calls off his assistant. Here is another ex-lover, who does the opposite of what the wretched syphilitic did, even at the cost of her own skin. This woman suddenly shines against her environment, and the Doctor sees her clearly. He does not know why the scene calls to mind the first time he saw Bora's almond-shaped eyes at the brothel.

"I am confiscating this," he says, turning toward Karola with the tin box. "It is evidence. You have collaborated with escaped convicts, and that is a serious matter. Did you provide clothes on other occasions? You can tell me the truth."

Karola is surprised by this almost encouraging tone. She is close to confessing everything. But she merely shakes her head: No, she did not. The Special Investigator takes her at her word.

Judging by the clothes lying all over the room, he concludes that the fugitives are now trying to pass for respectable middle-class citizens, as long as their clean shaves last. (He is correct on two counts out of three.) They may still have some funds left. And at least at the start they were heading north.

He issues a stern warning to Karola Gombocz never again to give clothes to a known criminal, not for love or money, because he will have her locked up. Later, in the cab, he will reflect that there is no use denying, he was lenient toward this woman because she refused to betray her lover to the police. Strange are the ways of the Lord.

He makes sure the corrected version of the circular is distributed.

At dawn two men wearing respectable clothes arrive at Szent-Endre, the fishing village north of Buda. One of them is limping slightly; he had to stuff paper in his shoes, which are too large. The men have avoided populated places on their way. At the Danube's edge they stop to deliberate. "Do you know how to swim?" the Greek asks Baumgarten. If not, he would be in a jam. But luckily he does. It is a skill they will have to resort to often in their long journey across our land, so rich in rivers and streams. (In Central Europe, progressing in an east-west direction, one must ford a major river on average every forty miles. Invading armies provide for this contingency by pontoon bridges and amphibian tanks, according to Little Kovács, who had been enlisted, and made a study of it.)

About two hundred yards upstream, at the ferry crossing, fishermen stand around the plainclothes detective who just arrived by cab from the capital, to inquire after any suspicious travelers. He glimpses the pair downstream, and yells out to them.

"Hey! You two! Hold it!" He starts running in their direction, screaming at the fishermen as he runs, "What are you waiting for? Catch them!"

The two fugitives quickly shed their clothes, bundle them up and, using their belts, tie the packs to their heads before wading into the river.

"Help me catch those fugitives at once! In the name of the law! I order you!" But the detective shouts in vain.

In the capital the police have more authority than here. The oldest fisherman, shuffling his feet, mutters something about not being in their pay (nor would he accept it if offered). Let the gentleman give his orders to his paid underlings. He is a good fisherman, a wise man, and his fellow fishermen of Szent-Endre usually heed his words. (The "Sándor Rózsa syndrome" at work.)

The two fugitives grab a floating log and, in plain sight of the detective screaming and fuming back on shore, they reach the other side, where they disappear in a thicket of willows. The small bag of Szeged paprika did not even get wet on top of the floating log.

Around noon at police headquarters, another cab-driver is found, another trail turns up, the result of all the routine work that never ceases. He states that he had a strange fare last night. The non-communicative individual flagged him down near a small hotel out on Kerepesi Road, under suspicious circumstances. Consider the late hour. The well-dressed man in a poor district. No sign of a hotel porter or servant; he was carrying his luggage himself. An elegant yellow pigskin suitcase and a shoulder bag of the same material. He gave a one-forint tip. After asking to be taken to the Southern Railroad Terminal he said not another word. He kept his face in the shadows and refused the driver's offer to carry his suitcase to the train. He was of medium height, with a springy walk.

At this very moment the traveler with the yellow suitcase is seemingly thinking about purchasing some of the illustrated papers at the Szabadka train station on the southern railroad line. Actually he is deliberating his next move. He is careful not to show his face too much. He would like to be beyond the border as soon as possible.

The two runaways, once across the Danube, dress themselves and smooth out their clothes.

"They gave me the slip," reports the detective back at headquarters, where he shows up late in the afternoon, with a fine, leisurely, home-cooked Szent-Endre luncheon under his belt. Dajka opens his office door and calls in all those present. He points at the detective for all to see.

"Take a good look, everyone. Go on, my good man, step up to the wall. Show your face. And now tell us what it is that a police detective cannot do, but an international safe-cracker and a train thief can? Was it beneath the dignity of Your Excellency to jump into the river after them? Or perhaps your courage failed you? Or is it that you *cannot swim*?! Perhaps you should seek employment as a crown prince or as a university professor. Get this into your heads, once and for all: It takes a policeman who is stronger, craftier and quicker than the thief to catch him!"

The strong, the crafty and the quick are on their way toward Vecsés, crossing the country eastward. The question marks multiply in the Special Investigator's notebook. Where are they heading? What are their plans? That way lies Galicia, and the Russian border.

Their clothes still announce them as decent folk, which is contrary to the truth. The pickpocket stops at a village on the way to purchase bread and bacon, and the first persons he meets are a pair of gendarmes, who greet him courteously, judging him by his clothes. After this, the fugitives make sure to give wide berth to populated areas.

The next twenty-four hours are crucial in the Budapest investigation. At the Southern Terminal no porter or conductor remembers seeing the gentleman burglar with the yellow leather luggage. When the ticket-booth girls are interrogated one by one, sure enough, one of them reports that the previous night she sold a discount round trip ticket to Szabadka. The purchaser was a solitary young woman, which is why the ticket seller remembers her. No, the woman was not dressed in black, and she was not wearing a veil.

Dajka thinks that if this is what Karola Gombocz was hiding from them, then her secret did not last very long. The next train on the southern line to Szabadka leaves at midnight, exactly twenty-four hours after the fugitive's train. Dajka tells his assistant not to bother with confronting Karola and the ticket seller. To himself, he rationalizes this as unnecessary, for clearly the woman was not going to testify against her ex-lover. Nor is it likely that she knew much more than what she was told, to buy a ticket to Szabadka. A criminal of this caliber does not as a rule leave much gratuitous information in his wake.

He has Inspector Marton buy two tickets. Dajka's faith is shaken in his detectives, and he decides to go after this noblest game in person. He takes a cab home to Bath Street, to pack his things and say goodbye to his wife.

That night, as if longing to be back, he shows up at the Kitty with his luggage, to smoke one final cigar. He sits at his table until the last minute, when duty calls him to the train station. He cannot forget that he still has some unfinished business here.

Inspector Marton is awaiting him with the tickets. During his absence, Dajka leaves the investigation in the hands of Chief Inspector Axaméthy. Dajka and Marton enter their sleeper compartment, but sleep does not come easily.

The two runaways avoid villages and towns and camp out under the open sky. They make do with the food purchased by Baumgarten, and augment their diet with roadside field pears, plums, and forest berries. This is one aspect we did not anticipate when we prepared for our great coup. I did not know we would work for a whole year only to lose the entire take and have to run with nothing but our last reserves.

They reach the River Tisza, white with mayflies. The great river winds in languorous loops, just as it did back in the days when this region temporarily went by the name of Vilayet of Buda, occupied by a foreign army obeying the call of a different faith. Those are the things that pass.

But not the river; it is here to stay. My friends, colleagues and confrères are worn, unshaven and hopeful. They look on with awe at the unbroken white stretch of the river, a spectacle of only a day or two each summer. (We believed it eternal, and then it was gone. The changes that came were greater than ephemeral mayflies, a mere occupation.)

They feel it is a good omen that the river awaited them dressed in white. Burglars and thieves are all superstitious, haven't I said that already?

So they walk on toward the east. They sleep in haystacks, and with each passing day their beards grow, their clothes become more and more creased.

Dajka and Marton get off the train at each stop of the southern line, and ask questions in the station house. The sleeping car's conductor stands ready to hand down their luggage through the window at a moment's notice.

In Szabadka, in a second-floor room of the the Golden Lamb Inn, the internationally hunted fugitive shoulders his bag and picks up his light suitcase. Only ten minutes before, he went downstairs in his dressing-gown to order, drowsily and in French, a full breakfast, to be placed in front of his door. Now he steps out through the window on the broad ledge outside. He has made sure to pay his bill for the next day, for he still has some money left. After all, he is a respectable safe-cracker; it would be beneath his dignity to take advantage of the good innkeeper by skipping out on him. Yes, this is a more primitive world, with different manners.

It still has not occurred to the proprietor that his guest kept his face out of view.

The international express train is scheduled for a three-minute stop in Szabadka. The officers of the law spend the first minute finding someone from whom they can obtain reliable information. During the second minute the station-master is able to confirm that there was indeed a passenger on yesterday's train who got off carrying a suitcase and shoulder bag of yellow leather. For this is a small town, where strangers are noticed. Not surprisingly, no one can provide a description of the traveler. In the third and last minute the conductor rapidly hands down their luggage. And in that third minute, on the other side of the tracks, their prey quietly opens the door of one of the first-class cars, and boards the train, suitcase in hand. He walks down the corridor in search of a seat as the train lurches off. As the two policemen ride to town in a cab they can see smoke curling up from the departing train.

At the police station on the main square the local chief lends them his one and only plainclothes detective, who takes them straight to the local cab stables. The trail is obvious and leads to the Golden Lamb Inn, where the man with the yellow suitcase checked in. The proprietor tells them that his guest went back to sleep; he was planning to leave the next day. The guest spoke French, but the innkeeper did not think the man was French. He seemed to keep his face averted all the time.

Since the guest had not left the inn, he should still be in his room.

No one answers the door. The soft-boiled eggs have cooled on the tray in front of the door. The owner's passkey goes to work. The eyes of the two officers from the capital, and of the local detective follow the same route: one ashtray has been used, the bed is in disarray, the drawers have been emptied and the window is open.

They will be able to travel on only by next morning's express train. The fugitive could not have gone back north, into the hornets' nest; he could only have continued his journey south on the train that brought them here. He gained a full twenty-four hour advantage. Yes, this is one adversary who merits Dajka's full personal attention.

The Doctor makes use of the enforced delay to rest and to exchange telegrams. There is no news of the other two fugitives.

They keep walking. Within the last two days they had to remove their clothes three times already, and bundle them up to wade and swim across this white river that keeps playfully reappearing in front of them, although they are heading directly due east. With each crossing, fragments of dead mayflies gather on their dark clothes.

The universal taboo of borders, so crippling for the

law-abiding citizen, is not observed by the outlaw. (This is still a time of tolerant conventions, without *self-adjusting* mortars, and Hiram Maxim's machine gun is not yet in use to enforce the taboo.) My accomplices at this moment are aiming to cross the border between Hungary and Galicia, and, by cutting across Galicia, to leave the Austro-Hungarian Dual Monarchy at their earliest opportunity.

Belgrade. The gentleman with yellow luggage is at the train station ticket booth. He buys a ticket to Milan, shifting the course of his journey westward.

Dajka and his assistant are optimistic as their train rattles on toward the Balkans. They still have a long way to go, but the trail they are following is a clear one. They are bound to inactivity by the plush comforts of the sleeping car as it traverses the distances of Europe. The Special Investigator finds himself with time on his hands. He sees the face of that girl with the Tatar eyes, her silent blank stare hovering in front of him in the misty window of the compartment. The only way he can free himself of the apparition is by concentrating all of his powers on the task ahead. He eggs on his junior officer.

They compose a circular to be sent by telegram to all railway junctions of Southern Europe, informing the local police forces about their manhunt. German has been the lingua franca of this time and place ever since the retreat of the Turk. They will send the telegrams, from the next stop.

After midnight the senior of the two men blows out the lamp, and they turn in for some sleep on the narrow beds of the compartment.

The fugitive's train arrives in Parma. He is planning to get off here, when he glimpses the carabinieri patrol proceeding along the platform, checking each car. For once, the escaped man loses his sang-froid. He grabs his yellow suitcase from the luggage rack. Hunted and fatigued, he makes a decisive mistake; as he jumps off on the other side to disappear in the crowds, he leaves behind a message that will not only betray his itinerary to his pursuers, but also offer both explanation and evidence of the Chicago-style safe jobs, and will even let them know that he is nearing the end of his funds.

Dajka and his assistant leave the train at Zimony (for you, Novo-Belgrade), where the hottest temperature in the country was recorded on the day of the "brick affair". Here they put up for a couple of days, across the river from Nándorfehérvár, and get in touch with their local colleagues. (Nándorfehérvár is Beograd in Serbian. The Turks called it *Dar ul Jihad* - City of the Holy War. Which was fought against us, the frontier bastion opposing the Turk. In Central Europe each ethnic group considers itself as the human barrier that stopped the progress of the Turk, thereby preventing West Europe from becoming a land of mosques and veiled women. And probably they all have a right to the claim. But let us remember that when the noontime bells sound from Tierra del Fuego to Lappland, it is to commemorate the Nándorfehérvár-Belgrado victory of János Hunyadi and Giovanni da Capistrano (after whom the small town of San Juan Capistrano in Southern California has been named) in the war against the Turk. Take a look at the map, at the places we have been to, and the places we are no longer in, within the Basin. The events seemed to go in this order: slaughter, re-settlement, annexation. Fact. Who will keep track of it, if we won't?)

On the evening of the second day a police courier brings to their hotel room a flat yellow leather shoulder bag. It was opened up by an unsuspecting clerk in the Lost and Found office of the Italian Royal Railways, in the hope of finding an address inside. The bag resembles a jeweler's *étui*, and its velvet-padded interior contains leather compartments holding a set of tempered steel burglar's tools of unprecedented workmanship. The Special Investigator emits a low whistle of admiration at this sight (as Marton was to tell me later).

Yes, these tools could indeed cut a round hole through a double-walled steel Wiese-Wertheim safe. Next to the tools are a fistful of crumpled hundred-forint banknotes, sixty forints in nickel twenty-fillér coins, rolled up in paper, and some picture postcards of resort areas on the French Riviera. A side pocket contains two roughly cut steel disks.

The amount of money - barely two thousand forints - does not make sense. Dajka had expected close to thirty thousand, but for the moment he sets this discrepancy aside. He hurries to compare the two cardboard disks, which he keeps with him everywhere, and ascertains that they indeed match the metal ones. These will now serve as material evidence, connecting the Bush Street cellar safe with Odessa, and linking both to the one at the Grand Bazaar in Budapest, and all of them with the leader of the gang, who is running barely one step ahead of them. This is the kind of proof that will be accepted even by the exacting Royal Hungarian courts.

Now only one thing remains to be done: to catch the thief. To find the cart that goes with the horse.

The Special Investigator proceeds to spell out his late-night cogitations.

"We intend to catch him in person, correct?" He thinks aloud for Marton. "But the nature of the railroads and timetables is such that even if we were to follow him flawlessly, we would never catch up with him." (And, lest you forget, trains are the fastest way to get anywhere.) "The crimefighter must know a little of everything. He must be a tamer of souls, if need be. He must be able to get inside the mind of the scoundrel he is chasing, and learn to think like him. Or else he must get inside his pocket, depending on where the rogue's decisions are made." (Didn't I tell you? Detective work is like writing fiction. Retroactively, we could claim the Doctor as a colleague, provided he would accept us as colleagues.) "So, what are we to do, Marton?"

Marton completes the train of thought. "His train is the Padua-Milan."

"Bravo." It looks like Dajka will have a competent successor, after all. "So we know his line of flight. It is up to our Italian counterparts to find out how far on the line his ticket will carry him. So compose that telegram, my son. It's all right if it is in French. You don't know any French? How about Italian? No? Then I advise you to learn, as soon as you can. I won't be around forever."

That night the two weary walkers come up against the Tisza,

for the fourth time. Yesterday's white-clad river is now whipped up by a relentless black rain. Both men are soaked to the skin, and only that bag of paprika is still dry, sheltered under the shirt of its carrier. They at last find a ferry, but it is abandoned. In the course of time the river has repeatedly shifted east and west on the plain. Now the ferry is only a stone's throw from the point where, on a summer day a long time ago, the fishermen, seeing the approaching alien army, fled in panic leaving their boats and nets behind.

The ferryboat is there, but the oars have been removed. The drenched, exhausted travelers are not up to this last setback. They must recoup their strength somehow. They enter Puhl's tavern, just outside the nearby village.

The tavern-keeper is a talkative, inquisitive type. It is so rare to see strangers coming this way. He settles in a chair next to the newcomers and tries some cheerful banter. One of them orders a shot of brandy. Both of them are morose and taciturn.

At last one of them speaks up. "We want to hire a boat."

When the kitchen girl goes past with a bowl of steaming goulash, Puhl notices the guests' wide-eyed interest in the food.

"Wouldn't you like some of that good warm soup?" And he right away places an order on their behalf. "So where are you heading?"

"We would like to cross the river."

The tavern-keeper nods; he understands. They have no luggage; they are too hungry, their appearance too neglected. Once they are on a boat, they could just drift downstream, and reach the Serbian border past Titel. He is incorrect in his assumptions, but it is not really his business. He steps out into the storm, to rouse a boat from a neighboring fisherman.

He bumps into a pair of gendarmes coming in for shelter from the rainstorm.

"Where are you off to, Mr. Puhl? Won't you join us for a word or two?" They shake the water from their hats and settle in at a table.

The two rain-soaked strangers, unnoticed by the gendarmes until now, jump up and race out into the rain. The gendarmes stare after them, one fires a shot in the air, but they soon give up with a shrug, and resume their seats at the table. One of them takes out the list of wanted criminals and licks his thumb, preparing to leaf through it.

At the hotel in Zimony, Marton has the reply telegram from the Italian police within twenty-four hours. The subject of the manhunt purchased a ticket from Milan to Genoa. The ticket seller said he spoke French, but it did not seem to be his native tongue. It is their man all right. He had to scrape up his last remaining change to buy a third-class ticket.

"That's all right, Safe King, you can hide your auburn locks all you want. For I don't think you have much money left after what you lost with the *étui*," says Marton, who is ready to second-guess his man. (Back home he will study foreign languages, for he is an earnest law officer, with a sense of mission.)

The Safe King's share has been captured with him; this must have been his last reserve, left with Karola Gombocz.

"What do you think he will do next?"

"Try to obtain some money."

"How?"

"Another safe job? Unlikely. He is alone, left his tools behind... But there are those postcards. The Riviera!"

The majority of the postcards found in the shoulder bag are from Nice, Marseille and Monte Carlo. The Safe King is an educated man, he belongs to the so-called "intellectual criminal" type. He is in a bind, without accomplices, informants or tools. And he does not have much time. He has been to the Riviera before; this is where the gang spent those good times after the Odessa job.

It is just possible: he could be heading for Monte Carlo, the only place in Europe where gambling is permitted. He would want to try his luck at the roulette and chemin de fer tables, like any other good citizen. He could still win. And all he could lose are his chains.

"Well, why don't we gamble as well. Let's put everything on this card." And the Special Investigator sends Marton to buy two tickets all the way to Monte Carlo, in the principality of

Monaco. His assistant obeys, a lingering doubt mixed with his amazement. His mentor is either mad, or a genius.

(NOW: BAG-LADY. LIMNED EFFIGIES)

Last week your cross-country coach kicked you off the team.

In our private movie we have come to the personal order of magnitude. This is what we are bound to spend the most time on. And it intertwines, mixes in with the historical. Suddenly our interest intensifies; we are getting closer to our one-time-only selves.

I spent yesterday afternoon straightening out the cross-country situation for you, this one last time. I could see in your eyes the pain of being left out. I know that feeling well. The others all get together every Thursday. Cecil *gets lost*. Ottilia slips her legs into nylon and she competes in junior events. On Sunday they board a train in their warm-up suits, each with her military green compass, and set out for the hills and woods, where the deer run. They enter in the N 13 category (girls under thirteen).

Note from the edge of the world: Spaceship Earth is again traversing the colder regions. For millions of years the average annual temperature had been twenty-two degrees (Centigrade; there are other systems), now it drops to fourteen.

You deserved to be thrown off the cross-country team, and you know it. You have missed practice twice in a row, and you lost your compass in the chaos of your room. As a meek spectator, I have come to like cross-country running. (And I usually cannot bear to watch sports. It is a personal limitation. It dates back to the days of the early 'fifties, to the year of the Newtown Festival, when we were locked up inside our own borders, and only athletes were allowed to travel abroad. I remember when the announcement of our prime minister Imre Nagy's execution was announced around the time of the soccer World Cup. Those in power deemed that people would be involved heart and soul with the pigskin ball and our golden-footed lads - and *they got away with it*.) Now a cross-country race is not merely mindless running, but a subtle interplay of strategy and tactics, making choices about directions and solutions. And it is a thoroughly amateur sport. Your Vargha grandparents must have looked like this, in that generation between the wars, when they donned their hiking boots or tennis outfits. A glass of raspberry soda is the only prize after the race. We even had a Hungarian world champion. Once, when I saw all of you with your glowing, flushed faces, I considered trying it myself - if I had had more faith in my ability to make decisions. I was concerned from the outset that the necessity for speedy decisions made you hesitant about training and racing; it did not really suit your temperament. Sooner or later this will make you drop out of cross-country running, regardless of my talk with the bimbo who is your coach.

All I asked for was that you be given one more chance. You and I have made our agreement beforehand. I will pay for the compass; what else can we do, you don't have an income. You promise that for one whole year you will not quit, regardless. Like we did once before, when you took violin lessons. And if you miss another session, they can throw you off the team.

I am beset by a perennial fear that you are not going to acquire good work habits, and as a result your life will be endless misery.

You were waiting for the results at a fast food restaurant, across from the former Café Nicoletti on Octagon Place. They took you back, you were given another chance. It was the first real winter day, and it came early; you have not seen its like in your twelve years. This is what I really wanted to talk about. About the beggar woman who staggered in from the cold.

Each of her extremities had a plastic bag tied around the rags that kept her warm; around the midriff of her bloated body a string was tied over a strip of plastic that served as the belt of her coat. She stood behind your back, wordlessly. The platinum-blonde waitress turned to the coal-blackhaired waitress:

"Here comes the little mamma."

And these two gave us the present of a moment of warmth. Yes, these two waitresses, who, one would assume, were well-developed specimens of the latest alienating wave in our homeland, the "hot-dog vendor" syndrome. It seemed a fitting celebration of your reinstatement. The black-haired one sliced off a large hunk of bread, and took a generous portion of meat from her grill. She abundantly doused the bread with gravy, placed the meat on top, and putting it all on a clean plate, handed it to the bag lady. She did not shove it at her. The bag lady accepted it without a word, and started eating. I realize that it was not food the waitress had brought from home, and that ultimately the customers were paying for it. But still: that was one piece she would not take home.

You were eating ice cream. You did not allow such trivialities as the weather to come between you and your enjoyment. Since you had your back to the events, I reported to you in a soft undertone.

They had instituted the daily theft of bread and meat for the old woman. It had become unwritten law. About those other slices, I don't really care.

But that wasn't all. As we went out into the freezing night, we saw the bag lady sitting in a taxi waiting at the stand. She was somewhat slumped in the front seat. The driver, whose role, by its very nature, has to be a dense distillate of this new-fangled loathsomeness compounded of bribe-taking and baksheesh-hunting had let her in, to keep herself warm in his idling cab. *Invited* her in.

I had to re-evaluate everything, and be more careful from now on about making superficial judgements. I basked in the warmth of recognizing that I had been idiotically mistaken. All along, these reserves have been there, hiding inside platinum-dyed waitresses and tip-hungry taxi drivers. So the next time someone pours gasoline over schoolchildren in a hijacked bus, let us remember the bag lady in the winter night. The current goes both ways.

We felt good about this for a long time.

In our private movie we reach the point where Little Kovács's future, prominent cheek bones are determined.

The Turk, at last, conquers Belgrade, which is no longer the last line of defense against Islam. Soon it will be Buda's turn to become the last outpost of Islam against the West. As it happens, it is our birthplace. From here on we would become the bastion of defence, for one or another of the warring parties, although we did not volunteer for the job. Lately historians have been traveling to the Istanbul archives to research Hungarian history. They will be going to other capitals as well, as soon as they are allowed access to the libraries.

Historical time flies over our heads at a giddy speed. In troubled times existence seems to be more fraught with happenings.

A work entitled *Concerning the Revolutions of the Heavenly Spheres* is published in the West. It tells us that we are not at the center of the heavens or of the universe, not even in the center of our Solar System. Since then, scientific knowledge has been made possible.

The plague sweeps through the country.

In our history, this is the age of stormy, far-reaching encounters.

The Turks are at Buda's gates. The order of magnitude here is personal, and it blends into the historical. You think this strange. But we have already caught a glimpse of the procession climbing up the river's banks; we are nearby. From our grassy, tree-shaded seat up here, behind which, like an eyebrow, overhangs the opening to a cave, we are able to observe the mounted raiders herding the Hungarian slaves, the cart with its solid wheels. We are going to come even closer, until we can make out the features of individual slaves, the handle of the smithy's hammer, the network of creases at the tip of a single finger. Four people: the girl, her brother, the enslaved smith and the Iron Man. We shall meet these four again.

We speed up, and take another look from far away, from

where we can make out tiny movements, against the background heartbeat of the cosmos. Then we want to slow down again, to close in on local flashes:

The multitudes of the town of Londinium, the old pirate with ear-ring and bandanna. We feast on hot roast leg of mutton. See the newborn calf, with two heads and eight legs. The Italian girl, whose eyes stir the blood, melt the bone marrow, my lasting betrothal to the storm-tossed life of itinerant mountebanks.

Wandering student, minstrel, I see a witch burned at the stake in the town of Berlin on the banks of the River Spree. She is taken in a procession, followed by a screaming, cursing hypocritical mob, down an unpaved street lined on both sides by piles of excrement left there by strumpets. The executioner in his scarlet robe, red feather in his hat. His apprentice headsmen also in red shirts. They drug the pallid female on a creaking oak cart, her face besmirched by the blood and soot of nocturnal torture. Toward the red, orange and blue flames of the pyre, toward the hour of dying screams drowned in the sizzle and sweet stink of scorched human flesh.

Then homewards on galleons, coaches, crossing the waters and plains. As an itinerant minstrel playing my lute throughout the Transdanubian region, at border castles besieged by the troops of the Pashas of Buda, Esztergom, Fehérvár. For my livelihood I sing songs of my own making: about how the Sultan captured our Buda in 'Forty-one without firing one shot. I help build frontier forts, unroofed, hedged by wattle and daub; I lug stones, sweep the yard, stand guard in rain and frost. I learn the builder's trade, the placement of reeds, rafters, planks. Until at last the fort is ready, stocked with provisions, gunpowder aplenty.

At the time of the Little Ice Age I find my way back to Pest in the guise of a Dutch trader, a roving night moth. The church is now a jami, the cross replaced by the crescent, houses are turned into stables for the janissaries' horses. Between leaning, swaying fences patched up with mud, in the middle of town a great ditch, a miasma of trickling sewage. Now our Buda is the chief western stronghold of the Mahometan empire. Abandoned churches, ashes of burnt houses. Motley lean-tos, vendors' stalls. Loud voices proclaim the teachings of Al-Koran, and the Hungarians are beaten everywhere.

I am the castle marketplace showman, displaying limned effigies, painted cloth on sticks, and sell booklets at ten dinars each, bemoaning the Turk lording over us, and the German emperor's troops burning and looting, while our nation dwindles.

I see the Papist lord of the castle who raids the neighboring heretic village, gladder to wrangle with his Calvinist neighbor than with the heathen. Elsewhere the Protestant swears he would sooner fight the Pope than the Turk. Not enough to have heathen, plague, cold and misery - our Hungarian robber barons ravage the poor's land, and convert by butchery, strappado, and fire. I will not be a part of this.

Laying aside my lute and painted images, I take my stand behind the palisades against the heathen. I shall not kill, that I'll never do, but I will do back-breaking work. (This solution worked well in several of my jobs; somebody has to get the work done, and, at this price, I could arrange my life according to my lights.) Hard labor: lime-baking, brick-laying. I bring back two shiploads from the town of Vienna: two hundred iron shovels and spades, one hundred wheelbarrows. In thirty days we raise the stone walls against the besieging troops of the Pasha of Buda, who builds his own earthworks, and aims his guns at our walls, bombarding us night and day. His cannonballs shoot the roof off our gunpowder storehouse. And they attack us with siege ladders and with howls, climbing the walls, pouring through the opening. The heathen believes that his Almighty God is fighting on his side. I ask myself, which of the opposing Gods is going to prove mightier? Our defenders allow in some of the Turks through the holes, then fall on them and overcome the brave vanguard. At last, on September 1st, according to the new calendar, the Turk retreats from our fort, and the serfs can clear away the bodies of the dead and the carrion under our walls. I set out again with a new song on my lute.

With the passing of the Turk, in the Christian Buda, the German *Hetzmeister* is in charge of bull-fights and bear-baiting. I stand at the cross-roads of Europe's trade routes on Bomb Square (for you, Batthyány, named after our other executed prime minister) and offer *Hetzen*-songs at home again, in peacetime. The bumbling bear's paw gropes after the fattened white duck in the pond. White feathers scatter. The hurdy-gurdy caterwauls. Baiters with pitchforks urge a pack of dogs at a toothless old lion, and the bloodthirsty crowd rejoices at the sight of torn bits of dog flying about.

At Carnival time, a fake blind beggar, I sing for the slowly Magyarizing town, on the ice of the lesser Danube branch by Rabbits' Island. I sell forbidden broadsides, Hungarian songs for four pence. The poor folk pinch each penny, tempted by nearby puppeteers performing a fable. I stamp my feet in the bitter cold; these are our winters in the Age of Beech. My eyes are always open now, I am on the lookout for her, week after week on the ice, scattered with straw, sprinkled with water refrozen again and again, so that it can support a loaded cart. A merry-go-round whirls to music. Gentlemen clad in armour shoot firearms into the air, firecrackers go off, rockets fly. Peasants gobble barbecued meat, quaff down beer and wine. The perilous warm wind splits the ice, I throw away my beggar's stave, helter-skelter stampede up the river bank. The screams of the drowning mingle with the roar of cracking ice.

I recite to the accompaniment of my three-stringed lute, and sell to the St. Medardus Day market crowds my printed broadsides that lie on the canvas here at Haymarket Place. (Calvin Place for you.) "Hang it on your rafters, stick it in your mirror frame, good people. Sweeter than honey. Two pence apiece." On my left the Punch and Judy show; on my right, the mechanical dolls.

Again I am showing painted effigies, eight pictures on each side of the canvas, the pointer in my hand, eyeglasses on the bridge of my nose (made of clear glass, for a scholarly effect). Vendors of knick-knacks in their booths, trained dogs and revolving stage shows, fortune teller. "There are no more winter nights!" I must keep up a patter, to rivet their attention and make them buy. Penny dreadfuls on the trestle table, in the wicker basket, on the tarpaulin, next to potions against the gout and lumbago.

And all of a sudden: we are back on the Danube quay, where enormous, sharp-pointed girders are piled up like pencils belonging to titans; serpentine coils of ropes, hawsers, tarpaulin-covered crates, barrels, basalt cobblestones in heaps, door and window-frames lying in the city's gateway, through which we ship, piece by piece, our roadways and sidewalks, our theaters and brothels.

The weave of events is now palpably tighter. Our native city is teeming with varicolored life, into the midst of which you will eventually arrive, where we shall roam, love and learn. Where, in the age of the electric trains, you will find Old Buda, the focus of our stories, a few hundred steps from Bomb Square, crossroads of Europe, where the streetcar stops in front of the Little Bear Bar, complete with Kovács, the street toughs, Sándorka and Piros.

· Land where life is a movable feast, and the Black Land. Lineal forebears: ancestors of the gang leader Alva Ráz. Of Laboda, Mr. Rudi, and Mia, who will shout "At half past eleven!" at the bar. Little Kovács's grandfather and Dani's great-grandfather. Etelka Hannauer, the Witch, as well as your Great-grandmother Vargha, the future teacher, who is not afraid of anyone. The adventurer Richard Edelman, the Whale's grandfather. The ancestors of Roland, the Brick. And Ferke, in person.

We may move in to take a closer look at the Safe King and at Special Investigator Dajka, at Bora's Russian prince on the Nevski Prospekt, at Maria and Julia Haldek, train thieves and prostitutes, the Jewish pickpocket Baumgarten, Rókus Láncz, the fence and the Armenian, Agap Kevorg.

The city re-building, after all the destruction and decay.

The smell of fresh brown and white paint on door and window frames of brand new apartment buildings. The original gray facets of cobblestones covering the grand network of new avenues. I sit on the box of a coach, overhearing conversations, I am not ashamed. A nightclub is being built on Rose Square. I work on construction sites, lugging bricks and mortar for the master mason. A Slovak glazier teaches me how to make a kaleidoscope. Later, the shadowy figures of the demimonde, to whom I am attracted by their rough-hewn, colorful life, lead me to learn a thing or two about the labors of a Dutch master diamond cutter, and the order placed by a respected Budapest jeweler.

Crowds blacken Radius Avenue; on the wood blocks of the roadway pound mounted processions from each county, hussars with powder pouches; endless lines of carriages, a mastodon of an omnibus, advertising Bensdorp's Dutch cocoa on its yellow billboard. The cheerful billed caps of veloci-pedists.   A court equipage.   National tricolors, endless buntings. Sixty thousand electric lights illuminate the Little Constantinople amusement park, designed by the English engineer Paine. Deep in our hearts we have not accepted the new name of Istambul, just as we reject the new names for Radius Avenue and Váci Street. For entertainment, we have built a "Turkish Buda" in the Park   we can afford to, now that the Turk is gone home.

Whirling dervishes whirl, howling dervishes howl at the summer festivities of the National Exposition. At night, four hundred musicians play taps. Horse-traders, army officers, make-believe soubrettes gape at our Bora in the disenchanting light of the back section of this smoky, stifling nightclub.

It was predictable: the only thing remembered about the case of the brick murder at the Silly Kitty is that the police have been unable to solve it. Most of the time people pass by the truly important events of their days with closed eyes. Instead, the sensational news of the day is the other, spectacular crime, which is eagerly discussed everywhere, from the urine-scented yards of taverns behind the Central Train Terminal to the salons of the mansions of Radius Avenue, lit by the unprecedented brilliance of the first fifteen-watt lightbulbs with tungsten filaments.

They talk about the international gang of safe-crackers, and the daring escape of these *Apaches*. This must mean that our city has at last attained the rank of a true metropolis, in the floodlight of European civilization, at the vanguard of international progress.

No one has seen the fugitives.

One of them is traveling third-class to the French Riviera, followed by the Special Investigator and Marton. Or rather, preceded by them.

They stop only long enough to change trains, and do not rest in Trieste, Milan or Genoa. Two days later they arrive at the town of Monte Carlo, a mile and a half from the town of Monaco. My fellow criminal is right behind them, on a speeding express train. Who is chasing whom? This question sounds familiar, as familiar as the notion of relativity.

By now the other two fugitives are so deep in the wilderness that they are beginning to feel safe. At night they lie down to sleep on a bed of moss. In the morning they wake to a bird's trills.

GALICIA AND THE RUSSIAN BORDER

For days on end, they have no idea where they are. They have been avoiding settled areas. Ever since their run-in with the gendarmes they have been haunted by premonitions.

On this morning they wake on a bed of pine needles, stretch their numb, stiff limbs, and descend into the valley to complete their brisk toilette in the icy water of a swiftly coursing stream.

It feels as if they have already left the country behind, but a painted sign of the royal forest administration informs them that they are in fact in the border county of Máramaros at the easternmost edge of the land. Beyond this lies Galicia, a territory of Austria (Austria on our *east*, as well: strange though it seems, these days), and east of that is the Russian Empire.

At the forest's edge they survey the land: out in the clearing, a pair of gendarmes with fixed bayonets, rooster feathers fluttering in their hats, are evidently returning from border patrol. The fugitives are close to deliverance.

In Monte Carlo the two detectives divide the town's hotels between themselves. (These are the kind of casino-resorts that

the Baroness had dreamed of in the hills of Buda.) At each
hotel they stop to talk to the doorman for a few minutes. After
that, they return to their own modest hostel, where they can
only wait and see if they had bet on a winning card. The
Doctor is aware of his junior colleague's eyes on him. If his
hunch proves incorrect, the burglar will have put half of
Europe between them by now, gaining an insurmountable
lead. But Dajka is confident that his gamble will pay off.
Meanwhile the tension mounts, hour by hour.

The fugitives walk the forest paths all day, trying to stay out
of sight until they cross the border. The railroad thief is badly
hobbled; his feet are blistered raw by the oversized shoes
taken from the archival clerk.

In Monte Carlo, toward evening, the resplendently uniformed head doorman of the Hotel Cléopatra on the Quai des
Anglais knocks on the door of the room occupied by the two
detectives.
"I think your man has arrived."
Marton's admiration for his superior at this moment reaches
new heights. They make sure to take handcuffs with them as
they hurry over to the Cléopatra. From here on Marton will
not have much time for amazement. They find the room
empty, with the freshly ironed cutaway, shirtfront, collar,
bowtie all laid out on the bed, in readiness for the evening's
visit to the gambling casino. They quickly search the remaining
yellow suitcase. Besides clothes, they find assorted Hungarian
Royal Postage stamps worth two-hundred twenty-five forints,
and five rolls of nickel twenties. Fifteen minutes later, led by
the gold-braided doorman, they are making the rounds of the
likely cafés where a recently arrived foreigner might be
expected to spend the afternoon hour, before the croupier's
exhilarating call is sounded: *"Rien ne va plus! Faites vos jeux,
mesdames et messieurs!"* This is it, ladies and gentlemen,
place your bets.

The fugitives nearing Hungary's eastern border can only
guess at the menacing reality of their situation. At every train

station in the country, male passengers are asked to identify
themselves. (But this was not done the way people today are
asked to produce their I.D. cards. It was enough to show a
postcard addressed to you, or a birth certificate, or a business
card - whatever happened to be in your wallet. We are in
Europe, after all - as the adventurer Edelman, the Whale's
grandfather, likes to put it.) The only reason the runaways
could get this far was that, even after being spotted at
Szent-Endre, no one would have thought they would choose to
hike across the length and breadth of the country. However, in
the border villages, their portraits have been posted, and their
descriptions have been announced at the marketplaces to the
sound of drumbeat.

And for the past few days in these villages peasants and
magistrates alike have been hoping to encounter the fugitives.
Some are motivated by the primeval, intoxicating instinct for
the hunt, calling from the depths of the chinless Black
Grandfather's epoch. Others simply look forward to helping
out, with a slice of bread, a shirt, or directions. Peasant and
magistrate are found in equal numbers on both sides.

At the end of their rope, utterly worn out, the runaways are
bound to make a mistake. Outside the village of Széle-Lonka,
before they know it, they find themselves out in an open field.

Back to the Mediterranean coast of France. At eight in the
evening a recent arrival in town is having dinner at a
strategically located window seat of the Restaurant Galatoire.
It is a fine eatery, with an atmosphere of its own. An oyster
vendor goes from table to table, offering his delicacies from a
tray. The guest is eating his meal with a lordly nonchalance,
but his eyes never leave the street, which leads to both the
main and the service entrances of the restaurant. He spent a
long time looking for a restaurant that fit this bill. He is well
dressed; his French is that of a cultivated foreigner - a
common type in this Mecca of gambling. But not even the
slickest old *roué* of a head waiter would be able to notice that
this customer is carefully tallying the price of each course,
making sure that after he pays the price of the meal, complete
with a generous tip, he will have just enough money for one

sizeable bet - which will have to be a winner.

But, alas, there will be no occasion for that tip, or for that daring bet. Three minutes past eight our elegant diner notices a strange procession approaching the restaurant. It is led by a ridiculously costumed individual, whose uniform would be the envy of a generalissimo presiding over some latter-day banana republic on the day of the coup. Gold stripes on the trousers, saucer-size fringed epaulettes, a tangle of gilded braids, and a scarlet overcoat hiding an awe-inspiring paunch. And behind him, the altogether too familiar faces of the two Hungarian police officers. Our man takes his time to dab his lips with the linen napkin. As he rises from the table, he even stops to bestow a most Hungarianly playful tap on the busboy's head, before disappearing in the direction of the lavatory, in the wake of the oyster vendor.

At precisely five minutes and fifty seconds past eight, Dajka's hand lashes out like a cobra, and collars the stooped oyster-seller trying to sneak past his back.

"I've got you, King!"

The two men who unintentionally emerge from the woods into the open meadow at Széle-Lonka have dark rings of sleeplessness under their eyes. Their bodies and clothes reflect the hardships of recent days. Their emaciated, weary faces are badly sunburned and peeling where not covered by wild growth of beard. By the time they realize where they are, they are surrounded by a group of Ruthenian peasants, who look on them with friendly curiosity. These are peaceful folk who toil all day in the fields, ready to shift along and show them the way to the border. But it is too late by then.

"King, *hein*?" says a familiar voice with a foreign accent behind the guise of the oyster vendor at the Restaurant Galatoire in Monte Carlo. Even at the moment of capture, this voice exudes triumph.

Indeed this is a surprise. At first Dr. Dajka cannot hide his disappointment, on glimpsing the handsome, olive-com-plexioned face of Socrates instead of Jankó the Safe King's. But in the end he cannot resist acknowledging, with a click of the tongue, the ability of this gang to produce surprises to the end. After all, he has been led around on a wild goose chase halfway across Europe, under the impression that he was after the King. The gang had confused the trail; Karola purchased a round-trip ticket for the Greek, who was traveling with the King's luggage, wearing the other man's clothes. He too spoke French, with a foreign accent. He stayed true to the part to the very last, even to the point of that little tap on the busboy's head, a typically Hungarian gesture. The Safe King, back home, said as little as possible, making it seem like he was the Greek, trying to hide his foreign accent. The latter, with his swarthy looks, had a better chance to blend in and stay inconspicuous in the Southern European setting. There had not been any descriptions of his person, for a ticket seller would see nothing remarkable in a black-haired, olive-skinned traveler, who looked like most of the natives.

Whereas the King is right at home now, whichever direction he might be escaping in.

But the stainless steel bracelets fit this prisoner just as well.

The authentic oyster vendor has to be freed from an awkward spot: he is found in the locked lavatory, crouching with nothing but his underwear on. He had been gagged with a handkerchief, slightly scented with a man's cologne, and bearing the initials of the King, M.J. (For our escape plans had included detailed provisions for the worst mishaps.)

The oyster man could not move, for his wrists, tied in the back, were fastened to the toilet flushing mechanism, so that with each movement he made, the rumble of rushing water would drown out his moans for help. A self-sustaining system improvised by a bright mind that could have been put to better use. Had it not been for Dajka, the elderly oyster vendor would have stayed a while longer, imprisoned in the lavatory.

The Special Investigator confiscates all of the remaining valuables in the Greek's possession, to be restored to the damaged parties. The Maître d'Hôtel waves a considerable dinner bill at him.

On the eastern border, the Safe King and the pickpocket observe a man who looks like an overseer sauntering in their direction.

"Good evening, gentlemen," the man greets them, and smacks his highly polished boots with a willow switch.

"Good evening," replies Baumgarten trying to be courteous, his voice enfeebled by hunger. The King mumbles something unintelligible; he is still trying to conceal his identity. Both men are at a loss; their customary quick wits abandon them. But the safe-cracker reaches in his pocket, a routine he had practised often, and unties the string of the small linen bag.

Their clothes were second-hand to start with, when they put them on an eon ago, in the Kerepesi Road slum. Since then, they have swum across the Danube at Szent-Endre, swum across the mayfly-covered Tisza three times, then a fourth time after their encounter at the inn; they have slept on the forest floor, have been burnt by the sun and soaked by the rain. They have never really managed to brush out the white mayfly fragments from their hair or from their clothes, which have repeatedly been rolled up at each river crossing.

"Well, what wind brings you gentlemen to these out-of-the-way parts?" asks the newcomer in a kindly voice. He motions with his stick, toward the peasants who are stacking hay at the other end of the clearing, to come closer. They all line up in a semicircle behind him, holding their pitchforks. Now the overseer continues in a different tone. "And who may you be? My name is Nemes-Trókay, magistrate of Széle-Lonka." He has already recognized the man with the limp, from the wanted posters that had been circulated. The pickpocket's feet are blistered raw by the archival clerk's shoes. And the other man also fits the descriptions. "Identify yourselves."

A gendarme patrol is approaching across the fields. At the sight of the scene they take their rifles in hand.

The King again reaches into the pocket of his worn black jacket, grabs a handful of red-hot paprika, and before any of the bystanders have a chance to realize what is happening, throws it in their eyes with a broad gesture of the sower of seeds.

They are on the run again, heading back toward the woods. The magistrate can only curse and rub his eyes. The gendarmes fire into the air, and run after the pair. The peasants are also off on the chase.

Baumgarten, in his ill-fitting shoes, keeps stumbling and begins to fall behind.

"I'm going to get caught," he yells after the King, who, seeing his comrade's plight, turns back and lifts him up. The pickpocket shakes his head, and hands over the small wallet containing his remaining money. "You can use this. Run!"

One of the fieldhands grabs Israel's foot, and holds on. The pickpocket falls down. Seeing there is nothing else to be done, the King dashes off, with a bounding stride. Baumgarten lies down; at last he can rest. He looks up at the evening sky, the green treetops, and his soul rejoices seeing his companion reach the forest and vanish in the wilderness.

The magistrate is still washing the paprika from his eyes by the stream. Apparently no great harm has been done, because it is with a laugh that he inquires from his men if they had captured the scoundrel with the paprika. But it would appear that he must be satisfied with the one lame, ragged fugitive.

"Where the hell could that other scoundrel be heading?" Nemes-Trókay wants to know, but Baumgarten does not reply. "Where were you two heading? Where was your rendezvous? What were you up to in Russia? Huh?" But the prisoner only shakes his head.

"Don't waste your breath, Your Honor. I won't say anything even if you kill me."

"Kill you?" Nemes-Trókay laughs heartily. "Who said anything about killing? We'll just ship you off to the capital, and you'll do your time in jail." And no one lays a finger on the pickpocket, for he is, after all, in the custody of the law, and enjoys its protection, in a civilized, European country.

Socrates, accompanied by his escort, travels through Milan and Vienna back to Budapest, where a special cell is waiting for him.

The pickpocket is taken to the village of Taracköz, where he is soon identified at the jail.

The local police chief decides not to place the exhausted

man in irons. The prisoner asks, in a weary voice, if he could shave. The policeman has his own prized Swedish steel razor brought from home, along with brush, soap and towel. He stands guard as the prisoner shaves, and makes sure that the railroad thief does not do himself harm. The policeman sends an order to the local inn for a double portion of Wiener schnitzel, pitcher of beer, bread, at his own cost. The innkeeper delivers the food in person, and spreads a freshly ironed white linen tablecloth in the cell - it is not every day that the village entertains such an illustrious guest. At last the prisoner can go to sleep on his bunk. The police chief checks up on him late at night; he adjusts the blanket on the sleeping captive.

A wire is sent to Budapest: the wanted escaped convict Baumgarten has been captured and will be transported to Budapest within seventy-two hours. His companion has temporarily eluded his pursuers in the vicinity of the village of Széle-Lonka; the manhunt continues.

Baumgarten is transferred to the jail at Máramarossziget, where his reception is not quite so cordial. In spite of Israel's vigorous resistance, four guards hold down his arms and legs while a fifth places heavy irons on him. At last he grows calm, and reconciled, as it were. From here on he remains quiet, almost serene.

Still exhausted, he sleeps through the night in his irons. Next morning he is sent off, in a separate car by himself, like a foreign minister; an entire third-class car is reserved for the prisoner and his guards. His face gradually assumes a beatific expression as he looks out of the window at the beautiful open country alternating with mountains and pine forests. He dreams of his earlier journeys, when all this beauty went hand in hand with his professional activities.

THE GENIUS OF SIR FRANCIS

The two policemen returning with their handcuffed prisoner from the shores of the Mediterranean have barely enough time to catch their breath before the delivery of the re-captured pickpocket.

First of all Dajka takes action at headquarters to withdraw the wanted circulars regarding the two captured fugitives. Neglecting to do this would mean violation of the prisoners' rights. Dajka has fond hopes of soon being able to do the same for the Safe King, who is still at large.

He proceeds to the prison, where a new order has been instituted. The teamster Wlastimir has been given notice; no more outside entrepreneurs are allowed to set foot within the prison gates.

The cell is large and well-lit, but the prisoner is confined hands and feet in irons. Previously the jailers had made sure that there were no hidden hollows in the cell by tapping every square inch of the walls and floors. He has been divested of his civilian clothes and now must wear the government-issued prison uniform. The recently appointed chief warden hands a long, sturdy nail to Dajka, and takes pride in reporting that it was found sewn into the lining of the Greek's jacket. That is all he would have needed to effect his escape again. (This is how mankind's great myths usually originate.)

At this point the captured members of the gang are the sole link to the bird that still flies free. They are the ones who know the planned escape routes, the prearranged meeting places.

They do indeed.

The Greek gruffly withdraws into himself. The adventure of the escape has used up all his strength, and by now he is reconciled to his fate. With or without an interpreter, he will say no more. Nor will our lookout, Bódog Haluska, who has been dug up from oblivion for the occasion.

Instead of resting, the Doctor shows up at the Kitty during rehearsal on the afternoon of his return. He will stay until the early morning hours, to do something that he has been thinking about for some time.

My initial mistakes have come to take their toll, as you know.

But my gravest error, as I was to learn later, has been

something accumulating all along. It is not a mere error; it is a crime. The crime of ignorance. If you take a job as a bartender, you find out beforehand what a Tom Collins is, and how it is mixed. If you find yourself working on a newspaper, you are bound to know the meaning of "justified" or that "cicero" stands for a twelve-point type, not an author of antiquity. And if you decide to be a safe-breaker, you had better familiarize yourself with the crime-fighting technology of your day. All of it. It would not have been too difficult. If I had only been aware of Sir Francis Galton's work, I would not have fallen victim to the most transparent ploy, and everything would have happened otherwise. I am not referring to Galton's work in eugenics, but to his other, more factual contribution.

The Special Investigator pushes his way through the clouds of cologne and the sourish, titillating scent of sweat emanating from the chorus girls who are primping themselves around me, and leans on my piano with a confidential air.

His expression is conspiratorial. "Mr. Piano Man, I need your help." At this point I still do not know that the Greek has been recaptured in Monte Carlo, and the pickpocket caught in Máramaros. These pieces of the mosaic will fall in place only after Marton will summarize the case for me, at a much later date. We will soon get to that. "I need your help in a scientific experiment that we are trying on everyone here," the Doctor adds, somewhat superfluously.

"At your service, Your Excellency," and I bow with apish insolence, rushing headlong to top my earlier mistakes with a new one. "I am honoured to be able to help."

At the end of the measure, and not a whit sooner, he closes the cover of my piano.

"Please follow me. Take a break!" he adds high-handedly, for the benefit of the girls. He leads me to the Baroness' office between floors. Next to the desk there is a compartmented champagne crate, with one oil lamp cylinder in it. Dajka turns to Baroness Vad: "Do you have any more lamp sleeves?" And, after the uncomprehending Baroness has another dozen brought in, he asks her to screw one into a lamp and light it. When the oil lamp is burning, he turns to me. "Tell me, can your hand tolerate touching a hot object?"

"Of course," I reply, stupidly showing off. And I firmly grasp the glass cylinder, looking at the officer like some proud schoolboy. And as long as we share the intimacy of collaborating in the same scientific experiment, I feel emboldened to ask a question. "If I am not prying, Your Excellency, can you tell me the reason for your continued interest in our humble establishment?"

"You are prying." And we leave it at that.

The glass was not that hot. Dajka now blows out the lamp and unscrews the cylinder, cautiously handling it with two fingers, and places it next to the other one in the Veuve Cliquot crate. Everything had been prepared. He has a patrolman take away the two glass cylinders, and asks the Baroness, "Do you happen to have any fine flour in your kitchen?"

What a question, in her household! She has a pound of flour brought up, while Dajka screws a fresh cylinder into the lamp.

"Please ask the chorus girls to come in, one by one." I realize that the Baroness has already been asked to do the same as I, and feel reassured that I have not been singled out. I am lulled into thinking that the procedure is not aimed at me personally. Blind, I would believe that I see.

"In due time you will learn the results of our experiment."

Dajka goes next door, and I return to my piano and the rehearsal.

As Marton was to tell me later, the Special Investigator, as soon as he is in the neighboring room, lifts the glass cylinder out of the crate, while it is still warm. He places it on the table and sprinkles it with the fine, powdery flour. After a moment, he blows away the flour, leaving finely spaced white lines.

If I could have seen and understood the implications at the time, I would not have continued to plink at my piano with such self-satisfaction.

Dajka, after using all the lamp cylinders on hand, sends for more to be purchased at the store on the corner of Danube Street, where the Baroness had bought the shopping baskets for her Hunchback. The procession of employees to the office goes on all night. Each emerges after a minute or two inside.

It is five a.m. by the clock of the Central Train Terminal when the gendarmes from Máramarossziget arrive with their prisoner. The corporal looks around sheepishly for the men of the state police who were supposed to meet them at the station. It looks like they have forgotten to show up. At six a.m. he goes outside, on Kerepesi Road. He is near the spot where, centuries before, fugitives had clambered over the crumbling stone wall around King Matthias' game preserve. In the same spot, at a future time, drug-traffickers are going to stage a fake police raid among some Arabs in Budapest. There the corporal stands with his gendarmes and their prisoner in chains, as the street is already getting crowded in the cool early morning hour, teeming with coaches, carts, wheelbarrows and gaping apprentice lads. It is all very dismaying for the gendarme, who has never been to the capital city before. At long last he decides to send one of his men to summon two cabs from a nearby stand. In the meantime, one of those weasel-faced figures with rings under their eyes, who sleep on the waiting room benches, sidles over to appraise the highly conspicuous group.

"Where is the Safe King?" he asks furtively.

"He gave us the slip," one of the honest gendarmes replies.

"You idiot!" But the corporal's admonition is too late. This is all the tramp needs to know. By the time the cabs arrive, a smallish crowd has gathered around the prisoner: revelers after an all-night spree, porters with nothing to do, cab drivers, and the occasional working lad. In the course of the past week the whole country has been avidly following the extraordinary bravado of the burglars' escape. So that the captured pickpocket receives a round of applause now, and a chorus of voices sends up loud cheers for the Safe King who again outsmarted the police.

The public demonstration lives up to the worst big-city fears of the gendarme corporal. With hurried gestures he shoves his prisoner into the waiting cab.

The news that at least one of the safe-crackers is still at large gets around town with incredible speed. The morning editions are not yet out when I hear the news as I leave the Kitty through the back door on Hat Street on my way home. I still do not know which of my partners has been caught.

At the Pest Regional Penitentiary the pickpocket is also locked up in a solitary cell; he has achieved a permanent new rank, it seems. Here he can resume his hard-earned rest.

The Special Investigator returns home only to find his assistant's message waiting him on Bath Street: Baumgarten has arrived in custody of the Máramarossziget gendarmes. This promises a fresh lead this morning. So Dajka bolts his breakfast, and somewhat refreshed, he takes a cab back to interrogate his returned prodigal.

Baumgarten exudes amazement. "Your Honour, I seem to have become an important man. Imagine, even the neighboring cells have been emptied. I take up as much room as a whole band of outlaws. And no use to rap on the walls, there is no one to hear me." This wing of the prison has recently been equipped with the most modern central steam heating, and the inmates, by virtue of their situation, were quicker than their keepers to discover that messages tapped out on heating pipes can go past empty cells - a fact Baumgarten wisely refrains from disclosing. When asked about the direction of the Safe King's escape, the pickpocket can reply only with a gentle smile, "Your Honour, it is enough if I suffer for the two of us."

"So why didn't you stay out of it?"

"Strange question," counters Baumgarten. "Is there a mother's son in here who would not want to be free? Your Excellency would have done the same in my place."

"If I were in your place," says Dajka, unable to contain his smile.

In the end, the railroad thief decides to make a statement; after all, he too has ambitions to be a good subject, a solid citizen, a star student, and a model prisoner. There were no accomplices; the whole escape was his work. He hand-filed the passkeys from the iron grill of his window.

"And who opened the oak door leading to the corridor of the archives?"

"I did."

"How did you do it?"

"How would I, now?" The prisoner shrugs. "That's the kind of thing I do best. I have worked the railroads long enough. I just stick that key in the slot, from the bottom up, slanting into that hole, feel around in there, feel out the mechanism, find the way it works in there, just like we learned in thief school...please don't write that down, I was only kidding about the school... So I opened the door, it creaked a wee little bit. But Your Honor knows it all better, anyway."

"That's right," nods Dajka. "See, my friend, I have caught you. The lock on that door was a Wertheim type, and you could not have opened it with your passkey. So you are lying to me."

"That's right, I am lying. You have found me out. But what would Your Excellency expect, from a convicted thief?"

"That door was open when you got there."

"It was, why deny it."

"But who opened it?" Baumgarten is silent. "You are covering for someone. Who is it?" But Baumgarten is silent.

The Doctor is looking for the inside accomplice. He will receive part of the answer sooner than he expects, when, a few days later, after the investigation has reached a certain stage, the suspended prison guard commits suicide, using his own service weapon, percussion lock, carbine round, leaving three orphans. This answer is deceptively complete, implying there is no further need to look for an inside accomplice.

The actual solution took a long time to reach Dajka, as did so many other things, in this complicated case.

He informs both prisoners that they will not be penalized for their attempted escape. The law takes into consideration this most natural instinct of prisoners to seek freedom. You see, Israel tells him, what I said was in line with the law.

He will be taken in chains by two armed guards to the Sopron penitentiary, where he will complete the rest of the Royal Judiciary's sentence.

There is nothing more I can do for them. Two escapes in a row are the stuff fairy tales are made of. We are going to lose sight of them, just as we did with our other accomplices. I am afraid we must save our own skins.

Dajka's last encounter with the pickpocket was related to me by Marton, years after the events. It occurred several days later, when the prisoner, his handcuffs removed, was eating his farewell civilian meal at the cafeteria of the Central Train Station, in the company of his armed escort. The Special Investigator suddenly shows up at the tableside. The convict had ordered matzoh-ball soup, braised beef, sour pickles and a pitcher of beer.

"I am going to starve in prison," Baumgarten announces, with a rueful look. "I am already fed up with it."

"Márton Jankó has escaped, because you refused to collaborate with us," says the Special Investigator.

"And so did the others," Baumgarten ripostes, with head raised high.

"That's right," nods the Special Investigator. "But now your King is going to have to rough it, all alone in the wilderness. He is exhausted, and he does not know the region. The border guard has been alerted. It's only a matter of time before he is caught. And instead of the maximum security prison you could have received more lenient treatment, with much better food, in return for a complete confession... I can still arrange it for you. Take care, for I am not going to ask you again: where was your rendezvous?"

A strange glint appears in Baumgarten's eyes, one that will be long remembered by Dr. Dajka, who had already tried the same gambit with the Greek and Haluska, but without result.

"Na-ah," says the thief, rapidly shaking his head. "If you are going to catch him anyway, what difference would it make?"

"When and where were you going to meet?"

"Na-ah." Again the headshake.

"All right. So be it. You choose the penitentiary. I am going to ask you something else now; you can answer this question, and there is no reward for it. Tell me, Israel, why do you still cover for the man?" At this point, unwittingly, he begins to address the prisoner with more formal respect.

Now the prisoner gives a straight answer. "Your Honor, I may be only a small-time *Yiddische* pickpocket. But when I meet greatness, I can recognize it. You know, all my life I wanted to be like the King... A safe-cracker in the grand style, a gentleman burglar. But I did not have what it takes. These people accepted me as one of them. For seven days and seven nights we shared bread. They needed me. Perhaps this will make you understand. And I pray God to keep him out of Your Excellency's hands."

Our preparations were extensive and thorough, our execution meticulous - and still the results turned out to be oddly inconsistent. For the goal of all our back-breaking efforts, the diamond known as the Blue Blood, and the accompanying consignment of jewels, in the end brought us not one penny. I could almost feel as much, that one time when I held the ice-cold brilliance of the Stone in my hand, and it scattered its rainbow in my eyes. When it was ours, for a moment. When I sensed its fickleness, sensed how little it had in common with existing things. Yet in the end, the most important one among my fellow burglars, the one who proved so worthy of his regal title, no matter how his later life would turn out, was never caught by Dr. Dajka. I had my share of the rest of the loot, exactly as much as the Special Investigator had so expertly calculated; and I know where Lori lives, where another share remains. There will be one more reapportionment of shares, by way of compensation. Some day, the ones who had to go to jail will receive their well-earned shares. And whatever is left for us, will be enough to see us through.

The Safe King will disappear without a trace on our eastern border. As Inspector Marton would tell me, the pickpocket's prayers were heard, and no policeman ever laid hand on Márton Jankó.

From here on my fate would be decided by the outcome of a battle of wits with Dajka. We shall see who is quicker, craftier. Luckier.

The Doctor will insist on finding the inside accomplice in the case at the Kitty, reaping the rewards of his long, at times Sisyphean labors. In the afternoon the Doctor delivers at the criminological laboratory crateloads of lamp cylinders bearing minuscule white lines.

He wants to know if it is possible to make three-to-fourfold photographic enlargements so the lines can be seen clearly.

"Naturally," the specialist replies, as he bends over his camera. Dajka looks on at the man, who is an expert photographic print-maker. "It will take a bit of time," the technician says. "And by the way, I have examined the handtowel from the nightclub washroom." He looks up at Dajka, and, timing his announcement with the air of one who knows how it will be received, slowly says, "It had been washed by a woman."

PART FIVE

THE WAY IT WAS

THAT BEAUTIFUL AND HECTIC SUMMER

"A woman!" Dajka growls in the laboratory on that Saturday afternoon. "Please explain to me how you arrived at that conclusion." His eyes are fierce. "What kind of eyeglasses do you have that see into the past? What is your miracle method? What on earth would tell you that the person who washed out the towel wore a skirt and not trousers?"

"It is what I did not find, sir. It is what I did not find." The technician is smiling. "I had expected you would ask."

It was the will of Fate that I could be there, on a much later day, when Chief Inspector Marton, equipped with all available hindsight, assembled the pieces of the mosaic, as one continuous narrative. From time to time his story was amplified by Judge Dajka, long ago retired, sitting by the marble fireplace of his small house in Budaörs. Lady Maria, who had herself been the unprompted participant in these bygone events, would contribute beyond a nod, or a shake of the head, an occasional word or two to this account of her husband's great "twin case" of yore; meanwhile she brought us frequent servings of fresh tea. Overhead came the roar of airplanes taking off and landing, but the two old people had gotten used to the noise that went with living near the airport.

Even at this late date, but without much expectation, they still hoped to be enlightened about more than one mysterious, unanswered aspect of the case.

At times you have asked me, how could I know so much about something or another, if I was not there. I begged your indulgence. Literary theoreticians claim that the narrator can no longer be divinely omniscient and omnipresent - these days. This is their livelihood; telling us what goes *these days*. They also say that the novel is dead. Well, rest in peace; I will mourn it when I have time. Meanwhile I have things to do; I have a novel to write. It needs to be fed; it is my business to know everything that belongs in it, and to be present everywhere. For example, the two of them, Marton and Dajka, told me what these two cases looked like from the side of the law, at the time. I am not going to explain each detail separately. There are ways and means; <u>life is always more multi-dimensional than the theories of literary esthetics.</u>

The laboratory technician had found no trace of blood in the towel. He was a professional, confident of his expertise, the kind that Dajka liked to work with. He reasoned backward, starting from the condition of the object he was presented with. It had been washed out in a hurry, and had not been ironed. Now, a fresh blood stain is relatively easy to wash out with cold water. On the other hand, washing in warm water leaves traces that are impossible to get rid of. Women, on account of their monthly cycles, are aware of this fact from early adolescence. Whereas men, obeying the dictates of some superficial logic, consider warm water to be more effective in removing any kind of stain.

If the hand towel had been washed in the course of that chaotic night, there had to be a reason. A most weighty reason. There can be only one reason weighty enough: a bloodstain. But there were no bloodstains found. Now in the washroom in question, directly behind the stage, the sink has both hot and cold water taps. If someone used only the cold water, that person had to be a woman. Q.E.D.

This is the moment when the Special Investigator experiences an initial change of heart regarding the new-fangled laboratory techniques. His cocksure rejection of these methods founders. His mind, trained in logical thinking, is disarmed by the elegance of this chain of deductive reasoning, by which an expert is able to establish something - *that is not there*. He will receive an even greater surprise from this quarter, but, fortunately for us, a bit too late. At any rate he is glad now to have always complied, even somewhat against his convictions, with his prescribed duties and standard operating procedures, as in the case of the lamp cylinders, for example.

The laboratory findings jibe with his own conclusions. Like a red thread running through most of his cases he finds the same maxim: look for the woman. And so he must, in this case as well, find a woman, along with a brick and a corpse.

This turning point revives the Doctor. He has plenty of time. He has not forgotten about this case: it has always been that proverbial fly in his ointment. Because of Bora. "My feeling responsible for that cat taken in from the rain," adds Judge Dajka to the Chief Inspector's narrative, in the course of this later meeting. Marton goes on with his account.

At police headquarters the rumors were getting louder that the Chief had gotten entangled in a personal affair, and there was a woman involved.

At this point, Chief Inspector Marton directed an apologetic glance at the occupant of the corner armchair. "Go on, Marton, you can tell it all," said Dajka's wife. "There are no secrets between us." Here she looked at me, to see if I understood. I did not want to say that there was no need to translate each word for me.

Marton felt free to speak at length now. He described how depressed the Special Investigator had been at the time, after the introduction of the new program at the Kitty. He had never seen him this way before. Asleep and awake he was haunted by the apparition of that woman whose hair turned white in the course of a single night, by the weird beauty of her face with its porcelain complexion, by her almond eyes staring vacantly into space.

He requested the prosecutor's permission to start the investigation all over. He decided to give no heed to the whispers behind his back; it had never been his style to worry about petty rumors.

He could cite the recently discovered new evidence. But in reality he was propelled by that intangible sixth sense that develops in a policeman or man of the law after a thousand cases. There could be no clue too trivial or dropped word too insignificant for him not to follow its trail. So he started anew that very Saturday.

On that Saturday, when I remain blithely unaware of his sudden self-assurance after months of frustration.

He surprises me by returning to us in the midst of his Europe-wide manhunt.

As a symbol of his determination, as he leaves home he slips in his pocket his army officer's service revolver - an otherwise superfluous gesture.

He brings only Inspector Marton. "I will accept a Turkish coffee," he says to the somewhat sulky Baroness. "After that I don't want anyone disturbing me."

For a half an hour we do not hear from him. Everyone goes on with his or her own business. We all detest the Special Investigator by now, despise his monomaniacal quest, and we have all given up expecting any results from him. He roots about in the storage rooms, in linen closets, in wardrobes; he keeps asking too many questions.

He has at last found the missing foothold he needed. The mistake he had been looking for. I watch him, and still I am not seized by a justifiable fear.

"He has always been a teacher to me," Marton went on with his account. "At this point he asked me to recapitulate the case. To go over it step by step, as if this were the first time. What happened, where, when, with whom, how and why? From the very beginning."

Yes, it seemed to be a most ordinary love triangle. Marton did not look in Maria's direction this time. "My poor Martzi," she said, stroking her husband's white hair. This was the first time I ever heard Dajka's familial nickname.

Most ordinary, from the police point of view, I thought. But there are some who would consider it otherwise.

Maria, it appeared, had helped to apportion the income earned by the deranged Bora Clarendon. It was her idea to open savings accounts for the singer's children, and she never failed to remind her husband each month when it was time to send the payments to Grinzing. It was no secret. Now, many years after the demolition of the Silly Kitty, I realized that Maria had known ever since the first raid at Mrs. Tremmel's that her Martzi's emotions toward his protégée were not purely paternal. Her female instincts knew the meaning of the more frequent late-night homecomings, the long thoughtful silences. And she did something that the white-haired retired judge only found out about then, in front of my eyes. Some years later, when Dajka sent a larger amount of money meant as a final payment, Maria had pawned her family jewels, in a fitting afterword to this case that has already involved several pieces of jewelry. "My husband is a very good man," said the Lady Maria in a gentle voice. "And that is why he fell, if he did, for the almond eyes of that poor woman." Back then they were expecting their first son (she explained, at a time when that son was already an officer of the general staff, and his brothers also settled in careers defending the peaceful dreams of ordinary citizens). So there was no extra money available to her. But her faith in her husband had not been shaken for a moment. And rightly so. After her husband had sent that last larger sum, she sent other "last" payments, and kept sending them until the envelope was returned stamped "Addressee unknown - *Inconnue*". They found out that Bora had met her fate at home. They adopted her children.

"So let us go back in time, to understand the events better," Marton continued. Going back a few years, when Keresztély Dajka, with his brand-new doctorate in political science and law, received his first appointment as a municipal clerk in the capital, much to the delight of his father, a police constable. Márton Jankó, the talented and charismatic offspring of a good family, enrolled in the Department of Mechanical Engineering as a first-year student at the Budapest Polytechnic Institute. The dark-haired, Tatar-eyed little daughter of a ropemaker was learning embroidery at the Ursulines at the time.

He wove into his narrative people, places and events that were not directly involved in the case of the brick murder. We know he had his reasons for doing so. There are ways and means.

The more information is available for the eventual compiler of the story, the more inevitable the logic of the events will seem to be. By the time of this belated conversation, many more facts had been made available to the retired judge and his former assistant than were accessible that Saturday, when they decided to resume the investigation.

Still later on, Little Kovács came across certain facts that could not have been available even to the excellent Special

Investigator, no matter how superb his professional expertise, no matter how extensive his access to the resources of other European police forces.

Little Kovács, the photographer, is an outstanding person. The Special Investigator is an outstanding person. And still, the story has certain threads that can be told only by the participant. So you know more than any one of them.

The old gentleman, growling and wheezing, filled another pipe by the fireplace. His wife Maria replenished our translucent *grain-de-ris* Chinese teacups.

I was a cab driver stationed at the stand in front of the National Casino. The Hunchback who was to be the doorman was a master stonecutter at the time in the uplands by Lake Balaton.

As a junior clerk, Dajka came into repeated conflict with the Chief of Police, who had gotten to be a frequent guest at Rézi Luft's infamous dive, located in the bog among the empty lots and lumber yards on the outskirts of town, beyond the pale of the boulevards. In this confrontation, the subordinate was bound to lose. Nowadays the Comic Theater stands on the lot where the dive used to be, added Marton for my benefit.

He need not have bothered. That used to be on our homeward route before we moved out here to the Angel-land district. That was where the cars could turn off the former Leopold Boulevard on to the former Valero Street by going up the driveway of the theater. Every taxi driver in the city knows this trick.

Back then the ropemaker's daughter was not as yet called Bora, and she had not set out on the roundabout trail that would lead to her fateful meeting with an auburn-haired ladykiller.

Back then the young Jankó was in love with mechanical engineering. But he found student life slow, and too book-bound. It was not for him to apply for a scholarship, and commit himself to years of government service. He felt that he was destined for greater things - a feeling that has motivated many a great career in art, politics, and burglary.

In the Cape Colony, a Sotho diamond miner found a hundred-carat stone. Since his reward was not quite enough for the full purchase price of a steed and complete accoutrements, he used it to buy himself a broad-hipped, fertile wife.

In Budapest, the police chief whose life had gotten entangled in the underworld soon came to an ugly end. The junior clerk Dajka was promoted. Veron Czérna traveled to Paris, from where she would be swept away by Colonel Archaroff.

Alone at night in the woods or in a nightclub one must look out for oneself. Veronika Czérna had not learned this lesson.

She gave birth to her first illegitimate child by the prince in Petersbourg.

Young Jankó, the pride of his professors and the joy of several café cashier lovelies, decided to put away his books. Soon afterwards, the legend of a mysterious safe-cracker was afoot.

Dr. Dajka was promoted to Inspector.

Erzsike Csorba, who would eventually come to title herself the Baroness, was still back in Bártfa, bestowing happiness on an overweight mill-owner.

Within a year or two, Jankó turned into the Safe King. Nor did the underworld know much more about him than the world at large. After the cash-register lady came the flower-girl. Then one fine day, it was time to leave the capital. He never said a word in farewell to his jilted lover.

Dajka became the youngest magistrate in the country. From a distance he kept a passionate, almost sympathetic watch on the career of the King. The Great Crime was still missing from his life. And back in those days, said Chief Inspector Marton wistfully, it still meant something to be a policeman. Everything was different in Hungary back then. The great international gangs began their careers here, and often ended here, as well.

The Turkish prison.

Bora's second child by the prince.

On a Wednesday, Erzsike received her inheritance, and on a Thursday, she boarded the train to Budapest. In a train compartment she enjoyed a brief but profound encounter with an officer of the Imperial uhlans who called himself Baron Ormund Freiherr von Berchtesgaden zu Neumannthal. She applied to the Ministry of the Interior to have her name legally changed to Agnes Vad. Enormous billboards hid the window-less salon between floors in the high-roofed old building on Rose Square. Inspector Axaméthy's group kept an eye on the club from the day of its opening.

In another prison, in another country the Safe King met the Greek, who was the father of locks and keys. After the reduction of his sentence for good behavior, he was released early.

The good old days on Cemetery Street. The King paid for a license and set up Karola in the second-hand clothes business. The Greek arrived in town.

Béres was hired as doorman at the newly opened Silly Kitty.

In my two-horse cab, ambling on Váci Boulevard, I heard Baron Vay pronounce the name Blue Blood. I signed up as day-laborer at one of the construction sites on sunny Grand Boulevard.

Jankó rented a room at the watchmaker Lápos' apartment. He had cards printed. Women, champagne, luxurious carriages.

They picked up the unemployed bricklayer, who became their lookout. Péterffy's on New World Street, Sonnenschein's on Idol Street.

The "Vengerka" was expelled from the Russian Empire. Vienna and the morphine syringe. The dairy shop in the Stone Quarry district. The children left behind in Grinzing. Rooms by the month, then by the day; finally the last stop: Mrs. Tremmel's brothel.

The burglars also hit Vienna. Esterhazy Street on the eve of Epiphany.

Hamburg, two safe-breaks in one night. Saint Petersburg

(Leningrad under the Soviets). Königsberg. Bucharest, Nagyvárad, Belgrade. Constantinople. Munich. Prague. Back home again, then Vienna, which was almost home. High rewards were offered for their capture.

After Saint Petersburg they established business relations with Agap Kevorg, who always paid in cash.

Keresztély Dajka received his appointment as Special Investigator directly from the King (His Royal Apostolic Majesty).

That beautiful and hectic summer, when one night there were two midnights in Budapest, and the first automobile huffed and puffed its way across the capital.

Dajka kept a running tab on the unsolved burglaries.

Bubbles found employment as cleaning woman at Mrs. Tremmel's brothel.

The Doctor liberated Bora Clarendon. "Oh, that twelve-year-old girl", hissed his wife Maria with flashing eyes, at this point in the story. "And that old man with the silver grayhound knob on his walking stick." She knew all about it, and she was proud of her husband.

The girl called Bubbles ran in panic.

Here I almost interrupted the Chief Inspector. She was far from being panicked; after all, she already had a protector, who looked out for her. But I was not in a position to make revelations.

Zara.

This was where the fourth man must have made his appearance. The police had practically no information on him. Only guesswork. I almost felt sorry here, unable to express my appreciation.

These were the professionals I had been looking for, ever since hearing about the extraordinary prize heading for Budapest. But I was not aware of their existence, so I could not look for them specifically.

That afternoon they spoke Hungarian in that harborside tavern by the Adriatic Sea. That very night I could hold in my hand their bright steel jimmy.

The Special Investigator was able to identify the gang's

signature. No one could have known about the Safe King, since he did not have a police record. "That's what we thought at the time," said the Chief Inspector many years later, with a shrug.

The Special Investigator started to keep four separate files.

In Amsterdam, the young diamond cutter came to a decision about the Stone's final form.

A few weeks later Jankó placed his fate and his wallet in my hands.

Drilling deep into his memory I come up with the name of the jewelers Hatvanger and Bócz. The Viennese guests arrive for the Exposition; the Stone is heading our way.

We conduct our experiment.

The Swiss engineer sends us a wire from the other side of the ocean: *Sutruroy*.

I find life's richest variety along the cobblestone streets of our capital city, where the lives of my associates unfold.

Our circus caravan, Odessa. At the Russian savings bank we did not touch any glass or metal surfaces, nor would we have known their significance. And Dr. Dajka, back home, was not particularly persistent in his search for bright and polished surfaces.

Homeward in our caravan. At the end of the long arc of our journey: the Hungarian capital. In the meantime, Lilia and Alma, and the silences.

I arrive home a few hours before my troupe, to set in motion our great coup.

"Experts are well aware of the burglar's habit of casing a joint before a larger score," said Inspector Marton, years later from his vantage beyond the events. The international gang zeroes in on an alcoholic house servant.

The tailor Knorr's apartment in a building with an elevator near the Circle train line; the rumble of nearby mills.

In the evenings my act in the Park earns loud proletarian applause and a smattering of coins on the tarpaulin.

"Uncle Martzi saw the fire-swallowing act of the man who was to become the piano player," said Chief Inspector Marton at this point in his narrative. He was the only other person on the face of the earth who could call Dajka by that nickname. By now he was pushing sixty, and he was like a son to the old couple.

Dajka saw me at the Park. Of course, I did not know who he was, nor did he know who I was.

I caught sight of Bubbles.

From that moment on I was not surprised by any success. I followed her to the house on Rose Square, and did not want to lose sight of her, ever. She came within a hair's breadth of deflecting me from my path.

I bequeathed the troupe to Kodel, "You are the boss."

At Muratti's I told my partners about our target.

By then my companions were ready to go through fire and water for me, with their own arrogant outlaw strides. That night at the red salon. The King. The girl, with the tray suspended from her neck. She was the only one I cared about.

THE HEAVY FOOT OF FATE

Bora Clarendon, when she no longer expected anything from life, was swept away by the miracle of a new love. She had already given up morphine. The King began to take her up to the apartment on Pannonia Street.

This placed our headquarters in jeopardy.

But life went on, as they say in popular TV soap operas. Fate has merely put one heavy-booted foot inside the door.

Then the Safe King, the spoiled darling of so many women, fell head over heels in love with Bubbles, the bread-girl with the pretty face.

And Bubbles, like so many women before her, got singed by

this man's fire, as she so meekly confessed to the Special Investigator at her first interrogation.

By speaking the truth, she told the biggest lie. It was all lies, from her virginal bed linen to her impish little face. For she had to be an active participant in that love affair. At that time it was still a novel notion for us, that love is the supreme power, overwhelming individual willpower, making it useless to struggle against it. Nor would we want to; we yearn to be swept away by love, come what may. We have learned to embrace our allotted destiny.

So the two of them hid their affair from the singer.

In Amsterdam the Stone was being set in platinum.

I first saw him and Bubbles on the canopied terrace of the hotel. I am not a believer in coincidences. How could there be any coincidences, after all that waiting and searching. Life was taking shape, filling out, like a masterpiece.

The jilted woman followed in their tracks, half mad with jealousy. Her last chance for happiness in life was melting away in front of my eyes.

The Chief Inspector went on with his retrospective analysis. According to him, Márton Jankó throughout his career measured his success, his status as the King, by the pampering he received from women. The only way he could terminate a liaison was by having the next woman in line forcing it. He preferred to wait, and let his women fight it out among themselves.

Men are often like that. In their everyday lives they may be fearless, ready to oppose the entire machinery of the state, armies, prisons and forced labor camps with their bare fists. But they do not dare to confront a woman when it is time to tell her that it is all over. (My friend, the Fráter, belongs in this category. A barely audible cry of anguish on his behalf arises in me at times: how can anyone divide his courage into two compartments? I am pulling for him. You are not aware of these things about him, because we do not discuss this sort of thing, not yet. In a few years' time.) So that the King, this world-class performer, a man bright and hard as a diamond, who endured years of imprisonment in a Turkish dungeon without once mentioning where he was from, or speaking his native language, was now, to put it simply and crudely, afraid.

The cast iron figureheads on the railing by the Danube (which you and I can recognize, from the movie about the Prague Spring).

The King has flouted the basic rules of security.

The singer followed the two of them to the love-nest she had known.

Shingle-roofed barges, millions of brand-new bricks. "Who is that woman?" I brood over Bubbles' recklessness. The soles of my shoes are coated with mud.

The givens of our situation change radically. The mud dries to a whitish color on my shoes. That night at the red salon. The Safe King, in the role of lover, is waiting for Bora.

"Our raid squad," said the Chief Inspector on reaching this point of the story in his later recapitulation, "was just leaving on its mission to clean up the capital's night life."

Bora steps on stage in front of the chorus line. By the time of our later conversation, Marton knew more about her.

In this familiar environment I recognized her at once. I tried to imagine her earlier that evening, looking up at the top floor of the apartment house, seeing the light go on in that room, where, as in a sideshow shadow play, the lovers' silhouettes were outlined on the curtain. From the sidewalk, she watched the intertwining forms of a man and a woman, until they were swallowed up by the voluptuous darkness. I imagined her turning and walking down to the quay. Her hand, as if in a trance, coming to rest on one of the bricks lying on top of a stacked pyramid. Clutching it with such force that her knuckles turn white. She does not know yet what she will do with it - if she will do anything. She slips it into her handbag. Her boots and the hem of her skirt are getting all muddy.

She strikes out at the table where her lover, the King, is sitting.

"We could never understand, in the light of the later

developments, why no one was able to prevent what happened," said the Chief Inspector, on that later occasion.

I could see the weight pulling her handbag down. I could see the white mud caked on her boots. I knew what she was going to do.

My eyes were looking for Bubbles. We could not afford to have her tangled up in a police investigation.

When the singer, brick in hand, did not move in her direction, my wound-up nerves and muscles relaxed momentarily.

The Baroness was standing by the stage. She could see the brick grasped by the singer's black-gloved hand, although she would never admit this. It was never proved that she witnessed the blow that was delivered.

The wind was still rising.

And Bora sang her song. To the Baroness, the audience, and later to the police, this seemed to be the first manifestation of her derangement.

The singer's button boots leave mudprints on the white shirtfront of the man lying on the floor.

A soft-spoken "Alley-oop!" heard only by Bubbles: it is time for some legerdemain. I pull down the circuit breaker.

Marton said: "The service entrance was padlocked; the front was watched by the old cashier woman, who had to leave her post for a minute."

It was as if my dream came to life. My leap into action had its effect: the doorman recognized me, and Bubbles was also on hand. One minute she was still smoothing out her apron with a mindless, innocent gesture; in the next instant, she was off and running. She was the third person who acted immediately in this emergency.

The singer caught a glimpse of my hand in the flickering light of a candle. Bubbles went ahead of me.

In the corridor the Hunchback caught up with me, he held the brick in his hand. He was no longer a cripple: his left shoulder was at normal height, as if he were winking at me, with his intact, imposing body. I stood there, somewhat at a loss amidst chaos and screams, with the body of the limp

Safe King in my arms, and I could not suppress a wide, clownish grin. Our collaborating had a natural ease, as if we had been working together all our lives. I recognized him, although I had never seen his face before.

It felt as if with each passing second the King's body was getting lighter. I feared for him, for I had grown to love him.

The roar of emptiness beyond the palisade of the outside passage.

Bubbles and I exchanged a single glance in her room, by the light of a candle, but it spoke volumes. She was waiting there for me, and I had been counting on her.

The doorman tossed two pebbles out the window, at the neighboring hut. Now he was the Hunchback again. Already he was scurrying out, still holding the brick and fumbling with his large bunch of keys.

The girl was looking at me with enormous, questioning eyes.

"Yes, he is alive," I nodded to her.

She got busy. Taking out a crisp fresh sheet from her wardrobe, she ripped it into bandage-size strips. We each did what we had to do, as if we had rehearsed this moment before.

The blood had clotted at the edges of the lacerated head wound.

Bubbles placed her palm on the King's drenched forehead. She loosened her lover's necktie. Her earlier nursing experience gained the upper hand now; it was like swimming - once you have learned it, you never forget. When the wounded man opened his eyes, the first thing he saw was his lover's anxious glance. He started to breathe more evenly. He calmed down, then lapsed into another swoon. He told me about this many times.

The doorman returned and handed me a key, nodding in the direction of the steel doors opening on the courtyard. Then he hurried back to the salon, where his presence was needed. He carried his hulking body with a remarkably soft, light tread.

I stroked Bubbles' hair.

"Everything will be all right now."

She pointed at her dresser drawer. "The cologne is there. I had ironed the sheet on the inside of the fold."

The wounded man regained consciousness and moaned. I put my finger on his lips.

I had to move him on the table, and this started the bleeding again. I stepped to the open door to peek out. The draft blew the tablecloth aside and a few drops of blood fell in a place where, at the right moment, they would give new impetus to the investigation.

"Holy Mother of God!" Sitting at my little piano I can hear the Special Investigator's cry resounding throughout the whole floor on that Saturday afternoon when he decides to start his investigation all over. He leaps up and runs upstairs, taking the steps three at a time. "Three hours and ten minutes! I have forgotten about the passage of three hours and ten minutes!" He yells back at Marton, who is unable to keep up with him.

He has not reckoned with one simple fact, and he has taken one assumption for granted.

If this Saturday had not been such a windy day, and if, at this hour of the afternoon - when the service entrance was already padlocked, for usually there were no deliveries at this time - there had not been a shipment of French champagne delivered from the railroad station, then the affair of the brick would never have been seen in this new light. But the wind was blowing. And the champagne has to be delivered just then, when the Special Investigator, who realizes he has left a hundred ninety minutes unaccounted for, reaches the corner room upstairs - and the two steel doors are again open at the same time.

The key to the room is in the lock outside. He turns it. His glance passes over the broad bed. The bed that receives no visitors, he recalls. His nose becomes aware of an aroma reminiscent of drying hay and he recalls the smell of wildflowers on his last visit here. Even now, there is a bouquet of wilting wildflowers in a vase. The policeman's trained eyes take inventory. Two piles of assorted Danube pebbles on the window sill. He muses for a moment about why on earth should this uncomplicated creature develop these eccentric traits: pebbles on the window sill and wildflowers that most simple folk consider to be mere weeds.

A small night stand, a chest of drawers. A narrow wardrobe. A wash stand with a basin. Used bathwater. For some reason this bothers him, the nearly crystal-clear surface of the water, and the greyish soapy residue at the bottom. Before leaving the room, he comes to the oversized oak table covered by the tablecloth that reaches to the floor. He opens the door to call out to his assistant.

He thinks he saw some movement at the edge of his field of vision. Closing the door, he turns back, his eyes scanning the room. Nothing. Once again. The third time, he opens the door and looks back again. This time, everything is different.

The draft blows the tablecloth aside.

Some barely perceptible disorder on the carpet disturbs his sense of symmetry. He leans closer, he gets down on the floor, as far down as only little boys and Special Investigators are likely to get.

Now he can clearly distinguish a dark stain on the rug's pattern, mostly in the brown crenellated area. The policeman's reflexes go to work; he categorizes the stain according to color, shape, substance. Blood. Old, dried blood. In all likelihood, human blood.

He does not touch anything. He shuts the door and stares at the floor. He opens it again. He closes it. "For a moment I thought that this time the chief had really lost his mind. Actually, he was never more in command," said Marton later, turning toward the fireplace with a somewhat apologetic chuckle.

Dajka posts Marton to guard the door. "No one, absolutely no one is to enter. If need be, use your weapon," and he hands Marton the ancient service revolver he brought with him.

They will have to question the room's occupant.

He takes a look at the usually locked area of the palisaded passageway, where delivery men are staggering in now, lugging crates of champagne. The Hunchback stands inside by the second steel door, where they put down their loads. After locking up, the doorman takes the crates in.

When both of the steel doors are open, the Doctor, standing at the top of the stairs, has a clear view through them, and can see the small huts on the opposite side of the courtyard, built against the wall of the neighboring building at No. 2 Leopold Street.

He calls out to the Hunchback, asking him to leave both doors open. "The only way that is allowed is if I stand by," the doorman replies. "Well then, stand by!" The Special Investigator returns to the corner room. He has to smile, seeing the hesitation on Marton's face, as he tries to interpret his orders. "It did occur to me," said Marton when he was Chief Inspector, "whether my order was supposed to include the Special Investigator himself." But he wisely refrains from using the revolver.

"We are on track," the Doctor tells him. He opens the door, and observes the tablecloth and the stain on the carpet. He nods, with a satisfied air.

But he is not quite sure yet about the significance of what he has found.

Twenty steps away, as the crow flies, I am plinking away on my little piano, for the afternoon rehearsal. And I am blissfully unaware of this latest find. If I knew, I would immediately go to find Bubbles somewhere on the outskirts of town, and we would be out of the country in a flash.

Squatting on the corridor floor, Dajka opens his black pocket notebook to the page containing his notes taken at the time of his first inspection of the premises.

"Here we are," he points it out to his assistant. "'In the upstairs rooms, nothing.' And here it says in parentheses, '(12:36 a.m.; Marton).' But this is all my fault. There is an arrow pointing from this to the *Facts* column: '3:46 a.m. Detailed inspection. Found nothing.'" A fact!

The wounded man stirred and mumbled something in his delirium.

I spread some of the bed linen under his head. I had to transcend the anxious flurry of this moment. It was not difficult to do - I was never able to rush non-stop along with the rest of humanity. I shut my eyes, squeezed my eyelids together, and paid strict attention to the task at hand. I felt his head around the wound. He certainly had a hard head, which was encouraging; the blow did not fracture the skull.

Then I placed my left palm over the unconscious man's mouth, and with a swift gesture of my right hand I poured cologne over the open wound. His whole body thrashed on the tabletop and my palm stifled a scream.

The room now reeked of the scent of meadow grass and wildflower exuded by Bubbles' cheap cologne.

Within a few seconds the King swooned back into benevolent unconsciousness. I snipped out an untouched, folded section of the sheet, with the ironed side up. I pulled the edges of the wound close together and applied a linen padding, then tied a temporary bandage around his temple. I would have to take care of the wound in a more effective manner within a few hours.

I was not amazed for a moment that Bubbles turned out to be a trained nurse. She had even laughed at me, on this day of so many laughs. Then she scurried back downstairs, so she would be in the salon when the lights came back on.

Time was running out.

I decided to abandon our Pannonia Street headquarters.

"Watch this, son," said the Special Investigator in the quiet corner room. "I open the door, like this. The draft blows the tablecloth aside. I shut the door, and the creased tablecloth covers up the stain. Blood once dripped here, from the table. There must have been an injured body lying on it. It was a windy day, like today. And both steel doors had to be open, as they are now."

He shouts orders to the doorman to shut the doors. "See, there is no draft now, the tablecloth hides the stain. That bloodstain has been waiting for us. Until we could give it another try. Yes, the hand towel had been bloodied, and there had to be blood elsewhere. Now we've found it. I am sure that our man must have dribbled it all over. By the time you hurried through the rooms, he had removed the body. But there must still be a few drops of blood around here, on the floor, on the basin, on the coverlet, on the bedlinen.

"Under ordinary circumstances, the two steel doors are never open at the same time. Whoever carried the body outside had to have an inside accomplice."

Only the doorman and the Baroness had keys for the steel doors.

They go over the doorman's statement again, then the Baroness'. They re-interrogate them, without results. They are looking for the unknown accomplice.

"Or unknown accomplices," added the Doctor from his fireside armchair. After all, at that late date, they at last knew as much as they were going to know, which was not everything. We will get to that. But you already know more than they did.

Again I peeked out on the corridor. Bubbles would have to clean up whatever traces I left in her room.

With the bandaged man in my arms, I stepped out into the courtyard. Suddenly the wind stopped.

My next encounter. With the man who had rescued Bubbles from the clutches of Mrs. Tremmel. The Special Investigator would never find out about him.

By the time the storm broke, I was back in the building. The time was ten fifty-five. By the light of a candle I inspected my clothes: they were disheveled, but only my hands were bloody.

Dr. Dajka had assumed until this day that the room Marton had seen was identical with that of his own more thorough-going inspection.

Whereas in the meantime three hours and ten minutes had elapsed.

"Well, call in that girl," he calls out on the corridor. He now has a fresh impetus to his search and to his questions. The time has arrived to conduct his lamp-sleeve experiment on the occupant of the corner room. He must interrogate her in the light of the newly uncovered facts.

"At the time he did not realize how close he was to the solution," said Marton, looking at the old man in the armchair.

"In the meantime, send a cab to headquarters, and have my bag brought in," Dajka said to Marton. "And ask the cab driver to wait."

He has a drawing of the stain made on a piece of tracing paper on which he indicates the cardinal points and the location of the furniture. The whole carpet is rolled up and taken down to the cab. On seeing the sour look in the Baroness' eyes, he simply says:

"The alternative was to cut the stain out with a pair of scissors."

He requests the laboratory chemist to determine whether the stain contains human blood.

The empty *Facts* column in his notebook is starting to fill up.

For a short while after the removal of the body, there was a likelihood that the singer would get Bubbles involved in the affair. It was my task to prevent this.

The doorman ripped out the wire leading to the circuit breaker, and he took his time repairing the damage. The salon was flooded by the electric lights again. I slipped him the key.

When I stepped out from behind the curtain, my eyes met Bora's, who, at this moment, was still in command of all her faculties.

Before I sat down to start playing the piano, I quietly called out to Bubbles, "The room." She nodded; she knew what she had to do. "The bedlinens. And the hand towel here in the washroom."

She slipped out of the harness of her bread tray and looked around in confusion. Anyone could see that she was the embodiment of the loyal employee, a silly little goose.

Downstairs the second show went on.

The situation was getting more complicated. The storm was raging outside, and the police boots were leaving amoeba-like puddles on the parquet of the dance floor.

The Special Investigator was very upset by the music. From the very first minute this piano man rubbed him the wrong way.

Bora said, with the instinctive certainty of lovers and madmen, that the body had been taken up to that slut's room.

In the room of the slut (who happened to be many things, but not that) at this moment the floor was still bloody in places. And there were wavy auburn hairs to be found on the floor; upon close microscopic examination, the police expert would have concluded they came from a Caucasian male, judging by their circular cross section. There were pebbles on the windowsill, but there was no vase of flowers on the table.

Dr. Dajka sent Marton up for a preliminary look.

The storm settled down to a steady rain.

They inspected the shoes of every person present at the scene of the crime. Somehow they skipped mine. Luck was definitely on our side. Perhaps it was the gods. Or it was in the stars. Or it was our presence of mind - it all depends on your worldview.

The more time passes before I sew up the wound, the nastier the scar would be; I was aware of that. But at least there was no danger of inflammation.

The *corpus delicti*, and the corpse, were missing.

The Special Investigator, in reactivating the case, wants to establish a secure foothold based on facts. Again, the almond-eyed singer's mental state comes under scrutiny.

"There was a flood of vague and contradictory statements," said Chief Inspector Marton, much later. "Suppositions, the screams of a madwoman. She was shouting that she had killed her lover. She also claimed that the piano player washed his hands, that the body had been spirited away. Yes, the hand towel had been washed out, and the victim's body had indeed been taken up to the corner room in the course of the night."

How much of Bora's delirious raving could be taken at face value? For she was deranged, beyond a doubt.

But she was not out of her mind throughout the entire night. What had unhinged her, if it was not that blow she struck at her lover?

And what was the role of the circus-showman-turned-piano-player in the affair? His hands were too clean.

At this later occasion, in front of the fireplace, I involuntarily inserted two fingers behind my necktie and loosened my collar, which suddenly felt too tight. Chief Inspector Marton raised a tobacco-stained finger. "The Special Investigator's task was to find out at precisely what point in the night did the singer's mind lose that delicate balance we like to call sanity."

(Superficially. And we take it for granted, as our rightful property.)

Selfishness has unfathomable depths. "No, I did not wash my hands. Not at all." With these few words, I achieve my purpose; Dr. Dajka will not have a chance. I am not proud of this solution. I hope you will make sure to do no irrevocable wrongs; always pay close attention to the other person, much closer than I did.

Resuming his investigation at the Kitty, Dajka reasons backward, starting with a few bare facts. The singer had shouted, "He has blood on his hands!" After that she never spoke again. By the time of our conversation years later, the Special Investigator realized that as long as Bora talked, her words made sense.

But the stain remained on the fake oriental rug. That was the mistake the police officer had been waiting for.

I was able to cover for Bubbles, and I could not think of anything else. I had to make sure that she would remain just one of the many girls at the Kitty.

As soon as her interrogation was over, she was free to move about the building without creating suspicion. She at once washed out the hand towel in cold water, and put it back on the rack in the washroom. Then she was gone for ten minutes while she cleaned up her room. She filched a large bouquet of wildflowers from the corridor, and, wrapping it in her humble little apron, took it to her room, where she put the flowers in a vase. Using cold water, she scrubbed away all traces of our having been there. At least what seemed like all traces. Then she was back in her place, with the tray hanging from her neck. Later, many witnesses said that she stayed in the salon throughout the entire night.

The Chief Inspector continued. "Now we discovered microscopic traces of single drops of blood here and there, in the cracks of the floorboards. The room had not been cleaned in a while.

"When the blood dripped under the table, the wind had been blowing. Therefore someone must have looked out on the corridor before the start of the storm."

On that later day I was listening to him put the details of the story together, piece by piece. "We found the steel doors all locked," he said.

After my interrogation I was free to go, like anyone else. The police guard let me out through the main entrance on Rose Square. I set out on Town Hall Street toward the north, in the direction of Váci Street. The rain had drawn a solid black veil over the Inner City.

If the Special Investigator decided to search the little huts in the courtyard before the King's wound healed enough for him to be be moved, then it would have been all over for us. The process could take five to seven days.

Reaching Town Hall Square, where I was no longer in view of the police guard, I turned left on Serpent Street, then cutting through Sebastian Street I approached Rose Square again. I went past the alley-like Lock Street, and a moment later I was scouting the scene from the far end of Hat Street. There was no guard posted at the carriage entrance. I walked along the stone wall and I was back where I had started from. I softly knocked under the wooden eaves of the hut. Domokos - the name which the tenant of the hovel went by at the time - opened the door.

The wounded man was still unconscious. We drew the curtains so that not one ray of light should betray us.

Next to the bed on which the wounded man lay was the brick and a doctor's bag with the bare essentials. A white linen sheet was spread over a large table, and water was boiling on the stove. A baking pan served as an autoclave for the syringe. There was a bottle of pure alcohol. Domokos poured water into a basin. He peeled away the armor-like shirtfront from the wounded man, while I started to wash his forehead around the edges of the wound, with slow, long-ago learned movements. I disinfected the blades of a pair of nail scissors, and carefully clipped the hair around the wound. The wavy auburn locks fell in profusion. I washed my fingertips with a cotton ball dipped in alcohol, and pulled the loosely flopping piece of skin over the wound.

The wounded man had inherited a hard skull from our ancestors who once were the scourge of Europe. The brick had not broken any bone, and I had to rely on my somewhat rusty training as a barber to put some stitches in. Sutures would not have been sufficient, nor did I have access to them. We sterilized the scissors, the curved needle, the tweezers and the syringe. There were no disposable syringes in this era, although there were morphine addicts. And there was no deadly AIDS, spread by shared needles. (Many, many years later, during the summer of our Kolozsvár-Bucharest-Black Sea trip - by which time our cobblestones were ripe for another turning, although their seventh life was still not used up - I contracted only infectious hepatitis when we volunteered for work at the Mohács flood, and the trained medical personnel injected thirty of us with the same un-sterilized needle. The period of incubation covered the time it took to rebuild the peasant houses, the travel time, and those Twelve Days of Autumn.)

The patient did not regain consciousness on the kitchen table. For anaesthesia, I injected cocaine and, after a half night's delay, and without running water, I sewed him up, using five figure-eight stitches. I did not have the competent hands of Bubbles to assist me; my host did the honors by handing me the instruments. I was praying that the bedsheets were clean.

At dawn, when the Special Investigator was through with

the interrogations, he personally examined the upstairs rooms.

In the corner room the scent of wildflowers disguised the reek of cologne. From then on Bubbles would always keep a bouquet of wildflowers in her room; who would keep track of when she had acquired this silly eccentricity of hers? The wet floor had dried in the elapsed three hours and ten minutes.

In the city's dawn I was received by the calm after the storm. I wanted to catch my breath after these great encounters. The sky was still cloudy. The rising sun radiated its early morning warmth only here and there over the cobblestones and asphalt of the Inner City streets.

The abandoning of the Pannonia Street apartment could wait, I reflected, almost as an afterthought.

Only my feet knew where they were taking me. I suddenly realized I was standing at the Grand Bazaar, with a lit Partagas cigar in my mouth, staring at the window display of the jewelers Hatvanger and Bócz, and laughing aloud at my reflection.

As fate would have it, we would now have enough time to acquaint ourselves with the routines and goings on at the jewelry store.

"We worked until dawn. The Special Investigator got to go home only in the morning," said Marton at our later meeting.

I sent a postcard to the tailor Knorr from the post office at the Western Train Station.

The diamond cutter mailed the Stone to Paris in a plain, worn envelope.

By noon the next day the edges of the wound turned a bright red. I could steal into the small hovel under cover of the continuing rain. The invalid had not yet woken, but his constitution ("strong as an ox") promised a speedy, assured recovery. He would need a few days' undisturbed rest. In the dark, Bubbles would be able to slip outside to change his bandages. I told them where they could find me in the neighborhood of the new House of Parliament. Besides the two of them, only the doorman was allowed to know my address.

I left the bloodied blanket for Domokos to take care of. I hid the brick, together with the waiter's napkin and the strips of bedlinen, under my cape.

That morning the Special Investigator tossed and turned in a restless, sweat-drenched sleep.

I went for an afternoon walk on Margaret Bridge. I waited until there was no one nearby; from the banks of the river I could not be seen. I flung the bundle containing the shoes, the bloodied strips of linen and the waiter's napkin into the Danube. By the time it floated down to Mohács, not much would be left of the package.

"For example, that brick was never found - if it was a brick," reminisced Marton.

I did not have the heart to throw it into the Danube; for some reason the dangerous temptation of elegant solutions gained the upper hand in me. But at least this time it did not lead to any complications, I can tell you in advance.

In advance?

Or in hindsight?

I went to the quay at Ujpest where I carefully placed that brick on top of a pyramid of bricks. I imagined it to be the one where Bora found it. That was absurd, of course.

They should have looked for it there, where it had come from. Where millions of stacked bricks formed a city for the eyes of all who walked that way. One brick had a bloody edge, but the rain washed away the last brownish smear, on the same day. And much later, when, around the time of the renovation of the whole vicinity of the Silly Kitty (and Agnes Vad would never get to build her palatial resort hotel in its place), the brick was built into the wall of one of the many four-storey apartment buildings, where it continued its motionless brick existence until one fine autumn day, during the season of the violent demise of so many Budapest buildings, it was knocked loose while whistling bombs were dropping. Eventually it would fit into another stack of loose bricks, and be built into some renovation. Let us assume. But this could only happen much later, by which time the Baroness, whose platinum blonde hair would never show gray, had long breathed her last in the arms of her faithful, stalwart lover, whose posture was again ramrod straight.

The streets were still wet. I could clean my shoes again.

"The Special Investigator would not allow them to close down the Kitty." In the glance cast by Chief Inspector Marton at his former mentor I could still detect the admiration of the young acolyte. Dajka was never one to abide by axiomatic assumptions or prevailing prejudices, such as safe-breakers having no home, and was thereby in a better position to catch them. He made sure he could gather all available clues, without sacrificing them on the altar of the hypocrisy that demanded the club be closed. Someone was struck down at the Silly Kitty; the body was removed through one of the three exits. He was unwilling to leave the case unsolved, a case in which he had gotten personally entangled, willy-nilly. He was both conservative and open-minded at the same time. A gentleman, for such did exist. He strove to preserve the original setting at the time of the crime, for he preferred to work with facts. (The man called Brick, at the Little Bear Bar, with his feminine, jagged mouth and anxious forehead, followed totally different principles. He claimed there were three types that he could always detect even at night, in the shadows, in the light of a fifteen-watt bulb: bushwahs, gays and gypsies. "He says 'bushwah' but he means Jews," my photographer friend Little Kovács informed me. The Brick blamed these types for his being out of work, for his cirrhosis of the liver, and for the winter cold. "What are you staring at me for with those bug-eyes," was how he tried to woo our vocalist, the Whale. She was easygoing and somewhat loose; if she liked a man, she would go to bed with him. But she did not like this one. "Oh, you botched-up nigger," he went on with his courtship. The Whale was called Olga Edelman; her father was a Jewish Hungarian, her mother a non-Jewish Hungarian. "Why don't you leave your boyfriend," the Brick continued. "Come over to my place, I've got ten inches for you." He received no response, so he grew pale, then red in the face. "Do you know the song that goes, 'I won't drink three glasses of red wine...'" No response. He pinched the Whale's fleshy nose between two fingers. "You think I don't know you are half Jewish? You know you've got to learn these songs so you can hide your origins." Olga the Whale now deigned to answer him. "You overestimate me. As far as you are concerned, I am all Jewish. And my mother was a Wallachian Gypsy. And I know every song, but I don't sing all of them." All kinds of things happened at the Little Bear in connection with this incident. The Brick, who used to drink there in the company of two two-hundred-pound coal haulers, insisted that the band play his song, and pulled out his butcher knife. Mátyás, our piano player, immediately broke into the first measures of "Just don't tell me the jail is cool/ And at night the stars shine behind bars". The two coalmen rose to their feet, and Laboda, who was second violin in the Alva Ráz gang, placed his hand on the Brick's paw and said, "No need for that." The rest of the gang showed up out of nowhere. Mr. Rudi, the boss, expelled the Brick from the premises, but received a message the next day, that the man's presence there was dictated by higher interests. But back to the reason I am telling this. Gyurika, the guitarist with the pockmarked face, on the night of the above episode put his hand on the Whale's shoulder. "Don't feel bad. He was totally blotto." "Oh, he was just saying what was on his mind," answered the Whale, with a deceptive smile. Gyurika loved peace and quiet. "Look," he said thoughtfully, as if in his mind's eye he were reviewing all of the migrations, conquests, rapes and tumbles in the hay, that went into the making of the crowd that was sitting, standing, eating, drinking, buzzing in the place, as if to illustrate the point. "I'm also a mix of so many strains: Hungarian, Serbian, German, even Jew. You know, nothing bad happened, really. The man was drunk, and it spilled out of him. It doesn't matter. The simplest thing is to acknowledge that, deep in his subconscious every Hungarian, no matter how open-minded, has a pinch of anti-semitism." "Every Hungarian?" Olga the Whale paused for a moment, to look around at all of us. At the piano player, who faced the butcher knife, at Little Kovács, who stood up to the two coalmen, one of whom could have flattened him with one hand tied behind his back; at Alva Ráz and the Old Buda gang. "You know, I can prove you wrong at once." And her swollen, biblical lips pronounced the unappealable sentence: "There is none in me.") But the Special Investigator was more careful with his facts, and this had given him an immeasurable advantage in his work. As if there existed some higher justice somewhere, a movable feast, the highest attainable mark. This way, as a side benefit, he accomplished the preservation of Bora's bread and shelter. His wife Maria nodded. That was the Christian thing to do.

And he looked askance at the piano player. He did not mind keeping an eye on him.

So he secured my job for me, unwittingly. I could observe the progress of the investigation. He was always in view.

Domokos got rid of the bloody blanket. Within forty-eight hours the invalid was past all serious danger. We could take him away on the fifth day.

The Special Investigator found time to inspect the small huts and their tenants at the end of the first week.

He found only a scholarly man with a patched sleeve among his books.

Well after this visit, Domokos moved from the place. By then he had rented another little house for himself.

I wrote a letter to the Armenian, *poste restante*, stating that my firm requested a revision in our contract, regarding the forty-two fake Persian carpets. This warned him not to travel this way under any circumstances for six weeks.

The King was speedily recovering. We lay low. Bubbles kept on selling bread and rolls and little cigars. She had worried about the King; she was head over heels in love.

The Special Investigator was firm in his determination to see justice done in the case.

I observed Bora day after day. She sang; she was a harmless madwoman. When she saw me, she stared at me, and her eyes asked, "Why?" Only her mortal shell walked in our midst; her fully human existence ended on that stormy summer night.

I was the only one who knew when, and why. And I had to live with that knowledge.

(NOW: FUNERAL, THE COUNTESS. FIRE HYDRANTS. AIDS)

Over the weekend two friends helped the Countess Pálma with her husband's funeral. She dissuaded us from attending. Today, three days later, she came over and had a good cry on my shoulder. Now we are her only family, so we had better act accordingly.

The world keeps on changing around us, as it always does. At times I fantasize about buying a computer, to give you a chance to get to know, if you feel like it, this new mode of thought. I would not buy computer games, though; they are only a distraction. A machine with a 64K memory would do just fine, but of course we cannot even afford a 16K one. Piros, who has a way of pretending to be a dumb cluck, asked a friend, "But what is it good for, besides multiplying and dividing?" "Your human contacts will become more multi-dimensional," he answered.

The apartment next door has been used as an office by a miracle doctor who offered Chinese acupuncture to lure patients eager to lose weight or stop smoking. Who knows what else he promised them. We saw him arriving once, a man with a greasy, crude, aggressive face, sporting three huge gold chains that flopped over his black shirt, unbuttoned down to his hairy belly. Sluggish young men and overweight women filled our little corner of the corridor. They smoked cigarettes while four-inch-long needles hung from their earlobes, nostrils, eyebrows. He charged five hundred forints for sticking them in; it is incredible what some people will believe. The other day the tax inspectors showed up to seal the apartment he rented; the quack had disappeared. When I snuggled my prickly unshaven face next to yours, you started to giggle, "Help! Papapuncture!"

New fire hydrants have been installed on Markó Street in front of the courthouse and by the central ambulance building. They are a new touch of color in our city, after the yellow street cars, blue and silver buses, and black telephones. In time, they will be all over, on the Grand Boulevard, on Váci Street, and in Buda. Now we too are able to say that our fire hydrants are red, they stand by the curbside, and there is no parking in front of them.

Another change will unfold only over the coming years. I have come across some specific information about AIDS. I was having a quick lunch at the fast-food place on the boulevard. Meat with rice that was quite delicious, each grain of rice well-steamed and separate. The lunch would have been a memorable experience if I had not visited the washroom, before leaving. This way it became even more memorable, and I am afraid I will remember it for a long time. These frequently repainted toilet doors are uncensored message and news centers of the city. (The censorship covers those things that the citizen dares not admit even to himself, walking the streets or squatting on the toilet seat. If you think that there is no such thing, just you wait. Grow up. Unfortunately I cannot expect our world to become much better by then.) Once upon a time Imola used to give me reports of uncensored graffiti in ladies' rooms. She was a real partner to me.

"Attention! You get AIDS only if you take it in the ass." That was the message. "I love sweet, bratty snotty kids. To pet, to lick and eat, to suck and fuck." This is the background noise. The epidemic itself is in its initial stages in our country. The disease is still restricted to homosexual men and to drug addicts who share needles. There are no Haitians here. There are people infected through blood transfusions, and among them, the first mortality.

THE THICKENED TRUNKS OF THE TREES ON THE BOULEVARD

The police were busy all over Europe. In Port Said the Turkish police uncovered an entire network of smugglers and dealers in stolen goods, and the reverberations of this operation would eventually affect our fate. Meanwhile, we went on with our preparations, unsuspecting. When I removed the stitches from the nearly healed wound, a cold sweat broke out on his forehead, but he made not a sound. The hair was already growing back around the wound. By the time he went back to work, there would be no visible trace of that love-propelled brick.

As a porter, Bódog Haluska was getting quite used to doing an honest day's work.

The Greek was chasing pretty women.

I timed the rounds of the night patrol.

Our tools were ready and waiting.

"On Monday nights my Martzi would come home late," the white-haired Lady Maria dreamily reminisced, when the trunks of those boulevard trees had grown much thicker than in the Kitty's day. By then our footsteps were wearing down the fifth basalt facet of the city's built-in cobblestone clock, and horse-drawn streetcars had become a thing of the past. Yes, the highly respected Special Investigator used to frequent that Kitty. "It was work," said the retired judge. Yes, that too.

We were waiting to receive the word about our approaching prize.

One windy Saturday afternoon I went out to make a wax imprint of the outside lock.

We intercepted the letter sent by the jewelers, and I could set our deadline. We sent a telegram to Agap Kevorg.

The Saturday afternoon the investigation at the Kitty is resumed, after receiving her personal effects, Bubbles is released from prison, and she sets out for home. At the cab

stand on Rose Square, she bumps into Máli, who had been
released a few hours earlier. The two friends hug each other.

"Guess what," prattles Máli. "The Special Investigator is at
it again, all day he's been at the Kitty. I just don't know what
he could still be looking for..."

And Bubbles, this young flibbertigibbet of a girl, who does
not have one quarter of my experience, proves to have a
hundred times more sense than I do. Then and there she turns
around and leaves. She leaves behind, in an upstairs wardrobe,
her finest pearl-gray dress and her wine-red Lyons parasol.
She does not go back for them. And don't think these items
are not important to her. But she hurries off on foot toward
Tollhouse Square.

The Viennese guests of the Exposition arrive in Budapest,
and the Stone is delivered in the mail. The day of the diamond
has arrived.

Monday. Dinner at Agnes Vad's institute. The Special
Investigator by now wants to create the impression that he has
decided to give up the inquiry.

The youngest Knorr girl is peeping at the tenant.

I was only a half-hearted participant at the burglary. Having
left the dinner table, I hurried home on the sidestreets, and
changed.

We left no ashes, blankets or cash at the store.

One by one we returned to our headquarters. I took off my
cape full of metal shavings and stains, rolled it around the
crowbar that the bungling Greek had dropped on the street,
and I, the bungler, hid the package up on a rafter.

Bódog Haluska tossed into the blue Danube a soft suitcase
containing a page from an accounting book filled with ashes,
several shredded green horse blankets, a brush and a broom.
The King proudly saved his trophy, the steel disk.

The Special Investigator had been waiting for this burglary.
He could not have known when or where it would occur, but
he knew how it would be done. It was not this gang's style to

grab the jewelry off the princess' neck. Every criminal has a modus operandi. Telling the story, Marton was again re-infected by the excitement of those bygone days. "The Chief knew very well that these people had to challenge stronger and stronger safes so they could triumph after manly struggles." Listening to the Chief Inspector's account, I thought that Dajka's reasoning evinced a deep understanding of the psyche, and was a homegrown, peasant equivalent of the theories of his Viennese contemporary, Professor Freud.

The moment had arrived to find the answer to the unresolved cases. The Special Investigator flung himself into the chase after the safe-breakers, with his faithful assistant Marton by his side. Those were invaluable years of schooling for the future Chief Inspector.

The Armenian in Port Said, the King at Karola Gombocz's.

I kept playing those sentimental waltzes. I placed myself on public display, just like that brick on the quay.

I have noted that in general destiny may have more smoke than fire, especially if one takes charge of one's life. And yet, I never really believed that we would get away with it. Perhaps this resignation was one of my many mistakes. My associates were still at large, when I was already making plans for their escape. I was able to work out the strategy for the Pest Regional Penitentiary - if and when they would be imprisoned there.

"Our methodical work began to show results," said the Chief Inspector.

We, too, worked hard, and not without a system. Bubbles witnessed the arrest of Rókus Láncz in Old Buda, and was able to warn me in time. Dajka found the cape that did not fit any of his prisoners, and although he came across the horse blankets that matched the green shreds, he was never able to identify the source of the white linen fragments collected in an envelope.

We did not bungle everything.

The humane Dr. Dajka, on the strength of sheer talent, compiles his album of criminals, which, paradoxically, became the harbinger of a much less humane epoch. In your lifetime this may sound almost incredible, but back then there were no I.D. cards. There were no Social Security numbers. Mug-shots and fingerprints were the exception. This was of great help to us later, when we were playing for different stakes. We common criminals were instrumental in evolving the techniques that were later used to keep track of law-abiding citizens.

All of the safe-crackers except one were collared by the police. When Chief Inspector Marton later told me about the little old lady across the street who saw their comings and goings on the afternoon of their capture, I shuddered at the thought of what would have happened if she had seen Bubbles, and had described her to the police.

They could not find the owner of the cape. The Special Investigator summarized it: from that very first night, when a folded note summoned him to look into the brick murder at the Kitty, he always arrived too late. Somebody was one step ahead of him.

Now he wanted to anticipate the villain. He wanted to be at the site of the next crime, waiting for him.

The time arrived for using our last reserves.

By the time it was necessary to organize their escape, I was well prepared. I approached the task on a theoretical basis. Prison is an institution that prevents getting out. But getting in is no problem. The rest was mere detail.

The Jewish pickpocket was caught and incarcerated at the Pest Regional Penitentiary.

With Bubbles in there as well, I knew I had to wait at least thirty days until she was released.

"The bread-girl did not return, Your Excellency," reported János Suk on that Saturday afternoon.

And the Baroness added, "She should be here by now, because her thirty days are up."

"What thirty days?" The Special Investigator looks up slowly from his notebook. He still does not know.

"Incarceration, I humbly report," says Suk, snapping to attention. "For disturbing the peace and creating a public nuisance."

The Doctor jerks up his head.

"And no one told me?" Apparently in this place everyone except him knew about the girl's jail sentence. That was why the soapy residue had settled so clearly in the wash basin in the girl's room. That is why the wildflowers had all dried up. "Didn't anyone realize that I was conducting an *inquiry* here?" His voice grew softer. "It could be most ominous at such times," said Chief Inspector Marton much later. Whoever stood in his vicinity trembled in the presence of such wrath. The long-retired judge now cast an almost apologetic look at his wife Maria. He had been most attentively following each word said by his former subordinate, and from time to time he would turn to the white-haired Maria, who hung on every detail of the narrative, and explain a thing or two.

"So her thirty days are up today. Well then, don't even bother to look for her," and with a curt gesture the Special Investigator motions Suk to stay in the room.

At this unfortunate moment, Dajka's face is lit up by the sheer intellectual delight at finding the missing piece of a puzzle, on glimpsing a clear ray of the light of reason through this tangled mess of mysteries.

"I have a well-worn penny that says she was incarcerated at the Pest Regional Penitentiary," he says, almost smiling.

"That's right," say the Baroness. "So you knew about it after all?"

No, he did not. But the bystanders were light-years behind him in grasping the events. Marton is eagerly waiting for his next word. Patrolman Suk gapes at his Chief in silent amazement. The man is a magician. His mind, like Roentgen's X-rays, can penetrate distances and walls of steel.

The Doctor senses that chance has just put him on the right track. He had pursued in vain, by land and sea, on the Riviera and through the Hungarian flatlands. The mystery woman was found, at last. And lost, as soon as found.

"She's gone by now."

On thinking it over, he shakes his head and laughs. That little bread-girl, who would have thought it. She lied when she said she had been a servant girl. That childish naturalness with which she admitted that the handsome customer had stolen her heart. She would go far in a career in crime, unless he stopped her now. She got herself locked up near the safe-crackers. Now, having done her thirty days, her job well done, she is out on the streets.

"Can't you see it?" He looks at his underlings. "Monday night she was off from the Kitty."

The internationally-bruited jewelry theft is tied in with the scene of his inconclusive private investigation. So it was not for nothing that he pursued the two inquiries side by side. That so-called sixth sense. He does not know whether to laugh or cry.

"The two cases are one," the Doctor says. But no one sees what he means, not at the time.

You have known it all along.

But he has them call the penitentiary, for formality's sake. The bread-girl had been released three hours previously, when she left for home. Eventually Máli tells how they got in jail. Fortunately for us, the police never inquire into who helped her find the job at the Kitty.

Such thirty-day sentences were not unusual among the girls who worked for her, so Baroness Vad never gave it a second thought, much less thought it worthwhile to mention to the police officer. Bubbles had just about total freedom of movement within the penitentiary; she could do whatever she wanted with the gold napoleons and the Swedish needle file left over from the engineer's workshop. Her petticoats were never searched. She located the pickpocket. The prison guard allowed the glittering gold to persuade him to deliver a cutting iron to an insignificant railroad thief, and to leave one door leading to a corridor unlocked. Afterwards he must have had occasion to meditate on whether honesty is divisible into greater or lesser parts.

Here Chief Inspector Marton paused briefly. I was thinking about the prison guard who committed suicide. Another victim left in our wake.

"And on that Saturday we still did not know about the coffee cake," Marton went on. The coffee cake that could have been sliced as thin as cigarette paper. There was nothing hidden inside it because the cake itself was the message, announcing that the bread-girl had found her way inside the penitentiary.

The King and the Greek both turned cooperative.

Karola Gombocz, in her Cemetery Road apartment, had all along kept the King's fine black suit freshly cleaned and ironed. Now it was time for her gently to cut and shave Jankó's beard and mustache. She bought the train ticket for the Southern line. Socrates had to learn to say three Hungarian words without a trace of accent: *A Déli Pályaud-varra* ("To the South Station"). We kept after him until his pronunciation was flawless, so that any cab driver would have thought he was a native speaker.

One after another we lost touch with Rókus Láncz and Bódog Haluska, left behind in the dungeons of police headquarters.

I had no word of the fate of the others until the pickpocket was finally recaptured in Máramaros.

At last the Greek was nabbed on the Riviera. "He led us on a merry chase all the way to Monte Carlo," said the Chief Inspector.

He had executed our carefully laid escape plans in a precise and professional manner.

The one thing the police officers could not understand was: how could such an internationally accomplished gang become involved in a cheap romantic nightclub melodrama just before their great coup? Chief Inspector Marton cast a glance at the old retired Judge Dajka, as if to signal that he would like to respect the older man's sensitivities, but still, facts were facts.

But it should have been easy enough to predict that if the Safe King Márton Jankó was going to do anything beyond his professional activities, it would be something to do with women.

TWO PORTIONS INTO SIX

"By now we had caught their international dealer in stolen goods," continued Chief Inspector Marton with his recapitulation. "We had recovered the diamond known as Blue Blood, and the jewels that were in the House of Hapsburg consignment." And here he grew meditative. "But two portions of the cash in their loot were never recovered."

I went to visit Lori, the seamstress on Seminary Street, on that Saturday afternoon just about the same time when the police officers at the Kitty at last discovered the identity of the woman who had accompanied the Safe King shopping for shirts and underwear, and to Gerenday's hardware store; the woman who washed the blood out of the hand towel.

Lori proves to be a simple, timid little creature; at first glance you would not guess her to be the Greek's wonder woman. I lay out my share on a Singer sewing machine. I ask her to produce the Greek's share. I tell her, "See this? It's all we have left. For all of us. Almost sixty thousand, with a little rounding off. I'm adding the amount needed to round it off. And now, we're going to divide it up again. Six shares, everyone gets ten thousand. Now it's up to you to take care of this money, don't let anyone find out that you have it. The Greek will be released from prison one day, and he will look you up. He will know who the other three shares belong to, and how to get it to them. Tell him I took two shares; he will understand."

The police never found out about Lori. She would do sewing at people's homes for a forint sixty an hour, while sitting on top of tens of thousands. The Greek and the others eventually received their rightful shares. (By rightful I do not mean the system of justice practised in our legislation-happy world.)

This is what we ended up with, for all our pains, for all our preparations and investments: ten thousand forints apiece. Still, I do not consider the enterprise a failure. I had found good friends, lived an adventure. Bubbles found her first love (regardless of how it turned out later).

And I had found my own people, once and for all; you can't ask for more.

Marton went on with his account. "Looking at that small bloodstain, the Chief took a deep breath, and began to explain to us its significance."

"If you have taken into account all the facts at your disposal," the Special Investigator said on that memorable Saturday, "and you have excluded the imposssible, then whatever is left, no matter how improbable, must be the solution you were looking for."

And a fresh piece of the puzzle falls into place.

"Call a cab at once!" Dajka shouts. On the way to the Pest Regional Penitentiary, he makes a mental note to update the circular. He runs up the stairs, taking the steps two at a time, and sweeps the prison doctor along with him. In the doctor's office, he asks for the escaped prisoners' medical records. This is where he must find the answer to the question that has been nagging him ever since the prison break.

He knows what he is looking for, and soon finds it.

Why would the Knorrs' tenant have left so suddenly for some unknown resort? All that time when he was interrogating the prisoners all he needed to do was reach out and brush those dashing auburn locks aside to reveal the freshly healed scar.

"The man whom we referred to as the victim of the brick murder," said Dajka to his assistant, "was, a few weeks later,

most effectively practising his profession, at the Grand
Bazaar."

There it was. He points out to the physician the sentence on
the medical admission sheet for the prisoner Márton Jankó:
"On the left frontal-temporal area of the skull, a healed
wound sewn up with five stitches."

"Do you happen to recall this?"

"With the kind we get here, things like that are about as
ordinary as clipping one's fingernails, for a law-abiding
citizen," says the doctor, with a shrug. "But, as it happens, I
remember this one."

Earlier, Dajka did not have time to digest the information
on the medical records, and did not include it on the circulars
sent out.

"How old would you say the wound was?"

It was the freshness of the scar that had called it to the
physician's attention.

"The final stage of healing, the formation of the epidermis,
must have been completed just before the examination, a few
days at most. The edge of the scar was still whiter than the
surrounding unaffected skin. At the maximum, the scar was
forty-five to forty-eight days old, and twenty-one at the
minimum."

The quack who treated this head wound without reporting it
to the police would probably never be found.

And I would have agreed, if they had asked me. But they
hadn't.

Dajka takes out his pocket notebook. He counts back, from
the day of the prison hospital admission. He takes into
account the few days it took to arrest the burglars. Six more
weeks before that - and we are back on the night of the brick
affair. The wounded Safe King had lain low somewhere,
convalescing at his leisure, sheltered by his inside and outside
accomplices.

"The stitching was done rather crudely," adds the prison
doctor. "Whoever did it used figure-eight stitches, which are
not indicated for a lacerated wound of this size."

Very funny. I would like to know how he would have

managed it, with all his expertise, by the light of a flickering oil lamp, on a dining table, with five hours' delay.

So the victim's body did not disappear. The corpse was not found for the simple reason that there had been no murder.

Dajka says an inward prayer of gratitude, for obeying his feelings at the time, possibly out of partiality; he would never be able to determine his motivation objectively. But he thanks God for not letting the deranged singer be committed to the Márianosztra prison, where she so self-destructively demanded to be taken. He thereby avoided a mistake that would have been tantamount to judicial murder.

"Because he is a good man, who followed the dictates of his heart," said his wife Maria.

"But I could not have done otherwise, anyway," added the retired judge, from his fireside chair. "Ours is an enlightened legal system; in cases involving a capital crime, the confession of the suspect, by itself, is not sufficient for a conviction. If the charges are not completely proven, independent of any confession, then the law prescribes acquittal. Guilt must be proven beyond a shadow of doubt."

"You are still a good-hearted person," insisted his wife, speaking with deep conviction.

But that frail little bread-girl could not have dragged a man's inert body away, without some help. All signs pointed to another inside accomplice. But who was it? And where did he hide?

The doctor's newly revived interest in the inquest made me very uneasy. On sleepless nights I would see his lamp cylinders dance in front of my eyes. I did not understand them, and I do not like what I cannot understand.

No sooner had I got home from Lori's, in the late afternoon, Domokos visited me at my room on Diver Street. This address, close to the new House of Parliament, would not be known to any of my colleagues, who would not be tempted to betray it when captured. Domokos came to tell me that Bubbles was staying at his place.

Well and good. I ask my visitor to enlighten me about the significance of a heated lamp cylinder. He knows all there is to know about the most unlikely topics.

He sits down, and asks for coffee, and a cigar. He wants to know all about it. Lately he has been using all of his time to do library research. He was the one who met that Austrian professor at the National Library, the one who assured him that every man has his price, in one or other of four ways.

He wants to know if anyone else handled the cylinder before me. And whether the lamp was blown out immediately afterward. "And the person who conducted the experiment was a policeman, right?"

"How did you know that?" I exclaim, almost aggressive in my surprise.

"Afterward he dusted it with flour, while it was still hot, so it could be photographed," says my friend, my brother.

Although I did not witness that part, I am certain that he knows what he is talking about. The cylinder had been taken out of the room without delay.

"It is the method recommended by Francis Galton," says my friend. "Oh yes. It is a very old observation - the Chinese have been aware of it for millennia. Recently it has seen use in the army in India, where the imprint of a soldier's three fingers is taken as verification of his identity." As he warms to the historical introduction of the subject, I am beginning to fidget. He notices this and in a few sentences tells me what I wanted to know. "That Britisher has certain theories about the tiny lines on our fingertips. One: each person has a unique configuration. Two: this remains the same for life. And three: on the basis of the above, anyone can be unmistakably identified by means of a fingerprint."

At last I understand the meaning of the Special Investigator's impromptu little experiment. And if I did not know about it sooner, it is my fault alone.

(NOW: ICE-HORSESHOES ON MY FEET, GLOVES ON MY HANDS)

We were away for eight days on a trip to visit Imola's relatives in Kolozsvár. They had never met you. Zoli had been in trouble, and we wanted to travel there while it was still possible.

Here at home the Fráter was still having a rough time with a sentence in his book. "Hungary was still there." They wanted this sentence out. We took coffee, soap, and three copies of an earlier book of his, to give away.

After we crossed the border the heat suddenly went off in the train; it was a cold spring night. The customs man in the door of our compartment reached into my bag, and found the three books. "Hungarian book? Periodical?" he asked, with a heavy accent. Everyone knows that condoms, heroin, and Hungarian books are not allowed across the border. He ticked them off on his finger. "None. None. None," he said. He placed his body so that it hid us from his colleague standing outside in the passage. Could he have been a secret Hungarian? That would have been an easy solution. I do not know of another story like this from that border; we shall never know what was the reason behind his leniency. We brought one copy for Zoli, the other for Peter, the poet - this profession seems to play an inordinately large role in our history. And the third copy was still looking for an owner.

The train kept climbing, higher and higher, toward the King's Pass, from where another train had descended with the railroad thief Baumgarten on board, in another time, on one of the railway arteries connecting the two lands of the Hungarian Crown, at the green forested rim of the Basin. I looked out through our fogged-up window at the mountains and forests, but could see only degrees of murkiness, and I tried to guess the direction in which the highway lay where Imola and I rode the bus the last time I met her relatives. That had been the first time she came back to her hometown since Great Carnage Number Two. That was a momentous summer in our lives. There had been a flood at Mohács, and an earthquake at Dunaharaszti; then came the brief weeks of the Second Age of Reform. After that, the twelve days of autumn - October, 1956 - changed not only our history, but that of the continent, and of the world, although seemingly things stayed the same as before.

We had no candidate for the third copy of the book. In the dark streets we looked for the Hotel Majestic which had the same name when the Safe King stayed in it between two professional engagements. Today it still has the same deep brown stairs and wooden banisters with reddish copper trim. The last time the threadbare red carpets were changed was when the town was temporarily returned to Hungary. The current dispensation allowed a single twenty-five watt bulb per household. But a hotel does not even qualify as a household, so that the fur-hatted, fur-coated porter had to show us to our room with a flashlight. There were no lights; the elevator was not working, there was no heat, and no discount on the price of the room. Zoli's wife Orsolya sent a friend of the family to greet us; I did not catch his name over the phone. He brought a bottle of Albanian cognac. We wrapped you up in a blanket, as a cognac-substitute, and we all warmed up. On the way out he inquired at the reception desk about the heat, and I was amazed that he spoke such fluent Romanian. He laughed with pride. "You didn't realize? I am Romanian. My name is Goga. Claudius Goga." I quickly pulled out the third signed copy of the Fráter's book and gave it to him. From then on I marvelled at his fluent Hungarian. I happen to be sensitive to languages, especially to my own.

He led us across the bridge over the Little Szamos, the roaring, foaming river that stumbles over rocks. We walked on zig-zag cobblestone streets toward where Zoli lived. It is a small town, and it felt as if one could walk anywhere on foot, and as if every path led through the Main Square.

We never got to see Zoli, although we went over to see Orsolya every day. They live in a huge, much-patched and reshaped loft-like room. That long-ago summer we had visited Zoli's parents there with Imola. Now every time we showed up Zoli's wife took the telephone out to the verandah, and, even out there, covered it with two cushions. Feeling that they had run out of breathing space, they had applied to emigrate - to Budapest, who would have believed it - the way people used to emigrate in the year of the Kitty. Within one week Zoli was drafted into the army, for three years. But now he was in a safe place, in prison. They had managed to bribe a soft-hearted Securitate officer who arrested him. Orsolya offered us brandy, and peeked in at the children, who were asleep in an alcove. She did not know when or how she would see her husband again.

Over and over, we came to the Main Square. I remembered an ice-cream parlor from long ago; one day we found it, for you. It is a square, such as you see in any Hungarian small town; in the middle there is a park, surrounded by streets on the four sides, lined with little shops. In the window displays we saw jars of preserves and green beans, brown canned goods, and brown Albanian cognac. One day you noticed they had bread. We had to eat, so we stood in line. The queue doubled back twice, like a writhing snake, and the policemen keeping order had uniforms like in some worker-peasant operetta, with strange, old-fashioned tommy guns slung over their shoulders. The food was mud-brown, so was the street, the wood fences, the gap-toothed boards of the wooden sidewalk. All the people wore gray, the more daring ones, brown - this is what we had had enough of, back home in the fall of '56, after Imola and I had returned from here.

Her school had organized the summer vacation trip, the first one abroad since the early 'fifties, and I was permitted to accompany them. We were strolling on Kolozsvár's Main Square, when some of Imola's male classmates were accosted by a group of local adolescents, and after a few words, were attacked. "You are in Romania, so speak Romanian," they were told, as we later found out from the teachers at the local secondary school. Our boys could not understand the words, not knowing any Romanian. There was a brawl then, for the locals - and not only the Hungarian-speaking locals - would not put up with that kind of talk. Back then, saying something like that created a scandal.

Around midnight, the teachers from the local Hungarian

secondary school came to serenade Imola's teacher. She took us on long hikes, and under the rock cliffs of the Torda Gorge she would describe to us the debates that were going on at the Petöfi Circle back home.* She lit a candle in her window to acknowledge the serenade. And we listened to their songs: "The Kolozsvár teachers are here / To wish you a good evening..." and, "Acacias by the roadside, summer eve, one Gypsy lad and a meadowlark...," that sort of nonsense.

The school touring bus did two thousand miles in ten days. It followed the same route taken by the Turk who drove Hungarian slaves across the Temesvár Vilayet at another time, past the forests at the rim of the Basin, far to the east. We saw the capital, we saw the sea, where the port was so different from anything Imola had seen in our landlocked Basin. There we sat, leaning on the unplaned table top; the flypaper hung in the middle of the ceiling, blackened with flies. There were flies in the air, flies on the tables, flies on our faces. Who knows how, but in that great orgy of grayness that held sway over half a continent, this town managed to retain part of its character: it was like ports anywhere on the globe, teeming with colors and fish-market smells. And at the most unexpected moments, at the end of some zig-zag alleyway, out popped a view of the Black Sea, with foreign flags, and ships. Yes, there were flies in the streets.

We swung back on the homeward leg, just as that traveling circus troupe did at another time. We stayed overnight at a strange town in the easternmost outpost of the Hungarian language, whose workers, both Hungarian and non-Hungarian speakers, had demanded, back in the early 'fifties, at the same time with the workers at Pentele and Katowice, that their communities be renamed after the foreigner with the big mustache.

We stayed at the huge dormitory of the Hungarian secondary school, sharing the local students' lot. We ate out of small tin basins held in our laps as we squatted by the walls of the long hall. Apparently the plates, tables, and chairs, so commonly found in student dormitories the world over, have

* The Petöfi Circle was the forum for reformist debate at the University of Budapest in 1956.

not been encouraged in this particular corner of the globe.

There were other things lacking, as well. Imola was the first to discover this, and I had trouble believing my eyes: the toilet seats were replaced by a pair of upturned, grooved metal boot soles. As if someone had stood on his head down there, wearing iron boots; as if some alien seven-headed Dragon had plunged him, head first, into concrete.

On the last day of our visit we met Imre, whose name, and very identity, I have been carrying ever since that fall, our great fall of '56. He bequeathed them to me like a suit of clothes. Before we left on our trip I was not even aware of his existence. We looked up Barna, the brother of my fatherly old friend, Kornél Vargha. (Whom you know as Grandfather Vargha; he had built a factory for the production of a certain prepared food he had developed, made out of brewer's yeast.) This way Imola had a chance to meet the young widow, whom you now call Grandma Vargha - for soon after, they became our adoptive family. I had met the Varghas earlier; they had helped me, with the naturalness typical of all great families, around the time of the Second Great Organized Slaughter: helped me with food and a room at their apartment by the Danube. Imre was the same age as Imola, seventeen; I could not have guessed that soon I would become closer to him than to anyone else. We walked and talked in the spacious courtyard of the Hungarian school. Both of us loved him at once, and after an hour's conversation the both of us realized, independently, that already at his early age he was a remarkable person. He was facing a great change in his life. Your Grandpa Vargha had already proposed to his widowed mother, and they were up to their necks in the bureaucratic tangles of marriage and emigration. The wait was tearing Imre apart - while he yearned to go out into the world, and to live in the Hungarian capital, it broke his heart to have to leave his birthplace. For it is natural to live out your days at home, where you were born; we know this truth from other times as well. When we said our good-byes, he promised we would meet in Budapest in the early fall.

The latter-day name-giver of the town was no longer alive, but dead men's beards keep on growing, and the town still kept his name. While alive, he had been immortal. Now fresh winds of change blew all over the continent. In the middle of the courtyard stood a gigantic loudspeaker intended to deliver marches, commands and inflammatory orations; on that day Radio Budapest was blaring its news. The three of us, with Imre, listened to it telling us that Hungary's satrap had resigned, citing illness, and had already left the country for the east. A historical era had ended; may oblivion descend on it.

This was Imola's last summer before graduation. She went to secondary school in Old Buda, where I lived; she was an Old Buda girl, and of course, a Kolozsvár girl as well. She was still a child, but between the two of us all the important things had already been decided - including, just about, even your arrival.

The next morning we clambered up into our bus, and started on our way home, back toward Kolozsvár, across lands populated by Hungarians. Her school had rented a brand new thirty-three-foot, rear-engined '55 Ikarusz bus. It grumbled as it climbed the serpentine mountain roads that were not built with such long vehicles in mind, and at some of the switchbacks we thought the bus would break in half as it turned. This was the first Hungarian vehicle in those parts since the war. We had to stop at each village; people came out and stood in front of their gates, they swarmed around us, they all wanted to give us something. Entire loaves of bread, and sides of bacon: we had to accept it all. Just before Kolozsvár a young peasant woman dressed in black invited all thirty-five students and escorts into her immaculate room, where we stood under the painted earthenware plates nailed on the walls, and watched her look at us with tears streaming down her face. That whole trip was like a painted picture, a kitschy lakeside sunset in iridescent purple, lilac, and orange - except that for these people it was their lives. Ever since then, when no one is listening, I'm always humming those kitschy, so-called "folk" songs, "Acacias by the Roadside" and "The Kolozsvár Hussars", even though I detest the genre.

At night we were back in the town where Imola spent her childhood. She took me to Farkas Street, where a manhole cover carried the inscription, "Ödön Fischer and Co. Machine

Works, Budapest". She took me to Torda Road, and pointed out an ivy-covered single-storey house, where she had lived while I was in Budapest, near the Danube. Her family fled there from Fogaras after the First Great War. Her grandfather, your great-grandfather, was assigned to Kolozsvár, where he was the Head Auditor of the town, with the rank of Chief Counsellor. "He would take me for long walks along Torda Road," Imola told me. "When I whined that I was tired, he would hire a horse-drawn cab to take us home. I was always tired. We had to get off one block from home, because my mother would get mad at him for spoiling me. This is where we waved from the gate at the soldiers who marched past singing, laden with flowers, to the battle at Torda Gorge." Some of those soldiers returned, without songs and flowers, muddy and bloody. Imola's father, who went through the years of the world cataclysm as a major in the air force, showed up with his single-engine biplane, packed in the whole family together with grandpa, put on his goggles, and the next time they saw his face was after landing at the Székesfehérvár military airport in Hungary. Imola would have liked to go inside the house, but was afraid that they would not understand what we wanted.

I took you to that building; in the meantime the ivy had died and the yard had overgrown with weeds. We found a rusty old street sign that said Torda Road. A true name, for it leads to Torda.

The last copy of the book was intended for the poet, Peter. Another poet, to keep the revolutionary consciousness alive, single-handedly, for all of us. This twenty-year-old young man has shouldered the responsibility, and dares to speak out. He speaks for village and city day-laborers who are isolated from the letters of their mother tongue, living with the steady erosion of language, perhaps incapable of articulate speech in any human tongue, to give words to their pain in an incomprehensible foreign environment. He is the kind of man that back here at home we have practically no need of. We had heard about his fearlessness, and I was curious to meet him. A burly, sluggish young man stepped out of the school's entrance; his face was soft and round, with pallid complexion. His trouser leg was too loose and kept hiking up, while his socks kept disappearing into his downtrodden shoes, forcing him repeatedly to bend down to pull them up.

When he saw us, and started to smile, I knew it was him. The one who refuses to be intimidated by prison, by midnight visitors or all-night interrogations.

He took us for a walk in the cemetery. I did not at first understand the reason. The plainclothes detective who was hovering on the other side of the street, dropped off at the cemetery's entrance. He probably knew that there was only one way out. We climbed slipping and sliding up the muddy hillside, with the rainwater running down the middle of the path. We found wooden grave markers that had been pulled up and piled in a heap; these we stuck back at random gravesites. Peter kept looking behind us. The crosses had Hungarian names on them. He told me that the local Romanian police paid street urchins fifty lei for each.

"Now I will show you something nice." We peeked out from behind a little mansion: it had been the family crypt of a great Humanist family famous for centuries of Hungarian history. We approached it through a ramshackle, neglected and overgrown section. It now carried a foreign family name in rich gilded lettering, inscribed in the new official language. Behind it, on the plain marble surface of a tombstone, a heavy-set, dark woman was arranging a tablecloth with great care. Placed on it, on a white kerchief over the recently dead, were a fresh loaf of bread, some fruit and flowers. The woman had black hair, black down over her upper lip, black clothes and stockings, and black mud on her brightly polished black shoes. Next to her stood other women, three children, a man. "They are not the ones who pull out the crosses from others' graves," said Peter. "They would not steal the past, for they know for sure that they have their own, like everyone, full of blood, poetry, gold, defeat and heroism." I thought, there is no bread in the stores for these people, either, and God only knows how they baked their bread, at the cost of what sacrifices, to observe their tradition for commemorating the dead. They probably do not even realize that we too had lived here. We found refuge here from the rapine of the pagan Turk, escaping from the walled town of Buda.

Fled to those parts of the two lands of the Hungarian Crown that lie beyond the King's Pass, where the pagan does not lord it and loot. In the morning, betimes, I rise from my bed of rustling fallen leaves, and set out in the direction of the town of Hatvan, six leagues from Pest. On my journey, to earn my food, I serve as beater at the hunt, or chop wood for peasants. I drink good wine at taverns. I arrive at a market town and try my luck, to find employment at a good master's smithy for copper and iron tools. But a wounded hand leaves me useless, so I must run on - from Eger onward it is the King's lands. I find day-work among carters, and go on from post to post, up on a coach, living on cold food, at times able to afford a bottle of wine, stashed away in the wicker framework. Past the town of Sárospatak, and from there one long haul through the Uplands, past Tokaj to Várad and into Transylvania.

Because of warfare, great is the misery and poverty all over the land. The Orient has pushed up this way from the Balkans, and spilled past our Buda. It is a miracle that we are still here. All my worldly goods are two pieces of gold. Only the Holy Ghost keeps my weeds together; my buskins are falling apart.

In the wintertime I hear news of the great Lady Homonnay, clad in silk finery, who had been imprisoned and raped by the Turk in Buda, giving birth to a dark-skinned man-child, offspring of one Moorish marauder among the dozens. She kept her affliction secret from her husband, only we ex-prisoners knew of it. Our Lord Homonnay received her back unknowing, not having to pay ransom, after her miraculous liberation from Turkish captivity by a band of peasant free-booters. The child was christened János after the Turk-beating Hunyadi; let him grow into a brave warrior, and a terror to the pagan. And that the child's father is not his true father, he will never know.

And I go on, by and by. When I reach the Székely land, the earth and water freeze like stone; ice horseshoes on my feet, frozen gloves on my hand. Some nights the snow covers my bed. When all I had left to eat was a handful of barley, I find room and board at my noble lord Benedek Bali's household in the village of Old Magyari, near Hunyad. There are men from Magyar land there aplenty, both common and nobles, running for their lives, just like myself. But there was enough to eat and drink for all.

And I am hired as manservant to accompany my young master Bali on his foreign peregrinations.

Years later we receive a letter from our good lord Bali at home, in Old Magyari, telling of how he had been bedridden by gout. His letter is full of news, about the wild rampage of the Turk, lording it over us. Their Emperor sent new armies to Transdanubia, where they pillage and burn. They destroy homes, enslaving many, plundering all their chattels. Scourged by starvation the people go into hiding and exile, fewer and fewer Magyars are left. So we set out for home, across the sea in galleys, overland in carts, post-haste. After thirty days in boat and cart, we arrive back in Old Magyari, where we find rich and poor wearing black mourning for our lord Bali, whose hour had come. Now my little master's peregrinations in foreign lands are over, and so are my happy adventures. My young lord buries his father with stately pomp and seemly obsequies, and now he is sole master of the demesne, comforter of the poor, at an age when his beard is barely sprouted. He does not want to let me go on my way. But we are, in our two lands, the crumbling ramparts of Europe's shores, dust and loess that is swept again and again by the storm of the foreigner's rage. To shore up this rampart with our own bodies, is our fate. While I ate my lord's bread, I had learned letters on the sly, and some Latin, and picked up a smattering of several disciplines. For which I shall remain beholden to him till the day I die. But my task, as it is everyone's, before any other, is to see how I can help to drive out the Turk. With this I take my leave of my lord Bali and the village of Old Magyari.

As long as we were in Transylvania, I wanted to see things. That summer we were here with Imola, we could see only the places where the school's bus took us. Now you and I mounted an overcrowded, cumbersome, angular, rattletrap bus at dawn. It stopped at a crossroads in the middle of the fields, without any sign of a village anywhere. A sixteen-year-old ruddy-faced, smart little Székely maid led us to the village; she said it was only ten miles away. I looked at you, but you waved it off: you are a cross-country runner, after all. On the way the girl told us the village was still all Hungarian-speaking; the three families who moved here from Wallachia had become Protestants and took on Hungarian ways. Only the policeman spoke Romanian.

We ate the food we had brought with us, walked around, inspected the village's two streets. The wife of the sacristan invited us into the blazing pure poverty of their little home. Table, chair, bench were all home-carved pieces; there was a stove under the tiny window; on the wall hung copper bowls and pottery, and a washbasin. At the other end of the room, which made up the whole house, was the marriage bed; at the foot of it, crosswise, the other bed for their three children.

Their church. The princely simplicity of those whitewashed timber walls. A balcony made of white timbers; spread out on it the coverlets embroidered with years of confirmation classes. The services offer a temporal meeting place for a simple, besieged community: the things to be done for children, for the school, for the church. What the expenses are. The embroidered Sunday wear of the girls is made of pink and light blue polyethylene yarn, with metal and glass star ornaments. When the Reverend talks about costs in lei, I realize where we are.

Farewell to the town. This time no one was listening to Radio Budapest on the Square. The windows of its antique little palazzos were all boarded up, as if the Turkish Buda had moved here, in its earlier wrecked state. This time the Torda Road and Farkas Street were no longer called by those names. I heard no Hungarian word spoken in the open air. As if, since that great summer of '56, someone had loaded up the inhabitants into huge moving vans, together with their mother tongue. But in the meantime, everyone really understood Hungarian, secretly and tacitly, whether they were natives of the town, or learned it after settling here. For this communal

crime this square, these historic buildings have been sentenced
to death.

Taking our official leave of the country. The taxi driver, on
hearing us speaking Hungarian, gave us change in paper
money in such hopelessly unusable condition as I had never
seen before. We could not even give it away to anyone
traveling in this direction. I asked the railroad man at the
station for the train to Budapest. He looked me over as if I
were a worm, and tossed some words at me. One of them was
"Romanian". He was probably telling me to speak his
language; this is what they usually say nowadays, and it no
longer causes a scandal. So I told him that I'm sorry, Mister,
but I do not speak the language. Believe me. And I know how
to be insistent. A local citizen would not have dared. He spat
at me in Hungarian, with every sign of revulsion, "Track two."
The train departed from track one.

On the way home, as I sipped Albanian cognac to wash
down the toast I munched on, and you huddled in my winter
coat, I thought of them.

That last morning before departure we went to the
marketplace; it's important to see the marketplace wherever
you travel. And we did have twelve hours of travel by train
ahead of us, so we needed food. It was as if it had been
another country. The peasant women all spoke Hungarian to
their clients. At one of the booths they were selling cottage
cheese out of a cloth, at three times the official price. We
stood in line. Soon there were people behind us, anxiously
peering to see if there would be enough left for them. You
said then that we should not buy any cottage cheese.
Tomorrow we could stroll into the store at home and buy as
much as we wanted. I felt bad that this had not occurred to
me, and I was happy that you thought of it.

I was thinking of them, the ones unable to travel, or stroll
into a store to go shopping. I thought of Peter, who might
decide, after another all-night interrogation, that he's had
enough. He would wander around with his broken face in the
early morning streets. He decides that they will not find him at
home the next time they come for him, and plunges into the

woods. In the area where they found the Hungarian priest, who preached too much, hanging from a tree. The very first night his feet are blistered, and he limps on, deeper in the wilderness, perhaps where the Iron Man had stumbled in an earlier time, before being picked up by the tribe of the Gypsy Voivode Shashtarash. He would live on nuts and seeds and green raspberries, and one day would glimpse a bear peering into his face peacefully from the other side of a bush, before lumbering away. At night he would lie on the fallen leaves. He would drag his bearish hulk clad in his loose city trousers, his pallid, chubby flesh would be exposed by his ever-slipping socks, and the undergrowth would pull him down, until one fine day his wounded feet would torment him no more, and he would look up at the high sky between the treetops and be free.

I thought of Orsolya, the way she looked after us that last time in her doorway. She is a very beautiful woman, timid, with glasses, modest and gentle. Her childlike face has a deep tinge; generations of husky, dark-haired frontiersmen gaze out from her eyes. Her parting glance was telling us that she was not sure what their fate would be, whether Zoli would stay in the safety of prison, or be released on some pretence, whether they would be able to stay in their family home, where they had lived in the light of the blessed sun and where even the roadside weeds were their familiars, or whether they would have to emigrate to the land of Canaan, flowing with milk and honey - to our country. She laughed at the notion. She wanted us to promise at all costs to return on a skiing trip to her mother's village, later this spring. You made enthusiastic plans; we would come back at the end of April, before the snow melted in the mountains. But, no matter how petty such considerations are next to her invitation, the truth is that I have no more vacation time, and you cannot take any more days off school, either. She gave us directions back to the hotel, waving after us in the evening light.

Back home the powers that be approved that sentence of the Fráter's: "Hungary was still there." It expressed the incredulous enlightenment felt by a traveler returning home through the surrounding nations. In the meantime, my friend

must have succeeded in proving the truth of that statement:
the country was still there. And I can testify to it that it is still
here.

TRAVELING LIGHT

Dajka knows he must act. For lack of other hard evidence,
he returns to his lamp cylinders. He requests his forensic
technician to match the prints taken at the nightclub with
those from the Zara bank robbery.
"How much time will you need?"
"We have more than thirty sets of fingerprints. This is
time-consuming work... I'll need at least two days."
"We don't have that much time. We don't have any time.
For now, why don't you skip the women. I want the results by
tomorrow morning."

I have some more questions for Domokos. He, too, wants to
know more: what happened, when and how. He does not ask
why, that is my business. I get to the Zara Italian-Hungarian
Bank in the course of my narrative. He wants to know about
what I did with my hands. Try to remember exactly. And I do.
I picked up that steel jimmy. And the steel jimmy was left
behind.
Because of Zara, I was included in the album of criminals.
At a conservative estimate, this would cost me years of my one
and only life. (To put it more precisely, it gave me years of
work. I firmly believe that human activity does not take away
from any life, but adds to it. To verify this, we would have to
prepare a catalogue of human actions. We can omit such
things as wrapping little girls tightly in rough night clothes, and
voting by means of blue absentee ballot slips in uncontested
elections.) By now, it is reasonable to hope, no more copies of
Dajka's album are to be found anywhere, and that is well and
good. We always did everything we could, then and later, so as
not to be entered in their books and computerized records.

And not solely for practical reasons: my innermost being rebels, and I find it revolting to have my life under bureaucratic scrutiny.

What happened here was my fault; now I must move on without the least hesitation.

"I will take Bubbles with me," I tell Domokos. "She's involved in this up to her neck."

He nods. "I am going to remain here." He has returned from a long journey not long ago. No one is after him; he will trust the girl to my care entirely. He needs peace and quiet; human knowledge is advancing by leaps and bounds, there is so much to research, and only at home can he have the opportunity for undisturbed work. Yes, I can see his point - I wish I could stay here, too. But we shall return some day.

He goes home to tell the girl. I ask him to say goodbye quickly, for we are ready to depart. Bubbles knows the schedule for each day of the week, the hour and the street corner where we are supposed to meet. Each day it is an hour later. On Saturday, it is the corner of Saint Peter and Hatvan streets. The same way, we have our rendezvous points worked out with the King, three countries and half a continent away in the west. It should still work, unless Socrates or Baumgarten the thief has betrayed us.

Domokos and I say our farewells, without sentimentality. It is not for eternity. Not ever again.

I will simply send him our address.

I cannot go back to the Kitty; events have overtaken it. I have no way of knowing if I have days or merely hours of freedom left. It takes me ten minutes to pack. I am accustomed to traveling light. In every life that is worthy to be called such, there comes a moment when one has to part with material possessions, without giving it a second thought. (Little Kovács knew this well, and made good use of it, when he based the strategy of his personal war of liberation on his opponent's pack-rat instincts, on her worship of material goods.) It wouldn't hurt if you too would make friends with this notion. And in case you believe that your books are not material objects, you should think again. Only human beings are irreplaceable.

I take a small bag which I can carry anywhere. One good suit of clothes and black shoes (these may be useful as working tools), my passport and my share, reduced by two thirds, is all I take with me.

I am going to owe my last month's rent. This will explain to the little old landlady why I chose to exit through the window, leaving behind my suitcase and other belongings. My large suitcase with all those splendid suits tailored for me by Kamarás will be left for the landlady. I made sure there are no telltale labels, or slips of paper left behind. She would never summon the police, as it later became apparent from Marton's account. For the police, my whereabouts were a mystery to the very end.

I let Domokos precede me out the window.

There is still one debt that, unlike my other debts, I am able to pay now. I have to go to the People's Park, past the Zoo

Late afternoon. Dajka is impatient, and stands behind the chemist, observing the man's precise and quick movements. The Special Investigator has grown somewhat unsure of his own conservative ways. He has decided he would like to learn some of these new-fangled scientific aspects of his profession.

The negative plate of the Zara fingerprints is in the photographic enlarger.

"The index finger of the left hand, of the fourth man in Zara," says the technician.

"NN 124," adds the Special Investigator.

The expert picks up the next photographic plate of a fingerprint from a lamp sleeve. The plates, carefully labeled by name, are lined up in the slots of a holder. For identification, they all bear the date of the brick affair. "Brick affair, and not brick murder," thinks the Special Investigator, and sighs.

"The pores of the sweat glands open onto the ridges," murmurs the laboratory technician, as he adjusts the magnifying lenses in their metal frames and tracks. "In primates. On soles, palms, and fingertips. You may observe the three basic patterns. Your Honor, take a look at this impression. The mountain-like formation is an arch." He forages about for another fingerprint. "This one is a loop, the name is self-explanatory. This point, where three ridges meet, is called a *triradius*." Some more rummaging, and another fingerprint is produced. "In this one, you can see a whorl, with two such points. From such a point one may count the ridges to the center of the pattern, and this way each individual fingerprint may be unequivocally described and classified. But since we have a basis for comparison, our work is somewhat easier." The next sample bears my name, the one I was using at the time. He picks out the photo of my left index finger. "All we need to do is enlarge this negative to the exact size of the photograph from Zara. Then, by projecting one image over the other, we are able to determine at a glance if there are any similarities."

"This Y-shaped scar..." The technician's sentence starts slowly, as the two projections are superimposed. "The similarity is amazing!"

"No," says the Special Investigator, placing his hand over the image.

The procedure is ingeniously simple and foolproof. To get an idea of what he sees, just look closely at the tip of your own index finger: all those delicate lines, curlicues, loops, meetings and separations, miniature whorls. The patterns are hereditary; what you see should look like the projected image.

Dr. Dajka has been primed for this moment by a whole year's work, in addition to the previously amassed data and his own abundant suspicions. He now has the benefit of science (as opposed to the crystal ball), and it will prove to be a decisive influence during the rest of his career. There can be no equivocation; the fingerprint belongs in the realm of direct perception. It could be the model of factual evidence. (Which is what we wish to work with, in this history.) It is measurable, comparable and provable. Photographable. We should keep it in mind, when we would consider more complicated phenomena. Even in the proximity of ultimate questions, ones that cannot be answered with a simple yes or no. (I have said that I do not take any certainties for granted: as soon as they show me unretouched photographs of the Virgin wearing a gray coat, I will give the miracle some thought.)

"Are you certain that you did not mix these up?" The

Doctor is forced to ask this question by a persistent conscientiousness. The technician can only give him a wounded look in reply.

The two images, when superimposed, are as if they were a single fingerprint. Dajka is ready to go: he has urgent business at the Kitty.

"No, these two fingerprints are not similar. They are identical."

"Whenever I was confronted by facts, I accepted them. This is what my life has been about," said the retired judge, by way of summary.

BA NN 124 has acquired a name. One of the Zara suspects is identified as that piano player at the Silly Kitty, whose face Dajka did not like from the beginning. He is the fourth man The Special Investigator reflects that, at first glance, he would have given the man five years. And his instinct was right.

Almost as lagniappe, he suddenly recalls that missing motif he has been racking his brains for all along. As he was heading home in the early morning after the affair with the brick, something jarred him on Huckster Street: a man, standing with his back to him. His posture seemed vaguely familiar. He was standing in front of the window of the jewelers, Hatvanger and Bócz, and this fact now acquires an unmistakable significance. The Special Investigator is appalled by the man's nerve: that this mountebank-turned-piano-player would be inspecting the scene of the upcoming burglary, only a few hours after having been interrogated.

He has already identified the Zara gang as the perpetrators of the Idol and New World Street jobs.

And of a series of safe burglaries all over Europe.

And finally, on the basis of their signature, as the perpetrators of the nearly forgotten Odessa burglary.

So this is the man who has been one step ahead of him, since the beginning. This is the man on whom the dusty, stained cape will be a perfect fit.

Here is the one who was washing his hands on the night of the brick affair at the Kitty. Yes, just as Bora accused him.

And what else can be pinned on him?

"Marton! See at once who is missing!"

It takes ten minutes to discover that no one at the nightclub knows where the piano man lives. By now Dajka is not surprised.

He asks for paper, pen and ink, and composes a new circular, for the arrest of the piano player and the bread-girl formerly employed at the Silly Kitty.

They may be accompanied by the fugitive convict Jankó, alias "Safe King", the perpetrator of the Grand Bazaar jewelry theft, and the subject of an earlier circular from the Budapest police.

Dajka is hard put to provide a verbal description of the quiet, unostentatious good looks of the bread-girl.

The piano player is easier. When last seen he was wearing a black suit, black shoes and hat. Short stature, fragile build, but suggestive of great physical strength. No beard or mustache, high forehead, straight black hair. Complexion, white; jaw, square. He has a strong growth of beard that needs to be shaved twice a day. Special identifying marks: a Y-shaped scar on the left index finger tip, on the medial surface.

"I would love to know how he got that scar," says Dajka to his assistant, on the way out.

He is thinking of the transfigured visage of Baumgarten, the petty thief, and for the first time in the course of the two investigations, there on the sidewalk of Leopold Street, it occurs to him that he may never catch us.

The last moment. The law is snapping at my heels, but that is the least of my worries. I can no longer take shelter in a showman's life, nor find refuge in the night; the world is growing more complex around us and is also shrinking. Everything is becoming bound to everything else.

Since my last return home, I have been moving about in all sorts of environments among the same half million people inhabiting the capital. It is soon apparent how small this beloved, promise-laden city of ours really is. The Special Investigator is not the only one to become familiar with my physiognomy, and with the unmistakable patterns of my gait and carriage. Very soon it could get too hot for me here. Any moment I could stumble on an aged Slovak glazier or that elderly Schwabian woman who wore a many-pleated skirt and lugged mortar by the basinful at a Grand Boulevard construction site. Or a customer could recognize the former cab driver. Someone else might recall that I was in show business, and greet me with effusive affection. I would insist, with sinking heart, that he must be mistaken. But the thoughtful glances, raised eyebrows, frowning faces would become more and more frequent. I must not wait that long.

And I set out on my long journey a better man this time. I will never again be alone; my people know me now. The ones that come with me as well as those who stay behind. We shall always know where to find one another.

It won't hurt Bubbles either, to be gone for a while. The hour has arrived; I meet her on the corner of Saint Peter Street. I take the risk and send a telegram in code from the Central Post Office: "WE ARE OFF ON THE LONG JOURNEY".

"Do you have your passport?" I ask her. After all, she is not a child any more. (Even though half the time I do not know whether to laugh or cry at her scatterbrained schemes. But then who am I to talk?) She keeps her passport handy in her small pack, ready to move on. (This is the kind of readiness you will have to develop for yourself, although we are not going to cross any borders the next time we move, that's for sure. We are going to find some other solution.) We will soon be seeing the King again, if his travels continue under the same lucky star as before - and I am a firm believer in it. I have made a promise to the girl who is so in love with him. The three of us will travel across the sea. So she should take her leave of Domokos. We shall come home one day, and there will be no more waiting then. She will bring only the bare minimum - her best things left at the Kitty, anyway. Our train departs at midnight from the Western Station, where I will be waiting for her.

Before then I have one more visit to make. I must be at the

People's Park by seven. In these past weeks I have been worried about the fate of my abandoned troupe. I will have to be careful there, for the police have singled them out for special attention, even in the midst of all those sideshows, circuses and mountebanks camped out past Zoo Circle.

My luggage is light, my feet are quick, and I can walk any distance in this city. I go on foot from the Danube's bank to the Park.

All the way down Radius Avenue with its wooden pavement, across the Exposition grounds, and over the bridge. I arrive in time, and take up a position at a safe distance from the tarpaulin. I watch the whole new program from the third row in the audience. It is quite good. These young men and women are after my heart; they chose the ever new call of the highway over the security of humdrum everyday life. Doubtless my life is no different. I can see that they have added new features to the enterprise: a shooting gallery with five air rifles, and even a Negro trumpeter who plays heart-rending blues from the black funerals of New Orleans. In my place it is Kodel who is the fire-eater now. His version is more mature. When the Pearl passes around that greasy old hat, the clinking coins fill it to the brim. I do not contribute, for I would have to shove my way to the front row for that. I watch from a safe distance as they fold up the tarpaulin. They have staked out an overgrown corner lot in this shantytown at the edge of the fairgrounds, and their circus caravans are parked so as to define their turf with their merry green boards.

A white water cart is parked by the roadside, with a somnolent dapple feeding from a nosebag. In its cover I take a solitary farewell of my birthplace. I know that I will never feel at home anywhere else, no matter what happens.

But I must leave for a while, leave behind this scintillating, colorful existence. I stare at the dapple with the star on its forehead and the feedbag around its neck, and at the street sweeper leaning on his brushwood besom. These brooms were introduced recently; and, if you think about it, there has not been anything more suitable invented until the busy little yellow street-sweeping machine that we used to see around the former Valero Street every day, before we moved to the

Angel-land district, where that kind of luxury is unknown.

Around the carts and tents there is a milling crowd of proletarians from the outskirts of town; I drift, unnoticed in their midst, until I am in front of the entrance to my troupe's campground.

In the open area surrounded by the caravans, a swing has been set up in the middle of a sea of black mud. Two grimy Rupucz children are arguing about whose turn it is. I know I have more important things to do, but I still get a little choked up, mostly because of my inconstancy. Together we had gone through the dust, the frost and burning sun of our eastern trek - and now they too will all drop out from my life.

A tiny toddler clambers down the steps of the corner coach, his bare white bottom flashing.

In the rectangular entry of the caravan stands Kodel, all washed and clean in his snow-white cotton shirt, with sleeves rolled up, watching the swirling, shifting crowds in the park.

He walks over to the naked child. He shoos the bigger ones away with a flick of his hand, puts the toddler on the swing and gives him a push. He is a tall, graceful man now, with a firm tread.

The days are getting shorter, the light is failing earlier. In the descending dusk the last thing I see is the muddy heel of the tot on the swing, kicking up over the skyline of caravan rooftops. On this day I will not have a chance to glimpse Lilia's marvelous breasts, or her sister Alma. The next time I meet Kodel will be a world war later, and he will be one-legged. The other leg will have been crushed by one of the first tanks in the trench warfare of the western front.

On this same evening there is a scene at the tailor Knorr's. I found out about it only many years later from the Chief Inspector.

By now the Special Investigator knows very well who owns the burglar's cape.

Obeying a sudden impulse, Dajka picks up the brand-new crowbar, wrapped in the cape, exactly the way it was stored in the locked cabinet at police headquarters.

He gets down from the cab at the apartment house on Pannonia Street where the Knorr family lives. He takes the elevator to the top floor, and knocks on the door.

"Tell me all you can about the owner of this cape," he says to the frightened little man. The tailor had hoped to have done with this case and to be left in peace; like any good Hungarian, he hates to deal with the police and the law. Have I said that already? We have not changed much, in this respect. Dajka puts the man at ease; he is here only to seek an expert opinion. He needs the tailor's help.

The tailor spreads out the duster, looks it over, draws his fingers along the seams, hemming and hawing. After about five minutes of scrutiny and mumbling, he points to the mend on the shoulder.

"That wasn't done by a tailor, Your Honor." He ignores the rest; the metal shavings, the oilstains are not his concern. The great personage did not come to consult him about those.

The Special Investigator finds this a strange opinion. "But now that you mention it, it looks to me like very even, fine stitching. Remarkably careful work."

"That's just it," nods Emil Knorr. He draws his finger along the minuscule, regular stitching. "I have worked in this trade thirty years, so you can believe me when I tell you: money can't buy work like this. Only love. This is a woman's handiwork, and she could only do this for her son, or for her true love."

"By that time the Chief knew very well who the woman was," said Marton. "But this did not mean we were any closer to catching her."

I was not present at the tailor's apartment. Nor did I hear about what happened there until much later. Had I known about it sooner, maybe I would have done certain things differently. Maybe. But I have learned not to regret anything I have done. Because then I might not even have you - of all people.

And what could have been known back then, was not known even by the woman who mended the cape. It was obvious only to the expert eyes of the little tailor Knorr.

The Doctor is all the more eager to look me in the eye; he yearns to grab me by the shoulder and give me a mighty shake. He imagines a thousand times how he would arrest me. He even knows what he would do before snapping the handcuffs on my wrists.

He outlines the procedure with gusto for Marton's benefit.

"I would start by politely requesting him to try on this worn but still serviceable cape. I would even help him with it."

Naturally, the cape would be a perfect fit, at last. And then, as if imposing an act of penitence for all his earlier arrogance, he would take a complete set of fingerprints, under laboratory conditions. He would compare these prints with the ones found on the Zara steel jimmy, and would present the results as evidence in court.

"*Ceterum censeo*," he says the next morning on arriving at the office. That is, above all else, the woman must be found. The circulars must be supplemented with the information about the piano player and the girl, and he orders Marton to do this immediately.

During that long Saturday night, Dajka keeps returning to the same question, "Who is this piano player, after all?"

A good question. I feel like saying, "Let me know when you find out." But naturally, I hold my peace. Who is a person, anyhow? Any person. Really and truly.

OH, THE OCEAN HAS NO BOTTOM

A sudden and unexpected turn of events at last brings the two criminal investigations to an acceptable resolution.

The beginning is promising. On a Wednesday, barely a week after an international circular has been dispatched for the arrest of the two fugitives from the Kitty, Special Investigator Dajka receives an early morning telegram from the Prefect of the Berlin police. It is addressed personally to him. According to unconfirmed reports, the three wanted individuals were seen together in the capital of the Prussian Kingdom and of the German Reich. In the wake of this first news comes the second dispatch, later in the day: the trail has been picked up; it only has to be followed to the boarding ramp of the next departing trans-Atlantic steamer. All indications point to Bremen, from where the steamer *Wotan* of the Nord-Deutsches Lloyd shipping line is due to depart on the second of the month. The German Imperial Police have taken steps to intercept the fugitives.

Two tense days of waiting follow.

Back in Budapest the grandiose series of Millennial festivities is winding down. The bridge builders at Tollhouse Square are working with redoubled efforts; the name of "St. Gellert's Bridge" has been proposed. In Vienna, Duchess Maria Dorothea and Archduke Joseph are engaged, and the Parliament in Budapest cables its wishes for the Almighty's blessings on the Royal couple. The dedication of the Kolozsvár statue of King Matthias is scheduled for this month, as is the unveiling of the Millennial monument on the border at Zimony. There is an international congress of Unitarianism (a faith that was born in Transylvania). The ceremonial opening of the Iron Gates on the Danube, recently made navigable, is attended by our king, and the kings of Romania and Serbia. (Your great-grandfather had finished his work in time. The other day Yugoslavia issued a formal protest to Romania for not respecting the Iron Gates hydroelectric plant agreement, and using more water than the stipulated amount. The matter is being dealt with by the two countries.) So-called history is being made in the wide world. The Russian Count Paul Suvalov, chief governor of Warsaw is felled by a stroke; his condition is serious, but not hopeless. At the Berlin industrial exposition the public, feeling its morals offended, attempts to disrupt a beauty contest. The police break up the righteous gathering with fixed bayonets. From London comes the sensational news that Captain Dreyfus, transported for life, has escaped from imprisonment at Cayenne. In Stamboul a bomb is thrown at the building of the Ottoman Bank, and Armenian hamals are suspected. The police, on the basis of traditional law, leave the settlement of the affair in the hands of the municipal rabble, armed with *uniform* bludgeons on the day before the massacre, which takes the lives of six thousand Armenians in the ensuing eight days. The police, together with the *Sheik-ül-Islam*, look on while the Armenians are clubbed to death.

The continuation is discouraging. At first comes the dispatch, from the Havas news agency, then from the correspondents of the larger domestic newspapers, dated the previous day, reporting the sighting in Berlin of the internationally wanted safe burglar, who, together with two accomplices, is also wanted by the Budapest police for questioning in connection with another serious crime. Then, on the afternoon of the same day, the headlines of the German papers report a terrible catastrophe at sea. Dr. Dajka receives a police telegram: only one boat sailed in the interim, the steamer *Wotan* of the Nord-Deutsches Lloyd Line, carrying emigrants. Ten hours after embarkation, between three and four in the morning, the *Wotan*, with a crew of fifty, and carrying three hundred fifty passengers on board, sank in the North Sea, thirty-one nautical miles from the Kristiansand lighthouse. The trail of the wanted piano player and bread-girl led beyond a doubt to this ship. Presumably the safe-breaker was traveling in their company. (Dajka agrees with this supposition.) There had been no opportunity to prevent their embarkation.

The supplement to the circular, together with the passport numbers, had arrived in Bremen with a one-day delay.

The beginning was encouraging, the continuation disheartening, and the end bleak. Little by little the news trickles in with details of the dreadful disaster. The superannuated *Wotan* had been plying the trans-Atlantic route between Germany and America for two decades; its timbers were rotten. The British steamer *Scavenger II*, on its roundabout way from Rotterdam to the Cape of Good Hope, in dense fog rammed into the side of the *Wotan*. At the time of the impact, the British ship sent up a flare. Within an hour the *Wotan* was submerged to the tip of its main mast.

It managed to launch only one of its lifeboats. Lost in the wreck were the ship's first engineer, steward, four stokers, seven seamen and two pilots, and one hundred eighty-six steerage passengers, all of them Slovak, Polish and Hungarian emigrants.

The Special Investigator is a methodical and thorough man. We know him well by now. For verification he telephones the Bremen police chief, whom he knows personally. The updated figures show more than two hundred passengers lost at sea. The crew of the *Scavenger II* rescued nineteen persons at the site. The lifeboat from the *Wotan*, with twenty-two aboard, landed around noon on the Norwegian coast near Teresfrot.

It takes another day or two to establish the identities of the rescued individuals, then follows the final official report. The records of the shipping company, and the eyewitness testimony of German emigration agents confirm that the piano player and the bread-girl boarded the *Wotan* under assumed names, disguised as steerage passengers. They were unable to erase or alter their passport numbers, and these were recorded by the German police. They were accompanied by another man whose person fits the description of the safe-cracker. It has been ascertained that there were no survivors from the steerage, where the Hungarian emigrants were sleeping. The stairs leading to the upper deck were too far away.

So their accomplices and carefully prepared network of contacts in the New World wait for them in vain, thinks Dr. Dajka. It would have been in vain anyway, but they were unaware of that. Criminals always forget that the arm of the Austro-Hungarian police can reach far indeed.

Here the retired Doctor took over the narrative on the occasion of our later meeting.

So it was done. He felt both relieved and, in some vague way, saddened. Such a senseless death for these international stars of a dark profession, who were able to make a fool of him until the last minute. Always one vital step ahead of him.

In the course of the past months, he had gotten to know these fellows personally; he was used to them, used to having them in his life. He felt empty. He missed them.

In the evening he went to a small tavern in the Tabán district, where nobody knew who he was, and he mourned the three victims. He drank enough of the house's own sour rosé to dull the pain. For the rest of his career he would never meet such worthy opponents.

"Oh, the ocean has no bottom," he murmurs on the way home as the hansom cab goes clip-clopping in the wee hours. "I didn't say anything, just keep driving," he growls at the jehu.

His mind's eye can see the inferno of the sinking ship. The temperature below freezing. The storm above, and the raging sea. In the impenetrable fog and mist the crests of waves two storeys tall rise over the ancient steamer, as freezing sleet and ice cover the decks. The lines have frozen stiff. Frail human figures are struggling against the tempest around the hoary cables and icicled lifeboats. He can see the three fugitives' brief, violent thrashing for air in the freezing, turbid flood that rises against them, sweeping along the wretched treasures of these searchers for a new life. A soldier's chest. A rag doll. The foot of the stairs is unreachable. He sees the upturned faces in their death throes. The bread-girl's beautiful long hair floating in her wake. Behind her the auburn locks of the King, now beardless. And the untameable blue-black stubble, on the deathly white face of the piano player.

So a higher judge has passed judgement on them. The case may be closed now, although in a different way than he would have hoped. As his mind clears momentarily in its bibulous haze, the Doctor is incapable of fathoming why he cannot truly set his heart at rest.

What would have happened if... Strange. What if I had spoken with the laboratory technician one day sooner. If I had found the bloodstain on Friday instead of Saturday. The same day I could have issued the circular, sending the two passport numbers after them that much sooner. They would have been captured in Bremen, prevented from boarding the *Wotan*. They would still be alive today.

He examines his conscience. In his mind he goes over each moment. There is no way he could have known sooner.

He thinks of his tomorrows on this grim dawn so crowded with unanswered questions. One after another he sees the characters that have filled the last two years of his life. He sees them, and he asks himself what will be their fate tomorrow. In the forefront is Bora, with her vacant, deranged stare and her white hair. Her two innocent children near Vienna. Something must be done for them. The Baroness, and her grandiose plans. The Hunchback, his crooked shoulder, his gleaming eyes, and the barely perceptible air of superiority in his smile. The elusive Outside Accomplice. The lookout Haluska and Israel Baumgarten, who knew how to stay silent once caught - and to what end. Socrates the Greek, at the lighthouse of Paros, after serving his prison sentence. All the witnesses, one by one. Muratti the restaurateur, and Viczián. The hardware merchant. The tailor Knorr and his lovelorn youngest daughter.

And the three fugitives. He would like to conjure up their familiar faces. He wants to know everything. He wants to see.

Fifteen days have elapsed since the ship disaster. In a narrow corridor the white paint of the ceiling reflects its light on the scene. The faces are still upturned, as if toward hope.

The once pretty face of Bubbles has been partially corroded by the salt water; the currents play hide and seek with her streaming hair, as it swirls in unison like the tentacles of luminous red medusas. The King's body, bent at the waist, is stuck in the rungs of steep iron stairs, as the calm frigid waters sway our hair, swing our arms and legs. We are surrounded by the living world of the cold sea; tiny, agile shrimp move in and out through my eye-sockets. Two weeks after the *Wotan*'s sinking, the Doctor keeps searching for some answer in our icy, watery grave a hundred fathoms deep: what could have happened to us?

But that is another story.

CONTENTS

THE SETUP

STEEL JIMMY

Near the safe - the first automobile - trees of the Grand Boulevard, cobblestones - a hundred carats - Bubbles - protégée.

Handwashing - the pre-AIDS era - cab driver - the final outcome.

Porta Marittima - darkest hour - in Hungarian - the first blunder.

THE SIGNATURE

Idol Street, New World Street - encysted ulcers - Suk!

Two years earlier - underworld grapevine - Bush Street - Cemetery Street - (for you,...) - tools.

Man in a loincloth - all of South Africa.

At the Ursulines - the youngest Special Investigator - Silly Kitty - youth in a brothel - made girls do filthy things - the Bosnian builder's crew - the Hunchback.

In the coach driver's seat by the National Casino - election issues, blackball - kaleidoscope, a Slovakian glassworker - this world was made.

Other facts, other people - a rash of safe-cracking - the depths of human existence.

Two midnights in Budapest - the appointed Millennium - cruising girlies - the Café Nicoletti - the pulse of the metropolis - four sets of footprints - a thin stranger - a new safe - foreign timetables - places of arrest.

NIGHTCLUBS AND BROTHELS

Pint mugs - deeper waters - forty-three brothels, Madame Tremmel - an earlier wave of Mongols - ninety kreuzers - two human arms and a leg in a sack - special empowerment - the Highest Wish.

Crime wave - a fingernail-size speck - Charles, the infamous buffoon - Not so fast! - the Yanomami Indians and Sir Francis - harmful genius - Teutonic and Hebrew barbarians - white slaves

(NOW: SAND IS SAND. 9 A.M. OCTOBER 23, 4004 B.C.)

Hatched-jawed, four foot-six - savanna, saber-toothed tiger - live lava - a little leg - lalalla, lala - the motivation of the popular novelist.

But how? - a hell of a good question - the escalator - like my fist - Whistling Zoli.

37 MEN: THE SOCIAL CONTRACT

Dream of a playful sexuality - Bubbles pretends to be busy - Dr. Dajka is angry - thirst for adventure - the man who stands by her - a whore's life - pulling their pants back on - decrepit voluptuary and innocent child.

Frau Bábi - the law of diminishing returns - health certificate, room by the day, legalized brothel - stupid bawd.

Our civilized European homeland - Socialist muckrakers - cat rescued from the rain - Veronica Czérna, singer.

A MATERIALISTIC ENTERPRISE

The Hunchback, the bread-girl - diamond dust - exploratory skirmishes - gentleman crook - worthy target - world class - the Baroness and her mate - nascent yellow journalism, the Safe King - patriotic optimism, Hajji - the giants - lovely days with Karola Gombocz - like bankers and journalists - aficionado of metal - inch-thick walls, hidden lock mechanism - the Great Coup - Chicago-style explosion - without capital - the second blunder - steel jimmy and rotary drill - with steel - night life.

THE MORAL CODE

The tribe of Voivode Shashtarash - flying squad at Newtown - Kodel and Murikeo the Pearl - Bora - marketplace and societal progress - fleshmarket - the Hunchback looks back.

Rough girls, laughter - one hundred visiting cards - nightlife rife with crisp banknotes - derbies, incognito - in the air at night - gambling - Gottfréd, Mech. Engineer - the ninety-nine cards - the names of ministers - Radius Avenue, Váci Street - the landsman of Abraham Ganz - the horrified fence - trial borings, the deep layers of memory - bedside smalltalk - aristocracies of blue blood and high finance - guests of the National Casino - knows too much, take care of him - bolt-studded handrail of the Chain Bridge - a Hungarian gentleman.

(NOW: UP, DOWN, STRANGE, CHARM. STONE DEAF ANGEL. GOAT TITS.)

In the former Valero Street - Imre, please - how is that? - The Second International Year of Physics - without Sneezy - when, where, how, what? - the patriot bites the dust, aleph followed by beth - your North African jellaba - the Fráter, in the village - Whoa!

THE CROWDED FAIR IN THE TOWN OF LONDINIUM

One thousand years later - enforced Gypsy welfare - covered wagon - three Gypsies, three Jews, three Slovaks.

In another time - itinerant - peddlers - pig Latin - a new world - two-headed calf - Italian girl, diamond eyes - beggars' songs, showing pictures - the Markó Street Courthouse - Lilia and Alma, snake girls.

WORLD PEACE

Oriental gentleman - East-West tilt - the Odessa Savings - Factory Street, Saracen Street - the safe in the cellar - the experiment - sooty faced devils - ninety minutes

Noise and message - New York, Second Avenue - Sutruroy.

DRESS REHEARSAL

Four covered wagons - across the two Hungarian domains - Agap Kevorg, Russian subject - abroad, good newspapers - dynamite in a portfolio - steel disk - double-entry bookkeeping and Biarritz - Muratti's Viennese beer hall - in the skies of the Continental criminal world.

Legends, the Odessa carnival - torrid, tender nocturnal threesomes - the Greater Russian Circuit, Evpatoria, Simferopol, Moscow, city of wooden houses - American gang - album of criminals - NN 124.

THAT WAS THE YEAR

The eventful year - the black man of Nazareth - fresh candidates for the brothels - Kishinev, Iassy, Kézdivásárhely, Kolozsvár.

(NOW: BEING BLACK. TRAIN STATION WATCHERS. HERMES AMBASSADOR)

Grass-green electric typewriter - five yards of pyjama elastic - rickety thin legs - saying your r's - Imola, your green-gold eyes - meat ration ticket - we are going to visit - bargaining with the Fráter - terminal, four pairs of tracks, Byzantium - plainclothesmen.

A MOVABLE FEAST...

Telephone news - a million Armenians - ten thousand dervishes - your forefathers negotiating territory - at the forefront of the world - Reedy Lake, Willow Lake, Fire Well - *Vaporetto* No. 4 and 6 - Chicago in Budapest - Tide Street, Angel-land - one-room hovels - potatoes, horse-meat and cheap brandy.

...AND THE BLACK LAND

Every road - assorted Jews and Gypsies - vague passions - the Whale's great-grandfather - for a few months, the occupiers - nightgown, of coarse material - self-polluter - gymnastics, hard board for a bed - sexless women and bricks - green meadow, many-colored balls - after Turk and Tatar - the folds of her mound of Venus, sweetly - Iron Gates, seventeen medals - our chaotic adoptive family - gunrunner, Grandpa Elek, dogskin.

(NOW: SWEDISH GIRLS, SWEDISH SUMMER)

Milky white sky - my cousin Kerstin - Pekinese palace poodles - Malcolm the Red's drum solo - whirlpools of incest.

GEMSTONE AND CESSPOOL

Jewelry, cash or children belonging to others - monkey circus - the future piano player - glitter and poverty - newspaper, public baths.

Human hodge-podge - new cobblestones - the dandified cab driver - layer of asphalt - there is an elevator - attic windows - double life - behind the new House of Parliament - Ministry of Produce Collection - empty lots, palings - bottled-up line of coaches - the blood curdles - platinum fire - mist and vapor.

STUDS AND FILLIES

A MAN

Stickball, penny-pitching, tag - ragamuffins - Fish Square (for you, nonexistent) - the dual nature of her establishment - dwarves and blackamoors - burst lamp cylinders - Danube Street - wicker hamper - hovels in the courtyard - voluminous bosom - four steel doors, with peepholes - service entrance - account books - world travelers, heartthrobs - bustling Hatvan Street - the blue scar, to infiltrate.

THE VENGERKA

The lucky ones of this world - dark, dog-like eyes - curlers and mustache-presses - the hostesses - Gypsies from Small Saltpeter Street - Mohammed Abdelkadar - spurious inflation - porcelain complexion, Asiatic eyes - at the Ursulines of Szentmihályfalva - daughter of the westernmost Eurasian steppe - terror in the dormer, bloodstains - dream prince, white automobile - demimondaine depths - *tout Petersbourg* - Cherkess danseuse - an early harbinger - unwed mother, the dreaded Ochrana - national misery, bitter defiance - little dancing sluts - first dose of morphine - abortionist - you know the rest.

RAGS, MUGS AND DOLLS

The safe-crackers, a year ago - ageing soubrettes - tomcats prowl - scarlet Lyons silk - the shadow of shutters.

So fine, all woman - canopied brass bed - sturdy nape - moist with desire.

Converging paths - the lookout is lugging - cutpurses, cat-burglars, pimps - blind horse, train carriages - polka-dot scarves, hurly-burly of fire-eaters.

ALLEY-OOP!

Always her - trivial little ballet - a telltale feminine mouth - alley-oop! - gliding blue strides - the moment of decision - farewell to the troupe.

Hermina Road - the seven wonders of the world - whirling and howling dervishes - occupation for a couple of hundred years - appetite - minstrel and public scribe - little Ice Age - wee Dutchmen, skating - Buda, a Mahommetan outpost - piteous wounds of my nation - pigs root, ramshackle fences, puddles - the yard-goods store on Deák Square - churches without priests - disappeared without a trace - stables, Turkish schools - a doll's-house Turkish Buda - wooden roadway, parading coaches - mastodon omnibus - velocipedists - traffic jam - public lavatory, "second class" - dogcart - Jews in silk yarmulkes - awnings like eyebrows - splashing and gargling - cable to Saint Petersburg - Muratti's Viennese beer hall.

In front of The King of Hungary - Merényi and Gombos, Mechanical Engineers, Dr. Bárán, Dentist - world power - teach the stones Hungarian.

(NOW: IMOLA'S FATHER, YOUR GRAND-FATHER; TRIBAL FEELINGS; JIGGLING ROTUNDITIES)

Rare bird, great man - continental head wind - so-called success - wherein I accept the law - naked little wife - messed-up life, red soup - beret-wearing guerrilla, bomb-throwing murderers - bums, need to travel - nothing for a hundred years - smaller than New York - fried snails, couscous under the willows - not likely - hovered like a Rubens.

HONKY-TONK PIANO

The workers' susceptible minds - European equivalent of the Bazaar - drying towels, curling irons - *chameuse excentrique.*

Upper crust - map - braised beef with macaroni - the name of .the Stone - seasoned rogues - pyromania - what they will testify - another star.

Cat costume - former chorus girls - embattled ladies - a broad female face - cut-glass carafes - titillating depravity - smart nightspots - prurient bourgeois - silver-haired head waiter - Hog-face - kitty-cat house, cobblestone song - Aladár - ventilation cowls - steel room - the labyrinth - the red salon - the third armpit - Bubbles - the chosen and the initiated - *homo sap. sap.* - crimson peace.

(NOW: UPPER FOREST ROW)

The Fráter - the novel before the first - the last remaining republic - no faking it - the comrade's private opinion - what will be in it?

BEFORE THE STORM

Ice cream - happy lovers - three weeks of Africa - Ofelioko, our deeply-pigmented companion - Soma and Adolf - a quick nap - Amsterdam: the Stone's setting - goldfish - toward the night-time drama - jungle love - innermost alarms - Buchwald chairs - iron figureheads - "Kalimagdora's Lover" - the occupiers - giant flagstones.

Silver theft - seventeen citations - homeless shelter - titanic schoolchildren - smell of distant ports - single-storey Pest - tomorrow's city, you and Imola - the old Theaters - a slum, geometric progression - steam mills on the Grand Boulevard - ant-like procession - a maze of paths - whitish mud - tuxedo, upturned collar - temporary lodgings on Cemetery Road - a sigh of relief: murderers, robbers and whores.

My showman's instinct - open and clandestine prostitution - the harnessed chorus line - the design, murder - tipsy Excellency - blowsy music - She's through!

(NOW: THE LARGEST PUBLIC SQUARE)

All the time in the world - megalomaniac era - as the wind, or thought? - learning ground - our ethnic group in the Basin - the name of nothingness, mustache, boots - this road is a non-road - sitting at the end of the world - rocky ledge, mulberry tree - newborn space-time bubbles - Thundering Dragon - the Seven-headed one - I smell a human - no green and no red - food, enemy, female - as one mountain would another - the poorman's youngest child - kingdom of the earth - Roentgen, Tivadar Puskás, the pioneers - what's left - hottest in Zimony - violence let loose.

"HEEYA HEY, HEEYA HO!"

A fury bursts in - her Grand Entrance - silver handbag - star singer - anticipating, ever since - I am there - red and gold, colors of the sun - hidden handle, hitch in the music - silly and torrid - sharpened senses, peripheral vision - he'll never be yours - princely bastards - splendid legs - lion and gazelle - loud and crystal clear.

ON A NEW JOB

ADRENALIN

Meadow full of dancers - Mindanao Trench - one more month - physical action - the horrid end - fat blockhead - the gunpowder of diligence - sift through the past - even from the devil - the swinging tray tips - bilingual - the blood of revolutionary heroes.

Streaks of lightning - downpour's fusillade - red sky near Tollhouse Square.

Washroom - patience - disappeared - weight of the unknown - police, newshounds - the future shines, nuggets - noises - doing his job - no need for the blotter - one gesture - a menial!

The Orpheum on Sailor Street - bloodstains - a finjan of Turkish coffee.

Water splashes - amoeba-like puddles - raving self-accusation - police boots - he knows - through the maze.

(NOW: RAZORBLADE, POLKA-DOT BANDANNA. LECSO. THE BEGINNING.)

Air Power, Carpet Bombers, Counterintelligence - New Europe, the old version - 'Rice - Technokol Rapid - Laci the Bear and the Thief.

Paddle forward in time - the beginning of it all - Dragons write a novel - the unspeakable, we say - 20 billion BC - ten to the minus thirtieth of a second - one blink, a million years - assuming - formations - the total number of baryons - three degrees Kelvin - to forget - light of dying suns - photos to prove it - white-bearded or close-shaven - Spindle Street, the 'pinach - until further data - twenty-two dimensions - everyday story, the poet Weöres - in blood and song - the other direction - cries out, on the beat - panning - the great stretch.

BUSY HANDS

Crazy - provocative piano - I killed him - let me see your eyes - your veins - the policeman's keen scent - my mug made his fingers itch - the red-head slut - jealousy - work as an opiate - blood and champagne - lioness with cubs - a hostess with a candle - it was me - confused - filthy, intolerable demands - dream of a resort hotel - When? Where? How? Who? What? - the famous steel chamber - bookworm - the call of nature - and for the Baroness? - cui prodest? - officers' shakos, patent leather boots - hide the evidence - bloody hand - gum Arabic - corns - the magnesium flash - dried mud - gallows, dungeons, coarse prison wear, Márianosztra - a man washed his hands - there is no brick - the end of their days - order: money and love - the last forkful of hay.

(NOW: CELLS, FACTIONS, HOT-DOG VENDORS. LIZARD)

Glorious cause, oppression - eighty-five dead - gasoline on bus seats - youth, armed men - paid to do it - heavy water, Nazis - victims or assassins - bloated whore, Calf Square - fight back - start to rebuild - paper giantess with six arms, two mouths - teeth - Uncle Ferenc dies - cauliflower in batter.

THE SANDOR ROZSA SYNDROME

The lower classes - mountebank - inspired modesty - my dubious physiognomy - green baize of society's table.

Routine work - Ofelioko, black wall of rain.

Alliance of accomplices - holier-than-thou mothers-in-law - 'Forty-nine - handsome man, got singed.

Childish naiveté - one girl per room - ailing creature - punishment - motive, occasion, method.

ENCOUNTERS

Empty shop-window - alley-oop! - a new helper - the body of her beloved - palisade, streaky light from the yard - to the back - young dandy - flapping curtains - bloody temple - pebbles - checkered tablecloth - candlelight - the outside accomplice - bear-like build - a man's kiss - the hovel's eaves - it was morning but the sun couldn't rise - Arabian veil, strict imam - something on Huckster Street.

Unexpectedly off to the spas - risks - the self-restraint of the press - an elderly nun - not common highwaymen - whiskbroom, clothes-brush - a dazzling female neck, sample without value - white-haired girl.

FROST-BITTEN FRUIT

Harmless - the tom-toms of the underworld - axe-murderer running amok - the bad girls are not so bad - battle charger, trumpet call - the next bit of sensational news - mature members of the House of Lords - madness and a fat take.

Epidemic of heart flutters - Life and Adventure, veiled lady - for weeks without a woman - marvelous little dame - the inspectable locks - Viennese guests of the National Casino - enter the Safe King - and pray, why not? - a visit with Uncle Safe - the silver overflows - a full selection of jewelry - natty dresser - Little Kovács: the eggshell of a provincial dialect - the Lali Gere types, the very set of their eyes - not born to be a servant - shining faith of murderers - stupid hick! - Bárán, Rákosszentmihály - hatreds - the republic of the street - the electrification of the horse-drawn train - the age of the already and the not-yet - rule of the masses, rapidly approaching - on location, siesta hour - a window on Knitter Street - the tear - the warm breeze of dreams - at the landing slip - taking inventory - a last cable - the Paris express - Clicquot's widow - secrecy a success - Amber, Russian subject.

My lady is understanding - compulsion to talk - passionate, playful and identical - screamed in my ears, peed in my lap - New World cowboy - six weeks ago.

Virginal white bed - pursuit to come - unrequited love - in the middle of the night - rumination, cigar and cognac.

(NOW: "CAISSON" AND "TUBING")

No valet - the Great Organized Blood Bath - "real abroad" - davay, kleba, ukase - the underground train - shot to rubble, tank treads, Imre - we, the living - handsome and thin.

THE SCENT OF WILDFLOWERS IN A ROOM

Professor Roentgen's X-rays - Porter No.56 - motive - warm, voluminous buttocks - at the borderline of light and shadow - wash-stand, oak table - crenellations on a carpet - a smooth pebble - the bread-girl, correct?

A bristle-mustachioed gentleman and the tipsy gent.

An object at a weekly wage - uniqueness - hindsight - ensuring family peace.

THE MORNING AFTER

Sparrows, bird hosannahs - behind the facade of the metropolis - Paradiso, the University Italian Department - steaming yellowish spheres - no need to go further! - the wife a true partner - stale tastes - officials - green wool shreds, white bed ticking - bloodless revolution - shoebox - the number of 100-forint notes - no sympathy - sandpaper - love at a higher rate of pay - chastushka, eastern origins - fences made of sausages - the First Wave of Immigration, and the Third.

Cape on a tie beam - from my interrogation, straight to the burglary.

BRAZEN RETURN

Steel instruments, velvet pockets - Marika's dowry - rasps,

augers - top to toe - gathering clouds - a passkey - superstitious lot - the cash drawer - the sixteenth minute - dynamite, blankets - the ashes from his Ibis - cigarillo - dull thud - object-oriented software design - the metal plate's flower petals - burglar-proof.

Gathering the loot - crystalline fire - Koh-i-Noor, Great Mogul - four ways to buy a man - soccer stars and pop singers - on the streetcar - debris, ashes, shreds - man's work.

The Russian Czar's scepter - endless versts.

The remnants of Odessa, through the Central Train Terminal.

Chopped-up body - a tidbit for the press - known fences - who, if not I?

Burglar fever - at Keresztes and Hácha's - whiny young lady - circles under his eyes - expertise - brocade and silk foulards - call for a manhunt - pension registration forms - a large-scale dragnet - the Fourth Man - let's leave them here.

CROSS-COUNTRY

WAITING

An old question - Amber, off to the east - newshounds - the inner soul of the underworld - firing mechanism - the lady Maria - metropolitan spawn - Jenö the Lisp, messenger - unknown big-timers - without receipt - (Inner Horsemarket Square - in rags - the French disease - vague queries) - No.56 - the better sort - How many is some? - (she grapples, used to be a woman - fleeting flowery springtime - a hundred years? or two? - putrescent flowers).

OPEN SEASON

To cooperate, or not - Gypsy complexion, crowbar - BA NN 210 - tailor Knorr is afraid - our goose cooking - diamond miner - fifty nickel coins - shares, money and women - fille de joie? - warm trail - hardware store genetics - barbarian land - giggling tart - one tavern, one pint - scar on the temple, NN 211 - drinking companion a gentleman - Agap Kevorg in Salonica - broken contacts - toward Switzerland - the cab is found.

Slow-witted detective - registration forms - grand cafés, plate-glass windows - English tweed, gold cufflinks - Agap rests - the lesson still remains - in the former Temesvár vilayet - the country gentleman's watch-chain - a Jewish pickpocket - Diri and Dongó - a décolletage - the speeding train - the realm of hired love - not Bora - telephone message - in full view - the Stamboul police, the trail, Salonica - the prisons - to the new House of Parliament - Dajka with us.

(NOW: THE MAP OF THE STORY, PLAY IN THE SAND)

I stop - iron horse, bawd, stews - counter-jumper, my fabled laziness - (where did those Mercedes ambulances go?) - Romanian bookshelves - work freak, the country and poverty - seven telex paper strips, monthly meat ration ticket, Manó Kogutowitz, the Earth, from Space - canned food poems - they love my mess - Imre-like smell - bachelor, with a child - play in the sand.

A NEEDLE IN A HAYSTACK

Marton: Inspector - house searches - a hair's breadth - (a woman - yearning - Imola) - pilfered silver - virgin tobacco - Bush Street, surprise - follow the scent - disguises, burglar's tools - green wool - Budapest-Odessa-Saint Petersburg - lawful receipt - *effendi*, good friend - my razor - each minute - the *poste restante* window - the Greek, Láncz in chains - the number of perpetrators - caricature figure, from the banks of the Homoród - Your Excellency is exaggerating - forty grams of gold.

From all over the field - informer, café owner - on a cab toward Pest - the Syndrome still lives - braised beef and macaroni - postcard from Leopoldstadt - aims ahead of us - M.J. - blessed with idiots - off to Pannonia Street - the facts stare at you - a man slips out - the elevator.

(NOW: TELEPHONE PECKING. BUBBLES. GRAPE CLUSTERS)

Mulberry tree, rocky ledge - Bang, if - Countess Pálma is 70 street game, hundred-forint coin - preachers, Communists - living crossword puzzle.

The perceivable Cosmos - our not-knowing - the chicken or the egg - let's skip - dark segments of space, a hundred fifty million light-years - assorted grape clusters, Vyatka Matryoshka dolls - the nearly perfect oval of our Basin - mountains, forests, plains, milk, honey - time-bigots - but hush, in space - the Little Bear, Greater Magellan Cloud, the Sculptor and the Dragon - Newtown in Old Buda - shore breeze - hands on the Moon - (not a soldier) - A I D and S, unpronounceable - a seventh-year elementary student's daddy, with women.

L'ESPRIT DE L'ESCALIER

Police raid - the black veil returns - workshop - the chimney-sweep's catwalk - stay for 30 days - stuffed wallets - handcuffs.

In unison - silk foulards, mouthwash - the hitch; seventy burglars - unrequited love - the right man in the right place - ladies' man - fresh linen shirt - (naked, excrement) - visitors, woman - lower-class man - engineer, cleanliness - skipped out - little old lady on a chair - get the chills - oxyhydrogen torch -

dinner with a bad girl - the notary's watch - flat key - any filth - well-practised collapse - dubious acquaintances, Zurich - the hand of fate - Vienna in a huff - two cases - shadowy struggle - ghosts and the independent Royal Hungarian courts.

(NOW: ANGEL-LAND, GLOBE STREET. EROTIC LITTLE HANDS)

Six million B.C. - knee-deep in the Pleistocene - my limits - coffee grounds, crystal ball, little green men on a saucer - black hair, gray overcoat - the psychiatrist's credibility - beyond the pale of human perception - their arrogant certainty - two feet.

Corn belt, Bible belt - Lord of the Texts - the forbidden and the compulsory, a T and a K - Pipe and Conduit, human habitation.

Gray matter - bands of twenty-five, swinging clubs - if you aim - cheaters - what makes us human - rich summer, lean winter - abundant tubers, fish and game - survivors - a new force at work - imagination, teardrop shape, fire - human nature - sixty thousand B.C. - beyond the final bourne, Cro-Magnon - Ildikó, bewitching on the Grand Boulevard - the Tata talisman - negroid features - our slower cousins - schools now and evermore - my atrophied instincts - homo paleohungaricus, close up - Buda Culture - gray-green Neolithic backdrop - alien female - tattered clouds, shivering water - long chase - raw scent of woman - hairy mass of flesh - mumbling - away from the instinctive, painfully - gray mane, tar - wriggles backward - custom of conquering man - theory, practice, embarrassing - we/they - us, them.

Cave, fire - caravans on foot - Lunar calendar - the seven movers - at "The Russians" - a wide open field.

SIMPLER TIMES

Prison entrepreneurs - Bubbles, flirtatious - a well-stuffed letter, gold napoleons - before the trial - crude iron locks -

(NOW: BIPEDS. LACTOSE INTOLERANCE)

tumbles in the hay - the eternal equilibrium of up and down - the Horde is Golden - in the middle of the highway - like a stray cat - the slant of Bora's eyes - folk migrations, violence, flowers in the girls' hair - the Lame One, a mountain of skulls - angel wings, Isonzo - piles of hair and heaps of crutches - after China - Modern times - the youngest monotheism - crescent and scimitar - on both sides of King's Pass - towns encircled by palisades - the twins, the lutanist - self-realization.

THE CART BEFORE THE HORSE

Manly farewell - red paprika - the western border stations - women, women - twitterings - ageless, noseless - once loved by the King - Cracklings, emperor of the rag trade - slums - ooze radar, two gold napoleons - truth finds its reward - pontoon, amphibious tank - not in the pay of the police - a taciturn gentleman - yellow - Szabadka, train station - Galicia and the Russian border - round-trip, at a discount - young woman - to the Kitty - the most noble beast - by the flowering Tisza - at the Golden Lamb - from the first minute to the third - the wanted man - French in the Bácska - the river's loops - good times, patience - Belgrade, train station - on the trail, to the Balkans - panic - Nándorfehérvár, Holy War, noontime bells - (San Juan de Capistrano and the order of annexation) - two disks - from Bush Street to Odessa - the cart before the horse - nothing quicker - same as novel-writing - you know nothing? - the wandering Tisza, black - the ferry, at another time - the tavern-keeper Puhl - rainstorm, gendarmes - shot in the air - Marton and languages - the Riviera, roulette - chemin-de-fer - only his chains - on one card.

(NOW: BAG-LADY. LIMNED EFFIGIES)

Cross-country, kicked out - the personal order of magnitude - the pain of exclusion - gets lost, enters junior events - Spaceship Earth - athletes - need to decide - Octagon Place, across from Nicoletti's - the little mama - a slice of meat on bread - the season, this trifle - they steal the meat; hidden reserves - Kovács's future cheekbones - slaves on the river bank - the girl, her brother, the enslaved blacksmith, the Iron Man - multitudes, witch to the stake - the minstrel, building forts, crumbling Pest, picture show, war against Papists - not to kill, one hundred wheelbarrows from Vienna, fighting Gods, hetzmeister, cracking ice, throw the beggar's staff away, eyeglasses, penny dreadfuls on the tarpaulin - theaters and bawdy houses - our native city, the Little Bear Bar - ancestors - brand-new apartment buildings - kaleidoscope, a Slovak glazier - we can afford it - illumination, 15 watts - on his trail, ahead of him.

GALICIA AND THE RUSSIAN BORDER

Dawn, birdsong - they ran out of the country - Máramaros, border county.

Monte Carlo, casino-resorts.

Széle-Lonka - peasants and gentry.

To the Cléopatra, handcuffs - gambler's blood - dinner, strategic point - only to win - doorman, banana republic - oyster vendor - thirty Ruthenian peasants - King, hein? - southern types - flushing mechanism.

Overseer - red hot - if they kill me - safe in the hands of the authorities - Taracköz, fatherly police captain - razor blade - Máramaros Sziget, a guard on each extremity - like foreign ministers.

THE GENIUS OF SIR FRANCIS

Wanted circulars - in irons - taciturn birds.

Cicero not an ancient author - spare lamp cylinders - I rush headlong - fine flour - white lines - where is the state police? - where the fugitives, the homeless - the glad news spreads - the found child - if you stay put - any mother's son - passkey from a window bar - railroad man - from a convicted scoundrel - a bullet finds its mark - natural instinct - the last meeting - alone in the wilderness - why do you cover for him? - a small-time pickpocket - may it be heard - inventory of the loot - without a trace.

The inside accomplice, at the Kitty - lamp cylinders, little lines - enlargements - the towel - washed by a woman.

THE WAY IT WAS

THAT BEAUTIFUL AND HECTIC SUMMER

A woman! - what he didn't find - later, the retired judge - the novel is dead, these days - blood and women - the red thread - cat in the rain - entangled - what will the concierge say - a Turkish coffee - justifiable fear - where, when, how, with whom, why - my Martzi - Bora's salary - belated realizations - from Mrs. Tremmel's - Inconnue.

Let's go back - Little Kovács - old gentleman - junior clerk - Rézi Luft's dive - student, little girl, Sotho miner - Prince Archaroff, safe-cracker - little Erzsi Csorba's dream - the youngest judge - the second love child - Baron Ormund Freiherr von and zu - another country, another prison - brilliant life - Epiphany - (under the Soviets) - special appointment - Bubbles, lily - not at all helter-skelter! - Zara, the fourth one - Sutruroy - shiny and smooth surfaces - covered wagon - Lilia, Alma and the quiet - the fire-eater - who am I? - only the girl.

THE HEAVY FOOT OF FATE

To lie the truth - impish little face - like a masterpiece - between two women - abandoned lovenest - raid - Bora's entrance - pyramid - police matters - mud on the shirtfront - dreams come alive - recognized, never seen - crisp, clean -

drenched forehead - "cologne, scissors" - drops.

Three hours and ten minutes - scent of hay, Danube pebbles, soapy residue - little boys and Special Investigators - delivery men - we are on track - in the afternoon, plinking away - to leave the moment - cheap cologne, open wound - the unknown - you know more - the courtyard - the Doctor's mistake - dangerous passage - quietly to Bubbles - bloodstain, hair from a male Caucasian - luck, gods and worldview - corpus delicti, corpse - what else was true - tight collar - that one faux pas - wild flowers - five to seven days - Domokos - scourge of Europe - infectious hepatitis - figure-eight stitches - in front of the Bazaar, Partagas - postcard - Margaret Bridge, to Mohács - in advance and in hindsight - from where it was taken - brick life - the Kitty's fate, Agnes Vad - gentleman - Brick at the Little Bear Bar - detects three types - courts - Olga the Whale - half and half - butcher knife, coal haulers, Mátyás, the Alva Ráz gang - nothing bad - none in me - highest mark - in full view - Why? - Bora's mortal shell.

(NOW: FUNERAL. THE COUNTESS. FIRE HYDRANTS. AIDS)

We, her family - thinking machine - miracle doctor - ours are red - uncensured news centers - in the ass - bratty kids - noise and information.

THE THICKENED TRUNKS OF THE TREES ON THE BOULEVARD

Port Said, European police - cold sweat - the girl is let out of jail - to Tollhouse Square - ashes, blankets and cash - the rafter, bungler - Professor Freud of Vienna - destiny's smoke and fire - harbinger of an epoch - the little old woman - the cape - never arrived - thirty days - don't look for her - light years - honesty divisible - in our wake - professionally, cheap nightclub melodrama.

TWO PORTIONS INTO SIX

To Lori's, on Seminary Street - a new apportionment - underworld justice - exclude the impossible - to the Pest Regional! - the frontal-temporal area - like clipping fingernails - amateurish stitching - prayer of thanks - our legal system - plenty of time - the Britisher's theories.

(NOW: ICE-HORSESHOES ON MY FEET, GLOVES ON MY HANDS)

Eight days - the Fráter's worries - condoms, heroin, Hungarian books - Imola, the great summer - storm lantern - Claudius - telephone, cushions - in a good place - always the Main Square - gray, brown, enough - corso, scandal - serenade - two thousand miles, the rim of the Basin - flies, flies, flies - outpost of the language - from a washbasin, squatting - head first into concrete - Imre, Barna and the widow - emigration - immortality - satrap - girl from Old Buda - '55 Ikarusz - sides of bacon - their lives - Torda Road - biplane - in place of us - fifty leis - the loaf on the stone - like everyone else - on the run - try my luck, find a good master - to Várad - buskins falling apart - my Lady's newborn - snow covers - running for their lives - outer lands - starvation - our Master's hour had come - our work in this world - Székely maid - Hungarianized - congregation - like a Turkish Buda - on track one - a market, let's not buy - free in the wilderness - to our Canaan, flowing with milk and honey - it was still there.

TRAVELING LIGHT

By next morning - a catalogue of human actions - in every life - (Little Kovács's winning strategy) - past the Zoo - NN 124 - photographs - arch, loop, whorl - photo of a gray coat - five years for me - who else is missing? - new circulars - description of the piano player.
Aged Slovak glazier, elderly Schwabian lady - pure space -

OH, THE OCEAN HAS NO BOTTOM

About the translator: John BÁTKI was born in 1942 in Miskolc, Hungary. Until November 1956 he lived in Budapest; early in 1957 he moved to the USA, becoming a U.S. citizen in 1962. Having completed his B.A. degree at Columbia University, he served in the U.S. Army Medical Corps Reserve, 1966-69. He completed an M.A. degree in English and American literature and creative writing at Syracuse University in 1969.

Mr Bátki has published two collections of his poetry: *The Mad Shoemaker* and *Falling Upwards*; and his stories and poems have appeared in many publications, including *The New Yorker*, *Ploughshares*, and *Antaeus*. His translations from Hungarian include *Attila Jozsef: Poems and Texts*; *Hungarian Art Nouveau*; *Zsolnay Porcelain*; as well as stories and novellas by László Csiki, Gyula Krúdy, Iván Mándy, Miklós Mészöly, Géza Ottlik, and István Örkény.

Mr Bátki lives in Syracuse, New York, where he writes and teaches. He is currently collaborating on a translation of a novel by the Hungarian writer Péter Esterházy.